PENGUIN BOO

LUCIA VICT

Edward Frederic Benson was born in 1867 at Wellington College, where his father Edward White Benson (later Archbishop of Canterbury) was headmaster. He was educated at Marlborough and King's College, Cambridge. His main interests were classics and archaeology and from 1892 to 1895 he studied and worked at the British School of Archaeology in Athens.

In 1893 his first novel *Dodo* had considerable success, and there followed a stream of novels and biographies, including his famous social comedies, the *Lucia* series, cult books since they were first published in the 1920s.

Mayor of Rye from 1934 to 1937, E. F. Benson was awarded the OBE and made an Honorary Fellow of Magdalene College, Cambridge. He died in 1940, having published over one hundred books.

LUCIA VICTRIX

MAPP AND LUCIA
LUCIA'S PROGRESS
TROUBLE FOR LUCIA

———————

E. F. BENSON

PENGUIN BOOKS

PENGUIN BOOKS

Published by the Penguin Group
Penguin Books Ltd, 80 Strand, London WC2R 0RL, England
Penguin Putnam Inc., 375 Hudson Street, New York, New York 10014, USA
Penguin Books Australia Ltd, 250 Camberwell Road, Camberwell, Victoria 3124, Australia
Penguin Books Canada Ltd, 10 Alcorn Avenue, Toronto, Ontario, Canada M4V 3B2
Penguin Books India (P) Ltd, 11 Community Centre, Panchsheel Park, New Delhi – 110 017, India
Penguin Books (NZ) Ltd, Cnr Rosedale and Airborne Roads, Albany, Auckland, New Zealand
Penguin Books (South Africa) (Pty) Ltd, 24 Sturdee Avenue, Rosebank 2196, South Africa

Penguin Books Ltd, Registered Offices: 80 Strand, London WC2R 0RL, England

www.penguin.com

Mapp and Lucia first published by Hodder & Stoughton Ltd, 1935
Lucia's Progress first published by Hodder & Stoughton Ltd, 1935
Trouble for Lucia first published by Hodder & Stoughton Ltd, 1939

This collection published under the title *Lucia Victrix* by Penguin Books 1991
12

Printed in England by Clays Ltd, St Ives plc
Filmset in Imprint

CONTENTS

Mapp and Lucia   1

Lucia's Progress   285

Trouble for Lucia   519

Mapp and Lucia

Though it was nearly a year since her husband's death, Emmeline Lucas (universally known to her friends as Lucia) still wore the deepest and most uncompromising mourning. Black certainly suited her very well, but that had nothing to do with this continued use of it, whatever anybody said. Pepino and she had been the most devoted couple for over twenty-five years, and her grief at his loss was heart-felt: she missed him constantly and keenly. But months ago now, she, with her very vital and active personality, had felt a most natural craving to immerse herself again in all those thrilling interests which made life at this Elizabethan village of Riseholme so exciting a business, and she had not yet been able to make up her mind to take the plunge she longed for. Though she had not made a luxury out of the tokens of grief, she had perhaps made, ever so slightly, a stunt of them.

For instance. There was that book-shop on the green, 'Ye Signe of ye Daffodille', under the imprint of which Pepino had published his severely limited edition of *Fugitive Lyrics* and *Pensieri Persi*. A full six months after his death Lucia had been walking past it with Georgie Pillson, and had seen in the window a book she would have liked to purchase. But next to it, on the shelf, was the thin volume of Pepino's *Pensieri Persi*, and, frankly, it had been rather stuntish of her to falter on the threshold and, with eyes that were doing their best to swim, to say to Georgie:

'I can't quite face going in, Georgie. Weak of me, I know, but there it is. Will you please just pop in, *caro*, and ask them to send me *Beethoven's Days of Boyhood*? I will stroll on.'

So Georgie had pressed her hand and done this errand for her, and of course he had repeated this pathetic little incident to others. Tasteful embroideries had been tacked on to it, and

3

it was soon known all over Riseholme that poor Lucia had gone into 'Ye Signe of ye Daffodille' to buy the book about Beethoven's boyhood, and had been so sadly affected by the sight of Pepino's poems in their rough brown linen cover with dark-green tape to tie them up with (although she constantly saw the same volume in her own house), that she had quite broken down. Some said that sal volatile had been administered.

Similarly, she had never been able to bring herself to have a game of golf, or to resume her Dante-readings, and having thus established the impression that her life had been completely smashed up it had been hard to decide that on Tuesday or Wednesday next she would begin to glue it together again. In consequence she had remained in as many pieces as before. Like a sensible woman she was very careful of her physical health, and since this stunt of mourning made it impossible for her to play golf or take brisk walks, she sent for a very illuminating little book, called *An Ideal System of Callisthenics for those no longer Young*, and in a secluded glade of her garden she exposed as much of herself as was proper to the invigorating action of the sun, when there was any, and had long bouts of skipping, and kicked, and jerked, and swayed her trunk, gracefully and vigorously, in accordance with the instructions laid down. The effect was most satisfactory, and at the very, very back of her mind she conceived it possible that some day she might conduct callisthenic classes for those ladies of Riseholme who were no longer young.

Then there was the greater matter of the Elizabethan fête to be held in August next, when Riseholme would be swarming with tourists. The idea of it had been entirely Lucia's, and there had been several meetings of the fête-committee (of which, naturally, she was President) before Pepino's death. She had planned the great scene in it: this was to be Queen Elizabeth's visit to the *Golden Hind*, when, on the completion of Francis Drake's circumnavigation of the world, Her Majesty went to dine with him on board his ship at Deptford and knighted him. The *Golden Hind* was to be moored in the pond on the village green; or, more accurately, a platform on piles

was to be built there, in the shape of a ship's deck, with masts
and rudder and cannons and bulwarks, and banners and ancients, particularly ancients. The pond would be an admirable
stage, for rows of benches would be put up all round it, and
everybody would see beautifully. The Queen's procession with
trumpeters and men-at-arms and ladies of the Court was
planned to start from the Hurst, which was Lucia's house, and
make its glittering and melodious way across the green to
Deptford to the sound of madrigals and medieval marches.
Lucia would impersonate the Queen, Pepino following her as
Raleigh, and Georgie would be Francis Drake. But at an early
stage of these incubations Pepino had died, and Lucia had
involved herself in this inextricable widowhood. Since then the
reins of government had fallen into Daisy Quantock's podgy
little hands, and she, in this as in all other matters, had come
to consider herself quite the Queen of Riseholme, until Lucia
could get a move on again and teach her better.

One morning in June, some seven weeks before the date
fixed for the fête, Mrs Quantock telephoned from her house a
hundred yards away to say that she particularly wanted to see
Lucia, if she might pop over for a little talk. Lucia had heard
nothing lately about the preparations for the fête, for the last
time that it had been mentioned in her presence, she had
gulped and sat with her hand over her eyes for a moment
overcome with the memory of how gaily she had planned it.
But she knew that the preparations for it must by this time be
well in hand, and now she instantly guessed that it was on this
subject that Daisy wanted to see her. She had premonitions of
that kind sometimes, and she was sure that this was one of
them. Probably Daisy wanted to address a moving appeal to
her that, for the sake of Riseholme generally, she should make
this fête the occasion of her emerging from her hermetic
widowhood. The idea recommended itself to Lucia, for before
the date fixed for it, she would have been a widow for over a
year, and she reflected that her dear Pepino would never have
wished her to make this permanent suttee of herself: also there
was the prestige of Riseholme to be considered. Besides, she
was really itching to get back into the saddle again, and depose

Daisy from her awkward, clumsy seat there, and this would be
an admirable opportunity. So, as was usual now with her, she
first sighed into the telephone, said rather faintly that she
would be delighted to see dear Daisy, and then sighed again.
Daisy, very stupidly, hoped she had not got a cough, and was
reassured on that point.

Lucia gave a few moments' thought as to whether she
would be found at the piano, playing the funeral march from
Beethoven's Sonata in A flat which she now knew by heart, or
be sitting out in Perdita's garden, reading Pepino's poems. She
decided on the latter, and putting on a shady straw hat with a
crêpe bow on it, and taking a copy of the poems from the shelf,
hurried out into Perdita's garden. She also carried with her a
copy of to-day's *Times*, which she had not yet read.

Perdita's garden requires a few words of explanation. It was
a charming little square plot in front of the timbered façade of
the Hurst, surrounded by yew-hedges and intersected with
paths of crazy pavement, carefully smothered in stone-crop,
which led to the Elizabethan sundial from Wardour Street in
the centre. It was gay in spring with those flowers (and no
others) on which Perdita doted. There were 'violets dim', and
primroses and daffodils, which came before the swallow dared
and took the winds (usually of April) with beauty. But now in
June the swallow had dared long ago, and when spring and the
daffodils were over, Lucia always allowed Perdita's garden a
wider, though still strictly Shakespearian scope. There was
eglantine (Penzance briar) in full flower now, and honeysuckle
and gillyflowers and plenty of pansies for thoughts, and yards
of rue (more than usual this year), and so Perdita's garden was
gay all the summer.

Here then, this morning, Lucia seated herself by the sundial,
all in black, on a stone bench on which was carved the motto
'Come thou north wind, and blow thou south, that my garden
spices may flow forth.' Sitting there with Pepino's poems and
The Times she obscured about one-third of this text, and fat
little Daisy would obscure the rest . . . It was rather annoying
that the tapes which tied the covers of Pepino's poems had got
into a hard knot, which she was quite unable to unravel, for

she had meant that Daisy should come up, unheard by her, in her absorption, and find her reading Pepino's lyric called 'Loneliness'. But she could not untie the tapes, and as soon as she heard Daisy's footsteps she became lost in reverie with the book lying shut on her lap, and the famous far-away look in her eyes.

It was a very hot morning. Daisy, like many middle-aged women who enjoyed perfect health, was always practising some medical regime of a hygienic nature, and just now she was a devoted slave to the eliminative processes of the body. The pores of the skin were the most important of these agencies, and, after her drill of physical jerks by the open window of her bedroom, she had trotted in all this heat across the green to keep up the elimination. She mopped and panted for a little.

'Made quite a new woman of me,' she said. 'You should try it, dear Lucia. But so good of you to see me, and I'll come to the point at once. The Elizabethan fête, you know. You see it won't be till August. Can't we persuade you, as they say, to come amongst us again? We all want you: such a fillip you'd give it.'

Lucia made no doubt that this request implied the hope that she might be induced to take the part of Queen Elizabeth, and under the spell of the exuberant sunshine that poured in upon Perdita's garden, she felt the thrill and the pulse of life bound in her veins. The fête would be an admirable occasion for entering the arena of activities again, and, as Daisy had hinted (delicately for Daisy), more than a year of her widowhood would have elapsed by August. It was self-sacrificing, too, of Daisy to have suggested this herself, for she knew that according to present arrangements Daisy was to take the part of the Virgin Queen, and Georgie had told her weeks ago (when the subject of the fête had been last alluded to) that she was already busy pricking her fingers by sewing a ruff to go round her fat little neck, and that she had bought a most sumptuous string of Woolworth pearls. Perhaps dear Daisy had realized what a very ridiculous figure she would present as Queen, and was anxious for the sake of the fête to retire from so laughable a role. But, however that might be, it was nice of her to volunteer abdication.

Lucia felt that it was only proper that Daisy should press her a little. She was being asked to sacrifice her personal feelings which so recoiled from publicity, and for the sake of Riseholme to rescue the fête from being a farce. She was most eager to do so, and a very little pressing would be sufficient. So she sighed again, she stroked the cover of Pepino's poems, but she spoke quite briskly.

'Dear Daisy,' she said, 'I don't think I could face it. I cannot imagine myself coming out of my house in silks and jewels to take my place in the procession without my Pepino. He was to have been Raleigh, you remember, and to have walked immediately behind me. The welcome, the shouting, the rejoicing, the madrigals, the Morris-dances and me with my poor desolate heart! But perhaps I ought to make an effort. My dear Pepino, I know, would have wished me to. You think so, too, and I have always respected the soundness of your judgment.'

A slight change came over Daisy's round red face. Lucia was getting on rather too fast and too far.

'My dear, none of us ever thought of asking you to be Queen Elizabeth,' she said. 'We are not so unsympathetic, for of course that would be far too great a strain on you. You must not think of it. All that I was going to suggest was that you might take the part of Drake's wife. She only comes forward just for a moment, and makes her curtsey to me – I mean to the Queen – and then walks backwards again into the chorus of ladies-in-waiting and halberdiers and things.'

Lucia's beady eyes dwelt for a moment on Daisy's rather anxious face with a glance of singular disdain. What a fool poor Daisy was to think that she, Lucia, could possibly consent to take any subordinate part in tableaux or processions or anything else at Riseholme where she had been Queen so long! She had decided in her own mind that with a very little judicious pressing she would take the part of the Queen, and thus make her superb entry into Riseholme life again, but all the pressure in the world would not induce her to impersonate anyone else, unless she could double it with the Queen. Was there ever anything so tactless as Daisy's tact? . . .

She gave a wintry smile, and stroked the cover of Pepino's poems again.

'Sweet of you to suggest it, dear,' she said, 'but indeed it would be quite too much for me. I was wrong to entertain the idea even for a moment. Naturally I shall take the greatest, the *very* greatest interest in it all, and I am sure you will understand if I do not even feel equal to coming to it, and read about it instead in the *Worcestershire Herald.*'

She paused. Perhaps it would be more in keeping with her empty heart to say nothing more about the fête. On the other hand, she felt a devouring curiosity to know how they were getting on. She sighed.

'I must begin to interest myself in things again,' she said. 'So tell me about it all, Daisy, if you would like to.'

Daisy was much relieved to know that even the part of Drake's wife was too much for Lucia. She was safe now from any risk of having the far more arduous part of the Queen snatched from her.

'All going splendidly,' she said. 'Revels on the green to open with, and madrigals and Morris-dances. Then comes the scene on the *Golden Hind* which was entirely your idea. We've only elaborated it a little. There will be a fire on the poop of the ship, or is it the prow?'

'It depends, dear, which end of the ship you mean,' said Lucia.

'The behind part, the stern. Poop, is it? Well, there will be a fire on the poop for cooking. Quite safe, they say, if the logs are laid on a sheet of iron. Over the fire we shall have an Elizabethan spit, and roast a sheep on it.'

'I wouldn't,' said Lucia, feeling the glamour of these schemes glowing in her. 'Half of it will be cinders and the rest blood.'

'No, dear,' said Daisy. 'It will really be roasted first at the Ambermere Arms, and then just hung over the fire on the *Golden Hind.*'

'Oh, yes: just to get a little kippered in the smoke,' said Lucia.

'Not to matter. Of course I shan't really eat any, because I never touch meat of any sort now: I shall only pretend to. But there'll be the scene of cooking going on for the Queen's dinner on the deck of the *Golden Hind*, just to fill up, while the Queen's procession is forming. Oh, I wonder if you would let us start the procession from your house rather than mine. The route would be so much more in the open: everyone will see it better. I would come across to dress, if you would let me, half an hour before.'

Lucia of course knew perfectly well that Daisy was to be the Queen, but she wanted to make her say so.

'Certainly start from here,' said Lucia. 'I am only too happy to help. And dress here yourself. Let me see: what are you going to be?'

'They've all insisted that I should be Queen Elizabeth,' said Daisy hurriedly. 'Where had we got to? Oh yes: as the procession is forming, the cooking will be going on. Songs of course, a chorus of cooks. Then the procession will cross the green to the *Golden Hind*, then dinner, and then I knight Drake. Such a lovely sword. Then Elizabethan games, running, jumping, wrestling and so on. We thought of baiting a bear, one out of some menagerie that could be trusted not to get angry, but we've given that up. If it didn't get angry, it wouldn't be baited, and if it did get angry it would be awful.'

'Very prudent,' said Lucia.

'Then I steal away into the Ambermere Arms which is quite close, and change into a riding-dress. There'll be a white palfrey at the door, the one that draws the milk-cart. Oh, I forgot. While I'm dressing, before the palfrey comes round, a rider gallops in from Plymouth on a horse covered with soap-suds to say that the Spanish Armada has been sighted. I think we must have a megaphone for that, or no one will hear. So I come out, and mount my palfrey, and make my speech to my troops at Tilbury. A large board, you know, with Tilbury written up on it like a station. That's quite in the Shakespearian style. I shall have to learn it all by heart, and just have Raleigh standing by the palfrey with a copy of my speech to prompt me if I forget.'

The old familiar glamour glowed brighter and brighter to Lucia as Daisy spoke. She wondered if she had made a mistake in not accepting the ludicrous part of Drake's wife, just in order to get a footing in these affairs again and attend committees, and, gradually ousting Daisy from her supremacy, take the part of the Queen herself. She felt that she must think it all over, and settle whether, in so advanced a stage of the proceedings, it could be done. At present, till she had made up her mind, it was wiser, in order to rouse no suspicions, to pretend that these things were all very remote. She would take a faint though kindly interest in them, as if some elderly person was watching children at play, and smiling pensively at their pretty gambols. But as for watching the fête when the date arrived, that was unthinkable. She would either be Queen Elizabeth herself, or not be at Riseholme at all. That was that.

'Well, you have got your work cut out for you, dear Daisy,' she said, giving a surreptitious tug at the knotted tape of Pepino's poems. 'What fun you will have, and, dear me, how far away it all seems!'

Daisy wrenched her mind away from the thought of the fête.

'It won't always, dear,' she said, making a sympathetic little dab at Lucia's wrist. 'Your joy in life will revive again. I see you've got Pepino's poems there. Won't you read me one?'

Lucia responded to this gesture with another dab.

'Do you remember the last one he wrote?' she said. 'He called it "Loneliness". I was away in London at the time. Beginning:

The spavined storm-clouds limp down the ruinous sky,
     While I sit alone.
Thick through the acid air the dumb leaves fly . . .

But I won't read it you now. Another time.'

Daisy gave one more sympathetic poke at her wrist, and rose to go.

'Must be off,' she said. 'Won't you come round and dine quietly to-night?'

'I can't, many thanks. Georgie is dining with me. Any news in Riseholme this morning?'

Daisy reflected for a moment.

'Oh, yes,' she said. 'Mrs Arbuthnot's got a wonderful new

apparatus. Not an ear-trumpet at all. She just bites on a small leather pad, and hears everything perfectly. Then she takes it out of her mouth and answers you, and puts it back again to listen.'

'No!' said Lucia excitedly. 'All wet?'

'Quite dry. Just between her teeth. No wetter anyhow than a pen you put in your mouth, I assure you.'

Daisy hurried away to do some more exercises and drink pints and pints of hot water before lunch. She felt that she had emerged safely from a situation which might easily have become menacing, for without question Lucia, in spite of her sighs and her wistful stroking of the covers of Pepino's poems, and her great crêpe bow, was beginning to show signs of her old animation. She had given Daisy a glance or two from that beady eye which had the qualities of a gimlet about it, she had shown eager interest in such topics as the roasting of the sheep and Mrs Arbuthnot's gadget, which a few weeks ago would not have aroused the slightest response from her stricken mind, and it was lucky, Daisy thought, that Lucia had given her the definite assurance that even the part of Drake's wife in the fête would be too much for her. For goodness only knew, when once Lucia settled to be on the mend, how swift her recuperation might be, or what mental horse-power in the way of schemings and domination she might not develop after this fallow period of quiescence. There was a new atmosphere about her to-day: she was like some spring morning when, though winds might still be chilly and the sun still of tepid and watery beams, the air was pregnant with the imminent birth of new life. But evidently she meant to take no hand in the fête, which at present completely filled Daisy's horizon. 'She may do what she likes afterwards,' thought Daisy, breaking into a trot, 'but I will be Queen Elizabeth.'

Her house, with its mulberry-tree in front and its garden at the back, stood next Georgie Pillson's on the edge of the green, and as she passed through it and out on to the lawn behind, she heard from the other side of the paling that tap-tap of croquet-mallet and ball which now almost without cessation punctuated the hours of any fine morning. Georgie had developed a craze for solitary croquet: he spent half the day practising all by himself, to the great neglect of his water-colour painting and his piano-playing. He seemed indeed, apart from croquet, to be losing his zest for life; he took none of his old interest in the thrilling topics of Riseholme. He had not been a bit excited at Daisy's description of Mrs Arbuthnot's new apparatus, and the prospect of impersonating Francis Drake at the forthcoming fête aroused only the most tepid enthusiasm in him. A book of Elizabethan costumes, full of sumptuous coloured plates, had roused him for a while from his lethargy, and he had chosen a white satin tunic with puffed sleeves slashed with crimson, and a cloak of rose-coloured silk, on the reproduction of which his peerless parlourmaid Foljambe was at work, but he didn't seem to have any keenness about him. Of course he had had some rather cruel blows of Fate to contend against lately: Miss Olga Bracely the prima donna to whom he had been so devoted had left Riseholme a month ago for a year's operatic tour in the United States and Australia, and that was a desolate bereavement for him, while Lucia's determination not to do any of all these things which she had once enjoyed so much had deprived him of all the duets they used to play together. Moreover, it was believed in Riseholme (though only whispered at present) that Foljambe, that paragon of parlourmaids, in whom the smoothness and comfort of his domestic life was centred, was walking out with Cadman, Lucia's chauffeur. It might not mean anything, but if it did, if Foljambe and he intended to get married and Foljambe left Georgie, and if Georgie had got wind of this, then indeed there would be good cause for that lack of zest, that air of gloom and apprehension which was now so often noticeable in him. All these causes, the blows Fate had already rained on him, and the anxiety concerning this possible catastrophe in the future, probably contributed to the eclipsed condition of his energies.

Daisy sat down on a garden-bench, and began to do a little deep-breathing, which was a relic of the days when she had studied Yoga. It was important to concentrate (otherwise the deep-breathing did no good at all), or rather to attain a complete blankness of mind and exclude from it all mundane interests which were Maya, or illusion. But this morning she found it difficult: regiments of topics grew up like mushrooms. Now she congratulated herself on having made certain that Lucia was not intending to butt into the fête, now she began to have doubts – these were disconcerting mushrooms – as to whether that was so certain, for Lucia was much brisker to-day than she had been since Pepino's death, and if that continued, her reawakened interest in life would surely seek for some outlet. Then the thought of her own speech to her troops at Tilbury began to leak into her mind: would she ever get it so thoroughly by heart that she could feel sure that no attack of nervousness or movement on the part of her palfrey would put it out of her head? Above all there was that disturbing tap-tap going on from Georgie's garden, and however much she tried to attain blankness of mind, she found herself listening for the next tap . . . It was no use and she got up.

'Georgie, are you there?' she called out.

'Yes,' came his voice, trembling with excitement. 'Wait a minute. I've gone through nine hoops and – Oh, how tarsome, I missed quite an easy one. What is it? I rather wish you hadn't called me just then.'

Georgie was tall, and he could look over the paling. Daisy pulled her chair up to it, and mounted on it, so that they could converse with level heads.

'So sorry, Georgie,' she said, 'I didn't know you were making such a break. Fancy! Nine! I wanted to tell you I've been to see Lucia.'

'Is that all? I knew that because I saw you,' said Georgie. 'I was polishing my bibelots in the drawing-room. And you sat in Perdita's garden.'

'And there's a change,' continued Daisy, who had kept her mouth open, in order to go on again as soon as Georgie stopped. 'She's better. Distinctly. More interested, and not so faint and die-away. Sarcastic about the roast sheep for instance.'

'What? Did she talk about the fête again?' asked Georgie. 'That is an improvement.'

'That was what I went to talk about. I asked her if she wouldn't make an effort to be Drake's wife. But she s id it would be too great a strain.'

'My dear, you didn't ask her to be Drake's wife?' said Georgie incredulously. 'You might as well have asked her to be a confused noise within. What can you have been thinking of?'

'Anyhow, she said she couldn't be anything at all,' said Daisy. 'I have her word for that. But if she is recovering, and I'm sure she is, her head will be full of plans again. I'm not quite happy about it.'

'What you mean is that you're afraid she may want to be the Queen,' observed Georgie acutely.

'I won't give it up,' said Daisy very firmly, not troubling to confirm so obvious an interpretation. 'I've had all the trouble of it, and very nearly learnt the speech to the troops, and made my ruff and bought a rope of pearls. It wouldn't be fair, Georgie. So don't encourage her, will you? I know you're dining with her to-night.'

'No, I won't encourage her,' said he. 'But you know what Lucia is, when she's in working order. If she wants a thing, she gets it somehow. It happens. That's all you can say about it.'

'Well, this one shan't happen,' said Daisy, dismounting from her basket-chair which was beginning to sag. 'It would be too mean. And I wish you would come across now and let us practise that scene where I knight you. We must get it very slick.'

'Not this morning,' said Georgie. 'I know my bit: I've only got to kneel down. You can practise on the end of a sofa. Besides, if Lucia is really waking up, I shall take some duets across this evening, and I must have a go at some of them. I've not touched my piano for weeks. And my shoulder's sore where you knighted me so hard the other day. Quite a bruise.'

Daisy suddenly remembered something more.

'And Lucia repeated me several lines out of one of Pepino's last poems,' she said. 'She couldn't possibly have done that a month ago without breaking down. And I believe she would have read one to me when I asked her to, but I'm pretty sure she couldn't undo one of those tapes that the book is tied up with. A hard knot. She was picking at it . . .'

'Oh, she must be better,' said he. 'Ever so much.'

So Georgie went in to practise some of the old duets in case Lucia felt equal to evoking the memories of happier days at the piano, and Daisy hit the end of her sofa some half-dozen times with her umbrella bidding it rise Sir Francis Drake. She still wondered if Lucia had some foul scheme in her head, but though there had ticked by some minutes, directly after their talk in Perdita's garden, which might have proved exceedingly dangerous to her own chance of being the Queen, these, by the time that she was knighting the sofa, had passed. For Lucia, still meditating whether she should not lay plots for ousting Daisy, had, in default of getting that knotted tape undone, turned to her unread *Times*, and scanned its columns with a rather absent eye. There was no news that could interest anybody, and her glance wandered up and down the lists of situations vacant and wanted, of the sailings of steamers, and finally of houses to be let for summer months. There was a picture of one with a plain pleasant Queen Anne front looking on to a cobbled street. It was highly attractive, and below it she read that Miss Mapp sought a tenant for her house in Tilling, called Mallards, for the months of August and September. Seven bedrooms, four sitting-rooms, h. & c. and an old-world garden. At that precise psychological moment Daisy's prospects of being Queen Elizabeth became vastly rosier, for this house to let started an idea in Lucia's mind which instantly took precedence of other schemes. She must talk to Georgie about it this evening: till then it should simmer. Surely also the name of Miss Mapp aroused faint echoes of memory in her mind: she seemed to remember a large woman with a wide smile who had stayed at the Ambermere Arms a few years ago, and had been very agreeable but slightly superior. Georgie would probably remember her . . . But the sun had become extremely powerful, and Lucia picked up her *Times* and her book of poems and went indoors to the cool lattice-paned parlour where her piano stood. By it was a book-case with volumes of bound-up music, and she drew from it one which contained the duets over which Georgie and she used to be so gay and so industrious. These were Mozart quartettes arranged for four hands, delicious, rippling airs: it was months since she had touched them, or since the music-room had resounded to anything but the most sombre and pensive strains. Now she opened the book and put it on the music-rest. '*Uno, due, tre,*' she said to herself and began practising the treble part which was the more amusing to play.

Georgie saw the difference in her at once when he arrived for dinner that evening. She was sitting outside in Perdita's garden and for the first time hailed him as of old in brilliant Italian.

'*Buona sera, caro,*' she said. '*Come sta?*'

'*Molto bene,*' he answered, 'and what a *caldo* day. I've brought a little music across with me in case you felt inclined. Mozartino.'

'What a good idea! We will have *un po' di musica* afterwards, but I've got *tanto, tanto* to talk to you about. Come in: dinner will be ready. Any news?'

'Let me think,' he said. 'No, I don't think there's much. I've got rather a bruised shoulder where Daisy knighted me the other day –'

'Dear Daisy!' said Lucia. 'A little heavy-handed sometimes, don't you find? Not a light touch. She was in here this morning talking about the fête. She urged me to take part in it. What part do you think she suggested, Georgie? You'll never guess.'

'I never should have, if she hadn't told me,' he said. 'The most ludicrous thing I ever heard.'

Lucia sighed.

'I'm afraid not much more ludicrous than her being Queen Elizabeth,' she said. 'Daisy on a palfrey addressing her troops! Georgie dear, think of it! It sounds like that rather vulgar game called "Consequences". Daisy, I am afraid, has got tipsy with excitement at the thought of being a queen. She is running amok, and she will make a deplorable exhibition of herself, and Riseholme will become the laughing-stock of all those American tourists who come here in August to see our lovely Elizabethan village. The village will be all right, but what of Elizabeth? *Tacete un momento*, Georgie. *Le domestiche.*'

Georgie's Italian was rusty after so much disuse, but he managed to translate this sentence to himself, and unerringly inferred that Lucia did not want to pursue the subject while Grosvenor, the parlourmaid, and her colleague were in the room.

'*Sicuro*,' he said, and made haste to help himself to his fish. The *domestiche* thereupon left the room again, to be summoned back by the stroke of a silver bell in the shape of a pomander which nestled among pepper- and mustard-pots beside Lucia. Almost before the door had closed on their exit, Lucia began to speak again.

'Of course after poor Daisy's suggestion I shall take no part myself in this fête,' she said; 'and even if she besought me on her knees to play Queen Elizabeth, I could not dream of doing so. She cannot deprive me of what I may call a proper pride, and since she has thought good to offer me the role of Drake's wife, who, she hastened to explain, only came on for one moment and curtsied to her, and then retired into the ranks of men-at-arms and ladies-in-waiting again, my sense of dignity, of which I have still some small fragments left, would naturally prevent me from taking any part in the performance, even at the end of a barge-pole. But I am sorry for Daisy, since she knows her own deficiencies so little, and I shall mourn for Riseholme if the poor thing makes such a mess of the whole affair as she most indubitably will if she is left to organize it herself. That's all.'

It appeared, however, that there was a little more, for Lucia quickly finished her fish, and continued at once.

'So after what she said to me this morning, I cannot myself offer to help her, but if you like to do so, Georgie, you can tell her – not from me, mind, but from your own impression – that you think I should be perfectly willing to coach her and make the best I can of her as the embodiment of great Queen Bess. Something might be done with her. She is short, but so was the Queen. She has rather bad teeth, but that doesn't matter, for the Queen had the same. Again she is not quite a lady, but the Queen also had a marked strain of vulgarity and bourgeoisie. There was a coarse fibre in the Tudors, as I have always maintained. All this, dear Georgie, is to the good. If dear Daisy will only not try to look tall, and if she will smile a good deal, and behave naturally these are advantages, real advantages. But in spite of them Daisy will merely make herself and Riseholme silly if she does not manage to get hold of some semblance of dignity and queenship. Little gestures, little turnings of the head, little graciousnesses; all that acting means. I thought it out in those dear old days when we began to plan it, and, as I say, I shall be happy to give poor Daisy all the hints I can, if she will come and ask me to do so. But mind, Georgie, the suggestion must not come from me. You are at liberty to say that you think I possibly might help her, but nothing more than that. *Capite?*'

This Italian word, not understood of the people, came rather late, for already Lucia had struck the bell, as, unconsciously, she was emphasizing her generous proposal, and Grosvenor and her satellite had been in the room quite a long time. Concealment from *le domestiche* was therefore no longer possible. In fact both Georgie and Lucia had forgotten about the *domestiche* altogether.

'That's most kind of you, Lucia,' said Georgie. 'But you know what Daisy is. As obstinate as –'

'As a palfrey,' interrupted Lucia.

'Yes, quite. Certainly I'll tell her what you say, or rather suggest what you might say if she asked you to coach her, but I don't believe it will be any use. The whole fête has become an awful bore. There are six weeks yet before it's held, and she wants to practise knighting me every day, and has processions up and down her garden, and she gets all the tradesmen in the place to walk before her as halberdiers and sea-captains, when they ought to be attending to their businesses and chopping meat and milking cows. Everyone's sick of it. I wish you would take it over, and be Queen yourself. Oh, I forgot, I promised Daisy I wouldn't encourage you. Dear me, how awful!'

Lucia laughed, positively laughed. This was an enormous improvement on the pensive smiles.

'Not awful at all, *Georgino mio*,' she said. 'I can well imagine poor Daisy's feverish fear that I should try to save her from being ridiculous. She loves being ridiculous, dear thing; it's a complex with her – that wonderful new book of Freud's which I must read – and subconsciously she pines to be ridiculous on as large a scale as possible. But as for my taking it over, that's quite out of the question. To begin with, I don't suppose I shall be here. Twelfth of August isn't it? Grouse-shooting opens in Scotland and bear-baiting at Riseholme.'

'No, that was given up,' said Georgie. 'I opposed it throughout on the committee. I said that even if we could get a bear at all, it wouldn't be baited if it didn't get angry –'

Lucia interrupted.

'And that if it did get angry it would be awful,' she put in.

'Yes. How did you know I said that?' asked Georgie. 'Rather neat, wasn't it?'

'Very neat indeed, *caro*,' said she. 'I knew you said it because Daisy told me she had said it herself.'

'What a cheat!' said Georgie indignantly.

Lucia looked at him wistfully.

'Ah, you mustn't think hardly of poor dear Daisy,' she said. 'Cheat is too strong a word. Just a little envious, perhaps, of bright clever things that other people say, not being very quick herself.'

'Anyhow, I shall tell her that I know she has bagged my joke,' said he.

'My dear, not worth while. You'll make quantities of others. All so trivial, Georgie, not worth noticing. Beneath you.'

Lucia leaned forward with her elbows on the table, quite in the old braced way, instead of drooping.

'But we've got far more important things to talk about than Daisy's little pilferings,' she said. 'Where shall I begin?'

'From the beginning,' said Georgie greedily. He had not felt so keen about the affairs of daily life since Lucia had buried herself in her bereavement.

'Well, the real beginning was this morning,' she said, 'when I saw something in *The Times*.'

'More than I did,' said Georgie. 'Was it about Riseholme or the fête? Daisy said she was going to write a letter to *The Times* about it?'

'I must have missed that,' said Lucia, 'unless by any chance they didn't put it in. No, not about the fête, nor about Riseholme. Very much not about Riseholme. Georgie, do you remember a woman who stayed at the Ambermere Arms one summer called Miss Mapp?'

Georgie concentrated.

'I remember the name, because she was rather globular, like a map of the world,' he said. 'Oh, wait a moment: something's coming back to me. Large, with a great smile. Teeth.'

'Yes, that's the one,' cried Lucia. 'There's telepathy going on, Georgie. We're suggesting to each other . . . Rather like a hyena, a handsome hyena. Not hungry now but might be.'

'Yes. And talked about a place called Tilling, where she had a Queen Anne house. We rather despised her for that. Oh, yes, and she came to a garden-party of mine. And I know when it was, too. It was that summer when you invented saying "Au reservoir" instead of *"Au revoir"*. We all said it for about a week and then got tired of it. Miss Mapp came here just about then; because she picked it up at my garden-party. She stopped quite to the end, eating quantities of red-currant fool, and saying that she had inherited a recipe from her grandmother which she would send me. She did, too, and my cook said it was rubbish. Yes: it was the au reservoir year, because she said au reservoir to everyone as they left, and told me she would take it back to Tilling. That's the one. Why?'

'Georgie, your memory's marvellous,' said Lucia. 'Now about the advertisement I saw in *The Times*. Miss Mapp is letting her Queen Anne house called Mallards, h. & c. and old-world garden, for August and September. I want you to drive over with me to-morrow and see it. I think that very likely, if it's at all what I hope, I shall take it.'

'No!' cried Georgie. 'Why of course I'll drive there with you to-morrow. What fun! But it will be too awful if you go away for two months. What shall I do? First there's Olga not coming back for a year, and now you're thinking of going away, and there'll be nothing left for me except my croquet and being Drake.'

Lucia gave him one of those glances behind which lurked so much purpose, which no doubt would be disclosed at the proper time. The bees were astir once more in the hive, and presently they would stream out for swarmings or stingings or honey-harvesting . . . It was delightful to see her looking like that again.

'Georgie, I want change,' she said, 'and though I'm much touched at the idea of your missing me, I think I must have it. I want to get roused up again and shaken and made to tick. Change of air, change of scene, change of people. I don't suppose anyone alive has been more immersed than I in the spacious days of Elizabeth, or more devoted to Shakespearian tradition and environment – perhaps I ought to except Sir Sidney Lee, isn't it? – than I, but I want for the present anyhow to get away from it, especially when poor Daisy is intending to make this deplorable public parody of all that I have held sacred so long.'

Lucia swallowed three or four strawberries as if they had been pills and took a gulp of water.

'I don't think I could bear to be here for all the rehearsals,' she said; 'to look out from the rue and honeysuckle of my sweet garden and see her on her palfrey addressing her lieges of Riseholme, and making them walk in procession in front of her. It did occur to me this morning that I might intervene, take the part of the Queen myself, and make a pageant such as I had planned in those happy days, which would have done honour to the great age and credit to Riseholme, but it would spoil the dream of Daisy's life, and one must be kind. I wash my hands of it all, though of course I shall allow her to dress here, and the procession to start from my house. She wanted that, and she shall have it, but of course she must state on the programmes that the procession starts from Mrs Philip Lucas's house. It would be too much that the visitors, if there are any, should think that my beautiful Hurst belongs to Daisy. And, as I said, I shall be happy to coach her, and see if I can do anything with her. But I won't be here for the fête, and I must be somewhere and that's why I'm thinking of Tilling.'

They had moved into the music-room where the bust of Shakespeare stood among its vases of flowers, and the picture of Lucia by Tancred Sigismund, looking like a chessboard with some arms and legs and eyes sticking out of it, hung on the wall. There were Georgie's sketches there, and the piano was open, and *Beethoven's Days of Boyhood* was lying on the table with the paper-knife stuck between its leaves, and there was animation about the room once more.

Lucia seated herself in the chair that might so easily have come from Anne Hathaway's cottage, though there was no particular reason for supposing that it did.

'Georgie, I am beginning to feel alive again,' she said. 'Do you remember what wonderful Alfred says in *Maud*? "My life hath crept so long on a broken wing." That's what my life has been doing, but now I'm not going to creep any more. And just for the time, as I say, I'm "off" the age of Elizabeth, partly poor Daisy's fault, no doubt. But there were other ages, Georgie, the age of Pericles, for instance. Fancy sitting at Socrates's feet or Plato's, and hearing them talk while the sun set over Salamis or Pentelicus. I must rub up my Greek, Georgie. I used to know a little Greek at one time, and if I ever manage any tableaux again, we must have the death of Agamemnon. And then there's the age of Anne. What a wonderful time, Pope and Addison! So civilized, so cultivated. Their routs and their tea-parties and rapes of the lock. With all the greatness and splendour of the Elizabethan age, there must have been a certain coarseness and crudity about them. No one reveres it more than I, but it is a mistake to remain in the same waters too long. There comes a tide in the affairs of men, which, if you don't nip it in the bud, leads on to boredom.'

'My dear, is that yours?' said Georgie. 'And absolutely impromptu like that! You're too brilliant.'

It was not quite impromptu, for Lucia had thought of it in her bath. But it would be meticulous to explain that.

'Wicked of me, I'm afraid,' she said. 'But it expresses my feelings just now. I do want a change, and my happening to see this notice of Miss Mapp's in *The Times* seems a very remarkable coincidence. Almost as if it was sent: what they call a leading. Anyhow, you and I will drive over to Tilling to-morrow and see it. Let us make a jaunt of it, Georgie, for it's a long way, and stay the night at an inn there. Then we shall have plenty of time to see the place.'

This was rather a daring project, and Georgie was not quite sure if it was proper. But he knew himself well enough to be certain that no passionate impulse of his would cause Lucia to regret that she had made so intimate a proposal.

'That'll be the greatest fun,' he said. 'I shall take my painting things. I haven't sketched for weeks.'

'*Cattivo ragazzo!*' said Lucia. 'What have you been doing with yourself?'

'Nothing. There's been no one to play the piano with, and no one, who knows, to show my sketches to. Hours of croquet, just killing the time. Being Drake. How that fête bores me!'

''Oo poor thing!' said Lucia, using again the baby-talk in which she and Georgie used so often to indulge. 'But me's back again now, and me will scold 'oo vewy vewy much if 'oo does not do your lessons.'

'And me vewy glad to be scolded again,' said Georgie. 'Me idle boy! Dear me, how nice it all is!' he exclaimed enthusiastically.

The clock on the old oak dresser struck ten, and Lucia jumped up.

'Georgie, ten o'clock already,' she cried. 'How time has flown. Now I'll write out a telegram to be sent to Miss Mapp first thing to-morrow to say we'll get to Tilling in the afternoon, to see her house, and then ickle *musica*. There was a Mozart duet we used to play. We might wrestle with it again.'

She opened the book that stood on the piano. Luckily that was the very one Georgie had been practising this morning. (So too had Lucia.)

'That will be lovely,' he said. 'But you mustn't scold me if I play vewy badly. Months since I looked at it.'

'Me too,' said Lucia. 'Here we are! Shall I take the treble? It's a little easier for my poor fingers. Now: *Uno, due, tre!* Off we go!'

2

They arrived at Tilling in the middle of the afternoon, entering it from the long level road that ran across the reclaimed marshland to the west. Blue was the sky overhead, complete with larks and small white clouds; the town lay basking in the hot June sunshine, and its narrow streets abounded in red-brick houses with tiled roofs, that shouted Queen Anne and George I in Lucia's enraptured ears, and made Georgie's fingers itch for his sketching-tools.

'Dear Georgie, perfectly enchanting!' exclaimed Lucia. 'I declare I feel at home already. Look, there's another lovely house. We must just drive to the end of this street, and then we'll inquire where Mallards is. The people, too, I like their looks. Faces full of interest. It's as if they expected us.'

The car had stopped to allow a dray to turn into the High Street from a steep cobbled way leading to the top of the hill. On the pavement at the corner was standing quite a group of Tillingites: there was a clergyman, there was a little round bustling woman dressed in a purple frock covered with pink roses which looked as if they were made of chintz, there was a large military-looking man with a couple of golf-clubs in his hand, and there was a hatless girl with hair closely cropped, dressed in a fisherman's jersey and knickerbockers, who spat very neatly in the roadway.

'We must ask where the house is,' said Lucia, leaning out of the window of her Rolls-Royce. 'I wonder if you would be so good as to tell me –'

The clergyman sprang forward.

'It'll be Miss Mapp's house you're seeking,' he said in a broad Scotch accent. 'Straight up the street, to yon corner, and it's richt there is Mistress Mapp's house.'

The odd-looking girl gave a short hoot of laughter, and they

25

all stared at Lucia. The car turned with difficulty and danced slowly up the steep narrow street.

'Georgie, he told me where it was before I asked,' said Lucia. 'It must be known in Tilling that I was coming. What a strange accent that clergyman had! A little tipsy, do you think, or only Scotch? The others too! All most interesting and unusual. Gracious, here's an enormous car coming down. Can we pass, do you think?'

By means of both cars driving on to the pavement on each side of the cobbled roadway, the passage was effected, and Lucia caught sight of a large woman inside the other, who in spite of the heat of the day wore a magnificent sable cloak. A small man with a monocle sat eclipsed by her side. Then, with glimpses of more red-brick houses to right and left, the car stopped at the top of the street opposite a very dignified door. Straight in front where the street turned at a right angle, a room with a large bow-window faced them; this, though slightly separate from the house, seemed to belong to it. Georgie thought he saw a woman's face peering out between half-drawn curtains, but it whisked itself away.

'Georgie, a dream,' whispered Lucia, as they stood on the doorstep waiting for their ring to be answered. 'That wonderful chimney, do you see, all crooked. The church, the cobbles, the grass and dandelions growing in between them . . . Oh, is Miss Mapp in? Mrs Lucas. She expects me.'

They had hardly stepped inside, when Miss Mapp came hurrying in from a door in the direction of the bow-window where Georgie had thought he had seen a face peeping out.

'Dear Mrs Lucas,' she said. 'No need for introductions, which makes it all so happy, for how well I remember you at Riseholme, your lovely Riseholme. And Mr Pillson! Your wonderful garden-party! All so vivid still. Red-letter days! Fancy your having driven all this way to see my little cottage! Tea at once, Withers, please. In the garden-room. Such a long drive, but what a heavenly day for it. I got your telegram at breakfast-time this morning. I could have clapped my hands for joy at the thought of possibly having such a tenant as Mrs Lucas of Riseholme. But let us have a cup of tea first. Your chauffeur? Of course he will have his tea here, too. Withers: Mrs Lucas's chauffeur. Mind you take care of him.'

Miss Mapp took Lucia's cloak from her, and still keeping up an effortless flow of hospitable monologue, led them through a small panelled parlour which opened on to the garden. A flight of eight steps with a canopy of wistaria overhead led to the garden-room.

'My little plot,' said Miss Mapp. 'Very modest, as you see, three-quarters of an acre at the most, but well screened. My flower-beds: sweet roses, tortoiseshell butterflies. Rather a nice clematis. My Little Eden I call it, so small, but so well beloved.'

'Enchanting!' said Lucia, looking round the garden before mounting the steps up to the garden-room door. There was a very green and well-kept lawn, set in bright flower-beds. A trellis at one end separated it from a kitchen-garden beyond, and round the rest ran high brick walls, over which peered the roofs of other houses. In one of these walls was cut a curved archway with a della Robbia head above it.

'Shall we just pop across the lawn,' said Miss Mapp, pointing to this, 'and peep in there while Withers brings our tea? Just to stretch the – the limbs, Mrs Lucas, after your long drive. There's a wee little plot beyond there which is quite a pet of mine. And here's sweet Puss-Cat come to welcome my friends. Lamb! Love-bird!'

Love-bird's welcome was to dab rather crossly at the caressing hand which its mistress extended, and to trot away to ambush itself beneath some fine hollyhocks, where it regarded them with singular disfavour.

'My little secret garden,' continued Miss Mapp as they came to the archway. 'When I am in here and shut the door, I mustn't be disturbed for anything less than a telegram. A rule of the house: I am very strict about it. The tower of the church keeping watch, as I always say over my little nook, and taking care of me. Otherwise not overlooked at all. A little paved walk round it, you see, flower-beds, a pocket-handkerchief of a lawn, and in the middle a pillar with a bust of good Queen Anne. Picked it up in a shop here for a song. One of my lucky days.'

'Oh Georgie, isn't it too sweet?' cried Lucia. *'Un giardino segreto. Molto bello!'*

Miss Mapp gave a little purr of ecstasy.

'How lovely to be able to talk Italian like that,' she said. 'So pleased you like my little . . . *giardino segreto*, was it? Now shall we have our tea, for I'm sure you want refreshment, and see the house afterwards? Or would you prefer a little whisky and soda, Mr Pillson? I shan't be shocked. Major Benjy – I should say Major Flint – often prefers a small whisky and soda to tea on a hot day after his game of golf, when he pops in to see me and tell me all about it.'

The intense interest in humankind, so strenuously cultivated at Riseholme, obliterated for a moment Lucia's appreciation of the secret garden.

'I wonder if it was he whom we saw at the corner of the High Street,' she said. 'A big soldier-like man, with a couple of golf-clubs.'

'How you hit him off in a few words,' said Miss Mapp admiringly. 'That can be nobody else but Major Benjy. Going off no doubt by the steam-tram (most convenient, lands you close to the links) for a round of golf after tea. I told him it would be far too hot to play earlier. I said I should scold him if he was naughty and played after lunch. He served for many years in India. Hindustanee is quite a second language to him. Calls *"Quai-hai"* when he wants his breakfast. Volumes of wonderful diaries, which we all hope to see published some day. His house is next to mine down the street. Lots of tiger-skins. A rather impetuous bridge-player: quite wicked sometimes. You play bridge of course, Mrs Lucas. Plenty of that in Tilling. Some good players.'

They had strolled back over the lawn to the garden-room where Withers was laying tea. It was cool and spacious, one window was shaded with the big leaves of a fig-tree, through which, unseen, Miss Mapp so often peered out to see whether her gardener was idling. Over the big bow-window looking on to the street one curtain was half-drawn, a grand piano stood near it, book-cases half-lined the walls, and above them hung many water-colour sketches of the sort that proclaims a domestic origin. Their subjects also betrayed them, for there was one of the front of Miss Mapp's house, and one of the secret garden, another of the crooked chimney, and several of the church tower looking over the house-roofs on to Miss Mapp's lawn.

Though she continued to spray on her visitors a perpetual shower of flattering and agreeable trifles, Miss Mapp's inner attention was wrestling with the problem of how much a week, when it came to the delicate question of terms for the rent of her house, she should ask Lucia. The price had not been mentioned in her advertisement in *The Times*, and though she had told the local house-agent to name twelve guineas a week, Lucia was clearly more than delighted with what she had seen already, and it would be a senseless Quixotism to let her have the house for twelve, if she might, all the time, be willing to pay fifteen. Moreover, Miss Mapp (from behind the curtain where Georgie had seen her) was aware that Lucia had a Rolls-Royce car, so that a few additional guineas a week would probably be of no significance to her. Of course, if Lucia was not enthusiastic about the house as well as the garden, it might be unwise to ask fifteen, for she might think that a good deal, and would say something tiresome about letting Miss Mapp hear from her when she got safe away back to Riseholme, and then it was sure to be a refusal. But if she continued to rave and talk Italian about the house when she saw over it, fifteen guineas should be the price. And not a penny of that should Messrs Woolgar & Pipstow, the house-agents, get for commission, since Lucia had said definitely that she saw the advertisement in *The Times*. That was Miss Mapp's affair: nothing to do with Woolgar & Pipstow. Meantime she begged Georgie not to look at those water-colours on the walls.

'Little daubs of my own,' she said, most anxious that this should be known. 'I should sink into the ground with shame, dear Mr Pillson, if you looked at them, for I know what a great artist you are yourself. And Withers has brought us our tea . . . You like the one of my little *giardino segreto*? (I must remember that beautiful phrase.) How kind of you to say so! Perhaps it isn't quite so bad as the others, for the subject inspired me,

and it's so important, isn't it, to love your subject? Major
Benjy likes it too. Cream, Mrs Lucas? I see Withers has picked
some strawberries for us from my little plot. Such a year for
strawberries! And Major Benjy was chatting with friends I'll
be bound, when you passed him.'

'Yes, a clergyman,' said Lucia, 'who kindly directed us to
your house. In fact he seemed to know we were going there
before I said so, didn't he, Georgie? A broad Scotch accent.'

'Dear Padre!' said Miss Mapp. 'It's one of his little ways to
talk Scotch, though he came from Birmingham. A very good
bridge-player when he can spare time as he usually can. Reverend Kenneth Bartlett. Was there a teeny little thin woman with
him like a mouse? It would be his wife.'

'No, not thin, at all,' said Lucia thoroughly interested.
'Quite the other way round: in fact round. A purple coat and a
skirt covered with pink roses that looked as if they were made
of chintz.'

Miss Mapp nearly choked over her first sip of tea, but just
saved herself.

'I declare I'm quite frightened of you, Mrs Lucas,' she said.
'What an eye you've got. Dear Diva Plaistow, whom we're all
devoted to. Christened Godiva! Such a handicap! And they
were chintz roses, which she cut out of an old pair of curtains
and tacked them on. She's full of absurd delicious fancies like
that. Keeps us all in fits of laughter. Anyone else?'

'Yes, a girl with no hat and an Eton crop. She was dressed in
a fisherman's jersey and knickerbockers.'

Miss Mapp looked pensive.

'Quaint Irene,' she said. 'Irene Coles. Just a touch of uncon-
ventionality, which sometimes is very refreshing, but can be
rather embarrassing. Devoted to her art. She paints strange
pictures, men and women with no clothes on. One has to be
careful to knock when one goes to see quaint Irene in her
studio. But a great original.'

'And then when we turned up out of the High Street,' said
Georgie eagerly, 'we met another Rolls-Royce. I was afraid we
shouldn't be able to pass it.'

'So was I,' said Miss Mapp unintentionally betraying the

fact that she had been watching from the garden-room. 'That car is always up and down this street here.'

'A large woman in it,' said Lucia. 'Wrapped in sables on this broiling day. A little man beside her.'

'Mr and Mrs Wyse,' said Miss Mapp. 'Lately married. She was Mrs Poppit, MBE. Very worthy, and such a crashing snob.'

As soon as tea was over and the inhabitants of Tilling thus plucked and roasted, the tour of the house was made. There were charming little panelled parlours with big windows letting in a flood of air and sunshine and vases of fresh flowers on the tables. There was a broad staircase with shallow treads, and every moment Lucia became more and more enamoured of the plain well-shaped rooms. It all looked so white and comfortable, and, for one wanting a change, so different from the Hurst with its small latticed windows, its steep irregular stairs, its single steps, up or down, at the threshold of every room. People of the age of Anne seemed to have a much better idea of domestic convenience, and Lucia's Italian exclamations grew gratifyingly frequent. Into Miss Mapp's own bedroom she went alone with the owner, leaving Georgie on the landing outside, for delicacy would not permit his looking on the scene where Miss Mapp nightly disrobed herself, and the bed where she nightly disposed herself. Besides, it would be easier for Lucia to ask that important point-blank question of terms, and for herself to answer it if they were alone.

'I'm charmed with the house,' said Lucia. 'And what exactly, how much I mean, for a period of two months –'

'Fifteen guineas a week,' said Miss Mapp without pause. 'That would include the use of my piano. A sweet instrument by Blumenfelt.'

'I will take it for August and September,' said Lucia.

'And I'm sure I hope you'll be as pleased with it,' said Miss Mapp, 'as I'm sure I shall be with my tenant.'

A bright idea struck her, and she smiled more widely than ever.

'That would not include, of course, the wages of my gardener, such a nice steady man,' she said, 'or garden-produce.

Flowers for the house by all means, but not fruit or vegetables.'

At that moment Lucia, blinded by passion for Mallards,
Tilling and the Tillingites, would have willingly agreed to pay
the water-rate as well. If Miss Mapp had guessed that, she
would certainly have named this unusual condition.

Miss Mapp, as requested by Lucia, had engaged rooms for
her and Georgie at a pleasant hostelry near by, called the
Trader's Arms, and she accompanied them there with Lucia's
car following, like an empty carriage at a funeral, to see that all
was ready for them. There must have been some misunderstanding of the message, for Georgie found that a double
bedroom had been provided for them. Luckily Lucia had
lingered outside with Miss Mapp, looking at the view over the
marsh, and Georgie with embarrassed blushes explained at the
bureau that this would not do at all, and the palms of his hands
got cold and wet until the mistake was erased and remedied.
Then Miss Mapp left them and they went out to wander about
the town. But Mallards was the magnet for Lucia's enamoured
eye, and presently they stole back towards it. Many houses
apparently were to be let furnished in Tilling just now, and
Georgie too grew infected with the desire to have one. Riseholme would be very dismal without Lucia, for the moment
the fête was over he felt sure that an appalling reaction after
the excitement would settle on it; he might even miss being
knighted. He had sketched everything sketchable, there would
be nobody to play duets with, and the whole place would
stagnate again until Lucia's return, just as it had stagnated
during her impenetrable widowhood. Whereas here there were
innumerable subjects for his brush, and Lucia would be installed in Mallards with a Blumenfelt in the garden-room, and,
as was already obvious, a maelstrom of activities whirling in
her brain. Major Benjy interested her, so did quaint Irene and
the Padre, all the group, in fact, which had seen them drive up
with such pre-knowledge, so it seemed, of their destination.

The wall of Miss Mapp's garden, now known to them from
inside, ran up to where they now stood, regarding the front of
Mallards, and Georgie suddenly observed that just beside

them was the sweetest little gabled cottage with the board announcing that it was to be let furnished.

'Look, Lucia,' he said. 'How perfectly fascinating! If it wasn't for that blasted fête, I believe I should be tempted to take it, if I could get it for the couple of months when you are here.'

Lucia had been waiting just for that. She was intending to hint something of the sort before long unless he did, and had made up her mind to stand treat for a bottle of champagne at dinner, so that when they strolled about again afterwards, as she was quite determined to do, Georgie, adventurous with wine, might find the light of the late sunset glowing on Georgian fronts in the town and on the levels of the surrounding country, quite irresistible. But how wise to have waited, so that Georgie should make the suggestion himself.

'My dear, what a delicious idea!' she said. 'Are you really thinking of it? Heavenly for me to have a friend here instead of being planted among strangers. And certainly it is a darling little house. It doesn't seem to be occupied, no smoke from any of the chimneys. I think we might really peep in through the windows and get some idea of what it's like.'

They had to stand on tiptoe to do this, but by shading their eyes from the westerly sun they could get a very decent idea of the interior.

'This must be the dining-room,' said Georgie, peering in.

'A lovely open fireplace,' said Lucia. 'So cosy.'

They moved on sideways like crabs.

'A little hall,' said Lucia. 'Pretty staircase going up out of it.'

More crab-like movements.

'The sitting-room,' said Georgie. 'Quite charming, and if you press your nose close you can see out of the other window into a tiny garden beyond. The wooden paling must be that of your kitchen-garden.'

They stepped back into the street to get a better idea of the topography, and at this moment Miss Mapp looked out of the bow-window of her garden-room and saw them there. She was as intensely interested in this as they in the house.

'And three bedrooms I should think upstairs,' said Lucia, 'and two attics above. Heaps.'

'I shall go and see the agent to-morrow morning,' said Georgie. 'I can imagine myself being very comfortable there!'

They strolled off into the disused graveyard round the church. Lucia turned to have one more look at the front of Mallards, and Miss Mapp made a low swift curtsey, remaining down so that she disappeared completely.

'About that old fête,' said Georgie, 'I don't want to throw Daisy over, because she'll never get another Drake.'

'But you can go down there for the week,' said Lucia who had thought it all out, 'and come back as soon as it's over. You know how to be knighted by now. You needn't go to all those endless rehearsals. Georgie, look at that wonderful clock on the church.'

'Lovely,' said Georgie absently. 'I told Daisy I simply would not be knighted every day. I shall have no shoulder left.'

'And I think that must be the Town Hall,' said Lucia. 'Quite right about not being knighted so often. What a perfect sketch you could do of that.'

'Heaps of room for us all in the cottage,' said Georgie. 'I hope there's a servants' sitting-room.'

'They'll be in and out of Mallards all day,' said Lucia. 'A lovely servants' hall there.'

'If I can get it, I will,' said Georgie. 'I shall try to let my house at Riseholme, though I shall take my bibelots away. I've often had applications for it in other years. I hope Foljambe will like Tilling. She will make me miserable if she doesn't. Tepid water, fluff on my clothes.'

It was time to get back to their inn to unpack, but Georgie longed for one more look at his cottage, and Lucia for one at Mallards. Just as they turned the corner that brought them in sight of these there was thrust out of the window of Miss Mapp's garden-room a hand that waved a white handkerchief. It might have been samite.

'Georgie, what can that be?' whispered Lucia. 'It must be a signal of some sort. Or was it Miss Mapp waving us good night?'

'Not very likely,' said he. 'Let's wait one second.'

He had hardly spoken when Miss Coles, followed by the

breathless Mrs Plaistow hurried up the three steps leading to the front door of Mallards and entered.

'Diva and quaint Irene,' said Lucia. 'It must have been a signal.'

'It might be a coincidence,' said Georgie. To which puerile suggestion Lucia felt it was not worth while to reply.

Of course it was a signal and one long prearranged, for it was a matter of the deepest concern to several householders in Tilling, whether Miss Mapp found a tenant for Mallards, and she had promised Diva and quaint Irene to wave a handkerchief from the window of the garden-room at six o'clock precisely, by which hour it was reasonable to suppose that her visitors would have left her. These two ladies, who would be prowling about the street below, on the look-out, would then hasten to hear the best or the worst.

Their interest in the business was vivid, for if Miss Mapp succeeded in letting Mallards, she had promised to take Diva's house, Wasters, for two months at eight guineas a week (the house being much smaller) and Diva would take Irene's house, Taormina (smaller still) at five guineas a week, and Irene would take a four-roomed labourer's cottage (unnamed) just outside the town at two guineas a week, and the labourer, who, with his family would be harvesting in August and hop-picking in September, would live in some sort of shanty and pay no rent at all. Thus from top to bottom of this ladder of lessors and lessees they all scored, for they all received more than they paid, and all would enjoy the benefit of a change without the worry and expense of travel and hotels. Each of these ladies would wake in the morning in an unfamiliar room, would sit in unaccustomed chairs, read each other's books (and possibly letters), look at each other's pictures, imbibe all the stimulus of new surroundings, without the wrench of leaving Tilling at all. No true Tillingite was ever really happy away from her town; foreigners were very queer untrustworthy people, and if you did not like the food it was impossible to engage another cook for an hotel of which you were not the proprietor. Annually in the summer this sort of ladder of house-letting was set up in Tilling and was justly popular. But it all depended on a successful letting of Mallards, for if Elizabeth Mapp did not let Mallards, she would not take Diva's Wasters nor Diva Irene's Taormina.

Diva and Irene therefore hurried to the garden-room where they would hear their fate; Irene forging on ahead with that long masculine stride that easily kept pace with Major Benjy's, the short-legged Diva with that twinkle of feet that was like the scudding of a thrush over the lawn.

'Well, Mapp, what luck?' asked Irene.

Miss Mapp waited till Diva had shot in.

'I think I shall tease you both,' said she playfully with her widest smile.

'Oh, hurry up,' said Irene. 'I know perfectly well from your face that you've let it. Otherwise it would be all screwed up.'

Miss Mapp, though there was no question about her being the social queen of Tilling, sometimes felt that there were ugly Bolshevistic symptoms in the air, when quaint Irene spoke to her like that. And Irene had a dreadful gift of mimicry, which was a very low weapon, but formidable. It was always wise to be polite to mimics.

'Patience, a little patience, dear,' said Miss Mapp soothingly. 'If you know I've let it, why wait?'

'Because I should like a cocktail,' said Irene. 'If you'll just send for one, you can go on teasing.'

'Well, I've let it for August and September,' said Miss Mapp, preferring to abandon her teasing than give Irene a cocktail. 'And I'm lucky in my tenant. I never met a sweeter woman than dear Mrs Lucas.'

'Thank God,' said Diva, drawing up her chair to the still uncleared table. 'Give me a cup of tea, Elizabeth. I could eat nothing till I knew.'

'How much did you stick her for it?' asked Irene.

'Beg your pardon, dear?' asked Miss Mapp, who could not be expected to understand such a vulgar expression.

'What price did you screw her up to? What's she got to pay you?' said Irene impatiently. 'Damage: dibs.'

'She instantly closed with the price I suggested,' said Miss

Mapp. 'I'm not sure, quaint one, that anything beyond that is what might be called your business.'

'I disagree about that,' said the quaint one. 'There ought to be a sliding-scale. If you've made her pay through the nose, Diva ought to make you pay through the nose for her house, and I ought to make her pay through the nose for mine. Equality, Fraternity, Nosality.'

Miss Mapp bubbled with disarming laughter and rang the bell for Irene's cocktail, which might stop her pursuing this subject, for the sliding-scale of twelve, eight and five guineas a week had been the basis of previous calculations. Yet if Lucia so willingly consented to pay more, surely that was nobody's affair but that of the high contracting parties. Irene, soothed by the prospect of her cocktail, pursued the dangerous topic no further, but sat down at Miss Mapp's piano and picked out God Save the King, with one uncertain finger. Her cocktail arrived just as she finished it.

'Thank you, dear,' said Miss Mapp. 'Sweet music.'

'Cheerio!' said Irene. 'Are you charging Lucas anything extra for use of a fine old instrument?'

Miss Mapp was goaded into a direct and emphatic reply.

'No, darling, I am not,' she said, 'as you are so interested in matters that don't concern you.'

'Well, well, no offence meant,' said Irene. 'Thanks for the cocktail. Look in to-morrow between twelve and one at my studio, if you want to see far the greater part of a well-made man. I'll be off now to cook my supper. Au reservoir.'

Miss Mapp finished the few strawberries that Diva had spared and sighed.

'Our dear Irene has a very coarse side to her nature, Diva,' she said. 'No harm in her, but just common. Sad! Such a contrast to dear Mrs Lucas. So refined: scraps of Italian beautifully pronounced. And so delighted with everything.'

'Ought we to call on her?' asked Diva. 'Widow's mourning, you know.'

Miss Mapp considered this. One plan would be that she should take Lucia under her wing (provided she was willing to go there), another to let it be known in Tilling (if she wasn't) that she did not want to be called upon. That would set Tilling's back up, for if there was one thing it hated it was anything that (in spite of widow's weeds) might be interpreted into superiority. Though Lucia would only be two months in Tilling, Miss Mapp did not want her to be too popular on her own account, independently. She wanted . . . she wanted to have Lucia in her pocket, to take her by the hand and show her to Tilling, but to be in control. It all had to be thought out.

'I'll find out when she comes,' she said. 'I'll ask her, for indeed I feel quite an old friend already.'

'And who's the man?' asked Diva.

'Dear Mr Georgie Pillson. He entertained me so charmingly when I was at Riseholme for a night or two some years ago. They are staying at the Trader's Arms, and off again to-morrow.'

'What? Staying there together?' asked Diva.

Miss Mapp turned her head slightly aside as if to avoid some faint unpleasant smell.

'Diva dear,' she said. 'Old friends as we are, I should be sorry to have a mind like yours. Horrid. You've been reading too many novels. If widow's weeds are not a sufficient protection against such innuendoes, a baby girl in its christening-robe wouldn't be safe.'

'Gracious me, I made no innuendo,' said the astonished Diva. 'I only meant it was rather a daring thing to do. So it is. Anything more came from your mind, Elizabeth, not mine. I merely ask you not to put it on to me, and then say I'm horrid.'

Miss Mapp smiled her widest.

'Of course I accept your apology, dear Diva,' she said. 'Fully, without back-thought of any kind.'

'But I haven't apologized and I won't,' cried Diva. 'It's for you to do that.'

To those not acquainted with the usage of the ladies of Tilling, such bitter plain-speaking might seem to denote a serious friction between old friends. But neither Elizabeth nor Diva had any such feeling: they would both have been highly surprised if an impartial listener had imagined anything so absurd. Such breezes, even if they grew far stronger than this, were no more than bracing airs that disposed to energy, or exercises to keep the mind fit. No malice.

'Another cup of tea, dear?' said Miss Mapp earnestly.

That was so like her, thought Diva: that was Elizabeth all over. When logic and good feeling alike had produced an irresistible case against her, she swept it all away, and asked you if you would have some more cold tea or cold mutton, or whatever it was.

Diva gave up. She knew she was no match for her and had more tea.

'About our own affairs then,' she said, 'if that's all settled –'

'Yes, dear: so sweetly so harmoniously,' said Elizabeth.

Diva swallowed a regurgitation of resentment, and went on as if she had not been interrupted.

'– Mrs Lucas takes possession on the first of August,' she said. 'That's to say, you would like to get into Wasters that day.'

'Early that day, Diva, if you can manage it,' said Elizabeth, 'as I want to give my servants time to clean and tidy up. I would pop across in the morning, and my servants follow later. All so easy to manage.'

'Then there's another thing,' said Diva. 'Garden-produce. You're leaving yours, I suppose.'

Miss Mapp gave a little trill of laughter.

'I shan't be digging up all my potatoes and stripping the beans and the fruit-trees,' she said. 'And I thought – correct me if I am wrong – that my eight guineas a week for your little house included garden-produce, which is all that really concerns you and me. I think we agreed as to that.'

Miss Mapp leant forward with an air of imparting luscious secret information, as that was settled.

'Diva: something thrilling,' she said. 'I happened to be glancing out of my window just by chance a few minutes before I waved to you, and there were Mrs Lucas and Mr Pillson peering, positively peering into the windows of Mallards Cottage. I couldn't help wondering if Mr Pillson is thinking of taking it. They seemed to be so absorbed in it. It is to let, for Isabel Poppit has taken that little brown bungalow with no proper plumbing out by the golf-links.'

'Thrilling!' said Diva. 'There's a door in the paling between that little back-yard at Mallards Cottage and your garden. They could unlock it –'

She stopped, for this was a development of the trend of ideas for which neither of them had apologized.

'But even if Mr Pillson is thinking of taking it, what next, Elizabeth?' she asked.

Miss Mapp bent to kiss the roses in that beautiful vase of flowers which she had cut this morning in preparation for Lucia's visit.

'Nothing particular, dear,' she said. 'Just one of my madcap notions. You and I might take Mallards Cottage between us, if it appealed to you. Sweet Isabel is only asking four guineas a week for it. If Mr Pillson happens – it's only a speculation – to want it, we might ask, say, six. So cheap at six.'

Diva rose.

'Shan't touch it,' she said. 'What if Mr Pillson doesn't want it? A pure speculation.'

'Perhaps it would be rather risky,' said Miss Mapp. 'And now I come to think of it, possibly, possibly rather stealing a march – don't they call it – on my friends.'

'Oh, decidedly,' said Diva. 'No "possibly possibly" about it.'

Miss Mapp winced for a moment under this smart rap, and changed the subject.

'I shall have little more than a month, then, in my dear house,' she said, 'before I'm turned out of it. I must make the most of it, and have a quantity of little gaieties for you all.'

Georgie and Lucia had another long stroll through the town after their dinner. The great celestial signs behaved admirably; it was as if the spirit of Tilling had arranged that sun, moon and stars alike should put forth their utmost arts of advertisement on its behalf, for scarcely had the fires of sunset ceased to blaze on its red walls and roofs and to incarnadine the thin skeins of mist that hung over the marsh, than a large punctual moon arose in the east and executed the most wonderful nocturnes in black and silver.

They found a great grey Norman tower keeping watch seaward, an Edwardian gate with drum towers looking out landward: they found a belvedere platform built out on a steep slope to the east of the town, and the odour of the flowering hawthorns that grew there was wafted to them as they gazed at a lighthouse winking in the distance. In another street there stood Elizabethan cottages of brick and timber, very picturesque, but of no interest to those who were at home in Riseholme. Then there were human interests as well: quaint Irene was sitting, while the sunset flamed, on a camp-stool in the middle of a street, hatless and trousered, painting a most remarkable picture, apparently of the Day of Judgment, for the whole world was enveloped in fire. Just as they passed her her easel fell down, and in a loud angry voice she said, 'Damn the beastly thing.' Then they saw Diva scuttling along the High Street carrying a bird-cage. She called up to an open window very lamentably, 'Oh, Dr Dobbie, please! My canary's had a fit!' From another window, also open and unblinded, positively inviting scrutiny, there came a baritone voice singing 'Will ye no' come back again?' and there, sure enough, was the Padre from Birmingham, with the little grey mouse tinkling on the piano. They could not tear themselves away (indeed there was quite a lot of people listening) till the song was over, and then they stole up the street, at the head of which stood Mallards, and from the house just below it came a muffled cry of 'Quai-hai', and Lucia's lips formed the syllables 'Major Benjy. At his diaries.' They tiptoed on past Mallards itself, for the garden-room window was open wide, and so past Mallards Cottage, till they were out of sight.

'Georgie, entrancing,' said Lucia. 'They're all being themselves, and all so human and busy –'

'If I don't get Mallards Cottage,' said Georgie, 'I shall die.'

'But you must. You shall. Now it's time to go to bed, though I could wander about for ever. We must be up early in order to get to the house-agents' as soon as it's open. Woggles & Pickstick, isn't it?'

'Now you've confused me,' said Georgie. 'Rather like it, but not quite.'

They went upstairs to bed: their rooms were next each other, with a communicating door. There was a bolt on Georgie's side of it, and he went swiftly across to this and fastened it. Even as he did so, he heard a key quietly turned from the other side of it. He undressed with the stealth of a burglar prowling about a house, for somehow it was shy work that he and Lucia should be going to bed so close to each other; he brushed his teeth with infinite precaution and bent low over the basin to eject (spitting would be too noisy a word) the water with which he had rinsed his mouth, for it would never do to let a sound of these intimate manoeuvres penetrate next door. When half-undressed he remembered that the house-agents' name was Woolgar & Pipstow, and he longed to tap at Lucia's door and proclaim it, but the silence of the grave reigned next door, and perhaps Lucia was asleep already. Or was she, too, being as stealthy as he? Whichever it was (particularly if it was the last) he must not let a betrayal of his presence reach her.

He got into bed and clicked out his light. That could be done quite boldly: she might hear that, for it only betokened that all was over. Then, in spite of this long day in the open air, which should have conduced to drowsiness, he felt terribly wide-awake, for the subject which had intermittently occupied his mind, shadowing it with dim apprehension, ever since Pepino's death, presented itself in the most garish colours. For years, by a pretty Riseholme fantasy, it had always been supposed that he was the implacably Platonic but devout lover of Lucia: somehow that interesting fiction had grown up, and Lucia had certainly abetted it as well as himself. She had let it be supposed that he was, and that she accepted this chaste fervour. But now that her year of widowhood was nearly over, there loomed in front of Georgie the awful fact that very soon there could be no earthly reason why he should not claim his reward for these years of devotion and exchange his passionate celibacy for an even more passionate matrimony. It was an unnerving thought that he might have the right before the summer was over, to tap at some door of communication like that which he had so carefully bolted (and she locked) and say, 'May I come in, darling?' He felt that the words would freeze on his tongue before he could utter them.

Did Lucia expect him to ask to marry her? There was the crux and his imagination proceeded to crucify him upon it. They had posed for years as cherishing for each other a stainless devotion, but what if, with her, it had been no pose at all, but a dreadful reality? Had he been encouraging her to hope, by coming down to stay at this hotel in this very compromising manner? In his ghastly midnight musing, it seemed terribly likely. He had been very rash to come, and all this afternoon he had been pursuing his foolhardy career. He had said that life wasn't worth living if he could not get hold of Mallards Cottage, which was less than a stone's throw (even he could throw a stone as far as that) from the house she was to inhabit alone. Really it looked as if it was the proximity to her that made the Cottage so desirable. If she only knew how embarrassing her proximity had been just now when he prepared himself for bed! . . .

And Lucia always got what she wanted. There was a force about her he supposed (so different from poor Daisy's violent yappings and scufflings), which caused things to happen in the way she wished. He had fallen in with all her plans with a zest which it was only reasonable she should interpret favourably: only an hour or two ago he had solemnly affirmed that he must take Mallards Cottage, and the thing already was as good as done, for they were to breakfast to-morrow morning at eight, in order to be at the house-agents' (Woggle & Pipsqueak, was it? He had forgotten again), as soon as it opened. Things happened like that for her: she got what she wanted. 'But never, never,' thought Georgie, 'shall she get me. I couldn't possibly marry her, and I won't. I want to live quietly and do my sewing and my sketching, and see lots of Lucia, and play any amount of duets with her, but not marry her. Pray God, she doesn't want me to!'

Lucia was lying awake, too, next door, and if either of them could have known what the other was thinking about, they would both instantly have fallen into a refreshing sleep, instead of tossing and turning as they were doing. She, too, knew that for years she and Georgie had let it be taken for granted that they were mutually devoted, and had both about equally encouraged that impression. There had been an interlude, it is true, when that wonderful Olga Bracely had shone (like evening stars singing) over Riseholme, but she was to be absent from England for a year; besides she was married, and even if she had not been would certainly not have married Georgie. 'So we needn't consider Olga,' thought Lucia. 'It's all about Georgie and me. Dear Georgie: he was so terribly glad when I began to be myself again, and how he jumped at the plan of coming to Tilling and spending the night here! And how he froze on to the idea of taking Mallards Cottage as soon as he knew I had got Mallards! I'm afraid I've been encouraging him to hope. He knows that my year of widowhood is almost over, and on the very eve of its accomplishment, I take him off on this solitary expedition with me. Dear me: it looks as if I was positively asking for it. How perfectly horrible!'

Though it was quite dark, Lucia felt herself blushing.

'What on earth am I to do?' continued these disconcerting reflections. 'If he asks me to marry him, I must certainly refuse, for I couldn't do so: quite impossible. And then when I say no, he has every right to turn on me, and say I've been leading him on. I've been taking moonlight walks with him, I'm at this moment staying alone with him in an hotel. Oh dear! Oh dear!'

Lucia sat up in bed and listened. She longed to hear sounds of snoring from the next room, for that would show that the thought of the fulfilment of his long devotion was not keeping him awake, but there was no sound of any kind.

'I must do something about it to-morrow,' she said to herself, 'for if I allow things to go on like this, these two months here with him will be one series of agitating apprehensions. I must make it quite clear that I won't before he asks me. I can't bear to think of hurting Georgie, but it will hurt him less if I show him beforehand he's got no chance. Something about the beauty of a friendship untroubled with

passion. Something about the tranquillity that comes with age
... There's that eternal old church clock striking three. Surely
it must be fast.'

Lucia lay down again: at last she was getting sleepy.

'Mallards,' she said to herself. 'Quaint Irene ... Woffles and
... Georgie will know. Certainly Tilling is fascinating ...
Intriguing, too ... characters of strong individuality to be
dealt with ... A great variety, but I think I can manage them
... And what about Miss Mapp? ... Those wide grins ... We
shall see about that ...'

Lucia awoke herself from a doze by giving a loud snore, and
for one agonized moment thought it was Georgie, whom she
had hoped to hear snoring, in alarming proximity to herself.
That nightmare-spasm was quickly over, and she recognized
that it was she that had done it. After all her trouble in not
letting a sound of any sort penetrate through that door!

Georgie heard it. He was getting sleepy, too, in spite of his
uneasy musings, but he was just wide-awake enough to realize
where that noise had come from.

'And if she snores as well ...' he thought, and dozed off.

3

It was hardly nine o'clock in the morning when they set out for the house-agents', and the upper circles of Tilling were not yet fully astir. But there was a town-crier in a blue frock-coat ringing a bell in the High Street and proclaiming that the water-supply would be cut off that day from twelve noon till three in the afternoon. It was difficult to get to the house-agents', for the street where it was situated was being extensively excavated and they had chosen the wrong side of the road, and though they saw it opposite them when half-way down the street, a long detour must be made to reach it.

'But so characteristic, so charming,' said Lucia. 'Naturally there is a town-crier in Tilling, and naturally the streets are up. Do not be so impatient, Georgie. Ah, we can cross here.'

There was a further period of suspense.

'The occupier of Mallards Cottage,' said Mr Woolgar (or it might have been Mr Pipstow), 'is wanting to let for three months, July, August and September. I'm not so sure that she would entertain –'

'Then will you please ring her up,' interrupted Georgie, 'and say you've had a firm offer for two months.'

Mr Woolgar turned round a crank like that used for starting rather old-fashioned motor-cars, and when a bell rang, he gave a number, and got into communication with the brown bungalow without proper plumbing.

'Very sorry, sir,' he said, 'but Miss Poppit has gone out for her sun-bath among the sand-dunes. She usually takes about three hours if fine.'

'But we're leaving again this morning,' said Georgie. 'Can't her servant, or whoever it is, search the sand-dunes and ask her?'

'I'll inquire, sir,' said Mr Woolgar sympathetically. 'But

there are about two miles of sand-dunes, and she may be any-where.'

'Please inquire,' said Georgie.

There was an awful period, during which Mr Woolgar kept on saying 'Quite', 'Just so', 'I see', 'Yes, dear', with the most tedious monotony, in answer to unintelligible quacking noises from the other end.

'Quite impossible, I am afraid,' he said at length. 'Miss Poppit only keeps one servant, and she's got to look after the house. Besides, Miss Poppit likes . . . likes to be private when she's enjoying the sun.'

'But how tarsome,' said Georgie. 'What am I to do?'

'Well, sir, there's Miss Poppit's mother you might get hold of. She is Mrs Wyse now. Lately married. A beautiful wedding. The house you want is her property.'

'I know,' broke in Lucia 'Sables and a Rolls-Royce Mr Wyse has a monocle.'

'Ah, if you know the lady, madam, that will be all right, and I can give you her address. Starling Cottage, Porpoise Street. I will write it down for you.'

'Georgie, Porpoise Street!' whispered Lucia in an entranced aside *'Com' e bello e molto characteristuoso!'*

While this was being done, Diva suddenly blew in, beginning to speak before she was wholly inside the office. A short tempestuous interlude ensued.

'– morning, Mr Woolgar,' said Diva, 'and I've let Wasters, so you can cross it off your books: such a fine morning.'

'Indeed, madam,' said Mr Woolgar. 'Very satisfactory. And I hope your dear little canary is better.'

'Still alive and in less pain, thank you, pip,' said Diva, and plunged through the excavations outside sooner than waste time in going round.

Mr Woolgar apparently understood that 'pip' was not a salutation but a disease of canaries, and did not say 'So long' or 'Pip pip'. Calm returned again.

'I'll ring up Mrs Wyse to say you will call, madam,' he said. 'Let me see: what name? It has escaped me for the moment.'

As he had never known it, it was difficult to see how it could have escaped.

'Mrs Lucas and Mr Pillson,' said Lucia. 'Where is Porpoise Street?'

'Two minutes' walk from here, madam. As if you were going up to Mallards, but first turning to the right just short of it.'

'Many thanks,' said Lucia, 'I know Mallards.'

'The best house in Tilling, madam,' said Mr Woolgar, 'if you were wanting something larger than Mallards Cottage. It is on our books, too.'

The pride of proprietorship tempted Lucia for a moment to say 'I've got it already,' but she refrained. The complications which might have ensued, had she asked the price of it, were endless . . .

'A great many houses to let in Tilling,' she said.

'Yes, madam, a rare lot of letting goes on about this time of year,' said Mr Woolgar, 'but they're all snapped up very quickly. Many ladies in Tilling like a little change in the summer.'

It was impossible (since time was so precious, and Georgie so feverishly apprehensive, after this warning, that somebody else would secure Mallards Cottage before him, although the owner was safe in the sand-dunes for the present) to walk round the excavations in the street, and like Diva they made an intrepid short cut among gas-pipes and water-mains and braziers and bricks to the other side. A sad splash of mud hurled itself against Georgie's fawn-coloured trousers as he stepped in a puddle, which was very tarsome, but it was useless to attempt to brush it off till it was dry. As they went up the now familiar street towards Mallards they saw quaint Irene leaning out of the upper window of a small house, trying to take down a board that hung outside it which advertised that this house, too, was to let: the fact of her removing it seemed to indicate that from this moment it was to let no longer. Just as they passed, the board, which was painted in the most amazing colours, slipped from her hand and crashed on to the pavement, narrowly missing Diva who simultaneously popped out of the front door. It broke into splinters at her feet, and she gave a shrill cry of dismay. Then perceiving Irene she called up, 'No harm done, dear,' and Irene, in a voice of fury, cried, 'No harm? My beautiful board's broken to smithereens. Why didn't you catch it, silly?'

A snort of infinite contempt was the only proper reply, and Diva trundled swiftly away into the High Street again.

'But it's like a game of general post, Georgie,' said Lucia excitedly, 'and we're playing too. Are they all letting their houses to each other? Is that it?'

'I don't care whom they're letting them to,' said Georgie, 'so long as I get Mallards Cottage. Look at this tarsome mud on my trousers, and I daren't try to brush it off. What will Mrs Wyse think? Here's Porpoise Street anyhow, and there's Starling Cottage. Elizabethan again.'

The door was of old oak, without a handle, but with a bobbin in the strictest style, and there was a thickly patinated green bronze chain hanging close by, which Georgie rightly guessed to be the bell-pull, and so he pulled it. A large bronze bell, which he had not perceived, hanging close to his head, thereupon broke into a clamour that might have been heard not only in the house but all over Tilling, and startled him terribly. Then bobbins and gadgets were manipulated from within and they were shown into a room in which two very diverse tastes were clearly exhibited. Oak beams crossed the ceiling, oak beams made a criss-cross on the walls: there was a large open fireplace of grey Dutch bricks, and on each side of the grate an ingle-nook with a section of another oak beam to sit down upon. The windows were latticed and had antique levers for their control: there was a refectory-table and a spice-chest and some pewter mugs and a Bible-box and a coffin-stool. All this was one taste, and then came in another, for the room was full of beautiful objects of a very different sort. The refectory-table was covered with photographs in silver frames: one was of a man in uniform and many decorations signed 'Cecco Faraglione', another of a lady in Court dress with a quantity of plumes on her head signed 'Amelia Faraglione'. Another was of the King of Italy, another of a man in a frock-coat signed 'Wyse'. In front of these, rather prominent, was an open purple morocco box in which reposed the riband and cross of a Member of the Order of the British Empire. There was a cabinet of china in one corner with a malachite vase above it: there was an occasional table with a marble mosaic top: there was a satinwood piano draped with a piece of embroidery: a palm-tree: a green velvet sofa over the end of which lay a sable coat, and all these things spoke of post-Elizabethan refinements.

Long before Lucia had time to admire them all, there came a jingling from a door over which hung a curtain of reeds and beads, and Mrs Wyse entered.

'So sorry to keep you waiting, Mrs Lucas,' she said, 'but they thought I was in the garden, and I was in my boudoir all the time. And you must excuse my deshabille, just my shopping-frock. And Mr Pillson, isn't it? So pleased. Pray be seated.'

She heaved the sable coat off the end of the sofa on to the window-seat.

'We've just been to see the house-agent,' said Georgie in a great hurry, as he turned his muddied leg away from the light, 'and he told us that you might help me.'

'Most happy I am sure, if I can. Pray tell me,' said Mrs Wyse, in apparent unconsciousness of what she could possibly help him about.

'Mallards Cottage,' said Georgie. 'There seems to be no chance of getting hold of Miss Poppit and we've got to leave before she comes back from her sun-bath. I so much want to take it for August and September.'

Mrs Wyse made a little cooing sound.

'Dear Isabel!' she said. 'My daughter. Out in the sand-dunes all morning! What if a tramp came along? I say to her. But no use: she calls it the Browning Society, and she must not miss a meeting. So quick and clever! Browning, not the poet but the action of the sun.'

'Most amusing!' said Georgie. 'With regard to Mallards Cottage –'

'The little house is mine, as no doubt Mr Woolgar told you,' said Mrs Wyse, forgetting she had been in complete ignorance of these manoeuvres, 'but you must certainly come and see over it, before anything is settled . . . Ah, here is Mr Wyse. Algernon: Mrs Lucas and Mr Pillson. Mr Pillson wants to take Mallards Cottage.'

Lucia thought she had never seen anyone so perfectly correct and polite as Mr Wyse. He gave little bows and smiles to each as he spoke to them, and that in no condescending manner, nor yet cringingly, but as one consorting with his high-bred equals.

'From your beautiful Riseholme, I understand,' he said to Lucia (bowing to Riseholme as well). 'And we are all encouraging ourselves to hope that for two months at the least the charm of our picturesque do you not find it so? – little Tilling will give Susan and myself the inestimable pleasure of being your neighbours. We shall look forward to August with keen anticipation. Remind me, dear Susan, to tell Amelia what is in store for us.' He bowed to August, Susan and Amelia and continued – 'And now I hear that Mr Pillson' (he bowed to Georgie and observed the drying spot of mud) 'is "after" as they say, after Mallards Cottage. This will indeed be a summer for Tilling.'

Georgie, during this pretty speech which Mr Wyse delivered in the most finished manner, was taking notes of his costume and appearance. His clean-shaven face, with abundant grey hair brushed back from his forehead, was that of an actor who has seen his best days, but who has given command performances at Windsor. He wore a brown velveteen coat, a Byronic collar and a tie strictured with a cameo-ring: he wore brown knickerbockers and stockings to match, he wore neat golfing shoes. He looked as if he might be going to play golf, but somehow it didn't seem likely . . .

Georgie and Lucia made polite deprecating murmurs.

'I was telling Mr Pillson he must certainly see over it first,' said Mrs Wyse. 'There are the keys of the cottage in my boudoir, if you'll kindly fetch them, Algernon. And the Royce is at the door, I see, so if Mrs Lucas will allow us, we will all drive up there together, and show her and Mr Pillson what there is.'

While Algernon was gone, Mrs Wyse picked up the photograph signed Amelia Faraglione.

'You recognize, no doubt, the family likeness,' she said to Lucia. 'My husband's sister Amelia who married the Conte di Faraglione, of the old Neapolitan nobility. That is he.'

'Charming,' said Lucia. 'And so like Mr Wyse. And that Order? What is that?'

Mrs Wyse hastily shut the morocco box.

'So like servants to leave that about,' she said. 'But they seem proud of it. Graciously bestowed upon me. Member of the British Empire. Ah, here is Algernon with the keys. I was showing Mrs Lucas, dear, the photograph of Amelia. She recognized the likeness at once. Now let us all pack in. A warm morning, is it not? I don't think I shall need my furs.'

The total distance to be traversed was not more than a hundred yards, but Porpoise Street was very steep, and the cobbles which must be crossed very unpleasant to walk on, so Mrs Wyse explained. They had to wait some little while at the corner, twenty yards away from where they started, for a van was coming down the street from the direction of Mallards, and the Royce could not possibly pass it, and then they came under fire of the windows of Miss Mapp's garden-room. As usual at this hour she was sitting there with the morning paper in her hand in which she could immerse herself if anybody passed whom she did not wish to see, but was otherwise intent on the movements of the street.

Diva Plaistow had looked in with the news that she had seen Lucia and Georgie at the house-agents', and that her canary still lived. Miss Mapp professed her delight to hear about the canary, but was secretly distrustful of whether Diva had seen the visitors or not. Diva was so imaginative; to have seen a man and a woman who were strangers was quite enough to make her believe she had seen Them. Then the Royce heaved into sight round the corner below, and Miss Mapp became much excited.

'I think, Diva,' she said, 'that this is Mrs Lucas's beautiful car coming. Probably she is going to call on me about something she wants to know. If you sit at the piano you will see her as she gets out. Then we shall know whether you really –'

The car came slowly up, barked loudly and instead of stopping at the front door of Mallards, turned up the street in the direction of Mallards Cottage. Simultaneously Miss Mapp caught sight of that odious chauffeur of Mrs Wyse's. She could not see more than people's knees in the car itself (that was the one disadvantage of the garden-room window being so high above the street), but there were several pairs of them.

'No, it's only Susan's great lumbering bus,' she said, 'filling up the street as usual. Probably she has found out that Mrs Lucas is staying at the Trader's Arms, and has gone to leave cards. Such a woman to shove herself in where she's not wanted *I* never saw. Luckily I told Mrs Lucas what a dreadful snob she was.'

'A disappointment to you, dear, when you thought Mrs Lucas was coming to call,' said Diva. 'But I did see them this morning at Woolgar's and it's no use saying I didn't!'

Miss Mapp uttered a shrill cry.

'Diva, they've stopped at Mallards Cottage. They're getting out. Susan first – so like her – and ... it's Them. She's got hold of them somehow ... There's Mr Wyse with the keys, bowing ... They're going in ... I was right, then, when I saw them peering in through the windows yesterday. Mr Pillson's come to see the house, and the Wyses have got hold of them. You may wager they know by now about the Count and Countess Faradiddleone, and the Order of the British Empire. I really didn't think Mrs Lucas would be so easily taken in. However, it's no business of mine.'

There could not have been a better reason for Miss Mapp being violently interested in all that happened. Then an idea struck her and the agitated creases in her face faded out.

'Let us pop in to Mallards Cottage, Diva, while they are still there,' she said. 'I should hate to think that Mrs Lucas should get her ideas of the society she will meet in Tilling from poor common Susan. Probably they would like a little lunch before their long drive back to Riseholme.'

The inspection of the cottage had taken very little time. The main point in Georgie's mind was that Foljambe should be pleased, and there was an excellent bedroom for Foljambe, where she could sit when unoccupied. The rooms that concerned him had been viewed through the windows from the street the evening before. Consequently Miss Mapp had hardly had time to put on her garden-hat, and trip up the street with Diva, when the inspecting party came out.

'Sweet Susan!' she said. 'I saw your car go by . . . Dear Mrs Lucas, good morning, I just popped across – this is Mrs Plaistow – to see if you would not come and have an early lunch with me before you drive back to your lovely Riseholme. Any time would suit me, for I never have any breakfast. Twelve, half-past twelve? A little something?'

'So kind of you,' said Lucia, 'but Mrs Wyse has just asked us to lunch with her.'

'I see,' said Miss Mapp, grinning frightfully. 'Such a pity. I had hoped – but there it is.'

Clearly it was incumbent on sweet Susan to ask her to join them at this early lunch, but sweet Susan showed no signs of doing anything of the sort. Off went Lucia and Georgie to the Trader's Arms to pack their belongings and leave the rest of the morning free, and the Wyses, after vainly trying to persuade them to drive there in the Royce, got into it themselves and backed down the street till it could turn in the slightly wider space opposite Miss Mapp's garden-room. This took a long time, and she was not able to get to her own front door till the manoeuvre was executed, for as often as she tried to get round the front of the car it took a short run forward, and it threatened to squash her flat against the wall of her own room if she tried to squeeze round behind it.

But there were topics to gloat over which consoled her for this act of social piracy on the part of the Wyses. It was a noble stroke to have let Mallards for fifteen guineas a week without garden-produce, and an equally brilliant act to have got Diva's house for eight with garden-produce, for Diva had some remarkably fine plum-trees, the fruit of which would be ripe during her tenancy, not to mention apples: Miss Mapp foresaw a kitchen-cupboard the doors of which could not close because of the jam-pots within. Such reflections made a happy mental background as she hurried out into the town, for there were businesses to be transacted without delay. She first went to the house-agents' and had rather a job to convince Mr Woolgar that the letting of Mallards was due to her own advertisement in *The Times*, and that therefore she owed no commission to his firm, but her logic proved irresistible. Heated but refreshed by that encounter, she paid a visit to her greengrocer and made a pleasant arrangement for the sale of the produce of her own kitchen-garden at Mallards during the months of August and September. This errand brought her to the east end of the High Street, and there was Georgie already established on the belvedere busy sketching the Landgate, before he went to breakfast (as those Wyses always called lunch) in Porpoise Street. Miss Mapp did not yet know whether he had taken Mallards Cottage or not, and that must be instantly ascertained.

She leaned on the railing close beside him, and moved a little, rustled a little, till he looked up.

'Oh, Mr Pillson, how ashamed of myself I am!' she said. 'But I couldn't help taking a peep at your lovely little sketch. So rude of me: just like an inquisitive stranger in the street. Never meant to interrupt you, but to steal away again when I'd had my peep. Every moment's precious to you, I know, as you're off this afternoon after your early lunch. But I must ask you whether your hotel was comfortable. I should be miserable if I thought that I had recommended it, and that you didn't like it.'

'Very comfortable indeed, thank you,' said Georgie.

Miss Mapp sidled up to the bench where he sat.

'I will just perch here for a moment before I flit off again,' she said, 'if you'll promise not to take any notice of me, but go on with your picky, as if I was not here. How well you've got the perspective! I always sit here for two or three minutes every morning to feast my eyes on the beauty of the outlook. What a pity you can't stay longer here! You've only had a glimpse of our sweet Tilling.'

Georgie held up his drawing.

'Have I got the perspective right, do you think?' he said. 'Isn't it tarsome when you mean to make a road go downhill and it will go up instead?'

'No fear of that with you!' ejaculated Miss Mapp. 'If I was a little bolder I should ask you to send your drawing to our Art Society here. We have a little exhibition every summer. Could I persuade you?'

'I'm afraid I shan't be able to finish it this morning,' said Georgie.

'No chance then of your coming back?' she asked.

'In August, I hope,' said he, 'for I've taken Mallards Cottage for two months.'

'Oh, Mr Pillson, that is good news!' cried Miss Mapp. 'Lovely! All August and September. Fancy!'

'I've got to be away for a week in August,' said Georgie, 'as we've got an Elizabethan fête at Riseholme. I'm Francis Drake.'

That was a trove for Miss Mapp and must be published at once. She prepared to flit off.

'Oh how wonderful!' she said. 'Dear me, I can quite see you. The *Golden Hind*! Spanish treasure! All the pomp and majesty. I wonder if I could manage to pop down to see it. But I won't interrupt you any more. So pleased to think it's only au reservoir and not good-bye.'

She walked up the street again, bursting with her budget of news. Only the Wyses could possibly know that Georgie had taken Mallards Cottage, and nobody that he was going to impersonate Francis Drake . . . There was the Padre talking to Major Benjy, no doubt on his way to the steam-tram, and there were Diva and Irene a little farther on.

'Good morning, Padre: good morning, Major Benjy,' said she.

'Good morrow, Mistress Mapp,' said the Padre. 'An' hoo's the time o' day wi' ye? 'Tis said you've a fair tenant for yon Mallards.'

Miss Mapp fired off her news in a broadside.

'Indeed, I have, Padre,' she said. 'And there's Mallards Cottage, too, about which you won't have heard. Mr Pillson has taken that, though he won't be here all the time as he's playing Francis Drake in a fête at Riseholme for a week.'

Major Benjy was not in a very good temper. It was

porridge-morning with him, and his porridge had been burned. Miss Mapp already suspected something of the sort, for there had been loud angry sounds from within as she passed his dining-room window.

'That fellow whom I saw with Mrs Lucas this morning with a cape over his arm?' he said scornfully. 'Not much of a hand against the Spaniards, I should think. Ridiculous! Tea-parties with a lot of old cats more in his line. Pshaw!' And away he went to the tram, shovelling passengers off the pavement.

'Porridge burned, I expect,' said Miss Mapp, thoughtfully, 'though I couldn't say for certain. Morning, dear Irene. Another artist is coming to Tilling for August and September.'

'Hoot awa', woman,' said Irene, in recognition of the Padre's presence. 'I ken that fine, for Mistress Wyse told me half an hour agone.'

'But he'll be away for a week, though of course you know that, too,' said Miss Mapp, slightly nettled. 'Acting Francis Drake in a fête at Riseholme.'

Diva trundled up.

'I don't suppose you've heard, Elizabeth,' she said in a great hurry, 'that Mr Pillson has taken Mallards Cottage.'

Miss Mapp smiled pityingly.

'Quite correct, dear Diva,' she said. 'Mr Pillson told me himself hours ago. He's sketching the Landgate now – a sweet picky – and insisted that I should sit down and chat to him while he worked.'

'Lor! How you draw them all in, Mapp,' said quaint Irene. 'He looks a promising young man for his age, but it's time he had his hair dyed again. Grey at the roots.'

The Padre tore himself away; he had to hurry home and tell wee wifie.

'Aweel, I mustn't stand daffing here,' he said, 'I've got my sermon to think on.'

Miss Mapp did a little more shopping, hung about on the chance of seeing Lucia again, and then went back to Mallards, to attend to her sweet flowers. Some of the beds wanted weeding, and now as she busied herself with that useful work and eradicated groundsel, each plant as she tore it up and flung it into her basket might have been Mr and Mrs Wyse. It was very annoying that they had stuck their hooks (so the process represented itself to her vigorous imagery) into Lucia, for Miss Mapp had intended to have no one's hook there but her own. She wanted to run her, to sponsor her, to arrange little parties for her, and cause Lucia to arrange little parties at her dictation, and, while keeping her in her place, show her off to Tilling. Providence, or whatever less beneficent power ruled the world, had not been considerate of her clear right to do this, for it was she who had been put to the expense of advertising Mallards in *The Times*, and it was entirely owing to that that Lucia had come down here, and wound up that pleasant machine of sub-letting houses, so that everybody scored financially as well as got a change. But there was nothing to be done about that for the present: she must wait till Lucia arrived here, and then be both benignant and queenly. A very sweet woman, up till now, was her verdict, though possibly lacking in fine discernment, as witnessed by her having made friends with the Wyses. Then there was Georgie: she was equally well disposed towards him for the present, but he, like Lucia, must be good, and recognize that she was the arbiter of all things social in Tilling. If he behaved properly in that regard she would propose him as an honorary member of the Tilling Art Society, and, as member of the hanging committee, see that his work had a conspicuous place on the walls of the exhibition, but it was worth remembering (in case he was not good) that quaint Irene had said that his hair was dyed, and that Major Benjy thought that he would have been very little use against the Spaniards.

But thinking was hungry work, and weeding was dirty work, and she went indoors to wash her hands for lunch after this exciting morning.

There was a dreadful block in Porpoise Street when Lucia's car came to pick up her and Georgie after their breakfast at Starling Cottage, for Mrs Wyse's Royce was already drawn up there. The two purred and backed and advanced foot by foot, they sidled and stood on pavements meant for pedestrians, and it was not till Lucia's car had gone backwards again round the corner below Miss Mapp's garden-room, and Mrs Wyse's forward towards the High Street, that Lucia's could come to the door, and the way down Porpoise Street lie open for their departure to Riseholme. As long as they were in sight, Susan stood waving her hand, and Algernon bowing.

Often during the drive Lucia tried, but always in vain, to start the subject which had kept them both awake last night, and tell Georgie that never would she marry again, but the moment she got near the topic of friendship, or even wondered how long Mrs Plaistow had been a widow or whether Major Benjy would ever marry, Georgie saw a cow or a rainbow or something out of the window and violently directed attention to it. She could not quite make out what was going on in his mind. He shied away from such topics as friendship and widowhood, and she wondered if that was because he was not feeling quite ready yet, but was screwing himself up. If he only would let her develop those topics she could spare him the pain of a direct refusal, and thus soften the blow. But she had to give it up, determining, however, that when he came to dine with her that evening, she would not be silenced by his irrelevances: she would make it quite clear to him, before he embarked on his passionate declaration that, with all her affection for him, she could never marry him . . . Poor Georgie!

She dropped him at his house, and as soon as he had told Foljambe about his having taken the house at Tilling (for that must be done at once), he would come across to the Hurst.

'I hope she will like the idea,' said Georgie very gravely, as he got out, 'and there is an excellent room for her, isn't there?'

Foljambe opened the door to him.

'A pleasant outing, I hope, sir,' said she.

'Very indeed, thank you, Foljambe,' said Georgie. 'And I've got great news. Mrs Lucas has taken a house at Tilling for August and September, and so have I. Quite close to hers. You could throw a stone.'

'That'll be an agreeable change,' said Foljambe.

'I think you'll like it. A beautiful bedroom for you.'

'I'm sure I shall,' said Foljambe.

Georgie was immensely relieved, and, as he went gaily across to the Hurst, he quite forgot for the time about this menace of matrimony.

'She likes the idea,' he said before he had opened the gate into Perdita's garden, where Lucia was sitting.

'Georgie, the most wonderful thing,' cried she. 'Oh, Foljambe's pleased, is she? So glad. An excellent bedroom. I knew she would. But I've found a letter from Adele Brixton; you know, Lady Brixton who always goes to America when her husband comes to England, and the other way about, so that they only pass each other on the Atlantic; she wants to take the Hurst for three months. She came down here for a Sunday, don't you remember, and adored it. I instantly telephoned to say I would let it.'

'Well, that is luck for you,' said Georgie. 'But three months – what will you do for the third?'

'Georgie, I don't know, and I'm not going to think,' she said. 'Something will happen: it's sure to. My dear, it's perfect rapture to feel the great tide of life flowing again. How I'm going to set to work on all the old interests and the new ones as well. Tilling, the age of Anne, and I shall get a translation of Pope's *Iliad* and of Plato's *Symposium* till I can rub up my Greek again. I have been getting lazy, and I have been getting – let us go into dinner – narrow. I think you have been doing the same. We must open out, and receive new impressions, and adjust ourselves to new conditions!'

This last sentence startled Georgie very much, though it might only apply to Tilling, but Lucia did not seem to notice his faltering step as he followed her into the panelled dining-room with the refectory-table, below which it was so hard to adjust the feet with any comfort, owing to the foot-rail.

'Those people at Tilling,' she said, 'how interesting it will all be. They seemed to me very much alive, especially the women, who appear to have got their majors and their padres completely under their thumbs. Delicious, isn't it, to think of the new interchange of experience which awaits us. Here, nothing happens. Our dear Daisy gets a little rounder and Mrs Arbuthnot a little deafer. We're in a rut: Riseholme is in a rut. We want, both of us, to get out of it, and now we're going to. Fresh fields and pastures new, Georgie . . . Nothing on your mind, my dear? You were so *distrait* as we drove home.'

Some frightful revivification, thought poor Georgie, had happened to Lucia. It had been delightful, only a couple of days ago, to see her returning to her normal interests, but this repudiation of Riseholme and the craving for the *Iliad* and Tilling and the *Symposium* indicated an almost dangerous appetite for novelty. Or was it only that having bottled herself up for a year, it was natural that, the cork being now out, she should overflow in these ebullitions? She seemed to be lashing her tail, goading herself to some further revelation of her mental or spiritual needs. He shuddered at the thought of what further novelty might be popping out next. The question perhaps.

'I'm sorry I was *distrait*,' said he. 'Of course I was anxious about how Foljambe might take the idea of Tilling.'

Lucia struck the pomander, and it was a relief to Georgie to know that Grosvenor would at once glide in . . . She laughed and laid her hand affectionately on his.

'Georgie, dear, you are' – she took refuge in Italian as Grosvenor appeared – 'you are *una vecchia signorina*.' (That means 'old maid', thought Georgie.) 'Wider horizons, Georgie: that is what you want. Put the rest of the food on the table, Grosvenor, and we'll help ourselves. Coffee in the music-room when I ring.'

This was ghastly: Lucia, with all this talk of his being an old maid and needing to adapt himself to new conditions, was truly alarming. He almost wondered if she had been taking monkey-gland during her seclusion. Was she going to propose to him in the middle of dinner? Never, in all the years of his friendship with her, had he felt himself so strangely alien. But he was still the master of his fate (at least he hoped so), and it should not be that.

'Shall I give you some strawberry fool?' he asked miserably. Lucia did not seem to hear him.

'Georgie, we must have ickle talk, before I ring for coffee,' she said. 'How long have you and I been dear friends? Longer than either of us care to think.'

'But all so pleasant,' said Georgie, rubbing his cold moist hands on his napkin . . . He wondered if drowning was anything like this.

'My dear, what do the years matter, if they have only deepened and broadened our friendship? Happy years, Georgie, bringing their sheaves with them. That lovely scene in Esmondi; Winchester Cathedral! And now we're both getting on. You're rather alone in the world, and so am I, but people like us with this dear strong bond of friendship between us can look forward to old age – can't we? – without any qualms. Tranquillity comes with years, and that horrid thing which Freud calls sex is expunged. We must read some Freud, I think; I have read none at present. That was one of the things I wanted to say all the time that you would show me cows out of the window. Our friendship is just perfect as it is.'

Georgie's relief when he found that Foljambe liked the idea of Tilling was nothing, positively nothing, to the relief he felt now.

'My dear, how sweet of you to say that,' he said. 'I, too, find the quality of our friendship perfect in every way. Quite impossible, in fact, to think of – I mean, I quite agree with you. As you say, we're getting on in years, I mean I am. You're right a thousand times.'

Lucia saw the sunlit dawn of relief in Georgie's face, and though she had been quite sincere in hoping that he would not be terribly hurt when she hinted to him that he must give up all hopes of being more to her than he was, she had not quite expected this effulgence. It was as if instead of pronouncing his sentence, she had taken from him some secret burden of terrible anxiety. For the moment her own satisfaction at having brought this off without paining him was swallowed up in surprise that he was so far from being pained. Was it possible that all his concern to interest her in cows and rainbows was due to apprehension that she might be leading up, *via* the topics of friendship and marriage, to something exceedingly different from the disclosure which had evidently gratified him rather than the reverse?

She struck the pomander quite a sharp blow.

'Let us go and have our coffee then,' she said. 'It is lovely that we are of one mind. Lovely! And there's another subject we haven't spoken about at all. Miss Mapp. What do you make of Miss Mapp? There was a look in her eye when she heard we were going to lunch with Mrs Wyse that amazed me. She would have liked to bite her or scratch her. What did it mean? It was as if Mrs Wyse – she asked me to call her Susan by the way, but I'm not sure that I can manage it just yet without practising – as if Mrs Wyse had pocketed something of hers. Most extraordinary. I don't belong to Miss Mapp. Of course it's easy to see that she thinks herself very much superior to all the rest of Tilling. She says that all her friends are angels and lambs, and then just crabs them a little. *Marcate mie parole, Georgino!* I believe she wants to run me. I believe Tilling is seething with intrigue. But we shall see. How I hate all that sort of thing! We have had a touch of it now and then in Riseholme. As if it mattered who took the lead! We should aim at being equal citizens of a noble republic, where art and literature and all the manifold interests of the world are our concern. Now let us have a little music.'

Whatever might be the state of affairs at Tilling, Riseholme during this month of July boiled and seethed with excitements. It was just like old times, and all circled, as of old, round Lucia. She had taken the plunge; she had come back (though just now for so brief a space before her entering upon Mallards) into her native centrality. Gradually, and in increasing areas, grey and white and violet invaded the unrelieved black in which she had spent the year of her widowhood; one day she wore a white belt, another there were grey panels in her skirt, another her garden-hat had a violet riband on it. Even Georgie, who had a great eye for female attire, could not accurately follow these cumulative changes: he could not be sure whether she had worn a grey cloak before, or whether she had had white gloves in church last Sunday. Then, instead of letting her hair droop in slack and mournful braids over her ears, it resumed its old polished and corrugated appearance, and on her pale cheeks (ashen with grief) there bloomed a little brown rouge, which made her look as if she had been playing golf again, and her lips certainly were ruddier. It was all intensely exciting, a series of subtle changes at the end of which, by the middle of July, her epiphany in church without anything black about her, and with the bloom of her vitality quite restored, passed almost unremarked.

These outward and visible signs were duly representative of what had taken place within. Time, the great healer, had visited her sick-room, laid his hand on her languid brow, and the results were truly astonishing. Lucia became as good as new, or as good as old. Mrs Arbuthnot and her tall daughters, Piggy and Goosie, Georgie and Daisy and her husband, greedy Robert, Colonel Boucher and his wife, and the rest were all bidden to dinner at the Hurst once more, and sometimes Lucia played to them the slow movement of the 'Moonlight' Sonata, and sometimes she instructed them in such elements of Contract Bridge as she had mastered during the day. She sketched, she played the organ in church in the absence of the organist who had measles, she sang a solo, 'O for the wings of a Dove' when he recovered and the leading chorister got chicken-pox, she had lessons in book-binding at 'Ye Signe of ye Daffodille', she sat in Perdita's garden, not reading Shakespeare, but Pope's *Iliad*, and murmured half-forgotten fragments of Greek irregular verbs as she went to sleep. She had a plan for visiting Athens in the spring ('"the violet-crowned", is not that a lovely epithet, Georgie?') and in compliment to Queen Anne regaled her guests with rich thick chocolate. The hounds of spring were on the winter traces of her widowhood, and snapped up every fragment of it, and indeed spring seemed truly to have returned to her, so various and so multi-coloured were the blossoms that were unfolding. Never at all had Riseholme seen Lucia in finer artistic and intellectual fettle, and it was a long time since she had looked so gay. The world, or at any rate Riseholme, which at Riseholme came to much the same thing, had become her parish again.

Georgie, worked to the bone with playing duets, with consulting Foljambe as to questions of linen and plate (for it appeared that Isabel Poppit, in pursuance of the simple life, slept between blankets in the back-yard, and ate uncooked vegetables out of a wooden bowl like a dog), with learning Vanderbilt conventions, with taking part in Royal processions across the

Green, with packing his bibelots and sending them to the bank, with sketching, so that he might be in good form when he began to paint at Tilling with a view to exhibiting in the Art Society, wondered what was the true source of these stupendous activities of Lucia's, whether she was getting fit, getting in training, so to speak, for a campaign at Tilling. Somehow it seemed likely, for she would hardly think it worth while to run the affairs of Riseholme with such energy, when she was about to disappear from it for three months. Or was she intending to let Riseholme see how dreadfully flat everything would become when she left them? Very likely both these purposes were at work; it was like her to kill two birds with one stone. Indeed, she was perhaps killing three birds with one stone, for multifarious as were the interests in which she was engaged there was one, now looming large in Riseholme, namely the Elizabethan fête, of which she seemed strangely unconscious. Her drive, her powers of instilling her friends with her own fervour, never touched that: she did not seem to know that a fête was being contemplated at all, though now a day seldom passed without a procession of some sort crossing the green or a Morris-dance getting entangled with the choristers practising madrigals, or a crowd of soldiers and courtiers being assembled near the front entrance of the Ambermere Arms, while Daisy harangued them from a chair put on the top of a table, pausing occasionally because she forgot her words, or in order to allow them to throw up their hats and cry 'God Save the Queen's Grace', 'To hell with Spain', and other suitable ejaculations. Daisy, occasionally now in full dress, ruff and pearls and all, came across to the gate of the Hurst, to wait for the procession to join her, and Lucia sitting in Perdita's garden would talk to her about Tilling or the importance of being prudent if you were vulnerable at contract, apparently unaware that Daisy was dressed up at all. Once Lucia came out of the Ambermere Arms when Daisy was actually mounting the palfrey that drew the milk-cart for a full-dress rehearsal, and she seemed to be positively palfrey-blind. She merely said 'Don't forget that you and Robert are dining with me to-night. Half-past seven, so that we shall get a good evening's bridge,' and went on her way . . . Or she would be passing the pond on which the framework of the *Golden Hind* was already constructed, and on which Georgie was even then kneeling down to receive the accolade amid the faint cheers of Piggy and Goosie, and she just waved her hand to Georgie and said: '*Musica* after lunch, Georgie?' She made no sarcastic comments to anybody, and did not know that they were doing anything out of the ordinary.

Under this pointed unconsciousness of hers, a species of blight spread over the scheme to which Riseholme ought to have been devoting its most enthusiastic energies. The courtiers were late for rehearsals, they did not even remove their cigarettes when they bent to kiss the Queen's hand, Piggy and Goosie made steps of Morris-dances when they ought to have been holding up Elizabeth's train, and Georgie snatched up a cushion, when the accolade was imminent, to protect his shoulder. The choir-boys droned their way through madrigals, sucking peppermints, there was no life, no keenness about it all, because Lucia, who was used to inspire all Riseholme's activities, was unaware that anything was going on.

One morning when only a fortnight of July was still to run, Drake was engaged on his croquet-lawn tapping the balls about and trying to tame his white satin shoes which hurt terribly. From the garden next door came the familiar accents of the Queen's speech to her troops.

'And though I am only a weak woman,' declaimed Daisy who was determined to go through the speech without referring to her book. 'Though I am only a weak woman, a weak woman –' she repeated.

'Yet I have the heart of a Prince,' shouted Drake with the friendly intention of prompting her.

'Thank you, Georgie. Or ought it to be Princess, do you think?'

'No: Prince,' said Georgie.

'Prince,' cried Daisy. 'Though I am only a weak woman, yet I have the heart of a Prince . . . Let me see . . . Prince.'

There was silence.

'Georgie,' said Daisy in her ordinary voice. 'Do stop your croquet a minute and come to the paling. I want to talk.'

'I'm trying to get used to these shoes,' said Georgie. 'They hurt frightfully. I shall have to take them to Tilling and wear them there. Oh, I haven't told you, Lady Brixton came down yesterday evening –'

'I know that,' said Daisy.

'– and she thinks that her brother will take my house for a couple of months, as long as I don't leave any servants. He'll be here for the fête, if he does, so I wonder if you could put me up. How's Robert's cold?'

'Worse,' she said. 'I'm worse too. I can't remember half of what I knew by heart a week ago. Isn't there some memory-system?'

'Lots, I believe,' said Georgie. 'But it's rather late. They don't improve your memory all in a minute. I really think you had better read your speech to the troops, as if it was the opening of Parliament.'

'I won't,' said Daisy, taking off her ruff. 'I'll learn it if it costs me the last breath of blood in my body – I mean drop.'

'Well it will be very awkward if you forget it all,' said Georgie. 'We can't cheer nothing at all. Such a pity, because your voice carries perfectly now. I could hear you while I was breakfasting.'

'And it's not only that,' said Daisy. 'There's no life in the thing. It doesn't look as if it was happening.'

'No, that's true,' said Georgie. 'These tarsome shoes of mine are real enough, though!'

'I begin to think we ought to have had a producer,' said Daisy. 'But it was so much finer to do it all ourselves, like – like Oberammergau. Does Lucia ever say anything about it? I think it's too mean for words of her to take no interest in it.'

'Well, you must remember that you asked her only to be my wife,' said Georgie. 'Naturally she wouldn't like that.'

'She ought to help us instead of going about as if we were all invisible,' exclaimed Daisy.

'My dear, she did offer to help you. At least, I told you ages ago, that I felt sure she would if you asked her to.'

'I feel inclined to chuck the whole thing,' said Daisy.

'But you can't. Masses of tickets have been sold. And who's

to pay for the *Golden Hind* and the roast sheep and all the costumes?' asked Georgie. 'Not to mention all our trouble. Why not ask her to help, if you want her to?'

'Georgie, will you ask her?' said Daisy.

'Certainly not,' said Georgie very firmly. 'You've been managing it from the first. It's your show. If I were you, I would ask her at once. She'll be over here in a few minutes, as we're going to have a music. Pop in.'

A melodious cry of '*Georgino mio!*' resounded from the open window of Georgie's drawing-room, and he hobbled away down the garden walk. Ever since that beautiful understanding they had arrived at, that both of them shrank, as from a cup of hemlock, from the idea of marriage, they had talked Italian or baby-language to a surprising extent from mere lightness of heart.

'Me tummin',' he called. ''Oo very good girl, Lucia. 'Oo *molto punctuale.*'

(He was not sure about that last word, nor was Lucia, but she understood it.)

'*Georgino! Che curiose scalpe!*' said Lucia, leaning out of the window.

'Don't be so *cattiva*. They are *cattivo* enough,' said Georgie. 'But Drake did have shoes exactly like these.'

The mere mention of Drake naturally caused Lucia to talk about something else. She did not understand any allusion to Drake.

'Now for a good practice,' she said, as Georgie limped into the drawing-room. 'Foljambe beamed at me. How happy it all is! I hope you said you were at home to nobody. Let us begin at once. Can you manage the *sostenuto* pedal in those odd shoes?'

Foljambe entered.

'Mrs Quantock, sir,' she said.

'Daisy darling,' said Lucia effusively. 'Come to hear our little practice? We must play our best, Georgino.'

Daisy was still in queenly costume, except for the ruff. Lucia seemed as usual to be quite unconscious of it.

'Lucia, before you begin –' said Daisy.

'So much better than interrupting,' said Lucia. 'Thank you, dear. Yes?'

'About this fête. Oh, for gracious' sake don't go on seeming to know nothing about it. I tell you there is to be one. And it's all nohow. Can't you help us?'

Lucia sprang from the music-stool. She had been waiting for this moment, not impatiently, but ready for it if it came, as she knew it must, without any scheming on her part. She had been watching from Perdita's garden the straggling procession smoking cigarettes, the listless halberdiers not walking in step, the courtiers yawning in Her Majesty's face, the languor and the looseness arising from the lack of an inspiring mind. The scene on the *Golden Hind*, and that of Elizabeth's speech to her troops were equally familiar to her, for though she could not observe them from under her garden-hat close at hand, her husband had been fond of astronomy and there were telescopes great and small, which brought these scenes quite close. Moreover, she had that speech which poor Daisy found so elusive by heart. So easy to learn, just the sort of cheap bombast that Elizabeth would indulge in: she had found it in a small history of England, and had committed it to memory, just in case . . .

'But I'll willingly help you, dear Daisy,' she said. 'I seem to remember you told me something about it. You as Queen Elizabeth, was it not, a roast sheep on the *Golden Hind*, a speech to the troops, Morris-dances, bear-baiting, no, not bear-baiting. Isn't it all going beautifully?'

'No! It isn't,' said Daisy in a lamentable voice. 'I want you to help us, will you? It's all like dough.'

Great was Lucia. There was no rubbing in: there was no hesitation, there was nothing but helpful sunny cordiality in response to this SOS.

'How you all work me!' she said, 'but I'll try to help you if I can. Georgie, we must put off our practice, and get to grips with all this, if the fête is to be a credit to Riseholme. *Addio, caro Mozartino* for the present. Now begin, Daisy, and tell me all the trouble.'

For the next week Mozartino and the *Symposium* and contract bridge were non-existent and rehearsals went on all day.

Lucia demonstrated to Daisy how to make her first appearance, and, when the trumpeters blew a fanfare, she came out of the door of the Hurst, and without the slightest hurry majestically marched down the crazy pavement. She did not fumble at the gate as Daisy always did, but with a swift imperious nod to Robert Quantock, which made him pause in the middle of a sneeze, she caused him to fly forward, open it, and kneel as she passed through. She made a wonderful curtsey to her lieges and motioned them to close up in front of her. And all this was done in the clothes of to-day, without a ruff or a pearl to help her.

'Something like that, do you think, dear Daisy, for the start of the procession?' she said to her. 'Will you try it like that and see how it goes? And a little more briskness, gentlemen, from the halberdiers. Would you form in front of me now, while Mrs Quantock goes into the house . . . Ah, that has more snap, hasn't it? Excellent. Quite like guardsmen. Piggy and Goosie, my dears, you must remember that you are Elizabethan Countesses. Very stately, please, and Countesses never giggle. Sweep two low curtsies, and while still down pick up the Queen's train. You opened the gate very properly, Robert. Very nice indeed. Now may we have that all over again. Queen, please,' she called to Daisy.

Daisy came out of the house in all the panoply of Majesty, and with the idea of not hurrying came so slowly that her progress resembled that of a queen following a hearse. ('A little quicker, dear,' called Lucia encouragingly. 'We're all ready.') Then she tripped over a piece of loose crazy pavement. Then she sneezed, for she had certainly caught Robert's cold. Then she forgot to bow to her lieges, until they had closed up in procession in front of her, and then bobbed to their backs.

'Hey ho, nonny, nonny,' sang Lucia to start the chorus. 'Off we go! Right, left – I beg your pardon, how stupid of me – Left, right. Crescendo, choir. Sing out, please. We're being Merrie England. Capital!'

Lucia walked by the side of the procession across the green, beating time with her parasol, full of encouragement and enthusiasm. Sometimes she ran on in front and observed their progress, sometimes she stood still to watch them go by.

'Open out a little, halberdiers,' she cried, 'so that we can get a glimpse of the Queen from in front. Hey nonny! Hold that top G, choir-boys! Queen, dear, don't attempt to keep step with the halberdiers. Much more royal to walk as you choose. The train a little higher, Piggy and Goosie. Hey nonny, nonny HEY!'

She looked round as they got near the *Golden Hind*, to see if the cooks were basting the bolster that did duty for the sheep, and that Drake's sailors were dancing their hornpipes.

'Dance, please, sailors,' she shrieked. 'Go on basting, cooks, until the procession stops, and then begins the chorus of sailors on the last "nonny Hey". Cooks must join in, too, or we shan't get enough body of sound. Open out, halberdiers, leave plenty of room for the Queen to come between you. Slowly, Elizabeth! "When the storm winds blow and the surges sweep." Louder! Are you ready, Georgie? No; don't come off the *Golden Hind*. You receive the Queen on the deck. A little faster, Elizabeth, the chorus will be over before you get here.'

Lucia clapped her hands.

'A moment, please,' she said. 'A wonderful scene. But just one suggestion. May I be Queen for a minute and show you the effect I want to get, dear Daisy? Let us go back, procession, please, twenty yards. Halberdiers still walking in front of Queen. Sailors' chorus all over again. Off we go! Now, halberdiers, open out. Half right and left turn respectively. Two more steps and halt, making an avenue.'

It was perfectly timed. Lucia moved forward up the avenue of halberdiers, and just as the last 'Yo ho' was yelled by cooks, courtiers and sailors, she stepped with indescribable majesty on to the deck of the *Golden Hind*. She stood there a moment quite still, and whispered to Georgie, 'Kneel and kiss my hand, Georgie. Now, everybody together! "God save the Queen". "Hurrah". Hats in the air. Louder, louder! Now die away! There!'

Lucia had been waving her own hat, and shrilly cheering herself, and now she again clapped her hands for attention, as she scrutinized the deck of the *Golden Hind*.

'But I don't see Drake's wife,' she said. 'Drake's wife, please.'

Drake's wife was certainly missing. She was also the grocer's wife, and as she had only to come forward for one moment, curtsey and disappear, she was rather slack at her attendance of rehearsals.

'It doesn't matter,' said Lucia. 'I'll take Drake's wife, just for this rehearsal. Now we must have that over again. It's one of the most important moments, this Queen's entry on to the *Golden Hind*. We must make it rich in romance, in majesty, in spaciousness. Will the procession, please, go back, and do it over again?'

This time poor Daisy was much too early. She got to the *Golden Hind* long before the cooks and the chorus were ready for her. But there was a murmur of applause when Mrs Drake (so soon to be Lady Drake) ran forward and threw herself at the Queen's feet in an ecstasy of loyalty, and having kissed her hand walked backwards from the Presence with head bent low, as if in adoration.

'Now step to the Queen's left, Georgie,' said Lucia, 'and take her left hand, holding it high and lead her to the banquet. Daisy dear, you *must* mind your train. Piggy and Goosie will lay it down as you reach the deck, and then you must look after it yourself. If you're not careful you'll tread on it and fall into the Thames. You've got to move so that it follows you when you turn round.'

'May I kick it?' asked Daisy.

'No, it can be done without. You must practise that.'

The whole company now, sailors, soldiers, courtiers and all were eager as dogs are to be taken out for a walk by their mistress, and Lucia reluctantly consented to come and look at the scene of the review at Tilbury. Possibly some little idea, she diffidently said, might occur to her; fresh eyes sometimes saw something, and if they all really wanted her she was at their disposal. So off they went to the rendezvous in front of the Ambermere Arms, and the fresh eyes perceived that according to the present grouping of soldiers and populace no spectator would see anything of the Queen at all. So that was rectified, and the mob was drilled to run into its proper places with due eagerness, and Lucia sat where the front row of spectators would be to hear the great speech. When it was over she warmly congratulated the Queen.

'Oh, I'm so glad you liked it,' said the Queen. 'Is there anything that strikes you?'

Lucia sat for a while in pensive silence.

'Just one or two little tiny things, dear,' she said, thoughtfully. 'I couldn't hear very well. I wondered sometimes what the mob was cheering about. And would it perhaps be safer to read the speech? There was a good deal of prompting that was quite audible. Of course there are disadvantages in reading it. It won't seem so spontaneous and inspiring if you consult a paper all the time. Still, I dare say you'll get it quite by heart before the time comes. Indeed, the only real criticism I have to make is about your gestures, your movements. Not quite, quite majestic enough, not inspiring enough. Too much as if you were whisking flies away. More breadth!'

Lucia sighed, she appeared to be lost in meditation.

'What kind of breadth?' asked Daisy.

'So difficult to explain,' said Lucia. 'You must get more variety, more force, both in your gestures and your voice. You must be fierce sometimes, the great foe of Spain, you must be tender, the mother of your people. You must be a Tudor. The daughter of that glorious cad, King Hal. Coarse and kingly. Shall I show you for a moment the sort of thing I mean? So much easier to show than to explain.'

Daisy's heart sank: she was full of vague apprehensions. But having asked for help, she could hardly refuse this generous granting of it, for indeed Lucia was giving up her whole morning.

'Very good of you,' she said.

'Lend me your copy of the speech, then,' said Lucia, 'and might I borrow your ruff, just to encourage myself. Now let me read through the speech to myself. Yes . . . yes . . . crescendo, and flare up then . . . pause again; a touch of tenderness . . . Well, as you insist on it I'll try to show you what I mean. Terribly nervous, though.'

Lucia advanced and spoke in the most ingratiating tones to her army and the mob.

'Please have patience with me, ladies and gentlemen,' she said, 'while I go through the speech once more. Wonderful words, aren't they? I know I shan't do them justice. Let me see: the palfrey with the Queen will come out from the garden of the Ambermere Arms, will it not? Then will the whole mob, please, hurry into the garden and then come out romping and cheering and that sort of thing in front of me. When I get to where the table is, that is to say, where the palfrey will stand as I make my speech, some of the mob must fall back, and the rest sit on the grass, so that the spectators may see. Now, please.'

Lucia stalked in from the garden, joining the mob now and then to show them how to gambol, and nimbly vaulted (thanks to callisthenics) on to the table on which was the chair where she sat on horseback.

Then with a great sweep of her arm she began to speak. The copy of the speech which she carried flew out of her hand, but that made no difference, for she had it all by heart, and without pause, except for the bursts of cheering from the mob, when she pointed at them, she declaimed it all, her voice now rising, now falling, now full of fire, now tender and motherly. Then she got down from the table, and passed along the line of her troops, beckoned to the mob – which in the previous scene had been cooks and sailors and all sorts of things – to close up behind her with shouts and cheers and gambollings, and went off down the garden path again.

'That sort of thing, dear Daisy, don't you think?' she said to the Queen, returning her ruff. 'So crude and awkwardly done I know, but perhaps that may be the way to put a little life into it. Ah, there's your copy of the speech. Quite familiar to me, I found. I dare say I learned it when I was at school. Now, I really must be off. I wish I could think that I had been any use.'

Next morning Lucia was too busy to superintend the re-hearsal: she was sure that Daisy would manage it beautifully, and she was indeed very busy watching through a field-glass in the music-room the muddled and anaemic performance. The halberdiers strolled along with their hands in their pockets.

Piggy and Goosie sat down on the grass, and Daisy knew less of her speech than ever. The collective consciousness of Riseholme began to be aware that nothing could be done without Lucia, and conspiratorial groups conferred stealthily, dispersing or dropping their voices as Queen Elizabeth approached and forming again when she had gone by. The choir which had sung so convincingly when Lucia was there with her loud 'Hey nonny nonny', never bothered about the high G at all, but simply left it out; the young Elizabethans who had gambolled like intoxicated lambkins under her stimulating eye sat down and chewed daisies; the cooks never attempted to baste the bolster; and the Queen's speech to her troops was received with the most respectful tranquillity.

Georgie, in Drake's shoes which were becoming less agonizing with use, lunched with Colonel and Mrs Boucher. Mrs Boucher was practically the only Riseholmite who was taking no part in the fête, because her locomotion was confined to the wheels of a bath-chair. But she attended every rehearsal and had views which were as strong as her voice.

'You may like it or not,' she said very emphatically, 'but the only person who can pull you through is Lucia.'

'Nobody can pull poor Daisy through,' said Georgie. 'Hopeless!'

'That's what I mean,' said she. 'If Lucia isn't the Queen, I say give it all up. Poor Daisy's bitten off, if you won't misunderstand me, as we're all such friends of hers, more than she can chew. My kitchen-cat, and I don't care who knows it, would make a better Queen.'

'But Lucia's going off to Tilling, next week,' said Georgie. 'She won't be here even.'

'Well, beg and implore her not to desert Riseholme,' said Mrs Boucher. 'Why, everybody was muttering about it this morning, army and navy and all. It was like a revolution. There was Mrs Arbuthnot; she said to me, "Oh dear, oh dear, it will never do at all," and there was poor Daisy standing close beside her; and we all turned red. Most awkward. And it's up to you, Georgie, to go down on your knees to Lucia and say "Save Riseholme!" There!'

'But she refused to have anything to do with it, after Daisy asked her to be my wife,' said Georgie Drake.

'Naturally she would be most indignant. An insult. But you and Daisy must implore her. Perhaps she could go to Tilling and settle herself in and then come back for the fête, for she doesn't need any rehearsals. She could act every part herself if she could be a crowd.'

'Marvellous woman!' said Colonel Boucher. 'Every word of the Queen's speech by heart, singing with the choir, basting with the cooks, dancing with the sailors. That's what I call instinct, eh? You'd have thought she had been studying it all the time. I agree with my wife, Georgie. The difficulty is Daisy. *Would* she give it up?'

Georgie brightened.

'She did say that she felt inclined to chuck the whole thing, a few days ago,' he said.

'There you are, then,' said Mrs Boucher. 'Remind her of what she said. You and she go to Lucia before you waste time over another rehearsal without her, and implore her. Implore! I shouldn't a bit wonder if she said yes. Indeed, if you ask me, I believe that she's been keeping out of it all until you saw you couldn't do without her. Then she came to help at a rehearsal, and you all saw what you could do when she was there. Why, I burst out cheering myself when she said she had the heart of a Prince. Then she retires again as she did this morning, and more than ever you see you can't do without her. I say she's waiting to be asked. It would be like her, you know.'

That was an illuminating thought; it certainly seemed tremendously like Lucia at her very best.

'I believe you're right. She's cleverer than all of us put together,' said Georgie. 'I shall go over to Daisy at once and sound her. Thank God, my shoes are better.'

It was a gloomy queen that Georgie found, a Queen of Sheba with no spirit left in her, but only a calmness of despair.

'It went worse than ever this morning,' she remarked. 'And I dare say we've not touched bottom yet. Georgie, what is to be done?'

It was more delicate to give Daisy the chance of abdicating herself.

'I'm sure I don't know,' said he. 'But something's got to be done. I wish I could think what.'

Daisy was rent with pangs of jealousy and of consciousness of her supreme impotence. She took half a glass of port, which her regime told her was deadly poison.

'Georgie! Do you think there's the slightest chance of getting Lucia to be the Queen and managing the whole affair?' she asked quaveringly.

'We might try,' said Georgie. 'The Bouchers are for it, and everybody else as well, I think.'

'Well, come quick then, or I may repent,' said Daisy.

Lucia had seen them coming, and sat down at her piano. She had not time to open her music, and so began the first movement of the 'Moonlight' Sonata.

'Ah, how nice!' she said. 'Georgie, I'm going to practise all afternoon. Poor fingers so rusty! And did you have a lovely rehearsal this morning? Speech going well, Daisy? I'm sure it is.'

'Couldn't remember a word,' said Daisy. 'Lucia, we all want to turn the whole thing over to you, Queen and all. Will you –'

'Please, Lucia,' said Georgie.

Lucia looked from one to the other in amazement.

'But, dear things, how can I?' she said. 'I shan't be here to begin with, I shall be at Tilling. And then all the trouble you've been taking, Daisy. I couldn't. Impossible. Cruel.'

'We can't do it at all without you,' said Daisy firmly. 'So that's impossible too. Please, Lucia.'

Lucia seemed quite bewildered by these earnest entreaties.

'Can't you come back for the fête?' said Georgie. 'Rehearse all day, every day, till the end of the month. Then go to Tilling, and you and I will return just for the week of the fête.'

Lucia seemed to be experiencing a dreadful struggle with herself.

'Dear Georgie, dear Daisy, you're asking a great sacrifice of me,' she said. 'I had planned my days here so carefully. My music, my Dante: all my lessons! I shall have to give them all up, you know, if I'm to get this fête into any sort of shape. No time for anything else.'

A miserable two-part fugue of 'Please, Lucia. It's the only chance. We can't do it unless you're Queen,' suddenly burst into the happy strains of 'It is good of you. Oh, thank you, Lucia,' and the day was won.

Instantly she became extremely business-like.

'No time to waste then,' she said. 'Let us have a full rehearsal at three, and after that I'll take the Morris-dancers and the halberdiers. You and Georgie must be my lieutenants, dear Daisy. We shall all have to pull together. By the way, what will you be now?'

'Whatever you like,' said Daisy recklessly.

Lucia looked at her fixedly with that gimlet eye, as if appraising, at their highest, her possibilities.

'Then let us see, dear Daisy,' she said, 'what you can make of Drake's wife. Quite a short part, I know, but so important. You have to get into that one moment all the loyalty, all the devotion of the women of England to the Queen.'

She rose.

'Let us begin working at once,' she said. 'This is the *Golden Hind*: I have just stepped on to it. Now go behind the piano, and then come tripping out, full of awe, full of reverence . . . Oh, dear me, that will never do. Shall I act it for you once more?' . . .

4

Lucia had come back to Tilling last night from the fêteful
week at Riseholme, and she was sitting next morning after
breakfast at the window of the garden-room in Miss Mapp's
house. It was a magic casement to anyone who was interested
in life, as Lucia certainly was, and there was a tide every
morning in the affairs of Tilling which must be taken at the
flood. Mrs Wyse's Royce had lurched down the street, Diva
had come out with her market-basket from quaint Irene's
house, of which she was now the tenant, Miss Mapp's (she was
already by special request 'Elizabeth') gardener had wheeled
off to the greengrocer his daily barrowful of garden-produce.
Elizabeth had popped in to welcome her on her return from
Riseholme and congratulate her on the fête of which the daily
illustrated papers had been so full, and, strolling about the
garden with her, had absently picked a few roses (Diva's had
green fly); the Padre passing by the magic casement had
wished her good morrow, Mistress Lucas, and finally Major
Benjy had come out of his house on the way to catch the tram
to the golf-links. Lucia called '*Quai-hai*' to him in silvery
tones, for they had made great friends in the days she had
already spent at Tilling, and reminded him that he was dining
with her that night. With great gallantry he had taken off his
cap, and bawled out that this wasn't the sort of engagement he
was in any danger of forgetting, au reservoir.

The tide had ebbed now, and Lucia left the window. There
was so much to think about that she hardly knew where to
begin. First her eyes fell on the piano which was no longer the
remarkable Blumenfelt belonging to Elizabeth on which she
had been granted the privilege to play, but one which she had
hired from Brighton. No doubt it was quite true that, as
Elizabeth had said, her Blumenfelt had been considered a

very fine instrument, but nobody, for the last twenty years or so, could have considered it anything but a remarkable curiosity. Some notes sounded like the chirping of canaries (Diva's canary was quite well again after its pip), others did not sound at all, and the *sostenuto* pedal was a thing of naught. So Lucia had hired a new piano, and had put the canary-piano in the little telephone-room off the hall. It filled it up, but it was still possible to telephone if you went in sideways. Elizabeth had shown traces of acidity about this when she discovered the substitution, and had rather pensively remarked that her piano had belonged to her dearest mamma, and she hoped the telephone-room wasn't damp. It seemed highly probable that it had been her mother's if not her grandmother's, but after all Lucia had not promised to play on it.

So much for the piano. There lay on it now a china bowl full of press-cuttings, and Lucia glanced at a few, recalling the triumphs of the past week. The fête, favoured by brilliant weather and special trains from Worcester and Gloucester and Birmingham, had been a colossal success. The procession had been cinematographed, so too had the scene on the *Golden Hind*, and the click of cameras throughout the whole performance had been like the noise of cicadas in the south. The Hurst had been the target for innumerable lenses (Lucia was most indulgent), and she was photographed at her piano and in Perdita's garden, and musing in an arbour, as Queen Elizabeth and as herself, and she had got one of those artists to take (rather reluctantly) a special photograph of Drake's poor wife. That had not been a success, for Daisy had moved, but Lucia's intention was of the kindest. And throughout, to photographers and interviewers alike, Lucia (knowing that nobody would believe it) had insisted that all the credit was due to Drake's wife, who had planned everything (or nearly) and had done all the spade-work.

There had nearly been one dreadful disaster. In fact there had been the disaster, but the amazing Lucia, quite impromptu, had wrung a fresh personal triumph out of it. It was on the last day of the fête, when the green would hardly contain the influx of visitors, and another tier of benches had been put up round the pond where the *Golden Hind* lay, that this excruciating moment had occurred. Queen Elizabeth had just left the deck where she had feasted on a plateful of kippered cinders, and the procession was escorting her away, when the whole of the stern of the *Golden Hind*, on which was the fire and the previously roasted sheep and a mast, streaming with ancients and the crowd of cheering cooks, broke off, and with a fearful splash and hiss fell into the water. Before anyone could laugh, Lucia (remembering that the water was only three feet deep at the most and so there was no danger of anyone drowning) broke into a ringing cry. 'Zounds and Zooks' she shouted. 'Thus will I serve the damned galleons of Spain,' and with a magnificent gesture of disdain at the cooks standing waist high in the water, she swept on with her procession. The reporters singled out for special notice this wonderful piece of symbolism. A few of the most highbrow deemed it not quite legitimate business, but none questioned the superb dramatic effect of the device, for it led on with such perfect fitness to the next topic, namely the coming of the Armada. The cooks waded ashore, rushed home to change their clothes, and were in time to take their places in the mob that escorted her white palfrey. Who would mind a ducking in the service of such a resourceful Queen? Of all Lucia's triumphs during the week that inspired moment was the crown, and she could not help wondering what poor Daisy would have done, if she had been on the throne that day. Probably she would have said: 'Oh dear, oh dear, they've all fallen into the water. We must stop.'

No wonder Riseholme was proud of Lucia, and Tilling which had been greedily devouring the picture papers was proud too. There was one possible exception, she thought, and that was Elizabeth, who in her visit of welcome just now had said, 'How dreadful all this publicity must be for you, dear! How you must shrink from it!'

But Lucia, as usual, had been quite up to the mark.

'Sweet of you to be so sympathetic, Elizabeth,' she had said. 'But it was my duty to help dear Riseholme, and I mustn't regard the consequences to myself.'

That put the lid on Elizabeth: she said no more about the fête.

*

Lucia, as these random thoughts suggested by that stack of press-cuttings flitted through her brain, felt that she would have soon to bring it to bear on Elizabeth, for she was becoming something of a problem. But first, for this was an immediate concern, she must concentrate on Georgie. Georgie at the present moment, unconscious of his doom, and in a state of the highest approbation with life generally, was still at Riseholme, for Adele Brixton's brother, Colonel Cresswell, had taken his house for two months and there were many bits of things, embroidery and sketches and little bottles with labels, 'For outward application only', which he must put away. He had been staying with Daisy for the fête, for Foljambe and the rest of his staff had come to Tilling at the beginning of August and it was not worth while taking them all back, though it would be difficult to get on without Foljambe for a week. Then he had stopped on for this extra day with Daisy after the fête was over, to see that everything was tidy and discreet and Lucia expected him back this morning.

She had very upsetting news for him: ghastly in fact. The vague rumours which had been rife at Riseholme were all too true, and Cadman, her chauffeur, had come to Lucia last night with the bomb-shell that he and Foljambe were thinking of getting married. She had seen Foljambe as well, and Foljambe had begged her to break the news to Georgie.

'I should take it very kind of you, ma'am, if you would,' Foljambe had said, 'for I know I could never bring myself to do it, and he wouldn't like to feel that I had made up my mind without telling him. We're in no hurry, me and Cadman, we shouldn't think of being married till after we got back to Riseholme in the autumn, and that'll give Mr Georgie several months to get suited. I'm sure you'll make him see it the right way, if anybody can.'

This handsome tribute to her tact had had its due weight, and Lucia had promised to be the messenger of these dismal tidings. Georgie would arrive in time for lunch to-day, and she was determined to tell him at once. But it was dreadful to think of poor Georgie on his way now, full of the pleasantest anticipations for the future (since Foljambe had expressed herself more than pleased with her bedroom) and rosy with the remarkable success of his Drake and the very substantial rent for which he had let his house for two months, with this frightful blow so soon to be dealt him by her hand. Lucia had no idea how he would take it, except that he was certain to be terribly upset. So, leaving the garden-room and establishing herself in the pleasant shade on the lawn outside, she thought out quite a quantity of bracing and valuable reflections.

She turned her thoughts towards Elizabeth Mapp. During those ten days before Lucia had gone to Riseholme for the fête, she had popped in every single day: it was quite obvious that Elizabeth was keeping her eye on her. She always had some glib excuse: she wanted a hot-water bottle, or a thimble or a screw-driver that she had forgotten to take away, and declining all assistance would go to look for them herself, feeling sure that she could put her hand on them instantly without troubling anybody. She would go into the kitchen wreathed in smiles and pleasant observations for Lucia's cook, she would pop into the servants' hall and say something agreeable to Cadman, and pry into cupboards to find what she was in search of. (It was during one of these expeditions that she had discovered her dearest mamma's piano in the telephone-room.) Often she came in without knocking or ringing the bell, and then if Lucia or Grosvenor heard her clandestine entry, and came to see who it was, she scolded herself for her stupidity in not remembering that for the present, this was not her house. So forgetful of her.

On one of these occasions she had popped out into the garden, and found Lucia eating a fig from the tree that grew against the garden-room, and was covered with fruit.

'Oh, you dear thief!' she said. 'What about garden-produce?'

Then seeing Lucia's look of blank amazement, she had given a pretty peal of laughter.

'Lulu, dear! Only my joke,' she cried. 'Poking a little fun at Queen Elizabeth. You may eat every fig in my garden, and I wish there were more of them.'

On another occasion Elizabeth had found Major Benjy

having tea with Lucia, and she had said, 'Oh, how disappointed I am! I had so hoped to introduce you to each other, and now someone else has taken that treat from me. Who was the naughty person?' But perhaps that was a joke too. Lucia was not quite sure that she liked Elizabeth's jokes, any more than she liked her informal visits.

This morning, Lucia cast an eye over her garden. The lawn badly wanted cutting, the flower-beds wanted weeding, the box-edgings to them wanted clipping, and it struck her that the gardener, whose wages she paid, could not have done an hour's work here since she left. He was never in this part of the garden at all, she seemed to remember, but was always picking fruit and vegetables in the kitchen-garden, or digging over the asparagus-bed, or potting chrysanthemums, or doing other jobs that did not concern her own interests but Elizabeth's. There he was now, a nice genial man, preparing a second basketful of garden-produce to take to the greengrocer's, from whom eventually Lucia bought it. An inquiry must instantly be held.

'Good morning, Coplen,' she said. 'I want you to cut the lawn to-day. It's got dreadfully long.'

'Very sorry, ma'am,' said he. 'I don't think I can find time to-day myself. I could get a man in perhaps to do it.'

'I should prefer that you should,' said Lucia. 'You can get a man in to pick those vegetables.'

'It's not only them,' he said. 'Miss Mapp she told me to manure the strawberry-beds to-day.'

'But what has Miss Mapp got to do with it?' said she. 'You're in my employment.'

'Well, that does only seem fair,' said the impartial Coplen. 'But you see, ma'am, my orders are to go to Miss Mapp every morning and she tells me what she wants done.'

'Then for the future please come to me every morning and see what I want done,' she said. 'Finish what you're at now, and then start on the lawn at once. Tell Miss Mapp by all means that I've given you these instructions. And no strawberry-bed shall be manured to-day, nor indeed until my garden looks less like a tramp who hasn't shaved for a week.'

Supported by an impregnable sense of justice but still dangerously fuming, Lucia went back to her garden-room, to tranquil-lize herself with an hour's practice on the new piano. Very nice tone; she and Georgie would be able to start their musical hours again now. This afternoon, perhaps, if he felt up to it after the tragic news, a duet might prove tonic. Not a note had she played during that triumphant week at Riseholme. Scales first then, and presently she was working away at a new Mozart, which she and Georgie would subsequently read over together.

There came a tap at the door of the garden-room. It opened a chink, and Elizabeth in her sweetest voice said:

'May I pop in once more, dear?'

Elizabeth was out of breath. She had hurried up from the High Street.

'So sorry to interrupt your sweet music, *Lucia mia*,' she said. 'What a pretty tune! What fingers you have! But my good Coplen has come to me in great perplexity. So much better to clear it up at once, I thought, so I came instantly though rather rushed to-day. A little misunderstanding, no doubt. Coplen is not clever.'

Elizabeth seemed to be labouring under some excitement which might account for this loss of wind. So Lucia waited till she was more controlled.

'– And your new piano, dear?' asked Elizabeth. 'You like it? It sounded so sweet, though not quite the tone of dearest mamma's. About Coplen then?'

'Yes, about Coplen,' said Lucia.

'He misunderstood, I am sure, what you said to him just now. So distressed he was. Afraid I should be vexed with him. I said I would come to see you and make it all right.'

'Nothing easier, dear,' said Lucia. 'We can put it all right in a minute. He told me he had not time to cut the lawn to-day because he had to manure your strawberry-beds, and I said "The lawn please, at once," or words to that effect. He didn't quite grasp, I think, that he's in my employment, so naturally I reminded him of it. He understands now, I hope.'

Elizabeth looked rather rattled at these energetic remarks, and Lucia saw at once that this was the stuff to give her.

'But my garden-produce, you know, dear Lulu,' said Elizabeth. 'It is not much use to me if all those beautiful pears are left to rot on the trees till the wasps eat them.'

'No doubt that is so,' said Lucia; 'but Coplen, whose wages I pay, is no use to me if he spends his entire time in looking after your garden-produce. I pay for his time, dear Elizabeth, and I intend to have it. He also told me he took his orders every morning from you. That won't do at all. I shan't permit that for a moment. If I had engaged your cook as well as your gardener, I should not allow her to spend her day in roasting mutton for you. So that's all settled.'

It was borne in upon Elizabeth that she hadn't got a leg to stand upon and she sat down.

'Lulu,' she said, 'anything would be better than that I should have a misunderstanding with such a dear as you are. I won't argue, I won't put my point of view at all. I yield. There! If you can spare Coplen for an hour in the morning to take my little fruits and vegetables to the greengrocer's I should be glad.'

'Quite impossible, I'm afraid, dear Elizabeth,' said Lucia with the greatest cordiality. 'Coplen has been neglecting the flower-garden dreadfully, and for the present it will take him all his time to get it tidy again. You must get someone else to do that.'

Elizabeth looked quite awful for a moment: then her face was wreathed in smiles again.

'Precious one!' she said. 'It shall be exactly as you wish. Now I must run away. Au reservoir. You're not free, I suppose, this evening to have a little dinner with me? I would ask Major Benjy to join us, and our beloved Diva, who has a passion, positively a passion for you. Major Benjy indeed too. He raves about you. Wicked woman, stealing all the hearts of Tilling.'

Lucia felt positively sorry for the poor thing. Before she left for Riseholme last week, she had engaged Diva and Major Benjy to dine with her to-night, and it was quite incredible that Elizabeth, by this time, should not have known that.

'Sweet of you,' she said, 'but I have a tiny little party myself to-night. Just one or two, dropping in.'

Elizabeth lingered a moment yet, and Lucia said to herself that the thumb-screw and the rack would not induce her to ask Elizabeth, however long she lingered.

Lucia and she exchanged kissings of the hand as Elizabeth emerged from the front door, and tripped down the street. 'I see I must be a little firm with her,' thought Lucia, 'and when I've taught her her place, then it will be time to be kind. But I won't ask her to dinner just yet. She must learn not to ask me when she knows I'm engaged. And she shall not pop in without ringing. I must tell Grosvenor to put the door on the chain.'

Lucia returned to her practice, but shovelled the new Mozart out of sight, when, in one of her glances out of the open window, she observed Georgie coming up the street, on his way from the station. He had a light and airy step, evidently he was in the best of spirits and he waved to her as he caught sight of her.

'Just going to look in at the cottage one second,' he called out, 'to see that everything's all right, and then I'll come and have a chat before lunch. Heaps to tell you.'

'So have I,' said Lucia, ruefully thinking what one of those things was. 'Hurry up, Georgie.'

He tripped along up to the cottage, and Lucia's heart was wrung for him, for all that gaiety would soon suffer a total eclipse, and she was to be the darkener of his day. Had she better tell him instantly, she wondered, or hear his news first, and outline the recent Manoeuvres of Mapp. These exciting topics might prove tonic, something to fall back on afterwards. Whereas, if she stabbed him straight away, they would be of no service as restoratives. Also there was stewed lobster for lunch, and Georgie who adored it would probably not care a bit about it if the blow fell first.

Georgie began to speak almost before he opened the door.

'All quite happy at the cottage,' he said, 'and Foljambe ever so pleased with Tilling. Everything in spick-and-span order and my paint-box cleaned up and the hole in the carpet mended quite beautifully. She must have been busy while I was away.'

('Dear, oh dear, she has,' thought Lucia.)

'And everything settled at Riseholme,' continued poor Georgie. 'Colonel Cresswell wants my house for three months, so I said yes, and now we're both homeless for October, unless we keep on our houses here. I had to put on my Drake clothes again yesterday, for the *Birmingham Gazette* wanted to photograph me. My dear, what a huge success it all was, but I'm glad to get away, for everything will be as flat as ditchwater now, all except Daisy. She began to buck up at once the moment you left, and I positively heard her say how quickly you picked up the part of the Queen after watching her once or twice.'

'No! Poor thing!' said Lucia with deep compassion.

'Now tell me all about Tilling,' said Georgie, feeling he must play fair.

'Things are beginning to move, Georgie,' said she, forgetting for the time the impending tragedy. 'Nightmarches, Georgie, manoeuvres. Elizabeth, of course. I'm sure I was right, she wants to run me, and if she can't (if!) she'll try to fight me. I can see glimpses of hatred and malice in her.'

'And you'll fight her?' asked Georgie eagerly.

'Nothing of the kind, my dear,' said Lucia. 'What do you take me for? Every now and then, when necessary, I shall just give her two or three hard slaps. I gave her one this morning: I did indeed. Not a very hard one, but it stung.'

'No! Do tell me,' said Georgie.

Lucia gave a short but perfectly accurate description of the gardener-crisis.

'So I stopped that,' she said, 'and there are several other things I shall stop. I won't have her, for instance, walking into my house without ringing. So I've told Grosvenor to put up the chain. And she calls me Lulu which makes me sick. Nobody's ever called me Lulu and they shan't begin now. I must see if calling her Liblib will do the trick. And then she asked me to dinner to-night, when she must have known perfectly well that Major Benjy and Diva are dining with me. You're dining too, by the way.'

'I'm not sure if I'd better,' said Georgie. 'I think Foljambe might expect me to dine at home the first night I get back. I know she wants to go through the linen and plate with me.'

'No, Georgie, quite unnecessary,' said she. 'I want you to help me to give the others a jolly comfortable evening. We'll play bridge and let Major Benjy lay down the law. We'll have a genial evening, make them enjoy it. And to-morrow I shall ask the Wyses and talk about Countesses. And the day after I shall ask the Padre and his wife and talk Scotch. I want you to come every night. It's new in Tilling I find, to give little dinners. Tea is the usual entertainment. And I shan't ask Liblib at all till next week.'

'But my dear, isn't that war?' asked Georgie. (It did look rather like it.)

'Not the least. It's benevolent neutrality. We shall see if she learns sense. If she does, I shall be very nice to her again and ask her to several pleasant little parties. I am giving her every chance. Also Georgie . . .' Lucia's eyes assumed that gimlet-like expression which betokened an earnest purpose, 'I want to understand her and be fair to her. At present I can't understand her. The idea of her giving orders to a gardener to whom I give wages! But that's all done with. I can hear the click of the mowing-machine on the lawn now. Just two or three things I won't stand. I won't be patronized by Liblib, and I won't be called Lulu, and I won't have her popping in and out of my house like a cuckoo clock.'

Lunch drew to an end. There was Georgie looking so prosperous and plump, with his chestnut-coloured hair no longer in the least need of a touch of dye, and his beautiful clothes. Already Major Benjy, who had quickly seen that if he wanted to be friends with Lucia he must be friends with Georgie too, had pronounced him to be the best-dressed man in Tilling, and Lucia, who invariably passed on dewdrops of this kind, had caused Georgie the deepest gratification by repeating this. And now she was about to plunge a dagger in his heart. She put her elbows on the table, so as to be ready to lay a hand of sympathy on his.

'Georgie, I've got something to tell you,' she said.

'I'm sure I shall like it,' said he. 'Go on.'

'No, you won't like it at all,' she said.

It flashed through his mind that Lucia had changed her mind about marrying him, but it could not be that, for she would never have said he wouldn't like it at all. Then he had a flash of intuition.

'Something about Foljambe,' he said in a quavering voice.

'Yes. She and Cadman are going to marry.'

Georgie turned on her a face from which all other expression except hopeless despair had vanished, and her hand of sympathy descended on his, firmly pressing it.

'When?' he said, after moistening his dry lips.

'Not for the present. Not till we get back to Riseholme.'

Georgie pushed away his untasted coffee.

'It's the most dreadful thing that's ever happened to me,' he said. 'It's quite spoiled all my pleasure. I didn't think Foljambe was so selfish. She's been with me fifteen years, and now she goes and breaks up my home like this.'

'My dear, that's rather an excessive statement,' said Lucia. 'You can get another parlourmaid. There are others.'

'If you come to that, Cadman could get another wife,' said Georgie, 'and there isn't another parlourmaid like Foljambe. I have suspected something now and then, but I never thought it would come to this. What a fool I was to leave her here when I went back to Riseholme for the fête! Or if only we had driven back there with Cadman instead of going by train. It was madness. Here they were with nothing to do but make plans behind our backs. No one will ever look after my clothes as she does. And the silver. You'll miss Cadman, too.'

'Oh, but I don't think he means to leave me,' said Lucia in some alarm. 'What makes you think that? He said nothing about it.'

'Then perhaps Foljambe doesn't mean to leave me,' said Georgie, seeing a possible dawn on the wreck of his home.

'That's rather different,' said Lucia. 'She'll have to look after his house, you see, by day, and then at night he'd – he'd like her to be there.'

'Horrible to think of,' said Georgie bitterly. 'I wonder what she can see in him. I've got a good mind to go and live in an hotel. And I had left her five hundred pounds in my will.'

'Georgie, that was very generous of you. Very,' put in Lucia, though Georgie would not feel the loss of that large sum after he was dead.

'But now I shall certainly add a codicil to say "if still in my service",' said Georgie rather less generously. 'I didn't think it of her.'

Lucia was silent a moment. Georgie was taking it very much to heart indeed, and she racked her ingenious brain.

'I've got an idea,' she said at length. 'I don't know if it can be worked, but we might see. Would you feel less miserable about it if Foljambe would consent to come over to your house say at nine in the morning and be there till after dinner? If you were dining out as you so often are, she could go home earlier. You see Cadman's at the Hurst all day, for he does odd jobs as well, and his cottage at Riseholme is quite close to your house. You would have to give them a charwoman to do the house-work.'

'Oh, that is a good idea,' said Georgie, cheering up a little. 'Of course I'll give her a charwoman or anything else she wants if she'll only look after me as before. She can sleep wherever she likes. Of course there may be periods when she'll have to be away, but I shan't mind that as long as I know she's coming back. Besides, she's rather old for that, isn't she?'

It was no use counting the babies before they were born, and Lucia glided along past this slightly indelicate subject with Victorian eyes.

'It's worth while seeing if she'll stay with you on these terms,' she said.

'Rather. I shall suggest it at once,' said Georgie. 'I think I shall congratulate her very warmly, and say how pleased I am, and then ask her. Or would it be better to be very cold and preoccupied and not talk to her at all? She'd hate that, and then when I ask her after some days whether she'll stop on with me, she might promise anything to see me less unhappy again.'

Lucia did not quite approve of this Machiavellian policy.

'On the other hand, it might make her marry Cadman instantly, in order to have done with you,' she suggested. 'You'd better be careful.'

'I'll think it over,' said Georgie. 'Perhaps it would be safer to be very nice to her about it and appeal to her better nature, if she's got one. But I know I shall never manage to call her Cadman. She must keep her maiden name, like an actress.'

Lucia duly put in force her disciplinary measures for the reduction of Elizabeth. Major Benjy, Diva and Georgie dined with her that night, and there was a plate of nougat chocolates for Diva, whose inordinate passion for them was known all over Tilling, and a fiery curry for the Major to remind him of India, and a dish of purple figs bought at the greengrocer's but plucked from the tree outside the garden-room. She could not resist giving Elizabeth ever so gentle a little slap over this, and said that it was rather a roundabout process to go down to the High Street to buy the figs which Coplen plucked from the tree in the garden, and took down with other garden-produce to the shop: she must ask dear Elizabeth to allow her to buy them, so to speak, at the pit-mouth. But she was genuinely astonished at the effect this little joke had on Diva. Hastily she swallowed a nougat chocolate entire and turned bright red.

'But doesn't Elizabeth give you garden-produce?' she asked in an incredulous voice.

'Oh no,' said Lucia, 'Just flowers for the house. Nothing else.'

'Well, I never!' said Diva. 'I fully understood, at least I thought I did –'

Lucia got up. She must be magnanimous and encourage no public exposure, whatever it might be, of Elizabeth's conduct, but for the pickling of the rod of discipline she would like to hear about it quietly.

'Let's go into the garden-room and have a chat,' she said. 'Look after Major Benjy, Georgie, and don't sit too long in bachelordom, for I must have a little game of bridge with him. I'm terribly frightened of him, but he and Mrs Plaistow must be kind to beginners like you and me.'

The indignant Diva poured out her tale of Elizabeth's iniquities in a turgid flood.

'So like Elizabeth,' she said. 'I asked her if she gave you

garden-produce, and she said she wasn't going to dig up her potatoes and carry them away. Well, of course I thought that meant she did give it you. So like her. Bismarck, wasn't it, who told the truth in order to deceive? And so of course I gave her my garden-produce and she's selling one and eating the other. I wish I'd known I ought to have distrusted her.'

Lucia smiled that indulgent Sunday-evening smile which meant she was thinking hard on week-day subjects.

'I like Elizabeth so much,' she said, 'and what do a few figs matter?'

'No, but she always scores,' said Diva, 'and sometimes it's hard to bear. She got my house with garden-produce thrown in for eight guineas a week and she lets her own without garden-produce for twelve.'

'No dear, I pay fifteen,' said Lucia.

Diva stared at her open-mouthed.

'But it was down in Woolgar's books at twelve,' she said. 'I saw it myself. She is a one: isn't she?'

Lucia maintained her attitude of high nobility, but this information added a little more pickling.

'Dear Elizabeth!' she said. 'So glad that she was sharp enough to get a few more guineas, I expect she's very clever, isn't she? And here come the gentlemen. Now for a jolly little game of bridge.'

Georgie was astonished at Lucia. She was accustomed to lay down the law with considerable firmness, and instruct partners and opponents alike, but to-night a most unusual humility possessed her. She was full of diffidence about her own skill and of praise for her partner's: she sought advice, even once asking Georgie what she ought to have played, though that was clearly a mistake, for next moment she rated him. But for the other two she had nothing but admiring envy at their declarations and their management of the hand, and when Diva revoked she took all the blame on herself for not having asked her whether her hand was bare of the suit. Rubber after rubber they played in an amity hitherto unknown in the higher gambling circles of Tilling; and when, long after the incredible hour of twelve had struck, it was found on the adjustment of accounts that Lucia was the universal loser, she said she had never bought experience so cheaply and pleasantly.

Major Benjy wiped the foam of his third (surreptitious and hastily consumed) whisky and soda from his walrus-moustache. 'Most agreeable evening of bridge I've ever spent in Tilling,' he said. 'Bless me, when I think of the scoldings I've had in this room for some little slip, and the friction there's been . . . Mrs Plaistow knows what I mean.'

'I should think I did,' said Diva, beginning to simmer again at the thought of garden-produce. 'Poor Elizabeth! Lessons in self-control are what she wants and after that a few lessons on the elements of the game wouldn't be amiss. Then it would be time to think about telling other people how to play.'

This very pleasant party broke up, and Georgie hurrying home to Mallards Cottage, thought he could discern in these comments the key to Lucia's unwonted humility at the card-table. For herself she had only kind words on the subject of Elizabeth as befitted a large-hearted woman, but Diva and Major Benjy could hardly help contrasting brilliantly to her advantage, the charming evening they had spent with the vituperative scenes which usually took place when they played bridge in the garden-room. 'I think Lucia has begun,' thought Georgie to himself as he went noiselessly upstairs so as not to disturb the slumbers of Foljambe.

It was known, of course, all over Tilling the next morning that there had been a series of most harmonious rubbers of bridge last night at Mallards till goodness knew what hour, for Diva spent half the morning in telling everybody about it, and the other half in advising them not to get their fruit and vegetables at the shop which dealt in the garden-produce of the Bismarckian Elizabeth. Equally well known was it that the Wyses were dining at Mallards to-night, for Mrs Wyse took care of that, and at eight o'clock that evening the Royce started from Porpoise Street, and arrived at Mallards at precisely one minute past. Georgie came on foot from the Cottage thirty yards away in the other direction, in the highest spirits, for Foljambe after consultation with her Cadman had settled to continue on day-duty after the return to Riseholme. So Georgie did not intend at present to execute that vindictive codicil to his will. He told the Wyses whom he met on the doorstep of Mallards about the happy termination of this domestic crisis, while Mrs Wyse took off her sables and disclosed the fact that she was wearing the order of the MBE on her ample bosom; and he observed that Mr Wyse had a soft crinkly shirt with a low collar, and velveteen dress clothes: this pretty costume caused him to look rather like a conjurer. There followed very polite conversations at dinner, full of bows from Mr Wyse; first he talked to his hostess, and when Lucia tried to produce general talk and spoke to Georgie, he instantly turned his head to the right, and talked most politely to his wife about the weather and the news in the evening paper till Lucia was ready for him again.

'I hear from our friend Miss Mapp,' he said to her, 'that you speak the most beautiful and fluent Italian.'

Lucia was quite ready to oblige.

'Ah, *che bella lingua!*' said she. '*Ma ho dimenticato tutto, non parla nessuno* in Riseholme.'

'But I hope you will have the opportunity of speaking it before long in Tilling,' said Mr Wyse. 'My sister Amelia, Contessa Faraglione, may possibly be with us before long and I shall look forward to hearing you and she talk together. A lovely language to listen to, though Amelia laughs at my poor efforts when I attempt it.'

Lucia smelled danger here. There had been a terrible occasion once at Riseholme when her bilingual reputation had been shattered by her being exposed to the full tempest of Italian volleyed at her by a native, and she had been unable to understand anything that he said. But Amelia's arrival was doubtful and at present remote, and it would be humiliating to confess that her knowledge was confined to a chosen though singularly limited vocabulary.

'Georgie, we must rub up our Italian again,' she said. 'Mr Wyse's sister may be coming here before long. What an opportunity for us to practise!'

'I do not imagine that you have much need of practice,' said Mr Wyse, bowing to Lucia. 'And I hear your Elizabethan fête' (he bowed to Queen Elizabeth) 'was an immense success. We so much want somebody at Tilling who can organize and carry through schemes like that. My wife does all she can, but she sadly needs someone to help, or indeed direct her. The hospital for instance, terribly in need of funds. She and I were talking as to whether we could not get up a garden fête with some tableaux or something of the sort to raise money. She has designs on you, I know, when she can get you alone, for indeed there is no one in Tilling with ability and initiative.'

Suddenly it struck Lucia that though this was very gratifying to herself, it had another purpose, namely to depreciate somebody else, and surely that could only be one person. But that name must not escape her lips.

'My services, such as they are, are completely at Mrs Wyse's disposal,' she said, 'as long as I am in Tilling. This garden for instance. Would that be a suitable place for something of the sort?'

Mr Wyse bowed to the garden.

'The ideal spot,' said he. 'All Tilling would flock here at your bidding. Never yet in my memory has the use of it been granted for such a purpose; we have often lamented it.'

There could no longer be much doubt as to the sub-current in such remarks, but the beautiful smooth surface must not be broken.

'I quite feel with you,' said Lucia. 'If one is fortunate enough, even for a short time, to possess a pretty little garden like this, it should be used for the benefit of charitable entertainment. The hospital: what more deserving object could we have? Some tableaux, you suggested. I'm sure Mr Pillson and I would be only too glad to repeat a scene or two from our fête at Riseholme.'

Mr Wyse bowed so low that his large loose tie nearly dipped itself in an ice pudding.

'I was trying to summon my courage to suggest exactly that,' he said. 'Susan, Mrs Lucas encourages us to hope that she will give you a favourable audience about the project we talked over.'

The favourable audience began as soon as the ladies rose,

and was continued when Georgie and Mr Wyse followed them. Already it had been agreed that the Padre might contribute an item to the entertainment, and that was very convenient, for he was to dine with Lucia the next night.

'His Scotch stories,' said Susan. 'I can never hear them too often, for though I've not got a drop of Scotch blood myself, I can appreciate them. Not a feature of course, Mrs Lucas, but just to fill up pauses. And then there's Mrs Plaistow. How I laugh when she does the sea-sick passenger with an orange, though I doubt if you can get oranges now. And Miss Coles. A wonderful mimic. And then there's Major Benjy. Perhaps he would read us portions of his diary.'

A pause followed. Lucia had one of those infallible presentiments that a certain name hitherto omitted would follow. It did.

'And if Miss Mapp would supply the refreshment department with fruit from her garden here, that would be a great help,' said Mrs Wyse.

Lucia caught in rapid succession the respective eyes of all her guests, each of whom in turn looked away. 'So Tilling knows all about the garden-produce already,' she thought to herself.

Bridge followed, and here she could not be as humble as she had been last night, for both the Wyses abased themselves before she had time to begin.

'We know already,' said Algernon, 'of the class of player that you are, Mrs Lucas,' he said. 'Any hints you will give Susan and me will be so much appreciated. We shall give you no game at all I am afraid, but we shall have a lesson. There is no one in Tilling who has any pretensions of being a player. Major Benjy and Mrs Plaistow and we sometimes have a well-fought rubber on our own level, and the Padre does not always play a bad game. But otherwise the less said about our bridge the better. Susan, my dear, we must do our best.'

Here indeed was a reward for Lucia's humility last night. The winners had evidently proclaimed her consummate skill, and was that, too, a reflection on somebody else, only once hitherto named, and that in connection with garden-produce?

To-night Lucia's hands dripped with aces and kings: she denuded her adversaries of all their trumps, and then led one more for safety's sake, after which she poured forth a galaxy of winners. Whoever was her partner was in luck, and to-night it was Georgie who had to beg for change for a ten-shilling note and leave the others to adjust their portions. He recked nothing of this financial disaster, for Foljambe was not lost to him. When the party broke up Mrs Wyse begged him to allow her to give him a lift in the Royce, but as this would entail a turning of that majestic car, which would take at least five minutes followed by a long drive for them round the church square and down into the High Street and up again to Porpoise Street, he adventured forth on foot for his walk of thirty yards and arrived without undue fatigue.

Georgie and Lucia started their sketching next morning. Like charity, they began at home, and their first subjects were each other's houses. They put their camp-stools side by side, but facing in opposite directions, in the middle of the street half-way between Mallards and Mallards Cottage; and thus, by their having different objects to portray, they avoided any sort of rivalry, and secured each other's companionship.

'So good for our drawing,' said Georgie. 'We were getting to do nothing but trees and clouds which needn't be straight.'

'I've got the crooked chimney,' said Lucia proudly. 'That one beyond your house. I think I shall put it straight. People might think I had done it crooked by accident. What do you advise?'

'I think I wouldn't,' said he. 'There's character in its crookedness. Or you might make it rather more crooked than it is: then there won't be any doubt . . . Here comes the Wyses' car. We shall have to move on to the pavement. Tarsome.'

A loud hoot warned them that that was the safer course, and the car lurched towards them. As it passed, Mr Wyse saw whom he had disturbed, stopped the Royce (which had so much better a right to the road than the artists) and sprang out, hat in hand.

'A thousand apologies,' he cried. 'I had no idea who it was, and for what artistic purpose, occupying the roadway. I am indeed distressed, I would instantly have retreated and gone round the other way had I perceived in time. May I glance? Exquisite! The crooked chimney! Mallards Cottage! The west front of the church!' He bowed to them all.

There followed that evening the third dinner-party when the Padre and wee wifie made the quartet. The Royce had called for him that day to take him to lunch in Porpoise Street (Lucia had seen it go by), and it was he who now introduced the subject of the proposed entertainment on behalf of the hospital, for he knew all about it and was ready to help in any way that Mistress Lucas might command. There were some Scottish stories which he would be happy to narrate, in order to fill up intervals between the tableaux, and he had ascertained that Miss Coles (dressed as usual as a boy) would give her most amusing parody of 'The boy stood on the burning deck', and that Mistress Diva said she thought that an orange or two might be procured. If not, a ripe tomato would serve the purpose. He would personally pledge himself for the services of the church choir to sing catches and glees and madrigals, whenever required. He suggested also that such members of the workhouse as were not bedridden might be entertained to tea, in which case the choir would sing grace before and after buns.

'As to the expense of that, if you approve,' he said, 'put another baubee on the price of admission, and there'll be none in Tilling to grudge the extra expense wi' such entertainment as you and the other leddies will offer them.'

'Dear me, how quickly it is all taking shape,' said Lucia, finding that almost without effort on her part she had been drawn into the place of prime mover in all this, and that still a sort of conspiracy of silence prevailed with regard to Miss Mapp's name, which hitherto had only been mentioned as a suitable provider of fruit for the refreshment department. You must form a little committee, Padre, for putting all the arrangements in hand at once. There's Mr Wyse who really thought of the idea, and you –'

'And with yourself,' broke in the Padre, 'that will make

three. That's sufficient for any committee that is going to do its work without any argle-bargle.'

There flashed across Lucia's mind a fleeting vision of what Elizabeth's face would be like when she picked up, as she would no doubt do next morning, the news of all that was becoming so solid.

'I think I had better not be on the committee,' she said, quite convinced that they would insist on it. 'It should consist of real Tillingites who take the lead among you in such things. I am only a visitor here. They will all say I want to push myself in.'

'Ah, but we can't get on wi'out ye, Mistress Lucas,' said the Padre. 'You must consent to join us. An' three, as I say, makes the perfect committee.'

Mrs Bartlett had been listening to all this with a look of ecstatic attention on her sharp but timid little face. Here she gave vent to a series of shrill minute squeaks which expressed a mouse-like merriment, quite unexplained by anything that had been actually said, but easily accounted for by what had not been said. She hastily drank a sip of water and assured Lucia that a crumb of something (she was eating a peach) had stuck in her throat and made her cough. Lucia rose when the peach was finished.

'To-morrow we must start working in earnest,' she said. 'And to think that I planned to have a little holiday in Tilling! You and Mr Wyse are regular slave-drivers, Padre.'

Georgie waited behind that night after the others had gone, and bustled back to the garden-room after seeing them off.

'My dear, it's getting too exciting,' he said. 'But I wonder if you're wise to join the committee.'

'I know what you mean,' said Lucia, 'but there really is no reason why I should refuse, because they won't have Elizabeth. It's not me, Georgie, who is keeping her out. But perhaps you're right, and I think to-morrow I'll send a line to the Padre and say that I am really too busy to be on the committee, and beg him to ask Elizabeth instead. It would be kinder. I can manage the whole thing just as well without being on the committee. She'll hear all about the entertainment to-morrow morning, and know that she's not going to be asked to do anything, except supply some fruit.'

'She knows a good deal about it now,' said Georgie. 'She came to tea with me to-day.'

'No! I didn't know you had asked her.'

'I didn't,' said Georgie. 'She came.'

'And what did she say about it?'

'Not very much, but she's thinking hard what to do. I could see that. I gave her the little sketch I made of the Landgate when we first came down here, and she wants me to send in another picture for the Tilling Art Exhibition. She wants you to send something too.'

'Certainly she shall have my sketch of Mallards Cottage and the crooked chimney,' said Lucia. 'That will show good will. What else did she say?'

'She's getting up a jumble-sale in aid of the hospital,' said Georgie. 'She's busy, too.'

'Georgie, that's copied from us.'

'Of course it is; she wants to have a show of her own, and I'm sure I don't wonder. And she knows all about your three dinner-parties.'

Lucia nodded. 'That's all right then,' she said. 'I'll ask her to the next. We'll have some duets that night, Georgie. Not bridge I think, for they all say she's a perfect terror at cards. But it's time to be kind to her.'

Lucia rose.

'Georgie, it's becoming a frightful rush already,' she said. 'This entertainment which they insist on my managing will make me very busy, but when one is appealed to like that, one can't refuse. Then there's my music, and sketching, and I haven't begun to rub up my Greek . . . And don't forget to send for your Drake clothes. Good night, my dear. I'll call to you over the garden-paling to-morrow if anything happens.'

'I feel as if it's sure to,' said Georgie with enthusiasm.

5

Lucia was writing letters in the window of the garden-room next morning. One, already finished, was to Adele Brixton asking her to send to Mallards the Queen Elizabeth costume for the tableaux: a second, also finished, was to the Padre, saying that she found she would not have time to attend committees for the hospital fête, and begging him to co-opt Miss Mapp. She would, however, do all in her power to help the scheme, and make any little suggestions that occurred to her. She added that the chance of getting fruit gratis for the refreshment department would be far brighter if the owner of it was on the board.

The third letter, firmly beginning 'Dearest Liblib' (and to be signed very large, LUCIA), asking her to dine in two days' time, was not quite done when she saw dearest Liblib, with a fixed and awful smile, coming swiftly up the street. Lucia, sitting sideways to the window, could easily appear absorbed in her letter and unconscious of Elizabeth's approach, but from beneath half-lowered eyelids she watched her with the intensest interest. She was slanting across the street now, making a bee-line for the door of Mallards ('and if she tries to get in without ringing the bell, she'll find the chain on the door,' thought Lucia).

The abandoned woman, disdaining the bell, turned the handle and pushed. It did not yield to her intrusion, and she pushed more strongly. There was the sound of jingling metal, audible even in the garden-room, as the hasp that held the end of the chain gave way; the door flew open wide, and with a few swift and nimble steps she just saved herself from falling flat on the floor of the hall.

Lucia, pale with fury, laid down her pen and waited for the situation to develop. She hoped she would behave like a lady, but was quite sure it would be a firm sort of lady. Presently up the steps to the garden-room came that fairy tread, the door was opened an inch, and that odious voice said:

'May I come in, dear?'

'Certainly,' said Lucia brightly.

'Lulu dear,' said Elizabeth, tripping across the room with little brisk steps. 'First I must apologize: so humbly. Such a stupid accident. I tried to open your front door, and gave it a teeny little push and your servants had forgotten to take the chain down. I am afraid I broke something. The hasp must have been rusty.'

Lucia looked puzzled.

'But didn't Grosvenor come to open the door when you rang?' she asked.

'That was just what I forgot to do, dear,' said Elizabeth. 'I thought I would pop in to see you without troubling Grosvenor. You and I such friends, and so difficult to remember that my dear little Mallards – Several things to talk about!'

Lucia got up.

'Let us first see what damage you have done,' she said with an icy calmness, and marched straight out of the room, followed by Elizabeth. The sound of the explosion had brought Grosvenor out of the dining-room, and Lucia picked up the dangling hasp and examined it.

'No, no sign of rust,' she said. 'Grosvenor, you must go down to the ironmonger and get them to come up and repair this at once. The chain must be made safer and you must remember always to put it on, day and night. If I am out, I will ring.'

'So awfully sorry, dear Lulu,' said Elizabeth, slightly cowed by this firm treatment. 'I had no idea the chain could be up. We all keep our doors on the latch in Tilling. Quite a habit.'

'I always used to in Riseholme,' said Lucia. 'Let us go back to the garden-room, and you will tell me what you came to talk about.'

'Several things,' said Elizabeth when they had settled themselves. 'First, I am starting a little jumble-sale for the hospital, and I wanted to look out some old curtains and rugs, laid away in cupboards, to give to it. May I just go upstairs and down-stairs and poke about to find them?'

'By all means,' said Lucia. 'Grosvenor shall go round with you as soon as she has come back from the ironmonger's.'

'Thank you, dear,' said Elizabeth, 'though there's no need to trouble Grosvenor. Then another thing. I persuaded Mr Georgie to send me a sketch for our picky exhibition. Promise me that you'll send me one too. Wouldn't be complete without something by you. How you get all you do into the day is beyond me; your sweet music, your sketching, and your dinner-parties every evening.'

Lucia readily promised, and Elizabeth then appeared to lose herself in reverie.

'There *is* one more thing,' she said at last. 'I have heard a little gossip in the town both to-day and yesterday about a fête which it is proposed to give in my garden. I feel sure it is mere tittle-tattle, but I thought it would be better to come up here to know from you that there is no foundation for it.'

'But I hope there is a great deal,' said Lucia. 'Some tableaux, some singing, in order to raise funds for the hospital. It would be so kind of you if you would supply the fruit for the refreshment booth from your garden. Apropos I should be so pleased to buy some of it every day myself. It would be fresher than if, as at present, it is taken down to the greengrocer and brought up again.'

'Anything to oblige you, dear Lulu,' said Elizabeth. 'But that would be difficult to arrange. I have contracted to send all my garden-produce to Twistevant's – such a quaint name, is it not? – for these months, and for the same reason I should be unable to supply this fête which I have heard spoken of. The fruit is no longer mine.'

Lucia had already made up her mind that, after this affair of the chain, nothing would induce her to propose that Elizabeth should take her place on the committee. She would cling to it through storm and tempest.

'I see,' she said. 'Perhaps then you could let us have some fruit from Diva's garden, unless you have sold that also.'

Elizabeth came to the point, disregarding so futile a suggestion.

'The fête itself, dear one,' she said, 'is what I must speak about. I cannot possibly permit it to take place in my garden. The rag-tag and bob-tail of Tilling passing through my hall and my sweet little sitting-room and spending the afternoon in my garden! All my carpets soiled and my flower-beds trampled on! And how do I know that they will not steal upstairs and filch what they can find?'

Lucia's blood had begun to boil: nobody could say that she was preserving a benevolent neutrality. In consequence she presented an icy demeanour, and if her voice trembled at all, it was from excessive cold.

'There will be no admission to the rooms in the house,' she said. 'I will lock all the doors, and I am sure that nobody in Tilling will be so ill bred as to attempt to force them open.'

That was a nasty one. Elizabeth recoiled for a moment from the shock, but rallied. She opened her mouth very wide to begin again, but Lucia got in first.

'They will pass straight from the front door into the garden,' she said, 'where we undertake to entertain them, presenting their tickets of admission or paying at the door. As for the carpet in your sweet little sitting-room, there isn't one. And I have too high an opinion of the manners of Tilling in general to suppose that they will trample on your flower-beds.'

'Perhaps you would like to hire a menagerie,' said Elizabeth, completely losing her self-control, 'and have an exhibition of tigers and sharks in the garden-room.'

'No: I should particularly dislike it,' said Lucia earnestly. 'Half of the garden-room would have to be turned into a sea-water tank for the sharks and my piano would be flooded. And the rest would have to be full of horse-flesh for the tigers. A most ridiculous proposal, and I cannot entertain it.'

Elizabeth gave a dreadful gasp as if she was one of the sharks and the water had been forgotten. She adroitly changed the subject.

'Then again, there's the rumour – of course it's only rumour – that there is some idea of entertaining such inmates of the workhouse as are not bedridden. Impossible.'

'I fancy the Padre is arranging that,' said Lucia. 'For my part, I'm delighted to give them a little treat.'

'And for my part,' said Miss Mapp, rising (she had become Miss Mapp again in Lucia's mind), 'I will not have my little home-sanctuary invaded by the rag-tag —'

'The tickets will be half a crown,' interposed Lucia.

'— and bob-tail of Tilling,' continued Miss Mapp.

'As long as I am tenant here,' said Lucia, 'I shall ask here whom I please, and when I please, and — and how I please. Or do you wish me to send you a list of the friends I ask to dinner for your sanction?'

Miss Mapp, trembling very much, forced her lips to form the syllables:

'But, dear Lulu —'

'Dear Elizabeth, I must beg you not to call me Lulu,' she said. 'Such a detestable abbreviation —'

Grosvenor had appeared at the door of the garden-room.

'Yes, Grosvenor, what is it?' asked Lucia in precisely the same voice.

'The ironmonger is here, ma'am,' she said, 'and he says that he'll have to put in some rather large screws, as they're pulled out —'

'Whatever is necessary to make the door safe,' said Lucia. 'And Miss Mapp wants to look into cupboards and take some things of her own away. Go with her, please, and give her every facility.'

Lucia, quite in the grand style, turned to look out of the window in the direction of Mallards Cottage, in order to give Miss Mapp the opportunity of a discreet exit. She threw the window open.

'Georgino! Georgino!' she called, and Georgie's face appeared above the paling.

'Come round and have ickle talk, Georgie,' she said. 'Sumfin' I want to tell you. Presto!'

She kissed her hand to Georgie and turned back into the room. Miss Mapp was still there, but now invisible to Lucia's eye. She hummed a gay bar of Mozartino, and went back to her table in the bow-window where she tore up the letter of resignation and recommendation she had written to the Padre, and the half-finished note to Miss Mapp, which so cordially asked her to dinner, saying that it was so long since they had met, for they had met again now. When she looked up she was alone, and there was Georgie tripping up the steps by the front door. Though it was standing open (for the ironmonger was already engaged on the firm restoration of the chain) he very properly rang the bell and was admitted.

'There you are,' said Lucia brightly as he came in. 'Another lovely day.'

'Perfect. What has happened to your front door?'

Lucia laughed.

'Elizabeth came to see me,' she said gaily. 'The chain was on the door, as I have ordered it always shall be. But she gave the door such a biff that the hasp pulled out. It's being repaired.'

'No!' said Georgie, 'and did you give her what for?'

'She had several things she wanted to see me about,' said Lucia, keeping an intermittent eye on the front door. 'She wanted to get out of her cupboards some stuff for the jumble-sale she is getting up in aid of the hospital, and she is at it now under Grosvenor's superintendence. Then she wanted me to send a sketch for the picture exhibition, I said I would be delighted. Then she said she could not manage to send any fruit for our fête here. She did not approve of the fête at all, Georgie. In fact, she forbade me to give it. We had a little chat about that.'

'But what's to be done then?' asked Georgie.

'Nothing that I know of, except to give the fête,' said Lucia. 'But it would be no use asking her to be on the committee for an object of which she disapproved, so I tore up the letter I had written to the Padre about it.'

Lucia suddenly focused her eyes and her attention on the front door, and a tone of warm human interest melted the deadly chill of her voice.

'Georgie, there she goes,' she said. 'What a quantity of things! There's an old kettle and a boot-jack, and a rug with a hole in it, and one stair-rod. And there's a shaving from the front door where they are putting in bigger screws, stuck to her skirt . . . And she's dropped the stair-rod . . . Major Benjy's picking it up for her.'

Georgie hurried to the window to see these exciting happenings, but Miss Mapp, having recovered the stair-rod, was already disappearing.

'I wish I hadn't given her my picture of the Landgate,' said he. 'It was one of my best. But aren't you going to tell me all about your interview? Properly, I mean: everything.'

'Not worth speaking of,' said Lucia. 'She asked me if I would like to have a menagerie and keep tigers and sharks in the garden-room. That sort of thing. Mere raving. Come out, Georgie. I want to do a little shopping. Coplen told me there were some excellent greengages from the garden which he was taking down to Twistevant's.'

It was the hour when the collective social life of Tilling was at its briskest. The events of the evening before, tea-parties and games of bridge had become known and were under discussion, as the ladies of the place with their baskets on their arms collided with each other as they popped in and out of shops and obstructed the pavements. Many parcels were being left at Wasters which Miss Mapp now occupied, for jumble-sales on behalf of deserving objects were justly popular, since everybody had a lot of junk in their houses, which they could not bear to throw away, but for which they had no earthly use. Diva had already been back from Taormina to her own house (as Elizabeth to hers) and had disinterred from a cupboard of rubbish a pair of tongs, the claws of which twisted round if you tried to pick up a lump of coal and dropped it on the carpet, but which were otherwise perfect. Then there was a scuttle which had a hole in the bottom, through which coal dust softly dribbled, and a candlestick which had lost one of its feet, and a glass inkstand once handsome, but now cracked. These treasures, handsome donations to a jumble-sale, but otherwise of no particular value, she carried to her own hall, where donors were requested to leave their offerings, and she learned from Withers, Miss Mapp's parlourmaid, the disagreeable news that the jumble-sale was to be held here. The thought revolted her; all the rag-tag and bob-tail of Tilling would come wandering about her house, soiling her carpets and smudging her walls. At this moment Miss Mapp herself came in carrying the tea kettle and the boot-jack and the other things. She had already thought of half a dozen withering retorts she might have made to Lucia.

'Elizabeth, this will never do,' said Diva. 'I can't have the jumble-sale held here. They'll make a dreadful mess of the place.'

'Oh no, dear,' said Miss Mapp, with searing memories of a recent inteview in her mind. 'The people will only come into your hall where you see there's no carpet, and make their purchases. What a beautiful pair of tongs! For my sale? Fancy! Thank you, dear Diva.'

'But I forbid the jumble-sale to be held here,' said Diva. 'You'll be wanting to have a menagerie here next.'

This was amazing luck.

'No, dear, I couldn't dream of it,' said Miss Mapp. 'I should hate to have tigers and sharks all over the place. Ridiculous!'

'I shall put up a merry-go-round in quaint Irene's studio at Taormina,' said Diva.

'I doubt if there's room, dear,' said Miss Mapp, scoring heavily again, 'but you might measure. Perfectly legitimate, of course, for if my house may be given over to parties for paupers, you can surely have a merry-go-round in quaint Irene's and I a jumble-sale in yours.'

'It's not the same thing,' said Diva. 'Providing beautiful tableaux in your garden is quite different from using my panelled hall to sell kettles and coal-scuttles with holes in them.'

'I dare say I could find a good many holes in the tableaux,' said Miss Mapp.

Diva could think of no adequate verbal retort to such coruscations, so for answer she merely picked up the tongs, the coal-scuttle, the candlestick and the inkstand, and put them back in the cupboard from which she had just taken them, and left her tenant to sparkle by herself.

Most of the damaged objects for the jumble-sale must have arrived by now, and after arranging them in tasteful groups Miss Mapp sat down in a rickety basket-chair presented by the

Padre for fell meditation. Certainly it was not pretty of Diva (no one could say that Diva was pretty) to have withdrawn her treasures, but that was not worth thinking about. What did demand her highest mental activities was Lucia's conduct. How grievously different she had turned out to be from that sweet woman for whom she had originally felt so warm an affection, whom she had planned to take so cosily under her wing, and administer in small doses as treats to Tilling society! Lucia had turned upon her and positively bitten the caressing hand. By means of showy little dinners and odious flatteries, she had quite certainly made Major Benjy and the Padre and the Wyses and poor Diva think that she was a very remarkable and delightful person and in these manoeuvres Miss Mapp saw a shocking and sinister attempt to set herself up as the Queen of Tilling society. Lucia had given dinner-parties on three consecutive nights since her return, she had put herself on the committee for this fête, which (however much Miss Mapp might say she could not possibly permit it) she had not the slightest idea how to stop, and though Lucia was only a temporary resident here, these weeks would be quite intolerable if she continued to inflate herself in this presumptuous manner. It was certainly time for Miss Mapp to reassert herself before this rebel made more progress, and though dinner-giving was unusual in Tilling, she determined to give one or two most amusing ones herself, to none of which, of course, she would invite Lucia. But that was not nearly enough: she must administer some frightful snub (or snubs) to the woman. Georgie was in the same boat and must suffer too, for Lucia would not like that. So she sat in this web of crippled fire-irons and napless rugs like a spider, meditating reprisals. Perhaps it was a pity, when she needed allies, to have quarrelled with Diva, but a dinner would set that right. Before long she got up with a pleased expression. 'That will do to begin with: she won't like that at all,' she said to herself and went out to do her belated marketing.

She passed Lucia and Georgie, but decided not to see them, and, energetically waving her hand to Mrs Bartlett, she popped into Twistevant's, from the door of which they had just come out. At that moment quaint Irene, after a few words with the Padre, caught sight of Lucia, and hurried across the street to her. She was hatless, as usual, and wore a collarless shirt and knickerbockers unlike any other lady of Tilling, but as she approached Lucia her face assumed an acid and awful smile, just like somebody else's, and then she spoke in a cooing velvety voice that was quite unmistakable.

'The boy stood on the burning deck, Lulu,' she said. 'Whence all but he had fled, dear. The flames that lit the battle-wreck, sweet one, shone round him --'

Quaint Irene broke off suddenly, for within a yard of her at the door of Twistevant's appeared Miss Mapp. She looked clean over all their heads, and darted across the street to Wasters, carrying a small straw basket of her own delicious greengages.

'Oh, lor!' said Irene. 'The Mapp's in the fire, so that's done. Yes. I'll recite for you at your fête. Georgie, what a saucy hat! I was just going to Taormina to rout out some old sketches of mine for the Art Show, and then this happens. I wouldn't have had it not happen for a hundred pounds.'

'Come and dine to-night,' said Lucia warmly, breaking all records in the way of hospitality.

'Yes, if I needn't dress, and you'll send me home afterwards. I'm half a mile out of the town and I may be tipsy, for Major Benjy says you've got jolly good booze, "*quai-hai*", the King, God bless him! Good-bye.'

'Most original!' said Lucia. 'To go on with what I was telling you, Georgie, Liblib said she would not have her little home-sanctuary – Good morning, Padre. Miss Mapp shoved her way into Mallards this morning without ringing, and broke the chain which was on the door, such a hurry was she in to tell me that she will not have her little home-sanctuary, as I was just saying to Georgie, invaded by the rag-tag and bob-tail of Tilling.'

'Hoots awa!' said the Padre. 'What in the world has Mistress Mapp got to do with it? An' who's holding a jumble-sale in Mistress Plaistow's? I keeked in just now wi' my bit o' rubbish

and never did I see such a mess. Na, na! Fair play's a jool, an'
we'll go richt ahead. Excuse me, there's wee wifie wanting me.'

'It's war,' said Georgie as the Padre darted across to the
Mouse, who was on the other side of the street, to tell her what
had happened.

'No, I'm just defending myself,' said Lucia. 'It's right that
people should know she burst my door-chain.'

Well, I feel like the fourth of August, 1914, said Georgie.
'What do you suppose she'll do next?'

'You may depend upon it, Georgie, that I shall be ready for
her whatever it is,' said Lucia. 'I shan't raise a finger against
her, if she behaves. But she *shall* ring the bell and I *won't* be
dictated to and I *won't* be called Lulu. However, there's no
immediate danger of that. Come, Georgie, let us go home and
finish our sketches. Then we'll have them framed and send
them to Liblib for the picture exhibition. Perhaps that will
convince her of my general good will, which I assure you is
quite sincere.'

The jumble-sale opened next day, and Georgie, having taken
his picture of Lucia's house and her picture of his to be framed
in a very handsome manner, went on to Wasters with the
idea of buying anything that could be of the smallest use for
any purpose, and thus showing more good will towards the
patroness. Miss Mapp was darting to and fro with lures for
purchasers, holding the kettle away from the light so that the
hole in its bottom should not be noticed, and she gave him a
smile that looked rather like a snarl, but after all very like the
smile she had for others. Georgie selected a hearth-brush,
some curtain-rings and a kettle-holder.

Then in a dark corner he came across a large cardboard tray,
holding miscellaneous objects with the label 'All 6d Each'.
There were thimbles, there were photographs with slightly
damaged frames, there were chipped china ornaments and
cork-screws, and there was the picture of the Landgate which
he had painted himself and given Miss Mapp. Withers, Miss
Mapp's parlourmaid, was at a desk for the exchange of custom
by the door, and he exhibited his purchases for her inspection.

'Ninepence for the hearth-brush and threepence for the curtain-rings,' said Georgie in a trembling voice 'and sixpence for the kettle-holder. Then there's this little picture out of the sixpenny tray, which makes just two shillings.'

Laden with these miscellaneous purchases he went swiftly up the street to Mallards. Lucia was at the window of the garden-room, and her gimlet eye saw that something had happened. She threw the sash up.

'I'm afraid the chain is on the door, Georgie,' she called out. 'You'll have to ring. What is it?'

'I'll show you,' said Georgie.

He deposited the hearth-brush, the curtain-rings and the kettle-holder in the hall, and hurried out to the garden-room with the picture.

'The sketch I gave her,' he said. 'In the sixpenny tray. Why, the frame cost a shilling.'

Lucia's face became a flint.

'I never heard of such a thing, Georgie,' said she. 'The monstrous woman!'

'It may have got there by mistake,' said Georgie, frightened at this Medusa countenance.

'Rubbish, Georgie,' said Lucia.

Pictures for the annual exhibition of the Art Society of which Miss Mapp was President had been arriving in considerable numbers at Wasters, and stood stacked round the walls of the hall where the jumble-sale had been held a few days before, awaiting the judgment of the hanging committee which consisted of the President, the Treasurer and the Secretary: the two latter were Mr and Mrs Wyse. Miss Mapp had sent in half a dozen water-colours, the Treasurer a study in still-life of a teacup, an orange and a wallflower, the Secretary a pastel portrait of the King of Italy, whom she had seen at a distance in Rome last spring. She had reinforced the vivid impression he had made on her by photographs. All these, following the precedent of the pictures of Royal Academicians at Burlington House, would be hung on the line without dispute, and there could not be any friction concerning them. But quaint Irene had sent some at which Miss Mapp felt lines must be drawn. They were, as usual, very strange and modern: there was one, harmless but insane, that purported to be Tilling church by moonlight: a bright green pinnacle all crooked (she supposed it was a pinnacle) rose up against a strip of purple sky and the whole of the rest of the canvas was black. There was the back of somebody with no clothes on lying on an emerald-green sofa: and, worst of all, there was a picture called 'Women Wrestlers', from which Miss Mapp hurriedly averted her eyes. A proper regard for decency alone, even if Irene had not mimicked her reciting 'The boy stood on the burning deck', would have made her resolve to oppose, tooth and nail, the exhibition of these shameless athletes. Unfortunately Mr Wyse had the most unbounded admiration for quaint Irene's work, and if she had sent in a picture of mixed wrestlers he would probably have said, 'Dear me, very powerful!' He was a hard man to resist, for if he and Miss Mapp had a very strong difference of opinion concerning any particular canvas he broke off and fell into fresh transports of admiration at her own pictures and this rather disarmed opposition.

The meeting of the hanging committee was to take place this morning at noon. Half an hour before that time, an errand-boy arrived at Wasters from the frame-maker's bringing, according to the order he had received, two parcels which contained Georgie's picture of Mallards and Lucia's picture of Mallards Cottage: they had the cards of their perpetrators attached. 'Rubbishy little daubs,' thought Miss Mapp to herself, 'but I suppose those two Wyses will insist.' Then an imprudent demon of revenge suddenly took complete possession of her, and she called back the boy, and said she had a further errand for him.

At a quarter before twelve the boy arrived at Mallards and rang the bell. Grosvenor took down the chain and received from him a thin square parcel labelled 'With care'. One minute afterwards he delivered a similar parcel to Foljambe at Mallards Cottage, and had discharged Miss Mapp's further errand. The two maids conveyed these to their employers, and Georgie and Lucia, tearing off the wrappers, found themselves simultaneously confronted with their own pictures. A typewritten slip accompanied each, conveying to them the cordial thanks of the hanging committee and its regrets that the limited wall-space at its disposal would not permit of these works of art being exhibited.

Georgie ran out into his little yard and looked over the paling of Lucia's garden. At the same moment Lucia threw open the window of the garden-room which faced towards the paling.

'Georgie, have you received –' she called.

'Yes,' said Georgie.

'So have I.'

'What are you going to do?' he asked.

Lucia's face assumed an expression eager and pensive, the far-away look with which she listened to Beethoven. She thought intently for a moment.

'I shall take a season ticket for the exhibition,' she said, 'and constantly –'

'I can't quite hear you,' said Georgie.

Lucia raised her voice.

'I shall buy a season ticket for the exhibition,' she shouted, 'and go there every day. Believe me, that's the only way to take it. They don't want our pictures, but we mustn't be small about it. Dignity, Georgie.'

There was nothing to add to so sublime a declaration and Lucia went across to the bow-window, looking down the street. At that moment the Wyses' Royce lurched out of Porpoise Street, and turned down towards the High Street. Lucia knew they were both on the hanging committee which had just rejected one of her own most successful sketches (for the crooked chimney had turned out beautifully), but she felt not the smallest resentment towards them. No doubt they had acted quite conscientiously and she waved her hand in answer to a flutter of sables from the interior of the car. Presently she went down herself to the High Street to hear the news of the morning, and there was the Wyses' car drawn up in front of Wasters. She remembered then that the hanging committee met this morning, and a suspicion, too awful to be credible, flashed through her mind. But she thrust it out, as being unworthy of entertainment by a clean mind. She did her shopping and on her return took down a pale straw-coloured sketch by Miss Mapp that hung in the garden-room, and put in its place her picture of Mallards Cottage and the crooked chimney. Then she called to mind that powerful platitude, and said to herself that time would show . . .

Miss Mapp had not intended to be present at the desecration of her garden by paupers from the workhouse and such low haunts. She had consulted her solicitor, about her power to stop the entertainment, but he assured her that there was no known statute in English law, which enabled her to prevent her tenant giving a party. So she determined, in the manner of Lucia and the Elizabethan fête at Riseholme, to be unaware of it, not to know that any fête was contemplated, and never afterwards to ask a single question about it. But as the day approached she suspected that the hot tide of curiosity, rapidly rising in her, would probably end by swamping and submerging her principles. She had seen the Padre dressed in a long black cloak, and carrying an axe of enormous size, entering Mallards; she had seen Diva come out in a white satin gown and scuttle down the street to Taormina, and those two prodigies taken together suggested that the execution of Mary Queen of Scots was in hand. (Diva as the Queen!) She had seen boards and posts carried in by the garden-door and quantities of red cloth, so there was perhaps to be a stage for these tableaux. More intriguing yet was the apparition of Major Benjy carrying a cardboard crown glittering with gold paper. What on earth did that portend? Then there was her fruit to give an eye to: those choir-boys, scampering all over the garden in the intervals between their glees, would probably pick every pear from the tree. She starved to know what was going on, but since she avoided all mention of the fête herself, others were most amazingly respectful to her reticence. She knew nothing, she could only make these delirious guesses, and there was *that* Lucia, being the centre of executioners and queens and choir-boys, instead of in her proper place, made much of by kind Miss Mapp, and enjoying such glimpses of Tilling society as she chose to give her. 'A fortnight ago,' thought kind Miss Mapp, 'I was popping in and out of the house, and she was Lulu. Anyhow, that was a nasty one she got over her picture, and I must bear her no grudge. I shall go to the fête because I can't help it, and I shall be very cordial to her and admire her tableaux. We're all Christians together, and I despise smallness.'

It was distressing to be asked to pay half a crown for admittance to her own Mallards, but there seemed positively no other way to get past Grosvenor. Very distressing, too, it was, to see Lucia in full fig as Queen Elizabeth, graciously receiving newcomers on the edge of the lawn, precisely as if this was her party and these people who had paid half a crown to come in, her invited guests. It was a bitter thought that it ought to be herself who (though not dressed in all that flummery, so unconvincing by daylight) welcomed the crowd; for to whom, pray, did Mallards belong, and who had allowed it (since she could not stop it) to be thrown open? At the bottom of the steps into the garden-room was a large placard 'Private', but of course that would not apply to her. Through the half-opened door, as she passed, she caught a glimpse of a familiar figure, though sadly travestied, sitting in a robe and a golden crown and pouring something into a glass: no doubt then the garden-room was the green-room of performers in the tableaux, who, less greedy of publicity than Lulu, hid themselves here till the time of their exposure brought them out. She would go in there presently, but her immediate duty, bitter but necessary, was to greet her hostess. With a very happy inspiration she tripped up to Lucia and dropped a low curtsey.

'Your Majesty's most obedient humble servant,' she said, and then trusting that Lucia had seen that this obeisance was made in a mocking spirit, abounded in geniality.

'My dear, what a love of a costume!' she said. 'And what a lovely day for your fête! And what a crowd! How the half-crowns have been pouring in! All Tilling seems to be here, and I'm sure I don't wonder.'

Lucia rivalled these cordialities with equal fervour and about as much sincerity.

'Elizabeth! How nice of you to look in!' she said. '*Ecco, le due Elizabethe!* And you like my frock? Sweet of you! Yes. Tilling has indeed come to the aid of the hospital! And your jumble-sale too was a wonderful success, was it not? Nothing left, I am told.'

Miss Mapp had a moment's hesitation as to whether she should not continue to stand by Lucia and shake hands with new arrivals and give them a word of welcome, but she decided she could do more effective work if she made herself independent and played hostess by herself. Also this mention of the jumble-sale made her slightly uneasy. Withers had told her that Georgie had bought his own picture of the Landgate from the sixpenny tray, and Lucia (for all her cordiality) might be about to spring some horrid trap on her about it.

'Yes, indeed,' she said. 'My little sale-room was soon as bare as Mother Hubbard's cupboard. But I mustn't monopolize you, dear, or I shall be lynched. There's a whole *queue* of people waiting to get a word with you. How I shall enjoy the tableaux! Looking forward to them so!'

She sidled off into the crowd. There were those dreadful old wretches from the workhouse, snuffy old things, some of them smoking pipes on her lawn and scattering matches, and being served with tea by Irene and the Padre's curate.

'So pleased to see you all here,' she said, 'sitting in my garden and enjoying your tea. I must pick a nice nosegay for you to take back home. How de do, Mr Sturgis. Delighted you could come and help to entertain the old folks for us. Good afternoon, Mr Wyse; yes, my little garden is looking nice, isn't it? Susan, dear! Have you noticed my bed of delphiniums? I must give you some seed. Oh, there is the town-crier ringing his bell! I suppose that means we must take our places for the tableaux. What a good stage! I hope the posts will not have made very big holes in my lawn. Oh, one of those naughty choir-boys is hovering about my fig-tree. I cannot allow that.'

She hurried off to stop any possibility of such depredation, and had made some telling allusions to the eighth commandment when on a second peal of the town-crier's bell, the procession of mummers came down the steps of the garden-room and advancing across the lawn disappeared behind the stage. Poor Major Benjy (so weak of him to allow himself to be dragged into this sort of thing) looked a perfect guy in his crown (who could he be meant for?) and as for Diva – Then there was Georgie (Drake indeed!), and last of all Queen Elizabeth with her train held up by two choir-boys. Poor Lucia! Not content with a week of mumming at Riseholme she had to go on with her processions and dressings-up here. Some people lived on limelight.

Miss Mapp could not bring herself to take a seat close to the stage, and be seen applauding – there seemed to be some hitch with the curtain: no, it righted itself, what a pity! – and she hung about on the outskirts of the audience. Glees were interposed between the tableaux; how thin were the voices of those little boys out of doors! Then Irene, dressed like a sailor, recited that ludicrous parody. Roars of laughter. Then Major Benjy was King Cophetua: that was why he had a crown. Oh dear, oh dear! It was sad to reflect that an elderly, sensible man (for when at his best, he was that) could be got hold of by a pushing woman. The final tableau, of course (anyone might have guessed that), was the knighting of Drake by Queen Elizabeth. Then amid sycophantic applause the procession of guys returned and went back into the garden-room. Mr and Mrs Wyse followed them, and it seemed pretty clear that they were going to have a private tea there. Doubtless she would be soon sought for among the crowd with a message from Lucia to hope that she would join them in her own garden-room, but as nothing of the sort came, she presently thought that it would be only kind to Lucia to do so, and add her voice to the general chorus of congratulation that was no doubt going on. So with a brisk little tap on the door, and the inquiry 'May I come in?' she entered.

There they all were, as pleased as children with dressing-up. King Cophetua still wore his crown, tilted slightly to one side like a forage cap, and he and Queen Elizabeth and Queen Mary were seated round the tea-table and calling each other your Majesty. King Cophetua had a large whisky and soda in front of him and Miss Mapp felt quite certain it was not his first. But though sick in soul at these puerilities she pulled herself together and made a beautiful curtsey to the silly creatures. And the worst of it was that there was no one left of her own intimate circle to whom she could in private express her disdain, for they were all in it, either actively or, like the Wyses, truckling to Lucia.

Lucia for the moment seemed rather surprised to see her, but she welcomed her and poured her out a cup of rather tepid tea, nasty to the taste. She must truckle, too, to the whole lot of them, though that tasted nastier than the tea.

'How I congratulate you all,' she cried. 'Padre, you looked too cruel as executioner, your mouth so fixed and stern. It was quite a relief when the curtain came down. Irene, quaint one, how you made them laugh! Diva, Mr Georgie, and above all our wonderful Queen Lucia. What a treat it has all been! The choir! Those beautiful glees. A thousand pities, Mr Wyse, that the Contessa was not here.'

There was still Susan to whom she ought to say something pleasant, but positively she could not go on, until she had eaten something solid. But Lucia chimed in.

'And your garden, Elizabeth,' she said. 'How they are enjoying it. I believe if the truth was known they are all glad that our little tableaux are over, so that they can wander about and admire the flowers. I must give a little party some night soon with Chinese lanterns and fairy-lights in the beds.'

'Upon my word, your Majesty is spoiling us all,' said Major Benjy. 'Tilling's never had a month with so much pleasure provided for it. Glorious.'

Miss Mapp had resolved to stop here if it was anyhow possible, till these sycophants had dispersed, and then have one private word with Lucia to indicate how ready she was to overlook all the little frictions that had undoubtedly arisen. She fully meant, without eating a morsel of humble pie herself, to allow Lucia to eat proud pie, for she saw that just for the present she herself was nowhere and Lucia everywhere. So Lucia should glut herself into a sense of complete superiority, and then it would be time to begin fresh manoeuvres. Major Benjy and Diva soon took themselves off: she saw them from the garden-window going very slowly down the street, ever so pleased to have people staring at them, and Irene, at the Padre's request, went out to dance a hornpipe on the lawn in her sailor clothes. But the two Wyses (always famous for sticking) remained and Georgie.

Mr Wyse got up from the tea-table and passed round behind Miss Mapp's chair. Out of the corner of her eye she could see he was looking at the wall where a straw-coloured picture of her own hung. He always used to admire it, and it was pleasant to feel that he was giving it so careful and so respectful a scrutiny. Then he spoke to Lucia.

'How well I remember seeing you painting that,' he said, 'and how long I took to forgive myself for having disturbed you in my blundering car. A perfect little masterpiece, Mallards Cottage and the crooked chimney. To the life.'

Susan heaved herself up from the sofa and joined in the admiration.

'Perfectly delightful,' she said. 'The lights, the shadows. Beautiful! What a touch!'

Miss Mapp turned her head slowly as if she had a stiff neck, and verified her awful conjecture that it was no longer a picture of her own that hung there, but the very picture of Lucia's which had been rejected for the Art Exhibition. She felt as if no picture but a bomb hung there, which might explode at some chance word, and blow her into a thousand fragments. It was best to hurry from this perilous neighbourhood.

'Dear Lucia,' she said, 'I must be off. Just one little stroll, if I may, round my garden, before I go home. My roses will never forgive me, if I go away without noticing them.'

She was too late.

'How I wish I had known it was finished!' said Mr Wyse. 'I should have begged you to allow us to have it for our Art Exhibition. It would have been the gem of it. Cruel of you, Mrs Lucas!'

'But I sent it in to the hanging committee,' said Lucia. 'Georgie sent his, too, of Mallards. They were both sent back to us.'

Mr Wyse turned from the picture to Lucia with an expression of incredulous horror, and Miss Mapp quietly turned to stone.

'But impossible,' he said. 'I am on the hanging committee myself, and I hope you cannot think I should have been such an imbecile. Susan is on the committee too: so is Miss Mapp. In fact, we are the hanging committee. Susan, that gem, that little masterpiece never came before us.'

'Never,' said Susan. 'Never. Never, never.'

Mr Wyse's eye transferred itself to Miss Mapp. She was still stone and her face was as white as the wall of Mallards Cottage in the masterpiece. Then for the first time in the collective memory of Tilling Mr Wyse allowed himself to use slang.

'There has been some hanky-panky,' he said. 'That picture never came before the hanging committee.'

The stone image could just move its eyes and they looked, in a glassy manner, at Lucia. Lucia's met them with one short gimlet thrust, and she whisked round to Georgie. Her face was turned away from the others, and she gave him a prodigious wink, as he sat there palpitating with excitement.

'*Georgino mio*,' she said. 'Let us recall exactly what happened. The morning, I mean, when the hanging committee met. Let me see: let me see. Don't interrupt me: I will get it all clear.'

Lucia pressed her hands to her forehead.

'I have it,' she said. 'It is perfectly vivid to me now. You had taken our little pictures down to the framer's, Georgie, and told him to send them in to Elizabeth's house direct. That was it. The errand-boy from the framer's came up here that very morning, and delivered mine to Grosvenor, and yours to Foljambe. Let me think exactly when that was. What time was it, Mr Wyse, that the hanging committee met?'

'At twelve, precisely,' said Mr Wyse.

'That fits in perfectly,' said Lucia. 'I called to Georgie out of the window here, and we told each other that our pictures had been rejected. A moment later, I saw your car go down to the High Street and when I went down there soon afterwards, it was standing in front of Miss – I mean Elizabeth's house. Clearly what happened was that the framer misunderstood

Georgie's instructions, and returned the pictures to us before the hanging committee sat at all. So you never saw them, and we imagined all the time – did we not, Georgie? – that you had simply sent them back.'

'But what must you have thought of us?' said Mr Wyse, with a gesture of despair.

'Why, that you did not conscientiously think very much of our art,' said Lucia. 'We were perfectly satisfied with your decision. I felt sure that my little picture had a hundred faults and feeblenesses.'

Miss Mapp had become unpetrified. Could it be that by some miraculous oversight she had not put into those parcels the formal, typewritten rejection of the committee? It did not seem likely, for she had a very vivid remembrance of the gratification it gave her to do so, but the only alternative theory was to suppose a magnanimity on Lucia's part which seemed even more miraculous. She burst into speech.

'How we all congratulate ourselves,' she cried, 'that it has all been cleared up! Such a stupid errand-boy! What are we to do next, Mr Wyse? Our exhibition must secure Lucia's sweet picture, and of course Mr Pillson's too. But how are we to find room for them? Everything is hung.'

'Nothing easier,' said Mr Wyse. 'I shall instantly withdraw my paltry little piece of still-life, and I am sure that Susan –'

'No, that would never do,' said Miss Mapp, currying favour all round. 'That beautiful wallflower, I could almost smell it: that King of Italy. Mine shall go: two or three of mine. I insist on it.'

Mr Wyse bowed to Lucia and then to Georgie.

'I have a plan better yet,' he said. 'Let us put – if we may have the privilege of securing what was so nearly lost to our exhibition – let us put these two pictures on easels as showing how deeply we appreciate our good fortune in getting them.'

He bowed to his wife, he bowed – was it quite a bow? – to Miss Mapp, and had there been a mirror, he would no doubt have bowed to himself.

'Besides,' he said, 'our little sketches will not thus suffer so much from their proximity to –' and he bowed to Lucia. 'And if Mr Pillson will similarly allow us –' he bowed to Georgie.

Georgie, following Lucia's lead, graciously offered to go round to the Cottage and bring back his picture of Mallards, but Mr Wyse would not hear of such a thing. He and Susan would go off in the Royce now, with Lucia's masterpiece, and fetch Georgie's from Mallards Cottage, and the sun should not set before they both stood on their distinguished easels in the enriched exhibition. So off they went in a great hurry to procure the easels before the sun went down and Miss Mapp, unable alone to face the reinstated victims of her fraud, scurried after them in a tumult of mixed emotions. Outside in the garden Irene, dancing hornpipes, was surrounded by both sexes of the enraptured youth of Tilling, for the boys knew she was a girl, and the girls thought she looked so like a boy. She shouted out 'Come and dance, Mapp,' and Elizabeth fled from her own sweet garden as if it had been a plague-stricken area, and never spoke to her roses at all.

The Queen and Drake were left alone in the garden-room.

'Well, I never!' said Georgie. 'Did you? She sent them back all by herself.'

'I'm not the least surprised,' said Lucia. 'It's like her.'

'But why did you let her off?' he asked. 'You ought to have exposed her and have done with her.'

Lucia showed a momentary exultation, and executed a few steps from a Morris-dance.

'No, Georgie, that would have been a mistake,' she said. 'She knows that we know, and I can't wish her worse than that. And I rather think, though he makes me giddy with so much bowing, that Mr Wyse has guessed. He certainly suspects something of the sort.'

'Yes, he said there had been some hanky-panky,' said Georgie. 'That was a strong thing for him to say. All the same –'

Lucia shook her head.

'No, I'm right,' she said. 'Don't you see I've taken the moral stuffing out of that woman far more completely than if I had exposed her?'

'But she's a cheat,' cried Georgie. 'She's a liar, for she sent back our pictures with a formal notice that the committee had rejected them. She hasn't got any moral stuffing to take out.'

Lucia pondered this.

'That's true, there doesn't seem to be much,' she said. 'But even then, think of the moral stuffing that I've put into myself. A far greater score, Georgie, than to have exposed her, and it must be quite agonizing for her to have that hanging over her head. Besides, she can't help being deeply grateful to me if there are any depths in that poor shallow nature. There may be: we must try to discover them. Take a broader view of it all, Georgie . . . Oh, and I've thought of something fresh! Send round to Mr Wyse for the exhibition your picture of the Landgate, which poor Elizabeth sold. He will certainly hang it and she will see it there. That will round everything off nicely.'

Lucia moved across to the piano and sat down on the treble music-stool.

'Let us forget all about these *piccoli disturbi*, Georgie,' she said, 'and have some music to put us in tune with beauty again. No, you needn't shut the door: it is so hot, and I am sure that no one else will dream of passing that notice of "Private", or come in here unasked. Ickle bit of divine Mozartino?'

Lucia found the duet at which she had worked quietly at odd moments.

'Let us try this,' she said, 'though it looks rather diffy. Oh, one thing more, Georgie. I think you and I had better keep those formal notices of rejection from the hanging committee just in case. We might need them some day, though I'm sure I hope we shan't. But one must be careful in dealing with that sort of woman. That's all I think. Now let us breathe harmony and loveliness again. *Uno, due* . . . pom.'

6

It was a mellow morning of October, the season, as Lucia reflected, of mists and mellow fruitfulness, wonderful John Keats. There was no doubt about the mists, for there had been several sea-fogs in the English Channel, and the mellow fruitfulness of the garden at Mallards was equally indisputable. But now the fruitfulness of that sunny plot concerned Lucia far more than it had done during August and September, for she had taken Mallards for another month (Adele Brixton having taken the Hurst, Riseholme, for three), not on those original Shylock terms of fifteen guineas a week, and no garden-produce – but of twelve guineas a week, and all the garden-produce. It was a wonderful year for tomatoes: there were far more than a single widow could possibly eat, and Lucia, instead of selling them, constantly sent little presents of them to Georgie and Major Benjy. She had sent one basket of them to Miss Mapp, but these had been returned and Miss Mapp had written an effusive note saying that they would be wasted on her. Lucia had applauded that; it showed a very proper spirit.

The chain of consequences, therefore, of Lucia's remaining at Mallards was far-reaching. Miss Mapp took Wasters for another month at a slightly lower rent, Diva extended her lease of Taormina, and Irene still occupied the four-roomed labourer's cottage outside Tilling, which suited her so well, and the labourer and his family remained in the hop-picker's shanty. It was getting chilly of nights in the shanty, and he looked forward to the time when, Adele having left the Hurst, his cottage could be restored to him. Nor did the chain of consequences end here, for Georgie could not go back to Riseholme without Foljambe, and Foljambe would not go back there and leave her Cadman, while Lucia remained at Mallards.

So Isabel Poppit continued to inhabit her bungalow by the sea, and Georgie remained in Mallards Cottage. With her skin turned black with all those sun-baths, and her hair spiky and wiry with so many sea-baths, Isabel resembled a cross between a kipper and a sea-urchin.

September had been full of events. The Art Exhibition had been a great success, and quantities of the pictures had been sold. Lucia had bought Georgie's picture of Mallards, Georgie had bought Lucia's picture of Mallards Cottage, Mr Wyse had bought his wife's pastel of the King of Italy, and sent it as a birthday present to Amelia, and Susan Wyse had bought her husband's teacup and wallflower and kept them herself. But the greatest gesture of all had been Lucia's purchase of one of Miss Mapp's six exhibits, and this had practically forced Miss Mapp, so powerful was the suggestion hidden in it, to buy Georgie's picture of the Landgate, which he had given her, and which she had sold (not even for her own benefit but for that of the hospital) for sixpence at her jumble-sale. She had had to pay a guinea to regain what had once been hers, so that in the end the revengeful impulse which had prompted her to put it in the sixpenny tray had been cruelly expensive. But she had still felt herself to be under Lucia's thumb in the whole matter of the exhibition (as indeed she was) and this purchase was of the nature of a propitiatory act. They had met one morning at the show, and Lucia had looked long at this sketch of Georgie's and then, looking long at Elizabeth, she had said it was one of the most charming and exquisite of his water-colours. Inwardly raging, yet somehow impotent to resist, Elizabeth had forked up. But she was now busily persuading herself that this purchase had something to do with the hospital, and that she need not make any further contributions to its funds this year: she felt there was a very good chance of persuading herself about this. No one had bought quaint Irene's pictures, and she had turned the women wrestlers into men.

Since then Miss Mapp had been very busy with the conversion of the marvellous crop of apples, plums and redcurrants in Diva's garden into jam and jelly. Her cook could not tackle so big a job alone, and she herself spent hours a day in the kitchen, and the most delicious odours of boiling preserves were wafted out of the windows into the High Street. It could not be supposed that they would escape Diva's sharp nose, and there had been words about it. But garden-produce (Miss Mapp believed) meant what it said, or would dear Diva prefer that she let the crop rot on the trees, and be a portion for wasps. Diva acknowledged that she would. And when the fruit was finished Miss Mapp proposed to turn her attention to the vegetable marrows, which, with a little ginger, made a very useful preserve for the household. She would leave a dozen of these pots for Diva.

But the jam-making was over now and Miss Mapp was glad of that, for she had scalded her thumb: quite a blister. She was even gladder that the Art Exhibition was over. All the import-ant works of the Tilling school (except the pastel of the King of Italy) remained in Tilling, she had made her propitiatory sacrifice about Georgie's sketch of the Landgate, and she had no reason to suppose that Lucia had ever repented of that moment of superb magnanimity in the garden-room, which had averted an exposure of which she still occasionally trembled to think. Lucia could not go back on that now, it was all over and done with like the jam-making (though, like the jam-making, it had left a certain seared and sensitive place behind) and having held her tongue then, Lucia could not blab after-wards. Like the banns in church, she must for ever hold her peace. Miss Mapp had been deeply grateful for that clemency at the time, but no one could go on being grateful indefinitely. You were grateful until you had paid your debt of gratitude, and then you were free. She would certainly be grateful again, when this month was over and Lucia and Georgie left Tilling, never, she hoped, to return, but for the last week or two she had felt that she had discharged in full every groat of gratitude she owed Lucia, and her mind had been busier than usual over plots and plans and libels and inductions with regard to her tenant who, with those cheese-paring ways so justly abhorred by Miss Mapp, had knocked down the rent to twelve guineas a week and grabbed the tomatoes.

But Miss Mapp did not yet despair of dealing Lucia some nasty blow, for the fact of the matter was (she felt sure of it) that Tilling generally was growing a little restive under Lucia's autocratic ways. She had been taking them in hand, she had been patronizing them, which Tilling never could stand, she had been giving them treats, just like that! She had sent out cards for an evening party (not dinner at all) with '*un po' di musica*' written in the left-hand corner. Even Mr Wyse, that notorious sycophant, had raised his eyebrows over this, and had allowed that this was rather an unusual inscription: '*musica*' (he thought) would have been more ordinary, and he would ask Amelia when she came. That had confirmed a secret suspicion which Miss Mapp had long entertained that Lucia's Italian (and, of course, Georgie's too) was really confined to such words as '*ecco*' and '*bon giorno*' and '*bello*' and she was earnestly hoping that Amelia would come before October was over, and they would all see what these great talks in Italian to which Mr Wyse was so looking forward, would amount to.

And what an evening that 'po-di-mu' (as it was already referred to with faint little smiles) had been! It was a wet night and in obedience to her command (for at that time Lucia was at the height of the ascendancy she had acquired at the hospital fête), they had all put mackintoshes over their evening clothes, and galoshes over their evening shoes, and slopped up to Mallards through the pouring rain. A couple of journeys of Lucia's car could have brought them all in comfort and dryness, but she had not offered so obvious a convenience. Mrs Wyse's Royce was being overhauled, so they had to walk too, and a bedraggled and discontented company had assembled. They had gone into the garden-room dripped on by the wistaria, and an interminable po-di-mu ensued. Lucia turned off all the lights in the room except one on the piano, so that they saw her profile against a black background, like the head on a postage stamp, and first she played the slow movement out of the 'Moonlight' Sonata. She stopped once, just after she had begun, because Diva coughed, and when she had finished there was a long silence. Lucia sighed and Georgie sighed, and everyone said 'Thank you' simultaneously. Major Benjy said he was devoted to Chopin and Lucia playfully told him that she would take his musical education in hand.

Then she had allowed the lights to be turned up again, and there was a few minutes' pause to enable them to conquer the poignancy of emotion aroused by that exquisite rendering of the 'Moonlight' Sonata, to disinfect it so to speak with cigarettes, or drown it, as Major Benjy did, in rapid whiskies and sodas, and when they felt braver the po-di-mu began again, with a duet, between her and Georgie, of innumerable movements by Mozart, who must indeed have been a most prolific composer if he wrote all that. Diva fell quietly asleep, and presently there were indications that she would soon be noisily asleep. Miss Mapp hoped that she would begin to snore properly, for that would be a good set-down for Lucia, but Major Benjy poked her stealthily on the knee to rouse her. Mr Wyse began to stifle yawns, though he sat as upright as ever, with his eyes fixed rather glassily on the ceiling, and ejaculated 'Charming' at the end of every movement. When it was all over there were some faintly murmured requests that Lucia would play to them again, and without any further pressing, she sat down. Her obtuseness was really astounding.

'How you all work me!' she said. 'A fugue by Bach then, if you insist on it, and if Georgie will promise not to scold me if I break down.'

Luckily amid suppressed sighs of relief, she did break down, and though she was still perfectly willing to try again, there was a general chorus of unwillingness to take advantage of her great good nature, and after a wretched supper, consisting largely of tomato-salad, they trooped out into the rain, cheered by the promise of another musical evening next week when she would have that beautiful fugue by heart.

It was not the next week but the same week that they had all been bidden to a further evening of harmony, and symptoms of revolt, skilfully fomented by Miss Mapp, were observable. She had just received her note of invitation one morning, when Diva trundled in to Wasters.

'Another po-di-mu already,' said she sarcastically. 'What are you –'

'Isn't it unfortunate?' interrupted Elizabeth, 'for I hope, dear Diva, you have not forgotten that you promised to come in that very night – Thursday, isn't it – and play piquet with me.'

Diva returned Elizabeth's elaborate wink. 'So I did,' she said. 'Anyhow, I do.'

'Consequently we shall have to refuse dear Lucia's invitation,' said Elizabeth regretfully. 'Lovely, wasn't it, the other night? And so many movements of Mozart. I began to think he must have discovered the secret of perpetual motion, and that we should be stuck there till Doomsday.'

Diva was fidgeting about the room in her restless manner. ('Rather like a spinning top,' thought Miss Mapp, 'bumping into everything. I wish it would die.')

'I don't think she plays bridge very well,' said Diva. 'She began, you know, by saying she was so anxious to learn, and that we all played marvellously, but now she lays down the law like anything, telling us what we ought to have declared, and how we ought to have played. It's quite like –'

She was going to say 'It's quite like playing with you,' but luckily stopped in time.

'I haven't had the privilege of playing with her. Evidently I'm not up to her form,' said Elizabeth, 'but I hear, only report, mind, that she doesn't know the elements of the game.'

'Well, not much more,' said Diva. 'And she says she will start a bridge class if we like.'

'She spoils us! And who will the pupils be?' asked Elizabeth.

'I know one who won't,' said Diva darkly.

'And one and one make two,' observed Elizabeth. 'A pity that she sets herself up like that. Saying the other night that she would take Major Benjy's musical education in hand! I always thought education began at home, and I'm sure I never heard so many wrong notes in my life.'

Diva ruminated a moment, and began spinning again. 'She offered to take the choir-practices in church, only the Padre wouldn't hear of it,' she said. 'And there's talk of a class to read Homer in Pope's translation.'

'She has every accomplishment,' said Elizabeth, 'including push.'

Diva bumped into another topic.

'I met Mr Wyse just now,' she said. 'Countess Amelia Faraglione is coming to-morrow.'

Miss Mapp sprang up.

'Not really?' she cried. 'Why, she'll be here for Lucia's po-di-mu on Thursday. And the Wyses will be going, that's certain, and they are sure to ask if they may bring the Faradidleone with them. Diva, dear, we must have our piquet another night. I wouldn't miss that for anything.'

'Why?' asked Diva.

'Just think what will happen! She'll be forced to talk Italian, for Mr Wyse has often said what a treat it will be to hear them talk it together, and I'm sure Lucia doesn't know any. I must be there.'

'But if she does know it, it will be rather a sell,' said Diva. 'We shall have gone there for nothing except to hear all that Mozart over again and to eat tomatoes. I had heart-burn half the night afterwards.'

'Trust me, Diva,' said Elizabeth. 'I swear she doesn't know any Italian. And how on earth will she be able to wriggle out of talking it? With all her ingeniousness, it can't be done. She can't help being exposed.'

'Well, that would be rather amusing,' said Diva. 'Being put down a peg or two certainly wouldn't hurt her. All right. I'll say I'll come.'

Miss Mapp's policy was now of course the exact reverse of what she had first planned. Instead of scheming to get all Tilling to refuse Lucia's invitation to listen to another po-di-mu, her object was to encourage everyone to go, in order that they might listen not so much to Mozart as to her rich silences or faltering replies when challenged to converse in the Italian language. She found that the Padre and Mrs Bartlett had hurriedly arranged a choir-practice and a meeting of the girl-guides respectively to take place at the unusual hour of half-past nine in the evening in order to be able to decline the po-di-mu, but Elizabeth, throwing economy to the winds, asked them both to dine with her on the fatal night, and come on to Lucia's delicious music afterwards. This added inducement prevailed, and off they scurried to tell choir-boys and girl-guides that the meetings were cancelled and would be held at the usual hour the day after. The curate needed no persuasion, for he thought that Lucia had a wonderful touch on the piano, and was already looking forward to more; Irene similarly had developed a violent *schwärm* for Lucia and had accepted, so that Tilling, thanks to Elizabeth's friendly offices, would now muster in force to hear Lucia play duets and fugues and not speak Italian. And when, in casual conversation with Mr Wyse, Elizabeth learned that he had (as she had anticipated) ventured to ask Lucia if she would excuse the presumption of one of her greatest admirers, and allow him to bring his sister Amelia to her *soirée* and that Lucia had sent him her most cordial permission to do so, it seemed that nothing could stand in the way of the fulfilment of Elizabeth's romantic revenge on that upstart visitor for presuming to set herself up as Queen of the social life of Tilling.

It was, as need hardly be explained, this aspect of the affair which so strongly appealed to the sporting instincts of the place. Miss Mapp had long been considered by others as well as herself the first social citizen of Tilling, and though she had often been obliged to fight desperately for her position, and had suffered from time to time manifold reverses, she had managed to maintain it, because there was no one else of so commanding and unscrupulous a character. Then, this alien from Riseholme had appeared and had not so much challenged her as just taken her sceptre and her crown and worn them now for a couple of months. At present all attempts to recapture them had failed, but Lucia had grown a little arrogant, she had offered to take choir-practice, she had issued her invitations (so thought Tilling) rather as if they had been commands, and Tilling would not have been sorry to see her suffer some set-back. Nobody wanted to turn out in the evening to hear her play Mozart (except the curate), no one intended to listen to her read Pope's translation of Homer's *Iliad*, or to be instructed how to play bridge, and though Miss Mapp was no favourite, they would have liked to see her score. But there was little partisanship; it was the sporting instinct which looked forward to witnessing an engagement between two well-equipped Queens, and seeing whether one really could speak Italian or not, even if they had to listen to all the fugues of Bach first. Everyone, finally, except Miss Mapp, wherever their private sympathies might lie, regretted that now in less than a month, Lucia would have gone back to her own kingdom of Riseholme, where it appeared she had no rival of any sort, for these encounters were highly stimulating to students of human nature and haters of Miss Mapp. Never before had Tilling known so exciting a season.

On this mellow morning, then, of October, Lucia, after practising her fugue for the coming po-di-mu, and observing Coplen bring into the house a wonderful supply of tomatoes, had received that appalling note from Mr Wyse, conveyed by the Royce, asking if he might bring Contessa Amelia di Faraglione to the musical party to which he so much looked forward. The gravity of the issue was instantly clear to Lucia, for Mr Wyse had made no secret about the pleasure it would give him to hear his sister and herself mellifluously converse in the Italian tongue, but without hesitation she sent back a note by the chauffeur and the Royce, that she would be charmed to see the Contessa. There was no getting out of that, and she must accept the inevitable before proceeding irresistibly to deal with it. From the window she observed the Royce backing and advancing and backing till it managed to turn and went round the corner to Porpoise Street.

Lucia closed the piano, for she had more cosmic concerns to think about than the fingerings of a fugue. Her party of course (that required no consideration) would have to be cancelled, but that was only one point in the problem that confronted her. For that baleful bilinguist the Contessa di Faraglione was not coming to Tilling (all the way from Italy) for one night but she was to stay here so Mr Wyse's note had mentioned, for 'about a week', after which she would pay visits to her relations the Wyses of Whitchurch and others. So for a whole week (or about) Lucia would be in perpetual danger of being called upon to talk Italian. Indeed, the danger was more than mere danger, for if anything in this world was certain, it was that Mr Wyse would ask her to dinner during this week, and exposure would follow. Complete disappearance from Tilling during the Contessa's sojourn here was the only possible plan, yet how was that to be accomplished? Her house at Riseholme was let, but even if it had not been, she could not leave Tilling to-morrow, when she had invited everybody to a party in the evening.

The clock struck noon: she had meditated for a full half-hour, and now she rose.

'I can only think of influenza,' she said to herself. 'But I shall consult Georgie. A man might see it from another angle.'

He came at once to her SOS.

'*Georgino mio*,' began Lucia, but then suddenly corrected herself. 'Georgie,' she said. 'Something very disagreeable. The Contessa Thingummy is coming to the Wyses to-morrow, and he's asked me if he may bring her to our *musica*. I had to say yes; no way out of it.'

Georgie was often very perceptive, He saw what this meant at once.

'Good Lord,' he said. 'Can't you put it off? Sprain your thumb.'

The man's angle was not being of much use so far.

'Not a bit of good,' she said. 'She'll be here about a week, and naturally I have to avoid meeting her altogether. The only thing I can think of is influenza.'

Georgie never smoked in the morning, but the situation seemed to call for a cigarette.

'That would do it,' he said. 'Rather a bore for you, but you could live in the secret garden a good deal. It's not over-looked.'

He stopped: the unusual tobacco had stimulated his percep-tive powers.

'But what about me?' he said.

'I'm sure I don't know,' said Lucia.

'You're not looking far enough,' said Georgie. 'You're not taking the long view which you so often talk to me about. I can't have influenza too, it would be too suspicious. So I'm bound to meet the Faraglione and she'll see in a minute I can't talk Italian.'

'Well?' said Lucia in a very selfish manner, as if he didn't matter at all.

'Oh, I'm not thinking about myself only,' said Georgie in self-defence. 'Not so at all. It'll react on you. You and I are supposed to talk Italian together, and when it's obvious I can't say more than three things in it, the fat's in the fire, however much influenza you have. How are you going to be supposed to jabber away in Italian to me when it's seen that I can't understand a word of it?'

Here indeed was the male angle, and an extremely awkward angle it was. For a moment Lucia covered her face with her hands.

'Georgie, what are we to do?' she asked in a stricken voice.

Georgie was a little ruffled at having been considered of such absolute unimportance until he pointed out to Lucia that her fate was involved with his, and it pleased him to echo her words.

'I'm sure I don't know,' he said stiffly.

Lucia hastened to smooth his smart.

'My dear, I'm so glad I thought of consulting you,' she said. 'I knew it would take a man's mind to see all round the question, and how right you are! I never thought of that.'

'Quite,' said Georgie. 'It's evident you haven't grasped the situation at all.'

She paced up and down the garden-room in silence, recoiling once from the window, as she saw Elizabeth go by and kiss her hand with that awful hyena grin of hers.

'Georgie, 'oo not cross with poor Lucia?' she said, resorting to the less dangerous lingo which they used in happier days. This softened Georgie.

'I was rather,' said Georgie, 'but never mind that now. What am I to do? *Che faro*, in fact.'

Lucia shuddered.

'Oh, for goodness' sake, don't talk Italian,' she said. 'It's that we've got to avoid. It's odd that we have to break ourselves of the habit of doing something we can't do . . . And you can't have influenza too. It would be too suspicious if you began simultaneously with me to-morrow. I've often wondered, now I come to think of it, if that woman, that Mapp, hasn't suspected that our Italian was a fake, and if we both had influenza exactly as the Faraglione arrived, she might easily put two and two together. Her mind is horrid enough for anything.'

'I know she suspects,' said Georgie. 'She said some word in Italian to me the other day, which meant paper-knife, and she looked surprised when I didn't understand, and said it in English. Of course, she had looked it out in a dictionary: it was a trap.'

A flood of horrid light burst in on Lucia.

'Georgie,' she cried. 'She tried me with the same word. I've forgotten it again, but it did mean paper-knife. I didn't know it either, though I pretended it was her pronunciation that puzzled me. There's no end to her craftiness. But I'll get the better of her yet. I think you'll have to go away, while the Faraglione is here and I have influenza.'

'But I don't want to go away,' began Georgie. 'Surely we can think of –'

Lucia paid no heed to this attempt at protest: it is doubtful if she even heard it, for the spark was lit now, and it went roaring through her fertile brain like a prairie fire in a high gale.

'You must go away to-morrow,' she said. 'Far better than influenza, and you must stop away till I send you a telegram, that the Faraglione has left. It will be very dull for me because I shall be entirely confined to the house and garden all the time you are gone. I think the garden will be safe. I cannot remember that it is overlooked from any other house and I shall do a lot of reading, though even the piano won't be possible . . . Georgie, I see it all. You have not been looking very well lately (my dear, you're the picture of health really, I have never seen you looking younger or better) and so you will have gone off to have a week at Folkestone or Littlestone, whichever you prefer. Sea air; you needn't bathe. And you can take my car, for I shan't be able to use it, and why not take

Foljambe as well to valet you, as you often do when you go for a jaunt? She'll have her Cadman: we may as well make other people happy, Georgie, as it all seems to fit in so beautifully. And one thing more: this little jaunt of yours is entirely undertaken for my sake, and I must insist on paying it all. Go to a nice hotel and make yourself thoroughly comfortable; half a bottle of champagne whenever you want it in the evening, and what extras you like, and I will telephone to you to say when you can come back. You must start to-morrow morning before the Faraglione gets here.'

Georgie knew it was useless to protest when Lucia got that loud, inspired, gabbling ring in her voice; she would cut through any opposition, as a steam saw buzzes through the most solid oak board till, amid a fountain of flying sawdust, it has sliced its way. He did not want to go away, but when Lucia exhibited that calibre of determination that he should, it was better to yield at once than to collapse later in a state of wretched exhaustion. Besides, there were bright points in her scheme. Foljambe would be delighted at the plan, for it would give her and Cadman leisure to enjoy each other's society; and it would not be disagreeable to stay for a week at some hotel in Folkestone and observe the cargoes of travellers from abroad arriving at the port after a billowy passage. Then he might find some bibelots in the shops, and he would listen to a municipal band, and have a bathroom next his bedroom, and do some sketches, and sit in a lounge in a series of those suits which had so justly earned him the title of the best-dressed man in Tilling. He would have a fine Rolls-Royce in the hotel garage, and a smart chauffeur coming to ask for orders every morning, and he would be seen, an interesting and opulent figure, drinking his half-bottle of champagne every evening and he would possibly pick up an agreeable acquaintance or two. He had no hesitation whatever in accepting Lucia's proposal to stand the charges of this expedition, for, as she had most truly said, it was undertaken in her interests, and naturally she paid (besides, she was quite rich) for its equipment.

The main lines of this defensive campaign being thus laid down, Lucia, with her Napoleonic eye for detail, plunged into minor matters. She did not, of course, credit 'that Mapp' with having procured the visit of the Faraglione, but a child could see that if she herself met the Faraglione during her stay here the grimmest exposure of her ignorance of the language she talked in such admired snippets must inevitably follow. 'That Mapp'· would pounce on this, and it was idle to deny that she would score heavily and horribly. But Georgie's absence (cheap at the cost) and her own invisibility by reason of influenza made a seemingly unassailable position and it was with a keen sense of exhilaration in the coming contest that she surveyed the arena.

Lucia sent for the trusty Grosvenor and confided in her sufficiently to make her a conspirator. She told her that she had a great mass of arrears to do in reading and writing, and that for the next week she intended to devote herself to them, and lead the life of a hermit. She wanted no callers, and did not mean to see anyone, and the easiest excuse was to say that she had influenza. No doubt there would be many inquiries, and so day by day she would issue to Grosvenor her own official bulletin. Then she told Cadman that Mr Georgie was far from well, and she had bundled him off with the car to Folkestone for about a week: he and Foljambe would accompany him. Then she made a careful survey of the house and garden to ascertain what freedom of movement she could have during her illness. Playing the piano, except very carefully with the soft pedal down, would be risky, but by a judicious adjustment of the curtains in the garden-room window, she could refresh herself with very satisfactory glances at the world outside. The garden, she was pleased to notice, was quite safe, thanks to its encompassing walls, from any prying eyes in the houses round: the top of the church tower alone overlooked it, and that might be disregarded, for only tourists ascended it.

Then forth she went for the usual shoppings and chats in the High Street and put in some further fine work. The morning tide was already on the ebb, but by swift flittings this way and that she managed to have a word with most of those who were coming to her po-di-mu to-morrow, and interlarded all she said to them with brilliant scraps of Italian. She just caught the Wyses as they were getting back into the Royce and said how *molto amabile* it was of them to give her the *gran' piacere* of seeing the Contessa next evening: indeed she would be a welcome guest, and it would be another *gran' piacere* to talk *la bella lingua* again. Georgie, alas, would not be there for he was *un po' ammalato*, and was going to spend a *settimana* by the *mare per stabilirsi*. Never had she been so fluent and idiomatic, and she accepted with *mille grazie* Susan's invitation to dine the evening after her music and renew the conversations to which she so much looked forward. She got almost tipsy with Italian ... Then she flew across the street to tell the curate that she was going to shut herself up all afternoon in order to get the Bach fugue more worthy of his critical ear, she told Diva to come early to her party in order that they might have a little chat first, and she just managed by a flute-like 'Cooee' to arrest Elizabeth as she was on the very doorstep of Wasters. With glee she learned that Elizabeth was entertaining the Padre and his wife and Major Benjy to dinner before she brought them on to her party, and then, remembering the trap which that woman had laid for her and Georgie over the Italian paper-knife, she could not refrain from asking her to dine and play bridge on the third night of her coming illness. Of course she would be obliged to put her off, and that would be about square ... This half-hour's active work produced the impression that, however little pleasure Tilling anticipated from to-morrow's po-di-mu, the musician herself looked forward to it enormously, and was thirsting to talk Italian.

From the window of her bedroom next morning Lucia saw Georgie and Cadman and Foljambe set off for Folkestone, and it was with a Lucretian sense of pleasure in her own coming tranquillity that she contemplated the commotion and general upset of plans which was shortly to descend on Tilling. She went to the garden-room, adjusted the curtains and brewed the tempest which she now sent forth in the shape of a series of notes charged with the bitterest regrets. They were written in pencil (the consummate artist) as if from bed, and were traced in a feeble hand not like her usual firm script. 'What a disappointment!' she wrote to Mrs Wyse. 'How cruel to have got the influenza – where could she have caught it? – on the very morning of her party, and what a blow not to be able to welcome the Contessa to-day or to dine with dear Susan to-morrow!' There was another note to Major Benjy, and others to Diva and quaint Irene and the curate and the Padre and Elizabeth. She still hoped that possibly she might be well enough for bridge and dinner the day after to-morrow, but Elizabeth must remember how infectious influenza was, and again she herself might not be well enough. That seemed pretty safe, for Elizabeth had a frantic phobia of infection, and Wasters had reeked of carbolic all the time the jumble-sale was being held, for fear of some bit of rubbish having come in contact with tainted hands. Lucia gave these notes to Grosvenor for immediate delivery and told her that the bulletin for the day in answer to callers was that there was no anxiety, for the attack though sharp was not serious, and only demanded warmth and complete quiet. She then proceeded to get both by sitting in this warm October sun in her garden, reading Pope's translation of the *Iliad* and seeing what the Greek for it was.

Three impregnable days passed thus. From behind the adjusted curtains of the garden-room she observed the coming of many callers and Grosvenor's admirable demeanour to them. The Royce lurched up the street, and there was Susan in her sables, and, sitting next her, a vivacious gesticulating woman with a monocle, who looked the sort of person who could talk at the most appalling rate. This without doubt was the fatal Contessa, and Lucia felt that to see her thus was like observing a lion at large from behind the bars of a comfortable cage. Miss Mapp on the second day came twice, and each time she glanced piercingly at the curtains, as if she knew that trick, and listened as if hoping to hear the sound of the piano. The Padre sent a note almost entirely in Highland dialect, the curate turned away from the door with evident relief in his face at the news he had received, and whistled the Bach fugue rather out of tune.

On the fifth day of her illness new interests sprang up for Lucia that led her to neglect Pope's *Iliad* altogether. By the first post there came a letter from Georgie, containing an enclosure which Lucia saw (with a slight misgiving) was written in Italian. She turned first to Georgie's letter.

The most wonderful thing has happened [wrote Georgie] and you will be pleased ... There's a family here with whom I've made friends, an English father, an Italian mother and a girl with a pig-tail. Listen! The mother teaches the girl Italian, and sets her little themes to write on some subject or other, and then corrects them and writes a fair copy. Well, I was sitting in the lounge this morning while the girl was having her lesson, and Mrs Brocklebank (that's her name) asked me to suggest a subject for the theme, and I had the most marvellous idea. I said 'Let her write a letter to an Italian Countess whom she has never seen before, and say how she regretted having been obliged to put off her musical party to which she had asked the Countess and her brother, because she had caught influenza. She was so sorry not to meet her, and she was afraid that as the Countess was only staying a week in the place, she would not have the pleasure of seeing her at all.' Mrs B. thought that would do beautifully for a theme, and I repeated it over again to make sure. Then the girl wrote it, and Mrs B. corrected it and made a fair copy. I begged her to give it me, because I adored Italian (though I couldn't speak it) and it was so beautifully expressed. I haven't told this very well, because I'm in a hurry to catch the post, but I enclose Mrs B.'s Italian letter, and you just see whether it doesn't do the trick too marvellously. I'm having quite a gay time, music and drives and seeing the Channel boat come in, and aren't I clever?

Your devoted,
Georgie

Foljambe and Cadman have had a row, but I'm afraid they've made it up.

Lucia, with her misgivings turned to joyful expectation, seized and read the enclosure. Indeed it was a miraculous piece of manna to one whom the very sight of it made hungry. It might have been the result of telepathy between Mrs Brocklebank and her own subconscious self, so aptly did that lady grasp her particular unspoken need. It expressed in the most elegant idiom precisely what met the situation, and she would copy out and send it to-day, without altering a single word. And how clever of Georgie to have thought of it. He deserved all the champagne he could drink.

Lucia used her highest art in making a copy (on Mallard paper) of this document, as if writing hastily in a familiar medium. Occasionally she wrote a word (it did not matter what), erased it so as to render it illegible to the closest scrutiny, and then went on with Mrs Brocklebank's manuscript; occasionally she omitted a word of it and then inserted it with suitable curves of direction above. No one receiving her transcript could imagine that it was other than her own extempore scribble. Mrs Brocklebank had said that in two or three days she hoped to be able to see her friends again, and that fitted beautifully, because in two or three days now the Contessa's visit would have come to an end, and Lucia could get quite well at once.

The second post arrived before Lucia had finished this thoughtful copy. There was a letter in Lady Brixton's handwriting, and hastily scribbling the final florid salutations to the Contessa, she opened this, and thereupon forgot Georgie and Mrs Brocklebank and everything else in the presence of the tremendous question which was brought for her decision. Adele had simply fallen in love with Riseholme; she affirmed that life was no longer worth living without a house there, and, of all houses, she would like best to purchase, unfurnished, the Hurst. Failing that there was another that would do, belonging to round red little Mrs Quantock, who, she had ascertained, might consider selling it. Could darling Lucia therefore let her know with the shortest possible delay whether she would be prepared to sell the Hurst? If she had no thought of doing so Adele would begin tempting Mrs Quantock at once. But if she had, let genteel indications about price be outlined at once.

There are certain processes of mental solidification which take place with extraordinary rapidity, because the system is already soaked and super-saturated with the issues involved. It

was so now with Lucia. Instantly, on the perusal of Adele's
inquiries her own mind solidified. She had long been obliquely
contemplating some such step as Adele's letter thrust in front
of her, and she was surprised to find that her decision was
already made. Riseholme, once so vivid and significant, had
during these weeks at Tilling been fading like an ancient
photograph exposed to the sun, and all its features, foregrounds
and backgrounds had grown blurred and dim. If she went back
to Riseholme at the end of the month, she would find there
nothing to occupy her energies, or call out her unique powers
of self-assertion. She had so swept the board with her management of the Elizabethan fête that no further progress was
possible. Poor dear Daisy might occasionally make some
minute mutinies, but after being Drake's wife (what a lesson
for her!) there would be no real fighting spirit left in her. It
was far better, while her own energies still bubbled within her,
to conquer this fresh world of Tilling than to smoulder at
Riseholme. Her work there was done, whereas here, as this
week of influenza testified, there was a very great deal to do.
Elizabeth Mapp was still in action and capable of delivering
broadsides; innumerable crises might still arise, volcanoes
smoked, thunder-clouds threatened, there were hostile and
malignant forces to be thwarted. She had never been better
occupied and diverted, the place suited her, and it bristled
with opportunities. She wrote to Adele at once saying that dear
as Riseholme (and especially the Hurst) was to her, she was
prepared to be tempted, and indicated a sum before which she
was likely to fall.

Miss Mapp by this fifth day of Lucia's illness was completely
baffled. She did not yet allow herself to despair of becoming
unbaffled, for she was certain that there was a mystery here,
and every mystery had an explanation if you only worked at it
enough. The coincidence of Lucia's illness with the arrival of
the Contessa and Georgie's departure, supported by the trap
she had laid about the paper-knife, was far too glaring to be
overlooked by any constructive mind, and there must be something behind it. Only a foolish ingenuous child (and Elizabeth

was anything but that) could have considered these as isolated phenomena. With a faith that would have removed mountains, she believed that Lucia was perfectly well, but all she had been able to do at present was to recite her creed to Major Benjy and Diva and others, and eagerly wait for any shred of evidence to support it. Attempts to pump Grosvenor and lynx-like glances at the window of the garden-room had yielded nothing, and her anxious inquiry addressed to Dr Dobbie, the leading physician of Tilling, had yielded a snub. She did not know who Lucia's doctor was, so with a view to ascertaining that, and possibly getting other information, she had approached him with her most winning smile, and asked how the dear patient at Mallards was.

'I am not attending any dear patient at Mallards,' had been his unpromising reply, 'and if I was I need hardly remind you that, as a professional man, I should not dream of answering any inquiry about my patients without their express permission to do so. Good morning.'

'A very rude man,' thought Miss Mapp, 'but perhaps I had better not try to get at it that way.'

She looked up at the church, wondering if she would find inspiration in that beautiful grey tower, which she had so often sketched, outlined against the pellucid blue of the October sky. She found it instantly, for she remembered that the leads at the top of it which commanded so broad a view of the surrounding country commanded also a perfectly wonderful view of her own little secret garden. It was a small chance, but no chance however small must be neglected in this famine of evidence, and it came to her in a flash that there could be no more pleasant way of spending the morning than making a sketch of the green, green marsh and the line of the blue, blue sea beyond. She hurried back to Wasters, pausing only at Mallards to glance at the garden-room where the curtains were adjusted in the most exasperatingly skilful manner, and to receive Grosvenor's assurance that the patient's temperature was quite normal to-day.

'Oh, that is good news,' said Miss Mapp. 'Then to-morrow perhaps she will be about again.'

'I couldn't say, miss,' said Grosvenor, holding on to the door.

'Give her my fondest love,' said Miss Mapp, 'and tell her how rejoiced I am, please, Grosvenor.'

'Yes, miss,' said Grosvenor, and before Miss Mapp could step from the threshold, she heard the rattle of the chain behind the closed door.

She was going to lunch that day with the Wyses, a meal which Mr Wyse, in his absurd affected fashion, always alluded to as breakfast, especially when the Contessa was staying with them. Breakfast was at one, but there was time for an hour at the top of the church tower first. In order to see the features of the landscape better, she took up an opera-glass with her sketching-things. She first put a blue watery wash on her block for the sky and sea, and a green one for the marsh, and while these were drying she examined every nook of her garden with the opera-glass. No luck, and she picked up her sketch again on which the sky was rapidly inundating the land.

Lucia had learned this morning *via* Grosvenor and her cook and Figgis, Mr Wyse's butler, that the week of the Contessa's stay here was to be curtailed by one day and that the Royce would convey her to Whitchurch next morning on her visit to the younger but ennobled branch of the family. Further intelligence from the same source made known that the breakfast to-day to which Miss Mapp was bidden was a Belshazzar breakfast, eight if not ten. This was good news: the period of Lucia's danger of detection would be over in less than twenty-four hours, and about the time that Miss Mapp at the top of the tower of Tilling Church was hastily separating the firmament from the dry land, Lucia wrote out a telegram to Georgie that he might return the following day and find all clear. Together with that she sent a request to Messrs Woolgar & Pipstow that they should furnish her with an order to view a certain house she had seen just outside Tilling, near quaint Irene's cottage, which she had observed was for sale.

She hesitated about giving Grosvenor the envelope addressed to Contessa di Faraglione, which contained the transcript, duly signed, of Mrs Brocklebank's letter to a Countess, and decided, on the score of dramatic fitness, to have it delivered shortly after one o'clock when Mrs Wyse's breakfast would be in progress, with orders that it should be presented to the Contessa at once.

Lucia was feeling the want of vigorous exercise, and bethought herself of the Ideal System of Callisthenics for those no longer Young. For five days she had been confined to house and garden, and the craving to skip took possession of her. Skipping was an exercise highly recommended by the ideal system, and she told Grosvenor to bring back for her, with the order to view from Messrs Woolgar & Pipstow, a simple skipping-rope from the toy-shop in the High Street. While Grosvenor was gone this desire for free active movement in the open air awoke a kindred passion for the healthful action of the sun on the skin, and she hurried up to her sick-room, changed into a dazzling bathing-suit of black and yellow, and, putting on a very smart dressing-gown gay with ribands, was waiting in the garden-room when Grosvenor returned, recalling to her mind the jerks and swayings which had kept her in such excellent health when grief forbade her to play golf.

The hour was a quarter to one when Lucia tripped into the secret garden, shed her dressing-gown and began skipping on the little lawn with the utmost vigour. The sound of the church clock immediately below Miss Mapp's eyrie on the tower warned her that it was time to put her sketching things away, deposit them at Wasters and go out to breakfast. During the last half-hour she had cast periodical but fruitless glances at her garden, and had really given it up as a bad job. Now she looked down once more, and there close beside the bust of good Queen Anne was a gay striped figure of waspish colours skipping away like mad. She dropped her sketch, she reached out a trembling hand for her opera-glasses, the focus of which was already adjusted to a nicety, and by their aid she saw that this athletic wasp who was skipping with such exuberant activity was none other than the invalid.

Miss Mapp gave a shrill crow of triumph. All came to him who waited, and if she had known Greek she would undoubtedly have exclaimed 'Eureka': as it was she only crowed.

It was all too good to be true, but it was all too distinct not to be. 'Now I've got her,' she thought. 'The whole thing is as clear as daylight. I was right all the time. She has not had influenza any more than I, and I'll tell everybody at breakfast what I have seen.' But the sight still fascinated her. What shameless vigour, when she should have been languid with fever! What abysses of falsehood, all because she could not talk Italian! What expense to herself in that unnecessary dinner to the Padre and Major Benjy! There was no end to it . . .

Lucia stalked about the lawn with a high prancing motion when she had finished her skipping. Then she skipped again, and then she made some odd jerks, as if she was being electrocuted. She took long deep breaths, she lifted her arms high above her head as if to dive, she lay down on the grass and kicked, she walked on tiptoe like a ballerina, she swung her body round from the hips. All this had for Miss Mapp the fascination that flavours strong disgust and contempt. Eventually, just as the clock struck one, she wrapped herself in her dressing-gown, the best was clearly over. Miss Mapp was already late, and she must hurry straight from the tower to her breakfast, for there was no time to go back to Wasters first. She would be profuse in pretty apologies for her lateness; the view from the church tower had been so entrancing (this was perfectly true) that she had lost all count of time. She could not show her sketch to the general company, because the firmament had got dreadfully muddled up with the waters which were below it, but instead she would tell them something which would muddle up Lucia.

The breakfast-party was all assembled in Mrs Wyse's drawing-room with its dark oak beams and its silver-framed photographs and its morocco case containing the order of the MBE, still negligently open. Everybody had been waiting, everybody was rather grumpy at the delay, and on her entry the Contessa had clearly said '*Ecco!* Now at last!'

They would soon forgive her when they learned what had really made her late, but it was better to wait for a little before imparting her news, until breakfast had put them all in a more appreciative mood. She hastened on this desired moment by little compliments all round: what a wonderful sermon the Padre had preached last Sunday: how well dear Susan looked: what a delicious dish these eggs *à la Capri* were, she must really be greedy and take a teeny bit more. But these dewdrops were only interjected, for the Contessa talked in a loud continuous voice as usual, addressing the entire table, and speaking with equal fluency whether her mouth was full or empty.

At last the opportunity arrived. Figgis brought in a note on an immense silver (probably plated) salver, and presented it to the Contessa: it was to be delivered at once. Amelia said *'Scusi'* which everybody understood – even Lucia might have understood that – and was silent for a space as she tore it open and began reading it.

Miss Mapp decided to tantalize and excite them all before actually making her revelation.

'I will give anybody three guesses as to what I have seen this morning,' she said. 'Mr Wyse, Major Benjy, Padre, you must all guess. It is about someone whom we all know, who is still an invalid. I was sketching this morning at the top of the tower, and happened to glance down into my pet little secret garden. And there was Lucia in the middle of the lawn. How was she dressed, and what was she doing? Three guesses each, shall it be?'

Alas! The introductory tantalization had been too long, for before anybody could guess anything the Contessa broke in again.

'But never have I read such a letter!' she cried. 'It is from Mrs Lucas. All in Italian, and such Italian! Perfect. I should not have thought that any foreigner could have had such command of idiom and elegance. I have lived in Italy for ten years, but my Italian is a bungle compared to this. I have always said that no foreigner ever can learn Italian perfectly, and Cecco too, but we were wrong. This Mrs Lucas proves it. It is composed by the ear, the spoken word on paper. *Dio mio!* What an escape I have had, Algernon! You had a plan to bring me and your Mrs Lucas together to hear us talk. But she would smile to herself, and I should know what she was thinking, for she would be thinking how very poorly I talk

Italian compared with herself. I will read her letter to you all, and though you do not know what it means you will recognize a fluency, a music . . .

The Contessa proceeded to do so, with renewed exclamations of amazement, and all that bright edifice of suspicion, so carefully reared by the unfortunate Elizabeth, that Lucia knew no Italian, collapsed like a house built of cards when the table is shaken. Elizabeth had induced everybody to accept invitations to the second po-di-mu in order that all Tilling might hear Lucia's ignorance exposed by the Contessa, and when she had wriggled out of that, Elizabeth's industrious efforts had caused the gravest suspicions to be entertained that Lucia's illness was feigned in order to avoid any encounter with one who did know Italian, and now not only was not one pane of that Crystal Palace left unshattered, but the Contessa was congratulating herself on her own escape.

Elizabeth stirred feebly below the ruins: she was not quite crushed.

'I'm sure it sounds lovely,' she said when the recitation was over. 'But did not you yourself, dear Mr Wyse, think it odd that anyone who knew Italian should put *un po' di musica* on her invitation-card?'

'Then he was wrong,' said the Contessa. 'No doubt that phrase is a little humorous quotation from something I do not know. Rather like you ladies of Tilling who so constantly say "au reservoir". It is not a mistake: it is a joke.'

Elizabeth made a final effort.

'I wonder if dear Lucia wrote that note herself,' she said pensively.

'Pish! Her parlourmaid, doubtless,' said the Contessa. 'For me, I must spend an hour this afternoon to see if I can answer that letter in a way that will not disgrace me.'

There seemed little more to be said on that subject and Elizabeth hastily resumed her tantalization.

'Nobody has tried to guess yet what I saw from the church tower,' she said. 'Major Benjy, you try! It was Lucia, but how was she dressed and what was she doing?'

There was a coldness about Major Benjy. He had allowed

himself to suspect, owing to Elizabeth's delicate hints, that there was perhaps some Italian mystery behind Lucia's influenza, and now he must make amends.

'Couldn't say, I'm sure,' he said. 'She was sure to have been very nicely dressed from what I know of her.'

'I'll give you a hint then,' said she. 'I've never seen her dressed like that before.'

Major Benjy's attention completely wandered. He made no attempt to guess but sipped his coffee.

'You then, Mr Wyse, if Major Benjy gives up,' said Elizabeth, getting anxious. Though the suspected cause of Lucia's illness was disproved, it still looked as if she had never had influenza at all, and that was something.

'My ingenuity, I am sure, will not be equal to the occasion,' said Mr Wyse very politely. 'You will be obliged to tell me. I give up.'

Elizabeth emitted a shrill little titter.

'A dressing-gown,' she said. 'A bathing-costume. And she was skipping! Fancy! With influenza!'

There was a dreadful pause. No babble of excited inquiry and comment took place at all. The Contessa put up her monocle, focused Elizabeth for a moment, and this pause somehow was like the hush that succeeds some slight *gaffe*, some small indelicacy that had better have been left unsaid. Her host came to her rescue.

'That is indeed good news,' said Mr Wyse. 'We may encourage ourselves to hope that our friend is well on the road to convalescence. Thank you for telling us that, Miss Mapp.'

Mrs Bartlett gave one of her little mouse-like squeals, and Irene said:

'Hurrah! I shall try to see her this afternoon. I am glad.'

That again was an awful thought. Irene no doubt, if admitted, would give an account of the luncheon-party which would lose nothing in the telling, and she was such a ruthless mimic. Elizabeth felt a sinking feeling.

'Would that be wise, dear?' she said. 'Lucia is probably not yet free from infection, and we mustn't have you down with it. I wonder where she caught it, by the way?'

'But your point is that she's never had influenza at all,' said Irene with that dismal directness of hers.

Choking with this monstrous dose of fiasco, Elizabeth made for the present no further attempt to cause her friends to recoil from the idea of Lucia's skippings, for they only rejoiced that she was sufficiently recovered to do so. The party presently dispersed, and she walked away with her sketching-things and Diva, and glanced up the street towards her house. Irene was already standing by the door, and Elizabeth turned away with a shudder, for Irene waved her hand to them and was admitted.

'It's all very strange, dear Diva, isn't it?' she said. 'It's impossible to believe that Lucia's been ill, and it's useless to try to do so. Then there's Mr Georgie's disappearance. I never thought of that before.'

Diva interrupted.

'If I were you, Elizabeth,' she said, 'I should hold my tongue about it all. Much wiser.'

'Indeed?' said Elizabeth, beginning to tremble.

'Yes. I tell you so as a friend,' continued Diva firmly. 'You got hold of a false scent. You made us think that Lucia was avoiding the Faraglione. All wrong from beginning to end. One of your worst shots. Give it up.'

'But there is something queer,' said Elizabeth wildly. 'Skipping –'

'If there is,' said Diva, 'you're not clever enough to find it out. That's my advice. Take it or leave it. I don't care. Au reservoir.'

7

Had Miss Mapp been able to hear what went on in the garden-
room that afternoon, as well as she had been able to see what
had gone on that morning in the garden, she would never have
found Irene more cruelly quaint. Her account of this
luncheon-party was more than graphic, for so well did she
reproduce the Contessa's fervid monologue and poor Elizabeth's teasings over what she wanted them all to guess, that it
positively seemed to be illustrated. Almost more exasperating
to Miss Mapp would have been Lucia's pitiful contempt for
the impotence of her malicious efforts.

'Poor thing!' she said. 'Sometimes I think she is a little mad.
Una pazza: un po' pazza ... But I regret not seeing the
Contessa. Nice of her to have approved of my scribbled note,
and I dare say I should have found that she talked Italian very
well indeed. To-morrow – for after my delicious exercise on
the lawn this morning, I do not feel up to more to-day – to-
morrow I should certainly have hoped to call – in the afternoon
– and have had a chat with her. But she is leaving in the
morning, I understand.'

Lucia, looking the picture of vigour and vitality, swept
across to the curtained window and threw back those screenings
with a movement that made the curtain-rings chime together.

'Poor Elizabeth!' she repeated. 'My heart aches for her, for I
am sure all that carping bitterness makes her wretched. I dare
say it is only physical: liver perhaps, or acidity. The ideal
system of callisthenics might do wonders for her. I cannot, as
you will readily understand, dear Irene, make the first ap-
proaches to her after her conduct to me, and the dreadful
innuendoes she has made, but I should like her to know that I
bear her no malice at all. Do convey that to her sometime.
Tactfully, of course. Women like her who do all they can on

every possible occasion to hurt and injure others are usually very sensitive themselves, and I would not add to the poor creature's other chagrins. You must all be kind to her.'

'My dear, you're too wonderful!' said Irene, in a sort of ecstasy. 'What a joy you are! But, alas, you're leaving us so soon. It's too unkind of you to desert us.'

Lucia had dropped on to the music-stool by the piano which had so long been dumb, except for a few timorous chords muffled by the *unsustenuto* pedal, and dreamily recalled the first bars of the famous slow movement.

Irene sat down on the cold hot-water pipes and yearned at her.

'You can do everything,' she said. 'You play like an angel, and you can knock out Mapp with your little finger, and you can skip and play bridge, and you've got such a lovely nature that you don't bear Mapp the slightest grudge for her foul plots. You are adorable! Won't you ask me to come and stay with you at Riseholme sometime?'

Lucia, still keeping perfect time with her triplets while this recital of her perfections was going on, considered whether she should not tell Irene at once that she had practically determined not to desert them. She had intended to tell Georgie first, but she would do that when he came back to-morrow, and she wanted to see about getting a house here without delay. She played a nimble arpeggio on the chord of C sharp minor and closed the piano.

'Too sweet of you to like me, dear,' she said, 'but as for your staying with me at Riseholme, I don't think I shall ever go back there myself. I have fallen in love with this dear Tilling, and I fully expect I shall settle here for good.'

'Angel!' said Irene.

'I've been looking about for a house that might suit me,' she continued when Irene had finished kissing her, 'and the house-agents have just sent me the order to view one which particularly attracts me. It's that white house on the road that skirts the marsh, half a mile away. A nice garden sheltered from the north wind. Right down on the level, it is true, but such a divine view. Broad, tranquil! A dyke and a bank just across the road, keeping back the high tides in the river.'

'But of course I know it; you mean Grebe,' cried Irene. 'The cottage I am in now adjoins the garden. Oh, do take it! While you're settling in, I'll let Diva have Taormina, and Diva will let Mapp have Wasters, and Mapp will let you have Mallards till Grebe's ready for you. And I shall be at your disposal all day to help you with your furniture.'

Lucia decided that there was no real danger of meeting the Contessa if she drove out there: besides the Contessa now wanted to avoid her for fear of showing how inferior was her Italian.

'It's such a lovely afternoon,' she said, 'that I think a little drive would not hurt me. Unfortunately Georgie, who comes back to-morrow, has got my car. I lent it him for his week by the sea.'

'Oh, how like you!' cried Irene. 'Always unselfish!'

'Dear Georgie! So pleased to give him a little treat,' said Lucia. 'I'll ring up the garage and get them to send me something closed. Come with me, dear, if you have nothing particular to do, and we'll look over the house.'

Lucia found much to attract her in Grebe. Though it was close to the road it was not overlooked, for a thick hedge of hornbeam made a fine screen: besides, the road did not lead anywhere particular. The rooms were of good dimensions, there was a hall and dining-room on the ground floor, with a broad staircase leading up to the first floor where there were two or three bedrooms and a long admirable sitting-room with four windows looking across the road to the meadows and the high bank bounding the river. Beyond that lay the great empty levels of the marsh, with the hill of Tilling rising out of it half a mile away to the west. Close behind the house was the cliff which had once been the coastline before the marshes were drained and reclaimed, and this would be a rare protection against northerly and easterly winds. All these pleasant rooms looked south, and all had this open view away seawards; they had character and dignity, and at once Lucia began to see herself living here. The kitchen and offices were in a wing by themselves, and here again there was character, for the kitchen had evidently been a coach-house, and still retained the big double doors appropriate to such. There had once been a road from it to the end of the kitchen garden, but with its disuse as a coach-house, the road had been replaced by a broad cinder path now bordered with beds of useful vegetables.

'*Ma molto conveniente*,' said Lucia more than once, for it was now perfectly safe to talk Italian again, since the Contessa, no less than she, was determined to avoid a duet in that language. '*Mi piace molto. E un bel giardino.*'

'How I love hearing you talk Italian,' ejaculated Irene, 'especially since I know it's the very best. Will you teach it me? Oh, I am so pleased you like the house.'

'But I am charmed with it,' said Lucia. 'And there's a garage with a very nice cottage attached which will do beautifully for Cadman and Foljambe.'

She broke off suddenly, for in the fervour of her enthusiasm for the house, she had not thought about the awful catastrophe which must descend on Georgie, if she decided to live at Tilling. She had given no direct thought to him, and now for the first time she realized the cruel blow that would await him, when he came back to-morrow, all bronzed from his week at Folkestone. He had been a real *Deus ex machino* to her: his stroke of genius had turned a very hazardous moment into a blaze of triumph, and now she was going to plunge a dagger into his domestic heart by the news that she and therefore Cadman and therefore Foljambe were not coming back to Riseholme at all . . .

'Oh, are they going to marry?' asked Irene. 'Or do you mean they just live together? How interesting!'

'Dear Irene, do not be so modern,' said Lucia, quite sharply. 'Marriage of course, and banns first. But never mind that for the present. I like those great double doors to the kitchen. I shall certainly keep them.'

'How ripping that you're thinking about kitchen-doors already,' said Irene. 'That really sounds as if you did mean to buy the house. Won't Mapp have a fit when she hears it! I must be there when she's told. She'll say' "Darling Lulu, what a joy," and then fall down and foam at the mouth.'

Lucia gazed out over the marsh where the level rays of

sunset turned a few low-lying skeins of mist to rose and gold. The tide was high and the broad channel of the river running out to sea was brimming from edge to edge. Here and there, where the banks were low, the water had overflowed on to adjacent margins of land; here and there, spread into broad lakes, it lapped the confining dykes. There were sheep cropping the meadows, there were seagulls floating on the water, and half a mile away to the west the red roofs of Tilling glowed as if molten not only with the soft brilliance of the evening light, but (to the discerning eye) with the intensity of the interests that burned beneath them . . . Lucia hardly knew what gave her the most satisfaction, the magic of the marsh, her resolve to live here, or the recollection of the complete discomfiture of Elizabeth.

Then again the less happy thought of Georgie recurred, and she wondered what arguments she could use to induce him to leave Riseholme and settle here. Tilling with all its manifold interests would be incomplete without him, and how dismally incomplete Riseholme would be to him without herself and Foljambe. Georgie had of late taken his painting much more seriously than ever before, and he had often during the summer put off dinner to an unheard-of lateness in order to catch a sunset, and had risen at most inconvenient hours to catch a sunrise. Lucia had strongly encouraged this zeal, she had told him that if he was to make a real career as an artist he had no time to waste. Appreciation and spurring-on was what he needed: perhaps Irene could help.

She pointed to the glowing landscape.

'Irene, what would life be without sunsets?' she asked. 'And to think that this miracle happens every day, except when it's very cloudy!'

Irene looked critically at the view.

'Generally speaking, I don't like sunsets,' she said. 'The composition of the sky is usually childish. But good colouring about this one.'

'There are practically no sunsets at Riseholme,' said Lucia. 'I suppose the sun goes down, but there's a row of hills in the way. I often think that Georgie's development as an artist is starved there. If he goes back there he will find no one to make him work. What do you think of his painting, dear?'

'I don't think of it at all,' said Irene.

'No? I am astonished. Of course your own is so different in character. Those wrestlers! Such movement! But personally I find very great perception in Georgie's work. A spaciousness, a calmness! I wish you would take an interest in it and encourage him. You can find beauty anywhere if you look for it.'

'Of course I'll do my best if you want me to,' said Irene. 'But it will be hard work to find beauty in Georgie's little valentines.'

'Do try. Give him some hints. Make him see what you see. All that boldness and freedom. That's what he wants . . . Ah, the sunset is fading. *Buona notte, bel sole!* We must be getting home too. *Addio, mia bella casa.* But Georgie must be the first to know, Irene, do not speak of it until I have told him. Poor Georgie: I hope it will not be a terrible blow to him.'

Georgie came straight to Mallards on his arrival next morning from Folkestone with Cadman and Foljambe. His recall, he knew, meant that the highly dangerous Contessa had gone, and his admission by Grosvenor, after the door had been taken off the chain, that Lucia's influenza was officially over. He looked quite bronzed, and she gave him the warmest welcome.

'It all worked without a hitch,' she said as she told him of the plots and counter-plots which had woven so brilliant a tapestry of events. 'And it was that letter of Mrs Brocklebank's which you sent me that clapped the lid on Elizabeth. I saw at once what I could make of it. Really, Georgie, I turned it into a stroke of genius.'

'But it was a stroke of genius already,' said Georgie. 'You only had to copy it out and send it to the Contessa.'

Lucia was slightly ashamed of having taken the supreme credit for herself: the habit was hard to get rid of.

'My dear, all the credit shall be yours then,' she said handsomely. 'It was your stroke of genius. I copied it out very carelessly as if I had scribbled it off without thought. That was a nice touch, don't you think? The effect? Colossal, so

Irene tells me, for I could not be there myself. That was only yesterday. A few desperate wriggles from Elizabeth, but of course no good. I do not suppose there was a more thoroughly thwarted woman in all Sussex than she.'

Georgie gave a discreet little giggle.

'And what's so terribly amusing is that she was right all the time about your influenza and your Italian and everything,' he said. 'Perfectly maddening for her.'

Lucia sighed pensively.

'Georgie, she was malicious,' she observed, 'and that never pays.'

'Besides, it serves her right for spying on you,' Georgie continued.

'Yes, poor thing. But I shall begin now at once to be kind to her again. She shall come to lunch to-morrow, and you of course. By the way, Georgie, Irene takes so much interest in your painting. It was news to me, for her style is so different from your beautiful, careful work.'

'No! That's news to me too,' said Georgie. 'She never seemed to see my sketches before: they might have been blank sheets of paper. Does she mean it? She's not pulling my leg?'

'Nothing of the sort. And I couldn't help thinking it was a great opportunity for you to learn something about more modern methods. There is something you know in those fierce canvases of hers.'

'I wish she had told me sooner,' said Georgie. 'We've only got a fortnight more here. I shall be very sorry when it's over, for I felt terribly pleased to be getting back to Tilling this morning. It'll be dull going back to Riseholme. Don't you feel that too? I'm sure you must. No plots: no competition.'

Lucia had just received a telegram from Adele concerning the purchase of the Hurst, and it was no use putting off the staggering moment. She felt as if she was Zeus about to discharge a thunderbolt on some unhappy mortal.

'Georgie, I'm not going back to Riseholme at all,' she said. 'I have sold the Hurst: Adele Brixton has bought it. And, practically, I've bought that white house with the beautiful garden, which we admired so much, and that view over the marsh (how I thought of you at sunset yesterday), and really charming rooms with character.'

Georgie sat open-mouthed, and all expression vanished from his face. It became as blank as a piece of sunburnt paper. Then slowly, as if he was coming round from an anaesthetic while the surgeon was still carving dexterously at living tissue, a look of intolerable anguish came into his face.

'But Foljambe, Cadman!' he cried. 'Foljambe can't come back here every night from Riseholme. What am I to do? Is it all irrevocable?'

Lucia bridled. She was quite aware that this parting (if there was to be one) between him and Foljambe would be a dagger; but it was surprising, to say the least, that the thought of the parting between herself and him should not have administered him the first shock. However, there it was. Foljambe first by all means.

'I knew parting from Foljambe would be a great blow to you,' she said, with an acidity that Georgie could hardly fail to notice. 'What a pity that row you told me about came to nothing! But I am afraid that I can't promise to live in Riseholme for ever in order that you may not lose your parlour-maid.'

'But it's not only that,' said Georgie, aware of this acidity and hastening to sweeten it. 'There's you as well. It will be ditchwater at Riseholme without you.'

'Thank you, Georgie,' said Lucia. 'I wondered if and when, as the lawyers say, you would think of that. No reason why you should, of course.'

Georgie felt that this was an unjust reproach.

'Well, after all, you settled to live in Tilling,' he retorted, 'and said nothing about how dull it would be without me. And I've got to do without Foljambe as well.'

Lucia had recourse to the lowest artifice.

'Georgie-orgie, 'oo not cwoss with me?' she asked in an innocent, childish voice.

Georgie was not knocked out by this sentimental stroke below the belt. It was like Lucia to settle everything in exactly the way that suited her best, and then expect her poor pawns to be stricken at the thought of losing their queen. Besides, the loss of Foljambe *had* occurred to him first. Comfort, like charity, began at home.

'No, I'm not cross,' he said, utterly refusing to adopt baby-talk which implied surrender. 'But I've got every right to be hurt with you for settling to live in Tilling and not saying a word about how you would miss me.'

'My dear, I knew you would take that for granted,' began Lucia.

'Then why shouldn't you take it for granted about me?' he observed.

'I ought to have,' she said. 'I confess it, so that's all right. But why don't you leave Riseholme too and settle here, Georgie? Foljambe, me, your career, now that Irene is so keen about your pictures, and this marvellous sense of not knowing what's going to happen next. Such stimulus, such stuff to keep the soul awake. And you don't want to go back to Riseholme: you said so yourself. You'd moulder and vegetate there.'

'It's different for you,' said Georgie. 'You've sold your house and I haven't sold mine. But there it is: I shall go back, I suppose, without Foljambe or you — I mean you or Foljambe. I wish I had never come here at all. It was that week when we went back for the fête, leaving Cadman and her here, which did all the mischief.'

There was no use in saying anything more at present, and Georgie, feeling himself the victim of an imperious friend and of a faithless parlourmaid, went sadly back to Mallards Cottage. Lucia had settled to leave Riseholme without the least thought of what injury she inflicted on him by depriving him at one fell blow of Foljambe and her own companionship. He was almost sorry he had sent her that wonderful Brocklebank letter, for she had been in a very tight place, especially when Miss Mapp had actually seen her stripped and skipping in the garden as a cure for influenza; and had he not, by his stroke of genius, come to her rescue, her reputation here might have suffered an irretrievable eclipse, and they might all have gone back to Riseholme together. As it was, he had established her on the most exalted pinnacle and her thanks for that boon were expressed by dealing this beastly blow at him.

He threw himself down, in deep dejection, on the sofa in the little parlour of Mallards Cottage, in which he had been so comfortable. Life at Tilling had been full of congenial pleasures, and what a spice all these excitements had added to it! He had done a lot of painting, endless subjects still awaited his brush, and it had given him a thrill of delight to know that quaint Irene, with all her modern notions about art, thought highly of his work. Then there was the diversion of observing and nobly assisting in Lucia's campaign for the sovereignty, and her wars, as he knew, were far from won yet, for Tilling certainly had grown restive under her patronizings and acts of autocracy, and there was probably life in the old dog (meaning Elizabeth Mapp) yet. It was dreadful to think that he would not witness the campaign that was now being planned in those Napoleonic brains. These few weeks that remained to him here would be blackened by the thought of the wretched future that awaited him, and there would be no savour in them, for in so short a time now he would go back to Riseholme in a state of the most pitiable widowerhood, deprived of the ministering care of Foljambe, who all these years had made him so free from household anxieties, and of the companion who had spurred him on to ambitions and activities. Though he had lain awake shuddering at the thought that perhaps Lucia expected him to marry her, he felt he would almost sooner have done that than lose her altogether. 'It may be better to have loved and lost,' thought Georgie, 'than never to have loved at all, but it's very poor work not having loved and also to have lost' . . .

There was Foljambe singing in a high buzzing voice as she unpacked his luggage in his room upstairs, and though it was a rancid noise, how often had it filled him with the liveliest satisfaction, for Foljambe seldom sang, and when she did, it meant that she was delighted with her lot in life and was planning fresh efforts for his comfort. Now, no doubt, she was planning all sorts of pleasures for Cadman, and not thinking of him at all. Then there was Lucia: through his open window he could already hear the piano in the garden-room, and that showed a horrid callousness to his miserable plight. She didn't care; she was rolling on like the moon or the car of Juggernaut. It was heartless of her to occupy herself with those gay tinkling tunes, but the fact was that she was odiously selfish, and cared about nothing but her own successes . . . He abstracted himself from those painful reflections for a moment and listened more attentively. It was clearly Mozart that she was practising, but the melody was new to him. 'I bet,' thought Georgie, 'that this evening or to-morrow, she'll ask me to read over a new Mozart, and it'll be that very piece that she's practising now.'

His bitterness welled up within him again, as that pleasing reflection faded from his mind, and almost involuntarily he began to revolve how he could pay her back for her indifference to him. A dark but brilliant thought (like a black pearl) occurred to him. What if he dismissed his own chauffeur, Dickie, at present in the employment of his tenant at Riseholme, and, by a prospect of a rise in wages, seduced Cadman from Lucia's service, and took him and Foljambe back to Riseholme? He would put into practise the plan that Lucia herself had suggested, of establishing them in a cottage of their own, with a charwoman, so that Foljambe's days should be his, and her nights Cadman's. That would be a nasty one for Lucia, and the idea was feasible, for Cadman didn't think much of Tilling, and might easily fall in with it. But hardly had this devilish device occurred to him than his better nature rose in revolt against it. It would serve Lucia right, it is true, but it was unworthy of him. 'I should be descending to her level,' thought Georgie very nobly, 'if I did such a thing. Besides, how awful it would be if Cadman said no, and then told her that I had tempted him. She would despise me for doing it, as much as I despise her, and she would gloat over me for having failed. It won't do. I must be more manly about it all somehow. I must be like Major Benjy and say "Damn the woman! Faugh!" and have a drink. But I feel sick at the idea of going back to Riseholme alone . . . I wish I had eyebrows like a paste-brush, and could say damn properly.'

With a view to being more manly he poured himself out a very small whisky and soda, and his eye fell on a few letters lying for him on the table, which must have come that morning.

There was one with the Riseholme postmark, and the envelope was of that very bright blue which he always used. His own stationery evidently, of which he had left a supply, without charge, for the use of his tenant. He opened it, and behold there was dawn breaking on his dark life, for Colonel Cresswell wanted to know if he had any thoughts of selling his house. He was much taken by Riseholme, his sister had bought the Hurst, and he would like to be near her. Would Georgie therefore let him have a line about this as soon as possible, for there was another house, Mrs Quantock's, about which he would enter into negotiations, if there was no chance of getting Georgie's . . .

The revulsion of feeling was almost painful. Georgie had another whisky and soda at once, not because he was depressed, but because he was so happy. 'But I mustn't make a habit of it,' he thought, as he seized his pen.

Georgie's first impulse when he had written his letter to Colonel Cresswell was to fly round to Mallards with this wonderful news, but now he hesitated. Some hitch might arise, the price Colonel Cresswell proposed might not come up to his expectations, though – God knew – he would not dream of haggling over any reasonable offer. Lucia would rejoice at the chance of his staying in Tilling but she did not deserve to have such a treat of pleasurable expectation for the present. Besides, though he had been manly enough to reject with scorn the wiles of the devil who had suggested the seduction of Cadman, he thought he would tease her a little even if his dream came true. He had often told her that if he was rich enough he would have a flat in London, and now, if this sale of his house came off, he would pretend that he was not meaning to live in Tilling at all, but would live in town, and he would see how she would take that. It would be her turn to be hurt, and serve her right. So instead of interrupting the roulades of Mozart that were pouring from the window of the garden-room, he walked briskly down to the High Street to see how Tilling was taking the news that it would have Lucia always with it, if her purchase of Grebe had become public property. If not, he would have the pleasure of disseminating it.

There was a hint of seafaring about Georgie's costume as befitted one who had lately spent so much time on the pier at Folkestone. He had a very nautical-looking cap, with a black shining brim, a dark-blue double-breasted coat, white trousers and smart canvas shoes: really he might have been supposed to have come up to Tilling in his yacht, and have landed to see the town ... A piercing whistle from the other side of the street showed him that his appearance had at once attracted attention, and there was Irene planted with her easel in the middle of the pavement, and painting a row of flayed carcasses that hung in the butcher's shop. Rembrandt had better look out ...

'Avast there, Georgie,' she cried. 'Home is the sailor, home from sea. Come and talk.'

This was rather more attention than Georgie had anticipated, but as Irene was quite capable of shouting nautical remarks after him if he pretended not to hear, he tripped across the street to her.

'Have you seen Lucia, Commodore?' she said. 'And has she told you?'

'About her buying Grebe?' asked Georgie. 'Oh, yes.'

'That's all right then. She told me not to mention it till she'd seen you. Mapp's popping in and out of the shops, and I simply must be the first to tell her. Don't cut in in front of me, will you? Oh, by the way, have you done any sketching at Folkestone?'

'One or two,' said Georgie. 'Nothing very much.'

'Nonsense. Do let me come and see them. I love your handling. Just cast your eye over this and tell me what's wrong with – There she is. Hi! Mapp!'

Elizabeth, like Georgie, apparently thought it more prudent to answer that summons and avoid further public proclamation of her name, and came hurrying across the street.

'Good morning, Irene mine,' she said. 'What a beautiful picture! All the poor skinned piggies in a row, or are they sheep? Back again, Mr Georgie? How we've missed you. And how do you think dear Lulu is looking after her illness?'

'Mapp, there's news for you,' said Irene, remembering the

luncheon-party yesterday. 'You must guess: I shall tease you. It's about your Lulu. Three guesses.'

'Not a relapse, I hope?' said Elizabeth brightly.

'Quite wrong. Something much nicer. You'll enjoy it tremendously.'

'Another of those beautiful musical parties?' asked Elizabeth. 'Or has she skipped a hundred times before breakfast?'

'No, much nicer,' said Irene. 'Heavenly for us all.'

A look of apprehension had come over Elizabeth's face, as an awful idea occurred to her.

'Dear one, give over teasing,' she said. 'Tell me.'

'She's not going away at the end of the month,' said Irene. 'She's bought Grebe.'

Blank dismay spread over Elizabeth's face.

'Oh, what a joy!' she said. 'Lovely news.'

She hurried off to Wasters, too much upset even to make Diva, who was coming out of Twistevant's, a partner in her joy. Only this morning she had been consulting her calendar and observing that there were only fifteen days more before Tilling was quit of Lulu, and now at a moderate estimate there might be at least fifteen years of her. Then she found she could not bear the weight of her joy alone and sped back after Diva.

'Diva dear, come in for a minute,' she said. 'I've heard something.'

Diva looked with concern at that lined and agitated face.

'What's the matter?' she said. 'Nothing serious?'

'Oh no, lovely news,' she said with bitter sarcasm. 'Tilling will rejoice. *She's* not going away. *She's* going to stop here for ever.'

There was no need to ask who 'she' was. For weeks Lucia had been 'she'. If you meant Susan Wyse, or Diva or Irene, you said so. But 'she' was Lucia.

'I suspected as much,' said Diva. 'I know she had an order to view Grebe.'

Elizabeth, in a spasm of exasperation, banged the door of Wasters so violently after she and Diva had entered, that the house shook and a note leaped from the wire letter-box on to the floor.

'Steady on with my front door,' said Diva, 'or there'll be some dilapidations to settle.'

Elizabeth took no notice of this petty remark, and picked up the note. The handwriting was unmistakable, for Lucia's study of Homer had caused her (subconsciously or not) to adopt a modified form of Greek script, and she made her 'a' like alpha and her 'e' like epsilon. At the sight of it Elizabeth suffered a complete loss of self-control, she held the note on high as if exposing a relic to the gaze of pious worshippers, and made a low curtsey to it.

'And this is from Her,' she said. 'Oh, how kind of Her Majesty to write to me in her own hand with all those ridiculous twiddles. Not content with speaking Italian quite perfectly, she must also write in Greek. I dare say she talks it beautifully too.'

'Come, pull yourself together, Elizabeth,' said Diva.

'I am not aware that I am coming to bits, dear,' said Elizabeth, opening the note with the very tips of her fingers, as if it had been written by someone infected with plague or at least influenza. 'But let me see what Her Majesty says . . . "Dearest Liblib" . . . the impertinence of it! Or is it Riseholme humour?'

'Well, you call her Lulu,' said Diva. 'Do get on.'

Elizabeth frowned with the difficulty of deciphering this crabbed handwriting.

'"Now that I am quite free of infection,"' she read – (Infection indeed. She never had flu at all) – '"of infection, I can receive my friends again, and hope so much you will lunch with me to-morrow. I hasten also to tell you of my change of plans, for I have so fallen in love with your delicious Tilling that I have bought a house here – (Stale news!) – and shall settle into it next month. An awful wrench, as you may imagine, to leave my dear Riseholme – (Then why wrench yourself?) – . . . and poor Georgie is in despair, but Tilling and all you dear people have wrapt yourselves round my heart. (Have we? The same to you!) – and it is no use my struggling to get free. I wonder therefore if you would consider letting me take your beautiful Mallards at the same rent for another month, while

Grebe is being done up, and my furniture being installed? I should be so grateful if this is possible, otherwise I shall try to get Mallards Cottage when my Georgie – (My!) – goes back to Riseholme. Could you, do you think, let me know about this to-morrow, if, as I hope, you will send me *un'amabile 'si'* – (What in the world is an *amabile si*?) – and come to lunch? *Tanti saluti*, Lucia."'

'I understand,' said Diva. 'It means "an amiable yes", about going to lunch.'

'Thank you, Diva. You are quite an Italian scholar too,' said Elizabeth. 'I call that a thoroughly heartless letter. And all of us, mark you, must serve her convenience. I can't get back into Mallards, because She wants it, and even if I refused, She would be next door at Mallards Cottage. I've never been so long out of my own house before.'

Both ladies felt that it would be impossible to keep up any semblance of indignation that Lucia was wanting to take Mallards for another month, for it suited them both so marvellously well.

'You are in luck,' said Diva, 'getting another month's let at that price. So am I too, if you want to stop here, for Irene is certain to let me stay on at her house, because her cottage is next to Grebe and she'll be in and out all day –'

'Poor Irene seems to be under a sort of spell,' said Elizabeth in parenthesis. 'She can think about nothing except that woman. Her painting has fallen off terribly. Coarsened ... Yes, dear, I think I will give the Queen of the Italian language an *amabile si* about Mallards. I don't know if you would consider taking rather a smaller rent for November. Winter prices are always lower.'

'Certainly not,' said Diva. 'You're going to get the same as before for Mallards.'

'That's my affair, dear,' said Elizabeth.

'And this is mine,' said Diva firmly. 'And will you go to lunch with her to-morrow?'

Elizabeth, now comparatively calm, sank down in the window-seat, which commanded so good a view of the High Street.

'I suppose I shall have to,' she said. 'One must be civil, whatever has happened. Oh, there's Major Benjy. I wonder if he's heard.'

She tapped at the window and threw it open. He came hurrying across the street and began to speak in a loud voice before she could get in a word.

'That amusing guessing game of yours, Miss Elizabeth,' he said, just like Irene. 'About Mrs Lucas. I'll give you three –'

'One's enough: we all know,' said Elizabeth. 'Joyful news, isn't it?'

'Indeed, it is delightful to know that we are not going to lose one who – who has endeared herself to us all so much,' said he very handsomely.

He stopped. His tone lacked sincerity; there seemed to be something in his mind which he left unsaid. Elizabeth gave him a piercing and confidential look.

'Yes, Major Benjy?' she suggested.

He glanced round like a conspirator to see there was no one eavesdropping.

'Those parties, you know,' he said. 'Those entertainments which we've all enjoyed so much. Beautiful music. But Grebe's a long way off on a wet winter night. Not just round the corner. Now if she was settling in Mallards –'

He saw at once what an appalling interpretation might be put on this, and went on in a great hurry.

'You'll have to come to our rescue, Miss Elizabeth,' he said, dropping his voice so that even Diva could not hear. 'When you're back in your own house again, you'll have to look after us all as you always used to. Charming woman, Mrs Lucas, and most hospitable, I'm sure, but in the winter, as I was saying, that long way out of Tilling, just to hear a bit of music, and have a tomato, if you see what I mean.'

'Why, of course I see what you mean,' murmured Elizabeth. 'The dear thing, as you say, is so hospitable. Lovely music and tomatoes, but we must make a stand.'

'Well, you can have too much of a good thing,' said Major Benjy, 'and for my part a little Mozart lasts me a long time, especially if it's a long way on a wet night. Then I'm told

there's an idea of callisthenic classes, though no doubt they
would be for ladies only –'

'I wouldn't be too sure about that,' said Elizabeth. 'Our dear
friend has got enough – shall we call it self-confidence? – to
think herself capable of teaching anybody anything. If you
aren't careful, Major Benjy, you'll find yourself in a skipping-
match on the lawn at Grebe, before you know what you're
doing. You've been King Cophetua already, which I, for one,
never thought to see.'

'That was just once in a way,' said he. 'But when it comes to
callisthenic classes –'

Diva, in an agony at not being able to hear what was going
on, had crept up behind Elizabeth, and now crouched close to
her as she stood leaning out of the window. At this moment,
Lucia, having finished her piano-practice, came round the
corner from Mallards into the High Street. Elizabeth hastily
withdrew from the window and bumped into Diva.

'So sorry: didn't know you were there, dear,' she said. 'We
must put our heads together another time, Major Benjy. Au
reservoir.'

She closed the window.

'Oh, do tell me what you're going to put your heads together
about,' said Diva. 'I only heard just the end.'

It was important to get allies: otherwise Elizabeth would
have made a few well-chosen remarks about eavesdroppers.

'It is sad to find that just when Lucia has settled never to
leave us any more,' she said, 'that there should be so much
feeling in Tilling about being told to do this and being made to
listen to that. Major Benjy – I don't know if you heard that
part, dear – spoke very firmly, and I thought sensibly about it.
The question really is if England is a free country or not, and
whether we're going to be trampled upon. We've been very
happy in Tilling all these years, going our own way, and living
in sweet harmony together, and I for one, and Major Benjy for
another, don't intend to put our necks under the yoke. I don't
know how you feel about it. Perhaps you like it, for after all
you were Mary Queen of Scots just as much as Major Benjy
was King Cophetua.'

'I won't go to any po-di-mus, after dinner at Grebe,' said
Diva. 'I shouldn't have gone to the last, but you persuaded us
all to go. Where was your neck then, Elizabeth? Be fair.'

'Be fair yourself, Diva,' said Elizabeth with some heat. 'You
know perfectly well that I wanted you to go in order that you
might all get your necks from under her yoke, and hear that
she couldn't speak a word of Italian.'

'And a nice mess you made of that,' said Diva. 'But never
mind. She's established now as a perfect Italian linguist, and
there it is. Don't meddle with that again, or you'll only prove
that she can talk Greek too.'

Elizabeth rose and pointed at her like one of Raphael's
Sibyls.

'Diva, to this day I don't believe she can talk Italian. It was
a conjuring trick, and I'm no conjurer but a plain woman, and
I can't tell you how it was done. But I will swear it was a trick.
Besides, answer me this! Why doesn't she offer to give us
Italian lessons if she knows it? She has offered to teach us
bridge and Homer and callisthenics and take choir-practices
and arranged tableaux. Why not Italian?'

'That's curious,' said Diva thoughtfully.

'Not the least curious. The reason is obvious. Everyone
snubbed me and scolded me, you among others, at that dreadful
luncheon-party, but I know I'm right, and some day the truth
will come out. I can wait. Meantime what she means to do is to
take us all in hand, and I won't be taken in hand. What is
needed from us all is a little firmness.'

Diva went home thrilled to the marrow of her bones at the
thought of the rich entertainment that these next months
promised to provide. Naturally she saw through Elizabeth's
rodomontade about yokes and free countries: what she meant
was that she intended to assert herself again, and topple Lucia
over. Two could not reign in Tilling, as everybody could see
by this time. 'All most interesting,' said Diva to herself. 'Elizabeth's got hold of Major Benjy for the present, and Lucia's
going to lose Georgie, but then men don't count for much in
Tilling: it's brains that do it. There'll be more bridge-parties
and teas this winter than ever before. Really, I don't know

which of them I would back. Hullo, there's a note from her. Lunch to-morrow, I expect . . . I thought so.'

Lucia's luncheon-party next day was to be of the nature of a banquet to celebrate the double event of her recovery and of the fact that Tilling, instead of mourning her approaching departure, was privileged to retain her, as Elizabeth had said, for ever and ever. The whole circle of her joyful friends would be there, and she meant to give them to eat of the famous dish of lobster *à la Riseholme*, which she had provided for Georgie, a few weeks ago, to act as a buffer to break the shock of Foljambe's engagement. It had already produced a great deal of wild surmise in the minds of the housewives at Tilling for no one could conjecture how it was made, and Lucia had been deaf to all requests for the recipe: Elizabeth had asked her twice to give it her, but Lucia had merely changed the subject without attempt at transition: she had merely talked about something quite different. This secretiveness was considered unamiable, for the use of Tilling was to impart its culinary mysteries to friends, so that they might enjoy their favourite dishes at each other's houses, and lobster *à la Riseholme* had long been an agonizing problem to Elizabeth. She had made an attempt at it herself, but the result was not encouraging. She had told Diva and the Padre that she felt sure she had 'guessed it', and, when bidden to come to lunch and partake of it, they had both anticipated a great treat. But Elizabeth had clearly guessed wrong, for lobster *à la Riseholme à la Mapp* had been found to consist of something resembling lumps of india-rubber (so tough that the teeth positively bounced away from them on contact) swimming in a dubious pink gruel, and both of them left a great deal on their plates, concealed as far as possible under their knives and forks, though their hostess continued manfully to chew, till her jaw-muscles gave out. Then Elizabeth had had recourse to underhand methods. Lucia had observed her more than once in the High Street, making herself suspiciously pleasant to her cook, and from the window of the garden-room just before her influenza, she had seen her at the back door of Mallards again in conversation with the lady of the kitchen. On this occasion, with an unerring conviction in her mind, she had sent for her cook and asked her what Miss Mapp wanted. It was even so: Elizabeth's ostensible inquiry was for an egg-whisk, which she had left by mistake at Mallards three months ago, but then she had unmasked her batteries, and, actually fingering a bright half-crown, had asked point-blank for the recipe of this lobster *à la Riseholme*. The cook had given her a polite but firm refusal, and Lucia was now more determined than ever that Elizabeth should never know the exquisite secret. She naturally felt that it was beneath her to take the slightest notice of this low and paltry attempt to obtain by naked bribery a piece of private knowledge, and she never let Elizabeth know that she was cognizant of it.

During the morning before Lucia's luncheon-party a telegram had come for Georgie from Colonel Cresswell making a firm and very satisfactory offer for his house at Riseholme, unfurnished. That had made him really busy: first he had to see Foljambe and tell her (under seal of secrecy, for he had his little plot of teasing Lucia in mind) that he was proposing to settle in Tilling. Foljambe was very pleased to hear it, and in a burst of most unusual feeling, had said that it would have gone to her heart to leave his service, after so many harmonious years, when he went back to Riseholme, and that she was very glad to adopt the plan, which she had agreed to, when it was supposed that they would all go back to Riseholme together. She would do her work all day in Georgie's house, and retire in the evening to the connubialities of the garage at Grebe. When this affecting interview was over, she went back to her jobs, and again Georgie heard her singing as she cleaned the silver. 'So that's beautiful,' he said to himself, 'and the cloud has passed for ever. Now I must instantly see about getting a house here.'

He hurried out. There was still an hour before he was due at the lobster lunch. Though he had left the seaside twenty-four hours ago, he put on his yachtsman's cap and, walking on air, set off for the house-agents'. Of all the houses in the place which he had seen, he was sure that none would suit him as well as this dear little Mallards Cottage which he now occupied; he liked it, Foljambe liked it, they all liked it, but he had no idea whether he could get a lease from kippered Isabel. As he crossed the High Street, a wild hoot from a motor-horn just behind him gave him a dreadful fright, but he jumped nimbly for the pavement, reached it unhurt, and though his cap fell off and landed in a puddle, he was only thankful to have escaped being run down by Isabel Poppit on her motor-cycle. Her hair was like a twisted mop, her skin incredibly tanned, and mounted on her cycle she looked like a sort of modernized Valkyrie in rather bad repair ... Meeting her just at this moment, when he was on his way to inquire about Mallards Cottage, seemed a good omen to Georgie, and he picked up his cap and ran back across the street, for in her natural anxiety to avoid killing him she had swerved into a baker's cart, and had got messed up in the wheels.

'I do apologize, Miss Poppit,' he said. 'Entirely my fault for not looking both ways before I crossed.'

'No harm done,' said she. 'Oh, your beautiful cap. I am sorry. But after all the wonderful emptiness and silence among the sand-dunes, a place like a town seems to me a positive nightmare.'

'Well, the emptiness and silence does seem to suit you,' said Georgie, gazing in astonishment at her mahogany face. 'I never saw anybody looking so well.'

Isabel, with a tug of her powerful arms, disentangled her cycle.

'It's the simple life,' said she, shaking her hair out of her eyes. 'Never again will I live in a town. I have taken the bungalow I am in now for six months more, and I only came in to Tilling to tell the house-agent to get another tenant for Mallards Cottage, as I understand that you're going back to Riseholme at the end of this month.'

Georgie had never felt more firmly convinced that a wise and beneficent Providence looked after him with the most amiable care.

'And I was also on my way to the house-agents',' he said, 'to see if I could get a lease of it.'

'Gracious! What a good thing I didn't run over you just now,' said Isabel, with all the simplicity derived from the emptiness and silence of sand-dunes. 'Come on to the agents'.'

Within half an hour the whole business was as good as settled. Isabel held a lease from her mother of Mallards Cottage, which had five years yet to run, and she agreed to transfer this to Georgie, and store her furniture. He had just time to change into his new mustard-coloured suit with its orange tie and its topaz tie-pin, and arrived at the luncheon-party in the very highest spirits. Besides, there was his talk with Lucia when other guests had gone, to look forward to. How he would tease her about settling in London!

Though Tilling regarded the joyful prospect of Lucia's never going away again with certain reservations, and, in the case of Elizabeth, with nothing but reservations, her guests vied with each other in the fervency of their self-congratulations, and Elizabeth outdid them all, as she took into her mouth small fragments of lobster, in the manner of a wine-taster, appraising subtle flavours. There was cheese, there were shrimps, there was cream: there were so many things that she felt like Adam giving names to the innumerable procession of different animals. She had helped herself so largely that when the dish came to Georgie there was nothing left but a little pink juice, but he hardly minded at all, so happy had the events of the morning made him. Then when Elizabeth felt that she would choke if she said anything more in praise of Lucia, Mr Wyse took it up, and Georgie broke in and said it was cruel of them all to talk about the delicious busy winter they would have, when they all knew that he would not be here any longer but back at Riseholme. In fact, he rather overdid his lamentations, and Lucia, whose acute mind detected the grossest insincerity in Elizabeth's raptures, began to wonder whether Georgie for some unknown reason was quite as woeful as he professed to be. Never had he looked more radiant, not a shadow of disappointment had come over his face when he inspected the casserole that had once contained his favourite dish, and found nothing left for him. There was something up – what on earth could it be? Had Foljambe jilted Cadman? – and just as Elizabeth was detecting flavours in the mysterious dish, so Lucia was trying to arrive at an analysis of the gay glad tones in which Georgie expressed his misery.

'It's too tarsome of you all to go on about the lovely things you're going to do,' he said. 'Callisthenic classes and Homer and bridge, and poor me far away, I shall tell myself every morning that I hate Tilling; I shall say like Coué, "Day by day in every way, I dislike it more and more," until I've convinced myself that I shall be glad to go.'

Mr Wyse made him a beautiful bow.

'We too shall miss you very sadly, Mr Pillson,' he said, 'and for my part I shall be tempted to hate Riseholme for taking from us one who has so endeared himself to us.'

'I ask to be allowed to associate myself with those sentiments,' said Major Benjy, whose contempt for Georgie and his sketches and his needlework had been intensified by the sight of his yachting cap, which he had pronounced to be only fit for a popinjay. It had been best to keep on good terms with him while Lucia was at Mallards, for he might poison her mind about himself, and now that he was going, there was no harm in these handsome remarks. Then the Padre said something Scotch and sympathetic and regretful, and Georgie found himself, slightly to his embarrassment, making bows and saying 'thank you' right and left in acknowledgment of these universal expressions of regret that he was so soon about to leave them. It was rather awkward, for within a few hours they would all know that he had taken Mallards Cottage unfurnished for five years, which did not look like an immediate departure. But this little deception was necessary if he was to bring off his joke against Lucia, and make her think that he meant to settle in London. And after all, since everybody seemed so sorry that (as they imagined) he was soon to leave Tilling, they ought to be very much pleased to find that he was doing nothing of the kind.

The guests dispersed soon after lunch and Georgie, full of mischief and naughtiness, lingered with his hostess in the garden-room. All her gimlet glances during lunch had failed to fathom his high good humour: here was he on the eve of parting with his Foljambe and herself, and yet his face beamed with content. Lucia was in very good spirits also, for she had seen Elizabeth's brow grow more and more furrowed as she strove to find a formula for the lobster.

'What a lovely luncheon-party, although I got no lobster at all,' said Georgie, as he settled himself for his teasing. 'I did enjoy it. And Elizabeth's rapture at your stopping here! She must have an awful blister on her tongue.'

Lucia sighed.

'Sapphira must look to her laurels, poor thing,' she observed pensively. 'And how sorry they all were that you are going away.'

'Wasn't it nice of them?' said Georgie. 'But never mind that now: I've got something wonderful to tell you. I've never felt happier in my life, for the thing I've wanted for so many years can be managed at last. You will be pleased for my sake.'

Lucia laid a sympathetic hand on his. She felt that she had shown too little sympathy with one who was to lose his parlour-maid and his oldest friend so soon. But the gaiety with which he bore his double stroke was puzzling . . .

'Dear Georgie,' she said, 'anything that makes you happy makes me happy. I am rejoiced that something of the sort has occurred. Really rejoiced. Tell me what it is instantly.'

Georgie drew a long breath. He wanted to give it out all in a burst of triumph like a fanfare.

'Too lovely,' he said. 'Colonel Cresswell has bought my house at Riseholme – such a good price – and now at last I shall be able to settle in London. I was just as tired of Riseholme as you, and now I shall never see it again or Tilling either. Isn't it a dream? Riseholme, stuffy little Mallards Cottage, all things of the past! I shall have a nice little home in London, and you must promise to come up and stay with me sometimes. How I looked forward to telling you! Orchestral concerts at Queen's Hall, instead of our fumbling little arrangements of Mozartino for four hands. Pictures, a club if I can afford it, and how nice to think of you so happy down at Tilling! As for all the fuss I made yesterday about losing Foljambe, I can't think why it seemed to me so terrible.'

Lucia gave him one more gimlet glance, and found she did not believe a single word he was saying except as regards the sale of his house at Riseholme. All the rest must be lies, for the Foljambe-wound could not possibly have healed so soon. But she instantly made up her mind to pretend to believe him, and clapped her hands for pleasure.

'Dear Georgie! What splendid news!' she said. 'I am pleased. I've always felt that you, with all your keenness and multifarious interests in life, were throwing your life away in these little backwaters like Riseholme and Tilling. London is the only place for you! Now, tell me: Are you going to get a flat or a house? And where is it to be? If I were you I should have a house!'

This was not quite what Georgie had expected. He had thought that Lucia would suggest that now that he was quit of Riseholme he positively must come to Tilling, but not only did she fail to do that, but she seemed delighted that no such thought had entered into his head.

'I haven't really thought about that yet,' he said. 'There's something to be said for a flat.'

'No doubt. It's more compact, and then there's no bother about rates and taxes. And you'll have your car, I suppose. And will your cook go with you? What does she say to it all?'

'I haven't told her yet,' said Georgie, beginning to get a little pensive.

'Really? I should have thought you would have done that at once. And isn't Foljambe pleased that you are so happy again?'

'She doesn't know yet,' said Georgie. 'I thought I would tell you first.

'Dear Georgie, how sweet of you,' said Lucia. 'I'm sure Foljambe will be as pleased as I am. You'll be going up to London, I suppose, constantly now till the end of this month, so that you can get your house or your flat, whichever it is, ready as soon as possible. How busy you and I will be, you settling into London and I into Tilling. Do you know, supposing you had thought of living permanently here, now that you've got rid of your house at Riseholme, I should have done my best to persuade you not to, though I know in my selfishness that I did suggest that yesterday. But it would never do, Georgie. It's all very well for elderly women like me, who just want a little peace and quietness, or for retired men like Major Benjy or for dilettantes like Mr Wyse, but for you, a thousand times no. I am sure of it.'

Georgie got thoughtfuller and thoughtfuller. It had been rather a mistake to try to tease Lucia, for so far from being teased she was simply pleased. The longer she went on like this, and there seemed no end to her expressions of approval, the harder it would be to tell her.

'Do you really think that?' he said.

'Indeed I do. You would soon be terribly bored with Tilling. Oh, Georgie, I am so pleased with your good fortune and your good sense. I wonder if the agents here have got any houses or flats in London on their books. Let's go down there at once and see. We might find something. I'll run and put on my hat.'

Georgie threw in his hand. As usual Lucia had come out on top.

'You're too tarsome,' he said. 'You don't believe a single word I've been telling you of my plans.'

'My dear, of course I don't,' said Lucia brightly. 'I never heard such a pack of rubbish. Ananias is not in it. But it is true about selling your Riseholme house, I hope?'

'Yes, that part is,' said Georgie.

'Then of course you're going to live here,' said she. 'I meant you to do that all along. Now how about Mallards Cottage? I saw that Yahoo in the High Street this morning, and she told me she wanted to let it for the winter. Let's go down to the agents' as I suggested, and see.'

'I've done that already,' said Georgie, 'for I met her too, and she nearly knocked me down. I've got a five years' lease of it.'

It was not in Lucia's nature to crow over anybody. She proved her quality and passed on to something else.

'Perfect!' she said. 'It has all come out just as I planned, so that's all right. Now, if you've got nothing to do, let us have some music.'

She got out the new Mozart which she had been practising.

'This looks a lovely duet,' she said, 'and we haven't tried it yet. I shall be terribly rusty, for all the time I had influenza, I hardly dared to play the piano at all.'

Georgie looked at the new Mozart.

'It does look nice,' he said. 'Tum-ti-tum. Why, that's the one I heard you practising so busily yesterday morning.'

Lucia took not the slightest notice of this.

'We begin together,' she said, 'on the third beat. Now . . . *Uno, due, TRE!*'

8

The painting and decorating of Grebe began at once. Irene offered to do all the painting with her own hands, and recommended as a scheme for the music-room, a black ceiling and four walls of different colours, vermilion, emerald green, ultramarine and yellow. It would take a couple of months or so to execute, and the cost would be considerable as lapis lazuli must certainly be used for the ultramarine wall, but she assured Lucia that the result would be unique and marvellously stimulating to the eye, especially if she would add a magenta carpet and a nickel-plated mantelpiece.

'It sounds too lovely, dear,' said Lucia, contemplating the sample of colours which Irene submitted to her, 'but I feel sure I shan't be able to afford it. Such a pity! Those beautiful hues!'

Then Irene besought her to introduce a little variety into the shape of the windows. It would be amusing to have one window egg-shaped, and another triangular, and another with five or six or seven irregular sides, so that it looked as if it was a hole in the wall made by a shell. Or how about a front door that, instead of opening sideways, let down like a portcullis?

Irene rose to more daring conceptions yet. One night she had dined on a pot of strawberry jam and half a pint of very potent cocktails, because she wanted her eye for colour to be at its keenest round about eleven o'clock when the moon would rise over the marsh, and she hoped to put the lid for ever on Whistler's naïve old-fashioned attempts to paint moonlight. After this salubrious meal she had come round to Mallards, waiting for the moon to rise and sat for half an hour at Lucia's piano, striking random chords, and asking Lucia what colour they were. These musical rainbows suggested a wonderful idea, and she shut down the piano with a splendid purple bang.

'Darling, I've got a new scheme for Grebe,' she said. 'I want you to furnish a room sideways, if you understand what I mean.'

'I don't think I do,' said Lucia.

'Why, like this,' said Irene very thoughtfully. 'You would open the door of the room and find you were walking about on wallpaper with pictures hanging on it. (I'll do the pictures for you.) Then one side of the room where the window is would be whitewashed as if it was a ceiling and the window would be the skylight. The opposite side would be the floor; and you would have the furniture screwed on to it. The other walls, including the one which would be the ceiling in an ordinary room, would be covered with wallpaper and more pictures and a book-case. It would all be sideways, you see: you'd enter through the wall, and the room would be at right angles to you; ceiling on the left, floor on the right, or vice versa. It would give you a perfectly new perception of the world. You would see everything from a new angle, which is what we want so much in life nowadays. Don't you think so?'

Irene's speech was distinct and clear cut, she walked up and down the garden-room with a firm unwavering step, and Lucia put from her the uneasy suspicion that her dinner had gone to her head.

'It would be most delightful,' she said, 'but slightly too experimental for me.'

'And then, you see,' continued Irene, 'how useful it would be if somebody tipsy came in. It would make him sober at once, for tipsy people see everything crooked, and so your sideways-room, being crooked, would appear to him straight, and so he would be himself again. Just like that.'

'That would be splendid,' said Lucia, 'but I can't provide a room where tipsy people could feel sober again. The house isn't big enough.'

Irene sat down by her, and passionately clasped one of her hands.

'Lucia, you're too adorable,' she said. 'Nothing defeats you. I've been talking the most abject nonsense, though I do think that there may be something in it, and you remain as calm as the moon which I hope will rise over the marsh before long, unless the almanack in which I looked it out is last year's. Don't tell anybody else about the sideways-room, will you, or they might think I was drunk. Let it be our secret, darling.'

Lucia wondered for a moment if she ought to allow Irene to spend the night on the marsh, but she was perfectly capable of coherent speech and controlled movements, and possibly the open air might do her good.

'Not a soul shall know, dear,' she said. 'And now if you're really going to paint the moon, you had better start. You feel quite sure you can manage it, don't you?'

'Of course I can manage the moon,' said Irene stoutly. 'I've managed it lots of times. I wish you would come with me. I always hate leaving you. Or shall I stop here, and paint you instead? Or do you think Georgie would come? What a lamb, isn't he? Pass the mint-sauce please, or shall I go home?'

'Perhaps that would be best,' said Lucia. 'Paint the moon another night.'

Lucia next day hurried up the firm to which she had entrusted the decoration of Grebe, in case Irene had some new schemes, and half-way through November, the house was ready to receive her furniture from Riseholme. Georgie simultaneously was settling into Mallards Cottage, and in the course of it went through a crisis of the most agitating kind. Isabel had assured him that by noon on a certain day men would arrive to take her furniture to the repository where it was to be stored, and as the vans with his effects from Riseholme had arrived in Tilling the night before, he induced the foreman to begin moving everything out of the house at nine next morning and bring his furniture in. This was done, and by noon all Isabel's tables and chairs and beds and crockery were standing out in the street ready for her van. They completely blocked it for wheeled traffic, though pedestrians could manage to squeeze by in single file. Tilling did not mind this little inconvenience in the least, for it was all so interesting, and tradesmen's carts coming down the street were cheerfully backed into the church-yard again and turned round in order to make a more circuitous route, and those coming up were equally obliging, while foot-passengers, thrilled with having the entire contents of a house exposed for their inspection, were unable to tear themselves away from so intimate an exhibition. Then Georgie's furniture was moved in, and there were dazzling and fascinating objects for inspection, pictures that he had painted, screens and bed-spreads that he had worked, very pretty woollen pyjamas for the winter and embroidered covers for hot-water bottles. These millineries roused Major Benjy's manliest indignation, and he was nearly late for the tram to take him out to play golf, for he could not tear himself away from the revolting sight. In a few hours Georgie's effects had passed into the house, but still there was no sign of anyone coming to remove Isabel's from the street, and, by dint of telephoning, it was discovered that she had forgotten to give any order at all about them, and the men from the repository were out on other jobs. It then began to rain rather heavily, and though Georgie called heaven and earth to witness that all this muddle was not his fault he felt compelled, out of mere human compassion, to have Isabel's furniture moved back into his house again. In consequence the rooms and passages on the ground floor were completely blocked with stacks of cupboards and tables piled high with books and crockery and saucepans, the front door would not shut, and Foljambe, caught upstairs by the rising tide, could not come down. The climax of intensity arrived when she let down a string from an upper window, and Georgie's cook attached a small basket of nourishing food to it. Diva was terribly late for lunch at the Wyses, for she was rooted to the spot, though it was raining heavily, till she was sure that Foljambe would not be starved.

But by the time that the month of November was over, the houses of the new-comers were ready to receive them, and a general post of owners back to their homes took place after a remunerative let of four months. Elizabeth returned to Mallards from Wasters, bringing with her, in addition to what she had taken there, a cargo of preserves made from Diva's garden of such bulk that Coplen had to make two journeys with her large wheelbarrow. Diva returned to Wasters from Taormina, quaint Irene came back to Taormina from the labourer's cottage with a handcart laden with striking canvases including that of the women wrestlers who had become men, and the labourer and his family were free to trek to their own abode from the hop-picker's shanty which they had inhabited so much longer than they had intended.

There followed several extremely busy days for most of the returning emigrants. Elizabeth in particular was occupied from morning till night in scrutinizing every corner of Mallards and making out a list of dilapidations against Lucia. There was a teacup missing, the men who removed Lucia's hired piano from the garden-room had scraped a large piece of paint off the wall, Lucia had forgotten to replace dearest mamma's piano which still stood in the telephone-room, and there was no sign of a certain egg-whisk. Simultaneously Diva was preparing a similar list for Elizabeth which would astonish her, but was pleased to find that the tenant had left an egg-whisk behind; while the wife of the labourer, not being instructed in dilapidations, was removing from the whitewashed wall of her cottage the fresco which Irene had painted there in her spare moments. It wasn't fit to be seen, that it wasn't, but a scrubbing-brush and some hot water made short work of all those naked people. Irene, for her part, was frantically searching among her canvases for a picture of Adam and Eve with quantities of the sons of God shouting for joy: an important work. Perhaps she had left it at the cottage, and then remembering that she had painted it on the wall, she hurried off there in order to varnish it against the inclemencies of weather. But it was already too late, for the last of the sons of God was even then disappearing under the strokes of the scrubbing-brush.

Gradually, though not at once, these claims and counter-claims were (with the exception of the fresco) adjusted to the general dissatisfaction. Lucia acknowledged the charge for the re-establishment of dearest mamma's piano in the garden-room, but her cook very distinctly remembered that on the day when Miss Mapp tried to bribe her to impart the secret of lobster *à la Riseholme*, she took away the egg-whisk, which had formed the gambit of Miss Mapp's vain attempt to corrupt her. So

Lucia reminded Elizabeth that not very long ago she had called at the back door of Mallards and had taken it away herself. Her cook believed that it was in two if not three pieces. So Miss Mapp, having made certain it had not got put by mistake among the pots of preserves she had brought from Wasters, went to see if she had left it there, and found not it alone, but a preposterous list of claims against her from Diva. But by degrees these billows, which were of annual occurrence, subsided, and apart from Elizabeth's chronic grievance against Lucia for her hoarding the secret of the lobster, they and other differences in the past faded away and Tilling was at leisure to turn its attention again to the hardly more important problems and perplexities of life and the menaces that might have to be met in the future.

Elizabeth, on this morning of mid-December, was quite settled into Mallards again, egg-whisk and all, and the window of her garden-room was being once more used by the rightful owner for the purpose of taking observations. It had always been a highly strategic position; it commanded, for instance, a perfect view of the front door of Taormina, which at the present moment quaint Irene was painting in stripes of salmon pink and azure. She had tried to reproduce the lost fresco on it, but there had been earnest remonstrances from the Padre, and also the panels on the door broke it up and made it an unsuitable surface for such a cartoon. She therefore was contenting herself with brightening it up. Then Elizabeth could see the mouth of Porpoise Street and register all the journeys of the Royce. These, after a fortnight's intermission, had become frequent again, for the Wyses had just come back from 'visiting friends in Devonshire', and though Elizabeth had strong reason to suspect that friends in Devonshire denoted nothing more than an hotel in Torquay, they had certainly taken the Royce with them, and during its absence the streets of Tilling had been far more convenient for traffic. Then there was Major Benjy's house as before, under her very eye, and now Mallards Cottage as well was a point that demanded frequent scrutiny. She had never cared what that distraught Isabel Poppit did, but with Georgie there it was different, and neither Major Benjy nor he (nor anybody else visiting them) could go in or out of either house without instant detection. The two most important men in Tilling, in fact, were powerless to evade her observation.

Nothing particular was happening at the moment, and Elizabeth was making a mental retrospect rather as if she was the King preparing his speech for the opening of Parliament. Her relations with foreign powers were excellent, and though during the last six months there had been disquieting incidents, there was nothing immediately threatening . . . Then round the corner of the High Street came Lucia's car and the King's speech was put aside.

The car stopped at Taormina. Quaint Irene instantly put down her painting paraphernalia on the pavement, and stood talking into the window of the car for quite a long time. Clearly therefore Lucia, though invisible, was inside it. Eventually Irene leaned her head forward into the car, exactly as if she was kissing something, and stepping back again upset one of her paint-pots. This was pleasant, but not of first-rate importance compared with what the car would do next. It turned down into Porpoise Street: naturally there was no telling for certain what happened to it there, for it was out of sight, but a tyro could conjecture that it had business at the Wyses', even if he had been so deaf as not to hear the clanging of that front-door bell. Then it came backing out again, went through the usual manoeuvres of turning, and next stopped at Major Benjy's. Lucia was still invisible, but Cadman got down and delivered a note. The tyro could therefore conjecture by this time that invitations were coming from Grebe.

She slid her chair a little farther back behind the curtain, feeling sure that the car would stop next at her own door. But it turned the corner below the window without drawing up, and Elizabeth got a fleeting glance into the interior, where Lucia was sitting with a large book open in her lap. Next it stopped at Mallards Cottage: no note was delivered there, but Cadman rang the bell, and presently Georgie came out. Like Irene, he talked for quite a long time into the window of the car, but, unlike her, did not kiss anything at the conclusion of the interview. The situation was therefore perfectly clear: Lucia had asked Irene and Major Benjy and Georgie and probably the Wyses to some entertainment, no doubt the house-warming of which there had been rumours, but had not asked her. Very well. The relations with foreign powers therefore had suddenly become far from satisfactory.

Elizabeth quitted her seat in the window, for she had observed enough to supply her with plenty of food for thought, and went back, in perfect self-control, to the inspection of her household books; adding up figures was a purely mechanical matter, which allowed the intenser emotions full play. Georgie would be coming in here presently, for he was painting a sketch of the interior of the garden-room; this was to be his Christmas present to Lucia (a surprise, about which she was to know nothing), to remind her of the happy days she had spent in it. He usually left his sketch here, for it was not worth while to take it backwards and forwards, and there it stood, propped up on the book-case. He had first tried an Irene-ish technique, but he had been obliged to abandon that, since the garden-room with this handling persisted in looking like Paddington Station in a fog, and he had gone back to the style he knew, in which book-cases, chairs and curtains were easily recognizable. It needed a few mornings' work yet, and now the idea of destroying it, and, when he arrived, of telling him that she was quite sure he had taken it back with him yesterday darted unbidden into Elizabeth's mind. But she rejected it, though it would have been pleasant to deprive Lucia of her Christmas present . . . and she did not believe for a moment that she had ordered a dozen eggs on Tuesday and a dozen more on Thursday. The butcher's bill seemed to be correct, though extortionate, and she must find out as soon as possible whether the Padre and his wife and Diva were asked to Grebe too. If they were – but she banished the thought of what was to be done if they were: it was difficult enough to know what to do even if they weren't.

The books were quickly done, and Elizabeth went back to finish reading the morning paper in the window. Just as she got there Georgie, with his little cape over his shoulders and his paint-box in his hand, came stepping briskly along from Mallards Cottage. Simultaneously Lucia's great bumping car returned round the corner by the churchyard, in the direction of Mallards.

An inspiration of purest ray serene seized Elizabeth. She waited till Georgie had rung the front-door bell, at which psychological moment Lucia's car was straight below the window. Without a second's hesitation Elizabeth threw up the sash, and, without appearing to see Lucia at all, called out to Georgie in a high cheerful voice, using baby-language.

''Oo is very naughty boy, Georgie!' she cried. 'Never ring Elizabeth's belly-pelly. 'Oo walk straight in always, and sing out for her. There's no chain up.'

Georgie looked round in amazement. Never had Elizabeth called him Georgie before, or talked to him in the language consecrated for his use and Lucia's. And there was Lucia's car close to him. She must have heard this affectionate welcome, and what would she think? But there was nothing to do but to go in.

Still without seeing (far less cutting) Lucia, Elizabeth closed the window again, positively dazzled by her own brilliance. An hour's concentrated thought could not have suggested to her anything that Lucia would dislike more thoroughly than hearing that gay little speech, which parodied her and revealed such playful intimacy with Georgie. Georgie came straight out to the garden-room, saying 'Elizabeth, Elizabeth' to himself below his breath, in order to get used to it, for he must return this token of friendship in kind.

'Good morning, Elizabeth,' he said firmly (and the worst was over until such time as he had to say it again in Lucia's presence).

'Good morning, Georgie,' she said by way of confirmation. 'What a lovely light for your painting this morning. Here it is ready for you, and Withers will bring you out your glass of water. How you've caught the feel of my dear little room!'

Another glance out of the window as she brought him his sketch was necessary, and she gasped. There was Cadman on the doorstep just handing Withers a note. In another minute she came into the garden-room.

'From Mrs Lucas,' she said. 'She forgot to leave it when she went by before.'

'That's about the house-warming, I'm sure,' said Georgie, getting his paint-box ready.

What was done, was done, and there was no use in thinking about that. Elizabeth tore the note open.

'A house-warming?' she said. 'Dear Lucia! What a treat that will be. Yes, you're quite right.'

'She's sending her car up for the Padre and his wife and Irene and Mrs Plaistow,' said Georgie, 'and asked me just now if I would bring you and Major Benjy. Naturally I will.'

Elizabeth's brilliant speech out of the window had assumed the aspect of a gratuitous act of war. But she could not have guessed that Lucia had merely forgotten to leave her invitation. The most charitable would have assumed that there was no invitation to leave.

'How kind of you!' she said. 'To-morrow night, isn't it? Rather short notice. I must see if I'm disengaged.'

As Lucia had asked the whole of the élite of Tilling, this proved to be the case. But Elizabeth still pondered as to whether she should accept or not. She had committed one unfriendly act in talking baby-language to Georgie, with a pointed allusion to the door-chain, literally over Lucia's head, and it was a question whether, having done that, it would not be wise to commit another (while Lucia, it might be guessed, was still staggering) by refusing to go to the house-warming. She did not doubt that there would be war before long: the only question was if she was ready now.

As she was pondering Withers came in to say that Major Benjy had called. He would not come out into the garden-room, but he would like to speak to her a minute.

'Evidently he has heard that Georgie is here,' thought Elizabeth to herself as she hurried into the house. 'Dear me, how men quarrel with each other, and I only want to be on good terms with everybody. No doubt he wants to know if I'm going to the house-warming – Good morning, Major Benjy.'

'Thought I wouldn't come out,' said this bluff fellow, 'as I heard your Miss Milliner Michael-Angelo, ha, was with you –'

'Oh Major Benjy, fie!' said Elizabeth. 'Cruel of you.'

'Well, leave it at that. Now about this party to-morrow. I think I shall make a stand straight away, for I'm not going to spend the whole of the winter evenings tramping through the mud to Grebe. To be sure it's dinner this time, which makes a difference.'

Elizabeth found that she longed to see what Lucia had made of Grebe, and what she had made of her speech from the window.

'I quite agree in principle,' she said, 'but a house-warming, you know. Perhaps it wouldn't be kind to refuse. Besides, Georgie –'

'Eh?' said the Major.

'Mr Pillson, I mean,' said Elizabeth, hastily correcting herself, has offered to drive us both down.'

'And back?' asked he suspiciously.

'Of course. So just for once, shall we?'

'Very good. But none of those after-dinner musicals, or lessons in bridge for me.'

'Oh, Major Benjy!' said Elizabeth. 'How can you talk so? As if poor Lucia would attempt to teach *you* bridge.'

This could be taken in two ways, one interpretation would read that he was incapable of learning, the other that Lucia was incapable of teaching. He took the more obvious one.

'Upon my soul she did, at the last game I had with her,' said he. 'Laid out the last three tricks and told me how to play them. Beyond a joke. Well, I won't keep you from your dressmaker.'

'O fie!' said Elizabeth again. 'Au reservoir.'

Lucia, meantime, had driven back to Grebe with that mocking voice still ringing in her ears, and a series of most unpleasant images, like some diabolical film, displaying themselves before her inward eye. Most probably Elizabeth had seen her when she called out to Georgie like that, and was intentionally insulting her. Such conduct called for immediate reprisals and she must presently begin to think these out. But the alternative, possible though not probable, that Elizabeth had not seen her, was infinitely more wounding, for it implied that Georgie was guilty of treacheries too black to bear looking at. Privately, when she herself was not present, he was on Christian-name terms with that woman, and permitted and enjoyed her obvious mimicry of herself. And what was Georgie doing popping in to Mallards like this, and being scolded in baby-voice for ringing the bell instead of letting himself in, with allusions of an absolutely unmistakable kind to that episode about the chain? Did they laugh over that together: did Georgie poke fun at his oldest friend behind her back? Lucia positively writhed at the thought. In any case, whether or no he was guilty of this monstrous infidelity, he must be in the habit of going into Mallards, and now she remembered that he had his paint-box in his hand. Clearly then he was going there to paint, and in all their talks when he so constantly told her what he had been doing, he had never breathed a word of that. Perhaps he was painting Elizabeth, for in this winter weather he could never be painting in the garden. Just now too, when she called at Mallards Cottage, and they had had a talk together, he had refused to go out and drive with her, because he had some little jobs to do indoors, and the moment he had got rid of her – no less than that – he had hurried off to Mallards with his paint-box. With all this evidence, things looked very dark indeed, and the worst and most wounding of these two alternatives began to assume probability.

Georgie was coming to tea with her that afternoon, and she must find out what the truth of the matter was. But she could not imagine herself saying to him: 'Does she really call you Georgie, and does she imitate me behind my back, and are you painting her?' Pride absolutely forbade that: such humiliating inquiries would choke her. Should she show him an icy aloof demeanour, until he asked her if anything was the matter? But that wouldn't do, for either she must say that nothing was the matter, which would not help, or she must tell him what the matter was, which was impossible. She must behave to him exactly as usual, and he would probably do the same. 'So how am I to find out?' said the bewildered Lucia quite aloud.

Another extremely uncomfortable person in tranquil Tilling that morning was Georgie himself. As he painted this sketch of the garden-room for Lucia, with Elizabeth busying herself with dusting her piano and bringing in chrysanthemums from her greenhouse, and making bright little sarcasms about Diva who was in ill odour just now, there painted itself in his mind, in colours growing ever more vivid, a most ominous picture of Lucia. If he knew her at all, and he was sure he did, she would say nothing whatever about that disconcerting scene on the doorstep. Awkward as it would be, he would be obliged to protest his innocence, and denounce Elizabeth. Most disagreeable, and who could foresee the consequences? For Lucia (if he knew her) would see red, and there would he war. Bloody war of the most devastating sort. 'But it will be rather exciting too,' thought he, 'and I back Lucia.'

Georgie could not wait for tea-time, but set forth on his uncomfortable errand soon after lunch. Lucia had seen him coming up the garden, and abandoned her musings and sat down hastily at the piano. Instantly on his entry she sprang up again, and plunged into mixed Italian and baby-talk.

'*Ben arrivato, Georgino,*' she cried. 'How early you are, and so we can have cosy ickle chat-chat before tea. Any newsy-pewsy?'

Georgie took the plunge.

'Yes,' he said.

'Tell Lucia, presto. 'Oo think me like it?'

'It'll interest you,' said Georgie guardedly. 'Now! When I was standing on Mallards doorstep this morning, did you hear what that old witch called to me out of the garden-room window?'

Lucia could not repress a sigh of relief. The worst could not be true. Then she became herself again.

'Let me see now!' she said. 'Yes. I think I did. She called you Georgie, didn't she: she scolded you for ringing. Something of that sort.'

'Yes. And she talked baby-talk like you and me,' interrupted Georgie, 'and she said the door wasn't on the chain. I want to tell you straight off that she never called me Georgie before, and that we've never talked baby-talk together in my life. I owe it to myself to tell you that.'

Lucia turned her piercing eye on to Georgie. There seemed to be a sparkle in it that boded ill for somebody.

'And you think she saw me, Georgie?' she asked.

'Of course she did. Your car was directly below her window.'

'I am afraid there is no doubt about it,' said Lucia. 'Her remarks, therefore, seem to have been directed at me. A singularly ill-bred person. There's one thing more. You were taking your paint-box with you –'

'Oh, that's all right,' said he. 'I'm doing a sketch of the garden-room. You'll know about that in time. And what are you going to do?' he asked greedily.

Lucia laughed in her most musical manner.

'Well, first of all I shall give her a very good dinner to-morrow, as she has not had the decency to say she was engaged. She telephoned to me just now telling me what a joy it would be, and how she was looking forward to it. And mind you call her Elizabeth.'

'I've done that already,' said Georgie proudly. 'I practised saying it to myself.'

'Good. She dines here then to-morrow night, and I shall be her hostess and shall make the evening as pleasant as I can to all my guests. But apart from that, Georgie, I shall take steps to teach her manners if she's not too old to learn. She will be sorry; she will wish she had not been so rude. And I can't see any objection to our other friends in Tilling knowing what occurred this morning, if you feel inclined to speak of it. I shan't, but there's no reason why you shouldn't.'

'Hurrah, I'm dining with the Wyses to-night,' said Georgie. 'They'll soon know.'

Lucia knitted her brows in profound thought.

'And then there's that incident about our pictures, yours and mine, being rejected by the hanging committee of the Art Club,' said she. 'We have both kept the forms we received saying that they regretted having to return them, and I think, Georgie, that while you are on the subject of Elizabeth Mapp, you might show yours to Mr Wyse. He is a member, so is Susan, of the committee, and I think they have a right to know that our pictures were rejected on official forms without ever coming before the committee at all. I behaved towards our poor friend with a magnanimity that now appears to me excessive, and since she does not appreciate magnanimity we will try her with something else. That would not be amiss.' Lucia rose.

'And now let us leave this very disagreeable subject for the present,' she said, 'and take the taste of it out of our mouths with a little music. Beethoven, noble Beethoven, don't you think? The fifth symphony, Georgie, for four hands. Fate knocking at the door.'

Georgie rather thought that Lucia smacked her lips as she said, 'this very disagreeable subject', but he was not certain, and presently Fate was knocking at the door with Lucia's firm fingers, for she took the treble.

They had a nice long practice, and when it was time to go home Lucia detained him.

'I've got one thing to say to you, Georgie,' she said, 'though not about that paltry subject. I've sold the Hurst, I've bought this new property, and so I've made a new will. I've left Grebe and all it contains to you, and also, well, a little sum of money. I should like you to know that.'

Georgie was much touched.

'My dear, how wonderful of you,' he said. 'But I hope it will be ages and ages before –'

'So do I, Georgie,' she said in her most sincere manner.

Tilling had known tensions before and would doubtless know them again. Often it had been on a very agreeable rack of suspense, as when, for instance, it had believed (or striven to believe) that Major Benjy might be fighting a duel with that old crony of his, Captain Puffin, lately deceased. Now there was a suspense of a more intimate quality (for nobody would have cared at all if Captain Puffin had been killed, nor much, if Major Benjy), for it was as if the innermost social guts of Tilling were attached to some relentless windlass, which, at any moment now, might be wound, but not relaxed. The High

Street next morning, therefore, was the scene of almost painful excitement. The Wyses' Royce, with Susan smothered in sables, went up and down, until she was practically certain that she had told everybody that she and Algernon had retired from the hanging committee of the Art Club, pending explanations which they had requested Miss (no longer Elizabeth) Mapp to furnish, but which they had no hope of receiving. Susan was perfectly explicit about the cause of this step, and Algernon who, at a very early hour, had interviewed the errand-boy at the frame-shop, was by her side, to corroborate all she said. His high-bred reticence, indeed, had been even more weighty than Susan's volubility. 'I am afraid it is all too true,' was all that could be got out of him. Two hours had now elapsed since their resignations had been sent in, and still no reply had come from Mallards.

But that situation was but an insignificant fraction of the prevalent suspense, for the exhibition had been open and closed months before, and if Tilling was to make a practice of listening to such posthumous revelations, life would cease to have any poignant interest, but be wholly occupied in retrospective retributions. Thrilling therefore as was the past, as revealed by the stern occupants of the Royce, what had happened only yesterday on the doorstep of Mallards was far more engrossing. The story of that, by 11.30 a.m., already contained several remarkable variants. The Padre affirmed that Georgie had essayed to enter Mallards without knocking, and that Miss Mapp (the tendency to call her Miss Mapp was spreading) had seen Lucia in her motor just below the window of the garden-room, and had called out 'Tum in, *Georgino mio*, no tarsome chains now that Elizabeth has got back to her own housie-pousie.' Diva had reason to believe that Elizabeth (she still stuck to that) had not seen Lucia in her motor, and had called out of the window to Georgie 'Ring the belly-pelly, dear, for I'm afraid the chain is on the door.' Mrs Bartlett (she was no use at all) said, 'All so distressing and exciting and Christmas Day next week, and very little good will, oh dear me!' Irene had said, 'That old witch will get what for.'

Again, it was known that Major Benjy had called at Mallards

soon after the scene, whatever it was, had taken place, and had refused to go into the garden-room, when he heard that Georgie was painting Elizabeth's portrait. Withers was witness (she had brought several pots of jam to Diva's house that morning, not vegetable marrow at all, but raspberry, which looked like a bribe) that the Major had said 'Faugh!' when she told him that Georgie was there. Major Benjy himself could not be cross-examined because he had gone out by the eleven o'clock tram to play golf. Lucia had not been seen in the High Street at all, nor had Miss Mapp, and Georgie had only passed through it in his car, quite early, going in the direction of Grebe. This absence of the principals, in these earlier stages of development, was felt to be in accordance with the highest rules of dramatic technique, and everybody, as far as was known, was to meet that very night at Lucia's house-warming. Opinion as to what would happen then was as divergent as the rumours of what had happened already. Some said that Miss Mapp had declined the invitation on the plea that she was engaged to dine with Major Benjy. This was unlikely, because he never had anybody to dinner. Some said that she had accepted, and that Lucia no doubt intended to send out a message that she was not expected, but that Georgie's car would take her home again. So sorry. All this, however, was a matter of pure conjecture, and it was work enough to sift out what had happened, without wasting time (for time was precious) in guessing what would happen.

The church clock had hardly struck half-past eleven (winter time) before the first of the principals appeared on the stage of the High Street. This was Miss Mapp, wreathed in smiles, and occupied in her usual shopping errands. She trotted about from grocer to butcher, and butcher to general stores, where she bought a mouse-trap, and was exceedingly affable to trades-people. She nodded to her friends, she patted Mr Woolgar's dog on the head, she gave a penny to a ragged individual with a lugubrious baritone voice who was singing 'The Last Rose of Summer', and said 'Thank you for your sweet music.' Then after pausing for a moment on the pavement in front of Wasters, she rang the bell. Diva, who had seen her from the window, flew to open it.

'Good morning, Diva dear,' she said. 'I just looked in. Any news?'

'Good gracious, it's I who ought to ask you that,' said Diva. 'What *did* happen really?'

Elizabeth looked very much surprised.

'How? When? Where?' she asked.

'As if you didn't know,' said Diva, fizzing with impatience. 'Mr Georgie, Lucia, paint-boxes, no chain on the door, you at the garden-room window, belly-pelly. Etcetera. Yesterday morning.'

Elizabeth put her finger to her forehead, as if trying to recall some dim impression. She appeared to succeed.

'Dear gossipy one,' she said, 'I believe I know what you mean. Georgie came to paint in the garden-room, as he so often does –'

'Do you call him Georgie?' asked Diva in an eager parenthesis.

'Yes, I fancy that's his name, and he calls me Elizabeth.'

'No!' said Diva.

'Yes,' said Elizabeth. 'Do not interrupt me, dear ... I happened to be at the window as he rang the bell, and I just popped my head out, and told him he was a naughty boy not to walk straight in.'

'In baby-talk?' asked Diva. 'Like Lucia?'

'Like any baby you chance to mention,' said Elizabeth. 'Why not?'

'But with her sitting in her car just below?'

'Yes, dear, it so happened that she was just coming to leave an invitation on me for her house-warming to-night. Are you going?'

'Yes, of course, everybody is. But how could you do it?'

Elizabeth sat wrapped in thought.

'I'm beginning to see what you mean,' she said at length. 'But what an absurd notion. You mean, don't you, that dear Lulu thinks – goodness, how ridiculous – that I was mimicking her.'

'Nobody knows what she thinks,' said Diva. 'She's not been seen this morning.'

'But gracious goodness me, what have I done?' asked Elizabeth. 'Why this excitement? Is there a law that only Mrs Lucas of Grebe may call Georgie, Georgie? So ignorant of me if there is. Ought I to call him Frederick? And pray, why shouldn't I talk baby-talk? Another law perhaps. I must get a book of the laws of England.'

'But you knew she was in the car just below you and must have heard.'

Elizabeth was now in possession of what she wanted to know. Diva was quite a decent barometer of Tilling weather, and the weather was stormy.

'Rubbish, darling,' she said. 'You are making mountains out of mole-hills. If Lulu heard – and I don't know that she did, mind – what cause of complaint has she? Mayn't I say Georgie? Mayn't I say "vewy naughty boy"? Let us hear no more about it. You will see this evening how wrong you all are. Lulu will be just as sweet and cordial as ever. And you will hear with your own ears how Georgie calls me Elizabeth.'

These were brave words, and they very fitly represented the stout heart that inspired them. Tilling had taken her conduct to be equivalent to an act of war, exactly as she had meant it to be, and if anyone thought that E. M. was afraid they were wrong . . . Then there was that matter of Mr Wyse's letter, resigning from the hanging committee. She must tap the barometer again.

'I think everybody is a shade mad this morning,' she observed, 'and I should call Mr Wyse, if anybody asked me to be candid, a raving lunatic. There was a little misunderstanding months and months ago – I am vague about it – concerning two pictures that Lulu and Georgie sent in to the art exhibition in the summer. I thought it was all settled and done with. But I did act a little irregularly. Technically I was wrong, and when I have been wrong about a thing, as you very well know, dear Diva, I am not ashamed to confess it.'

'Of course you were wrong,' said Diva cordially, 'if Mr Wyse's account of it is correct. You sent the pictures back, such beauties, too, with a formal rejection from the hanging committee when they had never seen them at all. So rash, too: I wonder at you.'

These unfavourable comments did not make the transaction appear any the less irregular.

'I said I was wrong, Diva,' remarked Elizabeth with some asperity, 'and I should have thought that was enough. And now Mr Wyse, raking bygones up again in the way he has, has written to me to say that he and Susan resign their places on the hanging committee.'

'I know: they told everybody,' said Diva. 'Awkward. What are you going to do?'

The barometer had jerked alarmingly downwards on this renewed tapping.

'I shall cry peccavi,' said Elizabeth, with the air of doing something exceedingly noble. 'I shall myself resign. That will show that whatever anybody else does, I am doing the best in my power to put right a technical error. I hope Mr Wyse will appreciate that, and be ashamed of the letter he wrote me. More than that, I shall regard his letter as having been written in a fit of temporary insanity, which I trust will not recur.'

'Yes; I suppose that's the best thing you can do,' said Diva. 'It will show him that you regret what you did, now that it's all found out.'

'That is not generous of you, Diva,' cried Elizabeth, 'I am sorry you said that.'

'More than I am,' said Diva. 'It's a very fair statement. Isn't it now? What's wrong with it?'

Elizabeth suddenly perceived that at this crisis it was unwise to indulge in her usual tiffs with Diva. She wanted allies.

'Diva, dear, we mustn't quarrel,' she said. 'That would never do. I felt I had to pop in to consult you as to the right course to take with Mr Wyse, and I'm so glad you agree with me. How I trust your judgment! I must be going. What a delightful evening we have in store for us. Major Benjy was thinking of declining, but I persuaded him it would not be kind. A house-warming, you know. Such a special occasion.'

The evening to which everybody had looked forward so much was, in the main, a disappointment to bellicose spirits. Nothing could exceed Lucia's cordiality to Elizabeth unless it was Elizabeth's to Lucia: they left the dining-room at the end of dinner with arms and waists intertwined, a very bitter sight. They then played bridge at the same table, and so loaded each other with compliments while deploring their own errors, that Diva began to entertain the most serious fears that they had been mean enough to make it up on the sly, or that Lucia in a spirit of Christian forbearance, positively unnatural, had decided to overlook all the attacks and insults with which Elizabeth had tried to provoke her. Or did Lucia think that this degrading display of magnanimity was a weapon by which she would secure victory, by enlisting for her the sympathy and applause of Tilling? If so, that was a great mistake; Tilling did not want to witness a demonstration of forgiveness or white feathers but a combat without quarter. Again, if she thought that such nobility would soften the malevolent heart of Mapp, she showed a distressing ignorance of Mapp's nature, for she would quite properly construe this as not being nobility at all but the most ignoble cowardice. There was Georgie under Lucia's very nose, interlarding his conversation with far more 'Elizabeths' than was in the least necessary to show that he was talking to her, and she volleyed 'Georgies' at him in return. Every now and then, when these discharges of Christian names had been particularly resonant, Elizabeth caught Diva's eye with a glance of triumph as if to remind her that she had prophesied that Lulu would be all sweetness and cordiality, and Diva turned away sick at heart.

On the other hand, there were still grounds for hope, and, as the evening went on, these became more promising: they were like small caps of foam and cats'-paws of wind upon a tranquil sea. To begin with, it was only this morning that the baseness of Elizabeth in that matter concerning the art committee had come to light. Georgie, not Lucia, had been directly responsible for that damning disclosure, but it must be supposed that he had acted with her connivance, if not with her express wish, and this certainly did not look so much like forgiveness as a nasty one for Elizabeth. That was hopeful, and Diva's eagle eye espied other signs of bad weather. Elizabeth, encouraged by Lucia's compliments and humilities throughout a long rubber, began to come out more in her true colours, and to

explain to her partner that she had lost a few tricks (no matter)
by not taking a finesse, or a whole game by not supporting her
declaration, and Diva thought she detected a certain dangerous
glitter in Lucia's eye as she bent to these chastisements. Surely,
too, she bit her lip when Elizabeth suddenly began to call her
Lulu again. Then there was Irene's conduct to consider: Irene
was fizzing and fidgeting in her chair, she cast glances of black
hatred at Elizabeth, and once Diva distinctly saw Lucia frown
and shake her head at her. Again, at the voluptuous supper
which succeeded many rubbers of bridge, there was the famous
lobster *à la Riseholme*. It had become, as all Tilling knew, a
positive obsession with Elizabeth to get the secret of that
delicious dish, and now, flushed with continuous victories at
bridge and with Lucia's persevering pleasantness, she made
another direct request for it.

'Lulu dear,' she said, 'it would be sweet of you to give me
the recipe for your lobster. So good . . .'

Diva felt this to be a crucial moment: Lucia had often
refused it before, but now if she was wholly Christian and
cowardly she would consent. But once more she gave no reply,
and asked the Padre on what day of the week Christmas fell.
So Diva heaved a sigh of relief, for there was still hope.

In spite of this rebuff, it was hardly to be wondered at that
Elizabeth felt in a high state of elation when the evening was
over. The returning revellers changed the order of their going,
and Georgie took back her and Diva. He went outside with
Diva, for, during the last half-hour, Mapp (as he now mentally
termed her in order to be done with Elizabeth) had grown like
a mushroom in complaisance and self-confidence, and he could
not trust himself, if she went on, as she would no doubt do, in
the same strain, not to rap out something very sharp. 'Let her
just wait,' he thought, 'she'll soon be singing a different tune.'

Georgie's precautions in going outside, well wrapped up in
his cap and his fur tippet and his fur rug, were well founded,
for hardly had Mapp kissed her hand for the last time to Lulu
(who would come to the door to see them off), and counted
over the money she had won, than she burst into staves of
intolerable triumph and condescension.

'So that's that!' she said, pulling up the window. 'And if I was to ask you, dear Diva, which of us was right about how this evening would go off, I don't think there would be very much doubt about the answer. Did you ever see Lulu so terribly anxious to please me? And did you happen to hear me say Georgie and him say Elizabeth? Lulu didn't like it, I am sure, but she had to swallow her medicine, and she did so with a very good grace, I am bound to say. She just wanted a little lesson, and I think I may say I've given it her. I had no idea, I will confess, that she would take it lying down like that. I just had to lean out of the window, pretend not to see her, and talk to Georgie in that silly voice and language and the thing was done.'

Diva had been talking simultaneously for some time, but Elizabeth only paused to take breath, and went on in a slightly louder tone. So Diva talked louder too, until Georgie turned round to see what was happening. They both broke off, and smiled at him, and then both began again.

'If you would allow me to get a word in edgeways,' said Diva, who had some solid arguments to produce, and, had she not been a lady, could have slapped Mapp's face in impotent rage –

'I don't think,' said Elizabeth, 'that we shall have much more trouble with her and her queenly airs. Quite a pleasant house-warming, and there was no doubt that the house wanted it, for it was bitterly cold in the dining-room, and I strongly suspect that chicken-cream of being rabbit. She only had to be shown that whatever Riseholme may have stood from her in the way of condescensions and graces, she had better not try them on at Tilling. She was looking forward to teaching us, and ruling us and guiding us. Pop! Elizabeth (that's me, dear!) has a little lamb, which lives at Grebe and gives a house-warming, so you may guess who *that* is. The way she flattered and sued to-night over our cards when but a few weeks ago she was thinking of holding bridge classes –'

'You were just as bad,' shouted Diva. 'You told her she played beauti –'

'She was "all over me", to use that dreadful slang expression of Major Benjy's,' continued Mapp. 'She was like a dog that has had a scolding and begs – so prettily – to be forgiven. Mind, dear, I do not say that she is a bad sort of woman by any means, but she required to be put in her place, and Tilling ought to thank me for having done so. Dear me, here we are already at your house. How short the drive has seemed!'

'Anyhow, you didn't get the recipe for the lobster *à la Riseholme*,' said Diva, for this was one of the things she most wanted to say.

'A little final wriggle,' said Mapp. 'I have not the least doubt that she will think it over and send it me to-morrow. Good night, darling. I shall be sending out invitations for a cosy evening of bridge some time at the end of this week.'

The baffled Diva let herself into Wasters in low spirits, so convinced and lucid had been Mapp's comments on the evening. It was such a dismal conclusion to so much excitement; and all that thrilling tension, instead of snapping, had relaxed into the most depressing slackness. But she did not quite give up hope, for there had been cats'-paws and caps of foam on the tranquil sea. She fell asleep visualizing these.

9

Though Georgie had thought that the garden-room would have to give him at least two more sittings before his sketch arrived at that high state of finish which he, like the Pre-Raphael-ites, regarded as necessary to any work of art, he decided that he would leave it in a more impressionist state, and sent it next morning to be framed. In consequence the glass of water which Elizabeth had brought out for him in anticipation of his now usual visit at eleven o'clock remained unsullied by wash-ings from his brush, and at twelve, Elizabeth, being rather thirsty in consequence of so late a supper the night before, drank it herself. On the second morning, a very wet one, Major Benjy did not go out for his usual round of golf, and again Georgie did not come to paint. But at a few minutes to one she observed that his car was at the door of Mallards Cottage; it passed her window, it stopped at Major Benjy's, and he got in. It was impossible not to remember that Lucia always lunched at one in the winter because a later hour for *colazione* made the afternoon so short. But it was a surprise to see Major Benjy driving away with Miss Milliner Michael-Angelo, and difficult to conjecture where else it was at all likely that they could have gone.

There was half an hour yet to her own luncheon, and she wrote seven post cards inviting seven friends to tea on Saturday, with bridge to follow. The Wyses, the Padres, Diva, Major Benjy and Georgie were the *destinataires* of these missives; these, with herself, made eight, and there would thus be two tables of agreeable gamblers. Lucia was not to be favoured: it would be salutary for her to be left out every now and then, just to impress upon her the lesson of which she had stood so sadly in need. She must learn to go to heel, to come when called, and to produce recipes when desired, which at present she had not done.

There had been several days of heavy rain, but early in the afternoon it cleared up, and Elizabeth set out for a brisk healthy walk. The field-paths would certainly make very miry going, for she saw from the end of the High Street that there was much water lying in the marsh, and she therefore kept to that excellent road, which, having passed Grebe, went nowhere particular. She was prepared to go in and thank Lucia for her lovely house-warming, in order to make sure whether Georgie and Major Benjy had gone to lunch with her, but no such humiliating need occurred, for there in front of the house was drawn up Georgie's motor-car, so (whether she liked it or not, and she didn't) *that* problem was solved. The house stood quite close to the road: a flagged pathway of half a dozen yards, flanked at the entrance-gate by thick hornbeam hedges on which the leaf still lingered, separated it from the road, and just as Elizabeth passed Georgie's car drawn up there, the front door opened, and she saw Lucia and her two guests on the threshold. Major Benjy was laughing in that fat voice of his, and Georgie was giving forth his shrill little neighs like a colt with a half-cracked voice.

The temptation to know what they were laughing at was irresistible. Elizabeth moved a few steps on and, screened by the hornbeam hedge, held her breath.

Major Benjy gave another great haw-haw and spoke.

''Pon my word, did she really?' he said. 'Do it again, Mrs Lucas. Never laughed so much in my life. Infernal impertinence!'

There was no mistaking the voice and the words that followed.

''Oo is vewy naughty boy, Georgie,' said Lucia. 'Never ring Elizabeth's belly-pelly –'

Elizabeth hurried on, as she heard steps coming down that short flagged pathway. But hurry as she might, she heard a little more.

''Oo walk straight in always and sing out for her,' continued the voice, repeating word for word the speech of which she had been so proud. 'There's no chain up' – and then came loathsome parody – 'now that Liblib has ritornata to Mallardino.'

It was in a scared mood, as if she had heard or seen a ghost, that Elizabeth hastened along up the road that led nowhere in particular, before Lucia's guests could emerge from the gate. Luckily at the end of the kitchen-garden the hornbeam hedge turned at right-angles, and behind this bastion she hid herself till she heard the motor move away in the direction of Tilling, the prey of the most agitated misgivings. Was it possible that her own speech, which she had thought had scarified Lucia's pride, was being turned into a mockery and a derision against herself? It seemed not only possible but probable. And how dare Mrs Lucas invent and repeat as if spoken by herself that rubbish about ritornata and Mallardino? Never in her life had she said such a thing.

When the coast was clear, she took the road again, and walked quickly on away from Tilling. The tide was very high, for the river was swollen with rain, and the waters overbrimmed its channel and extended in a great lake up to the foot of the bank and dyke which bounded the road. Perturbed as she was, Miss Mapp could not help admiring that broad expanse of water, now lit by a gleam of sun, in front of which to the westward, the hill of Tilling rose dark against a sky already growing red with the winter sunset. She had just turned a corner in the road, and now she perceived that close ahead of her somebody else was admiring it too in a more practical manner, for there by the roadside within twenty yards of her sat quaint Irene, with her mouth full of paint-brushes and an easel set up in front of her. She had not seen Irene since the night of the house-warming, when the quaint one had not been very cordial, and so, thinking she had walked far enough, she turned back. But Irene had quite evidently seen her, for she shaded her eyes for a moment against the glare, took some of the paint-brushes out of her mouth and called to her with words that seemed to have what might be termed a dangerous undertow.

'Hullo, Mapp,' she said. 'Been lunching with Lulu?'

'What a lovely sketch, dear,' said Mapp. 'No, just a brisk little walk. Not been lunching at Grebe to-day.'

Irene laughed hoarsely.

'I didn't think it was very likely, but thought I would ask,' she said. 'Yes; I'm rather pleased with my sketch. A bloody look about the sunlight, isn't there, as if the Day of Judgment was coming. I'm going to send it to the winter exhibition of the Art Club.'

'Dear girlie, what do you mean?' asked Mapp. 'We don't have winter exhibitions.'

'No, but we're going to,' said girlie. 'A new hanging committee, you see, full of pep and pop and vim. Haven't they asked you to send them something . . . Of course the space at their disposal is very limited.'

Mapp laughed, but not with any great exuberance. This undertow was tweaking at her disagreeably.

'That's news to me,' she said. 'Most enterprising of Mr Wyse and dear Susan.'

'Sweet Lulu's idea,' said Irene. 'As soon as you sent in your resignation, of course they asked her to be President.'

'That is nice for her,' said Mapp enthusiastically. 'She will like that. I must get to work on some little picky to send them.'

'There's that one you did from the church tower when Lucia had influenza,' said this awful Irene. 'That would be nice . . . Oh, I forgot. Stupid of me. It's by invitation: the committee are asking a few people to send pickies. No doubt they'll beg you for one. Such a good plan. There won't be any mistakes in the future about rejecting what is sent in.'

Mapp gave a gulp but rallied.

'I see. They'll be all Academicians together, and be hung on the line,' said she unflinchingly.

'Yes. On the line or be put on easels,' said Irene. 'Curse the light! It's fading. I must pack up. Hold these brushes, will you?'

'And then we'll walk back home together, shall we? A cup of tea with me, dear?' asked Mapp, anxious to conciliate and to know more.

'I'm going into Lucia's, I'm afraid. Wyses tummin' to play bridgey and hold a committee meeting,' said Irene.

'You are a cruel thing to imitate poor Lulu,' said Mapp. 'How well you've caught that silly baby-talk of hers. Just her voice. Bye-bye.'

'Same to you,' said Irene.

There was undoubtedly, thought Mapp, as she scudded swiftly homewards alone, a sort of mocking note about quaint Irene's conversation, which she did not relish. It was full of hints and awkward allusions; it bristled with hidden menace, and even her imitation of Lucia's baby-talk was not wholly satisfactory, for quaint Irene might be mimicking her imitation of Lucia, even as Lucia herself had done, and there was very little humour in that. Presently she passed the Wyses' Royce going to Grebe. She kissed her hand to a mound of sables inside, but it was too dark to see if the salute was returned. Her brisk afternoon's walk had not freshened her up; she was aware of a feeling of fatigue, of a vague depression and anxiety. And mixed with that was a hunger not only for tea but for more information. There seemed to be things going on of which she was sadly ignorant, and even when her ignorance was enlightened, they remained rather sad. But Diva (such a gossip) might know more about this winter exhibition, and she popped into Wasters. Diva was in, and begged her to wait for tea: she would be down in a few minutes.

It was a cosy little room, looking out on to the garden which had yielded her so many pots of excellent preserves during the summer, but dreadfully untidy, as Diva's house always was. There was a litter of papers on the table, notes half-thrust back into their envelopes, crossword puzzles cut out from the *Evening Standard* and partially solved: there was her own post card to Diva sent off that morning and already delivered, and there was a sheet of paper with the stamp of Grebe upon it and Lucia's monogram, which seemed to force itself on Elizabeth's eye. The most cursory glance revealed that this was a request from the Art Committee that Mrs Plaistow would do them the honour to send them a couple of her sketches for the forth-coming winter exhibition. All the time there came from Diva's bedroom, directly overhead, the sound of rhythmical steps or thumps, most difficult to explain. In a few minutes these ceased, and Diva's tread on the stairs gave Elizabeth sufficient warning to enable her to snatch up the first book that came to hand, and sink into a chair by the fire. She saw, with some feeling of apprehension similar to those which had haunted her all afternoon, that this was a copy of *An Ideal System of Callisthenics for those no longer Young*, of which she seemed to have heard. On the title-page was an inscription 'Diva from Lucia', and in brackets, like a prescription, 'Ten minutes at the exercises in Chapter I, twice a day for the present.'

Diva entered very briskly. She was redder in the face than usual, and, so Elizabeth instantly noticed, lifted her feet very high as she walked, and held her head well back and her breast out like a fat little pigeon. This time there was to be no question about getting a word in edgeways, for she began to talk before the door was fully open.

'Glad to see you, Elizabeth,' she said, 'and I shall be very pleased to play bridge on Saturday. I've never felt so well in my life, do you know, and I've only been doing them two days. Oh, I see you've got the book.'

'I heard you stamping and thumping, dear,' said Elizabeth. 'Was that them?'

'Yes, twice a day, ten minutes each time. It clears the head, too. If you sit down to a crossword puzzle afterwards you find you're much brighter than usual.'

'Callisthenics *à la Lucia*?' asked Elizabeth.

'Yes. Irene and Mrs Bartlett and I all do them, and Mrs Wyse is going to begin, but rather more gently. Hasn't Lucia told you about them?'

Here was another revelation of things happening. Elizabeth met it bravely.

'No. Dear Lulu knows my feelings about that sort of fad. A brisk walk such as I've had this afternoon is all I require. Such lovely lights of sunset and a very high tide. Quaint Irene was sketching on the road just beyond Grebe.'

'Yes. She's going to send it in and three more for the winter exhibition. Oh, perhaps you haven't heard. There's to be an exhibition directly after Christmas.'

'Such a good idea: I've been discussing it,' said Elizabeth.

Diva's eye travelled swiftly and suspiciously to the table where this flattering request to her lay on the top of the litter. Elizabeth did not fail to catch the significance of this.

'Irene told me,' she said hastily, 'I must see if I can find time to do them something.'

'Oh, then they have asked you,' said Diva with a shade of disappointment in her voice. 'They've asked me too –'

'No! Really?' said Elizabeth.

'– so of course I said yes, but I'm afraid I'm rather out of practice. Lucia is going to give an address on modern art at the opening, and then we shall all go round and look at each other's pictures.'

'What fun!' said Elizabeth cordially.

Tea had been brought in. There was a pot of greenish jam and Elizabeth loaded her buttered toast with it, and put it into her mouth. She gave a choking cry and washed it down with a gulp of tea.

'Anything wrong?' asked Diva.

'Yes, dear. I'm afraid it's fermenting,' said Elizabeth, laying down the rest of her toast. 'And I can't conceive what it's made of.'

Diva looked at the pot.

'You ought to know,' she said. 'It's one of the pots you gave me. Labelled vegetable marrow. So sorry it's not eatable. By the way, talking of food, did Lucia send you the recipe for the lobster?'

Elizabeth smiled her sweetest.

'Dear Lucia,' she said. 'She's been so busy with art and callisthenics. She must have forgotten. I shall jog her memory.'

The afternoon had been full of rather unpleasant surprises, thought Elizabeth to herself, as she went up to Mallards that evening. They were concerned with local activities, art and gymnastics, of which she had hitherto heard nothing, and they all seemed to show a common origin: there was a hidden hand directing them. This was disconcerting, especially since, only a few nights ago, she had felt so sure that that hand had been upraised to her, beseeching pardon. Now it rather looked as if that hand had spirited itself away and was very busy and energetic on its own account.

She paused on her doorstep. There was a light shining out through chinks behind the curtains in Mallards Cottage, and she thought it would be a good thing to pop in on Georgie and see if she could gather some further gleanings. She would make herself extremely pleasant: she would admire his needle-work if he was at it, she would praise the beautiful specklessness of his room, for Georgie always appreciated any compliment to Foljambe, she would sing the praises of Lucia, though they blistered her tongue.

Foljambe admitted her. The door of the sitting-room was ajar, and as she put down her umbrella, she heard Georgie's voice talking to the telephone.

'Saturday, half-past four,' he said. 'I've just found a post card. Hasn't she asked you?'

Georgie, as Elizabeth had often observed, was deafer than he knew (which accounted for his not hearing all the wrong notes she played in his duets with Lucia) and he had not heard her entry, though Foljambe spoke her name quite loud. He was listening with rapt attention to what was coming through and saying 'My dear!' or 'No!' at intervals. Now, however, he turned and saw her, and with a scared expression hung up the receiver.

'Dear me, I never heard you come in!' he said. 'How nice! I was just going to tell Foljambe to bring up tea. Two cups, Fol-jambe.'

'I'm interrupting you,' said Elizabeth. 'I can see you were just settling down to your sewing and a cosy bachelor evening.'

'Not a bit,' said Georgie. 'Do have a chair near the fire.' It was not necessary to explain that she had already, had tea with Diva, even if one mouthful of fermenting vegetable could properly be called tea, and she took the chair he pulled up for her.

'Such beautiful work,' she said, looking at Georgie's tambour of *petit point*, which lay near by. 'What eyes you must have to be able to do it.'

'Yes, they're pretty good yet,' said Georgie, slipping his spectacle-case into his pocket. 'And I shall be delighted to come to tea and bridge on Saturday. Thanks so much. Just got your invitation.'

Miss Mapp knew that already.

'That's charming,' she said. 'And how I envy you your Foljambe. Not a speck of dust anywhere. You could eat your tea off the floor, as they say.'

Georgie noticed that she did not use his Christian name. This confirmed his belief that the employment of it was reserved for Lucia's presence as an annoyance to her. Then the telephone-bell rang again.

'May I?' said Georgie.

He went across to it, rather nervous. It was as he thought: Lucia was at it again, explaining that somebody had cut her off. Listen as she might, Miss Mapp, from where she sat, could only hear a confused quacking noise. So to show how indifferent she was as to the conversation, she put her fingers close to her ears ready to stop them when Georgie turned round again, and listened hard to what he said.

'Yes . . . yes,' said Georgie. 'Thanks so much – lovely. I'll pick him up then, shall I? Quarter to eight, is it? Yes, her too. Yes, I've done them once to-day: not a bit giddy . . . I can't stop now, Lucia. Miss Ma – Elizabeth's just come in for a cup of tea . . . I'll tell her.'

Elizabeth felt she understood all this; she was an adept at telephonic reconstruction. There was evidently another party at Grebe. 'Him' and 'her' no doubt were Major Benjy and herself, whom Georgie would pick up as before. 'Them' were exercises, and Georgie's promise to tell 'her' clearly meant that he should convey an invitation. This was satisfactory: evidently Lucia was hoping to propitiate. Then Georgie turned round and saw Elizabeth smiling gaily at the fire with her hands over her ears. He moved into her field of vision and she uncorked herself.

'Finished?' she said. 'Hope you did not cut it short because of me.'

'Not at all,' said Georgie, for she couldn't (unless she was pretending) have heard him say that he had done precisely that. 'It was Lucia ringing up. She sends you her love.'

'Sweet of her, such a pet,' said Elizabeth, and waited for more about picking up and that invitation. But Lucia's love appeared to be all, and Georgie asked her if she took sugar. She did, and tried if he in turn would take another sort of sugar, both for himself and Lucia.

'Such a lovely house-warming,' she said, 'and how we all enjoyed ourselves. Lucia seems to have time for everything, bridge, those lovely duets with you, Italian, Greek (though we haven't heard much about that lately), a winter art exhibition, and an address (how I shall look forward to it!) on modern art, callisthenics –'

'Oh, you ought to try those,' said Georgie. 'You stretch and stamp and feel ever so young afterwards. We're all doing them.'

'And does she take classes as she threat – promised to do?' asked Elizabeth.

'She will when we've mastered the elements,' said Georgie. 'We shall march round the kitchen-garden at Grebe – cinder paths you know, so good in wet weather – keeping time, and then skip and flex and jerk. And if it's raining we shall do them in the kitchen. You can throw open those double doors, and have plenty of fresh air which is so important. There's that enormous kitchen-table too, to hold on to, when we're doing that swimming movement. It's like a great raft.'

Elizabeth had not the nerve to ask if Major Benjy was to be of that company. It would be too bitter to know that he, who had so sternly set his face against Lucia's domination, was in process of being sucked down in that infernal whirlpool of her energetic grabbings. Almost she wished that she had asked her to be one of her bridge-party tomorrow: but it was too late now. Her seven invitations – seven against Lucia – had gone forth, and not till she got home would she know whether her two bridge-tables were full.

'And this winter exhibition,' she asked. 'What a good idea! We're all so idle in the winter at dear old Tilling, and now there's another thing to work for. Are you sending that delicious picture of the garden-room? How I enjoyed our lovely chatty mornings when you were painting it!'

By the ordinary rules of polite conversation, Georgie ought to have asked her what she was sending. He did nothing of the kind; but looked a little uncomfortable. Probably then, as Irene had told her, the exhibition was to consist of pictures sent by request of the committee, and at present they had not requested her. She felt that she must make sure about that, and determined to send in a picture without being asked. That would show for certain what was going on.

'Weren't those mornings pleasant?' said the evasive Georgie. 'I was quite sorry when my picture was finished.'

Georgie appeared unusually reticent: he did not volunteer any more information about the winter exhibition, nor about Lucia's telephoning, nor had he mentioned that he and Major Benjy had lunched with her to-day. She would lead him in the direction of that topic . . .

'How happy dear Lucia is in her pretty Grebe,' she said. 'I took my walk along the road there to-day. Her garden, so pleasant! A high tide this afternoon. The beautiful river flowing down to the sea, and the tide coming up to meet it. Did you notice it?'

Georgie easily saw through that: he would talk about tides with pleasure, but not lunch.

'It looked lovely,' he said, 'but they tell me that in ten days' time the spring tides are on, and they will be much higher. The water has been over the road in front of Lucia's house sometimes.'

Elizabeth went back to Mallards more uneasy than ever.

Lucia was indeed busy arranging callisthenic classes and winter exhibitions and, clearly, some party at Grebe, but not a word had she said to her about any of these things, nor had she sent the recipe for lobster *à la Riseholme*. But there was nothing more to be done to-night except to take steps concerning the picture exhibition to which she had not been asked to contribute. The house was full of her sketches, and she selected quite the best of them and directed Withers to pack it up and send it, with her card, to the Committee of the Art Club, Grebe.

The winter bridge-parties in Tilling were in their main features of a fixed and invariable pattern. An exceedingly substantial tea, including potted-meat sandwiches, was served at half-past four, and, after that was disposed of, at least three hours of bridge followed. After such a tea, nobody, as was perfectly well known, dreamed of having dinner: and though round about eight o'clock, the party broke up, with cries of astonishment at the lateness of the hour, and said it must fly back home to dress, this was a mere fashion of speech. 'A tray' was the utmost refreshment that anyone could require, and nobody dressed for a solitary tray. Elizabeth was a great upholder of the dress-and-dinner fiction, and she had been known to leave a bridge-party at nine, saying that Withers would scold her for being so late, and that her cook would be furious.

So on this Saturday afternoon the party of eight (for all seven had accepted) assembled at Mallards. They were exceed-ingly cordial: it was as if they desired to propitiate their hostess for something presently to emerge. Also it struck that powerful observer that there was not nearly so much eaten as usual. She had provided the caviare sandwiches of which Mrs Wyse had been known absentmindedly to eat nine, she had provided the nougat chocolates of which Diva had been known to have eaten all, but though the chocolates were in front of Diva, and the caviare in front of Susan, neither of them exhibited any-thing resembling their usual greed. There was Scotch short-bread for the Padre, who, though he came from Birmingham, was insatiable with regard to that national form of biscuit, and there was whisky and soda for Major Benjy, who had no use for tea, and both of them, too, were mysteriously abstemious. Perhaps this wet muggy weather, thought Elizabeth, had made them all a trifle liverish, or very likely those callisthenics had taken away their appetites. It was noticeable, moreover, that throughout tea nobody mentioned the name of Lucia.

They adjourned to the garden-room where two tables were set out for bridge, and till half-past six nothing momentous occurred. At that hour Elizabeth was partner to Major Benjy, and she observed with dark misgivings that when she had secured the play of the hand (at a staggering sacrifice, as it was soon to prove) he did not as usual watch her play, but got up, and standing by the fire place indulged in some very antic movements. He bent down, apparently trying to touch his toes with his fingers and a perfect fusillade of small crackling noises from his joints (knee or hip it was impossible to tell) accompanied these athletic flexings. Then he whisked himself round to right and left as if trying to look down his back, like a parrot. This was odd and ominous conduct, this strongly suggested that he had been sucked into the callisthenic whirlpool, and what was more ominous yet was that when he sat down again he whispered to Georgie, who was at the same table, 'That makes my ten minutes, old boy.' Elizabeth did not like that at all. She knew now what the ten minutes must refer to, and that endearing form of address to Miss Milliner Michael-Angelo was a little worrying. The only consolation was that Georgie's attention was diverted from the game, and that he trumped his partner's best card. At the conclusion of the hand, Elizabeth was three tricks short of her contract, and another very puzzling surprise awaited her, for instead of Major Benjy taking her failure in very ill part, he was more than pleasant about it. What could be the matter with him?

'Very well played, Miss Elizabeth,' he said. 'I was afraid that after my inexcusable declaration we should lose more than that.'

Elizabeth began to feel more keenly puzzled as to why none of them had any appetites, and why they were all so pleasant to her. Were they rallying round her again, was their silence about Lucia a tactful approval of her absence? Or was there some hidden connection between their abstemiousness, their reticence and their unwontedly propitiatory attitude? If there was, it quite eluded her. Then as Diva dealt in her sloppy manner Lucia's name came up for the first time.

'Mr Georgie, you ought not to have led trumps,' she said. 'Lucia always says – Oh, dear me, I believe I've misdealt. Oh no, I haven't. That's all right.'

Elizabeth pondered this as she sorted her cards. Nobody inquired what Lucia said, and Diva's swift changing of the subject as if that name had slipped out by accident, looked as if possibly they none of them desired any allusion to be made to her. Had they done with her? she wondered. But if so, what about the callisthenics?

She was dummy now and was absorbed in watching Major Benjy's tragical mismanagement of the hand, for he was getting into a sadder bungle than anyone, except perhaps Lucia, could have involved himself in. Withers entered while this was going on, and gave Elizabeth a parcel. With her eye and her mind still glued to the cards, she absently unwrapped it, and took its contents from its coverings just as the last trick was being played. It was the picture she had sent to the art committee the day before and with it was a typewritten form to convey its regrets that the limited wall-space at its disposal would not permit of Miss Mapp's picture being exhibited. This slip floated out on to the floor, and Georgie bent down and returned it to her. She handed it and the picture and the wrappings to Withers, and told her to put them in the cupboard. Then she leaned over the table to her partner, livid with mixed and uncontrollable emotions.

'Dear Major Benjy, what a hash!' she said. 'If you had pulled out your cards at random from your hand, you could not, bar revokes, have done worse. I think you must have been having lessons from dear Lulu. Never mind: live and unlearn.'

There was an awful pause. Even the players at the other table were stricken into immobility and looked at each other with imbecile eyes. Then the most surprising thing of all happened.

''Pon my word, partner,' said Major Benjy, 'I deserve all the scoldings you can give me. I played it like a baby. I deserve to pay all our losings. A thousand apologies.'

Elizabeth, though she did not feel like it, had to show that she was generous too. But why didn't he answer her back in the usual manner?

'Naughty Major Benjy!' she said. 'But what does it matter? It's only a game, and we all have our ups and downs. I have them myself. That's the rubber, isn't it? Not very expensive after all. Now let us have another and forget all about this one.'

Diva drew a long breath, as if making up her mind to something, and glanced at the watch set with false pearls (Elizabeth was sure) on her wrist.

'Rather late to begin again,' she said. 'I make it ten minutes to seven. I think I ought to be going to dress.'

'Nonsense, dear,' said Elizabeth. 'Much too early to leave off. Cut, Major Benjy.'

He also appeared to take his courage in his hands, not very successfully.

'Well, upon my word, do you know, really Miss Elizabeth,' he babbled, 'a rubber goes on sometimes for a very long while, and if it's close on seven now, if, you know what I mean . . . What do you say, Pillson?'

It was Georgie's turn.

'Too tarsome,' he said, 'but I'm afraid personally that I must stop. Such a delightful evening. Such good rubbers . . .'

They all got up together, as if some common mechanism controlled their movements. Diva scuttled away to the other table, without even waiting to be paid the sum of one and threepence which she had won from Elizabeth.

'I'll see how they're getting on here,' she said. 'Why they're just adding up, too.'

Elizabeth sat where she was and counted out fifteen pennies. That would serve Diva right for going at ten minutes to seven. Then she saw that the others had got up in a hurry, for Susan Wyse said to Mrs Bartlett, 'I'll pay you later on,' and her husband held up her sable coat for her.

'Diva, your winnings,' said Elizabeth, piling up the coppers.

Diva whisked round, and instead of resenting this ponderous discharge of the debt, received it with enthusiasm.

'Thank you, Elizabeth,' she said. 'All coppers: how nice! So useful for change. Good night, dear. Thanks ever so much.'

She paused a moment by the door, already open, by which Georgie was standing.

'Then you'll call for me at twenty minutes to eight,' she said to him in the most audible whisper, and Georgie with a nervous glance in Elizabeth's direction gave a silent assent. Diva vanished into the night where Major Benjy had gone. Elizabeth rose from her deserted table.

'But you're not all going too?' she said to the others. 'So early yet.'

Mr Wyse made a profound bow.

'I regret that my wife and I must get home to dress,' he said. 'But one of the most charming evenings of bridge I have ever spent, Miss Mapp. So many thanks. Come along, Susan.'

'Delicious bridge,' said Susan. 'And those caviare sandwiches. Good night, dear. You must come round and play with us some night soon.'

'A grand game of bridge, Mistress Mapp,' said the Padre. 'Ah, wee wifie's callin' for me. Au reservoir.'

Next moment Elizabeth was alone. Georgie had followed on the heels of the others, closing the door very carefully, as if she had fallen asleep. Instead of that she hurried to the window and peeped out between the curtains. There were three or four of them standing on the steps while the Wyses got into the Royce, and they dispersed in different directions like detected conspirators, as no doubt they were.

The odd disconnected little incidents of the evening, the lack of appetites, the propitiatory conduct to herself, culminating in this unexampled departure a full hour before bridge-parties had ever been known to break up, now grouped themselves together in Elizabeth's constructive mind. They fitted on to other facts that had hitherto seemed unrelated, but now were charged with significance. Georgie, for instance, had telephoned the day and the hour of this bridge-party to Lucia, he had accepted an invitation to something at a quarter to eight: he had promised to call for 'him' and 'her'. There could be no reasonable doubt that Lucia had purposely broken up Elizabeth's party at this early hour by bidding to dinner the seven guests who had just slunk away to dress ... And her picture had been returned by the art committee, two of whom (though she did them the justice to admit that they were but the cat's-paws of a baleful intelligence) had hardly eaten any caviare sandwiches at all, for fear that they should not have good appetites for dinner. Hence also Diva's abstention from nougat chocolate, Major Benjy's from whisky, and the Padre's from shortbread. Nothing could be clearer.

Elizabeth was far from feeling unhappy or deserted, and very very far from feeling beaten. Defiance and hatred warmed her blood most pleasantly, and she spent half an hour sitting by the window, thoroughly enjoying herself. She meant to wait here till twenty minutes to eight, and if by that time she had not seen the Royce turning the corner of Porpoise Street, and Georgie's car calling at the perfidious Major Benjy's house, she would be ready to go barefoot to Grebe, and beg Lucia's pardon for having attributed to her so devilish a device. But no such humiliating pilgrimage awaited her, for all happened exactly as she knew it would. The great glaring head-lights of the Royce blazed on the house opposite the turning to Porpoise Street, its raucous fog-horn sounded, and the porpoise car lurched into view scaring everybody by its lights and its odious voice, and by its size making foot-passengers flatten themselves against the walls. Hardly had it cleared the corner into the High Street when Georgie's gay bugle piped out and his car came under the window of the garden-room, and stopped at Major Benjy's. Elizabeth's intellect, unaided by any direct outside information, except that which she had overheard on the telephone, had penetrated this hole-and-corner business, and ringing the bell for her tray, she ate the large remainder of caviare sandwiches and nougat chocolate and fed her soul with schemes of reprisals. She could not off-hand think of any definite plan of sufficiently withering a nature, and presently, tired with mental activity, she fell into a fireside doze and had a happy dream that Dr Dobbie had popped in to tell her that Lucia had developed undoubted symptoms of leprosy.

During the positively voluptuous week that followed Elizabeth's brief bridge-party, no fresh development occurred of the drama on which Tilling was concentrated, except that Lucia asked Elizabeth to tea and that Elizabeth refused. The rivals therefore did not meet, and neither of them seemed aware of the existence of the other. But both Grebe and Mallards had been inordinately gay; at Grebe there had been many lunches with bridge afterwards, and the guests on several occasions had hurried back for tea and more bridge at Mallards. Indeed, Tilling had never had so much lunch and tea in its life or enjoyed so brilliant a winter season, for Diva and the Wyses

and Mrs Padre followed suit in lavish hospitality, and Georgie
on one notable morning remembered that he had not had
lunch or tea at home for five days; this was a record that beat
Riseholme all to fits.

In addition to these gaieties there were celebrated the nup-
tials of Foljambe and Cadman, conducted from the bride's
home, and the disposition of Foljambe's time between days
with Georgie and nights with Cadman was working to admiration: everybody was pleased. At Grebe there had been other
entertainments as well; the callisthenic class met on alternate
days and Lucia in a tunic rather like Artemis, but with a
supplementary skirt and scarlet stockings, headed a remarkable
procession, consisting of Diva and the Wyses and Georgie and
Major Benjy and the Padres and quaint Irene, out on to the
cinder path of the kitchen-garden, and there they copied her
jerks and flexings and whirlings of the arms and touchings of
the toes to the great amazement of errand-boys who came
legitimately to the kitchen-door, and others who peered
through the hornbeam hedge. On wet days the athletes assembled in the kitchen with doors flung wide to the open air, and
astonished the cook with their swimming movements, an arm
and leg together, while they held on with the other hand to the
great kitchen-table. 'Uno, due, tre,' counted Lucia, and they all
kicked out like frogs. And quaint Irene in her knickerbockers,
sometimes stood on her head, but nobody else attempted that.
Lucia played them soothing music as they rested afterwards in
her drawing-room; she encouraged Major Benjy to learn his
notes on the piano, for she would willingly teach him: she
persuaded Susan to take up her singing again, and played 'La
ci darem' for her, while Susan sang it in a thin shrill voice, and
Mr Wyse said 'Brava! How I wish Amelia was here.' Sometimes Lucia read them Pope's translation of the Iliad as they
drank their lemonade and Major Benjy his whisky and soda,
and not content with these diversions (the wonderful creature)
she was composing the address on modern art which she was
to deliver at the opening of the exhibition on the day following
Boxing Day. She made notes for it and then dictated to her
secretary (Elizabeth Mapp's face was something awful to

behold when Diva told her that Lucia had a secretary) who took down what she said on a typewriter. Indeed, Elizabeth's face had never been more awful when she heard that, except when Diva informed her that she was quite certain that Lucia would be delighted to let her join the callisthenic class.

But though, during these days, no act of direct aggression like that of Lucia's dinner-party causing Elizabeth's bridge-party to break up had been committed on either side, it was generally believed that Elizabeth was not done for yet, and Tilling was on tiptoe, expectant of some 'view halloo' call to show that the chase was astir. She had refused Lucia's invitation to tea, and if she had been done for or gone to earth she would surely have accepted. Probably she took the view that the invitation was merely a test question to see how she was getting on, and her refusal showed that she was getting on very nicely. It would be absolutely unlike Elizabeth (to adopt a further metaphor) to throw up the sponge like that, for she had not yet been seriously hurt, and the bridge-party-round had certainly been won by Lucia; there would be fierce boxing in the next. It seemed likely that, in this absence of aggressive acts, both antagonists were waiting till the season of peace and good will was comfortably over and then they would begin again. Elizabeth would have a God-sent opportunity at the opening of the exhibition, when Lucia delivered her address. She could sit in the front row and pretend to go to sleep or suppress an obvious inclination to laugh. Tilling felt that she must have thought of that and of many other acts of reprisal unless she was no longer the Elizabeth they all knew and (within limits) respected, and (on numerous occasions) detested.

The pleasant custom of sending Christmas cards prevailed in Tilling, and most of the world met in the stationer's shop on Christmas Eve, selecting suitable salutations from the three-penny, the sixpenny and the shilling trays. Elizabeth came in rather early and had almost completed her purchases when some of her friends arrived, and she hung about looking at the backs of volumes in the lending-library, but keeping an eye on what they purchased. Diva, she observed, selected nothing from the shilling tray any more than she had herself; in fact, she thought that Diva's purchases this year were made entirely from the threepenny tray. Susan, on the other hand, ignored the threepenny tray and hovered between the sixpennies and the shillings and expressed an odiously opulent regret that there were not some 'choicer' cards to be obtained. The Padre and Mrs Bartlett were certainly exclusively threepenny, but that was always the case. However they, like everybody else, studied the other trays, so that when, next morning, they all received seasonable coloured greetings from their friends, a person must have a shocking memory if he did not know what had been the precise cost of all that were sent him. But Georgie and Lucia as was universally noticed, though without comment, had not been in at all, in spite of the fact that they had been seen about in the High Street together and going into other shops. Elizabeth therefore decided that they did not intend to send any Christmas cards and before paying for what she had chosen, she replaced in the threepenny tray a pretty picture of a robin sitting on a sprig of mistletoe which she had meant to send Georgie. There was no need to put back what she had chosen for Lucia, since the case did not arise.

Christmas Day dawned, a stormy morning with a strong gale from the south-west, and on Elizabeth's breakfast-table was a pile of letters, which she tore open. Most of them were threepenny Christmas cards, a sixpenny from Susan, smelling of musk, and none from Lucia or Georgie. She had anticipated that, and it was pleasant to think that she had put back into the threepenny tray the one she had selected for him, before purchasing it.

The rest of her post was bills, some of which must be stoutly disputed when Christmas was over, and she found it difficult to realize the jollity appropriate to the day. Last evening various choirs of amateur riff-raffs and shrill bob-tails had rendered the night hideous by repetitions of 'Good King Wenceslas' and the 'First Noël', church-bells borne on squalls of wind and rain had awakened her while it was still dark and now sprigs of holly kept falling down from the picture-frames where Withers had perched them. Bacon made her feel rather better, and she went to church, with a mackintosh against these driving gusts of rain, and a slightly blue nose against this boisterous wind. Diva was coming to a dinner-lunch: this was an annual institution held at Wasters and Mallards alternately.

Elizabeth hurried out of church at the conclusion of the service by a side door, not feeling equal to joining in the gay group of her friends who with Lucia as their centre were gathered at the main entrance. The wind was stronger than ever, but the rain had ceased, and she battled her way round the square surrounding the church before she went home. Close to Mallards Cottage she met Georgie holding his hat on against the gale. He wished her a merry Christmas, but then his hat had been whisked off his head; something very strange happened to his hair, which seemed to have been blown off his skull, leaving a quite bare place there, and he vanished in frenzied pursuit of his hat with long tresses growing from the side of his head streaming in the wind. A violent draught eddying round the corner by the garden-room propelled her into Mallards holding on to the knocker, and it was with difficulty that she closed the door. On the table in the hall stood a substantial package, which had certainly not been there when she left. Within its wrappings was a *terrine* of *pâté de foie gras* with a most distinguished label on it, and a card fluttered on to the floor, proclaiming that wishes for a merry Christmas from Lucia and Georgie accompanied it. Elizabeth instantly conquered the feeble temptation of sending this gift back again in the manner in which she had returned that basket of tomatoes from her own garden. Tomatoes were not *pâté*. But what a treat for Diva!

Diva arrived, and they went straight in to the banquet. The *terrine* was wrapped in a napkin, and Withers handed it to Diva. She helped herself handsomely to the truffles and the liver.

'How delicious!' she said. 'And such a monster!'

'I hope it's good,' said Elizabeth, not mentioning the donors. 'It ought to be. Paris.'

Diva suddenly caught sight of a small label pasted below the distinguished one. It was that of the Tilling grocer, and a flood of light poured in upon her.

'Lucia and Mr Georgie have sent such lovely Christmas presents to everybody,' she said. 'I felt quite ashamed of myself for only having given them threepenny cards.'

'How sweet of them,' said Elizabeth. 'What were they?'

'A beautiful box of hard chocolates for me,' said Diva. 'And a great pot of caviare for Susan, and an umbrella for the Padre – his blew inside out in the wind yesterday – and –'

'And this beautiful *pâté* for me,' interrupted Elizabeth, grasping the nettle, for it was obvious that Diva had guessed. 'I was just going to tell you.'

Diva knew that was a lie, but it was no use telling Elizabeth so, because she knew it too, and she tactfully changed the subject.

'I shall have to do my exercises three times to-day after such a lovely lunch,' she said, as Elizabeth began slicing the turkey. But that was not a well-chosen topic, for subjects connected with Lucia might easily give rise to discord and she tried again and again and again, bumping, in her spinning-top manner, from one impediment to another.

'Major Benjy can play the scale of C with his right hand' – (No, that wouldn't do). 'What an odd voice Susan's got: she sang an Italian song the other day at' – (Worse and worse). 'I sent two pictures to the winter exhibition' – (Worse if possible: there seemed to be no safe topic under the sun). 'A terrific gale, isn't it? There'll be three days of tremendous high tides for the wind is heaping them up. I should not wonder if the road by Grebe –' (she gave it up: it was no use) '– isn't flooded to-morrow.'

Elizabeth behaved like a perfect lady. She saw that Diva was doing her best to keep off disagreeable subjects on Christmas Day, but there were really no others. All topics led to Lucia.

'I hope not,' she said, 'for with all the field-paths soaked from the rain it is my regular walk just now. But not very likely, dear, for after the last time that the road was flooded, they built the bank opposite – opposite that house much higher.'

They talked for quite a long while about gales and tides and dykes in complete tranquillity. Then the proletarian diversions of Boxing Day seemed safe.

'There's a new film to-morrow at the Picture Palace about tadpoles,' said Elizabeth. 'So strange to think they become toads: or is it frogs? I think I must go.'

'Lucia's giving a Christmas-tree for the choir-boys in the evening, in that great kitchen of hers,' said Diva.

'How kind!' said Elizabeth hastily, to show she took no offence.

'And in the afternoon there's a whist drive at the Institute,' said Diva. 'I'm letting both my servants go, and Lucia's sending all hers too. I'm not sure I should like to be quite alone in a house along that lonely road. We in the town could scream from a top window if burglars got into our houses and raise the alarm.'

'It would be a very horrid burglar who was so wicked on Boxing Day,' observed Elizabeth sententiously. 'Ah, here's the plum pudding! Blazing beautifully, Withers! So pretty!'

Diva became justifiably somnolent when lunch was over, and after half an hour's careful conversation she went off home to have a nice long nap, which she expressed by the word exercises. Elizabeth wrote two notes of gratitude to the donors of the *pâté* and sat herself down to think seriously of what she could do. She had refused Lucia's invitation to tea a few days before, thus declaring her attitude, and now it seemed to her that that was a mistake, for she had cut herself off from the opportunities of reprisals which intercourse with her might have provided. She had been unable, severed like this, to devise anything at all effective; all she could do was to lie awake at night hating Lucia, and this seemed to be quite barren of results. It might be better (though bitter) to join that callisthenic class in order to get a foot in the enemy's territory. Her note of thanks for the *pâté* would have paved the way towards such a step, and though it would certainly be eating humble pie to ask to join an affair that she had openly derided, it would be pie with a purpose. As it was, for a whole week she had had no opportunities, she had surrounded herself with a smoke-cloud, she heard nothing about Lucia any more, except when clumsy Diva let out things by accident. All she knew was that Lucia, busier than any bee known to science, was undoubtedly supreme in all the social activities which she herself had been accustomed to direct, and to remain, like Achilles in his tent, did not lead to anything. Also she had an idea that Tilling expected of her some exhibition of spirit and defiance, and no one was more anxious than she to fulfil those expectations to the utmost. So she settled she would go to Grebe to-morrow, and, after thanking her in person for the *pâté*, ask to join the callisthenic class. Tilling, and Lucia too, no doubt would take that as a sign of surrender, but let them wait a while, and they should see.

'I can't fight her unless I get in touch with her,' reflected Elizabeth; 'at least I don't see how, and I'm sure I've thought enough.'

10

In pursuance of this policy Elizabeth set out early in the afternoon next day to walk out to Grebe, and there eat pie with a purpose. The streets were full of holiday folk, and by the railings at the end of the High Street, where the steep steps went down to the levels below, there was a crowd of people looking at the immense expanse of water that lay spread over the marsh. The south-westerly gale had piled up the spring tides, the continuous rains had caused the river to come down in flood, and the meeting of the two, the tide now being at its height, formed a huge lake, a mile and more wide, which stretched seawards. The gale had now quite ceased, the sun shone brilliantly from the pale blue of the winter sky, and this enormous estuary sparkled in the gleam. Far away to the south a great bank of very thick vapour lay over the horizon, showing that out in the Channel there was thick fog, but over Tilling and the flooded marsh the heavens overhead were of a dazzling radiance.

Many of Elizabeth's friends were there, the Padre and his wife (who kept exclaiming in little squeaks, 'Oh dear me, what a quantity of water!'), the Wyses who had dismounted from the Royce, which stood waiting, to look at the great sight, before they proceeded on their afternoon drive. Major Benjy was saying that it was nothing to the Jumna in flood, but then he always held up India as being far ahead of England in every way (he had even once said on an extremely frosty morning, that this was nothing to the bitterness of Bombay): Georgie was there and Diva. With them all Elizabeth exchanged the friendliest greetings, and afterwards, when the great catastrophe had happened, everyone agreed that they had never known her more cordial and pleasant, poor thing. She did not of course tell them what her errand was, for it would be rash to do that till she saw how Lucia received her, but merely said that she was going for her usual brisk walk on this lovely afternoon, and should probably pop into the Picture Palace to learn about tadpoles. With many flutterings of her hand and enough au reservoirs to provide water for the world, she tripped down the hill, through the Landgate, and out on to the road that led to Grebe and nowhere else particular.

She passed, as she neared Grebe, Lucia's four indoor servants and Cadman coming into the town, and, remembering that they were going to a whist drive at the Institute, wished them a merry Christmas and hoped that they would all win. (Little kindly remarks like that always pleased servants, thought Elizabeth; they showed a human sympathy with their pleasures, and cost nothing; so much better than Christmas boxes.) Her brisk pace made short work of the distance, and within quite a few minutes of her leaving her friends, she had come to the thick hornbeam hedge which shielded Grebe from the road. She stopped opposite it for a moment: there was that prodigious sheet of dazzling water now close to the top of the restraining bank to admire: there was herself to screw up to the humility required for asking Lucia if she might join her silly callisthenic class. Finally, coming from nowhere, there flashed into her mind the thought of lobster *à la Riseholme*, the recipe for which Lucia had so meanly withheld from her. Instantly that thought fructified into apples of Desire.

She gave one glance at the hornbeam hedge to make sure that she was not visible from the windows of Grebe. (Lucia used often to be seen spying from the windows of the garden-room during her tenancy of Mallards, and she might be doing the same thing here.) But the hedge was quite impenetrable to human eye, as Elizabeth had often regretfully observed already, and now instead of going in at the high wooden gate which led to the front door, she passed quickly along till she came to the far corner of the hedge bordering the kitchen-garden. So swift was thought to a constructive mind like hers already stung with desire, that, brisk though was her physical movement, her mind easily outstripped it, and her plan was laid before she got to the corner. Viz.:

The servants were all out – of that she had received ocular evidence but a few moments before – and the kitchen would certainly be empty. She would therefore go round to the gate at the end of the kitchen-garden and approach the house that way. The cinder path, used for the prancing of the callisthenic class in fine weather, led straight to the big coach-house doors of the kitchen, and she would ascertain by the simple device of trying the handle if these were unlocked. If they were locked, there was an end to her scheme, but if they were unlocked, she would quietly pop in, and see whether the cook's book of recipes was not somewhere about. If it was she would surely find in it the recipe for lobster *à la Riseholme*. A few minutes would suffice to copy it, and then tiptoeing out of the kitchen again, with the key to the mystery in her pocket, she would go round to the front door as cool as a cucumber, and ring the bell. Should Lucia (alone in the house and possibly practising for more po-di-mus) not hear the bell, she would simply postpone the eating of her humble pie till the next day. If, by ill chance, Lucia was in the garden and saw her approaching by this unusual route, nothing was easier than to explain that, returning from her walk, she thought she would look in to thank her for the *pâté* and ask if she might join her callisthenic class. Knowing that the servants were all out (she would glibly explain) she felt sure that the main gate on to the road would be locked, and therefore she tried the back way . . . The whole formation of the scheme was instantaneous; it was as if she had switched on the lights at the door of a long gallery, and found it lit from end to end.

Without hurrying at all she walked down the cinder path and tested the kitchen-door. It was unlocked, and she slipped in, closing it quietly behind her. In the centre of the kitchen, decked and ready for illumination, stood the Christmas-tree designed for the delectation of the choir-boys that evening, and the great kitchen-table, with its broad skirting of board half-way down the legs, had been moved away and stood on its side against the dresser in order to give more room for the tree. Elizabeth hardly paused a second to admire the tapers, the reflecting glass balls, the bright tinsely decorations, for she

saw a small shelf of books on the wall opposite, and swooped
like a merlin on it. There were a few trashy novels, there was a
hymn-book and a prayer-book, and there was a thick volume,
with no title on the back, bound in American cloth. She
opened it and saw at once that her claws had at last gripped the
prey, for on one page was pasted a cutting from the daily press
concerning *oeufs à l'aurore*, on the next was a recipe in manuscript for cheese straws. Rapidly she turned the leaves, and
there manifest at last was the pearl of great price, lobster *à la
Riseholme*. It began with the luscious words, 'Take two hen
lobsters.'

Out came her pencil; that and a piece of paper in which had
been wrapped a present for a choir-boy was all she needed. In
a couple of minutes she had copied out the mystic spell,
replaced the sacred volume on its shelf, and put in her pocket
the information for which she had pined so long. 'How odd,'
she cynically reflected, 'that only yesterday I should have said
to Diva that it must be a very horrid burglar who was so
wicked as to steal things on Boxing Day. Now I'll go round to
the front door.'

At the moment when this Mephistophelian thought came into
her mind, she heard with a sudden stoppage of her heart-beat, a
step on the crisp path outside, and the handle of the kitchen-door
was turned. Elizabeth took one sideways stride behind the gaudy
tree and peering through its branches, saw Lucia standing at the
entrance. Lucia came straight towards her, not yet perceiving
that there was a Boxing Day burglar in her own kitchen, and
stood admiring her tree. Then with a startled exclamation she
called out, 'Who's that?' and Elizabeth knew that she was
discovered. Further dodging behind the decorated fir would be
both undignified and ineffectual, however skilful her footwork.

'It's me, dear Lucia,' she said. 'I came to thank you in
person for that delicious *pâté* and to ask if –'

From somewhere close outside there came a terrific roar and
rush as of great water-floods released. Reunited for the moment
by a startled curiosity, they ran together to the open door, and
saw, already leaping across the road and over the hornbeam
hedge, a solid wall of water.

'The bank has given way,' cried Lucia. 'Quick, into the house through the door in the kitchen, and up the stairs.'

They fled back past the Christmas-tree, and tried the door into the house. It was locked: the servants had evidently taken this precaution before going out on their pleasuring.

'We shall be drowned,' wailed Elizabeth, as the flood came foaming into the kitchen.

'Rubbish,' cried Lucia. 'The kitchen-table! We must turn it upside down and get on to it.'

It was but the work of a moment to do this, for the table was already on its side, and the two stepped over the high boarding that ran round it. Would their weight be too great to allow it to float on the rushing water that now deepened rapidly in the kitchen? That anxiety was short-lived, for it rose free from the floor and bumped gently into the Christmas-tree.

'We must get out of this,' cried Lucia. 'One doesn't know how much the water will rise. We may be drowned yet if the table-legs come against the ceiling. Catch hold of the dresser and pull.'

But there was no need for such exertion, for the flood, eddying fiercely round the submerged kitchen, took them out of the doors that it had flung wide, and in a few minutes they were floating away over the garden and the hornbeam hedge. The tide had evidently begun to ebb before the bank gave way, and now the kitchen-table, occasionally turning round in an eddy, moved off in the direction of Tilling and of the sea. Luckily it had not got into the main stream of the river but floated smoothly and swiftly along, with the tide and the torrent of the flood to carry it. Its two occupants, of course, had no control whatever over its direction, but soon, with an upspring of hope, they saw that the current was carrying it straight towards the steep slope above the Landgate, where not more than a quarter of an hour ago Elizabeth had interchanged greetings and au reservoirs with her friends who had been looking at the widespread waters. Little had she thought that so soon she would be involved in literal reservoirs of the most gigantic sort – but this was no time for light conceits.

The company of Tillingites was still there when the bank

opposite Grebe gave way. All but Georgie had heard the rush and roar of the released waters, but his eyes were sharper than others, and he had been the first to see where the disaster had occurred.

'Look, the bank opposite Grebe has burst!' he cried. 'The road's under water, her garden's under water: the rooms downstairs must be flooded. I hope Lucia's upstairs, or she'll get dreadfully wet.'

'And that road is Elizabeth's favourite walk,' cried Diva. 'She'll be on it now.'

'But she walks so fast,' said the Padre, forgetting to speak Scotch. 'She'll be past Grebe by now, and above where the bank has burst.'

'Oh dear, oh dear, and on Boxing Day!' wailed Mrs Bartlett.

The huge flood was fast advancing on the town, but with this outlet over the fields, it was evident that it would get no deeper at Grebe, and that, given Lucia was upstairs and that Elizabeth had walked as fast as usual, there was no real anxiety for them. All eyes now watched the progress of the water. It rose like a wave over a rock when it came to the railway line that crossed the marsh and in a couple of minutes more it was foaming over the fields immediately below the town.

Again Georgie uttered woe like Cassandra.

'There's something coming,' he cried. 'It looks like a raft with its legs in the air. And there are two people on it. Now it's spinning round and round; now it's coming straight here ever so fast. There are two women, one without a hat. It's Them! It's Lucia and Miss Mapp! What *has* happened?'

The raft, with legs sometimes madly waltzing, sometimes floating smoothly along, was borne swiftly towards the bottom of the cliff, below which the flood was pouring by. The Padre, with his new umbrella, ran down the steps that led to the road below in order to hook it in, if it approached within umbrella-distance. On and on it came, now clearly recognizable as Lucia's great kitchen-table upside down, until it was within a yard or two of the bank. To attempt to wade out to it, for any effective purpose, was useless: the strongest would be swept away in such a headlong torrent, and even if he reached the raft there would be three helpless people on it instead of two and it would probably sink. To hook it with the umbrella was the only chance, for there was no time to get a boat-hook or a rope to throw out to the passengers. The Padre made a desperate lunge at it, slipped and fell flat into the water, and was only saved from being carried away by clutching at the iron railing alongside the lowest of the submerged steps. Then some fresh current tweaked the table and, still moving in the general direction of the flood-water, it sheered off across the fields. As it receded Lucia showed the real stuff of which she was made. She waved her hand and her clear voice rang out gaily across the waste of water.

'Au reservoir, all of you,' she cried. 'We'll come back: just wait till we come back,' and she was seen to put her arm round the huddled form of Mapp, and comfort her.

The kitchen-table was observed by the watchers to get into the main channel of the river, where the water was swifter yet. It twirled round once or twice as if waving a farewell, and then shot off towards the sea and that great bank of thick mist which hung over the horizon.

There was not yet any reason to despair. A telephone-message was instantly sent to the fishermen at the port, another to the coast-guards, another to the lifeboat, that a kitchen-table with a cargo of ladies on it was coming rapidly down the river, and no effort must be spared to arrest its passage out to sea. But, one after the other, as the short winter afternoon waned, came discouraging messages from the coast. The flood had swept from their moorings all the fishing boats anchored at the port or drawn up on the shore above high-water mark, and a coast-guardsman had seen an unintelligible object go swiftly past the mouth of the river before the telephone-message was received. He could not distinguish what it was, for the fog out in the Channel had spread to the coastline, and it had seemed to him more like the heads and necks of four sea-serpents playing together than anything else. But when interrogated as to whether it might be the legs of a kitchen-table upside down he acknowledged that the short glimpse which he obtained of it before it got lost in the fog would suit a kitchen-table as well as sea-serpents. He had said sea-serpents because it was in the sea, but it was just as like the legs of a kitchen-table, which had never occurred to him as possible. His missus had just such a kitchen-table – but as he seemed to be diverging into domestic reminiscences, the Mayor of Tilling, who himself conducted inquiries instead of opening the whist drive at the Institute with a short speech on the sin of gambling, cut him off. It was only too clear that this imaginative naturalist had seen – too late – the kitchen-table going out to sea.

The lifeboat had instantly responded to the SOS call on its services, and the great torrent of the flood having now gone by, the crew had been able to launch the boat and had set off to search the English Channel, in the blinding fog, for the table. The tide was setting west down the coast, the flood pouring out from the river mouth was discharged east, but they had gone off to row about in every direction, where the kitchen-table might have been carried. Rockets had been sent up from the station in case the ladies didn't know where they were. That, so the Mayor reflected, might conceivably show the ladies where they were, but it didn't really enable them to get anywhere else.

Dusk drew on and the friends of the missing went back to their respective houses, for there was no good in standing about in this dreadful cold fog which had now crept up from the marsh. Pneumonia wouldn't help matters. Four of them, Georgie and Major Benjy and Diva and quaint Irene, lived solitary and celibate, and the prospect of a lonely evening with only suspense and faint hopes to feed upon was perfectly ghastly. In consequence, when each of them in turn was rung up by Mr Wyse, who hoped, in a broken voice, that he might find them disengaged and willing to come round to his house for supper (not dinner), they all gladly accepted. Mr Wyse requested them not to dress as for dinner, and this was felt to show a great delicacy: not dressing would be a sort of symbol of their common anxiety. Supper would be at half-past eight, and Mr Wyse trusted that there would be encouraging news before that hour.

The Padre and Mrs Bartlett had been bidden as well, so that

there was a supper-party of eight. Supper began with the most. delicious caviare, and on the black oak mantelpiece were two threepenny Christmas cards. Susan helped herself plentifully to the caviare. There was no use in not eating.

'Dear Lucia's Christmas present to me,' she said. 'Hers and yours I should say, Mr Georgie.'

'Lucia sent me a wonderful box of nougat chocolates,' said Diva. 'She and you, I mean, Mr Georgie.'

Major Benjy audibly gulped.

'Mrs Lucia,' he said, 'if I may call her so, sent me half a dozen bottles of pre-war whisky.'

The Padre had pulled himself together by this time, and spoke Scotch.

'I had a wee mischance wi' my umbrella two days agone,' he said, 'and Mistress Lucia, such a menseful woman, sent me a new one. An' now that's gone bobbin' out to sea.'

'You're too pessimistic, Kenneth,' said Mrs Bartlett. 'An umbrella soon gets waterlogged and sinks, I tell you. The chances are it will be picked up in the marsh to-morrow, and it'll find its way back to you, for there's that beautiful silver band on the handle with your name engraved on it.'

'Eh, 'twould be a bonnie thing to recover it,' said her husband.

Mr Wyse thought that the conversation was getting a little too much concerned with minor matters; the recovery of an umbrella, though new, was a loss that might be lamented later. Besides, the other missing lady had not been mentioned yet. He pointed to the two threepenny Christmas cards on the mantelpiece.

'Our friend Elizabeth Mapp sent those to my wife and me yesterday,' he said. 'We shall keep them always among our most cherished possessions in case – I mean in any case. Pretty designs. Roofs covered with snow. Holly. Robins. She had a very fine artistic taste. Her pictures had always something striking and original about them.'

Everybody cudgelled their brains for something appropriate to say about Elizabeth's connection with Art. The effort was quite hopeless, for her ignoble trick in rejecting Lucia's and

Georgie's pictures for the last exhibition, and the rejection by the new committee of her own for the forthcoming exhibition were all that could occur to the most nimble brain, and while the artist was in direst peril on the sea, or possibly now at rest beneath it, it would be in the worst taste to recall those discordant incidents. A very long pause of silence followed, broken only by the crashing of toast in the mouths of those who had not yet finished their caviare.

Irene had eaten no caviare, nor hitherto had she contributed anything to the conversation. Now she suddenly burst into shrieks of hysterical laughter and sobs.

'What rubbish you're all talking,' she cried, wiping her eyes. 'How can you be so silly? I'm sure I beg your pardons, but there it is. I'll go home, please.'

She fled from the room and banged the front door so loudly that the house shook, and one of Miss Mapp's cards fell into the fireplace.

'Poor thing. Very excitable and uncontrolled,' said Susan. 'But I think she's better alone.'

There was a general feeling of relief that Irene had gone, and as Mrs Wyse's excellent supper progressed, with its cold turkey and its fried slices of plum pudding, its toasted cheese and its figs stuffed with almonds sent by Amelia from Capri, the general numbness caused by the catastrophe began to pass off. Consumed with anxiety as all were for the two (especially one of them) who had vanished into the Channel fogs on so unusual a vehicle, they could not fail to recognize what problems of unparalleled perplexity and interest were involved in what all still hoped might not turn out to be a tragedy. But whether it proved so or not, the whole manner of these happenings, the cause, the conditions, the circumstances which led to the two unhappy ladies whisking by on the flood must be discussed, and presently Major Benjy broke into this unnatural reticence.

'I've seen many floods on the Jumna,' he said, refilling his glass of port, 'but I never saw one so sudden and so – so fraught with enigmas. They must have been in the kitchen. Now we all know there was a Christmas-tree there –'

A conversational flood equal to the largest ever seen on the Jumna was unloosed; a torrent of conjectures, and reconstruction after reconstruction of what could have occurred to produce what they had all seen, was examined and rejected as containing some inherent impossibility. And then what did the gallant Lucia's final words mean, when she said, 'Just wait till we come back'? By now discussion had become absolutely untrammelled, the rivalry between the two, Miss Mapp's tricks and pointless meannesses, Lucia's scornful victories, and, no less, her domineering ways were openly alluded to.

'But "Just wait till we come back" is what we're talking about,' cried Diva. 'We must keep to the point, Major Benjy. I believe she simply meant "Don't give up hope. We *shall* come back." And I'm sure they will.'

'No, there's more in it than that,' said Georgie, interrupting. 'I know Lucia better than any of you. She meant that she had something frightfully interesting to tell us when she did come back, as of course she will, and I'd bet it was something about Elizabeth. Some new thing she'd found her out in.'

'But at such a solemn moment,' said the Padre, again forgetting his pseudo-Highland origin, 'when they were being whirled out to sea with death staring them in the face, I hardly think that such trivialities as those which had undoubtedly before caused between those dear ladies the frictions which we all deplored –'

'Nonsense, Kenneth,' said his wife, rather to his relief, for he did not know how he was to get out of this sentence, 'you enjoyed those rows as much as anybody.'

'I don't agree with you, Padre,' said Georgie. 'To begin with, I'm sure Lucia didn't think she was facing death and even if she did, she'd still have been terribly interested in life till she went phut.'

'Thank God I live on a hill,' exclaimed Major Benjy, thinking, as usual, of himself.

Mr Wyse held up his hand. As he was the host, it was only kind to give him a chance, for he had had none as yet. 'Your pardon,' he said, 'if I may venture to suggest what may combine the ideas of our reverend friend and of Mr Pillson' –

he made them two bows – 'I think Mrs Lucas felt she was facing death – who wouldn't? – but she was of that vital quality which never gives up interest in life, until, in fact (which we trust with her is not the case), all is over. But like a true Christian, she was, as we all saw, employed in comforting the weak. She could not have been using her last moments, which we hope are nothing of the sort, better. And if there had been frictions, they arose only from the contact of two highly vitalized –'

'She kissed Elizabeth too,' cried Mrs Bartlett. 'I saw her. She hasn't done that for ages. Fancy!'

'I want to get back to the kitchen,' said Diva. 'What could have taken Elizabeth to the kitchen? I've got a brilliant idea, though I don't know what you'll think of it. She knew Lucia was giving a Christmas-tree to the choir-boys, because I told her so yesterday –'

'I wonder what's happened to that,' said the Padre. 'If it wasn't carried away by the flood, and I think we should have seen it go by, it might be dried.'

Diva, as usual when interrupted, had held her mouth open, and went straight on.

'– and she knew the servants were out, because I'd told her that too, and she very likely wanted to see the Christmas-tree. So I suggest that she went round the back way into the kitchen – that would be extremely like her, you know – in order to have a look at it, without asking a favour of –'

'Well, I do call that clever,' interrupted Georgie admiringly. 'Go on. What happened next?'

Diva had not got further than that yet, but now a blinding brilliance illuminated her and she clapped her hands.

'I see, I see,' she cried. 'In she went into the kitchen and while she was looking at it, Lucia came in too, and then the flood came in too. All three of them. That would explain what was behind her words, "Just wait till we come back." She meant that she wanted to tell us that she'd found Elizabeth in her kitchen.'

It was universally felt that Diva had hit it, and after such a stroke of reconstructive genius, any further discussion must be bathos. Instantly a sad reaction set in, and they all looked at each other much shocked to find how wildly interested they had become in these trivial affairs, while their two friends were, to put the most hopeful view of the case, on a kitchen-table somewhere in the English Channel. But still Lucia had said that she and her companion were coming back, and though no news had arrived of the castaways, every one of her friends, at the bottom of their hearts, felt that these were not idle words, and that they must keep alive their confidence in Lucia. Miss Mapp alone would certainly have been drowned long ago, but Lucia, whose power of resource all knew to be unlimited, was with her. No one could suggest what she could possibly do in such difficult circumstances, but never yet had she been floored, nor failed to emerge triumphant from the most menacing situations.

Mrs Wyse's cuckoo clock struck the portentous hour of 1 a.m. They all sighed, they all got up, they all said good night with melancholy faces, and groped their ways home in the cold fog. Above Georgie's head as he turned the corner by Mallards there loomed the gable of the garden-room, where so often a chink of welcoming light had shone between the curtains, as the sound of Mozartino came from within. Dark and full of suspense as was the present, he could still, without the sense of something forever past from his life, imagine himself sitting at the piano again with Lucia, waiting for her *Uno, due, TRE* as they tried over for the first time the secretly familiar duets.

The whole of the next day this thick fog continued both on land and water, but no news came from seawards save the bleating and hooting of fog-horns, and as the hours passed, anxiety grew more acute. Mrs Wyse opened the picture exhibition on behalf of Lucia, for it was felt that in any case she would have wished that, but owing to the extreme inclemency of the weather only Mr Wyse and Georgie attended this inaugural ceremony. Mrs Wyse in the lamented absence of the authoress read Lucia's lecture on modern art from the typewritten copy which she had sent Georgie to look through and criticize. It lasted an hour and twenty minutes, and after Georgie's applause had died away at the end, Mr Wyse read the speech he had composed to propose a vote of thanks to Lucia for her most enthralling address. This also was rather long, but written in the most classical and urbane style. Georgie seconded this in a shorter speech, and Mrs Wyse (*vice* Lucia) read another longer speech of Lucia's which was appended in manuscript to her lecture, in which she thanked them for thanking her, and told them how diffident she had felt in thus appearing before them. There was more applause, and then the three of them wandered round the room and peered at each other's pictures through the dense fog. Evening drew in again, without news, and Tilling began to fear the worst.

Next morning there came a mute and terrible message from the sea. The fog had cleared, the day was of crystalline brightness, and since air and exercise would be desirable after sitting at home all the day before, and drinking that wonderful prewar whisky, Major Benjy set off by the eleven o'clock tram to play a round of golf with the Padre. Though hope was fast expiring, neither of them said anything definitely indicating that they no longer really expected to see their friends again, but there had been talk indirectly bearing on the catastrophe; the Major had asked casually whether Mallards was a freehold, and the Padre replied that both it and Grebe were the property of their occupiers and not held on lease; he also made a distant allusion to memorial services, saying he had been to one lately, very affecting. Then Major Benjy lost his temper with the caddie, and their game assumed a more normal aspect.

They had now come to the eighth hole, the tee of which was perched high like a pulpit on the sand-dunes and overlooked the sea. The match was most exciting: hole after hole had been halved in brilliant sixes and sevens, the players were both on the top of their form, and in their keenness had quite banished from their minds the overshadowing anxiety. Here Major Benjy topped his ball into a clump of bents immediately in front of the tee, and when he had finished swearing at his caddie for moving on the stroke, the Padre put his iron shot on to the green.

'A glorious day,' he exclaimed, and, turning to pick up his clubs, gazed out seawards. The tide was low, and an immense stretch of 'shining sands' as in Charles Kingsley's poem was spread in front of him. Then he gave a gasp.

'What's that?' he said to Major Benjy, pointing with a shaking finger.

'Good God,' said Major Benjy. 'Pick up my ball, caddie.' They scrambled down the steep dunes and walked across the sands to where lay this object which had attracted the Padre's attention. It was an immense kitchen-table upside down with its legs in the air, wet with brine but still in perfect condition. Without doubt it was the one which they had seen two days before whirling out to sea. But now it was by itself, no ladies were sitting upon it. The Padre bared his head.

'Shall we abandon our game, Major?' he said. 'We had better telephone from the Club-house to the Mayor. And I must arrange to get some men to bring the table back. It's far too heavy for us to think of moving it.'

The news that the table had come ashore spread swiftly through Tilling, and Georgie, hearing that the Padre had directed that when it had passed the Custom House it should be brought to the Vicarage, went round there at once. It seemed almost unfeeling in this first shock of bereavement to think about tables, but it would save a great deal of bother afterwards to see to this now. The table surely belonged to Grebe.

'I quite understand your point of view,' he said to the Padre, 'and of course what is found on the seashore in a general way belongs to the finder, if it's a few oranges in a basket, because nobody knows who the real owner is. But we all know, at least we're afraid we do, where this came from.'

The Padre was quite reasonable.

'You mean it ought to go back to Grebe,' he said. 'Yes, I agree. Ah, I see it has arrived.'

They went out into the street, where a trolley, bearing the table, had just drawn up. Then a difficulty arose. It was late, and the bearers demurred to taking it all the way out to Grebe to-night and carrying it through the garden.

'Move it in here then for the night,' said the Padre. 'You can get it through the back-yard and into the outhouse.'

Georgie felt himself bound to object to this: the table belonged to Grebe, and it looked as if Grebe, alas, belonged to him.

'I think it had better come to Mallards Cottage,' said he firmly. 'It's only just round the corner, and it can stand in my yard.'

The Padre was quite willing that it should go back to Grebe, but why should Georgie claim this object with all the painful interest attached to it? After all, he had found it.

'And so I don't quite see why you should have it,' he said a little stiffly.

Georgie took him aside.

'It's dreadful to talk about it so soon,' he said, 'but that is what I should like done with it. You see Lucia left me Grebe and all its contents. I still cling – can't help it – to the hope that neither it nor they may ever be mine, but in the interval which may elapse –'

'No! Really!' said the Padre with a sudden thrill of Tillingite interest which it was no use trying to suppress. 'I congrat – Well, well. Of course the kitchen-table is yours. Very proper.'

The trolley started again and by dint of wheedlings and cunning coaxings the sad substantial relic was induced to enter the back-yard of Mallards Cottage. Here for the present it would have to remain, but pickled as it was with long immersion in sea water, the open air could not possibly hurt it, and if it rained, so much the better, for it would wash the salt out.

Georgie, very tired and haggard with these harrowing arrangements, had a little rest on his sofa, when he had seen the table safely bestowed. His cook gave him a succulent and most nutritious dinner by way of showing her sympathy, and Foljambe waited on him with peculiar attention, constantly holding a pocket-handkerchief to the end of her nose, by way of expressing her own grief. Afterwards he moved to his sitting-room and took up his needlework, that 'sad narcotic exercise', and looked his loss in the face.

Indeed, it was difficult to imagine what life would be like without Lucia, but there was no need to imagine it, for he was experiencing it already. There was nothing to look forward to, and he realized how completely Lucia and her manoeuvres and her indomitable vitality and her deceptions and her greatnesses had supplied the salt to life. He had never been in the least in love with her, but somehow she had been as absorbing as any wayward and entrancing mistress. 'It will be too dull for anything,' thought he, 'and there won't be a single day in which I shan't miss her most dreadfully. It's always been like that: when she was away from Riseholme, I never seemed to care to paint or to play, except because I should show her what I had done when she came back, and now she'll never come back.'

He abandoned himself for quite a long time to despair with regard to what life would hold for him. Nobody else, not even Foljambe, seemed to matter at all. But then through the black, deep waters of his tribulation there began to appear little bubbles on the surface. It was like comparing a firefly with the huge night itself to weigh them against this all-encompassing darkness, but where for a moment each pricked the surface there was, it was idle to deny, just a spark that stood out momentarily against the blackness. The table, for instance: he would have a tablet fixed on to it, with a suitable inscription to record the tragic role it had played, a text, so to speak, as on a cenotaph. How would Lucia's last words do? 'Just wait till we come back.' But if this was a memorial table, it must record that Lucia was not coming back.

He fetched a writing-pad and began again. 'This is the table –' but that wouldn't do. It suggested 'This is the house that Jack built.' Then, 'It was upon this table on Boxing Day afternoon, 1930, that Mrs Emmeline Lucas, of Grebe, and Miss Elizabeth Mapp, of Mallards –' that was too prolix. Then, 'In memory of Emmeline Lucas and Elizabeth Mapp. They went to sea –' but that sounded like a nursery rhyme by Edward Lear, or it might suggest to future generations that they were sailors. Then he wondered if poetry would supply anything, and the lines, 'And may there be no sadness of farewell, when I embark,' occurred to him. But that wouldn't do: people would wonder why she had embarked on a kitchen-table, and even now, when the event was so lamentably recent, nobody actually knew.

'I hadn't any idea,' thought Georgie, 'how difficult it is to write a few well-chosen and heart-felt words. I shall go and look at the tombstones in the churchyard to-morrow. Lucia would have thought of something perfect at once.'

Tiny as were these bubbles and others (larger ones) which Georgie refused to look at directly, they made a momentary, an evanescent brightness. Some of them made quite loud pops as they burst, and some presented problems. This catastrophe had conveyed a solemn warning against living in a house so low-lying, and Major Benjy had already expressed that sentiment when he gave vent to that self-centred *cri du coeur* 'Thank God I live on a hill,' but for Georgie that question would soon become a practical one, though he would not attempt to make up his mind yet. It would be absurd to have two houses in Tilling, to be the tenant of Mallards Cottage, and the owner of Grebe. Or should he live in Grebe during the summer, when there was no fear of floods, and Mallards Cottage in the winter?

He got into bed: the sympathetic Foljambe, before going home, had made a beautiful fire, and his hot-water bottle was of such a temperature that he could not put his feet on it at all ... If he lived at Grebe she would only have to go back across the garden to her Cadman, if Cadman remained in his service. Then there was Lucia's big car. He supposed that would be included in the contents of Grebe. Then he must remember to put a black bow on Lucia's picture in the Art Exhibition. Then he got sleepy ...

II

Though Georgie had thought that there would be nothing interesting left in life now that Lucia was gone, and though Tilling generally was conscious that the termination of the late rivalries would take all thrill out of existence as well as eclipsing its gaieties most dreadfully, it proved one morning when the sad days had begun to add themselves into weeks, that there was a great deal for him to do, as well as a great deal for Tilling to talk about. Lucia had employed a local lawyer over the making of her will, and to-day Mr Causton (*re* the affairs of Mrs Emmeline Lucas) came to see Georgie about it. He explained to him with a manner subtly compounded of sympathy and congratulation that the little sum of money to which Lucia had alluded was no less than £80,000. Georgie was, in fact, apart from certain legacies, her heir. He was much moved.

'Too kind of her,' he said 'I had no idea –'

Mr Causton went on with great delicacy.

'It will be some months,' he said, 'before in the absence of fresh evidence, the death of my client can be legally assumed –'

'Oh, the longer, the better,' said Georgie rather vaguely, wiping his eyes, 'but what do you mean about fresh evidence?'

'The recovery, by washing ashore or other identification, of the lamented corpses,' said Mr Causton. 'In the interval the – the possibly late Mrs Lucas has left no provision for the contingency we have to face. If and when her death is proved, the staff of servants will receive their wages up to date and a month's notice. Until then the estate, I take it, will be liable for the out-goings and the upkeep of Grebe. I would see to all that, but I felt that I must get your authority first.'

'Of course, naturally,' said Georgie.

'But here a difficulty arises,' said Mr Causton. 'I have no authority for drawing on the late – or, we hope, the present Mrs Lucas's balance at the bank. There is, you see, no fund out of which the current expenses of the upkeep of the house can be paid. There is more than a month's food and wages for her servants already owing.'

George's face changed a little. A very little.

'I had better pay them myself,' he said. 'Would not that be the proper course?'

'I think, under the circumstances, that it would,' said Mr Causton. 'In fact, I don't see what else is to be done, unless all the servants were discharged at once, and the house shut up.'

'No, that would never do,' said Georgie. 'I must go down there and arrange about it all. If Mrs Lucas returns, how horrid for her to find all her servants who had been with her so long, gone. Everything must carry on as if she had only gone for a visit somewhere and forgotten to send a cheque for expenses.'

Here then, at any rate, was something to do already, and Georgie, thinking that he would like a little walk on this brisk morning, and also feeling sure that he would like a little conversation with friends in the High Street, put on his thinner cape, for a hint of spring was in the air, and there were snowdrops abloom in the flower-border of his little garden. Lucia, he remembered, always detested snowdrops: they hung their heads and were feeble; they typified for her slack though amiable inefficiency. In order to traverse the whole length of the High Street and get as many conversations as possible he went down by Mallards and Major Benjy's house. The latter, from the window of his study, where he so often enjoyed a rest or a little refreshment before and after his game of golf, saw him pass, and beckoned him in.

'Good morning, old boy,' he said. 'I've had a tremendous slice of luck: at least that is not quite the way to put it, but what I mean is – In fact, I've just had a visit from the solicitor of our lamented friend Elizabeth Mapp, God bless her, and he told me the most surprising news. I was monstrously touched by it: hadn't a notion of it, I assure you.'

'You don't mean to say,' began Georgie.

'Yes I do. He informed me of the provisions of that dear woman's will. In memory of our long friendship, these were the very words – and I assure you I was not ashamed to turn away and wipe my eyes, when he told me – in memory of our long friendship she has left me that beautiful Mallards and the sum of ten thousand pounds, which I understand was the bulk of her fortune. What do you think of that?' he asked, allowing his exultation to get the better of him for the moment.

'No!' said Georgie, 'I congratulate – at least in case –'

'I know,' said Major Benjy. 'If it turns out to be too true that our friends have gone for ever, you're friendly enough to be glad that what I've told you is too true, too. Eh?'

'Quite, and I've had a visit from Mr Causton,' said Georgie, unable to contain himself any longer, 'and Lucia's left me Grebe and eighty thousand pounds.'

'My word! What a monstrous fortune,' cried the Major with a spasm of chagrin. 'I congrat – Anyhow, the same to you. I shall get a motor instead of going to my golf on that measly tram. Then there's Mallards for me to arrange about. I'm thinking of letting it furnished, servants and all. It'll be snapped up at ten guineas a week. Why, she got fifteen last summer from the other poor corpse.'

'I wouldn't,' said Georgie. 'Supposing she came back and found she couldn't get into her house for another month because you had let it?'

'God grant she may come back,' said the Major, without falling dead on the spot. 'But I see your point: it would be awkward. I'll think it over. Anyhow, of course, after a proper interval, when the tragedy is proved, I shall go and live there myself. Till then I shall certainly pay the servants' wages and the upkeep. Rather a drain, but it can't be helped. Board wages of twelve shillings a week is what I shall give them: they'll live like fighting cocks on that. By jove, when I think of that terrible sight of the kitchen-table lying out there on the beach, it causes me such a sinking still. Have a drink: wonderful pre-war whisky.'

Georgie had not yet visited Grebe, and he found a thrilling

though melancholy interest in seeing the starting-point of the catastrophe. The Christmas-tree, he ascertained, had stuck in the door of the kitchen, and the Padre had already been down to look at it, but had decided that the damage to it was irreparable. It was lying now in the garden from which soil and plants had been swept away by the flood, but Georgie could not bear to see it there, and directed that it should be put up, as a relic, in an empty outhouse. Perhaps a tablet on that as well as on the table. Then he had to interview Grosvenor, and make out a schedule of the servants' wages, the total of which rather astonished him. He saw the cook and told her that he had the kitchen-table in his yard, but she begged him not to send it back, as it had always been most inconvenient. Mrs Lucas, she told him, had had a feeling for it; she thought there was luck about it. Then she burst into tears and said it hadn't brought her mistress much luck after all. This was all dreadfully affecting, and Georgie told her that in this period of waiting during which they must not give up hope, all their wages would be paid as usual, and they must carry on as before, and keep the house in order. Then there were some unpaid bills of Lucia's, a rather appalling total, which must be discharged before long, and the kitchen must be renovated from the effects of the flood. It was after dark when he got back to Mallards Cottage again.

In the absence of what Mr Causton called further evidence in the way of corpses, and of alibis in the way of living human bodies, the Padre settled in the course of the next week to hold a memorial service, for unless one was held soon, they would all have got used to the bereavement, and the service would lose point and poignancy. It was obviously suitable that Major Benjy and Georgie, being the contingent heirs of the defunct ladies, should sit by themselves in a front pew as chief mourners, and Major Benjy ordered a black suit to be made for him without delay for use on this solemn occasion. The church bell was tolled as if for a funeral service, and the two walked in side by side after the rest of the congregation had assembled, and took their places in a pew by themselves immediately in front of the reading-desk.

The service was of the usual character, and the Padre gave a most touching address on the text 'They were lovely and pleasant in their lives and in their death they were not divided.' He reminded his hearers how the two whom they mourned were as sisters, taking the lead in social activities, and dispensing to all who knew them their bountiful hospitalities. Their lives had been full of lovable energy. They had been at the forefront in all artistic and literary pursuits: indeed he might almost have taken the whole of the verse of which he had read them only the half as his text, and have added that they were swifter than eagles, they were stronger than lions. One of them had been known to them all for many years, and the name of Elizabeth Mapp was written on their hearts. The other was a newer comer, but she had wonderfully endeared herself to them in her briefer sojourn here, and it was typical of her beautiful nature that on the very day on which the disaster occurred, she had been busy with a Christmas-tree for the choristers in whom she took so profound an interest.

As regards the last sad scene, he need not say much about it, for never would any of them forget that touching, that ennobling, that teaching sight of the two, gallant in the face of death as they had ever been in that of life, being whirled out to sea. Mrs Lucas in the ordeal which they would all have to face one day, giving that humorous greeting of hers, 'au reservoir', which they all knew so well, to her friends standing in safety on the shore, and then turning again to her womanly work of comforting and encouraging her weaker sister. 'May we all,' said the Padre, with a voice trembling with emotion, 'go to meet death in that serene and untroubled spirit, doing our duty to the last. And now –'

This sermon, at the request of a few friends, he had printed in the Parish Magazine next week, and copies were sent to everybody.

It was only natural that Tilling should feel relieved when the ceremony was over, for the weeks since the stranding of the kitchen-table had been like the period between a death and a funeral. The blinds were up again now, and life gradually resumed a more normal complexion. January ebbed away into February, February into March, and as the days lengthened with the returning sun, so the mirths and squabbles of Tilling grew longer and brighter.

But a certain stimulus which had enlivened them all since Lucia's advent from Riseholme was lacking. It was not wholly that there was no Lucia, nor, wholly, that there was no Elizabeth, it was the intense reactions which they had produced together that everyone missed so fearfully. Day after day those who were left met and talked in the High Street, but never was there news of that thrilling kind which since the summer had keyed existence up to so exciting a level. But it was interesting to see Major Benjy in his new motor, which he drove himself, and watch his hairbreadth escapes from collisions at sharp corners and to hear the appalling explosions of military language if any other vehicle came within a yard of his green bonnet.

'He seems to think,' said Diva to Mrs Bartlett, as they met on shopping errands one morning, 'that now he has got a motor nobody else may use the road at all.'

'A trumpery little car,' said Mrs Bartlett, 'I should have thought, with ten thousand pounds as good as in his pocket, he might have got himself something better.'

They were standing at the corner looking up towards Mallards, and Diva suddenly caught sight of a board on Major Benjy's house, announcing that it was for sale.

'Why, whatever's that?' she cried. 'That must have been put up only to-day. Good morning, Mr Georgie. What about Major Benjy's house?'

Georgie still wore a broad black band on his sleeve.

'Yes, he told me yesterday that he was going to move into Mallards next week,' he said. 'And he's going to have a sale of his furniture almost immediately.'

'That won't be much to write home about,' said Diva scornfully. 'A few moth-eaten tiger-skins which he said he shot in India.'

'I think he wants some money,' said Georgie. 'He's bought a motor, you see, and he has to keep up Mallards' as well as his own house.'

'I call that very rash,' said Mrs Bartlett. 'I call that counting your chickens before they're hatched. Oh dear me, what a thing to have said! Dreadful!'

Georgie tactfully covered this up by a change of subject.

'I've made up my mind,' he said, 'and I'm going to put up a cenotaph in the churchyard to dear Lucia and Elizabeth.'

'What? Both?' asked Diva.

'Yes, I've thought it carefully over, and it's going to be both.'

'Major Benjy ought to go halves with you then,' said Diva. 'Well, I told him I was intending to do it,' said Georgie, 'and he didn't catch on. He only said "Capital idea," and took some whisky and soda. So I shan't say any more. I would really just as soon do it all myself.'

'Well, I do think that's mean of him,' said Diva. 'He ought anyhow to bear some part of the expense, considering everything. Instead of which he buys a motor-car which he can't drive. Go on about the cenotaph.'

'I saw, it down at the stonemason's yard,' said Georgie, 'and that put the idea into my head. Beautiful white marble on the lines, though of course much smaller, of the one in London. It had been ordered, I found, as a tombstone, but then the man who ordered it went bankrupt, and it was on the stonemason's hands.'

'I've heard about it,' said Mrs Bartlett, in rather a superior voice. 'Kenneth told me you'd told him, and we both think that it's a lovely idea.'

'The stonemason ought to let you have it cheap then,' said Diva.

'It wasn't very cheap,' said Georgie, 'but I've bought it, and they'll put it in its place to-day, just outside the south transept, and the Padre is going to dedicate it. Then there's the inscription. I shall have in loving memory of them, by me, and a bit of the Padre's text at the memorial service. Just "In death they were not divided."'

'Quite right. Don't put in about the eagles and the lions,' said Diva.

'No, I thought I would leave that out. Though I like that part,' said Georgie for the sake of Mrs Bartlett.

'Talking of whisky,' said Diva, flying back, as her manner was, to a remote allusion, 'Major Benjy's finished all the pre-war whisky that Lucia gave him. At least I heard him ordering some more yesterday. Oh, and there's the notice of his sale. Old English furniture – yes, that may mean two things, and I know which of them it is. Valuable works of Art. Well I never! A print of the "Monarch of the Glen" and a photograph of the "Soul's Awakening". Rubbish! Fine tiger-skins! The skins may be all right, but they're bald.'

'My dear, how severe you are,' said Georgie. 'Now I must go and see how they're getting on with the inscription. Au reservoir.'

Diva nodded at Evie Bartlett.

'Nice to hear that again,' she said. 'I've not heard it – well, since.'

The cenotaph with its inscription in bold leaded letters to say that Georgie had erected it in memory of the two undivided ladies, roused much admiration, and a full-page reproduction of it appeared in the Parish Magazine for April, which appeared on the last day of March. The stone-cutter had slightly miscalculated the space at his disposal for the inscription, and the words 'Elizabeth Mapp' were considerably smaller than the words 'Emmeline Lucas' in order to get them into the line. Though Tilling said nothing about that, it was felt that the error was productive of a very suitable effect, if a symbolic meaning was interpreted into it. Georgie was considered to have done it very handsomely and to be behaving in a way that contrasted most favourably with the conduct of Major Benjy, for whereas Georgie was keeping up Grebe at great expense, and restoring, all at his own charge, the havoc the flood had wrought in the garden, Major Benjy, after unsuccessfully trying to let Mallards at ten guineas a week, had moved into the house, and, with a precipitation that was as rash as it was indelicate, was already negotiating about the disposal of his own, and was to have a sale of his furniture on April the first. He had bought a motor, he had replenished the cellars of Mallards with strong wines and more pre-war whisky, he was spending money like water and on the evening of this last day of March he gave a bridge-party in the garden-room.

Georgie and Diva and Mrs Padre were the guests at this party: there had been dinner first, a rich elaborate dinner, and bridge afterwards up till midnight. It had been an uncomfortable evening, and before it was over they all wished they had not come, for Major Benjy had alluded to it as a house-warming, which showed that either his memory was going, or that his was a very callous nature, for no one whose perceptions were not of the commonest could possibly have used that word so soon. He had spoken of his benefactress with fulsome warmth, but it was painfully evident from what source this posthumous affection sprang. He thought of having the garden-room redecorated, the house wanted brightening up a bit, he even offered each of them one of Miss Mapp's water-colour sketches, of which was a profusion on the walls, as a memento of their friend, God bless her ... There he was straddling in the doorway with the air of a vulgar *nouveau riche* owner of an ancestral property, as they went their ways homeward into the night, and they heard him bolt and lock the door and put up the chain which Lucia in her tenancy had had repaired in order to keep out the uninvited and informal visits of Miss Mapp. 'It would serve him jolly well right,' thought Georgie, 'if she came back.'

12

It was a calm and beautiful night with a high tide that over-flowed the channel of the river. There was spread a great sheet of moonlit water over the submerged meadows at the margin, and it came up to the foot of the rebuilt bank opposite Grebe. Between four and five of the morning of April the first, a trawler entered the mouth of the river, and just at the time when the stars were growing pale and the sky growing red with the coming dawn, it drew up at the little quay to the east of the town, and was moored to the shore. There stepped out of it two figures clad in overalls and tarpaulin jackets.

'I think we had better go straight to Mallards, dear,' said Elizabeth, 'as it's so close, and have a nice cup of tea to warm ourselves. Then you can telephone from there to Grebe, and tell them to send the motor up for you.'

'I shall ring up Georgie too,' said Lucia. 'I can't bear to think that his suspense should last a minute more than is necessary.'

Elizabeth pointed upwards.

'See, there's the sun catching the top of the church tower,' she said. 'Little did I think I should ever see dear Tilling again.'

'I never had the slightest doubt about it,' said Lucia. 'Look, there are the fields we floated across on the kitchen-table. I wonder what happened to it.'

They climbed the steps at the south-east angle of the town, and up the slope to the path across the churchyard. This path led close by the south side of the church, and the white marble of the cenotaph gleamed in the early sunlight.

'What a handsome tomb,' said Elizabeth. 'It's quite new. But how does it come here? No one has been buried in the churchyard for a hundred years.'

Lucia gave a gasp as the polished lead letters caught her eye. 'But it's us!' she said.

They stood side by side in their tarpaulins, and together in a sort of chant read the inscription aloud.

THIS STONE WAS ERECTED BY
GEORGE PILLSON
IN LOVING MEMORY OF
EMMELINE LUCAS AND Elizabeth Mapp
LOST AT SEA ON BOXING DAY. 1930

'IN DEATH THEY WERE NOT DIVIDED.'

'I've never heard of such a thing,' cried Lucia. 'I call it most premature of Georgie, assuming that I was dead like that. The inscription must be removed instantly. All the same it was kind of him and what a lot of money it must have cost him! Gracious me, I suppose he thought – Let us hurry, Elizabeth.'

Elizabeth was still staring at the stone.

'I am puzzled to know why my name is put in such exceedingly small letters,' she said acidly. 'You can hardly read it. As you say, dear, it was most premature of him. I should call it impertinent, and I'm very glad dear Major Benjy had nothing to do with it. There's an indelicacy about it.'

They went quickly on past Mallards Cottage where the blinds were still down, and there was the window of the garden-room from which each had made so many thrilling observations, and the red-brick front, glowing in the sunlight, of Mallards itself. As they crossed the cobbled way to the front door, Elizabeth looked down towards the High Street and saw on Major Benjy's house next door the house-agents' board announcing that the freehold of this desirable residence was for disposal. There were bills pasted on the walls announcing the sale of furniture to take place there that very day.

Her face turned white, and she laid a quaking hand on Lucia's arm.

'Look, Major Benjy's house is for sale,' she faltered. 'Oh, Lucia, what has happened? Have we come back from the dead,

as it were, to find that it's our dear old friend instead? And to
think –' She could not complete the sentence.

'My dear, you mustn't jump at any such terrible conclusions,' said Lucia. 'He may, have changed his house –'

Elizabeth shook her head; she was determined to believe the
worst, and indeed it seemed most unlikely that Major Benjy
who had lived in the same house for a full quarter of a century
could have gone to any new abode but one. Meantime, eager to
put an end to this suspense, Elizabeth kept pressing the bell,
and Lucia plying the knocker of Mallards.

'They all sleep on the attic floor,' said Elizabeth, 'but I think
they must hear us soon if we go on. Ah, there's a step on the
stairs. Someone is coming down.'

They heard the numerous bolts on the door shot back, they
heard the rattle of the released chain. The door was opened
and there within stood Major Benjy. He had put on his dinner
jacket over his Jaeger pyjamas, and had carpet slippers on his
feet. He was sleepy and bristly and very cross.

'Now what's all this about, my men,' he said, seeing two
tarpaulined figures on the threshold. 'What do you mean by
waking me up with that infernal –'

Elizabeth's suspense was quite over.

'You wretch,' she cried in a fury. 'What do *you* mean? Why
are you in my house? Ah, I guess! He! He! He! You learned
about my will, did you? You thought you wouldn't wait to step
into a dead woman's shoes, but positively tear them off my
living feet. My will shall be revoked this day: I promise you
that . . . Now out you go, you horrid supplanter! Off to your
own house with you, for you shan't spend another minute in
mine.'

During this impassioned address Major Benjy's face changed
to an expression of the blankest dismay, as if he had seen
something much worse (as indeed he had) than a ghost. He
pulled pieces of himself together.

'But, my dear Miss Elizabeth,' he said. 'You'll allow me
surely, to get my clothes on, and above all to say one word of
my deep thankfulness that you and Mrs Lucas – it is Mrs
Lucas, isn't it? –'

'Get out!' said Elizabeth, stamping her foot. 'Thankfulness indeed! There's a lot of thankfulness in your face! Go away! Shoo!'

Major Benjy had faced wounded tigers (so he said) in India, but then he had a rifle in his hand. He could not face his benefactress, and, with first one slipper and then the other dropping off his feet, he hurried down the few yards of pavement to his own house. The two ladies entered: Elizabeth banged the door and put up the chain.

'So that's that,' she observed (and undoubtedly it was). 'Ah, here's Withers. Withers, we've come back, and though you ought never to have let the Major set foot in my house, I don't blame you, for I feel sure he bullied you into it.'

'Oh, miss!' said Withers. 'Is it you? Fancy! Well, that is a surprise!'

'Now get Mrs Lucas and me a cup of tea,' said Elizabeth, 'and then she's going back to Grebe. That wretch hasn't been sleeping in my room, I trust?'

'No, in the best spare bedroom,' said Withers.

'Then get my room ready, and I shall go to bed for a few hours. We've been up all night. Then, Withers, take all Major Benjy's clothes and his horrid pipes, and all that belongs to him, and put them on the steps outside. Ring him up, and tell him where he will find them. But not one foot shall he set in *my* house again.'

Lucia went to the telephone and rang up Cadman's cottage for her motor. She heard his exclamation of 'My Gawd', she heard (what she supposed was) Foljambe's cry of astonishment, and then she rang up Georgie. He and his household were all a-bed and asleep when the telephone began its summons, but presently the persistent tinkle penetrated into his consciousness, and made him dream that he was again watching Lucia whirling down the flood on the kitchen-table and ringing an enormous dinner-bell as she swept by the steps. Then he became completely awake and knew it was only the telephone.

'The tarsome thing!' he muttered. 'Who on earth can it be ringing one up at this time? Go on ringing then till you're tired. I shall go to sleep again.'

In spite of these resolutions, he did nothing of the kind. So ceaseless was the summons that in a minute or two he got out of bed, and putting on his striped dressing-gown (blue and yellow) went down to his sitting-room.

'Yes. Who is it? What do you want?' he said crossly.

There came a little merry laugh, and then a voice, which he had thought was silent for ever, spoke in unmistakable accents.

'Georgie! *Georgino mio!*' it said.

His heart stood still.

'What? What?' he cried.

'Yes, it's Lucia,' said the voice. 'Me's tum home, Georgie.'

Eighty thousand pounds (less death duties) and Grebe seemed to sweep by him like an avalanche, and fall into the gulf of the things that might have been. But it was not the cold blast of that ruin that filled his eyes with tears.

'Oh my dear!' he cried. 'Is it really you? Lucia, where are you? Where are you talking from?'

'Mallards. Elizabeth and I –'

'What, both of you?' called Georgie. 'Then – where's Major Benjy?'

'Just gone home,' said Lucia discreetly. 'And as soon as I've had a cup of tea I'm going to Grebe.'

'But I must come round and see you at once,' said Georgie. 'I'll just put some things on.'

'Yes, do,' said Lucia. 'Presto, presto, Georgie.'

Careless of his reputation for being the best-dressed man in Tilling, he put on his dress trousers and a pullover, and his thick brown cape, and did not bother about his *toupet*. The front door of Mallards was open, and Elizabeth's servants were laying out on the top step a curious collection of golf-clubs and tooth-brushes and clothes. From mere habit – everyone in Tilling had the habit – he looked up at the window of the garden-room as he passed below it, and was astonished to see two mariners in sou'wester caps and tarpaulin jackets kissing their hands to him. He had only just time to wonder who these could possibly be when he guessed. He flew into Lucia's arms, then wondered if he ought to kiss Elizabeth too. But there was a slight reserve about her which caused him to refrain. He was not brilliant enough at so early an hour to guess that she had seen the smaller lettering in which her loving memory was recorded.

There was but time for a few ejaculations and a promise from Georgie to dine at Grebe that night, before Lucia's motor arrived, and the imperturbable Cadman touched his cap and said to Lucia, 'Very pleased to see you back, ma'am,' as she picked her way between the growing deposits of socks and other more intimate articles of male attire which were now being ranged on the front steps. Georgie hurried back to Mallards Cottage to dress in a manner more worthy of his reputation, and Elizabeth up to her bedroom for a few hours' sleep. Below her oil-skins she still wore the ragged remains of the clothes in which she had left Tilling on Boxing Day, and now she drew out of the pocket of her frayed and sea-stained jacket, a half-sheet of discoloured paper. She unfolded it and having once more read the mystic words 'Take two hen lobsters', she stowed it safely away for future use.

Meantime Major Benjy next door had been the prey of the most sickening reflections; whichever way he turned, fate gave him some stinging blow that set him staggering and reeling in another direction. Leaning out of an upper window of his own house, he observed his clothes and boots and articles of toilet being laid out like a bird's breakfast on the steps of Mallards, and essaying to grind his teeth with rage he discovered that his upper dental plate must still be reposing in a glass of water in the best spare bedroom which he had lately quitted in such haste. To recover his personal property was the first necessity, and when from his point of observation he saw that the collection had grown to a substantial size, he crept up the pavement, seized a bundle of miscellaneous articles, as many as he could carry, then stole back again, dropping a nail-brush here and a sock-suspender there, and dumped them in his house. Three times he must go on these degrading errands, before he had cleared all the bird's breakfast away; indeed he was an early bird feeding on the worms of affliction.

Tilling was beginning to awake now: the milkman came clattering down the street and, looking in amazement at his

dishevelled figure, asked whether he wanted his morning
supply left at his own house or at Mallards: Major Benjy
turned on him so appalling a face that he left no milk at either
and turned swiftly into the less alarming air of Porpoise Street.
Again he had to make the passage of his Via Dolorosa to glean
the objects which had dropped from his overburdened arms,
and as he returned he heard a bumping noise behind him, and
saw his new portmanteau hauled out by Withers rolling down
the steps into the street. He emerged again when Withers had
shut the door, put more gleanings into it and pulled it into his
house. There he made a swift and sorry toilet, for there was
business to be done which would not brook delay. Already the
preparations for the sale of his furniture were almost finished;
the carpet and hearth-rug in his sitting-room were tied up
together and labelled Lot 1; the fire-irons and a fishing-rod
and a rhinoceros-hide whip were Lot 2; a kitchen tray with
packs of cards, a tobacco jar, a piece of chipped *cloisonné* ware
and a roll of toilet paper formed an unappetizing Lot 3. The sale
must be stopped at once and he went down to the auctioneer's
in the High Street and informed him that owing to circumstances over which he had no control he was compelled to
cancel it. It was pointed out to him that considerable expense
had already been incurred for the printing and display of the
bills that announced it, for the advertisements in the local
press, for the time and trouble already spent in arranging and
marking the lots, but the Major bawled out: 'Damn it all, the
things are mine and I won't sell one of them. Send me in your
bill.' Then he had to go to the house agents' and tell them to
withdraw his house from the market and take down his board,
and coming out of the office he ran into Irene, already on her
way to Grebe, who cried out: 'They've come back, old Benjy-
wenjy. Joy! Joy!'

The most immediate need of having a roof over his head and
a chair to sit on was now provided for, and as he had already
dismissed his own servants, taking those of Mallards, he must
go to another agency to find some sort of cook or charwoman
till he could get his establishment together again. They
promised to send an elderly lady, highly respectable though

rather deaf and weak in the legs, to-morrow if possible. Back
he came to his house with such cold comfort to cheer him, and
observed on the steps of Mallards half a dozen bottles of wine.
'My God, my cellar,' muttered the Major, 'there are dozens
and dozens of my wine and my whisky in the house!' Again he
crept up to the abhorred door and, returning with the bottles,
put a kettle on to boil, and began cutting the strings that held
the lots together. Just then the church bells burst out into a
joyful peal, and it was not difficult to conjecture the reason for
their unseemly mirth. All this before breakfast . . .

A cup of hot strong tea without any milk restored not only
his physical stability but also his mental capacity for suffering,
and he sat down to think. There was the financial side of the
disaster first of all, a thing ghastly to contemplate. He had
bought (but not yet paid for) a motor, some dozens of wine, a
suit of new clothes, as well as the mourning habiliments in
which he had attended the memorial service, quantities of
stationery with the Mallards stamp on it, a box of cigars and
other luxuries too numerous to mention. It was little comfort
to remember that he had refused to contribute to the cenotaph;
a small saving like that did not seem to signify. Then what
view, he wondered, would his benefactress, when she knew all,
take of his occupation of Mallards? She might find out (indeed
being who she was, she would not fail to do so) that he had
tried to let it at ten guineas a week and she might therefore
send him in a bill on that scale for the fortnight he had spent
there, together with that for her servants' wages, and for
garden-produce and use of her piano. Luckily he had only eaten
some beetroot out of the garden, and he had had the piano
tuned. But of all these staggering expenses, the only items
which were possibly recoverable were the wages he had paid to
the staff of Mallards between Boxing Day and the date of his
tenancy: these Elizabeth might consent to set against the debits.
Not less hideous than this financial débâcle that stared him in
the face, was the loss of prestige in Tilling. Tilling, he knew,
had disapproved of his precipitancy in entering into Mallards,
and Tilling, full, like Irene, of joy, joy for the return of the lost,
would simply hoot with laughter at him. He could visualize

with awful clearness the chatting groups in the High Street which would vainly endeavour to suppress their smiles as he approached. The day of swank was past and done, he would have to be quiet and humble and grateful to anybody who treated him with the respect to which he had been accustomed.

He unrolled a tiger-skin to lay down again in his hall: a cloud of dust and deciduous hair rose from it, pungent like snuff, and the remaining glass eye fell out of the socket. He bawled '*Quai-hai*' before he remembered that till tomorrow at least he would be alone in the house, and that even then his attendant would be deaf. He opened his front door and looked out into the street again, and there on the doorstep of Mallards was another dozen or so of wine and a walking-stick. Again he stole out to recover his property with the hideous sense that perhaps Elizabeth was watching him from the garden-room. His dental plate – thank God – was there too on the second step, all by itself, gleaming in the sun, and seeming to grin at him in a very mocking manner. After that throughout the morning he looked out at intervals as he rested from the awful labour of laying carpets and putting beds together, and there were usually some more bottles waiting for him, with stray golf-clubs, bridge-markers and packs of cards. About one o'clock just as he was collecting what must surely be the last of these bird-breakfasts, the door of Mallards opened and Elizabeth stepped carefully over his umbrella and a box of cigars. She did not appear to see him. It seemed highly probable that she was going to revoke her will.

Georgie, as well as Major Benjy, had to do a little thinking, when he returned from his visit at dawn to Mallards. It concerned two points, the cenotaph and the kitchen-table. The cenotaph had not been mentioned in those few joyful ejaculations he had exchanged with Lucia, and he hoped that the ladies had not seen it. So after breakfast he went down to the stonemason's and begged him to send a trolley and a hefty lot of men up to the churchyard at once, and remove the monument to the backyard of Mallards Cottage, which at present was chiefly occupied by the kitchen-table under a tarpaulin. But Mr Marble (such was his appropriate name) shook his head over this: the cenotaph had been dedicated, and he felt sure that a faculty must be procured before it could be removed. That would never do: Georgie could not wait for a faculty, whatever that was, and he ordered that the inscription, anyhow, should be effaced without delay: surely no faculty was needed to destroy all traces of a lie. Mr Marble must send some men up to chip, and chip and chip for all they were worth till those beautiful lead letters were detached and the surface of the stone cleared of all that erroneous information.

'And then I'll tell you what,' said Georgie, with a sudden splendid thought, 'why not paint on to it (I can't afford any more cutting) the inscription that was to have been put on it when that man went bankrupt and I bought the monument instead? He'll get his monument for nothing, and I shall get rid of mine, which is just what I want . . . That's beautiful. Now you must send a trolley to my house and take a very big kitchen-table, *the* one in fact, back to Grebe. It must go in through the door of the kitchen-garden and be put quietly into the kitchen. And I particularly want it done to-day.'

All went well with these thoughtful plans. Georgie saw with his own eyes the last word of his inscription disappear in chips of marble; and he carried away all the lead letters in case they might come in useful for something, though he could not have said what: perhaps he would have 'Mallards Cottage' let into the threshold of his house for that long inscription would surely contain the necessary letters. Rather a pretty and original idea. Then he ascertained that the kitchen-table had been restored to its place while Lucia slept, and he drove down at dinner-time feeling that he had done his best. He wore his white waistcoat with onyx buttons for the happy occasion.

Lucia was looking exceedingly well and much sun-burnt. By way of resting she had written a larger number of post cards to all her friends, both here and elsewhere, than Georgie had ever seen together in one place.

'Georgino,' she cried. 'There's so much to say that I hardly know where to begin. I think my adventures first, quite shortly, for I shall dictate a full account of them to my secretary, and have a party next week for all Tilling, and read them out to you. Two parties, I expect, for I don't think I shall be able to read it all in one evening. Now we go back to Boxing Day.

'I went into the kitchen that afternoon,' she said as they sat down to dinner, and there was Elizabeth. I asked her, naturally, don't you think? – why she was there, and she said, "I came to thank you for that delicious *pâté*, and to ask if –" That was as far as she got – I must return to that later – when the bank burst with a frightful roar, and the flood poured in. I was quite calm. We got on to, I should really say into the table – By the way, was the table ever washed up?'

'Yes,' said Georgie, 'it's in your kitchen now. I sent it back.'

'Thank you, my dear. We got into the kitchen-table, really a perfect boat, I can't think why they don't make more like it, flew by the steps – oh, did the Padre catch a dreadful cold? Such a splash it was, and that was the only drop of water that we shipped at all.'

'No, but he lost his umbrella, the one you'd given him,' said Georgie, 'and the Padre of the Roman Catholic church found it, a week afterwards, and returned it to him. Wasn't that a coincidence? Go on. Oh no, wait a minute. What did you mean by calling out "Just wait till we get back"?'

'Why of course I wanted to tell you that I had found Elizabeth in my kitchen,' said Lucia.

'Hurrah! I guessed you meant something of the kind,' said Georgie.

'Well, out we went – I've never been so fast in a kitchen-table before – out to sea in a blinding sea-fog. My dear; poor Elizabeth! No nerve of any kind! I told her that if we were rescued, there was nothing to cry about, and if we weren't all our troubles would soon be over.'

Grosvenor had put some fish before Lucia. She gave an awful shudder.

'Oh, take it away,' she said. 'Never let me see fish again, particularly cod, as long as I live. Tell the cook. You'll see why presently, Georgie. Elizabeth got hysterical and said she wasn't fit to die, so I scolded her – the best plan always with hysterical people – and told her that the longer she lived, the less fit she would be, and that did her a little good. Then it got dark, and there were fog-horns hooting all round us, and we called and yelled, but they had much more powerful voices than we, and nobody heard us. One of them grew louder and louder, until I could hardly bear it, and then we bumped quite gently into it, the fog-horn's boat I mean.'

'Gracious, you might have upset,' said Georgie.

'No, it was like a liner coming up to the quay,' said Lucia. 'No shock of any kind. Then when the fog-horn stopped, they heard us shouting, and took us aboard. It was an Italian trawler on its way to the cod-fishery (that's why I never want to see cod again) on the Gallagher Banks.'

'That was lucky too,' said Georgie, 'you could make them understand a little. Better than if they had been Spanish.'

'About the same, because I'm convinced, as I told Elizabeth, that they talked a very queer Neapolitan dialect. It was rather unlucky, in fact. But as the Captain understood English perfectly, it didn't matter. They were most polite, but they couldn't put us ashore, for we were miles out in the Channel by this time, and also quite lost. They hadn't an idea where the coast of England or any other coast was.'

'Wireless?' suggested Georgie.

'It had been completely smashed up by the dreadful gale the day before. We drifted about in the fog for two days, and when it cleared and they could take the sun again – a nautical expression, Georgie – we were somewhere off the coast of Devonshire. The captain promised to hail any passing vessel bound for England that he saw, but he didn't see any. So he continued his course to the Gallagher Banks, which is about as far from Ireland as it is from America, and there we were for two months. Cod, cod, cod, nothing but cod, and Elizabeth snoring all night in the cabin we shared together. Bitterly cold very often: how glad I was that I knew so many callisthenic exercises! I shall tell you all about that time at my lecture. Then we found that there was a Tilling trawler on the bank, and when it was ready to start home we trans-shipped – they call it – and got back, as you know, this morning. That's the skeleton.'

'It's the most wonderful skeleton I ever heard,' said Georgie. 'Do write your lecture quick.'

Lucia fixed Georgie with her gimlet eye. It had lost none of its penetrative power by being so long at sea.

'Now it's your turn for a little,' she said. 'I expect I know rather more than you think. First about that memorial service.'

'Oh, do you know about that?' he asked.

'Certainly. I found the copy of the Parish Magazine waiting for me, and read it in bed. I consider it to have been very premature. You attended it, I think.'

'We all did,' said Georgie. 'And after all, the Padre said extremely nice things about you.'

'I felt very much flattered. But all the same it was too early. And you and Major Benjy were chief mourners.'

Georgie considered for a moment.

'I'm going to make a clean breast of it,' he said. 'You told me you had left me Grebe, and a small sum of money, and your lawyer told me what that meant. My dear, I was too touched, and naturally, it was proper that I should be chief mourner. It was the same with Major Benjy. He had seen Elizabeth's will, so there we were.'

Suddenly an irresistible curiosity seized him.

'Major Benjy hasn't been seen all day,' he said. 'Do tell me what happened this morning at Mallards. You only said on the telephone that he had just gone home.'

'Yes, bag and baggage,' said Lucia. 'At least he went first and his bag and baggage followed. Socks and things, you saw some of them on the top step. Elizabeth was mad with rage, a perfect fishwife. So suitable after coming back from the Gallagher Banks. But tell me more. What was the next thing after the memorial service?'

The hope of keeping the knowledge of the cenotaph from Lucia became very dim. If Lucia had seen the February number of the Parish Magazine she had probably also seen the April number in which appeared the full-page reproduction of that monument. Besides, there was the gimlet eye.

'The next thing was that I put up a beautiful cenotaph to you and Elizabeth,' said Georgie firmly. '"In loving memory of by me." But I've had the inscription erased to-day.'

Lucia laid her hand on his.

'Dear Georgie, I'm glad you told me,' she said. 'As a matter of fact I knew, because Elizabeth and I studied it this morning. I was vexed at first, but now I think it's rather dear of you. It must have cost a lot of money.'

'It did,' said Georgie. 'And what did Elizabeth think about it?'

'Merely furious because her name was in smaller letters than mine,' said Lucia. 'So like the poor thing.'

'Was she terribly tarsome all these months?' asked Georgie.

'Tiresome's not quite the word,' said Lucia judicially. 'Deficient rather than tiresome, except incidentally. She had no idea of the tremendous opportunities she was getting. She never rose to her chances, nor forgot our little discomforts and that everlasting smell of fish. Whereas I learned such lots of things, Georgie: the Italian for starboard and port – those are the right and left sides of the ship – and how to tie an anchor-knot and a running noose, and a clove-hitch, and how to splice two ends of fishing-line together, and all sorts of things of the most curious and interesting kind. I shall show you some of them at my lecture. I used to go about the deck barefoot (Lucia had very pretty feet) and pull on anchors and capstans and things, and managed never to tumble out of my berth on to the floor when the ship was rolling frightfully, and not to be sea-sick. But poor Elizabeth was always bumping on to the floor, and sometimes being sick there. She had no spirit. Little moans and sighs and regrets that she ever came down the Tilling hill on Boxing Day.'

Lucia leaned forward and regarded Georgie steadfastly.

'I couldn't fathom her simply because she was so superficial,' she said. 'But I feel sure that there was something on her mind all the time. She used often to seem to be screwing herself up to confess something to me, and then not to be able to get it out. No courage. And though I can make no guess as to what it actually was, I believe I know its general nature.'

'How thrilling!' cried Georgie. 'Tell me!'

Lucia's eye ceased to bore, and became of far-off focus, keen still but speculative, as if she was Einstein concentrating on some cosmic deduction.

'Georgie, why did she come into my kitchen like a burglar on Boxing Day?' she asked. 'She told me she had come to thank me for that *pâté* I sent her. But that wasn't true: anyone could see that it wasn't. Nobody goes into kitchens to thank people for *pâtés*.'

'Diva guessed that she had gone there to see the Christmas-tree,' said Georgie. 'You weren't on very good terms at the time. We all thought that brilliant of her.'

'Then why shouldn't she have said so?' asked Lucia.

'I believe it was something much meaner and more under-hand than that. And I am convinced – I have those perceptions sometimes, as you know very well – that all through the months of our Odyssey she wanted to tell me why she was there, and was ashamed of doing so. Naturally I never asked her, because if she didn't choose to tell me, it would be beneath me to force a confidence. There we were together on the Gallagher Banks, she all to bits all the time, and I should have scorned myself for attempting to worm it out of her. But the more I think of it, Georgie, the more convinced I am, that what she had to tell me and couldn't, concerned that. After all, I had unmasked every single plot she made against me before, and I knew the worst of her up till that moment. She had something on her mind, and that something was why she was in my kitchen.'

Lucia's far-away prophetic aspect cleared.

'I shall find out all right,' she said. 'Poor Elizabeth will betray herself some time. But, Georgie, how in those weeks I missed my music! Not a piano on board any of the trawlers assembled there! Just a few concertinas and otherwise nothing except cod. Let us go, in a minute, into my music-room and have some Mozartino again. But first I want to say one thing.'

Georgie took a rapid survey of all he had done in his conviction that Lucia had long ago been drowned. But if she knew about the memorial service and the cenotaph there could be nothing more except the kitchen-table, and that was now in its place again. She knew all that mattered. Lucia began to speak baby-talk.

'Georgie,' she said. ''Oo have had dweffel disappointy –'

That was too much. Georgie thumped the table quite hard.

'I haven't,' he cried. 'How dare you say that?'

'Ickle joke, Georgie,' piped Lucia. 'Haven't had joke for so long with that melancholy Liblib. 'Pologize. 'Oo not angry wif Lucia?'

'No, but don't do it again,' said Georgie. 'I won't have it.'

'You shan't then,' said Lucia, relapsing into the vernacular of adults. 'Now all this house is spick and span, and Grosvenor tells me you've been paying all their wages, week by week.'

'Naturally,' said Georgie.

'It was very dear and thoughtful of you. You saw that my house was ready to welcome my return, and you must send me in all the bills and everything to-morrow and I'll pay them at once, and I thank you enormously for your care of it. And send me in the bill for the cenotaph too. I want to pay for it, I do indeed. It was a loving impulse of yours, Georgie, though, thank goodness, a hasty one. But I can't bear to think that you're out of pocket because I'm alive. Don't answer: I shan't listen. And now let's go straight to the piano and have one of our duets, the one we played last, that heavenly Mozartino.'

They went into the next room. There was the duet ready on the piano, which much looked as if Lucia had been at it already, and she slid on to the top music-stool.

'We both come in on the third beat,' said she. 'Are you ready? Now! *Uno, due, TRE!*'

13

The wretched Major Benjy, who had not been out all day except for interviews with agents and miserable traverses between his house and the doorsteps of Mallards, dined alone that night (if you could call it dinner) on a pork pie and a bottle of Burgundy. A day's hard work had restored the lots of his abandoned sale to their proper places, and a little glue had restored its eye to the bald tiger. He felt worse than bald himself, he felt flayed, and God above alone knew what fresh skinnings were in store for him. All Tilling must have had its telephone-bells (as well as the church bells) ringing from morning till night with messages of congratulation and suitable acknowledgments between the returned ladies and their friends, and he had never felt so much like a pariah before. Diva had just passed his windows (clearly visible in the lamplight, for he had not put up the curtains of his snuggery yet) and he had heard her knock on the door of Mallards. She must have gone to dine with the fatal Elizabeth, and what were they talking about now? Too well he knew, for he knew Elizabeth.

If in spirit he could have been present in the dining-room, where only last night he had so sumptuously entertained Diva and Georgie and Mrs Bartlett, and had bidden them punish the port, he would not have felt much more cheerful.

'In my best spare room, Diva, would you believe it?' said Elizabeth, 'with all the drawers full of socks and shirts and false teeth, wasn't it so, Withers? and the cellar full of wine. What he has consumed of my things, goodness only knows. There was that *pâté* which Lucia gave me only the day before we were whisked out to sea –'

'But that was three months ago,' said Diva.

'– and he used my coal and my electric light as if they were his own, not to mention firing,' said Elizabeth, going on exactly where she had left off, 'and a whole row of beetroot.'

Diva was bursting to hear the story of the voyage. She knew that Georgie was dining with Lucia, and he would be telling everybody about it to-morrow, but if only Elizabeth would leave the beetroot alone and speak of the other she herself would be another focus of information instead of being obliged to listen to Georgie.

'Dear Elizabeth,' she said, 'what does a bit of beetroot matter compared to what you've been through? When an old friend like you has had such marvellous experiences as I'm sure you must have, nothing else counts. Of course I'm sorry about your beetroot: most annoying, but I do want to hear about your adventures.'

'You'll hear all about them soon,' said Elizabeth, 'for to-morrow I'm going to begin a full history of it all. Then, as soon as it's finished, I shall have a big tea-party, and instead of bridge afterwards I shall read it to you. That's absolutely confidential, Diva. Don't say a word about it, or Lucia may steal my idea or do it first.'

'Not a word,' said Diva. 'But surely you can tell me some bits.'

'Yes, there is a certain amount which I shan't mention publicly,' Elizabeth said. 'Things about Lucia which I should never dream of stating openly.'

'Those are just the ones I should like to hear about most,' said Diva. 'Just a few little titbits.'

Elizabeth reflected a moment.

'I don't want to be hard on her,' she said, 'for after all we were together, and what would have happened if I had not been there, I can't think. A little off her head perhaps with panic: that is the most charitable explanation. As we swept by the town on our way out to sea she shrieked out – "Au reservoir: just wait till we come back." Diva, I am not easily shocked, but I must say I was appalled. Death stared us in the face and all she could do was to make jokes! There was I sitting quiet and calm, preparing myself to meet the solemn moment as a Christian should, with this screaming hyena for my companion. Then out we went to sea, in that blinding fog, tossing and pitching on the waves, till we went crash into the side of a ship which was invisible in the darkness.'

'How awful!' said Diva. 'I wonder you didn't upset.'

'Certainly it was miraculous,' said Elizabeth. 'We were battered about, the blows against the table were awful, and if I hadn't kept my head and clung on to the ship's side, we must have upset. They had heard our calls by then, and I sprang on to the rope-ladder they put down, without a moment's pause, so as to lighten the table for Lucia, and then she came up too.'

Elizabeth paused a moment.

'Diva, you will bear me witness that I always said, in spite of Amelia Faraglione, that Lucia didn't know a word of Italian, and it was proved I was right. It was an Italian boat, and our great Italian scholar was absolutely flummoxed, and the Captain had to talk to us in English. There!'

'Go on,' said Diva breathlessly.

'The ship was a fishing trawler bound for the Gallagher Banks, and we were there for two months, and then we found another trawler on its way home to Tilling, and it was from that we landed this morning. But I shan't tell you of our life and adventures, for I'm reserving that for my reading to you.'

'No, never mind then,' said Diva. 'Tell me intimate things about Lucia.'

Elizabeth sighed.

'We mustn't judge anybody,' she said, 'and I won't: but oh, the nature that revealed itself! The Italians were a set of coarse, lascivious men of the lowest type, and Lucia positively revelled in their society. Every day she used to walk about the deck, often with bare feet, and skip and do her callisthenics, and learn a few words of Italian; she sat with this one or that, with her fingers actually entwined with his, while he pretended to teach her to tie a knot or a clove-hitch or something that probably had an improper meaning as well. Such flirtation (at her age too), such promiscuousness, I have never seen. But I don't judge her, and I beg you won't.'

'But didn't you speak to her about it?' asked Diva.

'I used to try to screw myself up to it,' said Elizabeth, 'but her lightness positively repelled me. We shared a cabin about as big as a dog kennel, and oh, the sleepless nights when I used to be thrown from the shelf where I lay! Even then she wanted to instruct me, and show me how to wedge myself in. Always that dreadful superior attitude, that mania to teach everybody everything except Italian, which we have so often deplored. But that was nothing. It was her levity from the time when the flood poured into the kitchen at Grebe –'

'Do tell me about that,' cried Diva. 'That's almost the most interesting thing of all. Why had she taken you into the kitchen?'

Elizabeth laughed.

'Dear thing!' she said. 'What a lovely appetite you have for details! You might as well expect me to remember what I had for breakfast that morning. She and I had both gone into the kitchen; there we were, and we were looking at the Christmas-tree. Such a tawdry tinselly tree! Rather like her. Then the flood poured in, and I saw that our only chance was to embark on the kitchen-table. By the way, was it ever washed up?'

'Oh yes, without a scratch on it,' said Diva, thinking of the battering it was supposed to have undergone against the side of the trawler . . .

Elizabeth had evidently not reckoned on its having come ashore, and rose.

'I am surprised that it didn't go to bits,' she said. 'But let us go into the garden-room. We must really talk about that wretched sponger next door. Is it true he's bought a motor-car out of the money he hoped my death would bring him? And all that wine: bottles and bottles, so Withers told me. Oceans of champagne. How is he to pay for it all now with his miserable little income on which he used to pinch and scrape along before?'

'That's what nobody knows,' said Diva. 'An awful crash for him. So rash and hasty, as we all felt.'

They settled themselves comfortably by the fire, after Elizabeth had had one peep between the curtains.

'I'm not the least sorry for having been a little severe with him this morning,' she said. 'Any woman would have done the same.'

Withers entered with a note. Elizabeth glanced at the handwriting, and turned pale beneath the tan acquired on the cod-banks.

'From him,' she said. 'No answer, Withers.'

'Shall I read it?' said Elizabeth, when Withers had left the room, 'or throw it, as it deserves, straight into the fire.'

'Oh, read it,' said Diva, longing to know what was in it. 'You must see what he has to say for himself.'

Elizabeth adjusted her pince-nez and read it in silence.

'Poor wretch,' she said. 'But very proper as far as it goes. Shall I read it you?'

'Do, do, do,' said Diva.

Elizabeth read:

'My Dear Miss Elizabeth (if you will still permit me to call you so) –'

'Very proper,' said Diva.

'Don't interrupt, dear, or I shan't read it,' said Elizabeth.

'– call you so. I want first of all to congratulate you with all my heart on your return after adventures and privations which I know you bore with Christian courage.

'Secondly I want to tender you my most humble apologies for my atrocious conduct in your absence, which was unworthy of a soldier and Christian, and, in spite of all, a gentleman. Your forgiveness, should you be so gracious as to extend it to me, will much mitigate my present situation.

'Most sincerely yours (if you will allow me to say so),

'Benjamin Flint'

'I call that very nice,' said Diva. 'He didn't find that easy to write!'

'And I don't find it very easy to forgive him,' retorted Elizabeth.

'Elizabeth, you must make an effort,' said Diva energetically. 'Tilling society will all fly to smithereens if we don't take care. You and Lucia have come back from the dead, so that's a very good opportunity for showing a forgiving spirit and beginning again. He really can't say more than he has said.'

'Nor could he possibly, if he's a soldier, a Christian and a gentleman, have said less,' observed Elizabeth.

'No, but he's done the right thing.'

Elizabeth rose and had one more peep out of the window.
'I forgive him,' she said. 'I shall ask him to tea to-morrow.'

Elizabeth carried up to bed with her quantities of food for thought and lay munching it till a very late hour. She had got rid of a good deal of spite against Lucia, which left her head the clearer, and she would be very busy tomorrow writing her account of the great adventure. But it was the thought of Major Benjy that most occupied her. Time had been when he had certainly come very near making honourable proposals to her which she always was more than ready to accept. They used to play golf together in those days before that firebrand Lucia descended on Tilling; he used to drop in casually, and she used to put flowers in his buttonhole for him. Tilling had expected their union, and Major Benjy had without doubt been on the brink. Now, she reflected, was the precise moment to extend to him a forgiveness so plenary that it would start a new chapter in the golden book of pardon. Though only this morning she had ejected his golf-clubs and his socks and his false teeth with every demonstration of contempt, this appeal of his revived in her hopes that had hitherto found no fruition. There should be fatted calves for him as for a prodigal son, he should find in this house that he had violated a cordiality and a welcome for the future and an oblivion of the past that could not fail to undermine his celibate propensities. Discredited owing to his precipitate occupation of Mallards, humiliated by his degrading expulsion from it, and impoverished by the imprudent purchase of wines, motor-car and steel-shafted drivers, he would surely take advantage of the wonderful opportunity which she presented to him. He might be timid at first, unable to believe the magnitude of his good fortune, but with a little tact, a proffering of saucers of milk, so to speak, as to a stray and friendless cat, with comfortable invitations to sweet Pussie to be fed and stroked, with stealthy butterings of his paws, and with, frankly, a sudden slam of the door when sweet Pussie had begun to make himself at home, it seemed that unless Pussie was a lunatic, he could not fail to wish to domesticate himself. 'I think I can manage it,' thought Elizabeth, 'and then poor Lulu will only be a widow, and I a married woman with a well-controlled husband. How will she like that?'

Such sweet thoughts as these gradually lulled her to sleep.

It was soon evident that the return of the lost, an event in itself of the first magnitude, was instantly to cause a revival of those rivalries which during the autumn had rendered life at Tilling so thrilling a business. Georgie, walking down to see Lucia three days after her return, found a bill-poster placarding the High Street with notices of a lecture to be delivered at the Institute in two days' time by Mrs Lucas, admission free and no collection of any sort before, during or after. 'A modern Odyssey' was the title of the discourse. He hurried on to Grebe, and found her busy correcting the typewritten manuscript which she had been dictating to her secretary all yesterday with scarcely a pause for meals.

'Why, I thought it was to be just an after-dinner reading,' he said, straight off, without any explanation of what he was talking about.

Lucia put a paper-knife in the page she was at, and turned back to the first.

'My little room would not accommodate all the people who, I understand, are most eager to hear about what I went through,' she said. 'You see, Georgie, I think it is a duty laid upon those who have been privileged to pass unscathed through tremendous adventures to let others share, as far as is possible, their experiences. In fact that is how I propose to open my lecture. I was reading the first sentence. What do you think of it?'

'Splendid,' said Georgie. 'So well expressed.'

'Then I make some allusion to Nansen, and Stanley and Amundsen,' said Lucia, 'who have all written long books about their travels, and say that as I do not dream of comparing my adventure to theirs, a short verbal recital of some of the strange things that happened to me will suffice. I calculate that it will not take much more than two hours, or at most two and a half. I finished it about one o'clock this morning.'

'Well, you have been quick about it,' said Georgie. 'Why, you've only been back three days.'

Lucia pushed the pile of typewritten sheets aside.

'Georgie, it has been terrific work,' she said, 'but I had to rid myself of the incubus of these memories by writing them down. Aristotle, you know; the purging of the mind. Besides, I'm sure I'm right in hurrying up. It would be like Elizabeth to be intending to do something of the sort. I've hired the Institute anyhow –'

'Now that is interesting,' said Georgie. 'Practically every time that I've passed Mallards during these last two days Elizabeth has been writing in the window of the garden-room. Frightfully busy: hardly looking up at all. I don't know for certain that she is writing her Odyssey – such a good title – but she is writing something, and surely it must be that. And two of those times Major Benjy was sitting with her on the piano-stool and she was reading to him from a pile of blue foolscap. Of course I couldn't hear the words, but there were her lips going on like anything. So busy that she didn't see me, but I think he did.'

'No!' said Lucia, forgetting her lecture for the moment. 'Has she made it up with him then?'

'She must have. He dined there once, for I saw him going in, and he lunched there once, for I saw him coming out, and then there was tea, when she was reading to him, and I passed them just now in his car. All their four hands were on the wheel, and I think he was teaching her to drive, or perhaps learning himself.'

'And fancy his forgiving all the names she called him, and putting his teeth on the doorstep,' said Lucia. 'I believe there's more than meets the eye.'

'Oh, much more,' said he. 'You know she wanted to marry him and nearly got him, Diva says, just before we came here. She's having another go.'

'Clever of her,' said Lucia appreciatively. 'I didn't think she had so much ability. She's got him on the hop, you see, when he's ever so grateful for her forgiving him. But cunning, Georgie, rather low and cunning. And it's quite evident she's writing our adventures as hard as she can. It's a good thing I've wasted no time.'

'I should like to see her face when she comes back from her drive,' said Georgie. 'They were pasting the High Street with you, as I came. Friday afternoon, too: that's a good choice because it's early closing.'

'Yes, of course, that's why I chose it,' said Lucia. 'I don't think she can possibly be ready a whole day before me, and if she hires the Institute the day after me, nobody will go, because I shall have told them everything already. Then she can't have hired the Institute on the same day as I, because you can't have two lectures, especially on the same subject, going on in the same room simultaneously. Impossible.'

Grosvenor came in with the afternoon post.

'And one by hand, ma'am,' she said.

Lucia, of course, looked first at the one by hand. Nothing that came from outside Tilling could be as urgent as a local missive.

'Georgie!' she cried. 'Delicious complication! Elizabeth asks me – me – to attend her reading in the garden-room called "Lost to Sight", at three o'clock on Friday afternoon. Major Benjamin Flint has kindly consented to take the chair. At exactly that hour the Padre will be taking the chair at the Institute for me. I know what I shall do. I shall send a special invitation to Elizabeth to sit on the platform at my lecture, and I shall send another note to her two hours later as if I had only just received hers, to say that as I am lecturing myself that afternoon at the Institute, I much regret that, etc. Then she can't say I haven't asked her.'

'And when they come back from their drive this afternoon, she and Major Benjy,' cried Georgie, 'they'll see the High Street placarded with your notices. I've never been so excited before except when you came home.'

The tension next day grew very pleasant. Elizabeth, hearing that Lucia had taken the Institute, did her best to deprive her of an audience, and wrote personal notes not only to her friends of the immediate circle, but to chemists and grocers and auctioneers and butchers to invite them to the garden-room at Mallards at three o'clock on the day of battle in order to hear a *true* (underlined) account of her adventure. Lucia's reply to that was to make a personal canvass of all the shops, pay all her bills, and tell everyone that in the interval between the two sections of her lecture, tea would be provided gratis for the audience. She delayed this manoeuvre till Friday morning, so that there could scarcely be a counter-attack.

That same morning, the Padre, feeling that he must do his best to restore peace after the engagement that was now imminent, dashed off two notes to Lucia and Elizabeth, saying that a few friends (this was a lie because he had thought of it himself) had suggested to him how suitable it would be that he should hold a short service of thanksgiving for their escape from the perils of the sea and of cod-fisheries. He proposed therefore that this service should take place directly after the baptisms on Sunday afternoon. It would be quite short, a few prayers, the general thanksgiving, a hymn ('Fierce raged the tempest o'er the deep'), and a few words from himself. He hoped the two ladies would sit together in the front pew which had been occupied at the memorial service by the chief mourners. Both of them were charmed with the idea, for neither dared refuse for fear of putting herself in the wrong. So after about three forty-five on Sunday afternoon (and it was already two forty-five on Friday afternoon) there must be peace, for who could go on after that joint thanksgiving?

By three o'clock on Friday there was not a seat to be had at the Institute, and many people were standing. At the same hour every seat was to be had at the garden-room, for nobody was sitting down in any of them. At half-past three Lucia was getting rather mixed about the latitude and longitude of the Gallagher Bank, and the map had fallen down. At half-past three Elizabeth and Major Benjy were alone in the garden-room. It would be fatiguing for her, he said, to read again the lecture she had read him yesterday, and he wouldn't allow her to do it. Every word was already branded on his memory. So they seated themselves comfortably by the fire and Elizabeth began to talk of the loneliness of loneliness and of affinities. At half-past four Lucia's audience, having eaten their sumptuous tea, had ebbed away, leaving only Irene, Georgie, Mr and Mrs Wyse, and Mr and Mrs Padre to listen to the second half of the lecture. At half-past four in the garden-room Elizabeth and Major Benjy were engaged to be married. There was no reason for (in fact every reason against) a long engagement, and the banns would be put up in church next Sunday morning.

'So they'll all know about it, *Benjino mio*,' said Elizabeth, 'when we have our little thanksgiving service on Sunday afternoon, and I shall ask all our friends, Lucia included, to a cosy lunch on Monday to celebrate our engagement. You must send me across some of your best bottles of wine, dear.'

'As if you didn't know that all my cellar was at your disposal,' said he.

Elizabeth jumped up and clapped her hands.

'Oh, I've got such a lovely idea for that lunch,' she said. 'Don't ask me about it, for I shan't tell you. A splendid surprise for everybody, especially Lulu.'

Elizabeth was slightly chagrined next day, when she offered to read her lecture on practically any afternoon to the inmates of the workhouse, to find that Lucia had already asked all those who were not bedridden or deaf to tea at Grebe that very day, and hear an abridged form of what she had read at the Institute: an hour was considered enough, since perhaps some of them would find the excitement and the strain of a longer intellectual effort too much for them. But this chagrin was altogether wiped from her mind when on Sunday morning at the end of the second lesson the Padre published banns of marriage. An irrepressible buzz of conversation like a sudden irruption of bluebottle flies filled the church, and Lucia, who was sitting behind the choir and assisting the altos, said 'I thought so' in an audible voice. Elizabeth was assisting the trebles on the Cantoris side, and had she not been a perfect lady, and the scene a sacred edifice, she might have been tempted to put out her tongue or make a face in the direction of the Decani altos. Then in the afternoon came the service of thanksgiving, and the two heroines were observed to give each other a stage kiss. Diva, who sat in the pew immediately behind them, was certain that actual contact was not established. They resumed their seats, slightly apart.

As was only to be expected, notes of congratulation and acceptance to the lunch on Monday poured in upon the young couple. All the intimate circle of Tilling was there, the sideboard groaned with Major Benjy's most expensive wines, and everyone felt that the hatchet which had done so much interesting chopping in the past was buried, for never had two folk been so cordial to each other as were Lucia and Elizabeth.

They took their places at the table. Though it was only lunch there were menu cards, and written on them as the first item of the banquet was 'Lobster *à la Riseholme*'.

Georgie saw it first, though his claim was passionately disputed by Diva, but everybody else, except Lucia, saw it in a second or two and the gay talk dropped dead. What could have happened? Had Lucia, one day on the Gallagher Banks, given their hostess the secret which she had so firmly withheld? Somehow it seemed scarcely credible. The eyes of the guests, pair by pair, grew absorbed in meditation, for all were beginning to recall a mystery that had baffled them. The presence of Elizabeth in Lucia's kitchen when the flood poured in had never been fathomed, but surely ... A slight catalepsy seized the party, and all eyes were turned on Lucia who now for the first time looked at the menu. If she had given the recipe to Elizabeth, she would surely say something about it.

Lucia read the menu and slightly moistened her lips. She directed on Elizabeth a long penetrating gaze that mutely questioned her. Then the character of that look altered. There was no reproach in it, only comprehension and unfathomable contempt.

The ghastly silence continued as the lobster was handed round. It came to Lucia first. She tasted it and found that it was exactly right. She laid down her fork, and grubbed up the imperfectly buried hatchet.

'Are you sure you copied the recipe out quite correctly, *Elizabetha mia*?' she asked. 'You must pop into my kitchen some afternoon when you are going for your walk – never mind if I am in or not – and look at it again. And if my cook is out too, you will find the recipe in a book on the kitchen-shelf. But you know that, don't you?'

'Thank you, dear,' said Elizabeth. 'Sweet of you.'

Then everybody began to talk in a great hurry.

Lucia's Progress

I

Mrs Emmeline Lucas was walking briskly and elegantly up and down the cinder path which traversed her kitchen-garden and was so conveniently dry underfoot even after heavy rain. This house of hers, called 'Grebe', stood some quarter of a mile outside the ancient and enlightened town of Tilling, on its hill away to the west; in front there stretched out the green pasture-land of the marsh, flat and featureless, as far as the line of sand-dunes along the shore. She had spent a busy morning divided about equally between practising a rather easy sonata by Mozart and reading a rather difficult play by Aristophanes. There was the Greek on one page and an excellent English translation on the page opposite, and the play was so amusing that to-day she had rather neglected the Greek and pursued the English. At this moment she was taking the air to refresh her after her musical and intellectual labours, and felt quite ready to welcome the sound of that tuneful set of little bells in the hall which would summon her to lunch.

The January morning was very mild and her keen bird-like eye noted that several imprudent and precocious polyanthuses (she spoke and even thought of them as polyanthi) were already in flower, and that an even more imprudent tortoiseshell butterfly had been tempted from its hibernating quarters and was flitting about these early blossoms. Presently another joined it, and they actually seemed to be engaged in a decrepit dalliance quite unsuitable to their faded and antique appearance. The tortoiseshells appeared to be much pleased with each other, and Lucia was vaguely reminded of two friends of hers, both of mature years, who had lately married and with whom she was to play bridge this afternoon.

She inhaled the soft air in long breaths holding it in for five seconds according to the Yoga prescription and then expelling it all in one vigorous puff. Then she indulged in a few of those physical exercises, jerks and skippings and flexings which she found so conducive to health, pleased to think that a woman of her age could prance with such supple vigour. Another birthday would knock at her door next month, and if her birth certificate was correct (and there was no reason for doubting it) the conclusion was forced upon her that if for every year she had already lived, she lived another, she would then be a centenarian. For a brief moment the thought of the shortness of life and the all-devouring grave laid a chill on her spirit, as if a cold draught had blown round the corner of her house, but before she had time to shiver, her habitual intrepidity warmed her up again, and she resolved to make the most of the years that remained, although there might not be even fifty more in store for her. Certainly she would not indulge in senile dalliance, like those aged butterflies, for nothing made a woman so old as pretending to be young, and there would surely be worthier outlets for her energy than wantonness. Never yet had she been lacking in activity or initiative or even attack when necessary, as those ill-advised persons knew who from time to time had attempted to thwart her career, and these priceless gifts were still quite unimpaired.

It was a little over a year since the most remarkable adventure of her life so far had befallen her, when the great flood burst the river bank just across the road, and she and poor panic-stricken Elizabeth Mapp had been carried out to sea on the kitchen-table. They had been picked up by a trawler in the Channel and had spent three weird but very interesting months with a fleet of cod-fishers on the Gallagher Banks. Lucia's undefeated vitality had pulled them through, but since then she had never tasted cod. On returning home at grey daybreak on an April morning they had found that a handsome cenotaph had been erected to their memories in the churchyard, for Tilling had naturally concluded that they must be dead. But Tilling was wrong, and the cenotaph was immediately removed.

But since then, Lucia sometimes felt, she had not developed her undoubted horse-power to its full capacity. She had played

innumerable duets on the piano with Georgie Pillson: she had
constituted herself instructress in physical culture to the ladies
of Tilling, until the number of her pupils gradually dwindled
away and she was left to skip and flex alone: she had sketched
miles of marsh and been perfectly willing to hold classes in
contract bridge: she had visited the wards in the local hospital
twice a week, till the matron complained to Dr Dobbie that the
patients were unusually restless for the remainder of the day
when Mrs Lucas had been with them, and the doctor tactfully
told her that her vitality was too bracing for them (which was
probably the case). She had sung in the church choir; she had
read for an hour every Thursday afternoon to the inmates of
the workhouse till she had observed for herself that, long
before the hour was over, her entire audience was wrapped
in profound slumber; she had perused the masterpieces of
Aristophanes, Virgil and Horace with the help of a crib; she
had given a lecture on the 'Tendencies of Modern Fiction', at the
Literary Institute, and had suggested another on the 'Age of
Pericles', not yet delivered, as, most unaccountably, a suitable
date could not be arranged; but looking back on these multifarious activities, she found that they had only passed the time for
her without really extending her. To be sure there was the
constant excitement of social life in Tilling, where crises, plots
and counter-plots were endemic rather than epidemic, and
kept everybody feverish and with a high psychical temperature,
but when all was said and done (and there was always a great
deal to do, and a great deal more to say) she felt this morning,
with a gnawing sense of self-reproach, that if she had written
down all the achievements which, since her return from the
Gallagher Banks, were truly worthy of mention, the chronicle
would be sadly brief.

'I fear,' thought Lucia to herself, 'that the Recording Angel
will have next to nothing in his book about me this year. I've
been vegetating. *Molto cattiva!* I've been content (yet not
quite content: I will say that for myself) to be occupied with a
hundred trifles. I've been frittering my energies away over
them, drugging myself with the fallacy that they were important. But surely a woman in the prime of life like me could have

done all I have done as mere relaxations in her career. I must
do something more monumental (*monumentum œre perennius*,
isn't it?) in this coming year. I know I have the capacity for
high ambition. What I don't know is what to be ambitious
about. Ah, there's lunch at last.'

Lucia could always augur from the mode in which Grosvenor, her parlourmaid, played her prelude to food on those
tuneful chimes, in what sort of a temper she was. There were
six bells hung close together on a burnished copper frame, and
they rang the first six notes of an ascending major scale.
Grosvenor improvised on these with a small drumstick, and if
she was finding life a harmonious business she often treated
Lucia to charming dainty little tunes, quite a pleasure to listen
to, though sometimes rather long. Now and then there was an
almost lyrical outburst of melody, which caused Lucia a
momentary qualm of anxiety lest Grosvenor should have fallen
in love, and would leave. But if she felt morose or cynical, she
expressed her humour with realistic fidelity. To-day she struck
two adjoining bells very hard, and then ran the drumstick up
and down the peal, producing a most jangled effect, which
meant that she was jangled too. 'I wonder what's the matter:
indigestion perhaps,' thought Lucia, and she hurried indoors,
for a jangled Grosvenor hated to be kept waiting.

'Mr Georgie hasn't rung up?' she asked, as she seated herself.

'No, ma'am,' said Grosvenor.

'Nor Foljambe?'

'No, ma'am.'

'Is there no tomato sauce with the macaroni?'

'No, ma'am.'

Lucia knew better than to ask if she ached anywhere, for
Grosvenor would simply have said 'No, ma'am' again, and,
leaving her to stew in her own snappishness, she turned her
mind to Georgie. For over a fortnight now he had not been to
see her, and inquiries had only elicited the stark information
that he was keeping to the house, not being very well, but that
there was nothing to bother about. With Georgie such a
retirement might arise from several causes none of which need

arouse anxiety. Some little contretemps, thought Lucia: perhaps there was dental trouble, and change must be made in the furnishings of his mouth. Or he might have a touch of lumbago, and did not want to be seen hobbling and bent, instead of presenting his usual spry and brisk appearance. It was merely tactless when he assumed these invisibilities to ask the precise cause: he came out of them again with his hair more auburn than ever, or wreathed in smiles which showed his excellent teeth, and so one could guess.

But a fortnight was an unprecedentedly long seclusion, and Lucia determined to have a word with Foljambe when she came home in the evening. Foljambe was Georgie's peerless parlourmaid and also the wife of Lucia's chauffeur. She gave Cadman his early breakfast in the morning, and then went up to Georgie's house, Mallards Cottage, where she ministered all day to her master, returning home to her husband after she had served Georgie with his dinner. Like famous actresses who have married, she retained her maiden name, instead of becoming Mrs Cadman (which she undoubtedly was in the sight of God) since her life's work was Foljambizing to Georgie ... Then Grosvenor brought in the tomato sauce of which there were quantities, after Lucia had almost finished her macaroni, and by way of expressing penitence for her mistake, became more communicative, though hardly less morose.

'Foljambe won't say anything about Mr Georgie, ma'am,' she observed, 'except that he hasn't been outside his front door for over a fortnight nor seen anybody. Dr Dobbie has been in several times. You don't think it's something mental, ma'am, do you?'

'Certainly not,' said Lucia. 'Why should I think anything of the kind?'

'Well, my uncle was like that,' said Grosvenor. 'He shut himself up for about the same time as Mr Georgie, and then they took him away to the County Asylum, where he's thought himself to be the Prince of Wales ever since.'

Though Lucia poured scorn on this sinister theory, it made her more desirous of knowing what actually was the matter with Georgie. The news that the doctor had been to see him

disposed of the theory that a new chestnut-coloured *toupet* was
wanted, for a doctor would not have been needed for that,
while if he had been paying a round of visits to the dentist,
Foljambe would not have said that he had not been outside his
own front door, and an attack of lumbago would surely have
yielded to treatment before now. So, after telephoning to
Georgie suggesting, as she had often done before, that she
should look in during the afternoon, and receiving uncompromising discouragement, she thought she would walk
into Tilling after lunch and find what other people made of
this long retirement. It was Saturday and there would certainly
be a good many friends popping in and out of the shops.

Lucia looked at her engagement-book, and scribbled 'Mozart,
Aristophanes', as post-dated engagements for the morning of
to-day. She was due to play bridge at Mallards, next door to
Mallards Cottage, this afternoon at half-past three with Major
and Mrs Mapp-Flint: tea would follow and then more bridge.
For the last year contract had waged a deadly war with auction,
but the latter, like the Tishbites in King David's campaigns,
had been exterminated, since contract gave so much more
scope for violent differences of opinion about honour-tricks
and declarations and doublings and strong twos and takings-
out, which all added spleen and savagery to the game. There
were disciples of many schools of thought: one played Cul-
bertson, another one club, another two clubs, and Diva
Plaistow had a new system called 'Leeway', which she could
not satisfactorily explain to anybody, because she had not
any clearness about it herself. So, before a couple of tables
were started, there was always a gabble, as of priests of
various denominations reciting the articles of their faith. Mrs
Mapp-Flint was 'strong two', but her husband was 'one club'.
Consequently when they cut together their opponents had
to remember that when he declared one club, it meant that he
had strong outside suits, but possibly no club at all, but that when
his wife declared two clubs it meant that she certainly had
good clubs and heaps of other honour-tricks as well. Lucia
herself relied largely on psychic bids: in other words when she
announced a high contract in any suit, her partner had to guess

whether she held, say, a positive tiara of diamonds, or whether she was being psychic. If he guessed wrong, frightful disaster might result, and Elizabeth Mapp-Flint had once been justifiably sarcastic on the conclusion of one of these major débâcles. 'I see, dear,' she said, 'when you declare four diamonds, it means you haven't got any, and want to be taken out. So sorry: I shall know better another time.'

Lucia, as she walked up to Tilling, ran over in her head the various creeds of the rest of the players she was likely to meet. The Padre and his wife Evie Bartlett were sure to be there: he was even more psychic than herself, and almost invariably declared his weakest suit first, just to show he had not got any. Evie, his wife, was obliging enough to play any system desired by her partner, but she generally forgot what it was. Then Algernon and Susan Wyse would certainly be there: they need not be reckoned with, as they only declared what they thought they could get and meant what they said. The eighth would probably be Diva with her 'Leeway', of which, since she invariably held such bad cards, there was always a great deal to make up.

Lucia passed these systems in review, and then directed her stream of consciousness to her hostess, who, as Elizabeth Mapp, had been her timorous partner in the great adventure on the kitchen-table a year ago. She, at any rate, had not vegetated since their return, for she had married Major Benjamin Flint, and since he had only an Army Pension, and she was a woman of substance in every sense of the word, and owner of Mallards, it was only proper that she should hyphenate her surname with his. The more satirical spirits of Tilling thought she would have preferred to retain her maiden name like Foljambe and famous actresses. At the marriage service she had certainly omitted the word 'obey' when she defined what sort of wife she would make him. But the preliminary exhortation had been read in full, though the Padre had very tactfully suggested to the bride that the portion of it which related to children need not be recited: Elizabeth desired to have it all.

Immediately after the marriage the 'young couple' had left

Tilling, for Elizabeth had accepted the offer of a very good let for Mallards for the summer and autumn months, and they had taken a primitive and remote bungalow close to the golf-links two miles away, where they could play golf and taste romance in solitude. Mr and Mrs Wyse had been there to lunch occasionally and though Mr Wyse (such a gentleman) always said it had been a most enjoyable day, Susan was rather more communicative and let out that the food was muck and that no alcoholic beverage had appeared at table. On wet days the Major had occasionally come into Tilling by bus, on some such hollow pretext of having his hair cut, or posting a letter, and spent most of the afternoon at the Club where there was a remarkably good brand of port. Then Elizabeth's tenants had been so delighted with Mallards that they had extended their lease till the end of November, after which the Mapp-Flints, gorged with the gold of their rent-roll, had gone to the Riviera for the month of December, and had undoubtedly been seen by Mr Wyse's sister, the Contessa Faraglione, at the Casino at Monte Carlo. Thus their recent return to Tilling was a very exciting event, for nothing was really known as to which of them had established supremacy. Teetotalism at the bungalow seemed 'one up' to Elizabeth, for Benjy, as all Tilling knew, had a strong weakness in the opposite direction: on the other hand Mrs Wyse had hinted that the bride exhibited an almost degrading affection for him. Then which of them was the leading spirit in those visits to the Casino? Or were they both gamblers at heart? Altogether it was a most intriguing situation: the ladies of Tilling were particularly interested in the more intimate and domestic side of it, and expressed themselves with great delicacy.

Lucia came up the steep rise into the High Street and soon found some nice food for constructive observation. There was Foljambe just going into the chemist's, and Lucia, remembering that she really wanted a tooth-brush, followed her in, to hear what she ordered, for that might throw some light on the nature of Georgie's mysterious indisposition. But a packet of lint was vague as a clue, though it disposed of Grosvenor's dark suggestion that his illness was mental: lint surely never

cured lunacy. A little further on there was quaint Irene Coles
in trousers and a scarlet pullover, with her easel set up on the
pavement, so that foot-passengers had to step on to the roadway, making a highly impressionistic sketch of the street. Irene
had an almost embarrassing *schwärm* for Lucia, and she flung
her arms round her and upset her easel; but she had no news
of Georgie, and her conjecture that Foljambe had murdered
him and was burying him below the brick pillar in his back-
garden had nothing to support it.

'But it might be so, beloved,' she said. 'Such things do
happen, and why not in Tilling? Think of Crippen and Belle
Elmore. Let's suppose Foljambe gets through with the burial
to-day and replaces the pillar, then she'll go up there to-morrow
morning just as usual and tell the police that Georgie has
disappeared. Really I don't see what else it can be.'

Diva Plaistow scudded across the street to them. She always
spoke in the style of a telegram, and walked so fast that she
might be mistaken for a telegram herself. 'All too mysterious,'
she said, taking for granted what they were talking about. 'Not
seen since yesterday fortnight. Certainly something infectious.
Going to the Mapp-Flints, Lucia? Meet again then,' and she
whizzed away.

These monstrous suggestions did not arouse the least anxiety
in Lucia, but they vastly inflamed her curiosity. If Georgie's
ailment had been serious, she knew he would have told so old a
friend as herself: it must simply be that he did not want to be
seen. But it was time to go to the bridge-party, and she
retraced her steps a few yards (though with no definite scheme
in her mind) and turned up from the High Street towards the
church: this route, only a few yards longer, would lead her past
Mallards Cottage, where Georgie lived. It was dusk now, and
just as she came opposite that gabled abode, a light sprang up
in his sitting-room which looked on to the street. There was no
resisting so potent a temptation, and crossing the narrow
cobbled way she peered stealthily in. Foljambe was drawing
the curtains of the other window, and there was Georgie
sitting by the fire, fully dressed, with his head turned a little
away, doing his *petit point*. At that very moment he shifted in

his chair, and Lucia saw to her indescribable amazement that he had a short grey beard: in fact it might be called white. Just one glimpse she had, and then she must swiftly crouch down, as Foljambe crossed the room and rattled the curtains across the window into which she was looking. Completely puzzled but thrilled to the marrow, Lucia slid quietly away. Was he then in retirement only in order to grow a beard, feigning illness until it had attained comely if not venerable proportions? Common sense revolted at the notion, but common sense could not suggest any other theory.

Lucia rang the bell at Mallards, and was admitted into its familiar white-panelled hall which wanted painting so badly. On her first visit to Tilling, which led to her permanent residence here, she had taken this house for several months from Elizabeth Mapp and had adored it. Grebe, her own house, was very agreeable, but it had none of the dignity and charm of Mallards with its high-walled garden, its little square parlours, and, above all, with its entrancing garden-room, built a few yards away from the house itself, and commanding from its bow-window that unique view of the street leading down to the High Street, and, in the other direction, past Mallards Cottage to the church. The owner of Mallards ought not to let it for month after month and pig it in a bungalow for the sake of the rent. Mallards ought to be the centre of social life in Tilling. Really Elizabeth was not worthy of it: year after year she let it for the sake of the rent it brought her, and even when she was there she entertained very meagrely. Lucia felt very strongly that she was not the right person to live there, and she was equally strongly convinced as to who the right person was.

With a sigh she followed Withers out into the garden and up the eight steps into the garden-room. She had not seen the young couple since the long retirement of their honeymoon to the bungalow and to the garishness of Monte Carlo, and now even that mysterious phenomenon of Georgie with a grey, nearly white, beard faded out before the intense human interest of observing how they had adjusted themselves to matrimony . . .

'*Chérie!*' cried Mrs Elizabeth. 'Too lovely to see you again!

My Benjy-boy and I only got back two days ago, and since then it's been "upstairs and downstairs and in my lady's chamber", all day, in order to get things shipshape and comfy and *comme il faut* again. But now we're settled in, *n'est ce pas?'*

Lucia could not quite make up her mind whether these pretty Gallicisms were the automatic result of Elizabeth's having spent a month in France, or whether they were ironically allusive to her own habit of using easy Italian phrases in her talk. But she scarcely gave a thought to that, for the psychological balance between the two was so much more absorbing. Certainly Elizabeth and her Benjy-boy seemed an enamoured couple. He called her Liz and Girlie and perched himself on the arm of her chair as they waited for the rest of the gamblers to gather, and she patted his hand and pulled his cuff straight. Had she surrendered to him, Lucia wondered, had matrimony wrought a miraculous change in this domineering woman? The change in the room itself seemed to support the astounding proposition. It was far the biggest and best room in Mallards, and in the days of Elizabeth's virginity it had dripped with feminine knick-knacks, vases and china figures, and Tilling crockery pigs, screens set at angles, muslin blinds and riband-tied curtains behind which she sat in hiding to observe the life of the place. Here had been her writing-table close to the hot-water pipes and here her cosy corner by the fire with her work-basket. But now instead of her water-colours on the walls were heads of deer and antelopes, the spoil of Benjy's sporting expeditions in India, and a trophy consisting of spears and arrows and rhinoceros-hide whips and an apron made of shells, and on the floor were his moth-eaten tiger-skins. A stern business-table stood in the window, a leather chair like a hip-bath in her cosy corner, a gun stand with golf-clubs against the wall, and the room reeked of masculinity and stale cigar smoke. In fact, all it had in common with its old aspect was the big false book-case in the wall which masked the cupboard, in which once, for fear of lack of food during a coal strike, the prudent Elizabeth had stored immense quantities of corned beef and other nutritious provisions. All this change looked like surrender: Girlie Mapp had given up her best room to Benjy-boy Flint. Their little pats and tweaks at each other might have been put on merely as Company-manners suitable to a newly married couple, but the room itself furnished more substantial evidence.

The party speedily assembled: the Wyses' huge Rolls-Royce from their house fifty yards away hooted at the front door and Susan staggered in under the weight of her great sable coat, and the odour of preservatives from moth gradually overscored that of cigars. Algernon followed and made a bow and a polite speech to everybody. The Padre and Mrs Bartlett arrived next: he had been to Ireland for his holiday, and had acquired a touch of brogue which he grafted on to his Highland accent, and the effect was interesting, as if men of two nationalities were talking together of whom the Irishman only got in a word or two edgeways. Diva Plaistow completed the assembly and tripped heavily over the head of a one-eyed tiger. The other eye flew out at the shock of the impact and she put it, with apologies, on the chimneypiece.

The disposition of the players was easily settled, for there were three married couples to be separated, and Diva and Lucia made the fourth at each of the tables. Concentration settled down on the room like the grip of some intense frost, broken, at the end of each hand, as if by a sudden thaw, by torrential post mortems. At Lucia's table, she and Elizabeth were partners against Mr Wyse and the Padre. 'Begorra,' said he, 'the bhoys play the lassies. Eh, mon, there's a sair muckle job for the puir wee laddies agin the guid wives o' Tilling, begob.'

Though Elizabeth seemed to have surrendered to her Benjy-boy, it was clear that she had no thoughts of doing so to the other wee laddies, who, though vulnerable after the first hand, were again and again prevented from winning the rubber by preposterously expensive bids on Elizabeth's part.

'Yes, dear Lucia,' she said, 'three hundred down I'm afraid, but then it's worth six hundred to prevent the adversary from going out. Let me see, *qui donne?*'

'Key what?' asked the Padre.

'Who gives: I should say, who deals?'

'You do, dear Elizabeth,' said Lucia, 'but I don't know if it's worth quite so many three hundreds. What do you think?'

Lucia picked up a hand gleaming with high honours, but psychic silences were often as valuable as psychic declarations. The laddies, flushed with untold hundreds above, would be sure to declare something in order to net so prodigious a rubber, and she made no bid. Far more psychic to lure them on by modest overbidding and then crush them under a staggering double. But the timorous laddies held their tongues, the hands were thrown in and though Lucia tried to mingle hers with the rest of the pack, Elizabeth relentlessly picked it out and conducted a savage post mortem as if on the corpse of a regicide.

The rubber had to be left for the present, for it was long after tea-time. At tea a most intriguing incident took place, for it had been Major Benjy's invariable custom at these gatherings to have a whisky and soda or two instead of the milder refreshment. But to-day, to the desperate interest of those who, like Lucia, were intent on observing the mutual adjustments of matrimony, a particularly large cup was provided for him which, when everybody else was served, was filled to the brim by Elizabeth and passed to him. Diva noticed that, too, and paused in her steady consumption of nougat chocolates.

'And so *triste* about poor Mr Georgie,' said Elizabeth. 'I asked him to come in this afternoon, and he telephoned that he was too unwell: hadn't been out of his *maison* for more than a fortnight. What's the matter with him? You'll know, Lucia.'

Lucia and everybody else wondered which of them would have been left out if Georgie had come, or whether Elizabeth had asked him at all. Probably she had not.

'But indeed I don't know,' she said. 'Nobody knows. It's all very puzzling.'

'And haven't even you seen him? Fancy!' said Elizabeth. 'He must be terribly ill.'

Lucia did not say that actually she had seen him, nor did she mention his beard. She intended to find out what that meant before she disclosed it.

'Oh, I don't think that,' she said. 'But men like to be left quite alone when they're not the thing.'

Elizabeth kissed her finger-tips across the table to her husband. Really rather sickening.

'That's not the way of my little Benjy-boy,' she said. 'Why, he had a touch of chill out at Monte, and *pas un moment* did I get to myself till he was better. Wasn't it so, mischief?'

Major Benjy wiped his great walrus-moustache which had been dipped in that cauldron of tea.

'Girlie is a wizard in the sick-room,' he said. 'Bucks a man up more than fifty tonics. Ring Georgie up, Liz: say you'll pop in after dinner and sit with him.'

Lucia waited for the upshot of this offer with some anxiety. Georgie would certainly be curious to see Elizabeth after her marriage and it would be too shattering if he accepted this proposal after having refused her own company. Luckily nothing so lamentable happened. Elizabeth returned from the telephone in a very short space of time, a little flushed, and, for the moment, forgetting to talk French.

'Not up to seeing people,' she said, 'so Foljambe told me. A rude woman I've always thought: I wonder Mr Georgie can put up with her. Diva, dear, more chocolates? I'm sure there are plenty more in the cupboard. More tea, anybody? Benjy, dear, another cup? Shall we get back to our rubbers then? All so exciting!'

The wee laddies presently began to get as incautious as the guid wives. It was maddening to be a game up and sixty, and not to be allowed to secure one of the fattest scores above ever known in Sussex. Already it reached nearly to the top of the scoring-sheet, but now owing to penalties from their own overbidding, a second sky-scraper was mounting rapidly beside the first. Then the guid wives got a game, and the deadly process began again.

'*Très amusant!*' exclaimed Elizabeth, sorting her hand with a fixed smile, because it was so amusing, and a trembling hand because it was so agonizing. 'Now let me see; *que faire?*'

'Hold your hand a wee bitty higher, Mistress Mapp-Flint,' said the Padre, 'or sure I can't help getting a keek o't.'

'*Monsieur*, the more you keeked the less you'd like it,' said Elizabeth, scanning a hand of appalling rubbish. Quite legitimate to say that.

At this precise moment when Elizabeth was wondering whether it might not pay to be psychic for once, Major Benjy at the other table laid down his hand as dummy, and cast just one glance, quick as a lizard at the knotted face of his wife. 'Excuse me,' he said and quietly stole from the room. Elizabeth, so thought Diva, had not noticed his exit, but she certainly noticed his return, though she had got frightfully entangled in her hand, for Lucia had been psychic, too, and God knew what would happen . . .

'Not kept you waiting, I hope,' said Benjy stealing back. 'Just a telephone-message. Ha, we seem to be getting on, partner. Well, I must say, beautifully played.'

Diva thought these congratulations had a faint odour about them as if he had been telephoning to a merchant who dealt in spirituous liquors . . .

It was not till half-past seven that the great tussle came to an end, resulting in a complete wash-out, and the whole party, marvelling at the lateness of the hour, left in a great hurry so as not to keep dinner (or a tray) waiting. Mr Wyse vainly begged Lucia and Diva to be taken home in the Royce: it was such a dark night, he observed, but saw that there was a full moon, and it would be so wet underfoot, but he became aware that the pavements were bone-dry. So after a phrase or two in French from Elizabeth, in Italian from Lucia, in Scotch and Irish from the Padre, so that the threshold of Mallards resembled the Tower of Babel, Diva and Lucia went briskly down towards the High Street, both eager for a communing about the balance of the matrimonial equation.

'What a change, Diva!' began Lucia. 'It's quite charming to see what matrimony has done for Elizabeth. Miraculous, isn't it? At present there does not seem to be a trace left of her old cantankerousness. She seems positively to dote on him. Those little tweaks and dabs, and above all her giving up the garden-room to him: that shows there must be something real and heart-felt, don't you think? Fond eyes following him –'

'Not so sure about the fond eyes,' said Diva. 'Pretty sharp they looked when he came back from telephoning. Another kind of cup of tea was what he was after. That I'll swear to. Reeked!'

'No!' said Lucia. 'You don't say so!'

'Yes, I do. Teetotal lunches at the bungalow indeed! Rubbish. Whisky bottles, I bet, buried all over the garden.'

'Dear Diva, that's pure imagination,' said Lucia very nobly. 'If you say such things you'll get to believe them.'

'Ho! I believe them already,' said Diva. 'There'll be developments yet.'

'I hope they'll be happy ones, anyhow,' said Lucia. 'Of course, as the Padre would say, Major Benjy was apt to lift the elbow occasionally, but I shall continue to believe that's all done with. Such an enormous cup of tea: I never saw such a cup, and I think it's a perfect marriage. Perfect! I wonder –'

Diva chipped in.

'I know what you mean. They sleep in that big room overlooking the street. Withers told my cook. Dressing-room for Major Benjy next door; that slip of a room. I've seen him shaving at the window myself.'

Lucia walked quickly on after Diva turned into her house in the High Street. Diva was a little coarse sometimes, but in fairness Lucia had to allow that when she said 'I wonder', Diva had interpreted what she wondered with absolute accuracy. If she was right about the precise process of Major Benjy's telephoning, it would look as if matrimony had not wrought so complete a change in him as in his bride, but perhaps Diva's sense of smell had been deranged by her enormous consumption of chocolates.

Then like a faint unpleasant odour the thought of her approaching fiftieth birthday came back to her. Only this morning she had resolved to make a worthy use of the few years that lay in front of her and of the energy that boiled inside her, and to couple the two together and achieve something substantial. Yet, even while that resolve was glowing within her, she had frittered four hours away over tea and bridge, with vast expenditure of nervous force and psychic divination, and there was nothing to show for it except weariness of the brain, a few dubious conclusions as to the effect of matrimony on the middle-aged and a distaste for small cards ... Relaxation, thought Lucia in this sharp attack of moralizing, should be in itself productive. Playing duets with Georgie was productive because their fingers in spite of occasional errors, evoked the divine harmonies of Mozartino and Beethoven: when she made sketches of the twilight marsh her eye drank in the loveliness of Nature, but these hours of bridge, however strenuous, had not really enriched or refreshed her, and it was no use pretending that they had.

'I must put up in large capital letters over my bed "I am fifty",' she thought as she let herself into her house, 'and that will remind me every morning and evening that I've done nothing yet which will be remembered after I am gone. I've been busy (I will say that for myself) but beyond giving others a few hours of enchantment at the piano, and helping them to keep supple, I've done nothing for the world or indeed for Tilling. I must take myself in hand.'

The evening post had come in but there was nothing for her except a packet covered with seals which she knew must be her pass-book returned from the bank. She did not trouble to open it, and after a tray (for she had made a substantial tea) she picked up the evening paper, to see if she could find any hints about a career for a woman of fifty. Women seemed to be much to the fore: there was one flying backwards and forwards across the Atlantic, but Lucia felt it was a little late for her to take up flying: probably it required an immense amount of practice before you could, with any degree of confidence, start for New York alone, two or three thousand feet up in the air.

Then eight others were making a tour of pavilions and assembly rooms in towns on the South Coast, and entrancing everybody by their graceful exhibitions (in tights, or were their legs bare?) of physical drill; but on thinking it over, Lucia could not imagine herself heading a team of Tilling ladies, Diva and Elizabeth and Susan Wyse, with any reasonable hope of entrancing anybody. The pages of reviews of books seemed to deal entirely with novels by women, all of which were works of high genius. Lucia had long felt that she could write a marvellous novel, but perhaps there were enough geniuses already. Then there was a woman who, though it was winter, was in training to swim the Channel, but Lucia hated sea-bathing and could not swim. Certainly women were making a stir in the world, but none of their achievements seemed suited to the ambitions of a middle-aged widow.

Lucia turned the page. Dame Catherine Winterglass was dead at the age of fifty-five, and there was a long obituary notice of this remarkable spinster. For many years she had been governess to the children of a solicitor who lived at Balham, but at the age of forty-five she had been dismissed to make way for somebody younger. She had a capital of £500, and had embarked on operations on the Stock Exchange, making a vast fortune. At the time of her death she had a house in Grosvenor Square where she entertained Royalty, an estate at Mocomb Regis in Norfolk for partridge-shooting, a deer-forest in Scotland, and a sumptuous yacht for cruising in the Mediterranean; and from London, Norfolk, Ross-shire and the Riviera she was always in touch with the centres of finance. An admirable woman, too: hospitals, girl-guides, dogs' homes, indigent parsons, preventions of cruelty and propagations of the Gospel were the recipients of her noble bounty. No deserving case (and many undeserving) ever appealed to her in vain and her benefactions were innumerable. Right up to the end of her life, in spite of her colossal expenditure, it was believed that she grew richer and richer.

Lucia forgot all about nocturnal arrangements at Mallards, and read this account through again. What an extraordinary power money had! It enabled you not only to have everything you could possibly want yourself, but to do so much good, to relieve suffering, to make the world (as the Padre had said last Sunday) 'a better place'. Hitherto she had taken very little interest in money, being quite content every six months or so to invest a few hundred pounds from her constantly accruing balance in some gilt-edged security, the dividends from which added some negligible sum to her already ample income. But here was this woman who, starting with a total capital of a paltry five hundred pounds, had for years lived in Sybaritic luxury and done no end of good as well. 'To be sure,'.thought Lucia, 'she had the start of me by five years, for she was only forty-five when she began, but still . . .'

Grosvenor entered.

'Foljambe's back from Mr Georgie's ma'am,' she said. 'You told me you wanted to see her.'

'It doesn't matter,' said Lucia, deep in meditation about Dame Catherine. 'To-morrow will do.'

She let the paper drop, and fixed her gimlet eyes on the bust of Beethoven, for this conduced to concentration. She did not covet yachts and deer-forests but there were many things she would like to do for Tilling: a new organ was wanted at the church, a new operating-theatre was wanted at the hospital and she herself wanted Mallards. She intended to pass the rest of her days here, and it would be wonderful to be a great bene-factress to the town, a notable figure, a civic power and not only the Queen (she had no doubt about that) of its small social life. These benefactions and the ambitions for herself, which she had been unable to visualize before, outlined them-selves with distinctness and seemed wreathed together: the one twined round the other. Then the parable of the talents occurred to her. She had been like the unprofitable servant who, distrusting his financial ability, had wrapped it up in a napkin, for really to invest money in Government Stock was comparable with that, such meagre interest did it produce.

She picked up her paper again and turned to the page of financial news, and strenuously applied her vigorous mind to an article on the trend of markets by the City Editor. Those tedious gilt-edged stocks had fallen a little (as he had foreseen) but there was great activity in Industrials and in gold shares. Then there was a list of the shares which the City Editor had recommended to his readers a month ago. All of them (at least all that he quoted) had experienced a handsome rise: one had doubled in price. Lucia ripped open the sealed envelope contain-ing her pass-book and observed with a pang of retrospective remorse that it revealed that she had the almost indecent balance of twelve hundred pounds. If only, a month ago, she had invested a thousand of it in that share recommended by this clever City Editor each pound would have made another pound!

But it was no use repining, and she turned to see what the

wizard recommended now. Goldfields of West Africa were very promising, notably Siriami, and the price was eight to nine shillings. She did not quite know what that meant: probably there were two grades of shares, the best costing nine shillings, and a slightly inferior kind costing eight. Supposing she bought five hundred shares of Siriami and they behaved as those others had done, she would in a month's time have doubled the sum she had invested.

'I'm beginning to see my way,' she thought, and the way was so absorbing that she had not heard the telephone-bell ring, and now Grosvenor came in to say that Georgie wanted to speak to her. Lucia wondered whether Foljambe had seen her peeping in at his window this afternoon and had reported this intrusion, and was prepared, if this was the case and Georgie resented it, not exactly to lie about it, but to fail to understand what he was talking about until he got tired of explaining. She adopted that intimate dialect of baby-language with a peppering of Italian words in which they often spoke together.

'Is zat 'oo, *Georgino mio?*' she asked.

'Yes,' said Georgie in plain English.

'Lubly to hear your voice again. *Come sta?* Better I hope.'

'Yes, going on all right, but very slow. All too tarsome. And I'm getting dreadfully depressed seeing nobody and hearing nothing.'

Lucia dropped dialect.

'But, my dear, why didn't you let me come and see you before? You've always refused.'

'I know.'

There was a long pause. Lucia with her psychic faculties alert after so much bridge felt sure he had something more to say, and like a wise woman she refrained from pressing him. Clearly he had rung her up to tell her something, but found it difficult to bring himself to the point.

At last it came.

'Will you come in to-morrow then?'

'Of course I will. Delighted. What time?'

'Any time is the same to me,' said Georgie gloomily. 'I sit in this beastly little room all day.'

'About twelve then, after church?' she asked.

'Do. And I must warn you that I'm very much changed.'

('That's the beard,' thought Lucia.) She made her voice register deep concern.

'My dear, what do you mean?' she asked with a clever tremolo.

'Nothing to be anxious about at all, though it's frightful. I won't tell you because it's so hard to explain it all. Any news?'

That sounded better: in spite of this frightful change Georgie had his human interests alive.

'Lots: quantities. For instance, Elizabeth says *n'est ce pas* and *chérie*, because she's been to France.'

'No!' said Georgie with a livelier inflection. 'We'll have a good talk: lots must have happened. But remember there's a shocking change.'

'It won't shock *me*,' said Lucia. 'Twelve then, to-morrow. Good night, Georgino.'

'*Buona notte,*' said he.

2

Major Benjy was in church with his wife next morning: this was weighty evidence as regards her influence over him, for never yet had he been known to spend a fine Sunday morning except on the golf-links. He sat with her among the auxiliary choir sharing her hymn-book and making an underground sort of noise during the hymns. The Padre preached a long sermon in Scotch about early Christianity in Ireland which was somehow confusing to the geographical sense. After service Lucia walked away a little ahead of the Mapp-Flints, so that they certainly saw her ring the bell at Mallards Cottage and be admitted, and Elizabeth did not fail to remember that Georgie had said only yesterday afternoon that he was not up to seeing anybody. Lucia smiled and waved her hand as she went in to make sure Elizabeth saw, and Elizabeth gave a singularly mirthless smile in answer. As it was Sunday, she tried to feel pleased that he must be better this morning, but with only partial success. However, she would sit in the window of the garden-room and see how long Lucia stayed.

Georgie was not yet down and Lucia had a few minutes alone in his sitting-room among the tokens of his handiwork. There were dozens of his water-colour sketches on the walls, the sofa was covered with a charming piece of *gros point* from his nimble needle, and his new piece in *petit point*, not yet finished, lay on one of the numerous little tables. One window looked on to the street, the other on to a tiny square of flower-garden with a patch of crazy pavement surrounding a brick pillar on the top of which stood a replica of the Neapolitan Narcissus. Georgie had once told Lucia that he had just that figure when he was a boy, and with her usual tact she had assured him he had it still. There were large soft cushions in all the chairs, there was a copy of *Vogue*, a work-basket containing wools, a feather brush for dusting, a screen to shut off all draughts from the door, and a glass case containing his bibelots, including a rather naughty enamelled snuff-box: two young people – Then she heard his slippered tread on the stairs and in he came.

He had on his new blue suit: round his neck was a pink silk scarf with an amethyst pin to keep it in place, and above the scarf his face, a shade plumper than Narcissus's, thatched by his luxuriant auburn hair and decorated with an auburn moustache turned up at the ends, was now framed in a short grey, almost white beard.

'My dear, it's too dreadful,' he said. 'I know I'm perfectly hidjus, but I shan't be able to shave for weeks to come, and I couldn't bear being alone any longer. I tried to shave yesterday. Agonies!'

Dialectic encouragement was clearly the first thing to administer.

'Georgino! 'Oo vewy naughty boy not to send for me before,' said Lucia. 'If I'd been growing a *barba* – my dear, not *at all* disfiguring: rather dignified – do you think I should have said I wouldn't see you? But tell me all about it. I know nothing.'

'Shingles on my face and neck,' said Georgie. 'Blisters. Bandages. Ointments. Aspirin. Don't tell anybody. So degrading!'

'*Povero!* But I'm sure you've borne it wonderfully. And you're over the attack?'

'So they say. But it will be weeks before I can shave, and I can't go about before I do that. Tell me the news. Elizabeth rang me up yesterday, and offered to come and sit with me after dinner.'

'I know. I was there playing bridge and you, or Foljambe rather, said you weren't up to seeing people. But she saw me come in this morning.'

'No!' said Georgie. 'She'll hate that.'

Lucia sighed.

'An unhappy nature, I'm *afraid*,' she said. ' I waggled my hand and smiled at her as I stepped in, and she smiled back – how shall I say it? – as if she had been lunching on soused

mackerel and pickles instead of going to church. And all those
n'est ce pas-s as I told you yesterday.'

'But what about her and Benjy?' asked Georgie. 'Who wears
the trousers?'

'Georgie: it's difficult to say: I felt a man's eye was needed.
It looked to me as if they wore one trouser each. He's got the
garden-room as his sitting-room: horns and savage aprons on
the wall and bald tiger-skins on the floor. On the other hand
he had tea instead of whisky and soda at tea-time in an
enormous cup, and he was in church this morning. They dab
at each other about equally.'

'How disgusting!' said Georgie. 'You don't know how you
cheer me up.'

'So glad, Georgie. That's what I'm here for. And now I've
got a plan. No, it isn't a plan, it's an order. I'm not going to
leave you here alone. You're coming to stay with me at Grebe.
You needn't see anybody but me and me only when you feel
inclined. It's ridiculous your being cooped up here with no one
to talk to. Have your lunch and tell Foljambe to pack your
bags and order your car.'

Georgie required very little persuasion. It was a daring
proceeding to stay all alone with Lucia but that was not in its
disfavour. He was the professional *jeune premier* in social circles
at Tilling, smart and beautifully dressed and going to more
tea-parties than anybody else, and it was not at all amiss that he
should imperil his reputation and hers by these gay audacities.
Very possibly Tilling would never know, as the plan was that
he should be quite invisible till his clandestine beard was
removed, but if Tilling did then or later find out, he had no
objection. Besides, it would make an excellent opportunity for
his cook to have her holiday, and she should go off to-morrow
morning, leaving the house shut up. Foljambe would come up
every other day or so to open windows and air it.

So Lucia paid no long visit, but soon left Georgie to make
domestic arrangements. There was Elizabeth sitting at the
window of the garden-room, and she threw it open with
another soused mackerel smile as Lucia passed below.

'And how is our poor *malade*?' she asked. 'Better, I trust, since he is up to seeing friends again. I must pop in to see him after lunch.'

Lucia hesitated. If Elizabeth knew that he was moving to Grebe this afternoon, she would think it very extraordinary that she was not allowed to see him, but the secret of the beard must be inviolate.

'He's not very well,' she said. 'I doubt if he would see anybody else to-day.'

'And what's the matter exactly, *chérie*?' asked Elizabeth, oozing with the tenderest curiosity. Major Benjy, Lucia saw, had crept up to the window too. Lucia could not of course tell her that it was shingles, for shingles and beard were wrapped up together in one confidence.

'A nervous upset,' she said firmly. 'Very much pulled down. But no cause for anxiety.'

Lucia went on her way, and Elizabeth closed the window.

'There's something mysterious going on, Benjy,' she said. 'Poor dear Lucia's face had that guileless look which always means she's playing hokey-pokey. We shall have to find out what really is the matter with Mr Georgie. But let's get on with the crossword till luncheon: read out the next.'

By one of those strange coincidences, which admit of no explanation, Benjy read out:

'No. 3 down. A disease, often seen on the seashore.'

Georgie's move to Grebe was effected early that afternoon without detection, for on Sunday, during the hour succeeding lunch, the streets of Tilling were like a city of the dead. With his head well muffled up, so that not a hair of his beard could be seen, he sat on the front seat to avoid draughts, and, since it was not worth while packing all his belongings for so short a transit, Foljambe, sitting opposite him, was half buried under a loose moraine of coats, sticks, paint-boxes, music, umbrellas, dressing-gown, hot-water bottle and work-basket.

Hardly had they gone when Elizabeth, having solved the crossword except No. 3 down, which continued to baffle her, set about solving the mystery which, her trained sense assured her, existed, and she rang up Mallards Cottage with the inten-

tion of congratulating Georgie on being better, and of proposing to come in and read to him. Georgie's cook, who was going
on holiday next day and had been bidden to give nothing away,
answered the call. The personal pronouns in this conversation
were rather mixed as in the correspondences between Queen
Victoria and her Ministers of State.

'Could Mrs Mapp-Flint speak to Mr Pillson?'

'No, ma'am, she couldn't. Impossible just now.'

'Is Mrs Mapp-Flint speaking to Foljambe?'

'No, ma'am, it's me. Foljambe is out.'

'Mrs Mapp-Flint will call on Mr Pillson about 4.30.'

'Very good, ma'am, but I'm afraid Mr Pillson won't be able
to see her.'

The royal use of the third person was not producing much
effect, so Elizabeth changed her tactics, and became a com-
moner. She was usually an adept at worming news out of cooks
and parlourmaids.

'Oh, I recognize your voice, Cook,' she said effusively.
'Good afternoon. No anxiety, I hope, about dear Mr Georgie?'

'No, ma'am, not that I'm aware of.'

'I suppose he's having a little nap after his lunch.'

'I couldn't say, ma'am.'

'Perhaps you'd be so very kind as just to peep, oh, so
quietly, into his sitting-room and give him my message, if he's
not asleep.'

'He's not in his sitting-room, ma'am.'

Elizabeth rang off. She was more convinced than ever that
some mystery was afoot, and her curiosity passed from tender
oozings to acute inflammation. Her visit at 4.30 brought her
no nearer the solution, for Georgie's substantial cook blocked
the doorway, and said he was at home to nobody. Benjy on his
way back from golf met with no better luck, nor did Diva on
her way to evening church. All these kind inquiries were
telephoned to Georgie at Grebe: Tilling was evidently beginning to seethe, and it must continue to do so.

Lucia's household had been sworn to secrecy, and the two
passed a very pleasant evening. They had a grand duet on the
piano, and discussed the amazing romance of Dame Catherine

Winterglass who had become enshrined in Lucia's mind as a shining example of a conscientious woman of middle-age determined to make the world a better place.

'Really, Georgie,' she said, 'I'm ashamed of having spent so many years getting gradually a little richer without being a proper steward of my money. Money is a power, and I have been letting it lie idle, instead of increasing it by leaps and bounds like that wonderful Dame Catherine. Think of the good she did!'

'You might decrease it by leaps and bounds if you mean to speculate,' observed Georgie. 'It's supposed to be the quickest short cut to the workhouse, isn't it?'

'Speculation?' said Lucia. 'I abhor it. What I mean is studying the markets, working at finance as I work at Aristophanes, using one's brains, going carefully into all those prospectuses that are sent one. For instance, yesterday there was a strong recommendation in the evening paper to buy shares in a West African mine called Siriami, and this morning the City Editor of a Sunday paper gave the same advice. I collate those facts, Georgie. I reason that there are two very shrewd men recommending the same thing. Naturally I shall be very cautious at first, till I know the ropes, so to speak, and shall rely largely on my broker's advice. But I shall telegraph to him first thing tomorrow to buy me five hundred Siriami. Say they go up only a shilling – I've worked it all out – I shall be twenty-five pounds to the good.'

'My dear, how beautiful!' said Georgie. 'What will you do with it all?'

'Put it into something else, or put more into Siriami. Dame Catherine used to say that an intelligent and hard-working woman can make money every day of her life. She was often a bear. I must find out about being a bear.'

'I know what that means,' said Georgie. 'You sell shares you haven't got in order to buy them cheaper afterwards.'

Lucia looked startled.

'Are you sure about that? I must tell my broker to be certain that the man he buys my Siriami shares from has got them. I shall insist on that: no dealings with bears.'

Georgie regarded his needlework. It was a French design for a chair-back: a slim shepherdess in a green dress was standing among her sheep. The sheep were quite unmistakable but she insisted on looking like a stick of asparagus. He stroked the side of his beard which was unaffected by shingles.

'Tarsome of her,' he said. 'I must give her a hat or rip her clothes off and make her pink.'

'And if they went up two shillings I should make fifty pounds,' said Lucia absently.

'Oh, those shares: how marvellous!' said Georgie. 'But isn't there the risk of their going down instead?'

'My dear, the whole of life is a series of risks,' said Lucia sententiously.

'Yes, but why increase them? I like to be comfortable, but as long as I have all I want, I don't want anything more. Of course I hope you'll make tons of money, but I can't think what you'll do with it.'

'*Aspett'un po,' Georgino,'* said she. 'Why it's half-past ten. The invalid must go to bed.'

'Half-past ten: is it really?' said Georgie. 'Why, I've been going to bed at nine, because I was so bored with myself.'

Next morning Tilling seethed furiously. Georgie's cook had left before the world was a-stir, and Elizabeth, setting out with her basket about half-past ten to do her marketing in the High Street, observed that the red blinds in his sitting-room were still down. That was very odd: Foljambe was usually there at eight, but evidently she had not come yet: possibly she was ill, too. That distressing (but interesting) doubt was soon set at rest, for there was Foljambe in the High Street looking very well. Something might be found out from her, and Elizabeth put on her most seductive smile.

'Good morning, Foljambe,' she said. 'And how is poor Mr Georgie to-day?'

Foljambe's face grew stony, as if she had seen the Gorgon.

'Getting on nicely, ma'am,' she said.

'Oh, so glad! I was almost afraid you were ill, too, as his sitting-room blinds were down.'

'Indeed, ma'am,' said Foljambe, getting even more flintily petrified.

'And will you tell him I shall ring him up soon to see if he'd like me to look in?'

'Yes, ma'am,' said Foljambe.

Elizabeth watched her go along the street, and noticed she did not turn up in the direction of Mallards Cottage, but kept straight on. Very mysterious: where could she be going? Elizabeth thought of following her, but her attention was diverted by seeing Diva pop out of the hairdresser's establishment in that scarlet beret and frock which made her look so like a round pillar-box. She had taken the plunge at last after tortures of indecision, and had had her hair cropped quite close. The right and scathing thing to do, thought Elizabeth, was to seem not to notice any change in her appearance.

'Such a lovely morning, isn't it, dear Diva, for January,' she said. '*Si doux.* Any news?'

Diva felt there was enough news on her own head to satisfy anybody for one morning, and she wheeled so that Elizabeth should get a back view of it, where the change was most remarkable. 'I've heard none,' she said. 'Oh, there's Major Benjy. Going to catch the tram, I suppose.'

It was Elizabeth's turn to wheel. There had been a coolness this morning, for he had come down very late to breakfast, and had ordered fresh tea and bacon with a grumpy air. She would punish him by being unaware of him . . . Then that wouldn't do, because gossipy Diva would tell everybody they had had a quarrel, and back she wheeled again.

'Quick, Benjy-boy,' she called out to him, 'or you'll miss the tram. Play beautifully, darling. All those lovely mashies.'

Lucia's motor drew up close to them opposite the post-office. She had a telegraph form in her hand, and dropped it as she got out. It bowed and fluttered in the breeze, and fell at Elizabeth's feet. Her glance at it, as she picked it up, revealing the cryptic sentence: 'Buy five hundred Siriami shares,' was involuntary or nearly so.

'Here you are, dear,' she said. '*En route* to see poor Mr Georgie?'

Lucia's eye fell on Diva's cropped head.

'Dear Diva, I like it immensely!' she said. 'Ten years younger.'

Elizabeth remained profoundly unconscious.

'Well, I must be trotting,' she said. 'Such a lot of commissions for my Benjy. So like a man, bless him, to go off and play golf, leaving wifie to do all his jobs. Such a scolding I shall get if I forget any.'

She plunged into the grocer's, and for the next half-hour, the ladies of Tilling, popping in and out of shops, kept meeting on doorsteps with small collision of their baskets, and hurried glances at their contents. Susan Wyse alone did not take part in this ladies' chain, but remained in the Royce, and butcher and baker and greengrocer and fishmonger had to come out and take her orders through the window. Elizabeth felt bitterly about this, for, in view of the traffic, which would otherwise have become congested, tradesmen ran out of their shops, leaving other customers to wait, so that Susan's Royce might not be delayed. Elizabeth had addressed a formal complaint about it to the Town Council, and that conscientious body sent a reliable timekeeper in plain clothes down to the High Street on three consecutive mornings, to ascertain how long, on the average, Mrs Wyse's car stopped at each shop. As the period worked out at a trifle over twenty seconds they took the view that as the road was made for vehicular traffic, she was making a legitimate use of it. She could hardly be expected to send the Royce to the parking place by the Town Hall each time she stopped, for it would not nearly have got there by the time she was ready for it again. The rest of the ladies, not being so busy as Elizabeth, did not mind these delays, for Susan made such sumptuous orders that it gave you an appetite to hear them: she had been known, even when she and Algernon had been quite alone, to command a hen lobster, a pheasant, and a *pâté de foie gras* . . .

Elizabeth soon finished her shopping (Benjy-boy had only asked her to order him some shaving-soap), and just as she reached her door, she was astonished to see Diva coming rapidly towards her house from the direction of Mallards Cottage, thirty yards away, and making signs to her. After the severity with which she had ignored the Eton crop, it was clear that Diva must have something to say which overscored her natural resentment.

'The most extraordinary thing,' panted Diva as she got close, 'Mr Georgie's blinds –'

'Oh, is his sitting-room blind still down?' asked Elizabeth. 'I saw that an hour ago, but forgot to tell you. Is that all, dear?'

'Nowhere near,' said Diva. '*All* his blinds are down. Perhaps you saw that too, but I don't believe you did.'

Elizabeth was far too violently interested to pretend she had, and the two hurried up the street and contemplated the front of Mallards Cottage. It was true. The blinds of his dining-room, of the small room by the door, of Georgie's bedroom, of the cook's bedroom, were all drawn.

'And there's no smoke coming out of the chimneys,' said Diva in an awed whisper. 'Can he be dead?'

'Do not rush to such dreadful conclusions,' said Elizabeth. 'Come back to Mallards and let's talk it over.'

But the more they talked, the less they could construct any theory to fit the facts. Lucia had been very cheerful, Foljambe had said that Georgie was going on nicely, and even the two most ingenious women in Tilling could not reconcile this with the darkened and fireless house, unless he was suffering from some ailment which had to be nursed in a cold, dark room. Finally, when it was close on lunch-time, and it was obvious that Elizabeth was not going to press Diva to stay, they made their thoughtful way to the front door, still completely baffled. Till now, so absorbed had they been in the mystery, Diva had quite forgotten Elizabeth's unconsciousness of her cropped head. Now it occurred to her again.

'I've had my hair cut short this morning,' she said. 'Didn't you notice it?'

'Yes, dear, to be quite frank, since we are such old friends, I did,' said Elizabeth. 'But I thought it far kinder to say nothing about it. Far!'

'Ho!' said Diva, turning as red as her beret, and she trundled down the hill.

Benjy came back very sleepy after his golf, and in a foul
temper, for the Padre, who always played with him morning
and afternoon on Monday, to recuperate after the stress of
Sunday, had taken two half-crowns off him, and he was intending to punish him by not going to church next Sunday. In this
morose mood he took only the faintest interest in what might
or might not have happened to Georgie. Diva's theory seemed
to have something to be said for it, though it was odd that if he
was dead, there should not have been definite news by now.
Presently Elizabeth gave him a little butterfly kiss on his
forehead, to show she forgave him for his unpunctuality at
breakfast, and left him in the garden-room to have a good
snooze. Before his good snooze he had a good swig at a flask
which he kept in a locked drawer of his business-table.

Diva's theory was blown into smithereens next day, for Elizabeth from her bedroom window observed Foljambe letting
herself into Mallards Cottage at eight o'clock, and a short
stroll before breakfast showed her that blinds were up and
chimneys smoking, and the windows of Georgie's sitting-room
opened for an airing. Though the mystery of yesterday had not
been cleared up, normal routine had been resumed, and Georgie could not be dead.

After his sad lapse yesterday Benjy was punctual for breakfast
this morning. Half-past eight was not his best time, for during
his bachelor days he had been accustomed to get down about
ten o'clock, to shout 'Quai-hai' to show he was ready for his
food, and to masticate it morosely in solitude. Now all was
changed: sometimes he got as far as 'Quai', but Elizabeth
stopped her ears and said 'There is a bell, darling,' in her most
acid voice. And concerning half-past eight she was adamant:
she had all her household duties to attend to, and then after
she had minutely inspected the larder, she had her marketing
to do. Unlike him she was quite at her best and brightest
(which was saying a good deal) at this hour, and she hailed his
punctual advent to-day with extreme cordiality to show him
how pleased she was with him.

'Nice hot cup of tea for my Benjy,' she said, 'and dear me, what a disappointment – no, not disappointment: that wouldn't be kind – but what a surprise for poor Diva. Blinds up, chimneys smoking at Mr Georgie's, and there was she yesterday suggesting he was dead. Such a pessimist! I shan't be able to resist teasing her about it.'

Benjy had entrenched himself behind the morning paper, propping it up against the teapot and the maidenhair fern which stood in the centre of the table, and merely grunted. Elizabeth, feeling terribly girlish, made a scratching noise against it, and then looked over the top.

'Peep-o!' she said brightly. 'Oh, what a sleepy face! Turn to the City news, love, and see if you can find something called Siriami.'

A pause.

'Yes: West African mine,' he said. 'Got any, Liz? Shares moved sharply up yesterday: gained three shillings. Oh, there's a note about them. Excellent report received from the mine.'

'Dear me! how lovely for the shareholders, I wish I was one,' said Elizabeth with singular bitterness as she multiplied Lucia's five hundred shares by three and divided them by twenty. 'And what about my War Loan?'

'Down half a point.'

'That's what comes of being patriotic,' said Elizabeth, and went to see her cook. She had meant to have a roast pheasant for dinner this evening, but in consequence of this drop in her capital, decided on a rabbit. It seemed most unfair that Lucia should have made all that money (fifteen hundred shillings minus commission) by just scribbling a telegram, and dropping it in the High Street. Memories of a golden evening at Monte Carlo came back to her, when she and Benjy returned to their *pension* after a daring hour in the Casino with five hundred francs between them and in such a state of reckless elation that he had an absinthe and she a vermouth before dinner. They had resolved never to tempt fortune again, but next afternoon, Elizabeth having decided to sit in the garden and be lazy while he went for a walk, they ran into each other at the Casino, and an even happier result followed and there was more absinthe and vermouth. With these opulent recollections in her mind she bethought herself, as she set off with her market-basket for her shopping, of some little savings she had earmarked for the expenses of a rainy day, illness or repair to the roof of Mallards. It was almost a pity to keep them lying idle, when it was so easy to add to them . . .

Diva trundled swiftly towards her with Paddy, her great bouncing Irish terrier, bursting with news, but Elizabeth got the first word.

'All your gloomy anticipations about Mr Georgie quite gone phut, dear,' she said. 'Chimneys smoking, blinds up –'

'Oh, Lord, yes,' said Diva. 'I've been up to have a look already. You needn't have got so excited about it. And just fancy! Lucia bought some mining shares only yesterday, and she seems to have made hundreds and hundreds of pounds. She's telegraphing now to buy some more. What did she say the mine was? Syrian Army, I think.'

Elizabeth made a little cooing noise, expressive of compassionate amusement.

'I should think you probably mean Siriami, *n'est ce pas?*' she said. 'Siriami is a very famous gold mine somewhere in West Africa. *Mon vieux* was reading to me something about it in the paper this morning. But surely, dear, hundreds and hundreds of pounds is an exaggeration?'

'Well, quite a lot, for she told me so herself,' said Diva. 'I declare it made my mouth water. I've almost made up my mind to buy some myself with a little money I've got lying idle. Just a few.'

'I wouldn't if I were you, dear,' said Elizabeth earnestly. 'Gambling is such an insidious temptation. Benjy and I learned that at Monte Carlo.'

'Well, you made something, didn't you?' asked Diva.

'Yes, but I should always discourage anyone who might not be strong-minded enough to stop.'

'I'd back the strength of my mind against yours any day,' said Diva.

A personal and psychological discussion might have ensued, but Lucia at that moment came out of the post-office. She held in her hand a copy of the *Financial Post*.

'And have you bought some more Siriami?' asked Diva with a sort of vicarious greed.

Lucia's eyes wore a concentrated though far-away expression as if she was absorbed in some train of transcendent reasoning. She gave a little start as Diva spoke, and recalled herself to the High Street.

'Yes: I've bought another little parcel of shares,' she said. 'I heard from my broker this morning, and he agrees with me that they'll go higher. I find his judgment is usually pretty sound.'

'Diva's told me what a stroke of luck you've had,' said Elizabeth.

Lucia smiled complacently.

'No, dear Elizabeth, not luck,' she said. 'A little studying of the world-situation, a little inductive reasoning. The price of gold, you know: I should be much surprised if the price of gold didn't go higher yet. Of course I may be wrong.'

'I think you must be,' said Diva. 'There are always twenty shillings to the pound, aren't there?'

Lucia was not quite clear what was the answer to that. Her broker's letter, quite approving of a further purchase on the strength of the favourable news from the mine, had contained something about the price of gold, which evidently she had not grasped.

'Too intricate to explain, dear Diva,' she said indulgently. 'But I should be very sorry to advise you to follow my example. There is a risk. But I must be off and get back to Georgie.'

The moment she had spoken she saw her mistake. The only way of putting it right was to take the street that led up to Mallards Cottage and then get back to Grebe by a circuitous course, else surely Elizabeth would get on Georgie's track. Even as it was Elizabeth watched her till she had disappeared up the correct turning.

'So characteristic of the dear thing,' she said, 'making a lot of money in Siriami, and then advising you not to touch it! I shouldn't the least wonder if she wants to get all the shares herself and be created Dame Lucia Siriami. And then her airs, as if she was a great financier! Her views of the world-situation!

Her broker who agrees with her about the rising price of gold! Why she hadn't the slightest idea what it meant, anyone could see that. Diva, *c'est trop*! I shall get on with my humble marketing instead of buying parcels of gold.'

But behind this irritation with Lucia, Elizabeth was burning with the desire to yield to the insidious temptation of which she had warned Diva, and buy some Siriami shares herself. Diva might suspect her design if she went straight into the post-office, and so she crossed the street to the butcher's to get her rabbit. Out of the corner of her eye she saw Susan Wyse's car slowing up to stop at the same shop, and so she stood firm and square in the doorway, determined that that sycophantic vendor of flesh-food should not sneak out to take Susan's order before she was served herself, and that should take a long time. She would spin the rabbit out.

'Good morning, Mr Worthington,' she said in her most chatty manner. 'I just looked in to see if you've got anything nice for me to give the Major for his dinner tonight. He'll be hungry after his golfing.'

'Some plump young pheasants, ma'am,' said Mr Worthington. He was short, but by standing on tiptoe he could see that Susan's car had stopped opposite his shop, and that her large round face appeared at the window.

'Well, that does sound good,' said Elizabeth. 'But let me think. Didn't I give him a pheasant a couple of days ago?'

'Excuse me, ma'am, one moment,' said this harassed tradesman. 'There's Mrs Wyse –'

Elizabeth spread herself a little in the doorway with her basket to reinforce the barricade. Another car had drawn up on the opposite side of the street, and there was a nice congestion forming. Susan's chauffeur was hooting to bring Mr Worthington out and the car behind him was hooting because it wanted to get by.

'You haven't got a wild duck, I suppose,' said Elizabeth, gloating on the situation. 'The Major likes a duck now and then.'

'No ma'am. Mallards, if you'll excuse me, is over.'

More hoots and then an official voice.

'Move on, please,' said the policeman on point duty to Susan's chauffeur. 'There's a block behind you and nothing in front.'

Elizabeth heard the purr of the Royce as it moved on, releasing the traffic behind. Half-turning she could see that it drew up twenty yards further on and the chauffeur came back and waited outside the doorway which she was blocking so efficiently.

'Not much choice then,' said Elizabeth. 'You'd better send me up a rabbit, Mr Worthington. Just a sweet little bunny, a young one mind –'

'Brace of pheasants to Mrs Wyse,' shouted the chauffeur through the window, despairing of getting in.

'Right-o,' called Mr Worthington. 'One rabbit then, ma'am; thank you.'

'Got such a thing as a woodcock?' called the chauffeur.

'Not fit to eat to-day,' shouted Mr Worthington. 'Couple of snipe just come in.'

'I'll go and ask.'

'Oh, Mr Worthington, why didn't you tell me you'd got a couple of snipe?' said Elizabeth. 'Just what the Major likes. Well, I suppose they're promised now. I'll take my bunny with me.'

All this was cheerful work: she had trampled on Susan's self-assumed right to hold up traffic till she lured butchers out into the street to attend to her, and with her bunny in her basket she crossed to the post-office again. There was a row of little boxes like mangers for those who wanted to write telegrams, and she took one of these, putting her basket on the floor behind her. As she composed this momentous telegram for the purchase of three hundred Siriami shares and the denuding of the rainy-day fund, she heard a mixed indefinable hubbub at her back and looking round saw that Diva had come in with Paddy, and that Paddy had snatched bunny from the basket, and was playing with him very prettily. He tossed him in the air, and lay down with a paw on each side of him, growling in a menacing manner as he pretended to worry him. Diva who had gone to the counter opposite with a telegram in her hand was commanding Paddy to drop it, but Paddy leaped up, squeezed himself through the swing-door and mounted guard over his prey on the pavement. Elizabeth and Diva rushed out after him and by dint of screaming 'Trust, Paddy!' Diva induced her dog to drop bunny.

'So sorry, dear Elizabeth,' she said, smoothing the rumpled fur. 'Not damaged at all, I think.'

'If you imagine I'm going to eat a rabbit mangled by your disgusting dog –' began Elizabeth.

'You shouldn't have left it lying on the floor,' retorted Diva. 'Public place. Not my fault.'

Mr Worthington came nimbly across the street, unaware that he was entering a storm-centre.

'Mrs Wyse doesn't need that couple of snipe, ma'am,' he said to Elizabeth. 'Shall I send them up to Mallards?'

'I'm surprised at your offering me Mrs Wyse's leavings,' said Elizabeth. 'And charge the rabbit I bought just now to Mrs Plaistow.'

'But I don't want a rabbit,' said Diva. 'As soon eat rats.'

'All I can say is that it's not mine,' said Elizabeth.

Diva thought of something rather neat.

'Oh, well, it'll do for the kitchen,' she said, putting it in her basket.

'Diva dear, don't let your servants eat it,' said Elizabeth. 'As likely as not it would give them hydrophobia.'

'Pooh!' said Diva. 'Bet another dog carried it when it was shot. Oh, I forgot my telegram.'

'I'll pick out a nice young plump one for you, ma'am, shall I?' said Mr Worthington to Elizabeth.

'Yes, and mind you only charge one to me.'

The two ladies went back into the post-office with Paddy and the rabbit to finish the business which had been interrupted by that agitating scene on the pavement. Elizabeth's handwriting was still a little ragged with emotion when she handed her telegram in, and it was not (except the address which had been written before) very legible. In fact the young lady could not be certain about it.

'Buy "thin bunkered Simiawi" is it?' she asked.

'No, three hundred Siriami,' said Elizabeth, and Diva heard. Simultaneously Diva's young lady asked: 'Is it Siriami?' and Elizabeth heard. So both knew.

They walked back together very amicably as far as Diva's house, quite resolved not to let a rabbit wreck or even threaten so long-standing a friendship. Indeed there was no cause for friction any more, for Diva had no objection to an occasional rabbit for the kitchen, and Elizabeth saw that her bunny was far the plumper of the two. As regards Siriami, Diva had a distinct handle against her friend, in case of future emergencies, for she knew that Elizabeth had solemnly warned her not to buy them and had done so herself: she knew, too, how many Elizabeth had bought, in case she swanked about her colossal holding, whereas nobody but the young lady to whom she handed her telegram, knew how many she had bought. So they both quite looked forward to meeting that afternoon for bridge at Susan Wyse's.

Marketing had begun early this morning, and though highly sensational, had been brief. Consequently, when Elizabeth turned up the street towards Mallards, she met her Benjy just starting to catch the eleven o'clock tram for the golf-links. He held a folded piece of paper in his hand, which, when he saw her, he thrust into his pocket.

'Well, boy o' mine, off to your game?' she asked. 'Look, such a plump little bunny for dinner. And news. Lucia has become a great financier. She bought Siriami yesterday and again to-day.'

Should she tell him she had bought Siriami too? On the whole, not. It was her own private rainy-day fund she had raided, and if, by some inscrutable savagery of Providence, the venture did not prosper, it was better that he should not know. If, on the other hand, she made money, it was wise for a married woman to have a little unbeknownst store tucked away.

'Dear me, that's a bit of luck for her, Liz,' he said.

Elizabeth gave a gay little laugh.

'No, dear, you're quite wrong,' she said. 'It's inductive reasoning, it's study of the world-situation. How pleasant for her to have all the gifts. Bye-bye.'

She went into the garden-room, still feeling very sardonic about Lucia's gifts, and wondering in an undercurrent why Benjy had looked self-conscious. She could always tell when he was self-conscious, for instead of having a shifty eye, he had quite the opposite kind of eye; he looked at her, as he had done just now, with a sort of truculent innocence, as if challenging her to suspect anything. Then that piece of paper which he had thrust into his pocket, linked itself up. It was rather like a telegraph form, and instantly she wondered if he had been buying Siriami, too, out of his exiguous income. Very wrong of him, if he had, and most secretive of him not to have told her so. Sometimes she felt that he did not give her his full confidence, and that saddened her. Of course it was not actually proved yet that he had bought Siriami, but cudgel her brains as she might, she could think of nothing else that he could have been telegraphing about. Then she calculated afresh what she stood to win if Siriami went up another three shillings, and sitting down on the hot-water pipes in the window which commanded so wide a prospect, she let her thoughts stray back to Georgie. Even as she looked out she saw Foljambe emerge from his door, and without a shadow of doubt she locked it after her.

The speed with which Elizabeth jumped up was in no way due to the heat of the pipes. A flood of conjectures simply swept her off them. Lucia had gone up to see Georgie less than half an hour ago, so had Foljambe locked her and Georgie up together? Or had Foljambe (in case Lucia had already left) locked Georgie up alone with his cook? She hurried out for the second time that morning to have a look at the front of the house. All blinds were down.

3

Confidence was restored between the young couple at Mallards next morning in a manner that the most ingenious could hardly have anticipated. Elizabeth heard Benjy go thumping downstairs a full five minutes before breakfast-time, and peeping out from her bedroom door in high approval she called him a good laddie and told him to begin without her. Then suddenly she remembered something and made the utmost haste to follow. But she was afraid she would be too late.

Benjy went straight to the dining-room, and there on the table with *The Times* and *Daily Mirror,* were two copies of the *Financial Post.* He had ordered one himself for the sake of fuller information about Siriami, but what about the other? It seemed unlikely that the newsagent had sent up two copies when only one was ordered. Then hearing Elizabeth's foot on the stairs, he hastily sat down on one copy, which was all he was responsible for, and she entered.

'Ah, my *Financial Post,*' she said. 'I thought it would be amusing, dear, just to see what was happening to Lucia's gold mine. I take such an interest in it for her sake.'

She turned over the unfamiliar pages, and clapped her hands in sympathetic delight.

'Oh, Benjy-boy, isn't that nice for her?' she cried. 'Siriami has gone up another three shillings. Quite a fortune!'

Benjy was just as pleased as Elizabeth, though he marvelled at the joy that Lucia's enrichment had given her.

'No! That's tremendous,' he said. 'Very pleasant indeed.'

'Lovely!' exclaimed Elizabeth. 'The dear thing! And an article about West African mines. Most encouraging prospects, and something about the price of gold: the man expects to see it higher yet.'

Elizabeth grew absorbed over this, and let her poached egg get cold.

'I see what it means!' she said. 'The actual price of gold itself is going up, just as if it was coals or tobacco, so of course the gold they get out of the mine is worth more. Poor muddle-headed Diva, thinking that the number of shillings in a pound had something to do with it! And Diva will be pleased too. I know she bought some shares yesterday, after the rabbit, for she sent a telegram, and the clerk asked if a word was Siriami.'

'Did she indeed?' asked Benjy. 'How many?'

'I couldn't see. Ring the bell, dear, and don't shout *Quai-hai*. Withers has forgotten the pepper.'

Exultant Benjy forgot about his copy of the *Financial Post*, on which he was sitting, and disclosed it.

'What? Another *Financial Post*?' cried Elizabeth. 'Did you order one, too? Oh, Benjy, make a clean breast of it. Have you been buying Siriami as well as Lucia and Diva?'

'Well, Liz, I had a hundred pounds lying idle. And not such a bad way of using them after all. A hundred and fifty shares. Three times that in shillings. Pretty good.'

'Secretive one!' said Elizabeth. 'Naughty!'

Benjy had a brain-wave.

'And aren't you going to tell me how many you bought?' he asked.

Evidently it was no use denying the imputation. Elizabeth instinctively felt that he would not believe her, for her joy for Lucia's sake must already have betrayed her.

'Three hundred,' she said. 'Oh, what fun! And what are we to do next? They think gold will go higher. Benjy, I think I shall buy some more. What's the use of, say, a hundred pounds in War Loan earning three pound ten a year? I shouldn't miss three pound ten a year ... But I must get to my jobs. Not sure that I won't treat you to a woodcock to-night, if Susan allows me to have one.'

In the growing excitement over Siriami, Elizabeth got quite indifferent as to whether the blinds were up or down in the windows of Georgie's house. During the next week the shares continued to rise, and morning after morning Benjy appeared with laudable punctuality at breakfast, hungry for the *Financial Post*. An unprecedented extravagance infected both him and

Elizabeth: sometimes he took a motor out to the links, for what did a few shillings matter when Siriami was raining so many on him, and Elizabeth vied with Susan in luxurious viands for the table. Bridge at threepence a hundred, which had till lately aroused the wildest passions, failed to thrill, and next time the four gamblers, the Mapp-Flints and Diva and Lucia, met for a game, they all agreed to play double the ordinary stake, and even at that enhanced figure a recklessness in declaration, hitherto unknown, manifested itself. They lingered over tea discussing gold and the price of gold, the signification of which was now firmly grasped by everybody, and there were frightful searchings of heart on the part of the Mapp-Flints and Diva as to whether to sell out and realize their gains, or to invest more in hopes of a further rise. And never had Lucia shown herself more nauseatingly Olympian. She referred to her 'few shares' when everybody knew she had bought five hundred to begin with and had made one if not two more purchases since, and she held forth as if she was a City Editor herself.

'I was telephoning to my broker this morning,' she began.

'What? A trunk-call?' interrupted Diva. 'Half a crown, isn't it?'

'Very likely: and put my view of the situation about gold before him. He agreed with me that the price of gold was very high already, and that if, as I suggested, America might come off the gold standard – however, that is a very complicated problem; and I hope to hear from him to-morrow morning about it. Then we had a few words about English rails. Undeniably there have been much better traffic returns lately, and I am distinctly of the opinion that one might do worse –'

Diva was looking haggard. She ate hardly any chocolates, and had already confessed that she was sleeping very badly.

'Don't talk to me about English rails,' she said. 'The price of gold is worrying enough.'

Lucia spread her hands wide with a gesture of infinite capacity.

'You should enlarge your horizon, Diva,' she said. 'You should take a broad, calm view of world-conditions. Look at the markets, gold, industrials, rails as from a mountain height;

get a panoramic view. My few shares in Siriami have certainly given me a marvellous profit, and I am beginning to ask myself whether there is not more chance of capital-appreciation, if you follow me, elsewhere. Silver, for instance, is rising – nothing to do with the number of pennies in a shilling – one has to consider that. I feel very responsible, for Georgie has bought a little parcel – we call it – of Siriami on my advice. If one follows silver, I don't think one could do better – and my broker agrees – than to buy a few Burma Corporation. I am thinking seriously of clearing out of Siriami, and investing there. Wonderfully interesting, is it not?'

'It's so interesting that it keeps me awake,' said Diva. 'From one o'clock to two this morning, I thought I would buy more, and from six to seven I thought I would sell. I don't know which to do.'

Elizabeth rose. Lucia's lecture was quite intolerable. Evidently she was constituting herself a central bureau for the dispensing of financial instruction. So characteristic of her: she must boss and direct everybody. There had been her musical parties at which all Tilling was expected to sit in a dim light and listen to her and Georgie play endless sonatas. There had been her gymnastic class, now happily defunct, for the preservation of suppleness and slimness in middle-age, and when contract bridge came in she had offered to hold classes in that. True, she had been the first cause of the enrichment of them all by the purchase of Siriami, but no one could go on being grateful for ever, and Elizabeth's notable independence of character revolted against the monstrous airs she exhibited, and inwardly she determined that she would do exactly the opposite of anything Lucia recommended.

'Thank you, dear,' she said, 'for all you've told us. Most interesting and instructive. How wonderfully you've grasped it all! Now do you think we may go back to our bridge before it gets too late to begin another rubber? And I declare I haven't asked about *notre pauvre ami*, Mr Georgie. One hasn't seen him about yet, though Foljambe always tells me he's much better. And such odd things happen at his house. One day all his blinds will be down, as if the house was empty, and the next there'll be Foljambe coming at eight in the morning as usual.'

'No! What a strange thing!' said Lucia.

Diva managed to eat just one of those nougat chocolates of which she generally emptied the dish. It was lamentable how little pleasure it gave her, and how little she was thrilled by the mystery of those drawn blinds.

'I noticed that too,' she said. 'But then I forgot all about it.'

'Not before you suggested he was dead, dear,' said Elizabeth. 'I only hope Foljambe looks after him properly.'

'I saw him this morning,' said Lucia. 'He has everything he wants.'

The bridge was of a character that a week ago would have aroused the deepest emotions. Diva and Lucia played against the family and won three swift rubbers at these new dizzy points. There were neither vituperations between the vanquished nor crows of delight from the victors, and though at the end Diva's scoring, as usual, tallied with nobody's, she sacrificed a shilling without insisting that the others should add up again. There was no frenzy, there was no sarcasm even when Benjy doubled his adversaries out or when Elizabeth forgot he always played the club convention, and thought he had some. All was pale and passionless; the sense of the vast financial adventures going on made it almost a matter of indifference who won. Occasionally, at the end of a hand Lucia gave a short exposition of the psychic bid which had so flummoxed her opponents, but nobody cared.

Diva spent the evening alone without appetite for her tray. She took Paddy out for his stroll observing without emotion that someone, no doubt in allusion to him, had altered the notice of 'No Parking' outside her house to 'No Barking'. It scarcely seemed worth while to erase that piece of wretched bad taste, and as for playing patience to beguile the hour before bedtime, she could not bother to lay the cards out, but sat in front of her fire re-reading the City news in yesterday's and to-day's papers. She brooded over her note of purchase of Siriami shares: she made small addition sums in pencil on her blotting-paper: the greed for gold caused her to contemplate buying more: the instinct of prudence prompted her to write a telegram to her broker to sell out her entire holding. 'Which shall I do? Oh, which shall I do?' she muttered to herself. Ten struck and eleven: it was long after her usual bedtime on solitary evenings, and eventually she fell into a doze. From that she passed into deep sleep and woke with her fire out and her clock on the stroke of midnight, but with her mind made up. 'I shall sell two of my shares and keep the other three,' she said aloud.

For the first time for many nights she slept beautifully till she was called, and woke fresh and eager for the day. There on her dressing-table lay the three half-crowns which she had taken from Elizabeth the evening before. They had seemed then but joyless and negligible tokens: now they gleamed with their accustomed splendour. 'And to think that I won all that without really enjoying it,' thought Diva, as she performed a few of those salubrious flexes and jerks which Lucia had taught her. Just glancing at the *Financial Post* she saw that Siriami had gone up another sixpence, but she did not falter in her prudent determination to secure some part of her profits.

The same crisis which, for Diva, had sucked all the sweetness out of life but supplied Lucia with grist for the Imitation of Dame Catherine Winterglass. Georgie, with a white pointed beard (that clever Foljambe had trimmed it for him, as neatly as if she had been a barber all her life), came down to breakfast for the first time this morning, and pounced on the *Financial Post*.

'My dear, another sixpence up!' he exclaimed. 'What shall I do?'

Lucia already knew that: she had taken a swift glance at the paper before he came down, and had replaced it as if undisturbed. She shook a finger at him.

'Now, Georgie, what about my rule that we have no business-talk at meals? How are you? That's much more important.'

'Beautiful night,' said Georgie, 'except that I dreamt about a gold mine and the bottom fell out of it, and all the ore slid down to the centre of the earth.'

'That will never do, Georgie. You must not let money get on your mind. I'll attend to your interests when I get to work after breakfast. And are your face and neck better?'

'Terribly sore still. I don't know when I shall be able to shave.'

Lucia gave him a glance with head a little tilted, as if he was a landscape she proposed to paint. That neat beard gave character and distinction to his face. It hid his plump second chin and concealed the slightly receding shape of the first: another week's growth would give it a greater solidity. There was something Stuart-like, something Vandyckish about his face. To be sure the colour of his beard contrasted rather strangely with his auburn hair and moustache, in which not the faintest hint of grey was manifest, but that could be remedied. It was not time, however, to say anything about that yet.

'Don't think about it then,' she said. 'And now for to-day. I really think you ought to get some air. It's so mild and sunny. Wrap up well and come for a drive with me before lunch.'

'But they'll see me,' said Georgie.

'Not if you lean well back till we're out of the town. I shall walk up there when I've gone into my affairs and yours, for I'm sure to have a telegram to send, and the car shall take you and Foljambe straight up to your house. I shall join you, so that we shall appear to be starting from there. Now I must get to work. I see there's a letter from my broker.'

Lucia's voice had assumed that firm tone which Georgie knew well to betoken that she meant to have her way, and that all protest was merely a waste of nervous force. Off she went to the little room once known as the library, but now more properly to be called the Office. This was an inviolable sanctuary: Grosvenor had orders that she must never be disturbed there except under stress of some great emergency, such as a trunk-call from London. The table where Lucia used to sit with her Greek and Latin dictionaries and the plays of Aristophanes and the Odes of Horace with their English translations was now swept clean of its classical lore, and a ledger stood there, a bundle of prospectuses, some notes of purchase and a clip of communications from her broker. She opened the letter she had received this morning, and read it with great care. The rise in gold (and in consequence in gold mines) he thought had gone far enough and he repeated his suggestion that home-rails and silver merited attention. There lay the annual report of Burma Corporation, and a very confusing document she found it, for it dealt with rupees and annas instead of pounds and shillings, and she did not know the value of an anna or what relation it bore to a rupee: they might as well have been drachmas and obols. Then there was a statement about the earnings of the Great Western Railway (Lucia had no idea how many people went by train), and another about the Southern Railway showing much improved traffics. Once more she referred to her broker's last two letters, and then, with the dash and decision of Dame Catherine, made up her mind. She would sell out her entire holding in Siriami, and Burma Corporation and Southern Rails Preferred should enact a judgment of Solomon on the proceeds and each take half. She felt that she was slighting that excellent line, the Great Western, but it must get on without her support. Then she wrote out the necessary telegram to her broker, and touched the bell on her table. Grosvenor, according to orders, only opened the door an inch or two, and Lucia sent for Georgie.

Like a client he pulled a high chair up to the table.

'Georgie, I've gone very carefully into the monetary situation,' she said, 'and I am selling all my Siriami. As you and others in Tilling followed me in your little purchases, I feel it my duty to tell you all what I am doing.'

Georgie gave a sigh of relief, as when a very rapid movement in a piano duet came to an end.

'I shall sell, too, then,' he said. 'I'm very glad. I'm not up to the excitement after my shingles. It's been very pleasant because I've made fifty pounds, but I've had enough. Will you take a telegram for me when you go?'

Lucia closed her ledger, put a paper-weight on her prospectuses, and clipped Mammoncash's letter into its sheaf.

'I think – I say I think – that you're right, Georgie,' she said. 'The situation is becoming too difficult for me to advise about, and I am glad you have settled to clear out, so that I have no further responsibility. Now I shall walk up to Tilling – I find these great decisions very stimulating – and a quarter of an hour later, you will start in the car with Foljambe. I think – I say I think – that Mammoncash, my broker you know, telegraphic address, will approve my decision.'

As he had already strongly recommended this course, it was probable he would do so, and Lucia walked briskly up to the High Street. Then, seeing Benjy and Elizabeth hanging about outside the post-office, she assumed a slower gait and a rapt, financial face.

'*Bon jour, chérie*,' said Elizabeth, observing that she took two telegrams out of her bag. 'Those sweet Siriamis. Up another sixpence.'

Lucia seemed to recall her consciousness from an immense distance, and broke the transition in Italian.

'*Ah, si, si! Buono piccolo Siriami!* . . . So glad, dear Elizabeth and Major Benjy that my little pet has done well for you. But I've been puzzling over it this morning and I think the price of gold is high enough. That's my impression –'

Diva whizzed across the road from the greengrocer's. All her zest and brightness had come back to her.

'Such a relief to have made up my mind, Lucia,' she said. 'I've telegraphed to sell two-thirds of my Siriami shares, and I shall keep the rest.'

'Very likely you're right, dear,' said Lucia. 'Very likely I'm wrong, but I'm selling all my little portfolio of them.'

Diva's sunny face clouded over.

'Oh, but that's terribly upsetting,' she said. 'I wonder if I'm too greedy. Do tell me what you think.'

Lucia had now come completely out of her remote financial abstraction, and addressed the meeting.

'Far be it from me to advise anybody,' she said. 'The monetary situation is too complicated for me to take the responsibility. But my broker admits – I must say I was flattered – that there is a great deal to be said for my view, and since you all followed my lead in your little purchases of Siriami, I feel bound to tell you what I am doing to-day. Not one share of

Siriami am I keeping, and I'm reinvesting the whole – I beg of you all *not* to consider this advice in any way – in Burma Corporation and Southern Railway Preferred, Prefs as we call them. I have given some study to the matter, and while I don't think anyone would go far wrong in buying them, I should be sorry if any of you followed me blindly, without going into the matter for yourselves –'

Elizabeth simply could not stand it a moment longer.

'Sweet of you to tell us, dear,' she said, 'but pray don't make yourself uneasy about any responsibility for us. My Benjy and I have been studying too, and we've made up our minds to buy some more Siriami. So set your mind at ease.'

Diva moaned.

'Oh, dear me! Must begin thinking about it all over again,' she said, as Lucia, at this interruption from the meeting, went into the post-office.

Elizabeth waited till the swing-door had shut.

'I'm more and more convinced,' she said, 'that the dear thing has no more idea what she's talking about than when she makes psychic bids. I shall do the opposite of whatever she recommends.'

'Most confusing,' moaned Diva again. 'I wish I hadn't begun to make money at all.'

Elizabeth followed Lucia into the post-office, and Benjy went to catch the tram, while Diva, with ploughed and furrowed face, walked up and down the pavement in an agony of indecision as to whether to follow Lucia's example and sell her three remaining shares or to back Elizabeth and repurchase her two.

'Whatever I do is sure to be wrong,' she thought to herself, and then her attention was switched off finance altogether. Along the High Street came Lucia's motor. Cadman turned to go up the street leading to the church and Mallards Cottage, but had to back again to let Susan's Royce come down. Foljambe was sitting by her husband on the box, and for an instant there appeared at the window of the car the face of a man curiously like Georgie. Yet it couldn't be he, for he had a neat white beard. Perhaps Lucia had a friend staying with her, but, if so, it was very odd that nobody had heard about him. 'Most extraordinary,' thought Diva. 'Who can it possibly be?'

She got no second glimpse for the head was withdrawn in a great hurry, and Lucia came out of the post-office as calm as if she had been buying a penny stamp instead of conducting these vast operations.

'So that's done!' she said lightly, 'and now I must go and see whether I can persuade Georgie to come out for a drive.'

'Your car has just gone by,' said Diva.

'*Tante grazie*. I must hurry.'

Lucia went up to Mallards Cottage, and found Georgie had gone into his house, for fear that Elizabeth might peer into the car if she saw it standing there.

'And I was a little imprudent,' he said, 'for I simply couldn't resist looking out as we turned up from the High Street to see what was going on, and there was Diva standing quite close. But I don't think she could have recognized me.'

In view of this contingency, however, the re-embarkation was delayed for a few minutes, and then conducted with great caution. This was lucky, for Diva had told Elizabeth of that puzzling apparition at the window of the car, and Elizabeth, after a brilliant and sarcastic suggestion that it was Mr Montagu Norman who had come down to consult Lucia as to the right policy of the Bank of England in this world crisis, decided that the matter must be looked into at once. So the two ladies separated and Diva hurried up to the Church Square in case the car left Georgie's house by that route, while Elizabeth went up to Mallards, where, from the window of the garden-room, she could command the other road of exit . . . So, before Georgie entered the car again, Foljambe reconnoitred this way and that, and came back with the alarming intelligence that Diva was lurking in Church Square, and that Elizabeth was in her usual lair behind the curtains. Cadman and Foljambe therefore stood as a screen on each side of Georgie's doorstep while he, bending double, stole into the car. They passed under the window of the garden-room, and Lucia, leaning far forward to conceal Georgie, kissed and waved her hand to the half-drawn curtains to show Elizabeth that she was perfectly aware who was in ambush behind them.

'That's thwarted them,' she said, as she put down the window when danger-points were passed. 'Poor Elizabeth couldn't have seen you, and Diva may hide in Church Square till Doomsday. Let's drive out past the golf-links along the road by the sea and let the breeze blow away all these pettinesses.'

She sighed.

'Georgie, how glad I am that I've taken up finance seriously,' she said. 'It gives me real work to do at last. It's time I had some, for I'm fifty next week. Of course I shall give a birthday-party, and I shall have a cake with fifty-one candles on it, so as to prepare me for my next birthday. After all, it isn't the years that give the measure of one's age, but energy and capacity for enterprise. Achievement. Adventure.'

'I'm sure you were as busy as any woman could be,' said Georgie.

'Possibly, but about paltry things, scoring off Elizabeth when she was pushing and that *genus omne*. I shall give all that up. I shall dissociate myself from all the petty gossip of the place. I shall —'

'Oh, look,' interrupted Georgie. 'There's Benjy playing golf with the Padre. There! He missed the ball completely, and he's stamping with rage.'

'No! So it is!' cried Lucia, wildly interested. 'Pull up a minute, Cadman. There now he's hit it again into a sand-pit, and the Padre's arguing with him. I wonder what language he's talking.'

'That's the best of Tilling,' cried Georgie enthusiastically, throwing prudence to the sea-winds, and leaning out of the window. 'There's always something exciting going on. If it isn't one thing it's another, and very often both!'

Benjy dealt the sand-pit one or two frightful biffs and Lucia suddenly remembered that she had done with such paltry trifles.

'Drive on, Cadman,' she said. 'Georgie, I'm afraid Major Benjy's nature has not been broadened and enriched by marriage. Marriage, one hoped, might have brought that about, but I don't see the faintest sign of it. Indeed I can't make up my mind about their marriage at all. They dab and stroke each other, and they're Benjy-boy and Girlie, but is it more than lip-service and finger-tips? Some women, I know, have had their greatest triumphs when youth was long, long past: Diane de Poictiers was fifty, was she not, when she became the King's mistress, but she was an enchantress, and you could not reasonably call Elizabeth an enchantress. Of course you haven't seen them together yet, but you will at my birthday-party.'

Georgie gingerly fingered the portion of beard on the ailing side of his face.

'Not much chance of it,' he said. 'I don't suppose I shall get rid of this by then. Too tarsome.'

Lucia looked at him again with a tilted head.

'Well, we shall see,' she said. 'My dear, the sun glinting on the sea! Is that what Homer – or was it Aeschylus – meant by the "numberless laughter of ocean"? An immortal phrase.'

'I shouldn't wonder if it was,' said Georgie. 'But about Benjy and Elizabeth. I can't see how you could expect anybody to be broadened and enriched by marrying Elizabeth. Nor by marrying Benjy for that matter.'

'Perhaps I was too sanguine. I hope they won't come to grief over their speculations. They're ignorant of the elements of finance. I told them both this morning what I was going to do. So they went and did exactly the opposite.'

'It's marvellous the way you've picked it up,' said Georgie. 'I'm fifty pounds richer by following your advice –'

'No, Georgie, not advice. My lead, if you like.'

'Lead then. I'm not sure I shan't have another go.'

'I wouldn't,' said she. 'It began to get on your mind: you dreamed about gold mines. Don't get like Diva: she was wringing her hands on the pavement in agony as to what she should do.'

'But how can you help thinking about it?'

'I do think about it,' she said, 'but calmly, as if finance was a science, which indeed it is. I study, I draw my conclusions, I act. By the way, do you happen to know how much a rupee is worth?'

'No idea,' said Georgie, 'but not very much, I believe. If you have a great many of them, they make a lakh. But I don't know how many it takes, nor what a lakh is when they've made it.'

No startling developments occurred during the next week. Siriami shares remained steady, but the continued strain so told on Diva that, having bought seven more because the Mapp-Flints were making further purchases, she had a nervous crisis one morning when they went down sixpence, sold her entire holding (ten shares) and with the help of a few strychnine pills regained her impaired vitality. But she watched with the intensest interest the movements of the market, for once again, as so often before, a deadly duel was in progress between Elizabeth and Lucia, but now it was waged as on some vast battlefield consisting of railway lines running between the shafts of gold mines. Lucia, so to speak, on the footboard of an engine on the Southern Railway shrieked by, drawing a freight of Burma Corporation, while Elizabeth put lumps of ore from Siriami on the metals to wreck her train. For Southern Railway Prefs began to move: one morning they were one point up, another morning they were three, and at Mallards the two chagrined operators snatched up their copies of the *Financial Post* and ate with a poor appetite. It was known all over Tilling that this fierce fight was in progress, and when, next Sunday morning, the sermon was preached by a missionary who had devoted himself to the enlightenment of the heathen both in Burma and West Africa, Lucia, sitting among the auxiliary choir on one side of the church and the Mapp-Flints on the other, seemed indeed to be the incarnations of those dark countries. Mr Wyse, attending closely to the sermon, thought that was a most extraordinary coincidence: even missionary work in foreign lands seemed to be drawn into the vortex.

Next morning on the breakfast-table at Mallards was Lucia's invitation to the Mapp-Flints to honour her with their presence at dinner on Friday next, the occasion of her Jubilee. Southern Prefs had gone up again and Siriami down, but, so Elizabeth surmised, 'all Tilling' would be there, and if she and Benjy refused, which seemed the proper way to record what they felt about it, all Tilling would certainly conclude that they had not been asked.

'It's her *ways* that I find so hard to bear,' said Elizabeth, cracking the top of her boiled egg with such violence that the rather under-cooked contents streamed on to her plate. 'Her airs, her arrogance. Even if she says nothing about Siriami I shall know she's pitying us for not having followed her lead, and buying those wild-cat shares of hers. What has Bohemian Corporation, or whatever it is, been doing? I didn't look.'

'Up sixpence,' said Benjy, gloomily.

Elizabeth moistened her lips.

'I suspected as much, and you see I was right. But I suppose we had better go to her Jubilee, and perhaps we shall learn something of this mystery about Georgie. I'm sure she's keeping something dark: I feel it in my bones. Women of a certain age are like that. They know that they are getting on in years and have become entirely unattractive, and so they make mysteries in order to induce people to take an interest in them a little longer, poor things. There was that man with a beard whom Diva saw in her car; there's a mystery which has never been cleared up. Probably it was her gardener, who has a beard, dressed up, and she hoped we might think she had someone staying with her whom we were to know nothing about. Just a mystery.'

'Well, she made no mystery about selling Siriami and buying those blasted Prefs,' said Benjy.

'My fault then, I suppose,' said Elizabeth bitterly, applying the pepper-pot to the pool of egg on her plate, and scooping it up with her spoon. 'I see: I ought to have followed Lucia's lead, and have invested my money as she recommended. And curtsied, and said "Thank your gracious Majesty." Quite.'

'I didn't say you ought to have done anything of the kind,' said Benjy.

Elizabeth had applied pepper with too lavish a hand, and had a frightful fit of sneezing before she could make the obvious rejoinder.

'No, but you implied it, Benjy, which, if anything, is worse,' she answered hoarsely.

'No I didn't. No question of "ought" about it. But I wish to God I had done as she suggested. Southern Prefs have risen ten points since she told us.'

'We won't discuss it any further, please,' said Elizabeth.

Everyone accepted the invitation to the Jubilee, and now Lucia thought it time to put into action her scheme for getting Georgie to make his re-entry into the world of Tilling. He was quite himself again save for the pointed white beard which Foljambe had once more trimmed very skilfully, his cook was returning from her holiday next day, and he would be going back to shut himself up in his lonely little house until he could present his normal face to his friends. On that point he was immovable: nobody should see him with a little white beard, for it would be the end of his *jeune premier*-ship of Tilling: no *jeune premier* ever had a white beard, however little. And Dr Dobbie had told him not to think of 'irritating the nerve-ends' with the razor until they were incapable of resentment. In another three weeks or so, Dr Dobbie thought. This verdict depressed Georgie: there would be three weeks more of skulking out in his motor, heavily camouflaged, and of return to his dreary solitude in the evening. He wanted to hear the Padre mingle Irish with Scotch, he wanted to see Diva with her Eton crop, he wanted to study the effect of matrimony on Mapp and Flint, and what made him miss this daily bread the more was that Lucia was very sparing in supplying him with it, for she was rather strict in her inhuman resolve to have done with petty gossip. Taken unawares, she could still manifest keen interest in seeing Benjy hit a golf-ball into a bunker, but she checked herself in an annoying manner and became lofty again. Probably her inhumanity would wear off, but it was tarsome that when he so particularly thirsted for local news, she should be so parsimonious with it.

However, they dined very comfortably that night, though she had many far-away glances, as if at distant blue hills, which indicated that she was thinking out some abstruse problem: Georgie supposed it was some terrific financial operation of which she would not speak at meals. Then she appeared to have solved it, for the blue-hill-look vanished, she riddled him with several gimlet-glances, and suddenly gabbled about the modern quality of the Idylls of Theocritus. 'Yet perhaps modern is the wrong word,' she said. 'Let us call it the timeless quality, Georgie, *senza tempo* in fact. It is characteristic, don't you think of all great artists: Vandyck has it pre-eminently. What timeless distinction his portraits have! His Lady Castlemaine, the Kéroualle, Nell Gwyn –'

'But surely Vandyck was dead before their time,' began Georgie. 'Charles I, you know, not Charles II.'

'That may be so, possibly you are right,' said Lucia with her habitual shamelessness. 'But my proposition holds. Vandyck is timeless, he shows the dignity, the distinction which can be realized in every age. But I always maintain – I wonder if you will agree with me – that his portraits of men are far, far finer than his women. More perception: I doubt if he ever understood women really. But his men! That coloured print I have of his Gelasius in the next room by the piano. Marvellous! Have you finished your coffee? Let us go.'

Lucia strolled into the drawing-room, glanced at a book on the table, and touched a few notes on the piano as if she had forgotten all about Gelasius.

'Shall we give ourselves a holiday to-night, Georgie, and not tackle that dweful diffy Brahms?' she asked. 'I shall have to practise my part before I am fit to play it with you. Wonderful Brahms! As Pater says of something else, "the soul with all its maladies" has entered into his music.'

She closed the piano, and casually pointed to a coloured print that hung on the wall above it beside a false Chippendale mirror.

'Ah, there's the Gelasius I spoke of,' she said. 'Rather a dark corner. I must find a worthier place for him.'

Georgie came across to look at it. Certainly it was a most distinguished face: high eyebrowed with a luxuriant crop of auburn hair and a small pointed beard. A man in early middle life, perhaps forty at the most. Georgie could not remember having noticed it before, which indeed was not to be wondered at, since Lucia had bought it that very afternoon. She had seen the great resemblance to Georgie, and her whole magnificent scheme had flashed upon her.

'Dear me, what a striking face,' he said. 'Stupid of me never to have looked at it before.'

Lucia made no answer, and turning, he saw that she was eagerly glancing first at the picture and then at him, and then at the picture again. Then she sat down on the piano-stool and clasped her hands.

'Absolutely too *straordinario*,' she said as if speaking to herself.

'What is?' asked Georgie.

'*Caro*, do not pretend to be so blind! Why it's the image of you. Take a good look at it, then move a step to the right and look at yourself in the glass.'

Georgie did as he was told, and a thrill of rapture tingled in him. For years he had known (and lamented) that his first chin receded and that a plump second chin was advancing from below, but now his beard completely hid these blemishes.

'Well, I do see what you mean,' he said.

'Who could help it? Georgie, you *are* Gelasius, which I've always considered Vandyck's masterpiece. And it's your beard that has done it. Unified! Harmonized! And to think that you intend to shut yourself up for three weeks more and then cut it off! It's murder. Artistic murder!'

Georgie cast another look at Gelasius and then at himself. All these weeks he had taken only the briefest and most disgusted glances into his looking-glass because of the horror of his beard, and had been blind to what it had done for him. He felt a sudden stab of longing to be a permanent Gelasius, but there was one frightful snag in the way, irrespective of the terribly shy-making moment when he should reveal himself to Tilling so radically altered. The latter, with such added distinction to show them, he thought he could tone himself up to meet. But —

'Well?' asked Lucia rather impatiently. She had her part ready.

'What's so frightfully tarsome is that my beard's so grey that you might call it white,' he said. 'There's really not a grey hair on my head or in my moustache, and the stupid thing has come out this colour. No colour at all, in fact. Do you think it's because I'm run down?'

Lucia pounced on this: it was a brilliant thought of Georgie's, and made her part easier.

'Of course that's why,' she said. 'As you get stronger, your beard will certainly get its colour back. Just a question of time. I think it's beginning already.'

'But what am I to do till then?' asked Georgie. 'Such an odd appearance.'

She laughed.

'Fancy asking a woman that!' she said. 'Dye it, Georgino. Temporarily of course, just anticipating Nature. There's that barber in Hastings you go to. Drive over there to-morrow.'

Actually, Georgie had got a big bottle upstairs of the precise shade, and had been touching up with it this morning. But Lucia's suggestion of Hastings was most satisfactory. It implied surely that she had no cognizance of these hidden practices.

'I shouldn't quite like to do that,' said he.

Lucia had by now developed her full horse-power in persuasiveness. She could quite understand (knowing Georgie) why he intended to shut himself up for another three weeks, sooner than show himself to Tilling with auburn hair and a white beard (and indeed, though she personally had got used to it, he was a very odd object). Everyone would draw the inevitable conclusion that he dyed his hair, and though they knew it perfectly well already, the public demonstration of that fact would be intolerable to him, for the poor lamb evidently thought that this was a secret shared only by his bottle of hair-dye. Besides, she had now for over a fortnight concealed him like some Royalist giving a hiding place to King Charles, and while he had been there, she had not been able to ask a single one of her friends to the house, for fear they should catch a glimpse of him. Her kindliness revolted at the thought of his going back to his solitude, but she had had enough of his undiluted company. He had been a charming companion: she had even admitted to herself that it would be pleasant to have him always here, but not at the price of seeing nobody else . . . She opened the throttle.

'But how perfectly unreasonable,' she cried. 'Dyeing it is only a temporary measure till it resumes its colour. And the improvement! My dear, I never saw such an improvement. Diva's not in it! And how can you contemplate going back to solitary confinement, for indeed it's that, for weeks and weeks more, and then at the end to scrap it? The distinction, Georgie, the dignity, and, to be quite frank, the complete disappearance of your chin, which was the one weak feature in your face. And it's in your power to be a living Vandyck masterpiece, and you're hesitating whether you shall madly cast away, as the hymn says, that wonderful chance. Hastings to-morrow, directly after breakfast, I implore you. It will be dry by lunch-time, won't it? Why, a woman with the prospect of improving her appearance so colossally would be unable to sleep a wink to-night from sheer joy. Oh, *amico mio*,' she said, lapsing into the intimate dialect, ''Oo will vex *povera* Lucia vewy, vewy much if you shave off *vostra bella barba. Di grazia!* Georgie.'

'Me must fink,' said Georgie. He left his chair and gazed once more at Gelasius and then at himself, and wondered if he had the nerve to appear without warning in the High Street even if his beard was auburn.

'I believe you're right,' he said at length. 'Fancy all this coming out of my shingles. But it's a tremendous step to take . . . Yes, I'll do it. And I shall be able to come to your birthday-party after all.'

'It wouldn't be a birthday-party without you,' said Lucia warmly.

Georgie's cook having returned, he went back to his own house after the operation next morning. He had taken a little hand-glass with him to Hastings, and all the way home he had constantly consulted it in order to get used to himself, for he felt as if a total stranger with a seventeenth-century face was sharing the car with him, and his agitated consciousness suggested that anyone looking at him at all closely would conclude that this lately discovered Vandyck (like the Carlisle Holbein) was a very doubtful piece. It might be after Vandyck, but assuredly a very long way after. Foljambe opened the door of Mallards Cottage to him, and she considerably restored his shattered confidence. For the moment her jaw dropped, as if she had been knocked out, at the shock of this transformation, but then she recovered completely, and beamed up at him.

'Well, that is a pleasant change, sir,' she said, 'from your white beard, if you'll pardon me,' and Georgie hurried upstairs to get an ampler view of himself in the big mirror in his bedroom than the hand-glass afforded. He then telephoned to Lucia to say that the operation was safely over and she promised to come up directly after lunch and behold.

The nerve-strain had tired him and so did the constant excursions upstairs to get fresh impressions of himself. Modern costume was a handicap, but a very pretty little cape of his with fur round the neck had a Gelasian effect, and when Lucia arrived he came down in this. She was all applause: she walked slowly round him to get various points of view, ejaculating, 'My *dear*, what an improvement,' or 'My dear, *what* an improvement,' to which Georgie replied, 'Do you really like it?' until her iteration finally convinced him that she was sincere. He settled to rest for the remainder of the day after these fatigues, and to burst upon all Tilling at the marketing-hour next morning.

'And what do you seriously think they'll all think?' he asked. 'I'm terribly nervous as you may imagine. It would be good of you if you'd pop in to-morrow morning, and walk down with me. I simply couldn't pass underneath the garden-room window, with Elizabeth looking out, alone.'

'Ten forty-five, Georgie,' she said. '*What* an improvement!'

The afternoon and evening dragged after she was gone. It was pleasant to see his bibelots again, but he missed Lucia's companionship. Intimate as they had been for many years, they had never before had each other's undivided company for so long. A book, and a little conversation with Foljambe made dinner tolerable, but after that she went home to her Cadman, and he was alone. He polished up the naughty snuff-box, he worked at his *petit point* shepherdess. He had stripped her nakeder than Eve, and replaced her green robe with pink, and now instead of looking like a stick of asparagus she really might have been a young lady who, for reasons of her own, preferred to tend her sheep with nothing on; but he wanted to show her to somebody and he could hardly discuss her with his cook. Or a topic of interest occurred to him, but there was no one to share it with, and he played beautifully on his piano, but nobody congratulated him. It was dreary work to be alone, though no doubt he would get used to it again, and dreary to go up to bed with no chattering on the stairs. Often he used to linger with Lucia at her bedroom door, finishing their talk, and even go in with her by express invitation. To-night he climbed up the stairs alone, and heard his cook snoring.

Lucia duly appeared next morning, and they set off under the guns of the garden-room window. Elizabeth was there as usual, and after fixing on them for a moment her opera-glass which she used for important objects at a distance, she gave a squeal that caused Benjy to drop the *Financial Post* which recorded the ruinous fall of two shillings in Siriami.

'Mr Georgie's got a beard,' she cried, and hurried to get her hat and basket and follow them down to the High Street. Diva, looking out of her window, was the next to see him, and without the hint Elizabeth had had of observing his exit from his own house quite failed to recognize him at first. She had to go through an addition sum in circumstantial evidence before she arrived at his identity: he was with Lucia, he was of his own height and build, the rest of his face was the same and he had on the well-known little cape with the fur collar. QED. She whistled to Pat, she seized her basket, and taking a header into the street ran straight into Elizabeth who was sprinting down from Mallards.

'He's come out. Mr Georgie. A beard,' she said.

Elizabeth was out of breath with her swift progress.

'Oh yes, dear,' she panted. 'Didn't you know? Fancy! Where have they gone?'

'Couldn't see. Soon find them. Come on.'

Elizabeth, chagrined at not being able to announce the news to Diva, instantly determined to take the opposite line, and not show the slightest interest in this prodigious transformation.

'But why this excitement, dear?' she said. 'I cannot think of anything that matters less. Why shouldn't Mr Georgie have a beard? If you had one now –'

A Sinaitic trumpet-blast from Susan's Royce made them both leap on to the pavement, as if playing Tom Tiddler's ground.

'But don't you remember –' began Diva almost before alighting – 'there, we're safe – don't you remember the man with a white beard whom I saw in Lucia's car? Must be the same man. You said it was Mr Montagu Norman first and then Lucia's gardener disguised. The one we watched for, you at your window and me in Church Square.'

'Grammar, dear Diva. "I" not "me",' interrupted Elizabeth to gain time, while she plied her brain with crucial questions. For if Diva was right, and the man in Lucia's car had been Georgie (white beard), he must have been driving back to Mallards Cottage in Lucia's car from somewhere. Could he have been living at Grebe all the time while he pretended (or Lucia pretended for him) to have been at home too ill to see anybody? But if so, why, on some days, had his house appeared to be inhabited, and on some days completely deserted? Certainly Georgie (auburn beard) had come out of it this morning with Lucia. Had they been staying with each other alternately? Had they been living in sin? . . . Poor shallow Diva had not the slightest perception of these deep and probably grievous matters. Her feather-pated mind could get no further than the colour of beards. Before Diva could frame an adequate reply to this paltry grammatical point a positive eruption of thrills occurred. Lucia and Georgie came out of the post-office, Paddy engaged in a dog-fight, and the Padre and Evie Bartlett emerged from the side-street opposite, and, as if shot from a catapult, projected themselves across the road just in front of Susan's motor.

'Oh, dear me, they'll be run over!' cried Diva. 'PADDY! And there are Mr Georgie and Lucia. What a lot of things are happening this morning!'

'Diva, you're a little overwrought,' said Elizabeth with kindly serenity. 'What with white beards and brown beards and motor-accidents . . . Oh, *voilà*! There's Susan actually got out of

her car, and she's almost running across the road to speak to
Mr Georgie, and quaint Irene in shorts. What a fuss! For
goodness' sake let's be dignified and go on with our shopping.
The whole thing has been staged by Lucia, and I won't be a
super.'

'But I must go and say I'm glad he's better,' said Diva.

'*Certainement*, dear, if you happen to think he's been ill. I
believe it's all a hoax.'

But she spoke to the empty air for Diva had thumped Paddy
in the ribs with her market-basket and was whizzing away to
the group on the pavement where Georgie was receiving general congratulations on his recovery and his striking appearance. The verdict was most flattering, and long after his
friends had gazed their fill he continued to walk up and down
the High Street and pop into shops where he wanted nothing,
in order that his epiphany which he had been so nervous
about, and which he found purely enjoyable, might be manifest
to all. For a long time Elizabeth, determined to take no part in
a show which she was convinced was run by Lucia, succeeded
in avoiding him, but at last he ran her to earth in the greengrocer's. She examined the quality of the spinach till her back
ached, and then she had to turn round and face him.

'Lovely morning, isn't it, Mr Georgie,' she said. 'So pleased
to see you about again. Sixpennyworth of spinach, please, Mr
Twistevant. Looks so good!' and she hurried out of the shop,
still unconscious of his beard.

'Tarsome woman,' thought Georgie. 'If there is a fly anywhere about she is sure to put it in somebody's ointment' . . .
But there had been so much ointment on the subject that he
really didn't much mind about Elizabeth's fly.

4

Elizabeth Mapp-Flint had schemes for her husband and meant
to realize them. As a bachelor, with an inclination to booze and
a very limited income, inhabiting that small house next to
Mallards, it was up to him, if he chose, to spend the still
robust energies of his fifty-five years in playing golf all day and
getting slightly squiffy in the evening. But his marriage had
given him a new status: he was master, though certainly not
mistress, of the best house in Tilling; he was, through her, a
person of position, and it was only right that he should have a
share in municipal government. The elections to the Town
Council were coming on shortly, and she had made up her
mind, and his for him, that he must stand. The fact that, if
elected, he would make it his business to get something done
about Susan Wyse's motor causing a congestion of traffic
every morning in the High Street was not really a leading
motive. Elizabeth craved for the local dignity which his election
would give not only to him but her, and if poor Lucia (always
pushing herself forward) happened to turn pea-green with
envy, that would be her misfortune and not Elizabeth's fault.
As yet the programme which he should present to the electors
was only being thought out, but municipal economy (Major
Mapp-Flint and Economy) with reduction of rates would be the
ticket.

The night of Lucia's birthday-party was succeeded by a day
of pelting rain, and, no golf being possible, Elizabeth, having
sent her cook (she had a mackintosh) to do the marketing for
her, came out to the garden-room after breakfast for a chat.
She always knocked at the door, opening it a chink and saying,
'May I come in, Benjy-boy?' in order to remind him of her
nobility in giving it him. To-day a rather gruff voice answered
her, for economy had certainly not been the ticket at Lucia's

party, and there had been a frightful profusion of viands and wine: really a very vulgar display, and Benjy had eaten enormously and drunk far more wine than was positively necessary for the quenching of thirst. There had been a little argument as they drove home, for he had insisted that there were fifty-one candles round the cake and that it had been a remarkably jolly evening: she said that there were only fifty candles, and that it was a very mistaken sort of hospitality which gave guests so much more than they wanted to eat or should want to drink. His lack of appetite at breakfast might prove that he had had enough to eat the night before to last him some hours yet, but his extraordinary consumption of tea could not be explained on the same analogy. But Elizabeth thought she had made sufficient comment on that at breakfast (or tea as far as he was concerned) and when she came in this morning for a chat, she had no intention of rubbing it in. The accusation, however, that he had not been able to count correctly up to fifty or fifty-one, still rankled in his mind, for it certainly implied a faintly camouflaged connection with sherry, champagne, port and brandy.

'Such a pity, dear,' she said brightly, 'that it's so wet. A round of golf would have done you all the good in the world. Blown the cobwebs away.'

To Benjy's disgruntled humour, this seemed an allusion to the old subject, and he went straight to the point.

'There were fifty-one candles,' he said.

'*Cinquante*, Benjy,' she answered firmly. 'She is fifty. She said so. So there must have been fifty.'

'Fifty-one. Candles I mean. But what I've been thinking over is that you've been thinking, if you follow me, that I couldn't count. Very unjust. Perhaps you'll say I saw a hundred next. Seeing double, eh? And why should a round of golf do me all the good in the world to-day? Not more good than any other day, unless you want me to get pneumonia.'

Elizabeth sat down on the seat in the window as suddenly as if she had been violently hit behind the knees, and put her handkerchief up to her eyes to conceal the fact that there was not a vestige of a tear there. As he was facing towards the fire he did not perceive this manoeuvre and thought she had only gone to the window to make her usual morning observations. He continued to brood over the *Financial Post*, which contained the news that Siriami had been weak and Southern Prefs remarkably strong. These items were about equally depressing.

Elizabeth was doubtful as to what to do next. In the course of their married life, there had been occasional squalls, and she had tried sarcasm and vituperation with but small success. Benjy-boy had answered her back or sulked, and she was left with a sense of imperfect mastery. This policy of being hurt was a new one, and since the first signal had not been noticed she hoisted a second one and sniffed.

'Got a bit of a cold?' he asked pacifically.

No answer, and he turned round.

'Why, what's wrong?' he said.

'And there's a *jolie chose* to ask,' said Elizabeth with strangled shrillness. 'You tell me I want you to catch pneumonia, and then ask what's wrong. You wound me deeply.'

'Well, I got annoyed with your nagging at me that I couldn't count. You implied I was squiffy just because I had a jolly good dinner. And there were fifty-one candles.'

'It doesn't matter if there were fifty-one million,' cried Elizabeth. 'What matters is that you spoke to me very cruelly. I planned to make you so happy, Benjy, by giving up my best room to you and all sorts of things, and all the reward I get is to be told one day that I ought to have let Lucia lead me by the nose and almost the next that I hoped you would die of pneumonia.'

He came across to the window.

'Well, I didn't mean that,' he said. 'You're sarcastic, too, at times and say monstrously disagreeable things to me.'

'Oh, that's a wicked lie,' said Elizabeth violently. 'Never have I spoken disagreeably to you. *Jamais!* Firmly sometimes, but always for your good. *Toujours!* Never another thought in my head but your true happiness.'

Benjy was rather alarmed: hysterics seemed imminent.

'Yes, girlie, I know that,' he said soothingly. 'Nothing the matter? Nothing wrong?'

353

She opened her mouth once or twice like a gasping fish, and recovered her self-control.

'Nothing, dear, that I can tell you yet,' she said. 'Don't ask me. But never say I want you to get pneumonia again. It hurt me cruelly. There! All over! Look, there's Mr Georgie coming out in this pelting rain. Do you know, I like his beard, though I couldn't tell him so, except for that odd sort of sheen on it, like the colours on cold boiled beef. But I dare say that'll pass off. Oh, let's put up the window and ask him how many candles there were . . . Good morning, Mr Georgie. What a lovely, no, disgusting morning, but what a lovely evening yesterday! Do you happen to know for certain how many candles there were on Lucia's beautiful cake?'

'Yes, fifty-one,' said Georgie, 'though she's only fifty. She put an extra one, so that she may get used to being fifty-one before she is.'

'What a pretty idea! So like her,' said Elizabeth, and shut the window again.

Benjy with great tact pretended not to have heard, for he had no wish to bring back those hysterical symptoms. A sensational surmise as to the cause of them had dimly occurred to him, but surely it was impossible. So tranquillity being restored, they sat together 'ever so cosily', said Elizabeth, by the fire (which meant that she appropriated his hip-bath chair and got nearly all the heat) and began plotting out the campaign for the coming municipal elections.

'Better just get quietly to work, love,' said she, 'and not say much about it at first, for Lucia's sadly capable of standing, too, if she knows you are.'

'I'm afraid I told her last night,' said Benjy.

'Oh, what a blabbing boy! Well, it can't be helped now. Let's hope it'll put no jealous ambitions into her head. Now, *l'Économie* is the right slogan for you. Anything more reckless than the way the Corporation has been spending money I can't conceive. Just as if Tilling was Eldorado. Think of pulling down all those pretty little slums by the railway and building new houses! Fearfully expensive, and spoiling the town: taking all its quaintness away.'

'And then there's that new road they're making that skirts the town,' said Benjy, 'to relieve the congestion in the High Street.'

'Just so,' chimed in Elizabeth. 'They'd relieve it much more effectually if they didn't allow Susan to park her car, positively across the street, wherever she pleases, and as long as she pleases. It's throwing money about like that which sends up the rates by leaps and bounds; why, they're nearly double of what they were when I inherited Mallards from sweet Aunt Caroline. And nothing to show for it except a road that nobody wants and some ugly new houses instead of those picturesque old cottages. They may be a little damp, perhaps, but, after all, there was a dreadful patch of damp in my bedroom last year, and I didn't ask the Town Council to rebuild Mallards at the public expense. And I'm told all those new houses have got a bathroom in which the tenants will probably keep poultry. Then, they say, there are the unemployed. Rubbish, Benjy! There's plenty of work for everybody, only those lazy fellows prefer the dole and idleness. We've got to pinch and squeeze so that the so-called poor may live in the lap of luxury. If I didn't get a good let for Mallards every year we shouldn't be able to live in it at all, and you may take that from me. Economy! That's the ticket! Talk to them like that and you'll head the poll.'

A brilliant notion struck Benjy as he listened to this impassioned speech. Though he liked the idea of holding public office and of the dignity it conferred, he knew that his golf would be much curtailed by his canvassing, and, if he was elected, by his duties. Moreover, he could not talk in that vivid and vitriolic manner . . .

He jumped up.

'Upon my word, Liz, I wish you'd stand instead of me,' he said. 'You've got the gift of the gab; you can put things clearly and forcibly, and you've got it all at your fingers' ends. Besides, you're the owner of Mallards, and these rates and taxes press harder on you than on me. What do you say to that?'

The idea had never occurred to her before: she wondered why. How she would enjoy paying calls on all the numerous householders who felt the burden of increasing rates, and securing their votes for her programme of economy! She saw herself triumphantly heading the poll. She saw herself sitting in the Council Room, the only woman present, with sheaves of statistics to confute this spendthrift policy. Eloquence, compliments, processions to church on certain official occasions, a status, a doctorial-looking gown, position, power. All these enticements beckoned her, and from on high, she seemed to look down on poor Lucia as if at the bottom of a disused well, fifty years old, playing duets with Georgie, and gabbling away about all the Aristophanes she read and the callisthenics she practised, and the principles of psychic bidding, and the advice she gave her broker, while Councillor Mapp-Flint was as busy with the interests of the Borough. A lesson for the self-styled Queen of Tilling.

'Really, dear,' she said, 'I hardly know what to say. Such a new idea to me, for all this was the future I planned for you, and how I've lain awake at night thinking of it. I must adjust my mind to such a revolution of our plans. But there is something in what you suggest. That house-to-house canvassing: perhaps a woman is more suited to that than a man. A cup of tea, you know, with the mother and a peep at baby. It's true again that as owner of Mallards, I have a solider stake in property than you. Dear me, yes, I begin to see your point of view. Sound, as a man's always is. Then again what you call the gift of the gab – such a rude expression – perhaps forcible words do come more easily to me, and they'll be needful indeed when it comes to fighting the spendthrifts. But first you would have to promise to help me, for you know how I shall depend on you. I hope my health will stand the strain, and I'll gladly work myself to the bone in such a cause. Better to wear oneself out than rust in the scabbard.'

'You're cut out for the job,' said Benjy enthusiastically. 'As for wearing yourself out, hubby won't permit that!'

Once more Elizabeth recalled her bright visions of power and the reduction of rates. The prospect was irresistible.

'I give you your way as usual, Benjy-boy,' she said. 'How I spoil you! Such a bully! What? *Déjeuner* already, Withers? Hasn't the morning flown?'

The morning had flown with equal speed for Lucia. She had gone to her Office after breakfast, the passage to which had now been laid with india-rubber felting, so that no noise of footsteps outside could distract her when she was engaged in financial operations. This ensured perfect tranquillity, unless it so happened that she was urgently wanted, in which case Grosvenor's tap on the door startled her very much since she had not heard her approach; this risk, however, was now minimized because she had a telephone-extension to the Office. To-day there were entries to be made in the ledger, for she had sold her Southern Prefs at a scandalous profit, and there was a list of recommendations from that intelligent Mammoncash for the re-investment of the capital released.

She drew her chair up to the fire to study this. High-priced shares did not interest her much: you got so few for your money. 'The sort of thing I want,' she thought, 'is quantities of low-priced shares, like those angelic Siriamis, which nearly doubled their value in a few weeks,' but the list contained nothing to which Mammoncash thought this likely to happen. He even suggested that she might do worse than put half her capital into gilt-edged stock. He could not have made a duller suggestion: Dame Catherine Winterglass, Lucia felt sure, would not have touched Government Loans with the end of a barge-pole. Then there was 'London Transport "C"'. Taking a long view, Mammoncash thought that in a year's time there should be a considerable capital-appreciation . . .

Lucia found her power of concentration slipping from her, and her thoughts drifted away to her party last night. She had observed that Benjy had seldom any wine in his glass for more than a moment, and that Elizabeth's eye was on him. Though she had forsworn any interest in such petty concerns, food for serious thought had sprung out of this, for, getting expansive towards the end of dinner, he had told her that he was standing for the Town Council. He and Elizabeth both thought it was his duty. 'It'll mean a lot of work,' he said, 'but thank God, I'm not afraid of that, and something must be done to check this monstrous municipal extravagance. Less golf for me, Mrs

Lucas, but duty comes before pleasure. I shall hope to call on you before long and ask your support.'

Lucia had not taken much interest in this project at the time, but now ideas began to bubble in her brain. She need not consider the idea of his being elected – for who in his senses could conceivably vote for him? – and she found herself in violent opposition to the programme of economy which he had indicated. Exactly the contrary policy recommended itself: more work must somehow be found for the unemployed: the building of decent houses for the poor ought to be quickened up. There was urgent and serious work to be done, and, as she gazed meditatively at the fire, personal and ambitious day-dreams began to form themselves. Surely there was a worthy career here for an energetic and middle-aged widow. Then the telephone rang and she picked it off the table. Georgie.

'Such a filthy day: no chance of its clearing,' he said. 'Do come and lunch and we'll play duets.'

'Yes, Georgie, that will be lovely. What about my party last night?'

'Perfect. And weren't they all astonished when I told them about my shingles. Major Benjy was a bit squiffy. Doesn't get a chance at home.'

'I rather like to see people a little, just a little squiffy at my expense,' observed Lucia. 'It makes me feel I'm being a good hostess. Any news?'

'I passed there an hour ago,' said Georgie, 'and she suddenly threw the window up and asked me how many candles there were on your cake, and when I said there were fifty-one she banged it down again quite sharply.'

'No! I wonder why she wanted to know that and didn't like it when you told her,' said Lucia, intrigued beyond measure, and forgetting that such gossip could not be worth a moment's thought.

'Can't imagine. I've been puzzling over it,' said Georgie.

Lucia recollected her principles.

'Such a triviality in any case,' she said, 'whatever the explanation may be. I'll be with you at one-thirty. And I've got something very important to discuss with you. Something quite new: you can't guess.'

'My dear, how exciting! More money?'

'Probably less for all of us if it comes off,' said Lucia enigmatically. 'But I must get back to my affairs. I rather think, from my first glance at the report, that there ought to be capital appreciation in Transport "C".'

'Transport by sea?' asked Georgie.

'No, the other sort of sea. ABC.'

'Those tea-shops?' asked the intelligent Georgie.

'No, trams, buses, tubes.'

She rang off, but the moment afterwards so brilliant an idea struck her that she called him up again.

'Georgie: about the candles. I'm sure I've got it. Elizabeth believed that there were fifty. That's a clue for you.'

She rang off again, and meditated furiously on the future.

Georgie ran to the door when Lucia arrived and opened it himself before Foljambe could get there.

'– and Benjy said there were fifty-one and she thought he wasn't in a state to count properly,' he said all in one breath. 'Come in, and tell me at once about the other important thing. Lunch is ready. Is it about Benjy?'

Georgie at once perceived that Lucia was charged with weighty matter. She was rather overwhelming in these humours: sometimes he wished he had a piece of green baize to throw over her as over a canary, when it will not stop singing. ('Foljambe, fetch Mrs Lucas's baize,' he thought to himself.)

'Yes, indirectly about him, and directly about the elections to the Town Council. I think it's my duty to stand, Georgie, and when I see my duty clearly, I do it. Major Benjy is standing, you see; he told me so last night, and he's all out for the reduction of rates and taxes –'

'So am I,' said Georgie.

Lucia laid down her knife and fork, and let her pheasant get cold to Georgie's great annoyance.

'You won't be if you listen to me, my dear,' she said. 'Rates and taxes are high, it's true, but they ought to be ever so much higher for the sake of the unemployed. They must be given work, Georgie: I know myself how demoralizing it is not to have work to do. Before I embarked on my financial career, I was sinking into lethargy. It is the same with our poorer brethren. That new road, for instance. It employs a fair number of men, who would otherwise be idle and on the dole, but that's not nearly enough. Work helps everybody to maintain his – or her – self-respect: without work we should all go to the dogs. I should like to see that road doubled in width and – well in width, and however useless it might appear to be, the moral salvation of hundreds would have been secured by it. Again, those slums by the railway: it's true that new houses are being built to take the place of hovels which are a disgrace to any Christian town. But I demand a bigger programme. Those slums ought to be swept away, at once. All of them. The expense? Who cares? We fortunate ones will bear it between us. Here are we living in the lap of luxury, and just round the corner, so to speak, or, at any rate, at the bottom of the hill are those pig-sties, where human beings are compelled to live. No bathrooms, I believe; think of it, Georgie! I feel as if I ought to give free baths to anybody who cares to come and have one, only I suppose Grosvenor would instantly leave. The municipal building plans for the year ought to be far more comprehensive. That shall be my ticket: spend, spend, spend. I'm too selfish: I must work for others, and I shall send in my name as standing for the Town Council, and set about canvassing at once. How does one canvass?'

'You go from house to house asking for support I suppose,' said Georgie.

'And you'll help me, of course. I know I can rely on you.'

'But I don't want rates to be any higher,' said Georgie. 'Aren't you going to eat any pheasant?'

Lucia took up her knife and fork.

'But just think, Georgie. Here are you and I eating pheasant – *molto bene e bellissime* cooked – in your lovely little house, and then we shall play on your piano, and there are people in this dear little Tilling who never eat a pheasant or play on a piano from Christmas Day to New Year's Day, I mean the other way round. I hope to live here for the rest of my days, and I have a duty towards my neighbours.'

Lucia had a duty towards the pheasant, too, and wolfed it down. Her voice had now assumed the resonant tang of compulsion, and Georgie, like the unfortunate victim of the Ancient Mariner, 'could not choose but hear'.

'Georgie, you and I – particularly I – are getting on in years, and we shall not pass this way again. (Is it Kingsley, dear?) Anyhow we must help poor little lame dogs over stiles. Ickle you and me have been spoiled. We've always had all we wanted and we must do ickle more for others. I've got an insight into finance lately, and I can see what a power money is, what one can do with it unselfishly, like the wonderful Winterglass. I want to live, just for the few years that may still be left me, with a clear conscience, quietly and peacefully –'

'But with Benjy standing in the opposite interest, won't there be a bit of friction instead?' asked Georgie.

'Emphatically not, as far as I am concerned,' said Lucia, firmly. 'I shall be just as cordial to them as ever – I say "them", because of course Elizabeth's at the bottom of his standing – and I give them the credit for their policy of economy being just as sincere as mine.'

'Quite,' said Georgie, 'for if taxes were much higher, and if they couldn't get a thumping good let for Mallards every year, I don't suppose they would be able to live there. Have to sell.'

An involuntary gleam lit up Lucia's bird-like eyes, just as if a thrush had seen a fat worm. She instantly switched it off.

'Naturally I should be very sorry for them,' she said, 'if they had to do that, but personal regrets can't affect my principles. And then, Georgie, more schemes seem to outline themselves. Don't be frightened: they will bring only me to the workhouse. But they want thinking out yet. I seem to see – well, never mind. Now let us have our music. Not a moment have I had for practice lately, so you mustn't scold me. Let us begin with deevy Beethoven's fifth symphony. Fate knocking at the door. That's how I feel, as if there was one clear call for me.'

The window of Georgie's sitting-room, which looked out on to the street, was close to the front door. Lucia, as usual, had bagged the treble part, for she said she could never manage that difficult bass, omitting to add that the treble was far the more amusing to play, and they were approaching the end of the first movement, when Georgie, turning a page, saw a woman's figure standing on the doorstep.

'It's Elizabeth,' he whispered to Lucia. 'Under an umbrella. And the bell's out of order.'

'*Uno, due.* So much the better, she'll go away,' said Lucia with a word to each beat.

She didn't. Georgie occasionally glancing up saw her still standing there and presently the first movement came to an end.

'I'll tell Foljambe I'm engaged,' said Georgie, stealing from his seat. 'What can she want? It's too late for lunch and too early for tea.'

It was too late for anything. The knocker sounded briskly, and before Georgie had time to give Foljambe this instruction, she opened the door, exactly at the moment that he opened his sitting-room door to tell her not to.

'Dear Mr Georgie,' said Elizabeth. 'So ashamed, but I've been eavesdropping. How I enjoyed listening to that lovely music. Wouldn't have interrupted it for anything!'

Elizabeth adopted the motion she called 'scriggling'. Almost imperceptibly she squeezed and wriggled till she had got past Foljambe, and had a clear view into Georgie's sitting-room.

'Why! There's dear Lucia,' she said. 'Such a lovely party last night, *chéri*: all Tilling talking about it. But I know I'm interrupting. Duet wasn't it? May I sit in a corner, mum as a mouse, while you go on? It would be such a treat. That lovely piece: I seem to know it so well. I should never forgive myself if I broke into it, besides losing such a pleasure. *Je vous prie!*'

It was of course quite clear to the performers that Elizabeth had come for some purpose beyond that of this treat, but she sank into a chair by the fire, and assumed the Tilling musical face (Lucia's patent), smiling wistfully, gazing at the ceiling, and supporting her chin on her hand, as was the correct attitude for slow movements.

So Georgie sat down again, and the slow movement went on its long deliberate way, and Elizabeth was surfeited with her

treat pages before it was done. Again and again she hoped it
was finished, but the same tune (rather like a hymn, she
thought) was presented in yet another aspect, till she knew it
inside out and upside down: it was like a stage army passing
by, individually the same, but with different helmets, or kilts
instead of trousers. At long last came several loud thumps, and
Lucia sighed and Georgie sighed, and before she had time to
sigh too, they were off again on the next instalment. This was
much livelier and Elizabeth abandoned her wistfulness for a
mien of sprightly pleasure, and, in turn, for a mien of scarcely
concealed impatience. It seemed odd that two people should
be so selfishly absorbed in that frightful noise as to think that
she had come in to hear them practise. True, she had urged
them to give her a treat, but who could have supposed that
such a gargantuan feast was prepared for her? Bang! Bang!
Bang! It was over and she got up.

'Lovely!' she said. 'Bach was always a favourite composer of
mine. *Merci!* And such luck to have found you here, dear
Lucia. What do you think I came to see Mr Georgie about?
Guess! I won't tease you. These coming elections to the Town
Council. Benjy-boy and I both feel very strongly – I believe he
mentioned it to you last night – that something must be done
to check the monstrous extravagance that's going on. *Tout le
monde* is crippled by it: we shall all be bankrupt if it continues.
We feel it our duty to fight it.'

Georgie was stroking his beard: this had already become a
habit with him in anxious moments. There must be a disclosure
now, and Lucia must make it. It was no use being chivalrous
and doing so himself: it was her business. So he occupied
himself with putting on the rings he had taken off for fate
knocking at the door and stroked his beard again.

'Yes, Major Benjy told me something of his plans last night,'
said Lucia, 'and I take quite the opposite line. Those slums,
for instance, ought to be swept away altogether, and new
houses built *tutto presto*.'

'But such a vandalism, dear,' said Elizabeth. 'So picturesque
and, I expect, so cosy. As to our plans, there's been a little
change in them. Benjy urged me so strongly that I yielded, and

I'm standing instead of him. So I'm getting to work *toute suite*, and I looked in to get promise of your support, *monsieur*, and then you and I must convert dear Lucia.'

The time had come.

'Dear Elizabeth,' said Lucia very decisively, 'you must give up all idea of that. I am standing for election myself on precisely the opposite policy. Cost what it may we must have no more slums and no more unemployment in our beloved Tilling. A Christian duty. Georgie agrees.'

'Well, in a sort of way –' began Georgie.

'Georgie, *tuo buon' cuore* agrees,' said Lucia, fixing him with the compulsion of her gimlet eye. 'You're enthusiastic about it really.'

Elizabeth ignored Lucia, and turned to him.

'Monsieur Georgie, it will be the ruin of us all,' she said, 'the Town Council is behaving as I said *à mon mari* just now, as if Tilling was Eldorado and the Rand.'

'Georgie, you and I go to-morrow to see those cosy picturesque hovels of which dear Elizabeth spoke,' said Lucia, 'and you will feel more keenly than you do even now that they must be condemned. You won't be able to sleep a wink at night if you feel you're condoning their continuance. Whole families sleeping in one room. Filth, squalor, immorality, insanitation –'

In their growing enthusiasm both ladies dropped foreign tongues.

'Look in any time, Mr Georgie,' interrupted Elizabeth, 'and let me show you the figures of how the authorities are spending your money and mine. And that new road which nobody wants has already cost –'

'The unemployment here, Georgie,' said Lucia 'would make angels weep. Strong young men willing and eager to get work, and despairing of finding it, while you and dear Elizabeth and I are living in ease and luxury in our beautiful houses.'

Georgie was standing between these two impassioned ladies, with his head turning rapidly this way and that, as if he was watching lawn tennis. At the same time he felt as if he was the ball that was being slogged to and fro between these powerful players, and he was mentally bruised and battered by their alternate intensity. Luckily, this last violent drive of Lucia's diverted Elizabeth's attack to her.

'Dear Lucia,' she said. 'You, of course, as a comparatively new resident in Tilling can't know very much about municipal expenditure, but I should be only too glad to show you how rates and taxes have been mounting up in the last ten years, owing to the criminal extravagance of the authorities. It would indeed be a pleasure.'

'I'm delighted to hear they've been mounting,' said Lucia. 'I want them to soar. It's a matter of conscience to me that they should.'

'Naughty and reckless of you,' said Elizabeth, trembling a little. 'You've no idea how hardly it presses on some of us.'

'We must shoulder the burden,' said Lucia. 'We must make up our minds to economize.'

Elizabeth with that genial air which betokened undiluted acidity, turned to Georgie, and abandoned principles for personalities, which had become irresistible.

'Quite a coincidence, isn't it, Mr Georgie,' she said, 'that the moment Lucia heard that my Benjy-boy was to stand for the Town Council, she determined to stand herself.'

Lucia emitted the silvery laugh which betokened the most exasperating and child-like amusement.

'Dear Elizabeth!' she said. 'How can you be so silly?'

'Did you say "silly" dear?' asked Elizabeth, white to the lips. Georgie intervened.

'O, dear me!' he said. 'Let's all have tea. So much more comfortable than talking about rates. I know there are muffins.'

They had both ceased to regard him now: instead of being driven from one to the other, he lay like a ball out of court, while the two advanced to the net with brandished rackets.

'Yes, dear, I said "silly", because you are silly,' said Lucia, as if she was patiently explaining something to a stupid child. 'You certainly implied that my object in standing was to oppose Major Benjy *qua* Major Benjy. What made me determined to stand myself, was that he advocated municipal economy.

It horrified me. He woke up my conscience, and I am most grateful to him. Most. And I shall tell him so on the first opportunity. Let me add that I regard you both with the utmost cordiality and friendliness. Should you be elected, which I hope and trust you won't, I shall be the first to congratulate you.'

Elizabeth put a finger to her forehead.

'Too difficult for me, I'm afraid,' she said. 'Such niceties are quite beyond my simple comprehension . . . No tea for me, thanks, Mr Georgie, even with muffins. I must be getting on with my canvassing. And thank you for your lovely music. So refreshing. Don't bother to see me out, but do look in some time and let me show you my tables of figures.'

She gave a hyena-smile to Lucia, and they saw her hurry past the window, having quite forgotten to put up her umbrella, as if she welcomed the cooling rain. Lucia instantly and without direct comment sat down at the piano again.

'Georgino, a little piece of celestial Mozartino, don't you think, before tea?' she said. 'That will put us in tune again after those discords. Poor woman!'

The campaign began in earnest next day, and at once speculative investments, Lucia's birthday-party and Georgie's beard were, as topics of interest, as dead as Queen Anne. The elections were coming on very soon, and intensive indeed were the activities of the two female candidates. Lucia hardly set foot in her Office, letting Transport 'C' pursue its upward path unregarded, and Benjy, after brief, disgusted glances at the *Financial Post*, which gave sad news of Siriami, took over his wife's household duties and went shopping in the morning instead of her, with her market-basket on his arm. Both ladies made some small errors: Lucia, for instance, exercised all her powers of charm on Twistevant the greengrocer, and ordered unheard of quantities of forced mushrooms, only to find, when she introduced the subject of her crusade and spoke of those stinking (no less) pigsties where human beings were forced to dwell, that he was the owner of several of them and much resented her disparagement of his house property. 'They're very nice little houses indeed, ma'am,' he said, 'and I should be happy to live there myself. I will send the mushrooms round at once . . .' Again, Elizabeth, seeing Susan's motor stopping the traffic (which usually made her see red), loaded her with compliments on her sable cloak (which had long been an object of derision to Tilling) and made an appointment to come and have a cosy talk at six that afternoon, carelessly oblivious of the fact that, a yard away, Georgie was looking into the barber's window. Hearing the appointment made, he very properly told Lucia, who therefore went to see Susan at exactly the hour named. The two candidates sat and talked to her, though not to each other, about everything else under the sun for an hour and a half, each of them being determined not to leave the other in possession of the field. At half-past seven Mr Wyse joined them to remind Susan that she must go and dress, and the candidates left together without having said a single word about the election. As soon as they had got outside Elizabeth shot away up the hill, rocking like a ship over the uneven cobbles of the street. That seemed very like a 'cut', and when Lucia next day, in order to ascertain that for certain, met the mistress of Mallards in the High Street and wished her good morning, Elizabeth might have been a deaf mute. They were both on their way to canvass Diva, and crossed the road neck to neck, but Lucia by a dexterous swerve established herself on Diva's doorstep and rang the bell. Diva was just going out with her market-basket, and opened the door herself.

'*Diva mia*,' said Lucia effusively, 'I just popped in to ask you to dine to-morrow: I'll send the car for you. And have you two minutes to spare now?'

'I'll look in presently, sweet Diva,' called Elizabeth shrilly over Lucia's shoulder. 'Just going to see the Padre.'

Lucia hurried in and shut the door.

'May I telephone to the Padre?' she asked. 'I want to get him, too, for to-morrow night. Thanks. I'll give you a penny in a moment.'

'Delighted to dine with you,' said Diva, 'but I warn you –'

'Tilling 23, please,' said Lucia. 'Yes, Diva?'

'I warn you I'm not going to vote for you. Can't afford to pay higher rates. Monstrous already.'

'Diva, if you only saw the state of those houses – Oh, is that the Padre? I hope you and Evie will dine with me to-morrow. Capital. I'll send the car for you. And may I pop in for a minute presently? . . . Oh, she's with you now, is she. Would you ring me up at Diva's then, the moment she goes?'

'It's a squeeze to make ends meet as it is,' said Diva. 'Very sorry for unemployed, and all that, but the new road is sheer extravagance. Money taken out of my pocket. I shall vote for Elizabeth. Tell you frankly.'

'But didn't you make a fortune over my tip about Siriamis?' asked Lucia.

'That would be over-stating it. It's no use your canvassing me. Talk about something else. Have you noticed any change, any real change, in Elizabeth lately?'

'I don't think so,' said Lucia thoughtfully. 'She was very much herself the last time I had any talk with her at Georgie's a few days ago. She seemed to take it as a personal insult that anyone but herself should stand for the Town Council, which is just what one would expect. Perhaps a shade more acid than usual, but nothing to speak of.'

'Oh, I don't mean that,' said Diva, 'No change there: I told you about the rabbit, didn't I?'

'Yes, so characteristic,' said Lucia. 'One hoped, of course, that matrimony might improve her, mellow her, make a true woman of her, but eagerly as I've looked out for any signs of it, I can't say –'

Lucia broke off, for a prodigious idea as to what might be in Diva's mind had flashed upon her.

'Tell me what you mean,' she said, boring with her eye into the very centre of Diva's secret soul, 'Not – not *that*?'

Diva nodded her head eight times with increasing emphasis.

'Yes, that,' she said.

'But it can't be true!' cried Lucia. 'Quite impossible. Tell me precisely why you think so?'

'I don't see why it shouldn't be true,' said Diva, 'for I think she's not more than forty-three, though of course it's more likely that she's only trying to persuade herself of it. She was in here the other day. Twilight. She asked me what twilight sleep was. Then hurriedly changed the subject and talked about the price of soap. Went back to subject again. Said there were such pretty dolls in the toy-shop. Had a mind to buy one. It's odd her talking like that. May be something in it. I shall keep an open mind about it.'

The two ladies had sat down on the window-seat, where the muslin curtains concealed them from without, but did not obstruct from them a very fair view of the High Street. Their thrilling conversation was now suddenly broken by the loud ringing, as of a dinner-bell, not far away to the right.

'That's not the muffin-man,' said Diva. 'Much too sonorous and the town-crier has influenza, so it's neither of them. I think there are two bells, aren't there? We shall soon see.'

The bells sounded louder and louder, evidently there were two of them, and a *cortège* (no less) came into view. Quaint Irene led it. She was dressed in her usual scarlet pullover and trousers, but on her head she wore a large tin helmet, like Britannia on a penny, and she rang her dinner-bell all the time, turning round and round as she walked. Behind her came four ragged girls eating buns and carrying a huge canvas banner painted with an impressionist portrait of Lucia, and a legend in gold letters 'Vote for Mrs Lucas, the Friend of the Poor.' Behind them walked Lucy, Irene's six-foot maid, ringing a second dinner-bell and chanting in a baritone voice, 'Bring out your dead.' She was followed by four ragged boys, also eating buns, who carried another banner painted with a hideous rendering of Elizabeth and a legend in black, 'Down with Mrs Mapp-Flint, the Foe of the Poor.' The whole procession was evidently enjoying itself prodigiously.

'Dear me, it's too kind of Irene,' said Lucia in some agitation, 'but is it quite discreet? What will people think? I must ask her to stop it.'

She hurried out into the street. The revolving Irene saw her, and, halting her procession, ran to her.

'Darling, you've come in the nick of time,' she said. 'Isn't it noble? Worth hundreds of votes to you. We're going to march up and down through all the streets for an hour, and then burn the Mapp-Flint banner in front of Mallards. Three cheers for Mrs Lucas, the Friend of the Poor!'

Three shrill cheers were given with splutterings of pieces of bun and frenzied ringing of dinner-bells before Lucia could get a word in. It would have been ungracious not to acknowledge this very gratifying enthusiasm, and she stood smiling and bowing on the pavement.

'Irene, dear, most cordial and sweet of you,' she began when the cheers were done, 'and what a charming picture of me, but –'

'And three groans for the Foe of the Poor,' shouted Irene.

Precisely at that tumultuous moment Major Benjy came down one side-street from Mallards on his marketing errands, and Elizabeth down the next on her way from her canvassing errand to the Padre. She heard the cheers, she heard the groans, she saw the banners and the monstrous cartoon of herself, and beckoned violently to her Benjy-boy, who broke into a trot.

'The enemy in force,' shrieked Irene. ' Run, children.'

The procession fled down the High Street with bells ringing and banners wobbling frightfully. Major Benjy restrained an almost overwhelming impulse to hurl his market-basket at Lucy, and he and Elizabeth started in pursuit. But there was a want of dignity about such a race and no hope whatever of catching the children. Already out of breath, they halted, the procession disappeared round the far end of the street, and the clamour of dinner-bells died away.

Shoppers and shop-keepers, post-office clerks, errand-boys, cooks and house-maids and private citizens had all come running out into the street at the sound of the cheers and groans and dinner-bells, windows had been thrown open, and heads leaned out of them, goggle-eyed and open-mouthed. Everyone cackled and chattered: it was like the second act of *The Meistersinger*. By degrees the excitement died down, and the pulse of ordinary life, momentarily suspended, began to beat again. Cooks went back to their kitchens, house-maids to their brooms, shop-keepers to their customers, and goggle-faces were withdrawn and windows closed. Major Benjy, unable to face shopping just now, went to play golf instead, and there were left standing on opposite pavements of the High Street the Friend of the Poor and the Foe of the Poor, both of whom could face anything, even each other.

Lucia did not know what in the world to do. She was innocent of all complicity in Irene's frightful demonstration in her favour, except that mere good manners had caused her weakly to smile and bow when she was cheered by four small girls, but nothing was more certain than that Elizabeth would believe that she had got up the whole thing. But, intrepid to the marrow of her bones, she walked across the street to where a similar intrepidity was standing. Elizabeth fixed her with a steely glance, and then looked carefully at a point some six inches above her head.

'I just popped across to assure you,' said Lucia, 'that I knew nothing about what we have just seen until – well, until, I saw it.'

Elizabeth cocked her head on one side, but remained looking at the fixed point.

'I think I understand,' she said, 'you didn't see that pretty show until you saw it. Quite! I take your word for it.'

'And I saw it first when it came into the High Street,' said Lucia. 'And I much regret it.'

'I don't regret it in the least,' said Elizabeth with shrill animation. 'People, whoever they are, who demean themselves either to plan or to execute such gross outrages only hurt themselves. I may be sorry for them, but otherwise they are nothing to me. I do not know of their existence. *Ils n'existent pas pour moi.*'

'Nor for me either,' said Lucia, following the general sentiment rather than the precise application, '*Sono niente.*'

Then both ladies turned their backs on each other, as by some perfectly executed movement in a ballet, and walked away in opposite directions. It was really the only thing to do.

Two days still remained before the poll, and these two remarkable candidates redoubled (if possible) their activities. Major Benjy got no golf at all, for he accompanied his wife everywhere, and Georgie formed a corresponding bodyguard for Lucia: in fact the feuds of the Montagues and Capulets were but a faint historical foreshadowing of this municipal contest. The parties, even when they met on narrow pavements in mean streets, were totally blind to each other, and, pending the result, social life in Tilling was at a standstill. As dusk fell on the eve of the poll. Lucia and Georgie, footsore with so much tramping on uneven cobble-stones, dragged themselves up the hill to Mallards Cottage for a final checking of their visits and a reviving cup of tea. They passed below the windows of the garden-room, obscured by the gathering darkness, and there, quite distinctly against the light within, were the silhouettes of the enemy, and Elizabeth was drinking out of a wine-glass. The silhouette of Benjy with a half-bottle of champagne in his hand showed what the refreshment was.

'Poor Elizabeth, taken to drink,' said Lucia, in tones of the deepest pity. 'I always feared for Benjy's influence on her. Tired as I am, Georgie – and I can't remember ever being really tired before – have you ever known me tired?'

'Never!' said Georgie in a broken voice.

'Well, tired as I am, nothing would induce me to touch any sort of stimulant. Ah, how nice it will be to sit down.'

Foljambe had tea ready for them and Lucia lay down full length on Georgie's sofa.

'Very strong, please, Georgie,' she said. 'Stir the teapot up well. No milk.'

The rasping beverage rapidly revived Lucia; she drank two cups, the first out of her saucer, then she took her feet off the sofa, and the familiar gabbling *timbre* came back to her voice.

'Completely restored, Georgie, and we've got to think what will happen next,' she said. 'Elizabeth and I can't go on being totally invisible to each other. And what more can I do? I definitely told her that I had nothing to do with dear, loyal Irene's exhibition, and she almost as definitely told me that she didn't believe me. About the election itself I feel very confident, but if I get in at the top of the poll, and she is quite at the bottom, which I think more than likely, she'll be worse than ever. The only thing that could placate her would be if she was elected and I wasn't. But there's not the slightest chance of that happening as far as I can see. I have a *flair*, as Elizabeth would say, about such things. All day I have felt a growing conviction that there is a very large body of public opinion behind me. I can feel the pulse of the place.'

Sheer weariness had made Georgie rather cross.

'I dare say Elizabeth feels precisely the same,' he said, 'especially after her booze. As for future plans, for goodness' sake let us wait till we see what the result is.'

Lucia finished her tea.

'How right you are, Georgino,' she said. 'Let us dismiss it all. What about *un po' di musica?*'

'Yes, do play me something,' said Georgie. 'But as to a duet, I can't. Impossible.'

'*Povero!*' said Lucia. 'Is 'oo *fatigato?* Then 'oo shall rest. I'll be going back home, for I want two hours in my office. I've done hardly anything all this week. *Buon riposo.*'

The result of the poll was declared two mornings later with due pomp and circumstance. The votes had been counted in the committee-room of the King's Arms Hotel in the High Street, and thither at noon came the Mayor and Corporation in procession from the Town Hall clad in their civic robes and preceded by the mace-bearers. The announcement was to be made from the first-floor balcony overlooking the High Street. Traffic was suspended for the ceremony and the roadway was solid with folk, for Tilling's interest in the election, usually of the tepidest, had been vastly stimulated by the mortal rivalry between the two lady candidates and by Irene's riotous proceedings. Lucia and Georgie had seats in Diva's drawing-room window, for that would be a conspicuous place from which to bow to the crowd: Elizabeth and Benjy were wedged against the wall below, and that seemed a good omen. The morning was glorious, and in the blaze of the winter sun the scarlet gowns of Councillors, and the great silver maces dazzled the eye as the procession went into the hotel.

'Really a very splendid piece of pageantry,' said Lucia, the palms of whose hands, despite her strong conviction of success, were slightly moist. 'Wonderful effect of colour, marvellous maces; what a pity, Georgie, you did not bring your paint-box. I have always said that there is no more honourable and dignified office in the kingdom than that of the Mayor of a borough. The word "mayor", I believe, is the same as Major – poor Major Benjy.'

'There's the list of the Mayors of Tilling from the fifteenth century onwards painted up in the Town Hall,' said Georgie.

'Really! A dynasty indeed!' said Lucia. Her fingers had begun to tremble as if she was doing rapid shakes and trills on the piano. 'Look, there's Irene on the pavement opposite, smoking a pipe. I find that a false note. I hope she won't make any fearful demonstration when the names are read out, but I see she has got her dinner-bell. Has a woman ever been Mayor of Tilling, Diva?'

'Never,' said Diva. 'Not likely either. Here they come.'

The mace-bearers emerged on to the balcony, and the Mayor stepped out between them and advanced to the railing. In his hand he held a drawing-board with a paper pinned to it.

'That must be the list,' said Lucia in a cracked voice. The town-crier (not Irene) rang his bell.

'Citizens of Tilling,' he proclaimed. 'Silence for the Right Worshipful the Mayor.'

The Mayor bowed. There were two vacancies to be filled, he said, on the Town Council, and there were seven candidates. He read the list with the number of votes each candidate had polled. The first two had polled nearly three hundred votes each. The next three, all close together, had polled between a hundred and fifty and two hundred votes.

'Number six,' said the Mayor, 'Mrs Emmeline Lucas. Thirty-nine votes. Equal with her, Mrs Elizabeth Mapp-Flint, also thirty-nine votes. God save the King.'

He bowed to the assembled crowd and, followed by the mace-bearers, disappeared within. Presently the procession emerged again, and returned to the Town Hall.

'A most interesting ceremony, Diva. Quite medieval,' said Lucia. 'I am very glad to have seen it. We got a wonderful view of it.'

The crowd had broken up when she and Georgie came out into the street.

'That noble story of Disraeli's first speech in the House of Commons,' she began –

5

The cause that chiefly conduced to the reconciliation of these two ultimate candidates was not Christian charity so much as the fact that their unhappy estrangement wrecked the social gaieties of Tilling, for Georgie and Lucia would not meet Mallards and Mallards would not meet Irene as long as it continued, and those pleasant tea-parties for eight with sessions of bridge before and after, could not take place. Again, both the protagonists found it wearing to the optic nerve to do their morning's shopping with one eye scouting for the approach of the enemy, upon which both eyes were suddenly smitten with blindness. On the other hand the Padre's sermon the next Sunday morning, though composed with the best intentions, perhaps retarded a reconciliation, for he preached on the text, 'Behold, how good and joyful a thing it is, brethren, to dwell together in unity,' and his allusions to the sad dissensions which arose from the clash of ambitions, highly honourable in themselves, were unmistakable. Both protagonists considered his discourse to be in the worst possible taste, and Elizabeth entirely refused to recognize either him or Evie when next they met, which was another wedge driven into Tilling. But inconvenience, dropping like perpetual water on a stone, eventually wore down dignity, and when, some ten days after the election, the market-baskets of Lucia and Elizabeth came into violent collision at the door of the fishmonger's, Lucia was suddenly and miraculously healed of her intermittent blindness. 'So sorry, dear,' she said, 'quite my fault,' and Elizabeth, remembering with an effort that Lent was an appropriate season for self-humiliation, said it was quite hers. They chatted for several minutes, rather carefully, with eager little smiles, and Diva who had observed this interesting scene, raced up and down the street, to tell everybody that an armistice at least had been signed. So bridge-parties for eight were resumed with more than their usual frequency, to make up for lost time, and though Lucia had forsworn all such petty occupations, her ingenuity soon found a formula, which justified her in going to them much as usual.

'Yes, Georgie, I will come with pleasure this afternoon,' she said, 'for the most industrious must have their remissions. How wonderfully Horace puts it: "*Non semper arcum tendit Apollo.*" I would give anything to have known Horace. Terse and witty and wise. Half-past three then. Now I must hurry home, for my broker will want to know what I think about a purchase of Imperial Tobacco.'

That, of course, was her way of putting it, but put it as you liked, the fact remained that she had been making pots of money. An Industrial boom was on, and by blindly following Mammoncash's advice, Lucia was doing exceedingly well. She was almost frightened at the speed with which she had been growing richer, but remembered the splendid career of great Dame Catherine Winterglass, whose picture, cut out of an illustrated magazine, now stood framed on the table in her office. Dame Catherine had made a fortune by her own skill in forecasting the trend of the markets; that was not due to luck but to ability, and to be afraid of her own ability was quite foreign to Lucia's nature.

The financial group at Mallards, Mapp & Flint, was not displaying the same acumen, and one day it suffered a frightful shock. There had been a pleasant bridge-party at Diva's, and Elizabeth showed how completely she had forgiven Lucia, by asking her counsel about Siriami. The price of the shares had been going down lately, like an aneroid before a typhoon, and, as it dwindled, Elizabeth had continued to buy. What did Lucia think of this policy of averaging?

Lucia supported her forehead on her hand in the attitude of Shakespeare and Dame Catherine.

'Dear me, it is so long since I dealt in Siriami,' she said. 'A West African gold mine, I seem to recollect? The price of gold made me buy, I am sure. I remember reasoning it out and concluding that gold would go up. There were favourable reports from the mine too. And why did I sell? How you all work my poor brain! Ah! Eureka! I thought I should have to tie up my capital for a long time: my broker agreed with me, though I should say most decidedly that it is a promising lock-up. Siriami is still in the early stage of development, you see, and no dividend can be expected for a couple of years –'

'Hey, what's that?' asked Benjy.

'More than two years, do you think?' asked Lucia. 'I am rusty about it. Anyone who holds on, no doubt, will reap a golden reward in time.'

'But I shan't get any dividends for two years?' asked Elizabeth in a hollow voice.

'Ah, pray don't trust my judgment,' said Lucia. 'All I can say for certain, is that I made some few pounds in the mine, and decided it was too long a lock-up of my little capital.'

Elizabeth felt slightly unwell. Benjy had acquired a whisky and soda and she took a sip of it without it even occurring to her that he had no business to have it.

'Well, we must be off,' she said, for though the reconciliation was so recent, she felt it might be endangered if she listened to any more of this swank. 'Thanks, dear, for your views. All that four shillings mine? Fancy!'

It was raining hard when they left Diva's house, and they walked up the narrow pavement to Mallards in single file, with a loud and dismal tattoo drumming on their umbrellas, and streams of water pouring from the ends of the ribs. Arrived there, Elizabeth led the way out to the garden-room and put her dripping umbrella in the fender. It had been wet all afternoon and before going to Diva's, Benjy had smoked two cigars there.

'Of course, this is your room, dear,' said Elizabeth, 'and if you prefer it to smell like a pot-house, it shall. But would you mind having the window open a chink for a moment, for unless you do, I shall be suffocated.'

She fanned herself with her handkerchief, and took two or three long breaths of the brisker air.

'Thank you. Refreshed,' she said. 'And now we must talk Siriami. I think Lucia might have told us about its not paying dividends before, but don't let us blame her much. It merely isn't the way of some people to consider others –'

'She told you she was selling all the Siriami shares she held,' said Benjy.

'If you've finished championing her, Benjy, perhaps you'll allow me to go on. I've put two thousand pounds into that hole in the ground, for, as far as I can see, it's little more than that. And that means that for the next two years my income will be diminished by seventy pounds.'

'God bless me,' ejaculated Benjy. 'I had no idea you had invested so heavily in it.'

'I believe a woman, even though married, is allowed to do what she likes with her money,' said Elizabeth bitterly.

'I never said she wasn't. I only said that I didn't know it,' said Benjy.

'That was why I told you. And the long and short of it is that we had better let this house as soon as we can for as long as we can, because we can't afford to live here.'

'But supposing Mrs Lucas is wrong about it? I've known her wrong before now –'

'So have I,' interrupted Elizabeth, 'usually, in fact: but we must be prepared for her being right for once. As it is, I've got to let Mallards for three or four months in the year in order to live in it at all. I shall go to Woolgar & Pipstow's to-morrow and put it in their hands, furnished (all our beautiful things!) for six months. Perhaps with option of a year.'

'And where shall we go?' asked Benjy.

Elizabeth rose.

'Wherever we can. One of those little houses, do you think, which Lucia wanted to pull down. And then, perhaps, as I told you, there'll be another little mouth to feed, dear.'

'I wish you would go to Dr Dobbie and make sure,' he said.

'And what would Dr Dobbie tell me? "Have a good rest before dinner." Just what I'm going to do.'

With the re-establishment of cordial relations between the two leading ladies of Tilling, the tide of news in the mornings flowed on an unimpeded course, instead of being held up in the eddies of people who would speak to each other, and being blocked by those who wouldn't, and though as yet there was nothing definite on the subject to which Elizabeth and Benjy had thus briefly alluded, there were hints, there were signs and indications that bore on it, of the very highest significance. The first remarkable occurrence was that Major Benjy instead of going to play golf next morning, according to his invariable custom, came shopping with Elizabeth, as he had done when she was busy canvassing, and carried his wife's basket. There was a solicitous, a tender air about the way he gave her an arm as she mounted the two high steps into Twistevant's shop. Diva was the first to notice this strange phenomenon, and naturally she stood rooted to the spot in amazement, intent on further observation. When they came out there was not the shadow of doubt in her mind that Elizabeth had let out the old green skirt that everyone knew so well. It fell in much ampler folds than ever before, and Diva vividly recollected that strange talk about dolls and twilight sleep: how pregnant it seemed now, in every sense of the word! The two popped into another shop, and at that moment the Padre and Evie debouched into the High Street, a few yards away, and he went into the tobacconist's, leaving Evie outside. Diva uprooted herself with difficulty, hurried to her, and the two ladies had a few whispered remarks together. Then the Mapp-Flints came out again, and retraced their way, followed by four eager detective eyes.

'But no question whatever about the skirt,' whispered Evie, 'and she has taken Major Benjy's arm again. *So unusual.* What an event if it's really going to happen! Never such a thing before in our circle. She'll be quite a heroine. There's Mr Georgie. What a pity we can't tell him about it. What beautiful clothes!'

Georgie had on his fur-trimmed cape and a new bright blue beret which he wore a little sideways on his head. He was coming towards them with more than his usual briskness, and held his mouth slightly open as if to speak the moment he got near enough.

'Fiddlesticks, Evie,' said Diva. 'You don't expect that Mr Georgie, at his age, thinks they're found under gooseberry-bushes. Good morning, Mr Georgie. Have you seen Elizabeth –'

'Skirt,' he interrupted. 'Yes, of course. Three inches I should think.'

Evie gave a little horrified squeal at this modern lack of reticence in talking to a gentleman who wasn't your husband, on matters of such extreme delicacy, and took refuge in the tobacconist's.

'And Major Benjy carrying her basket for her,' said Diva. 'So it must be true, unless she's deceiving him.'

'Look, they've turned down Malleson Street,' cried Georgie. 'That's where Dr Dobbie lives.'

'So do Woolgar & Pipstow,' said Diva.

'But they wouldn't be thinking of letting Mallards as early as March,' objected Georgie.

'Well, it's not likely. Must be the doctor's. I'm beginning to believe it. At first when she talked to me about dolls and twilight sleep, I thought she was only trying to make herself interesting, instead of being so —'

'I never heard about dolls and twilight sleep,' said Georgie, with an ill-used air.

'Oh, here's Irene on her motor-bicycle, coming up from Malleson Street,' cried Diva. 'I wonder if she saw where they went. What a row she makes! And so rash. I thought she must have run into Susan's Royce, and what a mess there would have been.'

Irene, incessantly hooting, came thundering along the High Street, with foul fumes pouring from the open exhaust. She evidently intended to pull up and talk to them, but miscalculated her speed. To retard herself, she caught hold of Georgie's shoulder, and he tittuped along, acting as a brake, till she came to a standstill.

'My life-preserver!' cried Irene fervently, as she dismounted. 'Georgie, I adore your beard. Do you put it inside your bedclothes or outside? Let me come and see some night when you've gone to bed. Don't be alarmed, dear lamb, your sex protects you from any forwardness on my part. I was on my way to see Lucia. There's news. Give me a nice dry kiss and I'll tell you.'

'I couldn't think of it,' said Georgie. 'What would everybody say?'

'Dear old grandpa,' said Irene. 'They'd say you were a bold and brazen old man. That would be a horrid lie. You're a darling old lady, and I love you. What were we talking about?'

'You were talking great nonsense,' said Georgie, pulling his cape back over his shoulder.

'Yes, but do you know why? I had a lovely idea. I thought how enlightening it would be to live a day backwards. So when I got up this morning, I began backwards as if it was the end of the day instead of the beginning. I had two pipes and a whisky and soda. Then I had dinner backwards, beginning with toasted cheese, and I'm slightly tipsy. When I get home I shall have tea, and go out for a walk and then have lunch, and shortly before going to bed I shall have breakfast and then some salts. Do you see the plan? It gives you a new view of life altogether; you see it all from a completely different angle. Oh, I was going to tell you the news. I saw the Mapp-Flints going into the house-agents'. She appeared not to see me. She hasn't seen me since dinner-bell day. I hope you understand about living backwards. Let's all do it: one and all.'

'My dear, it sounds too marvellous,' said Georgie, 'but I'm sure it would upset me and I should only see it from the angle of being sick ... Diva, they were only going into Woolgar & Pipstow's.'

Diva had trundled up to them.

'Not the doctor's, then,' she said. 'I'm disappointed. It would have made it more conclusive.'

'Made what more conclusive?' asked Irene.

'Well, it's thought that Elizabeth's expecting –' began Diva.

'You don't say so!' said Irene. 'Who's the co-respondent? Georgie, you're blushing below your beard. Roguey-poguey-Romeo! I saw you climbing up a rope-ladder into the garden-room when you were supposed to be ill. Juliet Mapp opened the window to you, and you locked her in a passionate embrace. I didn't want to get you into trouble, so I didn't say anything about it, and now you've gone and got her into trouble, you wicked old Romeo, hoots and begorra. I must be godmother, Georgie, and now I'm off to tell Lucia.'

Irene leapt on to her bicycle and disappeared in a cloud of mephitic vapour in the direction of Grebe.

With the restoration of the free circulation of news, it was no wonder that by the afternoon it was universally known that this most interesting addition to the population of Tilling was expected. Neither of the two people most closely concerned spoke of it directly, but indirectly their conduct soon proclaimed it from the house-roofs. Benjy went strutting about with his wife, carrying her market-basket, obviously with the conscious pride of approaching fatherhood, pretty to see; and when he went to play golf, leaving her to do her marketing alone, Elizabeth, wreathed in smiles, explained his absence in hints of which it was impossible to miss the significance.

'I positively drove my Benjy-boy out to the links to-day,' she said to Diva. 'I insisted, though he was very loth to go. But where's the use of his hanging about? Ah, there's quaint Irene: foolish of me, but after her conduct at the elections, it agitates me a little to see her, though I'm sure I forgive her with all my heart. I'll just pop into the grocer's.'

Irene stormed by, and Elizabeth popped out again.

'And you may not have heard yet, dear,' she continued, 'that we want to let our sweet Mallards for six months or a year. Not that I blame anybody but myself for that necessity. Lucia perhaps might have told me that Siriami would not be paying any dividends for a couple of years, but she didn't. That's all.'

'But you were determined to do the opposite of whatever she advised,' said Diva. 'You told me so.'

'No, you're wrong there,' said Elizabeth, with some vehemence. 'I never said that.'

'But you did,' cried Diva. 'You said that if she bought Siriami, you would sell and versy-visa.'

Instead of passionately denying this, Elizabeth gave a faraway smile like Lucia's music smile over the slow movements of sonatas.

'We won't argue about it, dear,' she said. 'Have it all your own way.'

This suavity was most uncharacteristic of Elizabeth: was it a small piece of corroborative evidence?

'Anyhow, I'm dreadfully sorry you're in low water,' said Diva. 'Hope you'll get a good let. Wish I could take Mallards myself.'

'A little bigger than you're accustomed to, dear,' said Elizabeth with a touch of the old Eve. 'I don't think you'd be very comfortable in it. If I can't get a long let, I shall have to shut it up and store my furniture, to avoid those monstrous rates, and take a teeny-weeny house somewhere else. For myself I don't seem to mind at all, I shall be happy anywhere, but what really grieves me is that my Benjy must give up his dear garden-room. But as long as we're together, what does it matter, and he's so brave and tender about it . . . Good morning, Mr Georgie. I've news for you, which I hope you'll think is bad news.'

Georgie had a momentary qualm that this was something sinister about Foljambe, who had been very cross lately: there was no pleasing her.

'I don't know why you should hope I should think it bad news,' he said.

'I shall tease you,' said Elizabeth in a sprightly tone. 'Guess! Somebody going away: that's a hint.'

Georgie knew that if this meant Foljambe was going to leave, it was highly unlikely that she should have told Elizabeth and not him, but it gave him a fresh pang of apprehension.

'Oh, it's so tarsome to be teased,' he said. 'What is it?'

'You're going to lose your neighbours. Benjy and I have got to let Mallards for a long, long time.'

Georgie repressed a sigh of relief.

'Oh, I am sorry: that is bad news,' he said cheerfully. 'Where are you going?'

'Don't know yet. Anywhere. A great wrench, but there's so much to be thankful for. I must be getting home. My boyikins will scold me if I don't rest before lunch.'

Somehow this combination of financial disaster and great ex-pectations raised Elizabeth to a high position of respect and sympathy in the eyes of Tilling. Lucia, Evie and Diva were all

childless, and though Susan Wyse had had a daughter by her
first marriage, Isabel Poppit was now such a Yahoo, living
permanently in an unplumbed shack among the sand-dunes,
that she hardly counted as a human being at all. Even if she
was one, she was born years before her mother had come to
settle here, and thus was no Tillingite. In consequence Elizabeth became a perfect heroine; she was elderly (it was really
remarkably appropriate that her name was Elizabeth) and now
she was going to wipe the eye of all these childless ladies. Then
again her financial straits roused commiseration: it was sad for
her to turn out of the house she had lived in for so long and
her Aunt Caroline before her. No doubt she had been very
imprudent, and somehow the image presented itself of her and
Benjy being caught like flies in the great web Lucia had been
spinning, in the centre of which she sat, sucking gold out of
the spoils entangled there. The image was not accurate, for
Lucia had tried to shoo them out of her web, but the general
impression remained, and it manifested itself in little acts of
homage to Elizabeth at bridge-parties and social gatherings, in
care being taken that she had a comfortable chair, that she was
not sitting in draughts, in warm congratulations if she won her
rubbers and in sympathy if she lost. She was helped first and
largely at dinner, Susan Wyse constantly lent her the Royce
for drives in the country, so that she could get plenty of fresh
air without undue fatigue, and Evie Bartlett put a fat cushion
in her place behind the choir at church. Already she had
enjoyed precedence as a bride, but this new precedence quite
outshone so conventional a piece of etiquette. Benjy partook of
it too in a minor degree, for fatherhood was just as rare in the
Tilling circle as motherhood. He could not look down on
Georgie's head, for Georgie was the taller, but he straddled
before the fire with legs wide apart and looked down on the
rest of him and on the entire persons of Mr Wyse and Padre.
The former must have told his sister, the Contessa Faraglione,
who from time to time visited him in Tilling, of the happy
event impending, for she sent a message to Elizabeth of so
delicate a nature, about her own first confinement, that Mr
Wyse had been totally unable to deliver it himself, and en-

trusted it to his wife. The Contessa also sent Elizabeth a large
jar of Italian honey, notable for its nutritious qualities. As for
the Padre, he remembered with shame that he had suggested
that a certain sentence should be omitted from Elizabeth's
marriage service, which she had insisted should be read, and
he made himself familiar with the form for the Churching of
Women.

But there were still some who doubted. Quaint Irene was
one, in spite of her lewd observations to Georgie; in her coarse
way she offered to lay odds that she would have a baby before
Elizabeth. Lucia was another. But one morning Georgie,
coming out of Mallards Cottage, had seen Dr Dobbie's car
standing at the door of Mallards, and he had positively run
down to the High Street to disseminate this valuable piece of
indirect evidence, and in particular to tell Lucia. But she was
nowhere about, and, as it was a beautiful day, and he was less
busy than usual, having finished his piece of *petit point* yesterday, he walked out to Grebe to confront her with it. Just now,
being in the Office, she could not be disturbed, as Grosvenor
decided that a casual morning call from an old friend could not
rank as an urgency, and he sat down to wait for her in the
drawing-room. It was impossible to play the piano, for the
sound, even with the soft pedal down, would have penetrated
into the Great Silence, but he found on the table a fat volume
called *Health in the Home*, and saw at once that he could fill up
his time very pleasantly with it. He read about shingles and
decided that the author could never have come across as bad a
case as his own: he was reassured that the slight cough which
had troubled him lately was probably not incipient tuber-
culosis: he made a note of calomel, for he felt pretty sure that
Foljambe's moroseness was due to liver, and she might be
induced to take a dose. Then he became entirely absorbed in a
chapter about mothers. A woman, he read, often got mistaken
ideas into her head: she would sometimes think that she was
going to have a baby, but would refuse to see a doctor for fear
of being told that she was not. Then, hearing Lucia's step on
the stairs, he hastily tried to replace the book on the table, but
it slipped from his hand and lay open on the carpet, and there

was not time to pick it up before Lucia entered. She said not a word, but sank down in a chair, closing her eyes.

'My dear, you're not ill, are you?' said Georgie. Lucia kept her eyes shut.

'What time is it?' she asked in a hollow voice.

'Getting on for eleven. You are all right, are you?'

Lucia spread out her arms as if measuring some large object.

'Perfectly. But columns of figures, Georgie, and terrific decisions to make, and now reaction has come. I've been telephoning to London. I may be called up any moment. Divert my mind, while I relax. Any news?'

'I came down on purpose to tell you,' said Georgie, 'and perhaps even you will be convinced now. Dr Dobbie's car was waiting outside Mallards this morning.'

'No!' said Lucia, opening her eyes and becoming extremely brisk and judicial. 'That does look more like business. But still I can't say that I'm convinced. You see, finance makes one look at all possible sides of a situation. Consider. No doubt, it was the doctor's car: I don't dispute that. But Major Benjy may have had an upset. Elizabeth may have fallen downstairs, though I'm sure I hope she hasn't. Her cook may have mumps. Lots of things. No, Georgie, if the putative baby was an Industrial share – I put it badly – I wouldn't touch it.'

She pointed at the book on the floor.

'I see what that book is,' she said, 'and I feel sure you've been reading about it. So have I. A rather interesting chapter about the delusions and fancies of middle-aged women lately married. Sometimes, so it said, they do not even believe themselves, but are only acting a kind of charade. Elizabeth must have had great fun, supposing she has been merely acting, getting her Benjy-boy and you and others to believe her, and being made much of.'

Lucia cocked her head thinking she heard the telephone. But it was only a womanly fancy of her own.

'Poor dear,' she said. 'I am afraid her desire to have a baby may have led her to deceive others and perhaps herself, and then of course she likes being petted and exalted and admired. You must all be very kind and oblivious when the day comes that she has to give it up. No more twilight sleep or wanting to buy dolls or having the old green skirt let out – Ah, there's the telephone. Wait for me, will you, for I have something more to say.'

Lucia hurried out, and Georgie, after another glance at the medical book, applied his mind to the psychological aspect of the situation. Lucia had doubtless writhed under the growing ascendency of Elizabeth. She knew about the Contessa's honey, she had seen how Elizabeth was cossetted and helped first and listened to with deference, however abject her utterance, and she could not have liked the secondary place which the sentiment of Tilling assigned to herself. She was a widow of fifty, and Elizabeth in virtue of her approaching motherhood, had really become of the next generation, whose future lies before them. Everyone had let Lucia pass into eclipse. Elizabeth was the great figure, and was the more heroic because she was obliged to let the ancestral home of her Aunt. Then there was the late election: it must have been bitter to Lucia to be at the bottom of the poll and obtain just the same number of votes as Elizabeth. All this explained her incredulity . . . Then once more her step sounded on the stairs.

'All gone well?' asked Georgie.

'*Molto bene.* I convinced my broker that mine was the most likely view. Now about poor Elizabeth. You must all be kind to her, I was saying. There is, I am convinced, an awful anti-climax in front of her. We must help her past it. Then her monetary losses: I really am much distressed about them. But what can you expect when a woman with no financial experience goes wildly gambling in gold mines of which she knows nothing, and thinks she knows better than anybody? Asking for trouble. But I've made a plan, Georgie, which I think will pull her out of the dreadful hole in which she now finds herself. That house of hers, Mallards. Not a bad house. I am going to offer to take it off her hands altogether, to buy the freehold.'

'I think she only wants to let it furnished for a year if she can,' said Georgie, 'otherwise she means to shut it up.'

'Well, listen.'

Lucia ticked off her points with a finger of one hand on the fingers of the other.

'*Uno.* Naturally I can't lease it from her as it is, furnished with mangy tiger-skins, and hip-baths for chairs and Polynesian aprons on the walls and a piano that belonged to her grandmother. Impossible.'

'Quite,' said Georgie.

'*Due.* The house wants a thorough doing-up from top to bottom. I suspect dry rot. Mice and mildewed wallpaper and dingy paint, I know. And the drains must be overhauled. I don't suppose they've been looked at for centuries. I shall not dream of asking her to put it in order.'

'That sounds very generous so far,' said Georgie.

'That is what it is intended to be. *Tre.* I will take over from her the freehold of Mallards and hand to her the freehold of Grebe with a cheque for two thousand pounds, for I understand that is what she has sunk in her reckless speculations. If she accepts, she will step into this house all in apple-pie order and leave me with one which it will really cost a little fortune to make habitable. But I think I *ought* to do it, Georgie. The law of kindness. *Che pensate?*'

Georgie knew that it had long been the dream of Lucia's life to get Mallards for her own, but the transaction, stated in this manner, wore the aspect of the most disinterested philanthropy. She was evidently persuaded that it was, for she was so touched by the recital of her own generosity that the black bird-like brightness of her eyes was dimmed with moisture.

'We are all here to help each other, Georgie,' she continued, 'and I consider it a Providential privilege to be able to give Elizabeth a hand out of this trouble. There is other trouble in front of her, when she realizes how she has been deceiving others, and, as I say, perhaps herself, and it will make it easier for her if she has no longer this money worry and the prospect of living in some miserable little house. Irene burst into tears when I told her what I was going to do. So emotional.'

Georgie did not cry, for this Providential privilege of helping others, even at so great an expense, would give Lucia just what she wanted most. That consideration dried up, at its source, any real tendency to tears.

'Well, I think she ought to be very grateful to you,' he said.

'No, Georgie, I don't expect that; Elizabeth may not appreciate the benevolence of my intentions, and I shall be the last to point it out. Now let us walk up to the town. The nature of Dr Dobbie's visit to Mallards will probably be known by now and I have finished with my Office till the arrival of the evening post . . . Do you think she'll take my offer?'

Marketing was over before they got up to the High Street, but Diva made a violent tattoo on her window, and threw it open.

'All a wash-out about Dr Dobbie,' she called out. 'The cook scalded her hand, that's all. Saw her just now. Lint and oiled silk.'

'Oh, poor thing!' said Lucia. 'What did I tell you, Georgie?'

Lucia posted her philanthropic proposal to Elizabeth that very day. In consequence there was a most agitated breakfast duet at Mallards next morning.

'So like her,' cried Elizabeth, when she had read the letter to Benjy with scornful interpolations. 'So very like her. But I know her well enough now to see her meannesses. She has always wanted my house and is taking a low advantage of my misfortunes to try to get it. But she shan't have it. Never! I would sooner burn it down with my own hands.'

Elizabeth crumpled up the letter and threw it into the grate. She crashed her way into a piece of toast and resumed.

'She's an encroacher,' she said, 'and quite unscrupulous. I am more than ever convinced that she put the idea of those libellous dinner-bells into Irene's head.'

Benjy was morose this morning.

'Don't see the connection at all,' he said.

Elizabeth couldn't bother to explain anything so obvious and went on.

'I forgave her that for the sake of peace and quietness, and because I'm a Christian, but this is too much. Grebe indeed! Grab would be the best name for any house she lives in. A wretched villa liable to be swept away by floods, and you and me carried out to sea again on a kitchen-table. My answer is no, pass the butter.'

'I should't be too much in a hurry,' said Benjy. 'It's two thousand pounds as well. Even if you got a year's let for Mallards, you'd have to spend a pretty penny in doing it up. Any tenant would insist on that.'

'The house is in perfect repair in every respect,' said Elizabeth.

'That might not be a tenant's view. And you might not get a tenant at all.'

'And the wicked insincerity of her letter,' continued Elizabeth. 'Saying she's sorry I have to turn out of it. Sorry! It's what she's been lying in wait for. I have a good mind not to answer her at all.'

'And I don't see the point of that,' said Benjy. 'If you are determined not to take her offer, why not tell her so at once?'

'You're not very bright this morning, love,' said Elizabeth, who had begun to think.

This spirited denunciation of Lucia's schemings was in fact only a conventional prelude to reflection. Elizabeth went to see her cook; in revenge for Benjy's want of indignation, she ordered him a filthy dinner, and finding that he had left the dining-room, fished Lucia's unscrupulous letter out of the grate, slightly scorched, but happily legible, and read it through again. Then, though she had given him the garden-room for his private sitting-room, she entered, quite forgetting to knock and ask if she might come in, and established herself in her usual seat in the window, where she could observe the movements of society, in order to tune herself back to normal pitch. A lot was happening: Susan's great car got helplessly stuck, as it came out of Porpoise Street, for a furniture van was trying to enter the same street, and couldn't back because there was another car behind it. The longed-for moment therefore had probably arrived, when Susan would have to go marketing on foot. Georgie went by in his Vandyck cape and a new suit (or perhaps dyed), but what was quaint Irene doing? She appeared to be sitting in the air in front of her house on a level with the first-storey windows. Field-glasses had to be brought to bear on this: they revealed that she was suspended in a hammock slung from her bedroom window and (clad in pyjamas) was painting the sill in squares of black and crimson. Susan got out of her car and waddled towards the High Street. Georgie stopped and talked to Irene who dropped a paint-brush loaded with crimson on that blue beret of his. All quite satisfactory.

Benjy went to his golf: he had not actually required much driving this morning, and Elizabeth was alone. She had lately started crocheting a little white woollen cap, and tried it on. It curved downwards too sharply, as if designed for a much smaller head than hers, and she pulled a few rows out, and began it again in a flatter arc. A fresh train of musing was set up, and she thought, with strong distaste, of the day when Tilling would begin to wonder whether anything was going to happen, and, subsequently, to know that it wasn't. After all, she had never made any directly misleading statement: she had chosen (it was a free country) to talk about dolls and twilight sleep, and to let out her old green skirt, and Tilling had drawn its own conclusions. 'That dreadful gossipy habit,' she said to herself, 'if there isn't any news they invent it. And I know that they'll blame me for their disappointment. (Again she looked out of the window: Susan's motor had extricated itself, and was on its way to the High Street, and that was a disappointment too.) I must try to think of something to divert their minds when that time comes.'

Her stream of consciousness, eddying round in this depressing backwater, suddenly found an outlet into the main current, and she again read Lucia's toasted letter. It was a very attractive offer; her mouth watered at the thought of two thousand pounds, and though she had expressed to Benjy in unmistakable terms her resolve to reject any proposal so impertinent and unscrupulous, or, perhaps, in a fervour of disdain, not to answer it at all, there was nothing to prevent her accepting it at once, if she chose. A woman in her condition was always apt to change her mind suddenly and violently. (No: that would not do, since she was not a woman in her condition.) And surely here was a very good opportunity of diverting Tilling's attention. Lucia's settling into Mallards and her own move to Grebe would be of the intensest interest to Tilling's corporate mind, and that would be the time to abandon the role of coming motherhood. She would just give it up, just go shopping again with her usual briskness, just take in the green skirt and wear the enlarged woollen cap herself. She need make no explanations for she had said nothing that required them: Tilling, as usual, had done all the talking.

She turned her mind to the terms of Lucia's proposal. The blaze of fury so rightly kindled by the thought of Lucia possessing Mallards was spent, and the thought of that fat capital sum made a warm glow for her among the ashes. As Benjy had said, no tenant for six months or a year would take a house so sorely in need of renovation, and if Lucia was right in supposing that that wretched hole in the ground somewhere in West Africa would not be paying dividends for two years, a tenant for one year, even if she was lucky enough to find one, would only see her half through this impoverished period. No sensible woman could reject so open a way out of her difficulties.

The mode of accepting this heaven-sent offer required thought. Best, perhaps, just formally to acknowledge the unscrupulous letter, and ask for a few days in which to make up her mind. A little hanging back, a hint conveyed obliquely, say through Diva, that two thousand pounds did not justly represent the difference in values between her lovely Queen Anne house and the villa precariously placed so near the river, a heart-broken wail at the thought of leaving the ancestral home might lead to an increased payment in cash, and that would be pleasant. So, having written her acknowledgment Elizabeth picked up her market-basket and set off for the High Street.

Quaint Irene had finished her window-sill, and was surveying the effect of this brilliant decoration from the other side of the street. In view of the disclosure which must come soon, Elizabeth suddenly made up her mind to forgive her for the dinner-bell outrage for fear she might do something quainter yet: a cradle, for instance, with a doll inside it, left on the doorstep would be very unnerving, and was just the sort of thing Irene might think of. So she said:

'Good morning, love: what a pretty window-sill. So bright.'

Regardless of Elizabeth's marriage Irene still always addressed her as 'Mapp'.

'Not bad, is it, Mapp,' she said. 'What about my painting the whole of your garden-room in the same style? A hundred pounds down, and I'll begin to-day.'

'That *would* be very cheap,' said Mapp enthusiastically. 'But alas, I fear my days there are numbered.'

'Oh, of course; Lucia's offer. The most angelic thing I ever heard. I knew you'd jump at it.'

'No, dear, not quite inclined to jump,' said Mapp rather injudiciously.

'Oh, I didn't mean literally,' said Irene. 'That would be very rash of you. But isn't it like her, so noble and generous? I cried when she told me.'

'I shall cry when I have to leave my sweet Mallards,' observed Elizabeth. 'If I accept her offer, that is.'

'Then you'll be a crashing old crocodile, Mapp,' said Irene. 'You'll really think yourself damned lucky to get out of that old ruin of yours on such terms. Do you like my pyjamas? I'll give you a suit like them when the happy day –'

'Must be getting on,' interrupted Elizabeth. 'Such a lot to do.'

Feeling slightly battered, but with the glow of two thousand pounds comforting her within, Elizabeth turned into the High Street. Diva, it seemed, had finished her shopping, and was seated on this warm morning at her open window reading the paper. Elizabeth approached quite close unobserved, and with an irresistible spasm of playfulness said 'Bo!'

Diva gave a violent start.

'Oh, it's you, is it?' she said.

'No, dear, somebody quite different,' said Elizabeth skittishly. 'And I'm in such a state of perplexity this morning. I don't know what to do.'

'Benjy eloped with Lucia?' asked Diva. Two could play at being playful.

Elizabeth winced.

'Diva, dear, jokes on certain subjects only hurt me,' she said. '*Tiens! Je vous pardonne.*'

'What's perplexing you then?' asked Diva. 'Come in and talk if you want to, *tiens*. Can't go bellowing bad French into the street.'

Elizabeth came in, refused a low and comfortable chair and took a high one.

'Such an agonizing decision to make,' she said, 'and its coming just now is almost more than I can bear. I got *un petit lettre* from Lucia this morning offering to give me the freehold of Grebe and two thousand pounds in exchange for the freehold of Mallards.'

'I knew she was going to make you some offer,' said Diva. 'Marvellous for you. Where does the perplexity come in? Besides, you were going to let it for a year if you possibly could.'

'Yes, but the thought of never coming back to it. *Mon vieux*, so devoted to his garden-room, where we were engaged. Turning out for ever. And think of the difference between my lovely Queen Anne house and that villa by the side of the road that leads nowhere. The danger of floods. The distance.'

'But Lucia's thought of that,' said Diva, 'and puts the difference down at two thousand pounds. I should have thought one thousand was ample.'

'There are things like atmosphere that can't be represented in terms of money,' said Elizabeth with feeling. 'All the old associations. *Tante Caroline.*'

'Not having known your *Tante Caroline* I can't say what her atmosphere's worth,' said Diva.

'A saint upon earth,' said Elizabeth warmly. 'And Mallards used to be a second home to me long before it was mine.' (Which was a lie.) 'Silly of me, perhaps, but the thought of parting with it is agony. Lucia is terribly anxious to get it, *on m'a dit.*'

'She must be if she's offered you such a price for it,' said Diva.

'Diva, dear, we've always been such friends,' said Elizabeth, 'and it's seldom, *n'est ce pas*, that I've asked you for any favour. But I do now. Do you think you could let her know, quite casually, that I don't believe I shall have the heart to leave Mallards? Just that: hardly an allusion to the two thousand pounds.'

Diva considered this.

'Well, I'll ask a favour, too, Elizabeth,' she said, 'and it is that you should determine to drop that silly habit of putting easy French phrases into your conversation. So confusing. Besides everyone sees you're only copying Lucia. So ridiculous. All put on. If you will, I'll do what you ask. Going to tea with her this afternoon.'

'Thank you, sweet. A bargain then, and I'll try to break myself: I'm sure I don't want to confuse anybody. Now I must get to my shopping. Kind Susan is taking me for a drive this afternoon, and then a quiet evening with my Benjy-boy.'

'*Très agréable*,' said Diva ruthlessly. 'Can't you hear how silly it sounds? Been on my mind a long time to tell you that.'

Lucia was in her Office when Diva arrived for tea, and so could not possibly be disturbed. As she was actually having a sound nap, her guests, Georgie and Diva, had to wait until she happened to awake, and then, observing the time, she came out in a great hurry with a pen behind her ear. Diva executed her commission with much tact and casualness, but Lucia seemed to bore into the middle of her head with that penetrating eye. Having pierced her, she then looked dreamily out of the window.

'Dear me, what is that slang word one hears so much in the City?' she said. 'Ah, yes. Bluff. Should you happen to see dear Elizabeth, Diva, would you tell her that I just mentioned to you that my offer does not remain open indefinitely? I shall expect to hear from her in the course of to-morrow. If I hear nothing by then I shall withdraw it.'

'That's the stuff to give her,' said Georgie appreciatively. 'You'll hear fast enough when she knows that.'

But the hours of next day went by, and no communication came from Mallards. The morning post brought a letter from Mammoncash, which required a swift decision, but Lucia felt a sad lack of concentration, and was unable to make up her mind, while this other business remained undetermined. When the afternoon faded into dusk and still there was no answer, she became very anxious, and when, on the top of that, the afternoon post brought nothing her anxiety turned into sheer distraction. She rang up the house-agents' to ask whether Mrs Mapp-Flint had received any application for the lease of Mallards for six months or a year, but Messrs Woolgar & Pipstow, with much regret, refused to disclose the affairs of their client. She rang up Georgie to see if he knew anything, and received the ominous reply that as he was returning home just now, he saw a man, whom he did not recognize, being admitted into Mallards: Lucia in this tension felt convinced that it was somebody come to look over the house. She rang up Diva who had duly and casually delivered the message to Elizabeth at the marketing-hour. It was an awful afternoon, and Lucia felt that all the money she had made was dross if she could not get this coveted freehold. Finally after tea (at which she could not eat a morsel) she wrote to Elizabeth turning the pounds into guineas, and gave the note to Cadman to deliver by hand and wait for an answer.

Meantime, ever since lunch, Elizabeth had been sitting at the window of the garden-room, getting on with the conversion of the white crocheted cap into adult size, and casting frequent glances down the street for the arrival of a note from Grebe, to say that Lucia (terrified at the thought that she would not have the heart to quit Mallards) was willing to pay an extra five hundred pounds or so as a stimulant to that failing organ. But no letter came and Elizabeth in turn began to be terrified that the offer would be withdrawn. No sooner had Benjy swallowed a small (not the large) cup of tea on his return from his golf, than she sent him off to Grebe, with a note accepting Lucia's first offer, and bade him bring back the answer.

It was dark by now, and Cadman passing through the Landgate into the town met Major Benjy walking very fast in the direction of Grebe. The notes they both carried must therefore have been delivered practically simultaneously, and Elizabeth, in writing, had consented to accept two thousand pounds, and Lucia, in writing, to call them guineas.

6

This frightful discrepancy in the premium was adjusted by Lucia offering – more than equitably so she thought, and more than meanly thought the other contracting party – to split the difference, and the double move was instantly begun. In order to get into Mallards more speedily, Lucia left Grebe vacant in the space of two days, not forgetting the india-rubber felting in the passage outside the Office, for assuredly there would be another Temple of Silence at Mallards, and stored her furniture until her new house was fit to receive it. Grebe being thus empty, the vans from Mallards poured tiger-skins and Polynesian aprons into it, and into Mallards there poured a regiment of plumbers and painters and cleaners and decorators. Drains were tested, pointings between bricks renewed, floors scraped and ceilings whitewashed, and for the next fortnight other householders in Tilling had the greatest difficulty in getting any repairs done, for there was scarcely a workman who was not engaged on Mallards.

Throughout these hectic weeks Lucia stayed with Georgie at the Cottage, and not even he had ever suspected the sheer horse-power of body and mind which she was capable of developing when really extended. She had breakfasted before the first of her workmen appeared in the morning, and was ready to direct and guide them and to cancel all the orders she had given the day before, till everyone was feverishly occupied, and then she went back to the Cottage to read the letters that had come for her by the first post and skim the morning papers for world-movements. Then Mammoncash got his orders, if he had recommended any change in her investments, and Lucia went back to choose wallpapers, or go down into the big cellars that spread over the entire basement of the house. They had not been used for years, for a cupboard in the pantry had been adequate to hold such alcoholic refreshment as Aunt Caroline and her niece had wished to have on the premises, and bins had disintegrated and laths fallen, and rubbish had been hurled there, until the floor was covered with a foot or more of compacted debris. All this, Lucia decreed, must be excavated, and the floor-level laid bare, for both her distaste for living above a rubbish heap, and her passion for restoring Mallards to its original state demanded the clearance. Two navvies with pick-axe and shovel carried up baskets of rubbish through the kitchen where a distracted ironmonger was installing a new boiler. There were rats in this cellar, and Diva very kindly lent Paddy to deal with them, and Paddy very kindly bit a navvy in mistake for a rat. At last the floor-level was reached, and Lucia examining it carefully with an electric torch, discovered that there were lines of brickwork lying at an angle to the rest of the floor. The moment she saw them she was convinced that there was a Roman look about them, and secretly suspected that a Roman villa must once have stood here. There was no time to go into that just now: it must be followed up later, but she sent to the London Library for a few standard books on Roman remains in the South of England, and read an article during lunch-time in Georgie's Encyclopaedia about hypocausts.

After such sedentary mornings Lucia dug in the kitchen-garden for an hour or two clad in Irene's overalls. Her gardener vainly protested that the spring was not the orthodox season to manure the soil, but it was obvious to Lucia that it required immediate enrichment and it got it. There was a big potato-patch which had evidently been plundered quite lately, for only a few sad stalks remained, and the inference that Elizabeth, before quitting, had dug up all the potatoes and taken them to Grebe was irresistible. The greenhouse, too, was strangely denuded of plants: they must have gone to Grebe as well. But the aspect was admirable for peach-trees, and Lucia ordered half-a-dozen to be trained on the wall. Her gardening-book recommended that a few bumble-bees should always be domiciled in a peach-house for the fertilization of the blossoms, and after a long pursuit her gardener cleverly caught one in his cap. It was transferred with angry buzzings to the peach-house and immediately flew out through a broken pane in the roof.

A reviving cup of tea started Lucia off again, and she helped to burn the discoloured paint off the banisters of the stairs which were undoubtedly of oak, and she stayed on at this fascinating job till the sun had set and all the workmen had gone. While dressing for dinner she observed that the ground-floor rooms of Mallards that looked on to the street were brilliantly illuminated, as for a party, and realizing that she had left all the electric lights burning, she put a cloak over her evening gown and went across to switch them off. A ponderous parcel of books had arrived from the London Library and she promised herself a historical treat in bed that night. She finished dressing and hurried down to dinner, for Georgie hated to be kept waiting for his meals. Lucia had had little conversation all day, and now, as if the dam of a reservoir had burst, the pent waters of vocal intercourse carried all before them.

'Georgino, such an interesting day,' she said, 'but I marvel at the vandalism of the late owner. Drab paint on those beautiful oak banisters, and I feel convinced that I have found the remains of a Roman villa. I conjecture that it runs out towards the kitchen-garden. Possibly it may be a temple. My dear, what delicious fish! Did you know that in the time of Elizabeth – not this one – the Court was entirely supplied with fish from Tilling? A convoy of mules took it to London three times a week . . . In a few days more, I hope and trust, Mallards will be ready for my furniture, and then you must be at my beck and call all day. Your taste is exquisite: I shall want your sanction for all my dispositions. Shall the garden-room be my Office, do you think? But, as you know, I cannot exist without a music-room, and perhaps I had better use that little cupboard of a room off the hall as my Office. My ledgers and a telephone is all I want there, but double windows must be put in as it looks on to the street. Then I shall have my books in the garden-room: the Greek dramatists are what I shall chiefly work at this year. My dear, how delicious it would be to give some tableaux in the garden from the Greek tragedians! The

return of Agamemnon with Cassandra after the Trojan wars.
You must certainly be Agamemnon. Could I not double the
parts of Cassandra and Clytemnestra? Or a scene from Aristophanes. I began the *Thesmophoriazusae* a few weeks ago. About
the revolt of the Athenian women, from their sequestered and
blighted existence. They barricaded themselves into the Ac-
ropolis, exactly as the Pankhursts and the suffragettes pad-
locked themselves to the railings of the House of Commons and
the pulpit in Westminster Abbey. I have always maintained
that Aristophanes is the most modern of writers, Bernard
Shaw, in fact, but with far more wit, more Attic salt. If I
might choose a day in all the history of the world to live
through, it would be a day in the golden age of Athens. A talk
to Socrates in the morning; lunch with Pericles and Aspasia: a
matinée at the theatre for a new play by Aristophanes: supper
at Plato's Symposium. How it fires the blood!'

Georgie was eating a caramel chocolate and reply was impossible, since the teeth in his upper jaw were firmly glued to
those of the lower and care was necessary. He could only nod
and make massaging movements with his mouth, and Lucia,
like Cassandra, only far more optimistic, was filled with the
spirit of prophecy.

'I mean to make Mallards the centre of a new artistic and
intellectual life in Tilling,' she said, 'much as the Hurst was, if
I may say so without boasting, at our dear little placid Riseholme. My Attic day, I know, cannot be realized, but if there
are, as I strongly suspect, the remains of a Roman temple or
villa stretching out into the kitchen-garden, we shall have a
whiff of classical ages again. I shall lay bare the place, even if it
means scrapping the asparagus-bed. Very likely I shall find a
tesselated pavement or two. Then we are so near London,
every now and then I shall have a string quartet down, or get
somebody to lecture on an archaeological subject, if I am right
about my Roman villa. I am getting rather rich, Georgie, I
don't mind telling you, and I shall spend most of my gains on
the welfare and enlightenment of Tilling. I do not regard the
money I spent in buying Mallards a selfish outlay. It was
equipment: I must have some central house with a room like

the garden-room where I can hold my gatherings and symposia and so forth, and a garden for rest and refreshment and meditation. *Non e bella vista?*'

Georgie had rid himself of the last viscous strings of the caramel by the aid of a mouthful of hot coffee which softened them.

'My dear, what big plans you have,' he said. 'I always –' but the torrent foamed on.

'*Caro*, you know well that I have never cared for small interests and paltry successes. The broad sweep of the brush, Georgie: the great scale! Indeed it will be a change in the life-history of Mallards – I think I shall call it Mallards House – to have something going on there beyond those perennial spyings from the garden-room window to see who goes to the dentist. And I mean to take part in the Civic, the municipal government of the place: that too, is no less than a duty. Dear Irene's very ill-judged exhibition at the election to the Town Council deprived me, I feel sure, of hundreds of votes, though she meant so well. It jarred, it was not in harmony with the lofty aims I was hoping to represent. I *am* the friend of the poor, but a public pantomime was not the way to convince the electors of that. I shall be the friend of the rich, too. Those nice Wyses, for instance, their intellectual horizons are terribly bounded, and dear Diva hasn't got any horizons at all. I seem to see a general uplift, Georgie, an intellectual and artistic curiosity, such as that out of which all renaissances came. Poor Elizabeth! Naturally, I have no programme at present: it is not time for that yet. Well, there's just the outline of my plans. Now let us have an hour of music.'

'I'm sure you're tired,' said Georgie.

'Never fresher. I consider it is a disgrace to be tired. I was, I remember, after our last day's canvassing, and was much ashamed of myself. And how charming it is to be spending tranquil quiet evenings with you again. When you decided on a permanent beard after your shingles, and went to your own house again, the evenings seemed quite lonely sometimes. Now let us play something that will really test us.'

Lucia's fingers were a little rusty from want of practice and she had a few minutes of rapid scales and exercises. Then followed an hour of duets, and she looked over some samples of chintzes.

That night Georgie was wakened from his sleep by the thump of some heavy object on the floor of the adjoining bedroom. Lucia, so he learned from her next morning, had dropped into a doze as she was reading in bed one of those ponderous books from the London Library about Roman remains in the South of England, and it had slid on to the floor.

Thanks to the incessant spur and scourge of Lucia's presence, which prevented any of her workmen having a slack moment throughout the day, the house was ready incredibly soon for the reception of her furniture, and Cadman had been settled into a new garage and cottage near by, so that Foljambe's journeys between her home and Georgie's were much abbreviated. There was a short interlude during which fires blazed and hot-water pipes rumbled in every room in Mallards for the drying of newly hung paper and of paint. Lucia chafed at this inaction, for there was nothing for her to do but carry coal and poke the fires, and then a second period of feverish activity set in. The vans of her stored furniture disgorged at the door and Georgie was continually on duty so that Lucia might consult his exquisite taste and follow her own.

'Yes, that bureau would look charming in the little parlour upstairs,' she would say. 'Charming! How right you are! But somehow I seem to see it in the garden-room. I think I must try it there first.'

In fact Lucia saw almost everything in the garden-room, till a materialistic foreman told her that it would hold no more unless she meant it to be a lumber-room, in which case another table or two might be stacked there. She hurried out and found it was difficult to get into the room at all, and the piano was yet to come. Back came a procession of objects which were gradually dispersed among other rooms which hitherto had remained empty. Minor delays were caused by boxes of linen being carried out to the garden-room because she was sure they contained books, and boxes of books being put in the cellar because she was equally certain that they contained wine.

But by mid-April everything was ready for the house-warming lunch. All Tilling was bidden with the exception of quaint Irene, for she had another little disturbance with Elizabeth, and Lucia thought that their proximity was not a risk that should be taken on an occasion designed to be festive, for there were quite enough danger zones without that. Elizabeth at first was inclined to refuse her invitation: it would be too much of a heart-break to see her ancestral home in the hands of an alien, but she soon perceived that it would be a worse heart-break not to be able to comment bitterly on the vulgarity or the ostentation or the general uncomfortableness or whatever she settled should be the type of outrage which Lucia had committed in its hallowed precincts, and she steeled herself to accept. She had to steel herself also to something else, which it was no longer any use putting off; the revelation must be made, and, as in the case of Georgie's beard, everybody had better know together. Get it over.

Elizabeth had fashioned a very striking costume for the occasion. One of Benjy's tiger-skins was clearly not sufficiently strong to stand the wear and tear of being trodden on, but parts of it were excellent still, and she had cut some strips out of it which she hoped were sound and with which she trimmed the edge of the green skirt which had been exciting such interest in Tilling, and the collar of the coat which went with it. On her head she wore a white woollen crocheted cap, just finished: a decoration of artificial campanulas rendering its resemblance to the cap of a hydrocephalous baby less noticeable.

Elizabeth drew in her breath, wincing with a stab of mental anguish when she saw the dear old dingy panels in the hall, once adorned with her water-colour sketches, gleaming with garish white paint, and she and Benjy followed Grosvenor out to the garden-room. The spacious cupboard in the wall once concealed behind a false book-case of shelves ranged with leather simulacra of book-backs, 'Elegant Extracts' and 'Poems' and 'Commentaries', had been converted into a real book-case, and Lucia's library of standard and classical works filled it from top to bottom. A glass chandelier hung from the ceiling, Persian rugs had supplanted the tiger-skins and the walls were of dappled blue.

Lucia welcomed them.

'So glad you could come,' she said. 'Dear Elizabeth, what lovely fur! Tiger, surely.'

'So glad you like it,' said Elizabeth. 'And sweet of you to ask us. So here I am in my dear garden-room again. Quite a change.'

She gave Benjy's hand a sympathetic squeeze, for he must be feeling the desecration of his room, and in came the Padre and Evie, who after some mouse-like squeals of rapture began to talk very fast.

'What a beautiful room!' she said. 'I shouldn't have known it again, would you, Kenneth? How de do, Elizabeth. Bits of Major Benjy's tiger-skins, isn't it? Why that used to be the cupboard where you had been hoarding all sorts of things to eat in case the coal strike went on, and one day the door flew open and all the corned beef and dried apricots came bumping out. I remember it as if it was yesterday.'

Lucia hastened to interrupt that embarrassing reminiscence.

'Dear Elizabeth, pray don't stand,' she said. 'There's a chair in the window by the curtain, just where you used to sit.'

'Thanks, dear,' said Elizabeth, continuing slowly to revolve, and take in the full horror of the scene. 'I should like just to look round. So clean, so fresh.'

Diva trundled in. Elizabeth's tiger-trimmings at once caught her eye, but as Elizabeth had not noticed her cropped hair the other day, she looked at them hard and was totally blind to them.

'You've made the room lovely, Lucia,' she said. 'I never saw such an improvement, did you, Elizabeth? What a library, Lucia! Why that used to be a cupboard behind a false book-case. Of course, I remember –'

'And such a big chandelier,' interrupted Elizabeth, fearful of another recitation of that frightful incident. 'I should find it a little dazzling, but then my eyes are wonderful.'

'Mr and Mrs Wyse,' said Grosvenor at the door.

'Grosvenor, sherry at once,' whispered Lucia, feeling the tension. 'Nice of you to come, Susan. *Buon giono, Signor Sapiente.*'

Elizabeth, remembering her promise to Diva, just checked herself from saying '*Bon jour, Monsieur Sage,*' and Mr Wyse kissed Lucia's hand, Italian-fashion, as a proper reply to this elegant salutation, and put up his eye-glass.

'Genius!' he said. 'Artistic genius! Never did I appreciate the beautiful proportions of this room before; it was smothered – ah, Mrs Mapp-Flint! Such a pleasure, and a lovely costume if I may say so. That poem of Blake's: "Tiger, tiger, burning bright". I am writing to my sister Amelia to-day, and I must crave your permission to tell her about it. How she scolds me if I do not describe to her the latest fashions of the ladies of Tilling.'

'A glass of sherry, dear Elizabeth,' said Lucia.

'No, dear, not a drop, thanks. Poison to me,' said Elizabeth fiercely.

Georgie arrived last. He, of course, had assisted at the transformation of the garden-room, but naturally he added his voice to the chorus of congratulation which Elizabeth found so trying.

'My dear, how beautiful you've got the room!' he said. 'You'd have made a fortune over house-decorating. When I think what it was like – oh, good morning, Mrs Major Benjy. What a charming frock, and how ingenious. It's bits of the tiger that used to be the hearth-rug here. I always admired it so much.'

But none of these compliments soothed Elizabeth's savagery, for the universal admiration of the garden-room was poisoning her worse than sherry. Then lunch was announced, and it was with difficulty she was persuaded to lead the way, so used was she to follow other ladies as hostess, into the dining-room. Then, urged to proceed, she went down the steps with astonishing alacrity, but paused in the hall as if uncertain where to go next.

'All these changes,' she said. 'Quite bewildering. Perhaps Lucia has turned another room into the dining-room.'

'No, ma'am, the same room,' said Grosvenor.

More shocks. There was a refectory-table where her own round table had been, and a bust of Beethoven on the chimney-piece. The walls were of apple-green, and instead of being profusely hung with Elizabeth's best water-colours, there was nothing on them but a sconce or two for electric light. She determined to eat not more than one mouthful of any dish that might be offered her, and conceal the rest below her knife and fork. She sat down, stubbing her toes against the rail that ran round the table, and gave a little squeal of anguish.

'So stupid of me,' she said. 'I'm not accustomed to this sort of table. Ah, I see. I must put my feet over the little railing. That will be quite comfortable.'

Lobster *à la Riseholme* was handed round, and a meditative silence followed in its wake, for who could help dwelling for a moment on the memory of how Elizabeth, unable to obtain the recipe by honourable means, stole it from Lucia's kitchen? She took a mouthful, and then, according to plan, hid the rest of it under her fork and fish-knife. But her mouth began to water for this irresistible delicacy, and she surreptitiously gobbled up the rest, and then with a wistful smile looked round the desecrated room.

'An admirable shade of green,' said Mr Wyse, bowing to the walls. 'Susan, we must memorize this for the time when we do up our little *salle à manger*.'

'Begorra, it's the true Oirish colour,' said the Padre. 'I canna mind me what was the way of it before.'

'I can tell you, dear Padre,' said Elizabeth eagerly. 'Biscuit-colour, such a favourite tint of mine, and some of my little paintings on the walls. Quite plain and homely. Benjy, dear, how naughty you are: hock always punishes you.'

'Dear lady,' said Mr Wyse, 'surely not such nectar as we are now enjoying. How I should like to know the vintage. Delicious!'

Elizabeth turned to Georgie.

'You must be very careful of these treacherous spring days, Mr Georgie,' she said. 'Shingles are terribly liable to return, and the second attack is always much worse than the first. People often lose their eyesight altogether.'

'That's encouraging,' said Georgie.

Luckily Elizabeth thought that she had now sufficiently impressed on everybody what a searing experience it was to her to re-visit her ancestral home, and see the melancholy changes that had been wrought on it, and under the spell of the nectar her extreme acidity mellowed. The nectar served another purpose also: it bucked her up for the anti-maternal revelation which she had determined to make that very day. She walked very briskly about the garden after lunch. She tripped across the lawn to the *giardino segreto*: she made a swift tour of the kitchen-garden under her own steam, untowed by Benjy, and perceived that the ladies were regarding her with a faintly puzzled air: they were beginning to see what she meant them to see. Then with Diva she lightly descended the steps into the greenhouse and, diverted from her main purpose for the moment, felt herself bound to say a few words about Lucia's renovations in general, and the peach-trees in particular.

'Poor things, they'll come to nothing,' she said. 'I could have told dear hostess that, if she had asked me. You might as well plant cedars of Lebanon. And the dining-room, Diva! The colour of green apples, enough to give anybody indigestion before you begin! The glaring white paint in the hall! The garden-room! I feel that the most, and so does poor Benjy. I was prepared for something pretty frightful, but not as bad as this!'

'Don't agree,' said Diva. 'It's all beautiful. Should hardly have known it again. You'd got accustomed to see the house all dingy, Elizabeth, and smothered in cobwebs and your own water-colours and muck —'

That was sufficient rudeness for Elizabeth to turn her back on Diva, but it was for a further purpose that she whisked round and positively twinkled up those steep steps again. Diva gasped. For weeks now Elizabeth had leant on Benjy if there were steps to mount, and had walked with a slow and dignified gait, and all of a sudden she had resumed her nimble and rapid movement. And then the light broke. Diva felt she would burst unless she at once poured her interpretation of these phenomena into some feminine ear, and she hurried out of the greenhouse nearly tripping up on the steps that Elizabeth had so lightly ascended.

The rest of the party had gathered again in the garden-room, and by some feminine intuition Diva perceived in the eyes of the other women the knowledge which had just dawned on her. Presently the Mapp-Flints said good-bye, and Mr Wyse, who, with the obtuseness of a man, had noticed nothing, was pressing Elizabeth to take the Royce and go for a drive. Then came the first-hand authentic disclosure.

'So good for you,' said she, 'but Benjy and I have promised ourselves a long walk. Lovely party, Lucia: some day you must come and see your old house. Just looked at your peach-trees: I hope you'll have quantities of fruit. Come along, Benjy, or there won't be time for our tramp. Good-bye, sweet garden-room.'

They went out, and instantly there took place a species of manoeuvre which partook of the nature of a conjuring trick and a conspiracy. Evie whispered something to her Padre, and he found that he had some urgent district-visiting to do: Susan had a quiet word with her husband, and he recollected that he must get off his letter to Contessa Amelia Faraglione by the next post and Lucia told Georgie that if he could come back in half an hour she would be at leisure to try that new duet. The four ladies therefore were left, and Evie and Diva, as soon as the door of the garden-room was shut, broke into a crisp, unrehearsed dialogue of alternate sentences, like a couple of clergymen intoning the Commination service.

'She's given it up,' chanted Diva. 'She nipped up those steep steps from the greenhouse, as if it was on the flat.'

'But such a sell, isn't it,' cried Evie. 'It *would* have been exciting. Ought we to say anything about it to her? She must feel terribly disappointed –'

'Not a bit,' said Diva. 'I don't believe she ever believed it. Wanted us to believe it: that's all. Most deceitful.'

'And Kenneth had been going through the Churching of Women.'

'And she had no end of drives in your motor, Susan. False pretences, I call it. You'd never have lent her it at all, unless –'

'And all that nutritious honey from the Contessa.'

'And I think she's taken in the old green skirt again, but the strips of tiger-skin make it hard to be certain.'

'And I'm sure she was crocheting a baby-cap in white wool, and she must have pulled a lot of it out and begun again. She was wearing it.'

'And while I think of it,' said Diva in parenthesis, 'there'll be a fine mess of tiger-hairs on your dining-room carpet, Lucia. I saw clouds of them fly when she banged her foot.'

Susan Wyse had not had any chance at present of joining in this vindictive chant. Sometimes she had opened her mouth to speak, but one of the others had been quicker. At this point, as Diva and Evie were both a little out of breath, she managed to contribute.

'I don't grudge her her drives,' she said, 'but I do feel strongly about that honey. It was very special honey. My sister-in-law, the Contessa, took it daily when she was expecting her baby, and it weighed eleven pounds.'

'Eleven pounds of honey? O dear me, that is a lot!' said Evie.

'No, the baby –'

The chant broke out afresh.

'And so rude about the sherry,' said Diva, 'saying it was poison.'

'And pretending not to know where the dining-room was.'

'And saying that the colour of the walls gave her indigestion like green apples. She's enough to give anybody indigestion herself.'

The torrent spent itself: Lucia had been sitting with eyes half-closed and eyebrows drawn together as if trying to recollect something, and then took down a volume from her bookshelves of classical literature and rapidly turned over the pages. She appeared to find what she wanted, for she read on in silence a moment, and then replaced the book with a far-away sigh.

'I was saying to Georgie the other day,' she said, 'how marvellously modern Aristophanes was. I seemed to remember a scene in one of his plays – the *Thesmophoriazusae* – where a somewhat similar situation occurred. A woman, a dear, kind creature really, of middle-age or a little more, had persuaded her friends (or thought she had) that she was going to have a baby. Such Attic wit – there is nothing in English like it. I won't quote the Greek to you, but the conclusion was that it was only a "wind-egg". Delicious phrase, really untranslatable, but that is what it comes to. Shan't we all leave it at that? Poor dear Elizabeth! Just a wind-egg. So concise.'

She gave a little puff with her pursed lips, as if blowing the wind-egg away.

Rather awed by this superhuman magnanimity the conductors of the Commination service dispersed, and Lucia went into the dining-room to see if there was any serious deposit of tiger-hairs on her new carpet beside Elizabeth's place. Certainly there were some, though not quite the clouds of which Diva had spoken. Probably then that new pretty decoration would not be often seen again since it was moulting so badly.

'Everything seems to go wrong with the poor soul,' thought Lucia in a spasm of most pleasurable compassion, 'owing to her deplorable lack of foresight. She bought Siriami without ascertaining whether it paid dividends: she tried to make us all believe that she was going to have a baby without ascertaining whether there was the smallest reason to suppose she would, and with just the same blind recklessness she trimmed the old green skirt with tiger without observing how heavily it would moult when she moved.'

She returned to the garden-room for a few minutes' intensive practice of the duet she and Georgie would read through when he came back, and seating herself at the piano she noticed a smell as of escaping gas. Yet it could not be coal-gas, for there was none laid on now to the garden-room, the great chandelier and other lamps being lit by electricity. She wondered whether this smell was paint not quite dry yet, for during the renovation of the house her keen perception had noticed all kinds of smells incident to decoration: there was the smell of pear-drops in one room, and that was varnish: there was the smell of advanced corruption in another, and that was the best size: there was the smell of elephants in the cellar and that was rats.

So she thought no more about it, practised for a quarter of an hour, and then hurried away from the piano when she saw Georgie coming down the street, so that he should not find her poaching in the unseen suite by Mozart.

Georgie was reproachful.

'It was tarsome of you,' he said, 'to send me away when I longed to hear what you all thought about Elizabeth. I knew what it meant when I saw how she skipped and pranced and had taken in the old green skirt again –'

'Georgie, I never noticed that,' said Lucia. 'Are you sure?'

'Perfectly certain, and how she was going for a tramp with Benjy. The baby's off. I wonder if Benjy was an accomplice –'

'Dear Georgie!' remonstrated Lucia.

Georgie blushed at the idea that he could have meant anything so indelicate.

'Accomplice to the general deception was what I was going to say when you interrupted. I think we've all been insulted. We ought to mark our displeasure.'

Lucia had no intention of repeating her withering comment about the wind-egg. It was sure to get round to him.

'Why be indignant with the poor thing?' she said. 'She has been found out and that's quite sufficient punishment. As to her making herself so odious at lunch and doing her best, without any success, to spoil my little party, that was certainly malicious. But about the other, Georgie, let us remember what a horrid job she had to do. I foresaw that, you may remember, and expressed my wish that, when it came, we should all be kind to her. She must have skipped and pranced, as you put it, with an aching heart, and certainly with aching legs. As for poor Major Benjy, I'm sure he was putty in her hands, and did just what she told him. How terribly a year's marriage has aged him, has it not?'

'I should have been dead long ago,' said Georgie.

Lucia looked round the room.

'My dear, I'm so happy to be back in this house,' she said, 'and to know it's my own, that I would forgive Elizabeth almost anything. Now let us have an hour's harmony.'

They went to the piano where, most carelessly, Lucia had

left on the music-rack the duet they were to read through for the first time. But Georgie did not notice it. He began to sniff.

'Isn't there a rather horrid smell of gas?' he asked.

'I thought I smelled something,' said Lucia, successfully whisking off the duet. 'But the foreman of the gasworks is in the house now, attending to the stove in the kitchen. I'll get him to come and smell too.'

Lucia sent the message by Grosvenor, and an exceedingly cheerful young man bounded into the room. He smelt, too, and burst into a merry laugh.

'No, ma'am, that's not *my* sort of gas,' he said gaily. 'That'll be sewer-gas, that will. That's the business of the town surveyor and he's my brother. I'll ring him up at once and get him to come and see to it.'

'Please do,' said Lucia.

'He'll nip up in a minute to oblige Mrs Lucas,' said the gasman. 'Dear me, how we all laughed at Miss Irene's procession, if you'll excuse my mentioning it. But this is business now, not pleasure. Horrid smell that. It won't do at all.'

Lucia and Georgie moved away from the immediate vicinity of the sewer, and presently with a rap on the door, a second young man entered exactly like the first.

'A pleasure to come and see into your little trouble, ma'am,' he said. 'In the window my brother said. Ah, now I've got it.'

He laughed very heartily.

'No, no,' he said. 'Georgie's made a blooming error – beg your pardon, sir, I mean my brother – Let's have him in.'

In came Georgie of the gasworks.

'You've got something wrong with your nose-piece, Georgie,' said the sewer man. 'That's coal-gas, that is.'

'Get along, Percy!' said Georgie. 'Sewers. Your job, my lad.'

Lucia assumed her most dignified manner.

'Your immediate business, gentlemen,' she said, 'is to ascertain whether I am living (i) in a gas pipe or (ii) in a main drain.'

Shouts of laughter.

'Well, there's a neat way to put it,' said Percy appreciatively.

'We'll tackle it for you, ma'am. We must have a joint investigation, Georgie, till we've located it. It must be percolating through the soil and coming up through the floor. You send along two of your fellows in the morning, and I'll send two of the Corporation men, and we'll dig till we find out. Bet you a shilling it's coal-gas.'

'I'll take you. Sewers,' said Georgie.

'But I can't live in a room that's full of either,' said Lucia. 'One may explode and the other may poison me.'

'Don't you worry about that, ma'am,' said Georgie. 'I'll guarantee you against an explosion, if it's my variety of gas. Not near up to inflammatory point.'

'And I've workmen, ma'am,' said Percy, 'who spend their days revelling in a main drain, you may say, and live to ninety. We'll start to dig in the road outside in the morning, Georgie and me, for that's where it must come from. No one quite knows where the drains are in this old part of the town, but we'll get on to their scent if it's sewers, and then tally-ho. Good afternoon, ma'am. All OK.'

At an early hour next morning the combined exploration began. Up came the pavement outside the garden-room and the cobbles of the street, and deeper all day grew the chasm, while the disturbed earth reeked even more strongly of the yet unidentified smell. The news of what was in progress reached the High Street at the marketing hour, and the most discouraging parallels to this crisis were easily found. Diva had an uncle who had died in the night from asphyxiation owing to a leak of coal-gas, and Evie, not to be outdone in family tragedies, had an aunt, who, when getting into a new house (ominous), noticed a 'faint' smell in the dining-room, and died of blood-poisoning in record time. But Diva put eucalyptus on her handkerchief and Evie camphor and both hurried up to the scene of the excavation. To Elizabeth this excitement was a god-send, for she had been nervous as to her reception in the High Street after yesterday's revelation, but found that everyone was entirely absorbed in the new topic. Personally she was afraid (though hoping she might prove to be wrong) that the clearing out of the cellars at Mallards might somehow have tapped a reservoir of a far deadlier quality of vapour than either coal-gas or sewer-gas. Benjy, having breathed the polluted air of the garden-room yesterday, thought it wise not to go near the plague-spot at all, but after gargling with a strong solution of carbolic, fled to the links, with his throat burning very uncomfortably, to spend the day in the aseptic sea air. Georgie (not Percy's gay brother) luckily remembered that he had bought a gas-mask during the war, in case the Germans dropped pernicious bombs on Riseholme, and Foljambe found it and cleared out the cobwebs. He adjusted it (tarsome for the beard) and watched the digging from a little distance, looking like an elephant whose trunk had been cut off very short. The Padre came in the character of an expert, for he could tell sewer-gas from coal-gas, begorra, with a single sniff, but he had scarcely taken a proper sniff when the church clock struck eleven, and he had to hurry away to read matins. Irene, smoking a pipe, set up her easel on the edge of the pit and painted a fine impressionist sketch of navvies working in a crater. Then, when the dinner-hour arrived, the two gay brothers, Gas and Drains, leaped like Quintus Curtius into the chasm and shovelled feverishly till their workmen returned, in order that no time should be lost in arriving at a solution and the settlement of their bet.

As the excavation deepened Lucia with a garden-spud, raked carefully among the baskets of earth which were brought up, and soon had a small heap of fragments of pottery, which she carried into Mallards. Georgie was completely puzzled at this odd conduct, and, making himself understood with difficulty through the gas-mask, asked her what she was doing.

Lucia looked round to make sure she would not be overheard.

'Roman pottery without a doubt,' she whispered. 'I am sure they will presently come across some remains of my Roman villa –'

A burst of cheering came from the bowels of the earth. One of the gas workmen with a vigorous stroke of his pick at the side of the pit close to the garden-room brought down a slide of earth, and exposed the mouth of a tiled aperture some nine inches square.

'Drains and sewers it is,' he cried, 'and out we go,' and he and his comrade downed tools and clambered out of the pit, leaving the town surveyor's men to attend to the job now demonstrated to be theirs.

The two gay brethren instantly jumped into the excavation. The aperture certainly did look like a drain, but just as certainly there was nothing coming down it. Percy put his nose into it, and inhaled deeply as a Yogi, drawing a long breath through his nostrils.

'Clean as a whistle, Georgie,' he said, 'and sweet as a sugar-plum. Drains it may have been, old man, but not in the sense of our bet. We were looking for something active and stinkful —'

'But drains it is, Per,' said Georgie.

A broken tile had fallen from the side of it, and Percy picked it up.

'There's been no sewage passing along that for a sight of years,' he said. 'Perhaps it was never a drain at all.'

Into Lucia's mind there flashed an illuminating hypocaustic idea.

'Please give me that tile,' she called out.

'Certainly, ma'am,' said Percy, reaching up with it, 'and have a sniff at it yourself. Nothing there to make your garden-room stink. You might lay that on your pillow —'

Percy's sentence was interrupted by a second cheer from his two men who had gone on working, and they also downed tools.

''Ere's the gas pipe at last,' cried one. 'Get going at your work again, gas brigade!'

'And lumme, don't it stink,' said the other. 'Leaking fit to blow up the whole neighbourhood. Soil's full of it.'

They clambered out of the excavation, and stood with the gas workers to await further orders.

'Have a sniff at that, Georgie,' said Per encouragingly, 'and then hand me a bob. That's something like a smell, that is. Put that on your pillow and you'll sleep so as you'll never wake again.'

Georgie, though crestfallen, retained his sense of fairness, and made no attempt to deny that the smell that now spread freely from the disengaged pipe was the same as that which filled the garden-room.

'Seems like it,' he said, 'and there's your bob, not but what the other was a drain. We'll find the leak and have it put to rights now.'

'And then I hope you'll fill up that great hole,' said Lucia.

'No time to-day, ma'am,' said Georgie. 'I'll see if I can spare a couple of men to-morrow, or next day at the latest.'

Lucia's Georgie, standing on the threshold of Mallards, suddenly observed that the excavation extended right across the street, and that he was quite cut off from the Cottage. He pulled off his gas-mask.

'But, look, how am I to get home?' he asked in a voice of acute lamentation. 'I can't climb down into that pit and up on the other side.'

Great laughter from the brethren.

'Well, sir, that is awkward,' said Per. 'I'm afraid you'll have to nip round by the High Street and up the next turning to get to your little place. But it will be all right, come the day after to-morrow.'

Lucia carried her tile reverently into the house, and beckoned to Georgie.

'That square-tiled opening confirms all I conjectured about the lines of foundation in the cellar,' she said. 'Those wonderful Romans used to have furnaces underneath the floors of their houses and their temples – I've been reading about it – and the hot air was conveyed in tiled flues through the walls to heat them. Undoubtedly this was a hot-air flue and not a drain at all.'

'That would be interesting,' said Georgie. 'But the pipe seemed to run through the earth, not through a wall. At least there was no sign of a wall that I saw.'

'The wall may have perished at that point,' said Lucia after only a moment's thought. 'I shall certainly find it further on in the garden, where I must begin digging at once. But not a word to anybody yet. Without doubt, Georgie, a Roman villa stood here or perhaps a temple. I should be inclined to say a temple. On the top of the hill, you know: just where they always put temples.'

Dusk had fallen before the leak in the gas pipe was repaired, and a rope was put up round the excavation and hung with red lanterns. Had the pit been less deep, or the sides of it less precipitous, Lucia would have climbed down into it and continued her study of the hot-air flue. She took the tile to her bathroom and scrubbed it clean. Close to the broken edge of it there were stamped the letters SP.

She dined alone that night and went back to the garden-room from which the last odours of gas had vanished. She searched in vain in her books from the London Library for any mention of Tilling having once been a Roman town, but its absence made the discovery more important, as likely to prove a new chapter in the history of Roman Britain. Eagerly she turned over the pages: there were illustrations of pottery which fortified her conviction that her fragments were of Roman origin: there was a picture of a Roman tile as used in hot-air flues which was positively identical with her specimen. Then what could SP stand for? She ploughed through a list of inscriptions found in the South of England and suddenly gave a great crow of delight. There was one headed SPQR, which being interpreted meant *Senatus Populusque Romanus*, 'the Senate and the People of Rome'. Her instinct had been right: a private villa would never have borne those imperial letters; they were reserved for state-erected buildings, such as temples . . . It said so in her book.

7

For the next few days Lucia was never once seen in the streets of Tilling, for all day she supervised the excavations in her garden. To the great indignation of her gardener, she hired two unemployed labourers at very high wages in view of the importance of their work, and set them to dig a trench across the potato-patch which Elizabeth had despoiled and the corner of the asparagus-bed, so that she must again strike the line of the hot-air flue, which had been so providentially discovered at the corner of the garden-room. Great was her triumph when she hit it once more, though it was a pity to find that it still ran through the earth, and not, as she had hoped, through the buried remains of a wall. But the soil was rich in relics, it abounded in pieces of pottery of the same type as those she had decided were Roman, and there were many pretty fragments of iridescent, oxydized glass, and a few bones which she hoped might turn out to be those of red deer which at the time of the Roman occupation were common in Kent and Sussex. Her big table in the garden-room was cleared of its books and writing apparatus, and loaded with cardboard trays of glass and pottery. She scarcely entered the Office at all, and but skimmed through the communications from Mammoncash.

Georgie dined with her on the evening of the joyful day when she had come across the hot-air flue again. There was a slightly earthy odour in the garden-room where after dinner they pored over fragments of pottery, and vainly endeavoured to make pieces fit together.

'It's most important, Georgie,' she said, 'as you will readily understand, to keep note of the levels at which objects are discovered. Those in Tray D come from four feet down in the corner of the asparagus-bed: that is the lowest level we have reached at present, and they, of course, are the earliest.'

'Oh, and look at Tray A,' said Georgie. 'All those pieces of clay tobacco-pipes. I didn't know the Romans smoked. Did they?'

Lucia gave a slightly superior laugh.

'*Caro*, of course they didn't,' she said. 'Tray A: yes, I thought so. Tray A is from a much higher level, let me see, yes, a foot below the surface of the ground. We may put it down therefore as being subsequent to Queen Elizabeth when tobacco was introduced. At a guess I should say those pipes were Cromwellian. A Cromwellian look, I fancy. I am rather inclined to take a complete tile from the continuation of the air flue which I laid bare this morning, and see if it is marked in full SPQR. The tile from the street, you remember, was broken and had only SP on it. Yet is it a vandalism to meddle at all with such a fine specimen of a flue evidently *in situ*?'

'I think I should do it,' said Georgie, 'you can put it back when you've found the letters.'

'I will then. To-morrow I expect my trench to get down to floor-level. There may be a tesselated pavement like that found at Richborough. I shall have to unearth it all, even if I have to dig up the entire kitchen-garden. And if it goes under the garden-room, I shall have to underpin it, I think they call it. Fancy all this having come out of a smell of gas!'

'Yes, that was a bit of luck,' said Georgie stifling a yawn over Tray A, where he was vainly trying to make a complete pipe out of the fragments.

Lucia put on the kind, the indulgent smile suitable to occasions when Georgie did not fully appreciate her wisdom or her brilliance.

'Scarcely fair to call it entirely luck,' she said, 'for you must remember that when the cellar was dug out I told you plainly that I should find Roman remains in the garden. That was before the gas smelt.'

'I'd forgotten that,' said Georgie. 'To be sure you did.'

'Thank you, dear. And to-morrow morning, if you are strolling and shopping in the High Street, I think you might let it be known that I am excavating in the garden and that the results, so far, are most promising. Roman remains: you might go as far as that. But I do not want a crowd of sightseers yet: they will only impede the work. I shall admit nobody at present.'

Foljambe had very delicately told Georgie that there was a slight defect in the plumbing system at Mallards Cottage, and accordingly he went down to the High Street next day to see about this. It was pleasant to be the bearer of such exciting news about Roman remains, and he announced it to Diva through the window and presently met Elizabeth. She had detached the tiger-skin border from the familiar green skirt.

'Hope the smell of gas or drains or both has quite gone away now, Mr Georgie,' she said. 'I'm told it was enough to stifle anybody. Odd that I never had any trouble in my time nor Aunt Caroline in hers. Lucia none the worse?'

'Not a bit. And no smell left,' said Georgie.

'So glad! Most dangerous it must have been. Any news?'

'Yes: she's very busy digging up the kitchen-garden –'

'What? My beautiful garden?' cried Elizabeth shrilly. 'Ah, I forgot. Yes?'

'And she's finding most interesting Roman remains. A villa, she thinks, or more probably a temple.'

'Indeed! I must go up and have a peep at them.'

'She's not showing them to anybody just yet,' said Georgie. 'She's deep down in the asparagus-bed. Pottery. Glass. Air flues.'

'Well, that is news! Quite an archaeologist, and nobody ever suspected it,' observed Elizabeth smiling her widest. 'Padre, dear Lucia has found a Roman temple in my asparagus-bed.'

'Ye dinna say! I'll ring up, bedad.'

'No use,' said Elizabeth. 'Not to be shown to anybody yet.'

Georgie passed on to the plumbers. 'Spencer & Son' was the name of the firm, and there was the proud legend in the window that it had been established in Tilling in 1820 and undertook all kinds of work connected with plumbing and drains. Mr Spencer promised to send a reliable workman up at once to Mallards Cottage.

The news disseminated by Georgie quickly spread from end

to end of the High Street, and reached the ears of an enterprising young gentleman who wrote paragraphs of local news for the *Hastings Chronicle*. This should make a thrilling item, and he called at Mallards just as Lucia was coming in from her morning's digging, and begged to be allowed to communicate any particulars she could give him to the paper. There seemed no harm in telling him what she had allowed Georgie to reveal to Tilling (in fact she liked the idea) and told him briefly that she had good reason to hope that she was on the track of a Roman villa, or, more probably, a temple. It was too late for the news to appear in this week's issue, but it would appear next week, and he would send her a copy. Lucia lunched in a great hurry and returned to the asparagus-bed.

Soon after Georgie appeared to help. Lucia was standing in the trench with half of her figure below ground-level, like Erda in Wagner's justly famous opera. If only Georgie had not dyed his beard, he might have been Wotan.

'*Ben arrivato,*' she called to him in the Italian translation. 'I'm on the point of taking out a tile from my hot-air flue. I am glad you are here as a witness, and it will be interesting for you. This looks rather a loose one. Now.'

She pulled it out and turned it over.

'Georgie,' she cried. 'Here's the whole of the stamped letters of which I had only two.'

'Oh, how exciting,' said Georgie. 'I do hope there's a QR as well as the SP.'

Lucia rubbed the dirt off the inscription and then replaced the tile.

'What is the name of that plumber in the High Street established a century ago?' she asked in a perfectly calm voice.

Georgie guessed what she had found.

'My dear, how tarsome!' he said. 'I'm afraid it *is* Spencer.'

Lucia got nimbly out of the trench, and wiped her muddy boots against the box-edging of the path.

'Georgie, that is a valuable piece of evidence,' she said. 'No doubt this is an old drain. I confess I was wrong about it. Let us date it, tentatively, *circa* 1830. Now we know more about the actual levels. First we have the Cromwellian stratum: tobacco-pipes. Below again – what is that?'

There were two workmen in the trench, the one with a pick, the other shovelling the earth into a basket to dump it on to the far corner of the potato-patch uprooted by Elizabeth. Georgie was glad of this diversion (whatever it might be) for it struck him that the stratum which Lucia had assigned to Cromwell was far above the air-flue stratum, once pronounced to be Roman, but now dated *circa* 1830 . . . The digger had paused with his pick-axe poised in the air.

'Lovely bit of glass here, ma'am,' he said. 'I nearly went crash into it!'

Lucia jumped back into the trench and became Erda again. It was a narrow escape indeed. The man's next blow must almost certainly have shattered a large and iridescent piece of glass, which gleamed in the mould. Tenderly and carefully, taking off her gloves, Lucia loosened it.

'Georgie!' she said in a voice faint and ringing with emotion, 'take it from me in both hands with the utmost caution. A wonderful piece of glass, with an inscription stamped on it.'

'Not Spencer again, I hope,' said Georgie.

Lucia passed it to him from the trench, and he received it in his cupped hands.

'Don't move till I get out and take it from you,' said she. 'Not another stroke for the present,' she called to her workman.

There was a tap for the garden-hose close by. Lucia let the water drip very gently, drop by drop, on to the trove. It was brilliantly iridescent, of a rich greenish colour below the oxydized surface, and of curved shape. Evidently it was a piece of some glass vessel, ewer or bottle. Tilting it this way and that to catch the light she read the letters stamped on it.

'APOL,' she announced.

'It's like crosswords,' said Georgie. 'All I can think of is "Apology".'

Lucia sat down on a neighbouring bench, panting with excitement but radiant with triumph.

'Do you remember how I said that I suspected I should find the remains of a Roman temple?' she asked.

'Yes: or a villa,' said Georgie.

'I thought a temple more probable, and said so. Look at it, Georgie. Some sacrificial vessel – there's a hint for you – some flask for libations dedicated to a god. What god?'

'Apollo!' cried Georgie. 'My dear, how perfectly wonderful! I don't see what else it could be. That makes up for all the Spencers. And it's the lowest level of all, so that's all right anyhow.'

Reverently holding this (quite large) piece of the sacrificial vessel in her joined hands, Lucia conveyed it to the garden-room, dried the water off it with blotting-paper, and put it in a tray by itself, since the objects in Tray D, once indubitably Roman, had been found to be Spencerian.

'All important to find the rest of it,' she said. 'We must search with the utmost care. Let us go back and plan what is to be done. I think I had better lock the door of the garden-room.'

The whole system of digging was revised. Instead of the earth at the bottom of the trench being loosened with strong blows of the pick, Lucia, starting at the point where this fragment of a sacrificial vessel was found, herself dug with a trowel, so that no random stroke should crash into the missing pieces: when she was giddy with blood to the head from this stooping position, Georgie took her place. Then there was the possibility that missing pieces might have been already shovelled out of the trench, so the two workmen were set to turn over the mound of earth already excavated with microscopic diligence.

'It would be unpardonable of me,' said Lucia, 'if I missed finding the remaining portions, for they must be here, Georgie. I'm so giddy: take the trowel.'

'Something like a coin, ma'am,' sang out one of the workmen on the dump. 'Or it may be a button.'

Lucia vaulted out of the trench with amazing agility.

'A coin without doubt,' she said. 'Much weathered, alas, but we may be able to decipher it. Georgie, would you kindly put it – you have the key of the garden-room – in the same tray as the sacrificial vessel?'

For the rest of the afternoon the search was rewarded by no

further discovery. Towards sunset a great bank of cloud arose in the west, and all night long, the heavens streamed with torrential rain. The deluge disintegrated the dump, and the soil was swept over the newly planted lettuces, and on to the newly gravelled garden-path. The water drained down into the trench from the surface of the asparagus-bed, and next day work was impossible, for there was a foot of water in it, and still the rain continued. Driven to more mercenary pursuits, Lucia spent a restless morning in the Office, considering the latest advice from Mammoncash. He was strongly of opinion that the rise in the Industrial market had gone far enough: he counselled her to take the profits, of which he enclosed a most satisfactory list, and again recommended gilt-edged stock. Prices there had dwindled a good deal since the Industrial boom began, and the next week or two ought to see a rise. Lucia gazed at the picture of Dame Catherine Winterglass for inspiration, and then rang up Mammoncash (trunk-call) and assented. In her enthusiasm for archaeological discoveries, all this seemed tedious business: it required a great effort to concentrate on so sordid an aim as money-making, when further pieces of sacrificial vessels (or vessel) from a temple of Apollo must be lurking in the asparagus-bed. But the rain continued and at present they were inaccessible below a foot or more of opaque water enriched with the manure she had dug into the surrounding plots.

Several days elapsed before digging could be resumed, and Tilling rang with the most original reports about Lucia's discoveries. She herself was very cautious in her admissions, for before the complete 'Spencer' tile was unearthed, she had, on the evidence of the broken 'SP' tile, let it be known that she had found Roman remains, part of a villa or a temple, in the asparagus-bed, and now this evidence was not quite so conclusive as it had been. The Apolline sacrificial vessel, it is true, had confirmed her original theory, but she must wait for more finds, walls or tesselated pavement, before it was advisable to admit sightseers to the digging, or make any fresh announcement. Georgie was pledged to secrecy, all the gardener knew was that she had spoiled his asparagus-bed, and as for the coin (for coin it was and no button) the most minute scrutiny could not reveal any sort of image or superscription on its corroded surface: it might belong to the age of Melchizedeck or Hadrian or Queen Victoria. So since Tilling could learn nothing from official quarters, it took the obvious course, sanctified by tradition, of inventing discoveries for itself: a statue was hinted at and a Roman altar. All this was most fortunate for Elizabeth, for the prevailing excitement about the ancient population of Tilling following on the gas and sewer affair, had rendered completely obsolete its sense of having been cheated when it was clear that she was not about to add to the modern population, and her appearance in the High Street alert and active as usual ceased to rouse any sort of comment. To make matters square between the late and the present owner of Mallards, it was only right that, just as Lucia had never believed in Elizabeth's baby, so now Elizabeth was entirely incredulous about Lucia's temple.

Elizabeth, on one of these days of April tempest when digging was suspended, came up from Grebe for her morning's marketing in her rain-cloak and Russian boots. The approach of a violent shower had driven her to take shelter in Diva's house, who could scarcely refuse her admittance, but did not want her at all. She put down her market-basket, which for the best of reasons smelt of fish, where Paddy could not get at it.

'Such a struggle to walk up from Grebe in this gale,' she said. 'Diva, you could hardly believe the monstrous state of neglect into which the kitchen-garden there has fallen. Not a vegetable. A sad change for me after my lovely garden at Mallards where I never had to buy even a bit of parsley. But beggars can't be choosers, and far be it from me to complain.'

'Well, you took every potato out of the ground at Mallards before you left,' said Diva. 'That will make a nice start for you.'

'I said I didn't complain, dear,' said Elizabeth sharply. 'And how is the Roman Forum getting on? Any new temples? Too killing! I don't believe a single word about it. Probably poor Lucia has discovered the rubbish-heap of odds and ends I threw away when I left my beloved old home for ever.'

'Did you bury them in the ground where the potatoes had been?' asked Diva, intensely irritated at this harping on the old home.

Elizabeth, as was only dignified, disregarded this harping on potatoes.

'I'm thinking of digging up two or three old apple-trees at Grebe which can't have borne fruit for the last hundred years,' she said, 'and telling everybody that I've found the Ark of the Covenant or some Shakespeare Folios among their roots. Nobody shall see them, of course. Lucia finds it difficult to grow old gracefully: that's why she surrounds herself with mysteries, as I said to Benjy the other day. At that age nobody takes any further interest in her for herself, and so she invents Roman Forums to kindle it again. Must be in the limelight. And the fortune she's supposed to have made, the Office, the trunk-calls to London. More mystery. I doubt if she's made or lost more than half a crown.'

'Now that's jealousy,' said Diva. 'Just because you lost a lot of money yourself, and can't bear that she should have made any. You might just as well say that I didn't make any.'

'Diva, I ask you. *Did* you make any?' said Elizabeth, suddenly giving tongue to a suspicion that had long been a terrible weight on her mind.

'Yes. I did,' said Diva with great distinctness, turning a rich crimson as she spoke. 'And if you want to know how much, I tell you it's none of your business.'

'*Chérie* – I mean Diva,' said Elizabeth very earnestly, 'I warn you for your good, you're becoming a *leetle* mysterious, too. Don't let it grow on you. Let us be open and frank with each other always. No one would be more delighted than me if Lucia turns out to have found the Parthenon in the gooseberry-bushes, but why doesn't she let us see anything? It is these hints and mysteries which I deprecate. And the way she talks about finance, as if she was a millionaire. Pending further evidence, I say "Bunkum" all round.'

The superb impudence of Elizabeth of all women giving warnings against being mysterious and kindling waning interest by hinting at groundless pretensions, so dumbfounded Diva that she sat with open mouth staring at her. She did not trust herself to speak for fear she might say, not more than she meant but less. It was better to say nothing than not be adequate and she changed the subject.

'How's the tiger-skirt?' she asked. 'And collar.' Elizabeth rather mistakenly thought that she had quelled Diva over this question of middle-aged mysteriousness. She did not want to rub it in, and adopted the new subject with great amiability.

'Sweet of you to ask, dear, about my new little frock,' she said. 'Everybody complimented me on it, except you, and I was a little hurt. But I think – so does Benjy – that it's a wee bit smart for our homely Tilling. How I hate anybody making themselves conspicuous.'

Diva could trust herself to speak on this subject without fear of saying too little.

'Now Elizabeth,' she said, 'you asked me as a friend to be open and frank with you, and so I tell you that that's not true. The hair was coming off your new little frock – it was the old green skirt anyway – in handfuls. That day you lunched with Lucia and hit your foot against the table-rail it flew about. Grosvenor had to sweep the carpet afterwards. I might as well trim my skirt with strips of my doormat and then say it was too smart for Tilling. You'd have done far better to have buried that mangy tiger-skin and the eye I knocked out of it with the rest of your accumulations in the potato-patch. I should be afraid of getting eczema if I wore a thing like that, and I don't suppose that at this minute there's a single hair left on it. There!'

It was Elizabeth's turn to be dumbfounded at the vehemence of these remarks. She breathed through her nose and screwed her face up into amazing contortions.

'I never thought to have heard such words from you,' she said.

'And I never thought to be told that strips from a mangy tiger-skin were too smart to wear in Tilling,' retorted Diva. 'And pray, Elizabeth, don't make a face as if you were going to cry. Do you good to hear the truth. You think everybody else is being mysterious and getting into deceitful ways just because you're doing so yourself. All these weeks you've been given honey and driven in Susan's Royce and nobody's contradicted you because – oh, well, you know what I mean, so leave it at that.'

Elizabeth whisked up her market-basket and the door banged. Diva opened the window to get rid of that horrid smell of haddock.

'I'm not a bit sorry,' she said to herself. 'I hope it may do her good. It's done me good, anyhow.'

The weather cleared, and visiting the flooded trench one evening Lucia saw that the water had soaked away and that digging could be resumed. Accordingly she sent word to her two workmen to start their soil-shifting again at ten next morning. But when, awaking at seven, she found the sun pouring into her room from a cloudless sky, she could not resist going out to begin operations alone. It was a sparkling day, thrushes were scudding about the lawn listening with cocked heads for the underground stir of worms and then rapturously excavating for their breakfast: excavation, indeed, seemed like some beautiful law of Nature which all must obey. Moreover she wanted to get on with her discoveries as quickly as possible, for to be quite frank with herself, the unfortunate business of the Spencer-tile had completely exploded, sky-high, all her evidence, and in view of what she had already told the reporter from the *Hastings Chronicle*, it would give a feeling of security to get some more. To-day was Friday, the *Hastings Chronicle* came out on Saturday, and, with the earth soft for digging, with the example of the thrushes on the lawn and the intoxicating tonic of the April day, she had a strong presentiment that she would find the rest of that sacred bottle with the complete dedication to Apollo in time to ring up the *Hastings Chronicle* with this splendid intelligence before it went to press.

Trowel in hand Lucia jumped lightly into the trench. Digging with a trowel was slow work, but much safer than with pick and shovel, for she could instantly stop when it encountered any hard underground resistance which might prove to be a fragment of what she sought. Sometimes it was a pebble that arrested her stroke, sometimes a piece of pottery, and once her agonized heart leapt into her mouth when the blade of her instrument encountered and crashed into some brittle substance. But it was only a snail-shell: it proved to be a big brown one and she remembered a correspondence in the paper about the edible snails which the Romans introduced into Britain, so she put it carefully aside. The clock struck nine and Grosvenor stepping cautiously on the mud which the rain had swept on to the gravel path came out to know when she would want breakfast. Lucia didn't know herself, but would ring when she was ready.

Grosvenor had scarcely gone back again to the house, when once more Lucia's trowel touched something which she sensed to be brittle, and she stopped her stroke before any crash followed, and dug round the obstruction with extreme caution. She scraped the mould from above it, and with a catch in her breath disclosed a beautiful piece of glass, iridescent on the surface, and of a rich green in substance. She clambered out of the trench and took it to the garden tap. Under the drip of the water there appeared stamped letters of the same type as the APOL on the original fragment: the first four were LINA, and there were several more, still caked with a harder incrustation, to follow. She hurried to the garden-room, and laid the two pieces together. They fitted exquisitely, and the 'Apol' on the first ran straight on into the 'Lina' of the second.

'Apollina,' murmured Lucia. In spite of her Latin studies and her hunts through pages of Roman inscriptions, the name 'Apollina' (perhaps a feminine derivative from Apollo) was unfamiliar to her. Yet it held the suggestion of some name which she could not at once recall. Apollina . . . a glass vessel. Then a hideous surmise loomed up in her mind, and with brutal roughness regardless of the lovely iridescent surface of the glass, she rubbed the caked earth off the three remaining letters, and the complete legend 'Apollinaris' was revealed.

She sat heavily down and looked the catastrophe in the face. Then she took a telegraph form, and after a brief concentration addressed it to the editor of the *Hastings Chronicle*, and wrote: 'Am obliged to abandon my Roman excavations for the time.

Stop. Please cancel my interview with your correspondent as any announcement would be premature. Emmeline Lucas, Mallards House, Tilling.'

She went into the house and rang for Grosvenor.

'I want this sent at once,' she said.

Grosvenor looked with great disfavour at Lucia's shoes. They were caked with mud which dropped off in lumps on to the carpet.

'Yes, ma'am,' she said. 'And hadn't you better take off your shoes on the doormat? If you have breakfast in them you'll make an awful mess on your dining-room carpet. I'll bring you some indoor shoes and then you can put the others on again if you're going on digging after breakfast.'

'I shan't be digging again,' said Lucia.

'Glad to hear it, ma'am.'

Lucia breakfasted, deep in meditation. Her excavations were at an end, and her one desire was that Tilling should forget them as soon as possible, even as, in the excitement over them, it had forgotten about Elizabeth's false pretences. Oblivion must cover the memory of them, and obliterate their traces. Not even Georgie should know of the frightful tragedy that had occurred until all vestiges of it had been disposed of; but he was coming across at ten to help her, and he must be put off, with every appearance of cheerfulness so that he should suspect nothing. She rang him up, and her voice was as brisk and sprightly as ever.

'Dood morning, Georgino,' she said. 'No *excavazione* to-day.'

'Oh, I'm sorry,' said Georgie. 'I was looking forward to finding more glass vessel.'

'Me sorry, too,' said Lucia. 'Dwefful busy to-day, Georgie. We dine to-morrow, don't we, *alla casa dei sapienti*.'

'Where?' asked Georgie, completely puzzled.

'At the Wyses',' said Lucia.

She went out to the garden-room. Bitter work was before her but she did not flinch. She carried out, one after the other, trays A, B, C and D, to the scene of her digging, and cast their contents into the trench. The two pieces of glass that together formed a nearly complete Apollinaris bottle gleamed in the air as they fell, and the undecipherable coin clinked as it struck them. Back she went to the garden-room and returned to the London Library every volume that had any bearing on the Roman occupation of Britain. At ten o'clock her two workmen appeared and they were employed for the rest of the day in shovelling back into the trench every spadeful of earth which they had dug out of it. Their instructions were to stamp it well down.

Lucia had been too late to stop her brief communication to the reporter of the *Hastings Chronicle* from going to press, and next morning when she came down to breakfast she found a marked copy of it ('see page 2' in blue pencil). She turned to it and with a curdling of her blood read what this bright young man had made out of the few words she had given him.

'All lovers of art and archaeology will be thrilled to hear of the discoveries that Mrs Lucas has made in the beautiful grounds of her Queen Anne mansion at Tilling. The *châtelaine* of Mallards House most graciously received me there a few days ago, and in her exquisite *salon* which overlooks the quaint old-world street gave me, over "the cup that cheers but not inebriates", a brilliant little *résumé* of her operations up to date and of her hopes for the future. Mrs Lucas, as I need not remind my readers, is the acknowledged leader of the most exclusive social circles in Tilling, a first-rate pianist, and an accomplished scholar in languages, dead and alive.

'"I have long," she said, "been studying that most interesting and profoundly significant epoch in history, namely the Roman occupation of Britain, and it has long been my day-dream to be privileged to add to our knowledge of it. That day-dream, I may venture to say, bids fair to become a waking reality."

'"What made you first think that there might be Roman remains hidden in the soil of Tilling?" I asked.

'She shook a playful but warning finger at me. (Mrs Lucas's hands are such as a sculptor dreams of but seldom sees.)

'"Now I'm not going to let you into my whole secret yet," she said. "All I can tell you is that when, a little while ago, the street outside my house was dug up to locate some naughty leaking gas pipe, I, watching the digging closely, saw something unearthed that to me was indisputable evidence that under my *jardin* lay the remains of a Roman villa or temple. I had suspected it before: I had often said to myself that this hill of Tilling, commanding so wide a stretch of country, was exactly the place which those wonderful old Romans would have chosen for building one of their *castra* or forts. My intuition has already been justified, and, I feel sure, will soon be rewarded by even richer discoveries. More I cannot at present tell you, for I am determined not to be premature. Wait a little while yet, and I think, yes, I think you will be astonished at the results . . ."'

Grosvenor came in.

'Trunk-call from London, ma'am,' she said. 'Central News Agency.'

Lucia, sick with apprehension, tottered to the Office.

'Mrs Lucas?' asked a buzzing voice.

'Yes.'

'Central News Agency. We've just heard by phone from Hastings of your discovery of Roman remains at Tilling,' it said. 'We're sending down a special representative this morning to inspect your excavations and write –'

'Not the slightest use,' interrupted Lucia. 'My excavations have not yet reached the stage when I can permit any account of them to appear in the press.'

'But the London Sunday papers are most anxious to secure some material about them to-morrow, and Professor Arbuthnot of the British Museum, whom we have just rung up, is willing to supply them. He will motor down and be at Tilling –'

Lucia turned cold with horror.

'I am very sorry,' she said firmly, 'but it is quite impossible for me to let Professor Arbuthnot inspect my excavations at this stage, or to permit any further announcement concerning them.'

She rang off, she waited a moment, and, being totally unable to bear the strain of the situation alone, rang up Georgie. There was no Italian or baby-talk to-day.

'Georgie, I must see you at once,' she said.

'My dear, anything wrong about the excavations?' asked the intuitive Georgie.

'Yes, something frightful. I'll be with you in one minute.'

'I've only just begun my break –' said Georgie and heard the receiver replaced.

With the nightmare notion in her mind of some sleuth-hound of an archaeologist calling while she was out and finding no excavation at all, Lucia laid it on Grosvenor to admit nobody to the house under any pretext, and hatless, with the *Hastings Chronicle* in her hand, she scudded up the road to Mallards Cottage. As she crossed the street she heard from the direction of Irene's house a prolonged and clamorous ringing of a dinner-bell, but there was no time now even to conjecture what that meant.

Georgie was breakfasting in his blue dressing-gown. He had been touching up his hair and beard with the contents of the bottle that always stood in a locked cupboard in his bedroom. His hair was not dry yet, and it was most inconvenient that she should want to see him so immediately. But the anxiety in her telephone-voice was unmistakable, and very likely she would not notice his hair.

'All quite awful, Georgie,' she said, noticing nothing at all. 'Now first I must tell you that I found the rest of the Apollo-vessel yesterday, and it was an Apollinaris bottle.'

'My dear, how tarsome,' said Georgie sympathetically.

'Tragic rather than tiresome,' said Lucia. 'First the Spencer-tile then the Apollinaris bottle. Nothing Roman left, and I filled up the trench yesterday. *Finito!* Georgie, how I should have loved a Roman temple in my garden! Think of the prestige! Archaeologists and garden-parties with little lectures! It is cruel. And then as if the extinction of all I hoped for wasn't enough there came the most frightful complications. Listen to the *Hastings Chronicle* of this morning.'

She read the monstrous fabrication through in a tragic monotone.

'Such fibs, such inventions!' she cried. 'I never knew what a vile trade journalism was! I did see a young man last week – I can't even remember his name or what he looked like – for two minutes, not more, and told him just what I said you might tell Tilling. It wasn't in the garden-room and I didn't give him tea, because it was just before lunch, standing in the hall, and I never shook a playful forefinger at him or talked about day-dreams or naughty gas pipes, and I never called the garden *jardin*, though I may have said *giardino*. And I had hardly finished reading this tissue of lies just now, when the Central News rang me up and wanted to send down Professor Arbuthnot of the British Museum to see my excavations. Georgie, how I should have loved it if there had been anything to show him! I stopped that – the Sunday London papers wanted news too – but what am I to do about this revolting *Chronicle*?'

Georgie glanced through the paper again.

'I don't think I should bother much,' he said. 'The *châtelaine* of Mallards, you know, leader of exclusive circles, lovely hands, pianist and scholar: all very complimentary. What a rage Elizabeth will be in. She'll burst.'

'Very possibly,' said Lucia. 'But don't you see how this drags me down to her level? That's so awful. We've all been despising her for deceiving us and trying to make us think she was to have a baby, and now here am I no better than her, trying to make you all think I had discovered a Roman temple. And I did believe it much more than she ever believed the other. I did indeed, Georgie, and now it's all in print which makes it ever so much worse. Her baby was never in print.'

Georgie had absently passed his fingers through his beard, to assist thought, and perceived a vivid walnut stain on them. He put his hand below the tablecloth.

'I never thought of that,' he said. 'It is rather a pity. But think how very soon we forgot about Elizabeth. Why it was almost the next day after she gave up going to be a mother and took in the old green skirt again that you got on to your discoveries, and nobody gave a single thought to her baby any more. Can't we give them all something new to jabber about?'

Georgie had got up from the table and with his walnut hand still concealed strayed to the open window and looked out.

'If that isn't Elizabeth at the door of Mallards!' he said.

'She's got a paper in her hand: *Hastings Chronicle*, I bet. Grosvenor's opened the door, but not very wide. Elizabeth's arguing –'

'Georgie, she mustn't get in,' cried the agonized Lucia. 'She'll pop out into the garden, and see there's no excavation at all.'

'She's still arguing,' said Georgie in the manner of Brangaene warning Isolde. 'She's on the top step now . . . Oh, it's all right. Grosvenor's shut the door in her face. I could hear it, too. She's standing on the top step, thinking. Oh, my God, she's coming here, just as she did before, when she was canvassing. But there'll be time to tell Foljambe not to let her in.'

Georgie hurried away on this errand, and Lucia flattened herself against the wall so that she could not be seen from the street. Presently the door-bell tinkled, and Foljambe's voice was heard firmly reiterating, 'No, ma'am, he's not at home . . . No ma'am, he's not in . . . No, ma'am, he's out, and I can't say when he'll be in. Out.'

The door closed, and next moment Elizabeth's fell face appeared at the open window. A suspiciously minded person might have thought that she wanted to peep into Georgie's sitting-room to verify (or disprove) Foljambe's assertions, and Elizabeth, who could read suspicious minds like an open book, made haste to dispel so odious a supposition. She gave a slight scream at seeing him so close to her and in such an elegant costume.

'Dear Mr Georgie,' she said. 'I beg your pardon, but your good Foljambe was so certain you were out, and I, seeing the window was open, I – I just meant to pop this copy of the *Hastings Chronicle* in. I knew how much you'd like to see it. Lovely things about sweet Lucia, *châtelaine* of Mallards and Queen of Tilling and such a wonderful archaeologist. Full of surprises for us. How little one knows on the spot!'

Georgie, returning from warning Foljambe, had left the door ajar, and in consequence Lucia, flattening herself like a shadow against the wall between it and the window, was in a strong draught. The swift and tingling approach of a sneeze darted through her nose and it crashed forth.

'Thanks very much,' said Georgie in a loud voice to Elizabeth, hoping in a confused manner by talking loud to drown what had already resounded through the room. Instantly Elizabeth thrust her head a little further through the window and got a satisfactory glimpse of Lucia's skirt. That was enough: Lucia was there and she withdrew her head from its strained position.

'We're all agog about her discoveries,' she said. 'Such an excitement! You've seen them, of course.'

'Rather!' said Georgie with enthusiasm. 'Beautiful Roman tiles and glass and pottery. Exquisite!'

Elizabeth's face fell: she had hoped otherwise.

'Must be trotting along,' she said. 'We meet at dinner, don't we, at Susan Wyse's. Her Majesty is coming, I believe.'

'Oh, I didn't know she was in Tilling,' said Georgie. 'Is she staying with you?'

'Naughty! I only meant the Queen of Tilling.'

'Oh, I *see*,' said Georgie, 'Au reservoir.'

Lucia came out of her very unsuccessful lair.

'Do you think she saw me, Georgie?' she asked. 'It might have been Foljambe as far as the sneeze went.'

'Certainly she saw you. Not a doubt of it,' said Georgie, rather pleased at this compromising role which had been provided for him. 'And now Elizabeth will tell everybody that you and I were breakfasting in my dressing-gown – you see what I mean – and that you hid when she looked in. I don't know what she mightn't make of that.'

Lucia considered this a moment, weighing her moral against her archaeological reputation.

'It's all for the best,' she said decidedly. 'It will divert her horrid mind from the excavations. And did you ever hear such acidity in a human voice as when she said Queen of Tilling? A dozen lemons, well squeezed, were saccharine compared to it. But, my dear, it was most clever and most loyal of you to say you had seen my exquisite Roman tiles and glass. I appreciate that immensely.'

'I thought it was pretty good,' said he. 'She didn't like that.'

'*Caro*, it was admirable, and you'll stick to it, won't you? Now the first thing I shall do is to go to the newsagent's and buy up all their copies of the *Hastings Chronicle*. It may be useful to cut off her supplies . . . Oh, Georgie, your hand. Have you hurt it? Iodine?'

'Just a little sprain,' said Georgie. 'Nothing to bother about.'

Lucia picked up her hat at Mallards, and hurried down to the High Street. It was rather a shock to see a news-board outside the paper-shop with

MRS LUCAS'S ROMAN FINDS IN TILLING

prominent in the contents of the current number of the *Hastings Chronicle*, and a stronger shock to find that all the copies had been sold.

'Went like hot cakes, ma'am,' said the proprietor, 'on the news of your excavations, and I've just telephoned a repeat order.'

'Most gratifying,' said Lucia, looking the reverse of gratified . . . There was Diva haggling at the butcher's as she passed, and Diva ran out, leaving Paddy to guard her basket.

'Morning,' she said. 'Seen Elizabeth?'

Lucia thought of replying 'No, but she's seen me,' but that would entail lengthy explanations, and it was better first to hear what Diva had to say, for evidently there was news.

'No, dear,' she said. 'I've only just come down from Mallards. Why?'

Diva whistled to Paddy, who, guarding her basket, was growling ferociously at anyone who came near it.

'Mad with rage,' she said. '*Hastings Chronicle*. Seen it?'

Lucia concentrated for a moment, in an effort of recollection.

'Ah, that little paragraph about my excavations,' said she lightly. 'I did glance at it. Rather exaggerated, rather decorated, but you know what journalists are.'

'Not an idea,' said Diva, 'but I know what Elizabeth is. She told me she was going to expose you. Said she was convinced you'd not found anything at all. Challenging you. Of course

437

what really riled her was that bit about you being leader of social circles, etcetera. From me she went on to tell Irene, and then to call on you and ask you point-blank whether your digging wasn't all a fake, and then she was going on to Georgie . . . Oh, there's Irene.'

Diva called shrilly to her, and she pounded up to them on her bicycle on which was hung a paint-box, a stool and an immense canvas.

'Beloved!' she said to Lucia. 'Mapp's been to see me. She told me she was quite sure you hadn't found any Roman remains. So I told her she was a liar. Just like that. She went gabbling on, so I rang my dinner-bell close to her face until she could not bear it any more and fled. Nobody can bear a dinner-bell for long if it's rung like that: all nerve specialists will tell you so. We had almost a row, in fact.'

'Darling, you're a true friend,' cried Lucia, much moved.

'Of course I am. What else do you expect me to be? I shall bring my bell to the Wyses' this evening, in case she begins again. Good-bye, adored. I'm going out to a farm on the marsh to paint a cow with its calf. If Mapp annoys you any more I shall give the cow her face, though it's bad luck on the cow, and send it to our summer exhibition. It will pleasantly remind her of what never happened to her.'

Diva looked after her approvingly as she snorted up the High Street.

'That's the right way to handle Elizabeth, when all's said and done,' she remarked. 'Quaint Irene understands her better than anybody. Think how kind we all were to her, especially you, when she was exposed. You just said "Wind-egg". Never mentioned it again. Most ungrateful of Elizabeth, I think. What are you going to do about it? Why not show her a few of your finds, just to prove what a liar she is?'

Lucia thought desperately a moment, and then a warm, pitying smile dawned on her face.

'My dear, it's really beneath me,' she said, 'to take any notice of what she told you and Irene and no doubt others as well. I'm only sorry for that unhappy jealous nature of hers. Incurable, I'm afraid: chronic, and I'm sure she suffers dreadfully from it in her better moments. As for my little excavations, I'm abandoning them for a time.'

'That's a pity!' said Diva. 'Should have thought it was just the time to go on with them. Why?'

'Too much publicity,' said Lucia earnestly. 'You know how I hate that. They were only meant to be a modest little amateur effort, but what with all that *réclame* in the *Hastings Chronicle*, and the Central News this morning telling me that Professor Arbuthnot of the British Museum, who I understand is the final authority on Roman archaeology, longing to come down to see them –'

'No! from the British Museum?' cried Diva. 'I shall tell Elizabeth that. When is he coming?'

'I've refused. Too much fuss. And then my arousing all this jealousy and ill-feeling in – well, in another quarter, is quite intolerable to me. Perhaps I shall continue my work later on, but very quietly. Georgie, by the way, has seen my little finds, such as they are, and thinks them exquisite. But I stifle in this atmosphere of envy and malice. Poor Elizabeth! Good-bye, dear, we meet this evening at the Wyses', do we not?'

Lucia walked pensively back to Mallards, not displeased with herself. Irene's dinner-bell and her own lofty attitude would probably scotch Elizabeth for the present, and with Georgie as a deep-dyed accomplice and Diva as an ardent sympathizer, there was not much to fear from her. The *Hastings Chronicle* next week would no doubt announce that she had abandoned her excavations for the present, and Elizabeth might make exactly what she chose out of that. Breezy unconsciousness of any low libels and machinations was decidedly the right ticket.

Lucia quickened her pace. There had flashed into her mind the memory of a basket of odds and ends which she had brought from Grebe, but which she had not yet unpacked. There was a box of Venetian beads among them, a small ebony elephant, a silver photograph frame or two, some polished agates, and surely she seemed to recollect some pieces of pottery. She had no very distinct remembrance of them, but when she got home she unearthed (more excavation) this basket of dubious treasures from a cupboard below the stairs and found in her repository of objects suitable for a jumble-sale, a broken bowl and a saucer (patera) of red stamped pottery. Her intensive study of Roman remains in Britain easily enabled her to recognize them as being of 'Samian ware', not uncommonly found on sites of Roman settlements in this island. Thoughtfully she dusted them, and carried them out to the garden-room. They were pretty, they looked attractive casually but prominently disposed on the top of the piano. Georgie must be reminded how much he had admired them when they were found . . .

8

With social blood pressure so high, with such embryos of plots and counter-plots darkly developing, with, generally, an atmosphere so charged with electricity, Susan Wyse's party to-night was likely (to change the metaphor once more) to prove a scene of carnage. These stimulating expectations were amply fulfilled.

The numbers to begin with were unpropitious. It must always remain uncertain whether Susan had asked the Padre and Evie to dine that night, for though she maintained ever afterwards that she had asked them for the day after, he was equally willing to swear in Scotch, Irish and English that it was for to-night. Everyone, therefore, when eight people were assembled, thought that the party was complete, and that two tables of bridge would keep it safely occupied after dinner. Then when the door opened (it was to be hoped) for the announcement that dinner was ready, it proved to have been opened to admit these two further guests, and God knew what would happen about bridge. Susan shook hands with them in a dismayed and distracted manner, and slipped out of the room, as anyone could guess, to hold an agitated conference with her cook and her butler, Figgis, who said he had done his best to convince them that they were not expected, but without success. Starvation corner therefore was likely to be a Lenten situation, served with drumsticks and not enough soup to cover the bottom of the plate. Very embarrassing for poor Susan, and there was a general feeling that nobody must be sarcastic at her wearing the cross of a Member of the British Empire, which she had unwisely pinned to the front of her ample bosom, or say they had never been told that Orders would be worn. In that ten minutes of waiting, several eggs of discord (would that they had only been wind-eggs!) had been laid and there seemed a very good chance of some of them hatching.

In the main it was Elizabeth who was responsible for this clutch of eggs, for she set about laying them at once. She had a strong suspicion that the stain on Georgie's fingers, which he had been unable to get rid of, was not iodine but hair-dye, and asked him how he had managed to sprain those fingers all together: such bad luck. Then she turned to Lucia and inquired anxiously how her cold was: she hoped she had been having no further sneezing fits, for prolonged sneezing was so exhausting. She saw Georgie and Lucia exchange a guilty glance and again turned to him: 'We must make a plot, Mr Georgie,' she said, 'to compel our precious Lucia to take more care of herself. All that standing about in the wet and cold over her wonderful excavations.'

By this time Irene had sensed that these apparent dewdrops were globules of corrosive acid, though she did not know their precise nature, and joined the group.

'Such a lovely morning I spent, Mapp,' she said with an intonation that Elizabeth felt was very like her own. 'I've been painting a cow with its dear little calf. Wasn't it lovely for the cow to have a sweet baby like that?'

During this wait for dinner Major Benjy, screened from his wife by the Padre and Diva, managed to secure three glasses of sherry and two cocktails. Then Susan returned followed by Figgis, having told him not to hand either to her husband or her that oyster-savoury which she adored, since there were not enough oysters, and to be careful about helpings. But an abundance of wine must flow in order to drown any solid deficiencies, and she had substituted champagne for hock, and added brandy to go with the chestnut ice *à la Capri*. They went in to dinner: Lucia sat on Mr Wyse's right and Elizabeth on his left in starvation corner. On her other side was Georgie, and Benjy sat next to Susan Wyse on the same side of the table as his wife and entirely out of the range of her observation.

Elizabeth, a little cowed by Irene's artless story, found nothing to complain of in starvation corner, as far as soup went: indeed Figgis's rationing had been so severe on earlier recipients that she got a positive lake of it. She was pleased at having a man on each side of her, her host on her right, and Georgie on her left, whereas Lucia had quaint Irene on her right. Turbot came next; about that Figgis was not to blame, for people helped themselves, and they were all so inconsiderate that, when it came to Elizabeth's turn, there was little left but spine and a quantity of shining black mackintosh, and as for her first glass of champagne, it was merely foam. By this time, too, she was beginning to get uneasy about Benjy. He was talking in a fat contented voice, which she seldom heard at home, and neither by leaning back nor by leaning forward could she get any really informatory glimpse of him or his wine-glasses. She heard his gobbling laugh at the end of one of his own stories, and Susan said, 'Oh fie, Major, I shall tell of you.' That was not reassuring.

Elizabeth stifled her uneasiness and turned to her host.

'Delicious turbot, Mr Wyse,' she said. 'So good. And did you see the *Hastings Chronicle* this morning about the great Roman discoveries of the *châtelaine* of Mallards. Made me feel quite a dowager.'

Mr Wyse had clearly foreseen the deadly feelings that might be aroused by that article, and had made up his mind to be extremely polite to everybody, whatever they were to each other. He held up a deprecating hand.

'You will not be able to persuade your friends of that,' he said. 'I protest against your applying the word dowager to yourself. It has the taint of age about it. The ladies of Tilling remain young for ever, as my sister Amelia so constantly writes to me.'

Elizabeth tipped up her champagne-glass, so that he could scarcely help observing that there was really nothing in it.

'Sweet of the dear Contessa,' she said. 'But in my humble little Grebe, I feel quite a country mouse, so far away from all that's going on. Hardly Tilling at all: my Benjy-boy tells me I must call the house "Mouse-trap".'

Irene was still alert for attacks on Lucia.

'How about calling it Cat and Mouse trap, Mapp?' she inquired across the table.

'Why, dear?' said Elizabeth with terrifying suavity.

Lucia instantly engaged quaint Irene's attention, or something even more quaint might have followed, and Mr Wyse made signals to Figgis and pointed towards Elizabeth's wine-glass. Figgis thinking that he was only calling his notice to wine-glasses in general filled up Major Benjy's which happened to be empty, and began carving the chicken. The maid handed the plates and Lucia got some nice slices off the breast. Elizabeth receiving no answer from Irene, wheeled round to Georgie.

'What a day it will be when we are all allowed to see the great Roman remains,' she said.

'Won't it?' said Georgie.

A dead silence fell on the table except for Benjy's jovial voice.

'A saucy little customer she was. They used to call her the Pride of Poona. I've still got her photograph somewhere, by Jove.'

Rockets of conversation, a regular bouquet of them, shot up all round the table.

'And was Poona where you killed those lovely tigers, Major?' asked Susan. 'What a pretty costume Elizabeth made of the best bits. So ingenious. Figgis, the champagne.'

'Irene dear,' said Lucia in her most earnest voice, 'I think you must manage our summer picture exhibition this year. My hands are so full. Do persuade her to, Mr Wyse.'

Mr Wyse bowed right and left, particularly to Elizabeth.

'I see on all sides of me such brilliant artists and such competent managers –' he began.

'Oh, pray not me!' said Elizabeth. 'I'm quite out of touch with modern art.'

'Well, there's room for old masters and mistresses, Mapp,' said Irene encouragingly. 'Never say die.'

Lucia had just finished her nice slice of breast when a well-developed drumstick, probably from the leg on which the chicken habitually roosted, was placed before Elizabeth. Black roots of plucked feathers were dotted about in the yellow skin.

'Oh, far too much for me,' she said. 'Just a teeny slice after my lovely turbot.'

Her plate was brought back with a piece of the drumstick cut off. Chestnut ice with brandy followed, and the famous oyster-savoury, and then dessert, with a *compôte* of figs in honey.

'A little Easter gift from my sister Amelia,' explained Mr Wyse to Elizabeth. 'A domestic product of which the recipe is an heirloom of the mistress of Castello Faraglione. I think Amelia had the privilege of sending you a spoonful or two of the Faraglione honey not so long ago.'

The most malicious brain could not have devised two more appalling *gaffes* than this pretty speech contained. There was that unfortunate mention of the word 'recipe' again, and everyone thought of lobster, and who could help recalling the reason why Contessa Amelia had sent Elizabeth the jar of nutritious honey? The pause of stupefaction was succeeded by a fresh gabble of conversation, and a spurt of irrepressible laughter from quaint Irene.

Dinner was now over: Susan collected ladies' eyes, and shepherded them out of the room, while the Padre held the door open and addressed some bright and gallant little remark in three languages to each. In spite of her injunction to her husband that the gentlemen mustn't be long, or there would be no time for bridge, it was impossible to obey, for Major Benjy had a great number of very amusing stories to tell, each of which suggested another to him. He forgot the point of some, and it might have been as well if he had forgotten the point of others, but they were all men together, he said, and it was a sad heart that never rejoiced. Also he forgot once or twice to send the port on when it came to him, and filled up his glass again when he had finished his story.

'Most entertaining,' said Mr Wyse frigidly as the clock struck ten. 'A long time since I have laughed so much. You are a regular storehouse of amusing anecdotes, Major. But Susan will scold me unless we join the ladies.'

'Never do to keep the lil' fairies waiting,' said Benjy. 'Well, thanks, just a spot of sherry. Capital good dinner I've had. A married man doesn't often get much of a dinner at home, by Jove, at least I don't, though that's to go no further. Ha, ha! Discretion.'

Then arose the very delicate question of the composition of the bridge-tables. Vainly did Mr Wyse (faintly echoed by Susan) explain that they would both much sooner look on, for everybody else, with the same curious absence of conviction in their voices, said that they would infinitely prefer to do the same. That was so palpably false that without more ado cards were cut, the two highest to sit out for the first rubber. Lucia drew a king, and Elizabeth drew a knave, and it seemed for a little that they would have to sit out together, which would have been quite frightful, but then Benjy luckily cut a queen. A small sitting-room, opening from the drawing-room, would enable them to chat without disturbing the players, and Major Benjy gallantly declared that he would sooner have a talk with her than win two grand slams.

Benjy's sense of exuberant health and happiness was beginning to be overshadowed, as if the edge of a coming eclipse had nicked the full orb of the sun – perhaps the last glass or two of port had been an error in an otherwise judicious dinner – but he was still very bright and loquacious and suffused.

''Pon my word, a delightful little dinner,' he said, as he closed the door into the little sitting-room. 'Good talk, good friends, a glass of jolly good wine and a rubber to follow. What more can a man ask, I ask you, and Echo answers "Cern'ly not." And I've not had a pow-wow with you for a long time, *Signora*, as old Camelia Faradiddleone would say.'

Lucia saw that he had had about enough wine, but after many evenings with Elizabeth who wouldn't?

'No, I've been quite a hermit lately,' she said. 'So busy with my little jobs – oh, take care of your cigar, Major Benjy: it's burning the edge of the table.'

'Dear me, yes, monstrous stupid of me: where there's smoke there's fire! We've been busy, too, settling in. How do you think Liz is looking?'

'Very well, exceedingly well,' said Lucia enthusiastically. 'All her old energy, all her delightful activity seem to have returned. At one time –'

Major Benjy looked round to see that the door was closed and nodded his head with extreme solemnity.

'Quite, quite. Olive-branches. Very true,' he said. 'Marvellous woman, ain't she, the way she's put it all behind her. Felt it very much at the time, for she's mos' sensitive. Highly strung. Concert pitch. Liable to ups and downs. For instance, there was a paragraph in the Hastings paper this morning that upset Liz so much that she whirled about like a spinning top, butting into the tables and chairs. "Take it quietly, 'Lisbeth Mapp-Flint," I told her. Beneath you to notice it, or should I go over and punch the Editor's head?'

'Do you happen to be referring to the paragraph about me and my little excavations?' asked Lucia.

'God bless me, if I hadn't forgotten what it was about,' cried Benjy. 'You're right, Msslucas, the very first time. That's what it was about, if I may say so without prejudice. I only remembered there was something that annoyed 'Lisbeth Mapp-Flint, and that was enough for Major B, late of His Majesty's India forces, God bless him, too. If something annoys my wife, it annoys me, too, that's what I say. A husband's duty, Msslucas, is always to stand between her and any annoyances, what? Too many annoyances lately and often my heart's bled for her. Then it was a sad trial parting with her old home which she'd known ever since her aunt was a lil' girl, or since they were lil' girls together, if not before. Then that was a bad business about the Town Council and those dinner-bells. A dirty business I might call it, if there wasn't a lady present, though that mustn't go any further. Not cricket, hic. All adds up, you know, in the mind of a very sensitive woman. Twice two and four, if you see what I mean.'

Benjy sank down lower in his chair, and after two attempts to relight his cigar, gave it up, and the eclipse spread a little further.

'I'm not quite easy in my mind about 'Lisbeth,' he said, 'an' that's why it's such a privilege to be able to have quiet talk with you like this. There's no more sympathetic woman in Tilling, I tell my missus, than Msslucas. A thousand pities that you and she don't always see eye to eye about this or that, whether it's dinner-bells or it might be Roman antiquities or changing houses. First it's one thing and then it's another, and then it's something else. Anxious work.'

'I don't think there's the slightest cause for you to be anxious, Major Benjy,' said Lucia.

Benjy thumped the table with one hand, then drew his chair a little closer to hers, and laid the other hand on her knee.

'That reminds me what I wanted to talk to you about,' he said. 'Grebe, you know, our lil' place Grebe. Far better house in my opinion than poor ole Auntie's. I give you my word on that, and Major B's word's as good's his bond, if not better. Smelt of dry rot, did Auntie's house, and the paint peeling off the walls same as an orange. But 'Lisbeth liked it, Msslucas. It suited 'Lisbeth down to the ground. You give the old lady a curtain to sit behind an' something puzzling going on in the street outside, and she'll be azappy as a queen till the cows come home, if not longer. She misses that at our lil' place, Grebe, and it goes to my heart, Msslucas.'

He was rather more tipsy, thought Lucia, than she had supposed, but he was much better here, maundering quietly along than coming under Elizabeth's eye, for her sake as well as his, for she had had a horrid evening with nothing but foam to drink and mackintosh and muscular drumstick to eat, to the accompaniment of all those frightful *gaffes* about cat-traps and recipes and nutritious honey and hints about Benjy's recollections of the Pride of Poona, poor woman. Lucia sincerely hoped that the rubbers now in progress would be long, so that he might get a little steadier before he had to make a public appearance again.

'It gives 'Lisbeth the hump, does Grebe,' he went on in a melancholy voice. 'No little side-shows going on outside. Nothing but sheep and sea-gulls to squint at from behind a curtain at our lil' place. Scarcely worth getting behind a curtain at all, it isn't, and it's a sad come-down for her. I lie awake thinking of it, and I'll tell you what, Msslucas, though it mustn't go any further. Mum's the word, like what we had at dinner. I believe, though I couldn't say for certain, that she'd be willing to let you have Grebe, if you offered her thousan' pounds premium, and go back to Auntie's herself. Worth thinking about, or lemme see, do I mean that she'd give you thousan' pounds premium? Split the difference. Why, here's 'Lisbeth herself! There's a curious thing!'

Elizabeth stood in the doorway, and took him in from head to foot in a single glance, as he withdrew his hand from Lucia's knee as if it had been a live coal, and, hoisting himself with some difficulty out of his chair, brushed an inch of cigar-ash off his waistcoat.

'We're going home, Benjy,' she said. 'Come along.'

'But I want to have rubber of bridge, Liz,' said he. 'Msslucas and I've been waiting for our lil' rubber of bridge.'

Elizabeth continued to be as unconscious of Lucia as if they were standing for the Town Council again.

'You've had enough pleasure for one evening, Benjy,' said she, 'and enough –'

Lucia, crushing a natural even a laudable desire to hear what should follow, slipped quietly from the room and closed the door. Outside a rubber was still going on at one table, and at the other the Padre, Georgie and Diva were leaning forward discussing something in low tones.

'But she *had* quitted her card,' said Diva. 'And the whole rubber was only ninepence, and she's not paid me. Those hectoring ways of hers –'

'Diva, dear,' said Lucia, seating herself in the vacant chair. 'Let's cut for deal at once and go on as if nothing had happened. You and me. Laddies against lassies, Padre.'

They were still considering their hands when the door into the inner room opened again, and Elizabeth swept into the room followed by Benjy.

'Pray don't let anyone get up,' she said. 'Such a lovely evening, dear Susan! Such a lovely party! No, Mr Wyse, I insist. My Benjy tells me it's time for me to go home. So late. We shall walk and enjoy the beautiful stars. Do us both good. Galoshes outside in the hall. Everything.'

Mr Wyse got up and pressed the bell.

'But, my dear lady, no hurry, so early,' he said. 'A sandwich surely, a tunny sandwich, a little lemonade, a drop of whisky. Figgis: Whisky, sandwiches, galoshes!'

Benjy suddenly raised the red banner of revolt. He stood quite firmly in the middle of the room, with his hand on the back of the Padre's chair.

449

'There's been a lil' mistake,' he said. 'I want my lil' rubber of bridge. Fair play's a jewel. I want my tummy sandwich and mouthful whisky and soda. I want –'

'Benjy, I'm waiting for you,' said Elizabeth.

He looked this way and that but encountered no glance of encouragement. Then he made a smart military salute to the general company and marched from the room stepping carefully but impeccably, as if treading a tightrope stretched over an abyss, and shut the door into the hall with swift decision.

'Puir wee mannie,' said the Padre. 'Three no-trumps, Mistress Plaistow.'

'She *had* quitted the card,' said Diva still fuming. 'I saw the light between it and her fingers. Oh, is it me? Three spades, I mean four.'

9

Lucia and Georgie were seated side by side on the bench of the organ in Tilling church. The May sunshine streamed on to them through the stained glass of a south window, vividly colouring them with patches of the brightest hues, so that they looked like objects daringly camouflaged in war-time against enemy aircraft, for nobody could have dreamed that those brilliant Joseph-coats could contain human beings. The lights cast upon Lucia's face and white dress reached her through a picture of Elijah going up to heaven in a fiery chariot. The heat from this vehicle would presumably have prevented the prophet from feeling cold in interstellar space, for he wore only an emerald-green bathing-dress which left exposed his superbly virile arms and legs, and his snowy locks streamed in the wind. The horses were flame-coloured, the chariot was red-hot, and high above it in an ultramarine sky hung an orange sun which seemed to be the object of the expedition. Georgie came under the influence of the Witch of Endor. She was wrapped in an eau-de-Nil mantle, which made his auburn beard look livid. Saul in a purple cloak, and Samuel in a black dressing-gown made sombre stains on his fawn-coloured suit.

The organ was in process of rebuilding. A quantity of fresh stops were being added to it, and an electric blowing-apparatus had been installed. Lucia clicked on the switch which set the bellows working, and opened a copy of the 'Moonlight' Sonata.

'It sounds quite marvellous on the organ, Georgie,' she said. 'I was trying it over yesterday. What I want you to do is to play the pedals. Just those slow base notes: pom, pom. Quite easy.'

Georgie put a foot on the pedals. Nothing happened.

'Oh, I haven't pulled out any pedal stop,' said Lucia. By

mistake she pulled out the tuba, and as the pedals happened to be coupled to the solo organ a blast of baritone fury yelled through the church. 'My fault,' she said, 'entirely my fault, but what a magnificent noise! One of my new stops.'

She uncoupled the pedals and substituted the bourdon: Elijah and the Witch of Endor rattled in their leaded frames.

'That's perfect!' she said. 'Now with one hand I shall play the triplets on the swell, and the solo tune with the other on the *vox humana*! Oh, that tuba again! I thought I'd put it in.'

The plaintive throaty bleating of the *vox humana* was enervatingly lovely, and Lucia's America-cloth eyes grew veiled with moisture.

'So heart-broken,' she intoned, her syllables keeping time with the air. 'A lovely contralto tone. Like Clara Butt, is it not? The passionate despair of it. Fresh courage coming. So noble. No, Georgie, you must take care not to put your foot on two adjacent pedals at once. Now, listen! Do you hear that lovely crescendo? That I do by just opening the swell very gradually. Isn't it a wonderful effect? . . . I am surprised that no one has ever thought of setting this sonata for the organ . . . Go on pulling out stops on the great organ – yes, to your left there – in case I want them. One always has to look ahead in organ playing. Arrange your palette, so to speak. No, I shan't want them . . . It dies away, softer and softer . . . Hold on that bass C sharp till I say now . . . Now.'

They both gave the usual slow movement sigh. Then the volume of Beethoven tumbled on to the great organ on which Georgie had pulled out all the stops, and the open diapasons received it with a shout of rapture. Lucia slipped from the bench to pick it up. On the floor round about was an assemblage of small pipes.

'I think this lot is the cor anglais,' she said. 'I am putting in a beautiful cor anglais.'

She picked up one of the pipes, and blew through it.

'A lovely tone,' she said. 'It reminds one of the last act of *Tristan*, does it not, where the shepherd-boy goes on playing the cor anglais for ever and ever.'

Georgie picked up a pipe belonging to the flute. It happened to be a major third above Lucia's cor anglais, and they blew on them together with a very charming effect. They tried two others, but these happened to be a semitone apart, and the result was not so harmonious. Then they hastily put them down, for a party of tourists, being shown round the church by the Padre, came in at the north door. He was talking very strong Scots this morning, with snatches of early English in compliment to the architecture.

'The orrgan, ye see, is being renovated,' he said. ''Twill be a bonny instrument, I ken. Good morrow to ye, Mistress Lucas.'

Then, as she and Georgie passed him on their way out, he added in an audible aside:

'The leddy whose munificence has given it to the church. Eh, a grand benefaction. A thousand pounds and mair, what wi' lutes and psaltery, and a' the whustles.'

'I often go and have a little practice on my organ during the workmen's dinner-hour,' said Lucia as they stepped out into the hot sunshine. 'The organ, Georgie, I find is a far simpler instrument on which to get your effects than the piano. The stops supply expression: you just pull them out or push them in. That *vox humana*, for instance, with what ease one gets the singing tone, that's so difficult on the piano.'

'You've picked it up wonderfully quickly,' said Georgie. 'I thought you had a beautiful touch. And when will your organ be finished?'

'In a month or less, I hope. We must have a service of dedication and recital: the Padre, I know, will carry out my wishes about that. Georgie, I think I shall open the recital myself. I am sure that Tilling would wish it. I should play some little piece, and then make way for the organist. I might do worse than give them that first movement of the "Moonlight".'

'I'm sure Tilling would be much disappointed if you didn't,' said Georgie warmly. 'May I play the pedals for you?'

'I was going to suggest that, and help me with the stops. I have progressed, I know, and I'm glad you like my touch, but

I hardly think I could manage the whole complicated business alone yet. *Festina lente.* Let us practise in the dinner-hour every day. If I give the "Moonlight" it must be exquisitely performed. I must show them what can be done with it when the orchestral colour of the organ is added.'

'I promise to work hard,' said Georgie. 'And I do think, as the Padre said to the tourists just now, that it's a most munificent gift.'

'Oh, did he say that?' asked Lucia who had heard perfectly. 'That was why they all turned round and looked at me. But, as you know, it was always my intention to devote a great part, anyhow, of what I made on the Stock Exchange to the needs of our dear Tilling.'

'Very generous, all the same,' repeated Georgie.

'No, dear; simple duty. That's how I see it . . . Now what have I got to do this afternoon? That tea-party for the school-children: a hundred and twenty are coming. Tea in the garden in the shade, and then games and races. You'll be helping me all the time, won't you? Only four o'clock till seven.'

'Oh dear: I'm not very good with children,' said Georgie. 'Children are so sticky, particularly after tea, and I won't run a race with anybody.'

'You shan't run a race. But you'll help to start them, won't you, and find their mothers for them and that sort of thing. I know I can depend on you, and children always adore you. Let me see: do I dine with you to-night or you with me?'

'You with me. And then to-morrow's your great dinner-party. I tell you I'm rather nervous, for there are so many things we mustn't talk about, that there's scarcely a safe subject. It'll be the first complete party anyone's had since that frightful evening at the Wyses'.'

'It was clearly my duty to respond to Diva's appeal,' said Lucia, 'and all we've got to do is to make a great deal of poor Elizabeth. She's had a horrid time, most humiliating, Georgie, and what makes it worse for her is that it was so much her own fault. Four o'clock then, dear, this afternoon, or perhaps a little before.'

*

Lucia let herself into her house, musing at considerable length on the frightful things that had happened since that night at the Wyses' to which Georgie had alluded, when Elizabeth and Benjy had set out in their galoshes, to walk back to Grebe. That was an unwise step, for the fresh night air had made Benjy much worse and the curate returning home on the other side of the High Street after a meeting of the Band of Hope (such a contrast) had witnessed dreadful goings-on. Benjy had stood in the middle of the road, compelling a motor to pull up with a shriek of brakes, and asked to see the driver's licence, insisting that he was a policeman in plain clothes on point duty. When that was settled in a most sympathetic manner by a real policeman, Benjy informed him that Msslucas was a regular stunner, and began singing 'You are Queen of my heart to-night.' At that point the curate, pained but violently interested, reluctantly let himself into his house, and there was no information to be had with regard to the rest of their walk home to Grebe. Then the sad tale was resumed, for Withers told Foljambe (who told Georgie who told Lucia) that Major Mapp-Flint on arrival had, no doubt humorously, suggested getting his gun and shooting the remaining tiger-skins in the hall, but that Mrs Mapp-Flint wouldn't hear of it and was not amused. 'Rather the reverse,' said Withers . . . Bed.

The curate felt bound to tell his spiritual superior about the scene in the High Street and Evie told Diva, so that by the time Elizabeth came up with her market-basket next morning, this sad sequel to the Wyses' dinner-party was known everywhere. She propitiated Diva by paying her the ninepence which had been in dispute, and went so far as to apologize to her for her apparent curtness at the bridge-table last night. Then, having secured a favourable hearing, she told Diva how she had found Benjy sitting close to Lucia with his hand on her knee. 'He had had more to drink than he should,' she said, 'but never would he have done that unless she had encouraged him. That's her nature, I'm afraid: she can't leave men alone. She's no better than the Pride of Poona!'

So, when Diva met Lucia half an hour afterwards, she could not resist being distinctly 'arch' about her long *tête-à-tête* with Benjy during the first rubber. Lucia, not appreciating this archness, had answered not a word, but turned her back and went into Twistevant's. Diva hadn't meant any harm, but this truculent conduct (combined with her dropping that ninepence down a grating in the gutter) made her see red, and she instantly told Irene that Lucia had been flirting with Benjy. Irene had tersely replied, 'You foul-minded old widow.'

Then as comment spread, Susan Wyse was blamed for having allowed Benjy (knowing his weakness) to drink so much champagne, and Mr Wyse was blamed for being so liberal with his port. This was quite unfounded: it was Benjy who had been so liberal with his port. The Wyses adopted a lofty attitude: they simply were not accustomed to their guests drinking too much, and must bear that possibility in mind for the future: Figgis must be told. Society therefore once again, as on the occasion of the municipal elections, was rent. The Wyses were aloof, Elizabeth and Diva would not speak to Lucia, nor Diva to Irene, and Benjy would not speak to anybody because he was in bed with a severe bilious attack.

This haycock of inflammatory material would in the ordinary course of things soon have got dispersed or wet through or trodden into the ground, according to the Tilling use of disposing of past disturbances in order to leave the ground clear for future ones, but for the unexpected arrival of the Contessa Faraglione who came on a flying visit of two nights to her brother. He and Susan were still adopting their tiresome lofty, un-Tillingish attitude, and told her nothing at all exhaustive about Benjy's inebriation, Lucia's excavations, Elizabeth's disappointment and other matters of first-rate importance, and in the present state of tension thought it better not to convoke any assembly of Tilling society in Amelia's honour. But she met Elizabeth in the High Street who was very explicit about Roman antiquities, and she met Lucia, who was in a terrible fright lest she should begin talking Italian, and learned a little more, and she went to tea with Diva, who was quite the best chronicler in Tilling, and who poured into her madly interested ear a neat *résumé* of all previous rows, and had just got down to the present convulsion when the Padre popped in, and he and Diva began expounding it in alternate sentences after the manner of a Greek tragedy. Faradiddleone sat, as if hypnotized, alert and wide-eyed while this was going on, but when told of Elizabeth's surmise that Lucia had encouraged Benjy to make love to her, she most disconcertingly burst into peals of laughter. Muffins went the wrong way, she choked, she clapped her hands, her eyes streamed, and it was long before she could master herself for coherent speech.

'But you are all adorable,' she cried. 'There is no place like Tilling, and I shall come and live here for ever when my Cecco dies and I am dowager. My poor brother (such a prig!) and fat Susan were most discreet: they told me no more than that your great Benjy – he was my flirt here before, was he not, the man like a pink walrus – that he had a bilious attack, but of his tipsiness and of all those *gaffes* at dinner and of that scene of passion in the back drawing-room not a word. Thr-r-rilling! Imagine the scene. Your tipsy walrus. Your proud Lucia in her Roman blue stockings. She is a Duse, all cold alabaster without and burning with volcanic passion within. Next door is Mapp quarrelling about ninepence. What did the guilty ones do? I would have given anything to have been behind the curtain. Did they kiss? Did they embrace? Can you picture them? And then the entry of Mapp with her ninepence still in her pocket.'

'It's only fair to say that she paid me next morning,' said Diva scrupulously.

'Oh, stop me laughing,' cried Faradiddleone. 'Mapp enters. "Come home, Benjy," and then "Queen of my Heart" all down the High Street. The rage of the Mapp! If she could not have a baby she must invent for her husband a mistress. Who shall say it is not true, though? When his bilious attack is better will they meet in the garden at Mallards? He is Lothario of the tiger-skins. Why should it not be true? My Cecco has had a mistress for years – such a good-natured pretty woman – and why not your Major? *Basta!* I must be calm.'

This flippant and deplorably immoral view of the crisis had an inflammatory rather than a cooling effect. If Tilling was anything, it was intensely serious, and not to be taken seriously by this lascivious Countess made it far more serious. So, after a few days during which social intercourse was completely paralysed, Lucia determined to change the currents of thought by digging a new channel for them. She had long been considering which should be the first of those benefactions to Tilling which would raise her on a pinnacle of public pre-eminence and expunge the memory of that slight fiasco at the late municipal elections, and now she decided on the renovation and amplification of the organ on which she and Georgie had been practising this morning. The time was well chosen, for surely those extensive rents in the social fabric would be repaired by the universal homage rendered her for her munificence, and nothing more would be heard of Roman antiquities and dinner-bells and drunkenness and those odious and unfounded aspersions on the really untarnishable chastity of her own character. All would be forgotten.

Accordingly next Sunday morning the Padre had announced from the pulpit in accents trembling with emotion that through the generosity of a donor who preferred to remain anonymous the congregation's psalms and hymns of praise would soon be accompanied by a noble new relay of trumpets and shawms. Then, as nobody seemed to guess (as Lucia had hoped) who the anonymous donor was, she had easily been persuaded to let this thin veil of anonymity be withdrawn. But even then there was not such a tumultuous outpouring of gratitude and admiration as to sweep away all the hatchets that still lay perilously about: in fact Elizabeth who brought the news to Diva considered the gift a very ostentatious and misleading gesture.

'It's throwing dust in our eyes,' she observed with singular acidity. 'It's drawing a red herring across her Roman excavations and her abominable forwardness with Benjy on that terrible evening. As for the gift itself, I consider it far from generous. With the fortune she has made in gold mines and rails and all the rest of it, she doesn't feel the cost of it one atom. What I call generosity is to deprive yourself —'

'Now you're not being consistent, Elizabeth,' said Diva. 'You told me yourself that you didn't believe she had made more than half a crown.'

'No, I never said that, dear,' affirmed Elizabeth. 'You must be thinking of someone else you were gossiping with.'

'No, I mustn't,' said Diva. 'You did say it. And even if you hadn't, it would be very paltry of you to belittle her gift just because she was rich. But you're always carping and picking holes, and sowing discord.'

'I?' said Elizabeth, not believing her ears.

'Yes, you. Go back to that terrible evening as you call it. You've talked about nothing else since: you've been keeping the wound open. I don't deny that it was very humiliating for you to see Major Benjy exceed like that, and of course no woman would have liked her husband to go bawling out "Queen of my Heart" all the way home about some other woman. But I've been thinking it over. I don't believe Lucia made up to him any more than I did. We should be all settling down again happily if it wasn't for you, instead of being at loggerheads with each other. Strawberries will be in next week, and not one of us dares ask the rest to our usual summer bridge-parties for fear of there being more ructions.'

'Nonsense, dear,' said Elizabeth. 'As far as I am concerned it isn't a question of not daring at all, though of course I wouldn't be so rude as to contradict you about your own moral cowardice. It's simply that I prefer not to see anything of people like Lucia or Susan who on that night was neither more nor less than a bar-maid encouraging Benjy to drink until they've expressed regret for their conduct.'

'If it comes to expressions of regret,' retorted Diva, 'I think Major Benjy had better show the way and you follow. How you can call yourself a Christian at all is beyond me.'

'Benjy has expressed himself very properly to me,' said Elizabeth, 'so there's the end of that. As for my expressing regret I can't conceive what you wish me to express regret for. Painful though I should find it to be excommunicated by you, dear, I shall have to bear it. Or would you like me to apologize to Irene for all the wicked things she said to me that night?'

'Well I daren't ask our usual party,' said Diva, 'however brave you are. You may call it moral cowardice, but it's simply common sense. Lucia would refuse with some excuse that would be an insult to my intelligence, and Mr Georgie would certainly stick to her. So would Irene; besides she called me a foul-minded old widow. The Wyses won't begin, and I agree it wouldn't be any use your trying. The only person who's got the power or position or whatever you like to call it, to bring us all together again is Lucia herself. Don't look down your nose, Elizabeth, because it's true. I've a good mind to apologize to her for my bit of silly chaff about Major Benjy, and to ask her to do something for us.'

'I hope, dear,' said Elizabeth, rising, 'that you won't encourage her to think that Benjy and I will come to her house. That would only lead to disappointment.'

'By the way, how is he?' said Diva. 'I forgot to ask.'

'So I noticed, dear. He's better, thanks. Gone to play golf again to-day.'

Diva put her pride in her pocket and went up to Mallards that very afternoon and said that she was very sorry that a word of hers spoken really in jest, should have given offence to Lucia. Lucia, as might have been expected from her lofty and irritating ways, looked at her, smiling and a little puzzled, with her head on one side.

'Dear Diva, what do you mean?' she said. 'How can you have offended me?'

'What I said about Benjy and you,' said Diva. 'Just outside Twistevant's. Very stupid of me, but just chaff.'

'My wretched memory,' said Lucia. 'I've no recollection of it at all. I think you must have dreamed it. But so nice to see you, and tell me all the news. Heaps of pleasant little parties? I've been so busy with my new organ and so on, that I'm quite out of the movement.'

'There's not been a single party since that dinner at Susan's,' said Diva.

'You don't say so! And how is Major Benjy? I think somebody told me he had caught a chill that night, when he walked home. People who have lived much in the tropics are liable to them: he must take more care of himself.'

They had strolled out into the garden, awaiting tea, and

looked into the greenhouse where the peach-trees were covered with setting fruit. Lucia looked wistfully at the potato- and asparagus-beds.

'More treasures to be unearthed some time, I hope,' she said with really unparalleled nerve. 'But at present my hands are so full: my organ, my little investments, Georgie just dines quietly with me or I with him, and we make music or read. Happy busy days!'

Really she was quite maddening, thought Diva, pretending like this to be totally unaware of the earthquake which had laid in ruins the social life of Tilling. On she went.

'Otherwise I've seen no one but Irene, and just a glimpse of dear Contessa Faraglione, and we had a refreshing chat in Italian. I found I was terribly rusty. She told me that it was just a flying visit.'

'Yes, she's gone,' said Diva.

'Such a pity: I should have liked to get up an evening with *un po' di musica* for her,' said Lucia, who had heard from Georgie, who had it from the Padre, all about her monstrously immoral views and her maniac laughter. 'Ah, tea ready, Grosvenor? Tell me more Tilling news, Diva.'

'But there isn't any,' said Diva, 'and there won't be unless you do something for us.'

'I?' asked Lucia. 'Little hermit I?'

Diva could have smacked her for her lofty unconsciousness, but in view of her mission had to check that genial impulse.

'Yes, you, of course,' she said. 'We've all been quarrelling. Never knew anything so acute. We shall never get together again, unless you come to the rescue.'

Lucia sighed.

'Dear Diva, how you all work me, and come to me when there's trouble. But I'm very obedient. Tell me what you want me to do. Give one of my simple little parties, *al fresco*, here some evening?'

'Oh, *do!*' said Diva.

'Nothing easier. I'm afraid I've been terribly remiss, thinking of nothing but my busy fragrant life. Very naughty of me. And if, as you say, it will help to patch up some of your funny

little disagreements between yourselves, of which I know
nothing at all, so much the better. Let's settle a night at once.
My engagement-book, Grosvenor.'

Grosvenor brought it to her. There were no evening engagements at all in the future, and slightly tipping it up, so that
Diva could not see the fair white pages, she turned over a leaf
or two.

'This week, impossible, I'm afraid,' she said, with a noble
disregard of her own admission that she and Georgie dined
quietly together every night. 'But how about Wednesday next
week? Let me think – yes, that's all right. And whom am I to
ask? All our little circle?'

'Oh do!' said Diva. 'Start us again. Break the ice. Put out the
fire. They'll all come.'

Diva was right: even Elizabeth who had warned her that such
an invitation would only lead to disappointment accepted with
pleasure, and Lucia made the most tactful arrangements for
this *agapé*. Grosvenor was instructed to start every dish at
Mrs Mapp-Flint, and to offer barley-water as well as wine to
all the guests. They assembled before dinner in the garden-
room, and there, on the top of the piano, compelling notice,
were the bowl and saucer of Samian ware. Mr Wyse, with his
keen perception for the beautiful, instantly inquired what they
were.

'Just some fragments of Roman pottery,' said Lucia casually.
'So glad you admire them. They are pretty, but, alas, the bowl
as you see is incomplete.'

Evie gave a squeal of satisfaction: she had always believed in
Lucia's excavations.

'Oh, look, Kenneth,' she said to her husband. 'Fancy finding
those lovely things in an empty potato-patch.'

'Begorra, Mistress Lucia,' said he, ''twas worth digging up a
whole garden entoirely.'

Elizabeth cast a despairing glance at this convincing evidence, and dinner was announced.

Conversation was a little difficult at first; for there were so
many dangerous topics to avoid that to carry it on was like

crossing a quaking bog and jumping from one firm tussock to another over soft and mossy places. But Elizabeth's wintriness thawed, when she found that not only was she placed on Georgie's right hand who was acting as host, but that every dish was started with her, and she even asked Irene if she had been painting any of her sweet pictures lately. Dubious topics and those allied to them were quite avoided, and before the end of dinner, if Lucia had proposed that they should sing 'Auld Lang Syne', there would not have been a silent voice. Bridge, of so friendly a kind that it was almost insipid, followed, and it was past midnight before anyone could suppose that it was half-past ten. Then most cordial partings took place in the hall: Susan was loaded with her furs, Diva dropped a shilling and was distracted. Benjy found a clandestine opportunity to drink a strong whisky and soda, Irene clung passionately to Lucia, as if she would never finish saying good night, the Royce sawed to and fro before it could turn and set forth on its journey of one hundred yards, and the serene orbs of heaven twinkled benignly over a peaceful Tilling. This happy result (all but the stars) was Lucia's achievement: she had gone skimming up the pinnacle of social pre-eminence till she was almost among the stars herself.

Naturally nobody was foolish enough to expect that such idyllic harmony would be of long duration, for in this highly alert and critical society, with Elizabeth lynx-eyed to see what was done amiss, and Lucia, as was soon obvious, so intolerably conscious of the unique service she had done Tilling in having reconciled all those 'funny little quarrels' of which she pretended to be quite unaware, discord was sure to develop before long; but at any rate tea-parties for bridge were in full swing by the time strawberries were really cheap, and before they were over came the ceremony of the dedication of Lucia's organ.

She had said from the first that her whole function (and that a privilege) was to have made this little contribution to the beauty of the church services: that was all, and she began and ended there. But in a quiet talk with the Padre she suggested that the day of its dedication might be made to coincide with the annual confirmation of the young folk of the parish. The Bishop, perhaps, when his laying on of hands was done, would come to lunch at Mallards and take part in the other ceremony in the afternoon. The Padre thought that an excellent notion, and in due course the Bishop accepted Lucia's invitation and would be happy (DV) to dedicate the organ and give a short address.

Lucia had got her start: now like a great liner she cast off her tugs and began to move out under her own steam. There was another quiet talk in the garden-room.

'You know how I hate all fuss, dear Padre,' she said, 'but I do think, don't you, that Tilling would wish for a little pomp and ceremony. An idea occurred to me: the Mayor and Corporation perhaps might like to escort the Bishop in procession from here to the church after lunch. If that is their wish, I should not dream of opposing it. Maces, scarlet robes; there would be picturesqueness about it which would be suitable on such an occasion. Of course I couldn't suggest it myself, but, as Vicar, you might ascertain what they felt.'

'"I'would be a gran' sight,' said the Padre, quite distinctly seeing himself in the procession.

'I think Tilling would appreciate it,' said Lucia thoughtfully. 'Then about the service: one does not want it too long. A few prayers, a psalm, such as "I was glad when they said unto me": a lesson, and then, don't you think, as we shall be dedicating my organ, some anthem in praise of music? I had thought of that last chorus in Parry's setting of Milton's Ode on St Cecilia's Day, "Blest Pair of Sirens". Of course my organ would accompany the psalm and the anthem, but, as I seem to see it, unofficially incognito. After that, the Bishop's address: so sweet of him to suggest that.'

'Very menseful of him,' said the Padre.

'Then,' said Lucia, waving the Samian bowl, 'then there would follow the dedication of my organ, and its *official* appearance. An organ recital – not long – by our admirable organist to show the paces, the powers of the new instrument. Its scope. The tuba, the *vox humana* and the cor anglais: just a few of the new stops. Afterwards, I shall have a party in the garden here. It might give pleasure to those who have never seen it. Our dear Elizabeth, as you know, did not entertain much.'

The Mayor and Corporation welcomed the idea of attending the dedication of the new organ in state, and of coming to Mallards just before the service and conducting the Bishop in procession to the church. So that was settled, and Lucia, now full steam ahead, got to work on the organist. She told him, very diffidently, that her friends thought it would be most appropriate if, before his official recital (how she was looking forward to it!), she herself, as donor, just ran her hands, so to speak, over the keys. Mr Georgie Pillson, who was really a wonderful performer on the pedals, would help her, and it so happened that she had just finished arranging the first movement of Beethoven's 'Moonlight' Sonata for the organ. She was personally very unwilling to play at all, and in spite of all this pressure she had refused to promise to do so. But now as he added his voice to the general feeling she felt she must overcome her hesitation. It mustn't be mentioned at all: she wanted it to come as a little surprise to everybody. *Then* would follow the real, the skilled recital by him. She hoped he would then give them Falberg's famous 'Storm at Sea', that marvellous tone-poem with thunder on the pedals, and lightning on the diocton, and the choir of voices singing on the *vox humana* as the storm subsided. Terribly difficult, of course, but she knew he would play it superbly, and she sent him round a copy of that remarkable composition.

The day arrived, a hot and glorious morning, just as if Lucia had ordered it. The lunch at Mallards for the Bishop was very *intime*: just the Padre and his wife and the Bishop and his chaplain. Not even Georgie was asked, who, as a matter of fact, was in such a state of nerves over his approaching performance of the pedal part of the 'Moonlight' that he could not have eaten a morsel, and took several aspirin tablets instead. But Lucia had issued invitations broadcast for the garden-party afterwards, to the church choir, the Mayor and Corporation, and all her friends to meet the Bishop. RSVP; and there was not a single refusal. Tea for sixty.

The procession to church was magnificent, the sun poured down on maces and scarlet robes and on the Bishop, profusely perspiring, in his cope and mitre. Lucia had considered whether she should take part in the procession herself, but her hatred of putting herself forward in any way had caused her to abandon the idea of even walking behind the Bishop, and she followed at such a distance that not even those most critical of her conduct could possibly have accused her of belonging to the pageant, herself rather nervous, and playing triplets in the air to get her fingers supple. She took her seat close to the organ beside Georgie, so that they could slip into their places on the organ-bench while the Bishop was returning from the pulpit after his sermon. A tremendous bank of cloud had risen in the north, promising storm: it was lucky that it had held off till now, for umbrellas would certainly have spoiled the splendour of the procession.

The choir gave a beautiful rendering of the last chorus in 'Blest Pair of Sirens', and the Bishop a beautiful address. He made a very charming allusion to the patroness of organs, St Cecilia, and immediately afterwards spoke of the donor 'your distinguished citizeness' almost as if Lucia and that sainted musician were one. A slight stir went through the pews containing her more intimate friends: they had not thought of her like that, and Elizabeth murmured 'St Lucecilia' to herself for future use. During the address the church grew exceedingly dark, and the gloom was momentarily shattered by several vivid flashes of lightning followed by the mutter of thunder. Then standing opposite the organ, pastoral staff in hand, the Bishop solemnly dedicated it, and, as he went back to his seat in the chancel, Lucia and Georgie, like another blest pair of sirens, slid on to the organ-seat, unobserved in the gathering gloom, and were screened from sight by the curtain behind it. There was a momentary pause, the electric light in the church was switched on, and the first piece of the organ recital began. Though Lucia's friends had not heard it for some time, it was familiar to them and Diva and Elizabeth looked at each other, puzzled at first, but soon picking up the scent, as it were, of old associations. The scent grew hotter, and each inwardly visualized the picture of Lucia sitting at her piano with her face in profile against a dark curtain, and her fingers dripping with slow triplets: surely this was the same piece. Sacred edifice or not, these frightful suspicions had to be settled, and Elizabeth quietly rose and stood on tiptoe. She saw, quite distinctly, the top of Georgie's head and of Lucia's remarkable new hat. She sat down again, and in a hissing whisper said to Diva, 'So we've all been asked to come to church to hear Lucia and Georgie practise.' . . . Diva only shook her head sadly. On the slow movement went, its monotonous course relieved just once by a frightful squeal from the great organ as Georgie, turning over, put his finger on one of the top notes, and wailed itself away. The blest pair of sirens tiptoed round the curtain again, thereby completely disclosing themselves, and sank into their seats.

Then to show off the scope of the organ there followed

Falberg's famous tone-poem, 'Storm at Sea'. The ship evidently was having a beautiful calm voyage but then the wind began to whistle on swiftly ascending chromatic scales, thunder muttered on the pedals, and the diocton contributed some flashes of forked lightning. Louder grew the thunder, more vivid the lightning as the storm waxed fiercer. Then came a perfectly appalling crash, and the Bishop, who was perhaps dozing a little after his labours and his lunch, started in his seat and put his mitre straight. Diva clutched at Elizabeth, Evie gave a mouse-like squeal of admiring dismay, for never had anybody heard so powerful an instrument. Bang, it went again and then it dawned on the more perceptive that Nature herself was assisting at the dedication of Lucia's organ with two claps of thunder immediately overhead at precisely the right moment. Lucia herself sat with her music-face on, gazing dreamily at the vaulting of the church, as if her organ was doing it all. Then the storm at sea (organ solo without Nature) died away and a chorus presumably of sailors and passengers (*vox humana*) sang a soft chorale of thanksgiving. Diva gave a swift suspicious glance at the choir to make sure this was not another trick, but this time it was the organ. Calm broad chords, like sunshine on the sea, succeeded the chorale, and Elizabeth writhing in impotent jealousy called Diva's attention to the serene shafts of real sunshine that were now streaming through Elijah going up to heaven and the Witch of Endor.

Indeed it was scarcely fair. Not content with supplying that stupendous *obbligato* to the storm at sea, Nature had now caused the sun to burst brilliantly forth again, in order to make Lucia's garden-party as great a success as her organ, unless by chance the grass was too wet for it. But during the solemn melody which succeeded, the sun continued to shine resplendently, and the lawn at Mallards was scarcely damp. There was Lucia receiving her guests and their compliments: the Mayor in his scarlet robe and chain of office was talking to her as Elizabeth stepped into what she still thought of as her own garden.

'Magnificent instrument, Mrs Lucas,' he was saying. 'That storm at sea was very grand.'

Elizabeth was afraid that he thought the organ had done it all, but she could hardly tell him his mistake.

'Dear Lucia,' she said. 'How I enjoyed that sweet old tune you've so often played to us. Some of your new stops a little harsh in tone, don't you think? No doubt they will mellow. Oh, how sadly burned up my dear garden is looking!'

Lucia turned to the Mayor again.

'So glad you think my little gift will add to the beauty of our services,' she said. 'You must tell me, Mr Mayor, what next – Dear Diva, so pleased to see you. You liked my organ?'

'Yes, and wasn't the real thunderstorm a bit of luck?' said Diva. 'Did Mr Georgie play the pedals in the Beethoven? I heard him turn over.'

Lucia swerved again.

'Good of you to look in, Major Benjy,' she said. 'You'll find tea in the marquee, and other drinks in the *giardino segreto*.'

That was clever: Benjy ambled off in an absent-minded way towards the place of other drinks, and Elizabeth, whom Lucia wanted to get rid of, ambled after him, and towed him towards the less alcoholic marquee. Lucia went on ennobling herself to the Mayor.

'The unemployed,' she said. 'They are much and often on my mind. And the hospital. I'm told it is in sad need of new equipments. Really it will be a privilege to do something more before very long for our dear Tilling. You must spare me half an hour sometime and talk to me about its needs.'

Lucia gave her most silvery laugh.

'Dear me, what a snub I got over the election to the Town Council,' she said. 'But nothing discourages me, Mr Mayor . . . Now I think all my guests have come, so let us go and have a cup of tea. I am quite ashamed of my lawn to-day, but not long ago I had an entertainment for the school-children and games and races, and they kicked it up sadly, dear mites.'

As they walked towards the marquee, the Mayor seemed to Lucia to have a slight bias (like a bowl) towards the *giardino segreto* and she tactfully adapted herself to this change of direction. There were many varieties of sumptuous intoxicants, cocktails and sherry and whisky and hock-cup. Grosvenor was

serving, but just now she had a flinty face, for a member of the
Corporation had been addressing her as 'Miss', as if she was a
bar-maid. Then Major Benjy joined Grosvenor's group, having
given Elizabeth the slip while she was talking to the Bishop,
and drank a couple of cocktails in a great hurry before she
noticed his disappearance. Lucia was specially attentive to
members of the Corporation, making, however, a few slight
errors, such as recommending her greengrocer the strawberries
she had bought from him, and her wine merchant his own
sherry, for that was bringing shop into private life. Then
Elizabeth appeared with the Bishop in the doorway of the
giardino segreto, and with a wistful face she pointed out to him
this favourite spot in her ancestral home: but she caught sight of
Benjy at the bar and her wistfulness vanished, for she had found
something of her own again. Firmly she convoyed him to the less
alcoholic garden, and Lucia took the Bishop, who was interested
in Roman antiquities, to see the pieces of Samian ware in the
garden-room and the scene of her late excavations. 'Too sad,'
she said, 'to have had to fill up my trenches again, but digging
was terribly expensive, and the organ must come first.'

A group was posed for a photograph: Lucia stood between
the Mayor and the Bishop, and afterwards she was more than
affable to the reporter for the *Hastings Chronicle*, whose account
of her excavations had already made such a stir in Tilling. She
gave him hock-cup and strawberries, and sitting with him in a
corner of the garden, let him take down all she said in shorthand. Yes: it was she who had played the opening piece at the
recital (the first movement of the sonata in C sharp minor by
Beethoven, usually called the 'Moonlight'). She had arranged
it herself for the organ ('Another glass of hock-cup, Mr Meriton?') and hoped that he did not think it a vandalism to adapt
the Master. The Bishop had lunched with her, and had been
delighted with her little Queen Anne house and thought very
highly of her Roman antiquities. Her future movements this
summer? Ah, she could not tell him for certain. She would like
to get a short holiday, but they worked her very hard in
Tilling. She had been having a little chat with the Mayor
about some schemes for the future, but it would be premature

to divulge them yet . . . Elizabeth standing near and straining her ears, heard most of this frightful conversation and was petrified with disgust. The next number of the *Hastings Chronicle* would be even more sickening than the excavation number. She could bear it no longer and went home with Benjy, ordering a copy in advance on her way.

The number, when it appeared, justified her gloomiest anticipations. The Bishop's address about the munificent citizeness was given very fully, and there was as well a whole column almost entirely about Lucia. With qualms of nausea Elizabeth read about Mrs Lucas's beautiful family home that dated from the reign of Queen Anne, its panelled parlours, its garden-room containing its positively Bodleian library and rare specimens of Samian ware which she had found in the excavations in her old-world garden. About the lawn with the scars imprinted on its velvet surface by the happy heels of the school-children whom she had entertained for an afternoon of tea and frolics. About the Office with its ledgers and strip of noiseless india-rubber by the door, where the *châtelaine* of Mallards conducted her financial operations. About the secret garden (Mrs Lucas who spoke Italian with the same ease and purity as English referred to it as '*mio giardino segreto*') in which she meditated every morning. About the splendour of the procession from Mallards to the church with the Mayor and the maces and the mitre and the cope of the Lord Bishop, who had lunched privately with Mrs Lucas. About the masterly arrangement for the organ of the first movement of Beethoven's 'Moonlight' Sonata, made by Mrs Lucas, and her superb performance of the same. About her princely entertainment of the local magnates. About her hat and her hock-cup.

'I wonder how much she paid for that,' said Elizabeth, tossing the foul sheet across to Benjy as they sat at breakfast. It fell on his poached egg, in which he had just made a major incision, and smeared yolk on the clean tablecloth. She took up the *Daily Mirror*, and there was the picture of Lucia standing between the Mayor and the Bishop. She took up the *Financial Gazette*, and Siriami had slumped another shilling.

*

It was not only Elizabeth who was ill pleased with this sycophantic column. Georgie had ordered a copy, which he first
skimmed swiftly for the name of Mr G. Pillson: a more careful
reading of it showed him that there was not the smallest allusion
to his having played the pedals in the 'Moonlight'. Rather mean
of Lucia; she certainly ought to have mentioned that, for,
indeed, without the pedals it would have been a very thin
performance. 'I don't mind for myself,' thought Georgie, 'for
what good does it do me to have my name in a squalid provincial
rag, but I'm afraid she's getting grabby. She wants to have it all.
She wants to be on the top with nobody else in sight. Her
masterly arrangement of the 'Moonlight'? Rubbish! She just
played the triplets with one hand and the air with the other,
while I did the bass on the pedals. And her family house! It's
been in her family (only she hasn't got one) since April. Her
Italian, too! And the Samian ware from her excavations! That's a
whopper. All she got from her excavations was three-quarters of
an Apollinaris bottle. If she had asked my advice, I should have
told her that it was wiser to let sleeping dogs lie! . . . So instead
of popping into Mallards and congratulating her on her marvellous press, Georgie went straight down to the High Street
in a condition known as dudgeon. He saw the back of Lucia's
head in the Office, and almost hoped she would disregard
Mammoncash's advice and make some unwise investment.

There was a little group of friends at the corner, Diva and
Elizabeth and Evie. They all hailed him: it was as if they were
waiting for him, as indeed they were.

'Have you read it, Mr Georgie?' asked Diva. (There was no
need to specify what.)

'Her family home,' interrupted Elizabeth musingly. 'And
this is my family market-basket. It came into my family when
I bought it the day before yesterday and it's one of my most
cherished heirlooms. Did you *ever* Mr Georgie? It's worse
than her article about the Roman Forum, in the potato-bed.'

'And scarcely a word about Kenneth,' interrupted Evie. 'I
always thought he was Vicar of Tilling –'

'No, dear, we live and learn when we come up against the
châtelaine of Mallards,' said Elizabeth.

'After all, you and the Padre went to lunch, Evie,' said Diva who never let resentment entirely obliterate her sense of fairness. 'But I think it's so mean of her not to say that Mr Georgie played the pedals for her. I enjoyed them much more than the triplets.'

'What I can't understand is that she never mentioned the real thunderstorm,' said Elizabeth. 'I expected her to say she'd ordered it. Surely she did, didn't she? Such a beauty, too: she might well be prouder of it than of her hat.'

Georgie's dudgeon began to evaporate in these withering blasts of satire. They were ungrateful. Only a few weeks ago Lucia had welded together the fragments of Tilling society, which had been smashed up in the first instance by the tipsiness of Benjy. Nobody could have done it except her, strawberry-time would have gone by without those luscious and inexpensive teas and now they were all biting the hand that had caused them to be fed. It was bright-green jealousy, just because none of them had ever had a line in any paper about their exploits, let alone a column. And who, after all, had spent a thousand pounds on an organ for Tilling, and got a Bishop to dedicate it, and ordered a thunderstorm, and asked them all to a garden-party afterwards? They snatched at the benefits of their patroness, and then complained that they were being patronized. Of course her superior airs and her fibs could be maddening sometimes, but even if she did let a reporter think that she spoke Italian as naturally as English and had dug up Samian ware in her garden, it was 'pretty Fanny's way', and they must put up with it. His really legitimate grievance about his beautiful pedalling vanished.

'Well, I thought it was a wonderful day,' he said. 'She's more on a pinnacle than ever. Oh, look: here she comes.'

Indeed she did, tripping gaily down the hill with a telegraph form in her hand.

'*Buon giorno a tutti,*' she said. 'Such a nuisance: my telephone is out of order and I must go to the post-office. A curious situation in dollars and francs. I've been puzzling over it.'

Stony faces and forced smiles met her. She tumbled to it at once, the clever creature.

473

'And how good of you all to have rallied round me,' she said, 'and have made our little *festa* such a success. I was so anxious about it, but I needn't have been with so many dear loyal friends to back me up. The Bishop was enchanted with Mallards, Elizabeth: of course I told him that I was only an interloper. And what sweet things he said to me about the Padre, Evie.'

Lucia racked her brain to invent something nice which he said about Diva. So, though Paddy hadn't been at the party, how immensely the Bishop admired her beautiful dog!

'And how about a little bridge this afternoon?' she asked. 'Shan't invite you, Georgino: just a woman's four. Yes and yes and yes? Capital! It's so hot that we might play in the shelter in Elizabeth's secret garden. Four o'clock then. Georgie, come to the stationer's with me. I want you to help me choose a book. My dear, your pedalling yesterday! How enthusiastic the organist was about it. Au reservoir, everybody.

'Georgie, I must get a great big scrap-book,' she went on, 'to paste my press-notices into. They multiply so. That paragraph the other day about my *excavazioni*, and to-day a whole column, and the photograph in the *Daily Mirror*. It would be amusing perhaps, years hence, to turn over the pages and recall the past. I must get a handsome-looking book, morocco, I think. How pleased all Tilling seems to be about yesterday.'

The holiday season came round with August, and, as usual, the householders of the Tilling social circle let their own houses, and went to live in smaller ones, thereby not only getting a change of environment, but making, instead of spending, money on their holiday, for they received a higher rent for the houses they quitted than they paid for the houses they took. The Mapp-Flints were the first to move: Elizabeth inserted an advertisement in *The Times* in order to save those monstrous fees of house-agents and instantly got an inquiry from a most desirable tenant, no less than the widow of a Baronet. In view of her rank, Elizabeth asked for and obtained a higher rent than she had ever netted at Mallards, and, as on her honeymoon, she took a very small bungalow near the sea, deficient in plumbing, but otherwise highly salubrious, and as she touchingly remarked 'so near the golf-links for my Benjy-boy. He will be as happy as the day is long.' She was happy, too, for the rent she received for Grebe was five times what (after a little bargaining) she paid for this shack which would be so perfect for her Benjy-boy.

Her new tenant was interesting: she had forty-seven canaries, each in its own cage, and the noise of their pretty chirping could be heard if the wind was favourable a full quarter of a mile from the house. It was ascertained that she personally cleaned out all their cages every morning, which accounted for her not being seen in Tilling till after lunch. She then rode into the town on a tricycle and bought rape-seed and groundsel in prodigious quantities. She had no dealings with the butcher, so it was speedily known, and thus was probably a vegetarian; and Diva, prowling round Grebe one Friday morning, saw her clad in a burnous, kneeling on a carpet in the garden and prostrating herself in an eastward position. It might therefore be inferred that she was a Mahommedan as well.

This was all very satisfactory, a titled lady, of such marked idiosyncrasies, was evidently a very promising addition to Tilling society, and Diva, not wishing to interrupt her devotions, went quietly away, greatly impressed, and called next day, meaning to follow up this formality with an invitation to a vegetarian lunch. But even as she waited at the front door a window directly above was thrown open, and a shrill voice shouted 'Not at home. Ever.' So Diva took the tram out to the golf-links, and told Elizabeth that her tenant was certainly a lunatic. Elizabeth was much disturbed, and spent an hour every afternoon for the next three days in hiding behind the hornbeam hedge at Grebe, spying upon her. Lucia thought that Diva's odd appearance might have accounted for this chilling reception and called herself. Certainly nobody shouted at her, but nobody answered the bell and, after a while, pieces of groundsel rained down on her, probably from the same upper window ... The Padre let the vicarage for August and September, and took a bungalow close to the Mapp-Flints. He and Major Benjy played golf during the day and the four played hectic bridge in the evening.

Diva at present had not succeeded in letting her house, even at a very modest rental, and so she remained in the High Street. One evening horrid fumes of smoke laden with soot came into her bathroom where she was refreshing herself before dinner, and she found that they came down the chimney from the kitchen of the house next door. The leakage in the flue was localized, and it appeared that Diva was responsible for it, since, for motives of economy, which seemed sound at the time, she had caused the overflow pipe from her cistern to be passed through it. The owner of the house next door most obligingly promised not to use his range till Diva had the damage to the flue repaired, but made shift with his gas-ring, since he was genuinely anxious not to suffocate her when she was washing. But Diva could not bring herself to spend nine pounds (a frightful sum) on the necessary work on the chimney, and for the next ten days took no further steps.

Then Irene found a tenant for her house, and took that of Diva's neighbour. He explained to her that just at present, until Mrs Plaistow repaired a faulty flue, the kitchen-range could not be used, and suggested that Irene might put a little pressure on her, since this state of things had gone on for nearly a fortnight, and his repeated reminders had had no effect. So Irene put pressure, and on the very evening of the day she moved in, she and Lucy lit an enormous fire in her range, though the evening was hot, and waited to see what effect that would have. Diva happened to be again in her bath, musing over the terrible expense she would be put to: nine pounds meant the saving of five shillings a week for the best part of a year. These gloomy meditations were interrupted by volumes of acrid smoke pouring through the leak, and she sprang out of her bath, convinced that the house was on fire, and without drying herself she threw on her dressing-gown. She had left the bathroom door open: thick vapours followed her downstairs. She hastily dressed and with her servant and Paddy wildly barking at her heels flew into the High Street and hammered on Irene's door.

Irene, flushed with stoking, came upstairs.

'So I've smoked you out,' she said. 'Serve you right.'

'I believe my house is on fire,' cried Diva. 'Never saw such smoke in my life.'

'Call the fire-engine then,' said Irene. 'Good-bye: I must put some more damp wood on. And mind, I'll keep that fire burning day and night, if I don't get a wink of sleep, till you've had that flue repaired.'

'Please, please,' cried Diva in agony. 'No more damp wood, I beg. I promise. It shall be done to-morrow.'

'Well, apologize for being such a damned nuisance,' said Irene. 'You've made me and Lucy roast ourselves over the fire. Not to mention the expense of the firing.'

'Yes. I apologize. Anything!' wailed Diva. 'And I shall have to re-paper my bathroom. Kippered.'

'Your own fault. Did you imagine I was going to live on a gas-ring, because you wouldn't have your chimney repaired?'

Then Diva got a tenant in spite of the kippered bathroom, and moved to a dilapidated hovel close beside the railway line, which she got for half the rent which she received for her house. Passing trains shook its crazy walls and their whistlings woke her at five in the morning, but its cheapness gilded these inconveniences, and she declared it was delightful to be awakened betimes on these August days. The Wyses went out to Capri to spend a month with the Faragliones, and so now the whole of the Tilling circle, with the exception of Georgie and Lucia, were having change and holiday to the great advantage of their purses. They alone remained in their adjoining abodes and saw almost as much of each other as during those weeks when Georgie was having shingles and growing his beard in hiding at Grebe. Lucia gave her mornings to finance and the masterpieces of the Greek tragedians, and in this piping weather recuperated herself with a siesta after lunch. Then in the evening coolness they motored and sketched or walked over the field-paths of the marsh, dined together and had orgies of Mozartino. All the time (even during her siesta) Lucia's head was as full of plans as an egg of meat, and she treated Georgie to spoonfuls of it.

They were approaching the town on one such evening from the south. The new road, now finished, curved round the bottom of the hill on which the town stood: above it was a bare bank with tufts of coarse grass rising to the line of the ancient wall.

Lucia stood with her head on one side regarding it.

'An ugly patch,' she said. 'It offends the eye, Georgie. It is not in harmony with the mellow brick of the wall. It should be planted. I seem to see it covered with almond-trees; those late flowering ones. Pink blossom, a foam of pink blossom for *la bella Primavera*. I estimate that it would require at least fifty young trees. I shall certainly offer to give them to the town and see to them being put in.'

'That would look lovely,' said Georgie.

'It shall look lovely. Another thing. I'm going to stop my financial career for the present. I shall sell out my tobacco shares – realize them is the phrase we use – on which I have made large profits. I pointed out to my broker, that, in my opinion, tobaccos were high enough, and he sees the soundness of that.'

Georgie silently interpreted this swanky statement. It meant, of course, that Mammoncash had recommended their sale; but there was no need to express this. He murmured agreement.

'Also I must rid myself of this continual strain,' Lucia went on. 'I am ashamed of myself, but I find it absorbs me too much: it keeps me on the stretch to be always watching the markets and estimating the effect of political disturbances. The Polish corridor, Hitler, Geneva, the new American president. I shall close my ledgers.'

They climbed in silence up the steep steps by the Norman tower. They were in considerable need of repair, and Lucia, contemplating the grey bastion in front, stumbled badly over an uneven paving-stone.

'These ought to be looked to,' she said. 'I must make a note of that.'

'Are you going to have them repaired?' asked Georgie humorously.

'Quite possibly. You see, I've made a great deal of money, Georgie. I've made eight thousand pounds –'

'My dear, what a sum. I'd no notion.'

'Naturally one does not talk about it,' said Lucia loftily. 'But there it is, and I shall certainly spend a great deal of it, keeping some for myself – the labourer is worthy of his hire – on Tilling. I want – how can I put it – to be a fairy godmother to the dear little place. For instance, I expect the plans for my new operating-theatre at the hospital in a day or two. That I regard as necessary. I have told the Mayor that I shall provide it, and he will announce my gift to the Governors when they meet next week. He is terribly keen that I should accept a place on the Board: really he's always worrying me about it. I think I shall allow him to nominate me. My election, he says, will be a mere formality, and will give great pleasure.'

Georgie agreed. He felt he was getting an insight into Lucia's schemes, for it was impossible not to remember that after her gift of the organ she reluctantly consented to be a member of the Church Council.

'And do you know, Georgie,' she went on, 'they elected me only to-day to be President of the Tilling Cricket Club. Fancy!

Twenty pounds did that – I mean I was only too glad to give them the heavy roller which they want very much, and I was never more astonished in my life than when those two nice young fellows, the foreman of the gas works and the town surveyor –'

'Oh yes, Georgie and Per,' said he, 'who laughed so much over the smell in the garden-room, and started you on your Roman –'

'Those were their names,' said Lucia. 'They came to see me and begged me to allow them to nominate me as their President, and I was elected unanimously to-day. I promised to appear at a cricket-match they have to-morrow against a team they called the Zingâri. I hope they did not see me shudder, for as you know it should be "I Zingâri": the Italian for "gipsies". And the whole of their cricket-ground wants levelling and re-laying. I shall walk over it with them, and look into it for myself.'

'I didn't know you took any interest in any game,' said Georgie.

'Georgino, how you misjudge me! I've always held, always, that games and sport are among the strongest and most elevating influences in English life. Think of Lord's, and all those places where they play football, and the Lonsdale belt for boxing, and Wimbledon. Think of the crowds here, for that matter, at cricket- and football-matches on early closing days. Half the townspeople of Tilling are watching them: Tilling takes an immense interest in sport: they all tell me that people will much appreciate my becoming their President. You must come with me to-morrow to the match.'

'But I don't know a bat from a ball,' said Georgie.

'Nor do I, but we shall soon learn. I want to enter into every side of life here. We are too narrow in our interests. We must get a larger outlook, Georgie, a wider sympathy. I understand they play football on the cricket-ground in the winter.'

'Football's a sealed book to me,' said Georgie, 'and I don't intend to unseal it.'

They had come back to Mallards, and Lucia standing on the doorstep looked over the cobbled street with its mellow brick houses.

'*Bella piccola città!*' she exclaimed. 'Dinner at eight here, isn't it, and bring some *musica*. How I enjoy our little domestic evenings.'

'Domestic': just the word 'domestic' stuck in Georgie's mind as he touched up his beard, and did a little sewing while it dried, before he dressed for dinner. It nested in his head, like a woodpecker, and gave notice of its presence there by a series of loud taps at frequent intervals. No doubt Lucia was only referring to their usual practice of dining together and playing the piano afterwards, or sitting (even more domestically) as they often did, each reading a book in easy silence with casual remarks. Such a mode of spending the evening was infinitely pleasanter and more sensible than that they should sit, she at Mallards and he at the Cottage, over solitary meals and play long solos on their pianos instead of those adventurous duets. No doubt she had meant nothing more than that by the word.

The party from the bungalows, the Mapp-Flints and the Padre and his wife, came into Tilling next day to see the cricket-match. They mingled with the crowd and sat on public benches, and Elizabeth observed with much uneasiness how Lucia and Georgie were conducted by the town surveyor to reserved deck-chairs by the pavilion: she was afraid that meant something sinister. Lucia had put a touch of sun-burn rouge on her face, in order to convey the impression that she often spent a summer day watching cricket, and she soon learned the difference between bats and balls: but she should have studied the game a little more before she asked Per, when three overs had been bowled and no wicket had fallen, who was getting the best of it. A few minutes later a Tilling wicket fell and Per went in. He immediately skied a ball in the direction of long-on, and Lucia clapped her hands wildly. 'Oh, look, Georgie,' she said. 'What a beautiful curve the ball is describing! And so high. Lovely . . . What? Has he finished already?'

Tilling was out for eighty-seven runs, and between the inningses, Lucia, in the hat which the *Hastings Chronicle* had already described, was escorted out to look at the pitch by the merry brothers. She had learned so much about cricket in the last hour that her experienced eye saw at once that the greater part of the field ought to be levelled and the turf relaid. Nobody took any particular notice of Georgie, so while Lucia was inspecting the pitch he slunk away and lunched at home. She, as President of the Tilling Club, lunched with the two teams in the pavilion, and found several opportunities of pronouncing the word Zingâri properly.

The bungalow-party having let their houses picnicked on sandwiches and indulged in gloomy conjecture as to what Lucia's sudden appearance in sporting circles signified. Then Benjy walked up to the Club nominally to see if there were any letters for him and actually to have liquid refreshment to assuage the thirst caused by the briny substances which Elizabeth had provided for lunch, and brought back the sickening intelligence that Lucia had been elected President of the Tilling Cricket Club.

'I'm not in the least surprised,' said Elizabeth. 'I suspected something of the sort. Nor shall I be surprised if she plays football for Tilling in the winter. Shorts, and a jersey of Tilling colours. Probably that hat.'

Satire, it was felt, had said its last word.

The *Hastings Chronicle* on the next Saturday was a very painful document. It contained a large-print paragraph on its middle page headed 'Munificent Gift by Mrs Lucas of Mallards House, Tilling.' Those who felt equal to reading further then learnt that she had most graciously consented to become President of the Tilling Cricket Club, and had offered, at the Annual General Meeting of the Club, held after the XI's match against the Zingâri, to have the cricket-field levelled and relaid. She had personally inspected it (so said Mrs Lucas in her Presidential address) and was convinced that Tilling would never be able to do itself justice at the King of Games till this was done. She therefore considered it a privilege, as President of the Club, in which she had always taken so deep an interest, to undertake this work (loud and prolonged applause) . . . This splendid gift would benefit footballers as well as cricketers since they used the same ground, and the Committee of the Football Club, having ascertained Mrs Lucas's feelings on the subject, had unanimously elected her as President.

The very next week there were more of these frightful revelations. Again there was that headline, 'Munificent Gift, etc.' This time it was the Tilling hospital. At a meeting of the Governors the Mayor announced that Mrs Lucas (already known as the Friend of the Poor) had offered to build a new operating-theatre, and to finish it with the most modern equipment according to the plan and schedule which he now laid before them –

Elizabeth was reading this aloud to Benjy, as they lunched in the verandah of their bungalow, in an indignant voice. At this point she covered up with her hand the remainder of the paragraph.

'Mark my words, Benjy,' she said. 'I prophesy that what happened next was that the Governors accepted this gift with the deepest gratitude and did themselves the honour of inviting her to a seat on the Board.'

It was all too true, and Elizabeth finished the stewed plums in silence. She rose to make coffee.

'The *Hastings Chronicle* ought to keep "Munificent Gift by Mrs Lucas of Mallards House, Tilling" permanently set up in type,' she observed. 'And "House" is new. In my day and Aunt Caroline's before me, "Mallards" was grand enough. It will be "Mallards Palace" before she's finished with it.'

But with this last atrocity, the plague of munificences was stayed for the present. August cooled down into September, and September disgraced itself at the season of its spring tides by brewing a terrific south-west gale. The sea heaped up by the continued press of the wind broke through the shingle bank on the coast and flooded the low land behind, where some of the bungalows stood. That inhabited by the Padre and Evie was built on a slight elevation and escaped being inundated, but the Mapp-Flints were swamped. Nearly a foot of water covered the rooms on the ground floor, and until it subsided, the house was uninhabitable unless you treated it like a palazzo on the Grand Canal at Venice, and had a gondola moored to the banisters of the stairs. News of the disaster was brought to Tilling by the Padre when he bicycled in to take matins on Sunday morning. He met Lucia at the church door, and in a few vivid sentences described how the unfortunate couple had waded ashore. They had breakfasted with him and Evie and would lunch and sup there, but then they would have to wade back again to sleep, since he had no spare room. A sad holiday experience: and he hurried off to the vestry to robe.

The beauty of her organ wrought upon Lucia, for she had asked the organist to play Falberg's 'Storm at Sea' as a voluntary at the end of the service, and, as she listened, the inexorable might of Nature, of which the Mapp-Flints were victims, impressed itself on her. Moreover she really enjoyed dispensing benefits with a bountiful hand on the worthy and unworthy alike, and by the time the melodious storm was over she had made up her mind to give board and lodging to the refugees until the salt water had ebbed from their ground-floor rooms. Grebe was still let and resonant with forty-seven canaries, and she must shelter them, as Noah took back the dove sent out over the waste of waters, in the Ark of their old home . . . She joined softly in the chorale of passengers and sailors, and left the church with Georgie.

'I shall telephone to them at once, Georgie,' she said, 'and offer to take them in at Mallards House. The car shall fetch them after lunch.'

'I wouldn't,' said Georgie. 'Why shouldn't they go to an hotel?'

'*Caro*, simply because they wouldn't go,' said Lucia. 'They would continue to wade to their beds and sponge on the Padre. Besides if their bungalow collapsed – it is chiefly made of laths tied together with pieces of string and pebbles from the shore – and buried them in the ruins, I should truly regret it. Also I welcome the opportunity of doing a kindness to poor Elizabeth. Mallards House will always be at the service of the needy. I imagine it will only be for a day or two. You must promise to lunch and dine with me, won't you, as long as they are with me, for I don't think I could bear them alone.'

Lucia adopted the seignorial manner suitable to the donor of organs and operating-theatres. She instructed Grosvenor to telephone in the most cordial terms to Mrs Mapp-Flint, and wrote out what she should say. Mrs Lucas could not come to the telephone herself at that moment, but she sent her sympathy, and insisted on their making Mallards House their home, till the bungalow was habitable again: she thought she could make them quite comfortable in her little house. Elizabeth of course accepted her hospitality though it was odd that she had not telephoned herself. So Lucia made arrangements for the reception of her guests. She did not intend to give up her bedroom and dressing-room which they had occupied before, since it would be necessary to bring another bed in, and it would be very inconvenient to turn out herself. Besides, so it happily occurred to her, it would arouse very poignant emotion if they found themselves in their old nuptial chamber. Elizabeth should have the pleasant room looking over the garden, and Benjy the one at the end of the passage, and the little sitting-room next Elizabeth's should be devoted to their exclusive use. That would be princely hospitality, and thus the garden-room, where she always sat, would not be invaded during the day. After tea, they might play bridge there, and of course use it after dinner for more bridge or music. Then it was time to send Cadman with the motor to fetch them, and Lucia furnished it with a thick fur rug and a hot-water bottle in case they had caught cold with their wadings. She put a Sunday paper in their sitting-room, and strewed a few books about to give it an inhabited air, and went out as usual for her walk, for it would be more in the seignorial style if Grosvenor settled them in, and she herself casually returned about tea-time, certain that everything would have been done for their comfort.

This sumptuous *insouciance* a little miscarried, for though Grosvenor had duly conducted the visitors to their own private sitting-room, they made a quiet little pilgrimage through the house while she was unpacking for them, peeped into the Office, and were sitting in the garden-room when Lucia returned.

'So sorry to be out when you arrived, dear Elizabeth,' she said, 'but I knew Grosvenor would make you at home.'

Elizabeth sprang up from her old seat in the window. (What a bitter joy it was to survey from there again.)

'Dear Lucia,' she cried. 'Too good of you to take in the poor homeless ones. Putting you out dreadfully, I'm afraid.'

'Not an atom. *Tutto molto facile.* And there's the parlour upstairs ready for you, which I hope Grosvenor showed you.'

'Indeed she did,' said Elizabeth effusively. 'Deliciously cosy. So kind.'

'And what a horrid experience you must have had,' said Lucia. 'Tea will be ready: let us go in.'

'A waste of waters,' said Elizabeth impressively, 'and a foot deep in the dining-room. We had to have a boat to take our luggage away. It reminded Benjy of the worst floods on the Jumna.'

''Pon my word, it did,' said Benjy, 'and I shouldn't wonder if there's more to come. The wind keeps up, and there's the highest of the spring tides to-night. Total immersion of the Padre, perhaps. Ha! Ha! Baptism of those of Riper Years.'

'Naughty!' said Elizabeth. Certainly the Padre had been winning at bridge all this week, but that hardly excused levity over things sacramental, and besides he had given them lunch and breakfast. Lucia also thought his joke in poor taste and called attention to her dahlias. She had cut a new flower-bed, where there had once stood a very repulsive weeping-ash, which had been planted by Aunt Caroline, and which, to Elizabeth's pretty fancy, had always seemed to mourn for her. She suddenly felt its removal very poignantly, and not trusting herself to speak about that, called attention to the lovely red admiral butterflies on the buddleia. With which deft changes of subjects they went in to tea. Georgie and bridge, and dinner, and more bridge followed, and Lucia observed with strong misgivings that Elizabeth left her bag and Benjy his cigar-case in the garden-room when they went to bed. This seemed to portend their return there in the morning, so she called attention to their forgetfulness. Elizabeth on getting upstairs had a further lapse of memory, for she marched into Lucia's bedroom, which she particularly wanted to see, before she recollected that it was no longer her own.

Lucia was rung up at breakfast next morning by the Padre. There was more diluvial news from the shore, and his emotion caused him to speak pure English without a trace of Scotch or Irish. A tide, higher than ever, had caused a fresh invasion of the sea, and now his bungalow was islanded, and the gale had torn a quantity of slates from the roof. Georgie, he said, had kindly offered to take him in, as the Vicarage was still let, and he waited in silence until Lucia asked him where Evie was going. He didn't know, and Lucia's suggestion that she should come to Mallards House was very welcome. She promised to send her car to bring them in and rejoined her guests.

'More flooding,' she said, 'just as you prophesied, Major Benjy. So Evie is coming here, and Georgie will take the Padre. I'm sure you won't mind moving on to the attic floor, and letting her have your room.'

Benjy's face fell.

'Oh, dear me, no,' he said heartily. 'I've roughed it before now.'

'We shall be quite a party,' said Elizabeth without any marked enthusiasm, for she supposed that Evie would share their sitting-room.

Lucia went to see to her catering, and her guests to their room, taking the morning papers with them.

'I should have thought that Diva might have taken Evie in, or she might have gone to the King's Arms,' said Elizabeth musingly. 'But dear Lucia revels in being Lady Bountiful. Gives her real pleasure.'

'I don't much relish sleeping in one of those attics,' said Benjy. 'Draughty places with sloping roofs if I remember right.'

Elizabeth's pride in her ancestral home flickered up.

'They're better than any rooms in the house you had before we married, darling,' she said. 'And not quite tactful to have told her you had roughed it before now . . . Was your haddock at breakfast *quite* what it should be?'

'Perfectly delicious,' said Benjy hitting back. 'It's a treat to get decent food again after that garbage we've been having.'

'Thank you dear,' said Elizabeth.

She picked up a paper, read it for a moment and decided to make common cause with him.

'Now I come to think of it,' she said, 'it would have been easy enough for Lucia not to have skied you to the attics. You and I could have had our old bedroom and dressing-room, and there would have been the other two rooms for her and Evie. But we must take what's given us and be thankful. What I do want to know is whether we're allowed in the garden-room unless she asks us. She seemed to give you your cigar-case and me my bag last night rather purposefully. Not that this is a bad room by any means.'

'It'll get stuffy enough this afternoon,' said he, 'for it's going to rain all day and I suppose there'll be three of us here.'

Elizabeth sighed.

'I suppose it didn't occur to her to take this room herself, and give her guests the garden-room,' she said. 'Not selfish at all: I don't mean that, but perhaps a little wanting in imagination. I'll go down to the garden-room presently and see how the land lies ... There's the telephone ringing again. That's the third time since breakfast. She's arranging football-matches, I expect. Oh, the *Daily Mirror* has got hold of her gift to the hospital. "Most munificent": how tired I am of the word. Of course it's the silly season still.'

Had Elizabeth known what that third telephone-call was, she would have called the season by a more serious name than silly. The speaker was the Mayor, who now asked Lucia if she could see him privately for a few moments. She told him that it would be quite convenient, and might have added that it was also very exciting. Was there perhaps another Board which desired to have the honour of her membership? The Literary Institute? The Workhouse? The – Back she went to the garden-room and hurriedly sat down at her piano and began communing with Beethoven. She was so absorbed in her music that she gave a startled little cry when Grosvenor, raising her voice to an unusual pitch called out for the second time: 'The Mayor of Tilling!' Up she sprang.

'Ah, good morning, Mr Mayor,' she cried. 'So glad. Grosvenor, I'm not to be interrupted. I was just snatching a few minutes, as I always do after breakfast, at my music. It tunes me in – don't they call it – for the work of the day. Now, how can I serve you?'

His errand quite outshone the full splendour of Lucia's imagination. A member of the Town Council had just resigned, owing to ill-health, and the Mayor was on his way to an emergency meeting. The custom was, he explained, if such a vacancy occurred during the course of the year, that no fresh election should be held, but that the other members of the Council should co-opt a temporary member to serve till the next elections came round. Would she therefore permit him to suggest her name?

Lucia sat with her chin in her hand in the music attitude. Certainly that was an enormous step upwards from having been equal with Elizabeth at the bottom of the poll . . . Then she began to speak in a great hurry, for she thought she heard a footfall on the stairs into the garden-room. Probably Elizabeth had eluded Grosvenor.

'How I appreciate the honour,' she said. 'But – but how I should hate to feel that the dear townsfolk would not approve. The last elections, you know . . . Ah, I see what is in your mind. You think that since then they realize a little more the sincerity of my desire to forward Tilling's welfare to the best of my humble capacity.' (There came a tap at the door.) 'I see I shall have to yield and, if your colleagues wish it, I gladly accept the great honour.'

The door had opened a chink; Elizabeth's ears had heard the words 'great honour', and now her mouth (she *had* eluded Grosvenor) said:

'May I come in, dear?'

'*Entrate,*' said Lucia. 'Mr Mayor, do you know Mrs Mapp-Flint? You must! Such an old inhabitant of dear Tilling. Dreadful floods out by the links, and several friends, Major and Mrs Mapp-Flint and the Padre and Mrs Bartlett are all washed out. But such a treat for me, for I am taking them in, and have quite a party. Mallards House and I are always at the service of our citizens. But I mustn't detain you. You will let me know whether the meeting accepts your suggestion? I shall be eagerly waiting.'

Lucia insisted on seeing the Mayor to the front door, but returned at once to the garden-room, which had been thus violated by Elizabeth.

'I hope your sitting-room is comfortable, Elizabeth,' she said. 'You've got all you want there? Sure?'

The desire to know what those ominous words 'great honour' could possibly signify, consumed Elizabeth like a burning fire, and she was absolutely impervious to the hint so strongly conveyed to her.

'Delicious, dear,' she enthusiastically replied. 'So cosy, and Benjy so happy with his cigar and his paper. But didn't I hear the piano going just now? Sounded so lovely. May I sit mum as a mouse and listen?'

Lucia could not quite bring herself to say 'No, go away,' but she felt she must put her foot down. She had given her visitors a sitting-room of their own, and did not intend to have them here in the morning. Perhaps if she put her foot down on what she always called the *sostenuto* pedal, and played loud scales and exercises she could render the room intolerable to any listener.

'By all means,' she said. 'I have to practise very hard every morning to keep my poor fingers from getting rusty, or Georgie scolds me over our duets.'

Elizabeth slid into her familiar place in the window where she could observe the movements of Tilling, conducted chiefly this morning under umbrellas, and Lucia began. C major up and down till her fingers ached with their unaccustomed drilling: then a few firm chords in that jovial key.

'Lovely chords! Such harmonies,' said Elizabeth, seeing Lucia's motor draw up at Mallards Cottage and deposit the Padre and his suit-case.

C minor. This was more difficult. Lucia found that the upward scale was not the same as the downward, and she went over it half a dozen times, rumbling at first at the bottom end of the piano and then shrieking at the top and back again, before she got it right. A few simple minor chords followed.

'That wonderful funeral march,' said Elizabeth absently. Evie had thrust her head out of the window of the motor, and, to anybody who had any perception, was quite clearly telling Georgie, who had come to the door, about the flood, for she lowered and then raised her podgy little paw, evidently showing how much the flood had risen during the night.

As she watched, Lucia had begun to practise shakes, including that very difficult one for the third and fourth fingers.

'Like the sweet birdies in my garden,' said Elizabeth, still absently (though nothing could possibly have been less like), 'thrushes and blackbirds and . . .' Her voice trailed into silence as the motor moved on, down the street towards Mallards, minus the Padre and his suit-case.

'And here's Evie just arriving,' she said, thinking that Lucia would stop that hideous noise, and go out to welcome her guest. Not a bit of it: the scale of D major followed: it was markedly slower because her fingers were terribly fatigued. Then Grosvenor came in. She left the door open, and a strong draught blew round Elizabeth's ankles.

'Yes, Grosvenor?' said Lucia, with her hands poised over the keys.

'The Mayor has rung up, ma'am,' said Grosvenor, 'and would like to speak to you, if you are disengaged.'

The Mayoral call was irresistible, and Lucia went to the telephone in her Office. Elizabeth, crazy with curiosity, followed, and instantly became violently interested in the book-case in the hall, where she hoped she could hear Lucia's half, at any rate, of the conversation. After two or three gabbling, quacking noises, her voice broke jubilantly in.

'Indeed, I am most highly honoured, Mr Mayor –' she began. Then, unfortunately for the cause of the dissemination of useful knowledge, she caught sight of Elizabeth in the hall just outside with an open book in her hand, and smartly shut the Office door. Having taken this sensible precaution she continued:

'Please assure my colleagues, as I understand that the Town Council is sitting now, that I will resolutely shoulder the responsibility of my position.'

'Should you be unoccupied at the moment, Mrs Lucas,' said the Mayor, 'perhaps you would come and take part in the business that lies before us, as you are now a member of the Council.'

'By all means,' cried Lucia. 'I will be with you in a couple of minutes.'

Elizabeth had replaced the fourth volume of Pepys's Diary upside down, and had stolen up closer to the Office door, where her footfall was noiseless on the india-rubber. Simultaneously Grosvenor came into the hall to open the front door to Evie, and Lucia came out of the Office, nearly running into Elizabeth.

'Admiring your lovely india-rubber matting, dear,' said Elizabeth adroitly. 'So pussy-cat quiet.'

Lucia hardly seemed to see her.

'Grosvenor: my hat, my raincoat, my umbrella at once,' she cried. 'I've got to go out. Delighted to see you, dear Evie. So sorry to be called away. A little soup or a sandwich after your drive? Elizabeth will show you the sitting-room upstairs. Lunch at half-past one: begin whether I'm in or not. No, Grosvenor, my new hat –'

'It's raining, ma'am,' said Grosvenor.

'I know it is, or I shouldn't want my umbrella.'

Her feet twinkled nearly as nimbly as Diva's as she sped through the rain to the Mayor's parlour at the Town Hall. The assembled Council rose to their feet as she entered, and the Mayor formally presented them to the new colleague whom they had just co-opted: Per of the gasworks, and Georgie of the drains, and Twistevant the greengrocer. Just now Twistevant was looking morose, for the report of the town surveyor about his slum-dwellings had been received, and this dire document advised that eight of his houses should be condemned as insanitary, and pulled down. The next item on the agenda was Lucia's offer of fifty almond-trees (or more if desirable) to beautify in spring-time the bare grass slope to the south of the town. She said a few diffident words about the privilege of being allowed to make a little garden there, and intimated that she would pay for the enrichment of the soil and the planting of the trees and any subsequent upkeep, so that not a penny should fall on the rates. The offer was gratefully accepted with the applause of knuckles on the table, and as she was popular enough for the moment, she deferred announcing her project for the re-laying of the steps by the Norman tower. Half an hour more sufficed for the rest of the business before the Town Councillors.

Treading on air, Lucia dropped in at Mallards Cottage to tell Georgie the news. The Padre had just gone across to Mallards, for Evie and he had got into a remarkable muddle that morning packing their bags in such a hurry: he had to recover his shaving-equipment from hers, and take her a few small articles of female attire.

'I think I had better tell them all about my appointment at once, Georgie,' she said, 'for they are sure to hear about it very soon, and if Elizabeth has a bilious attack from chagrin, the sooner it's over the better. My dear, how tiresome she has been already! She came and sat in the garden-room, which I don't intend that anybody shall do in the morning, and so I began playing scales and shakes to smoke her out. Then she tried to overhear my conversation on the Office telephone with the Mayor –'

'And did she?' asked Georgie greedily.

'I don't think so. I banged the door when I saw her in the hall. You and the Padre will have all your meals with me, won't you, till they go, but if this rain continues, it looks as if they might be here till they get back into their own houses again. Let me sit quietly with you till lunch-time, for we shall have them all on our hands for the rest of the day.'

'I think we've been too hospitable,' said Georgie. 'One can overdo it. If the Padre sits and talks to me all morning, I shall have to live in my bedroom. Foljambe doesn't like it, either. He's called her "my lassie" already.'

'No!' said Lucia. 'She'd hate that. Oh, and Benjy looked as black as ink when I told him I must give up his room to Evie. But we must rejoice, Georgie, that we're able to do something for the poor things.'

'Rejoice isn't quite the word,' said Georgie firmly.

Lucia returned to Mallards a little after half-past one, and went up to the sitting-room she had assigned to her guests and tapped on the door before entering. That might convey to Elizabeth's obtuse mind that this was their private room, and she might infer, by implication, that the garden-room was Lucia's private room. But this little moral lesson was wasted, for the room was empty except for stale cigar-smoke. She went to the dining-room, for they might, as desired, have begun lunch. Empty also. She went to the garden-room, and even as she opened the door, Elizabeth's voice rang out.

'No, Padre, my card was *not* covered,' she said. 'Uncovered.'

'An exposed card whatever then, Mistress Mapp,' said the Padre.

'Come, come, Mapp-Flint, Padre,' said Benjy.

'Oh, there's dearest Lucia!' cried Elizabeth. 'I thought it was Grosvenor come to tell us that lunch was ready. Such a dismal morning; we thought we would have a little game of cards to pass the time. No card-table in our cosy parlour upstairs.'

'Of course you shall have one,' said Lucia.

'And you've done your little business?' asked Elizabeth.

Lucia was really sorry for her, but the blow must be dealt.

'Yes: I attended a meeting of the Town Council. But there was very little business.'

'The Town Council, did you say?' asked the stricken woman.

'Yes: they did me the honour to co-opt me, for a member has resigned owing to ill-health. I felt it my duty to fill the vacancy. Let us go in to lunch.'

It was not till a fortnight later that Georgie and Lucia were once more dining alone at Mallards House, both feeling as if they were recovering from some debilitating nervous complaint, accompanied by high blood-pressure and great depression. The attack, so to speak, was over, and now they had to pick up their strength again. Only yesterday had the Padre and Evie gone back to their bungalow, and only this morning had the Mapp-Flints returned to Grebe. They might have gone the day before, since the insane widow of the Baronet had left that morning, removing herself and forty-seven canaries in two gipsy-vans. But there was so much rape-seed scattered on the tiger-skins, and so many tokens of bird-life on curtains and tables and chairs that it had required a full day to clean up. Benjy on his departure had pressed a half-crown and a penny into Grosvenor's hand, one from himself and one from Elizabeth. This looked as if he had calculated the value of her services with meticulous accuracy, but the error had arisen because he had mixed up coppers and silver in his pocket, and he had genuinely meant to give her five shillings. Elizabeth gave her a sweet smile and shook hands.

Anyhow the fortnight was now over. Lucia had preserved the seignorial air to the end. Her car was always at the disposal of her guests, fires blazed in their bedrooms, she told them what passed at the meetings of the Town Council, she consulted their tastes at table. One day there was haggis for the Padre who was being particularly Scotch, and one day there were stewed prunes for Elizabeth, and fiery curry for Major Benjy in his more Indian moods, and parsnips for Evie who had a passion for that deplorable vegetable. About one thing only was Lucia adamant. They might take all the morning papers up to the guests' sitting-room, but until lunch-time they should not read them in the garden-room. *Verboten; défendu; non permesso.* If Elizabeth showed her nose there, or Benjy his cigar, or Evie her parish magazine, Lucia telephoned for Georgie, and they played duets till the intruder could stand it no more . . .

She pressed the pomander which rang the electric bell. Grosvenor brought in coffee, and now they could talk freely.

'That wonderful fourth round of the Inferno, Georgie,' said Lucia dreamily. 'The guests who eat the salt of their host, and *sputare* it on the floor. Some very unpleasant fate awaited them: I think they were pickled in brine.'

'I'm sure they deserved whatever it was,' said Georgie.

'She,' said Lucia, mentioning no name, 'she went to see Diva one morning and said that Grosvenor had no idea of valeting, because she had put out a sock for Benjy with a large hole in it. Diva said: "Why did you let it get like that?"'

'So that was that,' said Georgie.

'And Benjy told the Padre that Grosvenor was very sparing with the wine. Certainly I did tell her not to fill up his glass the moment it was empty, for I was not going to have another Wyse-evening every day of the week.'

'Quite right, and there was always plenty for anyone who didn't want to get tipsy,' said Georgie. And Benjy wasn't very sparing with my whisky. Every evening practically he came across to chat with me about seven, and had three stiff goes.'

'I thought so,' cried Lucia triumphantly, bringing her hand sharply down on the table. Unfortunately she hit the pomander, and Grosvenor re-entered. Lucia apologized for her mistake.

'Georgie, I inferred there certainly must be something of the sort,' she resumed when the door was shut again. 'Every evening round about seven Benjy used to say that he wouldn't play another rubber because he wanted a brisk walk and a breath of fresh air before dinner. Clever of him, Georgie. Though I'm sorry for your whisky I always applaud neat execution, however alcoholic the motive. After he had left the room, he banged the front door loud enough for her to hear it, so that she knew he had gone out and wasn't getting at the sherry in the dining-room. I think she suspected something, but she didn't quite know what.'

'I never knew an occasion on which she didn't suspect something,' said he.

Lucia crunched a piece of coffee-sugar in a meditative manner.

'An interesting study,' she said. 'You know how devoted I am to psychological research, and I learned a great deal this last fortnight. Major Benjy was not very clever when he wooed and won her, but I think marriage has sharpened his wits. Little bits of foxiness, little evasions, nothing, of course, of a very high order, but some inkling of ingenuity and contrivance. I can understand a man developing a certain acuteness if he knew Elizabeth was always just round the corner. The instinct of self-protection. There is a character in Theophrastus very like him: I must look it up. Dear me; for the last fortnight I've hardly opened a book.'

'I can imagine that,' said he. 'Even I, who had only the Padre in the house, couldn't settle down to anything. He was always coming in and out, wanting some ink in his bedroom, or a piece of string, or change for a shilling.'

'Multiply it by three. And she treated me all the time as if I was a hotel-keeper and she wasn't pleased with her room or her food, but made no formal complaint. Oh, Georgie, I must tell you, Elizabeth went up four pounds in weight the first week she was here. She shared my bathroom and always had her bath just before me in the evening, and there's a weighing-machine there, you know. Of course, I was terribly interested, but one day I felt I simply must thwart her, and so I hid the weights behind the bath. It was the only inhospitable thing I did the whole time she was here, but I couldn't bear it. So I don't know how much more she went up the second week.'

'I should have thought your co-option on to the Town Council would have made her thinner,' observed Georgie. 'But thrilling! She must have weighed herself without clothes, if she was having her bath. How much did she weigh?'

'Eleven stone twelve was the last,' said Lucia. 'But she has got big bones, Georgie. We must be fair.'

'Yes, but her bones must have finished growing,' said Georgie. They wouldn't have gone up four pounds in a week. Just fat.'

'I suppose it must have been. As for my co-option, it was frightful for her. Frightful. Let's go into the garden-room. My dear, how delicious to know that Benjy won't be there, smoking one of his rank cigars, or little Evie, running about like a mouse, so it always seemed to me, among the legs of chairs and tables.'

'Hurrah, for one of our quiet evenings again,' said he.

It was with a sense of restored well-being that they sank into their chairs, too content in this relief from strain to play duets. Georgie was sewing a border of lace on to some new doilies for finger-bowls, and Lucia found the 'Characters of Theophrastus', and read to him in the English version the sketch of Benjy's prototype. As their content worked inside them both, like tranquil yeast, they both became aware that a moment of vital import to them, and hardly less so to Tilling, was ticking its way nearer. A couple of years ago only, each had shuddered at the notion that the other might be thinking of matrimony, but now the prospect of it had lost its horror. For Georgie had stayed with her when he was growing his shingles-beard, and she had stayed with him when she was settling into Mallards, and those days of domestic propinquity had somehow convinced them both that nothing was further from the inclination of either than any species of dalliance. With that nightmare apprehension removed they could recognize that for a considerable portion of the day they enjoyed each other's society more than their own solitude: they were happier together than apart. Again, Lucia was beginning to feel that, in the career which was opening for her in Tilling, a husband would give her a certain stability: a Prince Consort, though emphatically not for dynastic purposes, would lend her weight and ballast. Georgie with kindred thoughts in his mind could see himself filling that eminent position with grace and effectiveness.

Georgie, not attending much to his sewing, pricked his finger: Lucia read a little more Theophrastus with a wandering mind and moved to her writing-table, where a pile of letters was kept in place by a pretty paper-weight consisting of a small electro-plate cricket bat propped against a football, which had been given her jointly by the two clubs of which she was President. The clock struck eleven: it surprised them both that the hours had passed so quickly: eleven was usually the close of their evening. But they sat on, for all was ready for the vital moment, and if it did not come now, when on earth could there be a more apt occasion? Yet who was to begin, and how?

Georgie put down his work, for all his fingers were damp, and one was bloody. He remembered that he was a man. Twice he opened his mouth to speak, and twice he closed it again. He looked up at her, and caught her eye, and that gimlet-like quality in it seemed not only to pierce but to encourage. It bored into him for his good and for his eventual comfort. For the third time, and now successfully, he opened his mouth.

'Lucia, I've got something I must say, and I hope you won't mind. Has it ever occurred to you that – well – that we might marry?'

She fiddled for a moment with the cricket bat and the football, but when she raised her eyes again, there was no doubt about the encouragement.

'Yes, Georgie: unwomanly as it may sound,' she said, 'it has. I really believe it might be an excellent thing. But there's a great deal for us to think over first, and then talk over together. So let us say no more for the present. Now we must have our talk as soon as possible: some time to-morrow.'

She opened her engagement-book. She had bought a new one, since she had become a Town Councillor, about as large as an ordinary blotting-pad.

'*Dio*, what a day!' she exclaimed. 'Town Council at half-past ten, and at twelve I am due at the slope by the Norman tower to decide about the planting of my almond-trees. Not in lines, I think, but scattered about: a little clump here, a single one there . . . Then Diva comes to lunch. Did you hear? A cinder from a passing engine blew into her cook's eye as she was leaning out of the kitchen window, poor thing. Then after lunch my football team are playing their opening match and I promised to kick off for them.'

'My dear, how wonderfully adventurous of you!' exclaimed Georgie. 'Can you?'

'Quite easily and quite hard. They sent me up a football and I've been practising in the *giardino segreto*. Where were we? Come to tea, Georgie – no, that won't do: my Mayor is bringing me the plans for the new artisan dwellings. It must be dinner then, and we shall have time to think it all over. Are you off? *Buona notte, caro: tranquilli* – dear me, what is the Italian for "sleep"? How rusty I am getting!'

Lucia did not go back with him into the house, for there were some agenda for the meeting at half-past ten to be looked through. But just as she heard the front door shut on his exit, she remembered the Italian for sleep, and hurriedly threw up the window that looked on the street.

'*Sonni*,' she called out, '*sonni tranquilli.*'

Georgie understood: and he answered in Italian.

'*I stessi a voi*, I mean, *te*,' he brilliantly shouted.

The half-espoused couple had all next day to let simmer in their heads the hundred arrangements and adjustments which the fulfilment of their romance would demand. Again and again Georgie cast his doily from him in despair at the magnitude and intricacy of them. About the question of connubialities, he meant to be quite definite: it must be a *sine qua non* of matrimony, the first clause in the marriage treaty, that they should be considered absolutely illicit, and he need not waste thought over that. But what was to happen to his house, for presumably he would live at Mallards? And if so, what was to be done with his furniture, his piano, his bibelots? He could not bear to part with them, and Mallards was already full of Lucia's things. And what about Foljambe? She was even more inalienable than his Worcester china, and Georgie felt that though life might be pretty much the same with Lucia, it could not be the same without Foljambe. Then he must insist on a good deal of independence with regard to the companionship his bride would expect from him. His mornings must be inviolably his own and also the time between tea and dinner as he would be with her from then till bedtime severed them. Again two cars seemed more than two people should require, but he could not see himself without his Armaud. And what if Lucia, intoxicated by her late success on the Stock Exchange, took to gambling and lost all her money? The waters on which they thought of voyaging together seemed sown with jagged reefs, and he went across to dinner the next night with a drawn and anxious face. He was rather pleased to see that Lucia looked positively haggard, for that showed that she realized the appalling conundrums that must be solved before any irretraceable step was taken. Probably she had got some more of her own.

They settled themselves in the chairs where they had been so easy with each other twenty-four hours ago and Lucia with an air of determination, picked up a paper of scribbled memoranda from her desk.

'I've put down several points we must agree over, Georgie,' she said.

'I've got some, too, in my head,' said he.

Lucia fixed her eyes on a corner of the ceiling, as if in a music-face, but her knotted brow showed it was not that.

'I thought of writing to you about the first point, which is the most important of all,' she said, 'but I found I couldn't. How can I put it best? It's this, Georgie. I trust that you'll be very comfortable in the oak bedroom.'

'I'm sure I shall,' interrupted Georgie eagerly.

'– and all that implies,' Lucia went on firmly. 'No caresses of any sort: none of those dreadful little dabs and pecks Elizabeth and Benjy used to make at each other.'

'You needn't say anything more about that,' said he. 'Just as we were before.'

The acuteness of her anxiety faded from Lucia's face.

'That's a great relief,' she said. 'Now what is my next point? I've been in such a whirl all day and scribbled them down so hastily that I can't read it. It looks like "Frabjious".'

'It sounds as if it might be Foljambe,' said Georgie. 'I've been thinking a lot about her. I can't part with her.'

'Nor can I part with Grosvenor, as no doubt you will have realized. But what will their respective positions be? They've both bossed our houses for years. Which is to boss now? And will the other one consent to be bossed?'

'I can't see Foljambe consenting to be bossed,' said Georgie.

'If I saw Grosvenor consenting to be bossed,' said Lucia, 'I merely shouldn't believe my eyes.'

'Could there be a sort of equality?' suggested Georgie. 'Something like King William III and Queen Mary?'

'Oh, Georgie, I think there might be a solution there,' said Lucia. 'Let us explore that. Foljambe will only be here during the day, just as she is now with you, and she'll be your valet, and look after your rooms, for you must have a sitting-room of your own. I insist on that. You will be her province, Georgie, where she's supreme. I shall be Grosvenor's. I don't suppose either of them wants to leave us, and they are friends. We'll put it to them to-morrow, if we agree about the rest.'

'Won't it be awful if they don't come to terms?' said Georgie. 'What are we to do then?'

'Don't let's anticipate trouble,' said Lucia. 'Then let me see. "Mallards Cottage" is my next entry. Naturally we shall live here.'

'I've been worrying terribly about that,' said Georgie. 'I quite agree we must live here, but I can't let the Cottage with all my things. I don't wish other people to sleep in my bed and that sort of thing. But if I let it unfurnished, what am I to do with them? My piano, my pictures and embroideries, my sofa, my particular armchair, my bed, my bibelots? I've got six occasional tables in my sitting-room, because I counted them. There's no room for them here, and things go to pot if one stores them. Besides there are a lot of them which I simply can't get on without. Heart's blood.'

A depressed silence followed, for Lucia knew what his household goods meant to Georgie. Then suddenly she sprang up, clapping her hands, and talking so weird a mixture of baby-language and Italian that none but the most intimate could have understood her at all.

'Georgino!' she cried. 'Ickle me vewy clever. Lucia's got a *molto bella* idea. Lucia knows how Georgino loves his *bibelotine*. Tink a minute: shut 'oo eyes and tink! Well, Lucia no tease you any more ... Georgino will have booful night-nursery here, bigger nor what he had in Cottagino. And booful *salone* bigger nor *salone* there. Now do you see?'

'No, I don't,' said Georgie firmly.

Lucia abandoned baby and foreign tongues.

'I'll send all the furniture in your bedroom and sitting-room here across to Mallards Cottage, and you shall fill them with your own things. More than enough room for the curtains and pictures and occasional tables which you really love. You wouldn't mind letting the Cottage if you had all your special things here?'

'Well, you are clever!' said Georgie.

An appreciative pause followed instead of that depressed silence, and Lucia referred to her notes.

'"Solitude" is my next entry,' she said. 'What can – Oh, I know. It sounds rather as if I was planning that we should see as little as possible of each other if and when we marry, but I don't mean that. Only, with all the welter of business which my position in Tilling already entails (and it will get worse rather than better) I must have much time to myself. Naturally we shall entertain a good deal: those quaint bridge-parties and so on, for Tilling society will depend on us more than ever. But ordinarily, when we are alone, Georgie, I must have my mornings to myself, and a couple of hours at least before dinner. Close times. Of course nothing hard or fast about it; very likely we shall often make music together then. But you mustn't think me unsociable if, as a rule, I have those hours to myself. My municipal duties, my boards and committees already take a great deal of time, and then there are all my private studies. A period of solitude every day is necessary for me. Is it not Goethe who says that we ripen in solitude?'

'I quite agree with him if he does,' said Georgie. 'I was going to speak about it myself if you hadn't.'

Most of the main dangers which threatened to render matrimony impossible had now been provided for and of these the Foljambe–Grosvenor complication alone remained. That, to be sure, was full of menace, for the problem that would arise if those two pillars of the house would not consent to support it in equal honour and stability, seemed to admit of no solution. But all that could be done at present was to make the most careful plans for the tactful putting of the proposition before William and Mary. It ought to be done simultaneously in both houses, and Lucia decided it would be quite legitimate if she implied (though not exactly stated) to Grosvenor that Foljambe thought the plan would work very well, while at the same moment Georgie was making the same implication to Foljambe. The earlier that was done, the shorter would be the suspense, and zero hour was fixed for ten next morning. It was late now, and Georgie went to bed. A random idea of kissing Lucia once, on the brow, entered his mind, but after what had been said about caresses, he felt she might consider it a minor species of rape.

Next morning at a quarter past ten Georgie was just going to the telephone with brisk tread and beaming face, when Lucia rang him up. The sparkle in her voice convinced him that all was well even before she said '*La domestica e molto contenta.*'

'So's mine,' said Georgie.

All obstacles to the marriage being now removed, unless Elizabeth thought of something and forbade the banns, there was no reason why it should not be announced. If Diva was told, no further dissemination was needful. Accordingly Lucia wrote a note to her about it, and by half-past eleven practically all Tilling knew. Elizabeth, on being told, said to Diva, 'Dear, how can you repeat such silly stories?' So Diva produced the note itself, and Elizabeth without a particle of shame said, 'Now my lips are unsealed. I knew a week ago. High time they were married, I should say.'

Diva pressed her to explain precisely what she meant with such ferocity that Paddy showed his teeth, being convinced by a dog's unfailing instinct that Elizabeth must be an enemy. So she explained that she had only meant that they had been devoted to each other for so long, and that neither of them would remain quite young much longer. Irene burst into tears when she heard it, but in all other quarters the news was received with great cordiality, the more so perhaps because

Lucia had told Diva that they neither of them desired any wedding-presents.

The date and manner of the wedding much exercised the minds of the lovers. Georgie, personally, would have wished the occasion to be celebrated with the utmost magnificence. He strongly fancied the prospective picture of himself in frock-coat and white spats waiting by the north door of the church for the arrival of the bride. Conscious that for the rest of his years he would be over-shadowed by the first citizeness of Tilling, his nature demanded one hour of glorious life, when the dominating role would be his, and she would promise to love, honour and obey, and the utmost pomp and circumstance ought to attend this brief apotheosis. To Lucia he put the matter rather differently.

'Darling,' he said (they had settled to allow themselves this verbal endearment), 'I think, no, I'm sure, that Tilling would be terribly disappointed if you didn't allow this to be a great occasion. You must remember who you are, and what you are to Tilling.'

Lucia was in no serious danger of forgetting that, but she had got another idea in her head. She sighed, as if she had herself just played the last chord of the first movement of the 'Moonlight'.

'Georgie,' she said, 'I was turning up only yesterday the account of Charlotte Brontë's wedding. Eight o'clock in the morning, and only two of her most intimate friends present. No one of the folk at Haworth even knew she was being married that day. So terribly *chic* somehow, when one remembers her world-wide fame. I am not comparing myself to Charlotte – don't think that – but I have got a touch of her exquisite delicacy in shunning publicity. My public life, darling, must and does belong to Tilling, but not my private life.'

'I can't quite agree,' said Georgie. 'It's not the same thing, for all Tilling knows you're going to be married, and it wouldn't be fair to them. I should like you to ask the Bishop to come again in cope and mitre –'

Lucia remembered that day of superb triumph.

'Oh, Georgie, I wonder if he would come,' she said. 'How Tilling enjoyed it before!'

'Try anyhow. And think of your organ. Really it ought to make a joyful noise at your wedding. Mendelssohn's "Wedding March": tubas.'

'No, darling, not that,' said Lucia. 'So lascivious don't you think?'

'Well, Chopin's then,' said Georgie.

'No, that's a funeral march,' said Lucia. 'Most unsuitable.'

'Well, some other march,' said Georgie. 'And the Mayor and Corporation would surely attend. You're a Town Councillor.'

The example of Charlotte Brontë's was fading out in Lucia's mind, vanishing in a greater brightness.

'And the *Hastings Chronicle*,' said Georgie pushing home his advantage. 'That would be a big cutting for your book. A column at least.'

'But there'll be no wedding-presents,' she said. 'Usually most of it is taken up with wedding-presents.'

'Another score for you,' said Georgie ingeniously. 'Tell your Mr Meriton that because of the widespread poverty and unemployment you begged your friends not to spend their money on presents. They'd have been very meagre little things in any case: two packs of patience cards from Elizabeth and a penwiper from Benjy. Much better to have none.'

Lucia considered these powerful arguments.

'I allow you have shaken my resolve, darling,' she said. 'If you really think it's my duty as –'

'As a Town Councillor and a fairy godmother to Tilling, I do,' said he. 'The football club, the cricket club. Everybody. I think you ought to sacrifice your personal feelings, which I quite understand.'

That finished it.

'I had better write to the Bishop at once then,' she said, 'and give him a choice of dates. Bishops I am sure are as busy as I.'

'Scarcely that,' said Georgie. 'But it would be as well.'

Lucia took a couple of turns up and down the garden-room. She waved her arms like Brünnhilde awakening on the mountain-top.

'Georgie, I begin to visualize it all,' she said. 'A procession from here would be out of place. But afterwards, certainly a reception in the garden-room, and a buffet in the dining-room. Don't you think? But one thing I must be firm about. We must steal away afterwards. No confetti or shoes. We must have your motor at the front door, so that everyone will think we are driving away from there, and mine at the little passage into Porpoise Street, with the luggage on.'

She sat down and took a sheet of writing-paper.

'And we must settle about my dress,' she said. 'If we are to have this great show, so as not to disappoint Tilling, it ought to be up to the mark. Purple brocade, or something of the sort. I shall have it made here, of course: that good little milliner in the High Street. Useful for her . . . "Dear Lord Bishop" is correct, is it not?'

The Bishop chose the earliest of the proffered dates, and the Mayor and Corporation thereupon signified their intention of being present at the ceremony, and accepted Lucia's invitation to the reception afterwards at Mallards. A further excitement for Tilling two days before the wedding was the sight of eight of the men whom now Lucia had come to call 'her unemployed' moving in opposite directions between Mallards and the Cottage like laden ants, observing the rules of the road. They carried the most varied burdens: a bed in sections came out of Mallards passing on its way sections of another bed from the Cottage: book-cases were interchanged and wardrobes: an ant festooned with gay water-colour sketches made his brilliant progress towards Mallards, meeting another who carried prints of Mozart at the age of four improvising on the spinet and of Beethoven playing his own compositions to an apparently remorseful audience. A piano lurched along from the Cottage, first sticking in the doorway, and thus obstructing the progress of other ants laden with crockery vessels, water-jugs and basins and other meaner objects, who had to stand with their intimate burdens in the street, looking a shade self-conscious, till their way was clear. Curtains and rugs and fire-irons and tables and chairs were interchanged, and Tilling puzzled itself into knots to know what these things meant.

As if this conundrum was not sufficiently agonizing, nobody

could ascertain where the happy pair were going for their honeymoon. They would be back in a week, for Lucia could not forsake her municipal duties for longer than that, but she had made concession enough to publicity, and this was kept a profound secret, for the mystery added to the *cachet* of the event. Elizabeth made desperate efforts to find out: she sprang all sorts of Jack-in-the-box questions on Lucia in the hope that she would startle her into revealing the unknown destination. Were there not very amusing plays going on in Paris? Was not the climate of Cornwall very agreeable in November? Had she ever seen a bull-fight? All no use: and completely foiled she expressed her settled conviction that they were not going away at all, but would immure themselves at Mallards, as if they had measles.

All was finished on the day before the wedding, and Georgie slept for the last time in the Cottage surrounded by the furniture from his future bedroom at Mallards, and clad in his frock-coat and fawn-coloured trousers had an early lunch, with a very poor appetite, in his unfamiliar sitting-room. He brushed his top-hat nervously from time to time, and broke into a slight perspiration when the church bells began to ring, yearning for the comfortable obscurity of a registry office, and wishing that he had never been born, or, at any rate, was not going to be married quite so soon. He tottered to the church.

The ceremony was magnificent, with cope and corporation and plenty of that astonishing tuba on the organ. Then followed the reception in the garden-room and the buffet in the dining-room, during which bride and bridegroom vanished, and appeared again in their going-away clothes, a brown Lucia with winter-dessert in her hat, and a bright mustard-coloured Georgie. The subterfuge, however, of starting from Porpoise Street *via* the back door was not necessary, since the street in front of Mallards was quite devoid of sightseers and confetti. So Georgie's decoy motor-car retreated, and Grosvenor ordered up Lucia's car from Porpoise Street. There was some difficulty in getting round that awkward corner, for there was a van in the way, and it had to saw backwards and forwards. The company crowded into the hall and on to the doorstep to see them off, and Elizabeth was quite certain that Lucia did not say a word to Cadman as she stepped in. Clearly then Cadman knew where they were going, and if she had only thought of that she might have wormed it out of him. Now it was too late: also her conviction that they were not going anywhere at all had broken down. She tried to persuade Diva that they were only going for a drive and would be back for tea, but Diva was pitilessly scornful.

'Rubbish!' she said. Or was all that luggage merely a blind? 'You're wrong as usual, Elizabeth.'

Lucia put the window half down: it was a warm afternoon.

'Darling, it all went off beautifully,' she said. 'And what fun it will be to see dear Riseholme again. It was nice of Olga Bracely to lend us her house. We must have some little dinners for them all.'

'They'll be thrilled,' said Georgie. 'Do you like my new suit?'

Lucia decided to take a rare half-holiday and spend this brilliant afternoon in mid-May, in strolling about Tilling with Georgie, for there was a good deal she wanted to inspect. They went across the churchyard pausing to listen to the great blare of melodious uproar that poured out through the open south door, for the organist was practising on Lucia's organ, and, after enjoying that, proceeded to the Norman tower. The flight of steps down to the road below had been relaid from top to bottom, and a most elegant hand-rail put up. A very modest stone tablet at the side of the top step recorded in quite small letters the name of the person to whom Tilling owed this important restoration.

'They were only finished yesterday, Georgie,' said Lucia hardly glancing at the tablet, since she had herself chosen the lettering very carefully and composed the inscription, 'and I promised the foreman to look at them. Nice, I think, and in keeping. And very evenly laid. One can walk down them without looking to one's feet.'

Half-way down she stopped and pointed.

'Georgie,' she cried. 'Look at the lovely blossom on my almond-trees! They are in flower at last, after this cold spring. I was wise to get well-grown trees: smaller ones would never have flowered their first year. Oh, there's Elizabeth coming up my steps. That old green skirt again. It seems quite imperishable.'

They met.

'Lovely new steps,' said Elizabeth very agreeably. 'Quite a pleasure to walk up them. Thank you, dear, for them. But those poor almond-trees. So sad and pinched, and hardly a blossom on them. Perhaps they weren't the flowering sort. Or do you think they'll get acclimatized after some years?'

'They're coming out beautifully,' said Lucia in a very firm voice. 'I've never seen such healthy trees in all my life. By next week they will be a blaze of blossom. Blaze.'

'I'm sure I hope you'll be right, dear,' said Elizabeth, 'but I don't see any buds coming myself.' Lucia took no further notice of her, and continued to admire her almond-trees in a loud voice to Georgie.

'And how gay the pink blossom looks against the blue sky, darling,' she said. 'You must bring your paint-box here some morning and make a sketch of them. Such a feast for the eye.'

She tripped down the rest of the steps, and Elizabeth paused at the top to read the tablet.

'You know Mapp is really the best name for her,' said Lucia, still slightly bubbling with resentment. 'Irene is quite right never to call her anything else. Poor Mapp is beginning to imitate herself: she says exactly the things which somebody taking her off would say.'

'And I'm sure she wanted to be pleasant just now,' said Georgie, 'but the moment she began to praise your steps she couldn't bear it, and found herself obliged to crab something else of yours.'

'Very likely. I never knew a woman so terribly in the grip of her temperament. Look, Georgie: they're playing cricket on my field. Let us go and sit in the pavilion for a little. It would be appreciated.'

'Darling, it's so dull watching cricket,' said Georgie. 'One man hits the ball away and another throws it back and all the rest eat daisies.'

'We'll just go and show ourselves,' said Lucia. 'We needn't stop long. As President I feel I must take an interest in their games. I wish I had time to study cricket. Doesn't the field look beautifully level now? You could play billiards on it.'

'Oh, by the way,' said Georgie, 'I saw Mr Woolgar in the town this morning. He told me he had a client, very desirable he thought, but he wasn't at liberty to mention the name yet, inquiring if I would let the Cottage for three months from the end of June. Only six guineas a week offered, and I asked eight. But even at that a three months' let would be pleasant.'

'The client's name is Mapp,' said Lucia with decision. 'Diva told me yesterday that the woman with the canaries had taken Grebe for three months from the end of June at twenty guineas a week.'

'That may be only a coincidence,' said Georgie.

'But it isn't,' retorted Lucia. 'I can trace the windings of her mind like the course of a river across the plain. She thinks she wouldn't get it for six guineas if you knew she was the client, for she had let out that she was getting twenty for Grebe. Stick to eight, Georgie, or raise it to ten.'

'I'm going to have tea with Diva,' said Georgie, 'and the Mapps will be there. I might ask her suddenly if she was going to take a bungalow again for the summer, and see how she looks.'

'Anyhow they can't get flooded out of Mallards Cottage,' observed Lucia.

They had skirted the cricket-ground and come to the pavilion, but since Tilling was fielding Lucia's appearance did not evoke the gratification she had anticipated, since none of the visiting side had the slightest idea who she was. The Tilling bowling was being slogged all over the field, and the fieldsmen had really no time to eat daisies with this hurricane hitting going on. One ball crashed on to the wall of the pavilion just above Georgie's head, and Lucia willingly consented to leave her cricket-field, for she had not known the game was so perilous. They went up into the High Street and through the churchyard again, and were just in sight of Mallards Cottage on which was a board: 'To be let Furnished or Sold', when the door opened, and Elizabeth came out, locking the door after her: clearly she had been to inspect it, or how could she have got the keys? Lucia knew that Georgie had seen her, and so did not even say 'I told you so.'

'You must promise to do a sketch of my almond-trees against the sky, Georgie,' she said. 'They will be in their full beauty by next week. And we must really give one of our omnibus dinner-parties soon. Saturday would do: I have nothing on Saturday evening, I think. I will telephone all round now.'

Georgie went upstairs to his own sitting-room to get a reposeful half-hour, before going to his tea-party. More and more he marvelled at Lucia's superb vitality: she was busier now than she had ever pretended to be, and her labours were but as fuel to feed her fires. This walk to-day, for instance, had for him necessitated a short period of quiescence before he set off again for fresh expenditure of force, but he could hear her voice crisp and vigorous as she rang up number after number, and the reason why she was not coming to Diva's party was that she had a class of girl-guides in the garden-room at half-past four, and a meeting of the Governors of the hospital at six. At 7.15 (for 7.30) she was to preside at the annual dinner of the cricket club. Not a very full day.

Lucia had been returned at the top of the poll in the last elections for the Town Council. Never did she miss a meeting, never did she fail to bring forward some fresh scheme for the employment of the unemployed, for the lighting of streets or the paving of roads or for the precedence of perambulators over pedestrians on the narrow pavements of the High Street. Bitter had been the conflict which called for a decision on that knotty question. Mapp, for instance, meeting two per-ambulators side by side had refused to step into the road and so had the nursery-maids. Instead they had advanced, chatting gaily together, solid as a phalanx and Mapp had been forced to retreat before them and turn up a side-street. 'What with Susan's great bus,' she passionately exclaimed, 'filling up the whole of the roadway, and perambulators sweeping all before them on the pavements, we shall have to do our shopping in aeroplanes.'

Diva, to whom she made this protest, had been sadly forget-ful of recent events, which, so to speak, had not happened and replied:

'Rubbish, dear Elizabeth! If you had ever had occasion to push a perambulator, you wouldn't have wheeled it on to the road to make way for the Queen.' . . . Then, seeing her error, Diva had made things worse by saying she hadn't meant *that*, and the bridge party to which Georgie was going this afternoon was to mark the reconciliation after the resultant coolness. The legislation suggested by Lucia to meet this traffic problem was a model of wisdom: perambulators had precedence on pavements, but they must proceed in single file. Heaps of room for everybody.

Georgie, resting and running over her activities in his mind, felt quite hot at the thought of them, and applied a little eau-de-cologne to his forehead. To-morrow she was taking all her girl-guides for a day by the sea at Margate: they were starting in a chartered bus at eight in the morning, but she expected to be back for dinner. The occupations of her day fitted into each other like a well-cut jigsaw puzzle, and not a piece was missing from the picture. Was all this activity merely the outpouring of her inexhaustible energy that spouted like the water from the rock when Moses smote it? Sometimes he wondered whether there was not an ulterior purpose behind it. If so, she never spoke of it, but drove relentlessly on in silence.

He grew a little drowsy; he dozed, but he was awakened by a step on the stairs and a tap at his door. Lucia always tapped, for it was his private room, and she entered with a note in her hand. Her face seemed to glow with some secret radiance which she repressed with difficulty: to mask it she wore a frown, and her mouth was working with thought.

'I must consult you, Georgie,' she said, sinking into a chair. 'There is a terribly momentous decision thrust upon me.'

Georgie dismissed the notion that Mapp had made some violent assault upon the infant occupiers of the perambulators as inadequate.

'Darling, what has happened?' he asked.

She gazed out of the window without speaking.

'I have just received a note from the Mayor,' she said at length in a shaken voice. 'While we were so light-heartedly looking at almond-trees, a private meeting of the Town Council was being held.'

'I see,' said Georgie, 'and they didn't send you notice. Outrageous. Anyhow, I think I should threaten to resign. After all you've done for them, too!'

She shook her head.

'No: you mustn't blame them,' she said. 'They were right,

for a piece of business was before them at which it was impossible I should be present.'

'Oh, something not quite nice?' suggested Georgie. 'But I think they should have told you.'

Again she shook her head.

'Georgie, they decided to sound me as to whether I would accept the office of Mayor next year. If I refuse, they would have to try somebody else. It's all private at present, but I had to speak to you about it, for naturally it will affect you very greatly.'

'Do you mean that I shall be something?' asked Georgie eagerly.

'Not officially, of course, but how many duties must devolve on the Mayor's husband!'

'A sort of Mayoress,' said Georgie with the eagerness clean skimmed off his voice.

'A thousand times more than that,' cried Lucia. 'You will have to be my right hand, Georgie. Without you I couldn't dream of undertaking it. I should entirely depend on you, on your judgment and your wisdom. There will be hundreds of questions on which a man's instinct will be needed by me. We shall be terribly hard-worked. We shall have to entertain, we shall have to take the lead, you and I, in everything, in municipal life as well as social life, which we do already. If you cannot promise to be always by me for my guidance and support, I can only give one answer. An unqualified negative.'

Lucia's eloquence, with all the practice she had had at Town Councils, was most effective. Georgie no longer saw himself as a Mayoress, but as the Power behind the Throne; he thought of Queen Victoria and the Prince Consort, and bright images bubbled in his brain. Lucia, with a few sideways gimlet-glances, saw the effect, and, wise enough to say no more, continued gazing out of the window. Georgie gazed too: they both gazed.

When Lucia thought that her silence had done as much as it could, she sighed, and spoke again.

'I understand. I will refuse then,' she said.

That, in common parlance, did the trick.

'No, don't fuss me,' he said. 'Me must fink.'

'*Si, caro: pensa seriosamente*,' said she. 'But I must make up my mind now: it wouldn't be fair on my colleagues not to. There are plenty of others, Georgie, if I refuse. I should think Mr Twistevant would make an admirable Mayor. Very business-like. Naturally, I do not approve of his views about slums and, of course, I should have to resign my place on the Town Council and some other bodies. But what does that matter?'

'Darling, if you put it like that,' said Georgie, 'I must say that I think it your duty to accept. You would be condoning slums almost, if you didn't.'

The subdued radiance in Lucia's face burst forth like the sun coming out from behind a cloud.

'If you think it's my duty, I must accept,' she said. 'You would despise me otherwise. I'll write at once.'

She paused at the door.

'I wonder what Elizabeth –' she began, then thought better of it, and tripped lightly downstairs.

Tilling had unanimously accepted Lucia's invitation for dinner and bridge on Saturday, and Georgie, going upstairs to dress, heard himself called from Lucia's bedroom.

He entered.

Her bed was paved with hats: it was a *parterre* of hats, of which the boxes stood on the floor, a rampart of boxes. The hats were of the most varied styles. There was one like an old-fashioned beaver hat with a feather in it. There was a Victorian bonnet with strings. There was a three-cornered hat, like that which Napoleon wore in the retreat from Moscow. There was a head-dress like those worn by nuns, and a beret made of cloth of gold. There was a hat like a full-bottomed wig with ribands in it, and a Stuart-looking head-dress like those worn by the ladies of the Court in the time of Charles I. Lucia sitting in front of her glass, with her head on one side, was trying the effect of a green turban.

'I want your opinion, dear,' she said. 'For official occasions as when the Mayor and Corporation go in state to church, or give a civic welcome to distinguished visitors, the Mayor, if a woman, has an official hat, part of her robes. But there are many semi-official occasions, Georgie, when one would not be wearing robes, but would still like to wear something distinctive. When I preside at Town Councils, for instance, or at all those committees of which I shall be chairman. On all those occasions I should wear the same hat: an undress uniform, you might call it. I don't think the green turban would do, but I am rather inclined to that beret in cloth of gold.'

Georgie tried on one or two himself.

'I like the beret,' he said. 'You could trim it with your beautiful seed-pearls.'

'That's a good idea,' said Lucia cordially. 'Or what about the thing like a wig. Rather majestic: the Mayor of Tilling, you know, used to have the power of life and death. Let me try it on again.'

'No, I like the beret better than that,' said Georgie critically. 'Besides the Mayor doesn't have the power of life and death now. Oh, but what about this Stuart-looking one? Rather Vandyckish, don't you think?'

He brought it to her, and came opposite the mirror himself, so that his face was framed there beside hers. His beard had been trimmed that day to a beautiful point.

'Georgino! Your beard: my hat,' cried Lucia. 'What a harmony! Not a question about it!'

'Yes, I think it does suit us,' said Georgie, blushing a little.

Trouble for Lucia

Lucia Pillson, the Mayor-Elect of Tilling and her husband Georgie were talking together one October afternoon in the garden-room at Mallards. The debate demanded the exercise of their keenest faculties. Viz.:

Should Lucia, when next month she entered on the supreme Municipal Office, continue to go down to the High Street every morning after breakfast with her market-basket, and make her personal purchases at the shops of the baker, the grocer, the butcher and wherever else the needs of the day's catering directed? There were pros and cons to be considered, and Lucia had been putting the case for both sides with the tedious lucidity of opposing counsel addressing the Court. It might be confidently expected that, when she had finished exploring the entire territory, she would be fully competent to express the verdict of the jury and the sentence of the judge. In anticipation of the numerous speeches she would soon be called upon to make as Mayor, she was cultivating, whenever she remembered to do so, a finished oratorical style, and a pedantic Oxford voice.

'I must be very careful, Georgie,' she said. 'Thoroughly democratic as you know I am in the truest sense of the word, I shall be entrusted, on the ninth of November next, with the duty of upholding the dignity and tradition of my high office. I'm not sure that I ought to go popping in and out of shops, as I have hitherto done, carrying my market-basket and bustling about just like anybody else. Let me put a somewhat similar case to you. Supposing you saw a newly appointed Lord Chancellor trotting round the streets of Westminster in shorts, for the sake of exercise. What would you feel about it? What would your reactions be?'

'I hope you're not thinking of putting on shorts, are you?' asked Georgie, hoping to introduce a lighter tone.

'Certainly not,' said Lucia. 'A parallel case only. And then there's this. It would be intolerable to my democratic principles that, if I went into the grocer's to make some small purchase, other customers already there should stand aside in order that I might be served first. That would never do. Never!'

Georgie surveyed with an absent air the pretty piece of needlework on which he was engaged. He was embroidering the Borough arms of Tilling in coloured silks on the back of the white kid gloves which Lucia would wear at the inaugural ceremony, and he was not quite sure that he had placed the device exactly in the middle.

'How tarsome,' he said. 'Well, it will have to do. I dare say it will stretch right. About the Lord Chancellor in shorts. I don't think I should mind. It would depend a little on what sort of knees he had. As for other customers standing aside because you were the Mayor, I don't think you need be afraid of that for a moment. Most unlikely.'

Lucia became violently interested in her gloves.

'My dear, they look too smart for anything,' she said. 'Beautiful work, Georgie. Lovely. They remind me of the jewelled gloves you see in primitive Italian pictures on the hands of kneeling Popes and adoring Bishops.'

'Do you think the arms are quite in the middle?' he asked.

'It looks perfect. Shall I try it on?'

Lucia displayed the back of her gloved hand, leaning her forehead elegantly against the finger-tips.

'Yes, that seems all right,' said Georgie. 'Give it me back. It's not quite finished. About the other thing. It would be rather marked if you suddenly stopped doing your marketing yourself, as you've done it every day for the last two years or so. Except Sundays. Some people might say that you were swanky because you were Mayor. Elizabeth would.'

'Possibly. But I should be puzzled, dear, to name off-hand anything that mattered less to me than what Elizabeth Mapp-Flint said, poor woman. Give me your opinion, not hers.'

'You might drop the marketing by degrees, if you felt it was undignified,' said Georgie yawning. 'Shop every day this week, and only on Monday, Wednesday and Friday next week –'

'No, dear,' interrupted Lucia. 'That would be hedging, and I never hedge. One thing or the other.'

'A hedge may save you from falling into a ditch,' said Georgie brilliantly.

'Georgino, how epigrammatic! What does it mean exactly? What ditch?'

'Any ditch,' said Georgie. 'Just making a mistake and not being judicious. Tilling is a mass of pitfalls.'

'I don't mind about pitfalls so long as my conscience assures me that I am guided by right principles. I must set an example in my private as well as my public life. If I decide to go on with my daily marketing I shall certainly make a point of buying very cheap, simple provisions. Cabbages and turnips, for instance, not asparagus.'

'We've got plenty of that in the garden when it comes in,' said Georgie.

'– plaice, not soles. Apples,' went on Lucia, as if he hadn't spoken. 'Plain living in private – everybody will hear me buying cheap vegetables – Splendour, those lovely gloves, in public. And high thinking in both.'

'That would sound well in your inaugural speech,' said Georgie.

'I hope it will. What I want to do in our dear Tilling is to elevate the tone, to make it a real centre of intellectual and artistic activity. That must go on simultaneously with social reforms and the well-being of the poorer classes. All the slums must be cleared away. There must be an end to overcrowding. Pasteurization of milk, Georgie; a strict censorship of the films; benches in sunny corners. Of course, it will cost money. I should like to see the rates go up by leaps and bounds.'

'That won't make you very popular,' said Georgie.

'I should welcome any unpopularity that such reforms might earn for me. The decorative side of life, too. Flower-boxes in the windows of the humblest dwellings. Cheap concerts of first-rate music. The revival of ancient customs, like beating the bounds. I must find out just what that is.'

'The Town Council went in procession round the boundaries of the parish,' said Georgie, 'and the Mayor was bumped on the boundary-stones. Hadn't we better stick to the question of whether you go marketing or not?'

Lucia did not like the idea of being bumped on boundary-stones . . .

'Quite right, dear. I lose myself in my dreams. We were talking about the example we must set in plain living. I wish it to be known that I do my catering with economy. To be heard ordering neck of mutton at the butcher's.'

'I won't eat neck of mutton in order to be an example to anybody,' said Georgie. 'And, personally, whatever you settle to do, I won't give up the morning shopping. Besides, one learns all the news then. Why, it would be worse than not having the wireless! I should be lost without it. So would you.'

Lucia tried to picture herself bereft of that eager daily interchange of gossip, when her Tilling circle of friends bustled up and down the High Street carrying their market-baskets and bumping into each other in the narrow doorways of shops. Rain or fine, with umbrellas and galoshes or with sunshades and the thinnest blouses, it was the bracing hour that whetted the appetite for the complications of life. The idea of missing it was unthinkable, and without the slightest difficulty she ascribed exalted motives and a high sense of duty to its continuance.

'You are right, dear,' she said. 'Thank you for your guidance! More than ever now in my new position, it will be incumbent on me to know what Tilling is thinking and feeling. My finger must be on its pulse. That book I was reading the other day, which impressed me so enormously – what on earth was it? A biography.'

'Catherine the Great?' asked Georgie. Lucia had dipped into it lately, but the suggestion was intended to be humorous.

'Yes: I shall forget my own name next. She always had her finger on the pulse of her people: that I maintain was the real source of her greatness. She used to disguise herself, you remember, as a peasant-woman – moujik, isn't it? – and let herself out of the back door of the Winter Palace, and sit in the bars and cafés or wherever they drink vodka and tea – samovars – and hear what the common people were saying, astonishing her Ministers with her knowledge.'

Georgie felt fearfully bored with her and this preposterous

rubbish. Lucia did not care two straws what 'the common people' were saying. She, in this hour of shopping in the High Street, wanted to know what fresh mischief Elizabeth Mapp-Flint was hatching, and what Major Benjy Mapp-Flint was at, and whether Diva Plaistow's Irish terrier had got mange, and if Irene Coles had obtained the sanction of the Town Surveying Department to paint a fresco on the front of her house of a nude Venus rising from the sea, and if Susan Wyse had really sat down on her budgerigar, squashing it quite flat. Instead of which she gassed about the duty of the Mayor-Elect of Tilling to have her finger on the pulse of the place, like Catherine the Great. Such nonsense was best met with a touch of sarcasm.

'That will be a new experience, dear,' he said. 'Fancy your disguising yourself as a gipsy-woman and stealing out through the back door, and sitting in the bars of public-houses. I do call that thorough.'

'Ah, you take me too literally, Georgie,' she said. 'Only a loose analogy. In some respects I should be sorry to behave like that marvellous woman. But what a splendid notion to listen to all that the moujiks said when their tongues were unloosed with vodka. *In vino veritas.*'

'Not always,' said Georgie. 'For instance, Major Benjy was sitting boozing in the Club this afternoon. The wind was too high for him to go out and play golf, so he spent his time in port . . . Putting out in a gale, you see, or stopping in port. Quite a lot of port.'

Georgie waited for his wife to applaud this pretty play upon words, but she was thinking about herself and Catherine the Great.

'Well, wine wasn't making him truthful, but just the opposite,' he went on. 'Telling the most awful whoppers about the tigers he'd shot and his huge success with women when he was younger.'

'Poor Elizabeth,' said Lucia in an unsympathetic voice.

'He grew quite dreadful,' said Georgie, 'talking about his bachelor days of freedom. And he had the insolence to dig me in the ribs and whisper "We know all about that, old boy, don't we? Ha ha. What?"'

'Georgie, how impertinent,' cried Lucia. 'Why, it's comparing Elizabeth with me!'

'And me with him,' suggested Georgie.

'Altogether most unpleasant. Any more news?'

'Yes; I saw Diva for a moment. Paddy's not got mange. Only a little eczema. And she's quite determined to start her tea-shop. She asked me if I thought you would perform the opening ceremony and drink the first cup of tea. I said I thought you certainly would. Such *éclat* for her if you went in your robes! I don't suppose there would be a muffin left in the place.'

Lucia's brow clouded, but it made her happy to be on Mayoral subjects again.

'Georgie, I wish you hadn't encouraged her to hope that I would,' she said. 'I should be delighted to give Diva such a magnificent send-off as that, but I must be very careful. Supposing next day somebody opens a new boot-shop I shall have made a precedent and shall have to wear the first pair of shoes. Or a hat-shop. If I open one, I must open all, for I will not show any sort of favouritism. I will gladly, ever so gladly, go and drink the first cup of tea at Diva's, as Mrs Pillson, but not officially. I must be officially incognita.'

'She'll be disappointed,' said Georgie.

'Poor Diva, I fear so. As for robes, quite impossible. The Mayor never appears in robes except when attended by the whole Corporation. I can hardly request my Aldermen and Councillors to have tea with Diva in state. Of course it's most enterprising of her, but I can't believe her little tea-room will resemble the gold mine she anticipates.'

'I don't think she's doing it just to make money,' said Georgie, 'though, of course she wouldn't mind that.'

'What then? Think of the expense of cups and saucers and tables and teaspoons. The trouble, too. She told me she meant to serve the teas herself.'

'It's just that she'll enjoy so much,' said Georgie, 'popping in and out and talking to her customers. She's got a raving passion for talking to anybody, and she finds it such silent work living alone. She'll have constant conversation if her tea-room catches on.'

'Well, you may be right,' said Lucia. 'Oh, and there's another thing. My Mayoral banquet. I lay awake half last night – perhaps not quite so much – thinking about it, and I don't see how you can come to it.'

'That's sickening,' said Georgie. 'Why not?'

'It's very difficult. If I ask you, it will certainly set a precedent –'

'You think too much about precedents,' interrupted Georgie. 'Nobody will care.'

'But listen. The banquet is entirely official. I shall ask the Mayors of neighbouring boroughs, the Bishop, the Lord Lieutenant, the Vicar, who is my Chaplain, my Aldermen and Councillors, and Justices of the Peace. You, dear, have no official position. We are, so to speak, like Queen Victoria and the Prince Consort.'

'You said that before,' said Georgie, 'and I looked it up. When she opened Parliament he drove with her to Westminster and sat beside her on a throne. A throne –'

'I wonder if that is so. Some of those lives of the Queen are very inaccurate. At that rate, the wife of the Lord Chancellor ought to sit on a corner of the Woolsack. Besides, where are you to be placed? You can't sit next me. The Lord Lieutenant must be on my right and the Bishop on my left –'

'If they come,' observed Georgie.

'Naturally they won't sit there if they don't. After them come the Mayors, Aldermen and Councillors. You would have to sit below them all, and that would be intolerable to me.'

'I shouldn't mind where I sat,' said Georgie.

'I should love you to be there, Georgie,' she said. 'But in what capacity? It's all official, I repeat. Think of tradition.'

'But there isn't any tradition. No woman has ever been Mayor of Tilling before: you've often told me that. However, don't let us argue about it. I expect Tilling will think it very odd if I'm not there. I shall go up to London that day, and then you can tell them I've been called away.'

'That would never do,' cried Lucia. 'Tilling would think it much odder if you weren't here on my great day.'

'Having dinner alone at Mallards,' said Georgie bitterly. 'The neck of mutton you spoke of.'

He rose.

'Time for my bath,' he said. 'And I shan't talk about it or think about it any more. I leave it to you.'

Georgie went upstairs, feeling much vexed. He undressed and put on his blue silk dressing-gown, and peppered his bath with a liberal allowance of verbena salts. He submerged himself in the fragrant liquid, and concentrated his mind on the subject he had resolved not to think about any more. Just now Lucia seemed able to apply her mind to nothing except herself and the duties or dignities of her coming office.

'"Egalo-megalo-mayoralo-mania", I call it,' Georgie said to himself in a withering whisper. 'Catherine the Great! Delirium! She thinks the whole town is as wildly excited about her being Mayor as she is herself. Whereas it's a matter of supreme indifference to them . . . All except Elizabeth, who trembles with rage and jealousy whenever she sees Lucia . . . But she always did that . . . Bother! I've dropped my soap and it slips away like an eel . . . All very tarsome. Lucia can't talk about anything else . . . Breakfast, lunch, tea and dinner, there's nothing but that . . . Mayoral complex . . . It's a crashing bore, that's What it is . . . Everlastingly reminding me that I've no official position . . . Hullo, who's that? No, you can't come in, whoever you are.'

A volley of raps had sounded at the door of the bathroom. Then Lucia's voice:

'No, I don't want to come in,' she said. 'But, eureka, Georgie. *Ho trovato: ho ben trovato!*'

'What have you found?' called Georgie, sitting up in his bath.

'It. Me. My banquet. You and my banquet. I'll tell you at dinner. Be quick.'

'Probably she'll let me hand the cheese,' thought Georgie, still feeling morose. 'I'm in no hurry to hear that.'

He padded back to his bedroom in his dressing-gown and green morocco slippers. A parcel had arrived for him while he was at his bath, and Foljambe, the parlourmaid valet had put it on his pink bed-quilt.

'It must be my new dinner-suit,' he said to himself. 'And with all this worry I'd quite forgotten about it.'

He cut the string and there it was: jacket and waistcoat and trousers of ruby-coloured velvet, with synthetic-onyx buttons, quite superb. It was Lucia's birthday-present to him; he was to order just what dinner-suit he liked, and the bill was to be sent to her. She knew nothing more, except that he had told her that it would be something quite out of the common and that Tilling would be astonished. He was thrilled with its audacious beauty.

'Now let me think,' he meditated. 'One of my pleated shirts, and a black butterfly tie, and my garnet solitaire. And my pink vest. Nobody will see it, but I shall know it's there. And red socks. Or daren't I?'

He swiftly invested himself in this striking creation. It fitted beautifully in front, and he rang the bell for Foljambe to see if it was equally satisfactory behind. Her masterful knock sounded on the door, and he said come in.

Foljambe gave a shrill ejaculation.

'Lor!' she said. 'Something fancy-dress, sir?'

'Not at all,' said Georgie. 'My new evening suit. Isn't it smart, Foljambe? Does it fit all right at the back?'

'Seems to,' said Foljambe, pulling his sleeve. 'Stand a bit straighter, sir. Yes, quite a good fit. Nearly gave me one.'

'Don't you like it?' asked Georgie anxiously.

'Well, a bit of a shock, sir. I hope you won't spill things on it, for it would be a rare job to get anything sticky out of the velvet, and you do throw your food about sometimes. But it is pretty now I begin to take it in.'

Georgie went into his sitting-room next door, where there was a big mirror over the fireplace, and turned on all the electric lights. He got up on a chair, so that he could get a more comprehensive view of himself, and revolved slowly in the brilliant light. He was so absorbed in his Narcissism that he did not hear Lucia come out of her bedroom. The door was ajar, and she peeped in. She gave a strangled scream at the sight of a large man in a glaring red suit standing on a chair with his back to her. It was unusual. Georgie whisked round at her cry.

'Look!' he said. 'Your delicious present. There it was when I came from my bath. Isn't it lovely?'

Lucia recovered from her shock.

'Positively Venetian, Georgie,' she said. 'Real Titian.'

'I think it's adorable,' said Georgie, getting down. 'Won't Tilling be excited? Thank you a thousand times.'

'And a thousand congratulations, Georgino,' she said. 'Oh, and my discovery! I am a genius, dear. There'll be a high table across the room at my banquet with two tables joining it at the corners going down the room. Me, of course, in the centre of the high table. We shall sit only on one side of these tables. And you can sit all by yourself exactly opposite me. Facing me. No official position, neither above or below the others. Just the Mayor's husband close to her materially, but officially in the air, so to speak.'

From below came the merry sound of little bells that announced dinner. Grosvenor, the other parlourmaid, was playing quite a sweet tune on them to-night, which showed she was pleased with life. When she was cross she made a snappy jangled discord.

'That solves everything!' said Georgie. 'Brilliant. How clever of you! I *did* feel a little hurt at the thought of not being there. Listen: Grosvenor's happy, too. We're all pleased.'

He offered her his beautiful velvet arm, and they went downstairs.

'And my garnet solitaire,' he said. 'Doesn't it go well with my clothes? I must tuck my napkin in securely. It would be frightful if I spilt anything. I am glad about the banquet.'

'So am I, dear. It would have been horrid not to have had you there. But I had to reconcile the feelings of private life with the etiquette of public life. We must expect problems of the sort to arise while I'm Mayor –'

'Such good fish,' said Georgie, trying to divert her from the eternal subject.

Quite useless.

'Excellent, isn't it,' said Lucia. 'In the time of Queen Elizabeth, Georgie, the Mayor of Tilling was charged with supplying fish for the Court. A train of pack-mules was despatched to

London twice a week. What a wonderful thing if I could get that custom restored! Such an impetus to the fishermen here.'

'The Court must have been rather partial to putrid fish,' said Georgie. 'I shouldn't care to eat a whiting that had been carried on a mule to London in hot weather, or in cold, for that matter.'

'Ah, I should not mean to go back to the mules,' said Lucia, 'though how picturesque to see them loaded at the river bank, and starting on their Royal errand. One would use the railway. I wonder if it could be managed. The Royal Fish Express.'

'Do you propose a special train full of soles and lobsters twice a week for Buckingham Palace or Royal Lodge?' he asked.

'A refrigerating van would be sufficient. I dare say if I searched in the archives I should find that Tilling had the monopoly of supplying the Royal table, and that the right has never been revoked. If so, I should think a petition to the King: 'Your Majesty's loyal subjects of Tilling humbly pray that this privilege be restored to them.' Or perhaps some preliminary inquiries from the Directors of the Southern Railway first. Such prestige. And a steady demand would be a wonderful thing for the fishing industry.'

'It's got enough demand already,' said Georgie. 'There isn't too much fish for us here as it is.'

'Georgie! Where's your political economy? Demand invariably leads to supply. There would be more fishing-smacks built, more men would follow the sea. Unemployment would diminish. Think of Yarmouth and its immense trade. How I should like to capture some of it for our Tilling! I mustn't lose sight of that among all the schemes I ponder over so constantly . . . But I've had a busy day: let us relax a little and make music in the garden-room.'

She rose, and her voice assumed a careless lightness. 'I saw to-day,' she said, 'in one of my old bound-up volumes of duets, an arrangement for four hands of Glazonov's "Bacchanal". It looked rather attractive. We might run through it.'

Georgie had seen it, too, a week ago, and though most of Lucia's music was familiar, he felt sure they had never tried this. He had had a bad cold in the head, and, not being up to their usual walk for a day or two, he had played over the bass part several times while Lucia was out taking her exercise: some day it might come in useful. Then this very afternoon, busy in the garden, he had heard a long-continued soft-pedalled tinkle, and rightly conjectured that Lucia was stealing a march on him in the treble part . . . Out they went to the garden-room, and Lucia found the 'Bacchanal'. His new suit made him feel very kindly disposed.

'You must take the treble, then,' he said. 'I could never read that.'

'How lazy of you, dear,' she said, instantly sitting down. 'Well, I'll try if you insist, but you mustn't scold me if I make a mess of it.'

It went beautifully. Odd trains of thought coursed through the heads of both. 'Why is she such a hypocrite?' he wondered. 'She was practising it half the afternoon.' . . . Simultaneously Lucia was saying to herself, 'Georgie can't be reading it. He must have tried it before.' At the end were mutual congratulations: each thought that the other had read it wonderfully well. Then bedtime. She kissed her hand to him as she closed her bedroom door, and Georgie made a few revolutions in front of his mirror before divesting himself of the new suit. By a touching transference of emotions, Lucia had vivid dreams of heaving seas of ruby-coloured velvet, and Georgie of the new Cunard liner, *Queen Mary*, running aground in the river on a monstrous shoal of whiting and lobsters.

There was an early autumnal frost in the night, though not severe enough to blacken the superb dahlias in Lucia's garden and soon melting. The lawn was covered with pearly moisture when she and Georgie met at breakfast, and the red roofs of Tilling gleamed bright in the morning sun. Lucia had already engaged a shorthand and typewriting secretary to get used to her duties before the heavy Mayoral correspondence began to pour in, but to-day the post brought nothing but a few circulars at once committed to the waste-paper basket. But it would not do to leave Mrs Simpson completely idle, so, before setting out for the morning marketing, Lucia dictated invitations to Mrs Bartlett and the Padre, to Susan and Mr Wyse, to Elizabeth Mapp-Flint and Major Benjy for dinner and bridge the following night. She would write in the invocations and signatures when she returned, and she apologized in each letter for the stress of work which had prevented her from writing with her own hand throughout.

'Georgie, I shall have to learn typing myself,' she said as they started. 'I can easily imagine some municipal crisis which would swamp Mrs Simpson, quick worker though she is. Or isn't there a machine called the dictaphone? . . . How deliciously warm the sun is! When we get back I shall make a watercolour sketch of my dahlias in the *giardino segreto*. Any night might see them blackened, and I should deplore not having a record of them. *Ecco*, there's Irene beckoning to us from her window. Something about the fresco, I expect.'

Irene Coles bounced out into the street.

'Lucia, beloved one,' she cried. 'It's too cruel! That lousy Town Surveying Department refuses to sanction my fresco-design of Venus rising from the sea. Come into my studio and look at my sketch of it, which they have sent back to me. Goths and Vandals and Mrs Grundys to a man and woman!'

The sketch was very striking. A nude, well-nourished, putty-coloured female, mottled with green shadows, was balanced on an oyster-shell, while a prize-fighter, representing the wind and sprawling across the sky, propelled her with puffed cheeks up a river towards a red-roofed town on the shore which presented Tilling with Pre-Raphaelite fidelity.

'Dear me! Quite Botticellian!' said Lucia.

'What?' screamed Irene. 'Darling, how can you compare my great deep-bosomed Venus, fit to be the mother of heroes, with Botticelli's anaemic flapper? What'll the next generation in Tilling be like when my Venus gets ashore?'

'Yes. Quite. So vigorous! So allegorical!' said Lucia. 'But, dear Irene, do you want everybody to be reminded of that whenever they go up and down the street?'

'Why not? What can be nobler than Motherhood?' asked Irene.

'Nothing! Nothing!' Lucia assured her. 'For a maternity home –'

Irene picked up her sketch and tore it across.

'I know what I shall do,' she said. 'I shall turn my wondrous Hellenic goddess into a Victorian mother. I shall dress her in a tartan shawl and skirt and a bonnet with a bow underneath her chin and button-boots and a parasol. I shall give my lusty South Wind a frock-coat and trousers and a top-hat, and send the design back to that foul-minded Department asking if I have now removed all objectionable features. Georgie, when next you come to see me, you won't need to blush.'

'I haven't blushed once!' said Georgie indignantly. 'How can you tell such fibs?'

'Dear Irene is so full of vitality,' said Lucia as they regained the street. 'Such ozone! She always makes me feel as if I was out in a high wind, and I wonder if my hair is coming down. But so easily managed with a little tact – Ah! There's Diva at her window. We might pop in on her for a minute, and I'll break it to her about a state-opening for her tea-rooms ... Take care, Georgie! There's Susan's Royce plunging down on us.'

Mrs Wyse's huge car, turning into the High Street, drew up directly between them and Diva's house. She let down the window and put her large round face where the window had been. As usual, she had on her ponderous fur coat, but on her head was a quite new hat, to the side of which, like a cockade, was attached a trophy of bright blue, green and yellow plumage, evidently the wings, tail and breast of a small bird.

'Can I give you a lift, dear?' she said in a mournful voice. 'I'm going shopping in the High Street. You, too, of course, Mr Georgie, if you don't mind sitting in front.'

'Many thanks, dear Susan,' said Lucia, 'but hardly worth while, as we are in the High Street already.'

Susan nodded sadly to them, put up the window, and signalled to her chauffeur to proceed. Ten yards brought her to the grocer's, and the car stopped again.

'Georgie, it was the remains of the budgerigar tacked to her hat,' said Lucia in a thrilled whisper as they crossed the street. 'Yes, Diva: we'll pop in for a minute.'

'Wearing it,' said Diva in her telegraphic manner as she opened the front door to them. 'In her hat.'

'Then is it true, Diva?' asked Lucia. 'Did she sit down on her budgerigar?'

'Definitely, I was having tea with her. Cage open. Budgerigar flitting about the room. A messy bird. Then Susan suddenly said "Tweet, tweet. Where's my Blue Birdie?" Not a sign of it. "It'll be all right," said Susan. "In the piano or somewhere." So we finished tea. Susan got up and there was Blue Birdie. Dead and as flat as a pancake. We came away at once.'

'Very tactful,' said Georgie. 'But the head wasn't on her hat, I'm pretty sure.'

'Having it stuffed, I expect. To be added later between the wings. And what about those new clothes, Mr Georgie?'

'How on earth did you hear that?' said Georgie in great astonishment. How news travelled in Tilling! Only last night, dining at home, he had worn the ruby-coloured velvet for the first time, and now, quite early next morning, Diva had heard about it. Really things were known in Tilling almost before they happened.

'My Janet was posting a letter, ten p.m.,' said Diva. 'Foljambe was posting a letter. They chatted. And are they really red?'

'You'll see before long,' said Georgie, pleased to know that interest in his suit was blazing already. 'Just wait and see.'

All this conversation had taken place on Diva's doorstep.

'Come in for a minute,' she said. 'I want to consult you about my parlour, when I make it into a tea-room. Shall take away those two big tables, and put in six little ones, for four at each. Then there's the small room at the back full of things I could never quite throw away. Bird-cages. Broken coal-scuttles. Old towel-horses. I shall clear them out now, as there's no rummage-sale coming on. Put that big cupboard there against the wall, and a couple of card-tables. People might like a rubber after their tea if it's raining. Me always ready to make a fourth if wanted. Won't that be cosy?'

'Very cosy indeed,' said Lucia. 'But may you provide facilities for gambling in a public place, without risking a police-raid?'

'Don't see why not,' said Diva. 'I may provide chess or draughts, and what's to prevent people gambling at them? Why not cards? And you will come in your robes, won't you, on Mayoring day, to inaugurate my tea-rooms?'

'My dear, quite impossible,' said Lucia firmly. 'As I told Georgie, I should have to be attended by my Aldermen and Councillors, as if it was some great public occasion. But I'll come as Mrs Pillson, and everyone will say that the Mayor performed the opening ceremony. But, officially, I must be incognita.'

'Well, that's something,' said Diva. 'And may I put up some posters to say that Mrs Pillson will open it?'

'There can be no possible objection to that,' said Lucia with alacrity. 'That will not invalidate my incognita. Just some big lettering at the top "Ye Olde Tea-House", and, if you think my name will help, big letters again for "Mrs Pillson" or "Mrs Pillson of Mallards". Quite. Any other news? I know that your Paddy hasn't got mange.'

'Nothing, I think. Oh yes, Elizabeth was in here just now, and asked me who was to be your Mayoress?'

'My Mayoress?' asked Lucia. 'Aren't I both?'

'I'm sure I don't know,' said Diva. 'But she says she's sure all Mayors have Mayoresses.'

'Poor Elizabeth: she always gets things muddled. Oh, Diva, will you – No nothing: I'm muddled, too. Good-bye, dear. All too cosy for words. A month to-day, then, for the opening. Georgie, remind me to put that down.'

Lucia and her husband passed on up the street.

'Such an escape!' she said. 'I was on the point of asking Diva to dine and play bridge to-morrow, quite forgetting that I'd asked the Bartletts and the Wyses and the Mapp-Flints. You know, our custom of always asking husbands and wives together is rather Victorian. It dates us. I shall make innovations when the first terrific weeks of office are over. If we always ask couples, single people like Diva get left out.'

'So shall I if the others do it, too,' remarked Georgie. 'Look, we've nearly caught up Susan. She's going into the post-office.'

As Susan, a few yards ahead, stepped ponderously out of the Royce, her head brushed against the side of the door, and a wing from the cockade of bright feathers, insecurely fastened, fluttered down on to the pavement. She did not perceive her loss, and went into the office. Georgie picked up the plume.

'Better put it back on the seat inside,' whispered Lucia. 'Not tactful to give it her in public. She'll see it when she gets in.'

'She may sit down on it again,' whispered Georgie. 'Oh, the far seat: that'll do. She can't miss it.'

He placed it carefully in the car, and they walked on.

'It's always a joy to devise those little unseen kindnesses,' said Lucia. 'Poulterer's first, Georgie. If all my guests accept for to-morrow, I had better bespeak two brace of partridges.'

'Delicious,' said Georgie, 'but how about the plain living? Oh I see: that'll be after you become Mayor . . . Good morning, Padre.'

The Reverend Kenneth Bartlett stepped out of a shop in front. He always talked a mixture of faulty Scots and spurious Elizabethan English. It had been a playful diversion at first, but now it had become a habit, and unless carried away by the conversation he seldom spoke the current tongue.

'Guid morrow, richt worshipful leddy,' he said. 'Well met, indeed, for there's a sair curiosity abroad, and 'tis you who can still it. Who's the happy wumman whom ye'll hae for your Mayoress?'

'That's the second time I've been asked that this morning,' said Lucia. 'I've had no official information that I must have one.'

'A'weel. It's early days yet. A month still before you need her. But ye mun have one: Mayor and Mayoress, 'tis the law o' the land. I was thinking –'

He dropped his voice to a whisper.

'There's that helpmate of mine,' he said. 'Not that there's been any colloquy betune us. She just passed the remark this morning: "I wonder who Mistress Pillson will select for her Mayoress," and I said I dinna ken and left it there.'

'Very wise,' said Lucia encouragingly.

The Padre's language grew almost anglicized.

'But it put an idea into my head, that my Evie might be willing to help you in any way she could. She'd keep you in touch with all Church matters which I know you have at heart, and Sunday Schools and all that. Mind. I don't promise that she'd consent, but I think 'tis likely, though I wouldn't encourage false hopes. All confidential, of course; and I must be stepping.'

He looked furtively round as if engaged in some dark conspiracy and stepped.

'Georgie, I wonder if there can be any truth in it,' said Lucia. 'Of course, nothing would induce me to have poor dear little Evie as Mayoress. I would as soon have a mouse. Oh, there's Major Benjy: he'll be asking me next who my Mayoress is to be. Quick, into the poulterer's.'

They hurried into the shop. Mr Rice gave her a low bow.

'Good morning, Your Worship –' he began.

'No, not yet, Mr Rice,' said Lucia. 'Not for a month yet. Partridges. I shall very likely want two brace of partridges tomorrow evening.'

'I've got some prime young birds, Your Worsh – ma'am,' said Mr Rice.

'Very well. Please earmark four birds for me. I will let you know the first thing to-morrow morning, if I require them.'

'Earmarked they are, ma'am,' said Mr Rice enthusiastically.

Lucia peeped cautiously out. Major Benjy had evidently seen them taking cover, and was regarding electric heaters in the shop next door with an absent eye. He saw her look out and made a military salute.

'Good morning,' he said cordially. 'Lovely day isn't it? October's my favourite month. Chill October, what? I was wondering, Mrs Pillson, as I strolled along, if you had yet selected the fortunate lady who will have the honour of being your Mayoress.'

'Good morning, Major. Oddly enough somebody else asked me that very thing a moment ago.'

'Ha! I bet five to one I know who that was. I had a word or

two with the Padre just now, and the subject came on the *tapis*, as they say in France. I fancy he's got some notion that that good little wife of his – but that would be too ridiculous –'

'I've settled nothing yet,' said Lucia. 'So overwhelmed with work lately. Certainly it shall receive my attention. Elizabeth quite well? That's good.'

She hurried away with Georgie.

'The question of the Mayoress is in the air like influenza, Georgie,' she said. 'I must ring up the Town Hall as soon as I get in, and find out if I must have one. I see no necessity. There's Susan Wyse beckoning again.'

Susan let down the window of her car.

'Just going home again,' she said. 'Shall I give you a lift up the hill?'

'No, a thousand thanks,' said Lucia. 'It's only a hundred yards.'

Susan shook her head sadly.

'Don't overdo it, dear,' she said. 'As we get on in life we must be careful about hills.'

'This Mayoress business is worrying me, Georgie,' said Lucia when Susan had driven off. 'If it's all too true, and I must have one, who on earth shall I get? Everyone I can think of seems so totally unfit for it. I believe, do you know, that it must have been in Major Benjy's mind to recommend me to ask Elizabeth.'

'Impossible!' said Georgie. 'I might as well recommend you to ask Foljambe.'

2

Lucia found on her return to Mallards that Mrs Simpson had got through the laborious task of typing three identical dinner-invitations for next day to Mrs Wyse, Mrs Bartlett and Mrs Mapp-Flint with husbands. She filled up in autograph 'Dearest Susan, Evie and Elizabeth' and was affectionately theirs. Rack her brains as she would she could think of no further task for her secretary, so Mrs Simpson took these letters to deliver them by hand, thus saving time and postage. 'And could you be here at nine-thirty to-morrow morning,' said Lucia, 'instead of ten in case there is a stress of work? Things turn up so suddenly, and it would never do to fall into arrears.'

Lucia looked at her engagement-book. Its fair white pages satisfied her that there were none at present.

'I shall be glad of a few days' quiet, dear,' she said to Georgie. 'I shall have a holiday of painting and music and reading. When once the rush begins there will be little time for such pursuits. Yet I know there was something very urgent that required my attention. Ah, yes! I must find out for certain whether I must have a Mayoress. And I must get a telephone-extension into the garden-room, to save running in and out of the house for calls.'

Lucia went in and rang up the clerk at the Town Hall. Yes: he was quite sure that every Mayor had a Mayoress, whom the Mayor invited to fill the post. She turned to Georgie with a corrugated brow.

'Yes, it is so,' she said. 'I shall have to find some capable obliging woman with whom I can work harmoniously. But who?'

The metallic clang of the flap of the letter-box on the front door caused her to look out of the window. There was Diva going quickly away with her scudding, bird-like walk. Lucia

opened the note she had left, and read it. Though Diva was
telegraphic in conversation, her epistolary style was flowing.

Dearest Lucia,

I felt quite shy of speaking to you about it to-day, for
writing is always the best, don't you think, when it's difficult to find the right words or to get them out when you
have, so this is to tell you that I am quite at your disposal,
and shall to find the right words or to get them out when
you have, so much longer in Tilling than you, dear, that
perhaps I can be of some use in all your entertainments and
other functions. Not that I would ask you to choose me as
your Mayoress, for I shouldn't think of such a thing. So
pushing! So I just want to say that I am quite at your
service, as you may feel rather diffident about asking me,
for it would be awkward for me to refuse, being such an old
friend, if I didn't feel like it. But I should positively enjoy
helping you, quite apart from my duty as a friend.

Ever yours,
Diva

'Poor dear, ridiculous little Diva!' said Lucia, handing
Georgie this artless epistle. 'So ambitious and so pathetic! And
now I shall hurry off to begin my sketch of the dahlias. I will
not be interrupted by any further public business this morning.
I must have a little time to myself – What's that?'

Again the metallic clang from the letter-box, and Lucia,
consumed with curiosity, again peeped out from a corner of
the window and saw Mr Wyse with his malacca cane and his
Panama hat and his black velveteen coat, walking briskly away.

'Just an answer to my invitation for to-morrow, I expect,'
she said. 'Susan probably doesn't feel up to writing after the
loss of her budgerigar. She had a sodden and battered look this
morning, didn't you think, like a cardboard box that has been
out in the rain. Flaccid. No resilience.'

Lucia had taken Mr Wyse's letter from the post-box, as she
made these tonic remarks. She glanced through it, her mouth
falling wider and wider open.

'Listen, Georgie!' she said:

Dear and Worshipful Mayor-Elect,

It has reached my ears (Dame Rumour) that during the coming year, when you have so self-sacrificingly consented to fill the highest office which our dear little Tilling can bestow, thereby honouring itself so far more than you, you will need some partner to assist you in your arduous duties. From little unconscious signs, little involuntary self-betrayals that I have observed in my dear Susan, I think I may encourage you to hope that she *might* be persuaded to honour herself and you by accepting the onerous post which I hear is yet unfilled. I have not had any word with her on the subject. Nor is she aware that I am writing to you. As you know, she has sustained a severe bereavement in the sudden death of her little winged companion. But I have ventured to say to her, '*Carissima sposa*, you must buck up. You must not let a dead bird, however dear, stand between you and the duties and opportunities of life which may present themselves to you.' And she answered (whether she guessed the purport of my exhortation, I cannot say), 'I will make an effort, Algernon.' I augur favourably from that.

Of the distinction which renders her so suitable for the post of Mayoress I need not speak, for you know her character so well. I might remind you, however, that our late beloved Sovereign himself bestowed on her the insignia of the Order of Member of the British Empire, and that she would therefore bring to her new office a *cachet* unshared by any of the otherwise estimable ladies of Tilling. And in this distressing estrangement which now exists between the kingdoms of England and Italy, the fact that my dear Susan is sister-in-law to my dear sister Amelia, Contessa di Faraglione, might help to heal the differences between the countries. In conclusion, dear lady, I do not think you could do better than to offer my Susan the post for which her distinction and abilities so eminently fit her, and you may be sure that I shall use my influence with her to get her to accept it.

A rivederci, illustrissima Signora, ed anche presto!

Algernon Wyse

PS: I will come round at any moment to confer with you.

PPS: I reopen this to add that Susan has just received your amiable invitation for to-morrow, which we shall both be honoured to accept.

Lucia and Georgie looked at each other in silence at the end of the reading of this elegant epistle.

'Beautifully expressed, I must allow,' she said. 'Oh, Georgie, it is a frightful responsibility to have patronage of this crucial kind in one's gift! It is mine to confer not only an honour but an influence for good of a most far-reaching sort. A line from me and Susan is my Mayoress. But good Susan has not the energy, the decision which I should look for. I could not rely on her judgment.'

'She put Algernon up to writing that lovely letter,' said Georgie. 'How they're all struggling to be Mayoress!'

'I am not surprised, dear, at that,' said Lucia, with dignity. 'No doubt also Evie got the Padre to recommend her –'

'And Diva recommended herself,' remarked Georgie, 'as she hadn't got anyone to do it for her.'

'And Major Benjy was certainly going to say a word for Elizabeth, if I hadn't cut him short,' said Lucia. 'I find it all rather ugly, though, poor things, I sympathize with their ambitions which in themselves are noble. I shall have to draft two very tactful letters to Diva and Mr Wyse, before Mrs Simpson comes to-morrow. What a good thing I told her to come at half-past nine. But just for the present I shall dismiss it all from my mind, and seek an hour's peace with my paint-box and my *belli fiori*. What are you going to do till lunch?'

'It's my day for cleaning my bibelots,' said Georgie. 'What a rush it all is!'

Georgie went to his sitting-room and got busy. Soon he thought he heard another metallic clang from the post-box, and hurrying to the window, he saw Major Benjy walking briskly away from the door.

'That'll be another formal application, I expect,' he said to himself, and went downstairs to see, with his wash-leather in his hand. There was a letter in the post-box, but to his surprise it was addressed not to Lucia, but himself. It ran:

My Dear Pillson,

My wife has just received Her Worship's most amiable invitation that we should dine *chez vous* to-morrow. I was on the point of writing to you in any case, so she begs me to say we shall be charmed.

Now, my dear old man (if you'll permit me to call you so) I've a word to say to you. Best always, isn't it, to be frank and open. At least that's my experience in my twenty-five years of service in the King's (God bless him) army. So listen. *Re Mayoress.* It will be a tremendous asset to your wife's success in her most distinguished post, if she can get a wise and levelling character, big-minded enough to disregard the little flurries and disturbances of her office, and above all one who has tact, and would never make mischief. Some of our mutual friends − I mention no names − are only too apt to scheme and intrigue and indulge in gossip and tittle-tattle. I can only put my finger on one who is entirely free from such failings, and that is my dear Elizabeth. I can't answer for her accepting the post. It's a lot to ask of any woman, but in my private opinion, if your wife approached Elizabeth in a proper spirit, making it clear how inestimable a help she (Elizabeth) would be to her (the Mayor), I think we might hope for a favourable reply. Perhaps to-morrow evening I might have a quiet word with you.

Sincerely yours,
Benjamin Mapp-Flint (Major)

Georgie with his wash-leather hurried out to the *giardino segreto* where Lucia was drawing dahlias. He held the letter out to her, but she scarcely turned her head.

'No need to tell me, dear, that your letter is on behalf of another applicant. Elizabeth Mapp-Flint, I believe. Read it me while I go on drawing. Such exquisite shapes: we do not look at flowers closely enough.'

As Georgie read it she plied a steady pencil, but when he came to the sentence about approaching Elizabeth in a proper spirit, her hand gave a violent jerk.

'Georgie, it isn't true!' she cried. 'Show me ... Yes. My india-rubber? Ah, there it is.'

Georgie finished the letter, and Lucia, having rubbed out the random line her pencil had made, continued to draw dahlias with concentrated attention.

'Lucia, it's too ridiculous of you to pretend to be absorbed in your sketch,' he said impatiently. 'What are you going to do?'

Lucia appeared to recall herself from the realms of peace and beauty.

'Elizabeth will be my Mayoress,' she said calmly. 'Don't you see, dear, she would be infinitely more tiresome if she wasn't? As Mayoress, she will be muzzled, so to speak. Officially, she will have to perform the tasks I allot to her. She will come to heel, and that will be very good for her. Besides, who else *is* there? Diva with her tea-shop? Poor Susan? Little mouse-like Evie Bartlett?'

'But can you see yourself approaching Elizabeth in a proper spirit?' he asked.

Lucia gave a gay trill of laughter.

'Certainly I cannot. I shall wait for her to approach me. She will have to come and implore me. I shall do nothing till then.'

Georgie pondered on this extraordinary decision.

'I think you're being very rash,' he said. 'And you and Elizabeth hate each other like poison –'

'Emphatically no,' said Lucia. 'I have had occasion sometimes to take her down a peg or two. I have sometimes felt it necessary to thwart her. But hate? Never. Dismiss that from your mind. And don't be afraid that I shall approach her in any spirit at all.'

'But what am I to say to Benjy when he asks me for a few private words to-morrow night?'

Lucia laughed again.

'My dear, they'll all ask you for a few private words to-morrow night. There's the Padre running poor little Evie.

There's Mr Wyse running Susan. They'll all want to know whom I'm likely to choose, and to secure your influence with me. Be like Mr Baldwin and say your lips are sealed, or like some other Prime Minister, wasn't it? who said "Wait and see." Counting Diva, there are four applicants now – remind me to tell Mrs Simpson to enter them all – and I think the list may be considered closed. Leave it to me; be discreet . . . And the more I think of it, the more clearly I perceive that Elizabeth Mapp-Flint must be my Mayoress. It is far better to have her on a lead, bound to me by ties of gratitude than skulking about like a pariah dog, snapping at me. True, she may not be capable of gratitude, but I always prefer to look for the best in people, like Mr Somerset Maugham in his delightful stories.'

Mrs Simpson arriving at half-past nine next morning had to wait a considerable time for Lucia's tactful letters to Diva and Mr Wyse; she and Georgie sat long after breakfast scribbling and erasing on half-sheets and envelopes turned inside out till they got thoroughly tactful drafts. Lucia did not want to tell Diva point-blank that she could not dream of asking her to be Mayoress, but she did not want to raise false hopes. All she could do was to thank her warmly for her offers of help ('So like you, dear Diva!') and to assure her that she would not hesitate to take advantage of them should occasion arise. To Mr Wyse she said that no one had a keener appreciation of Susan's great gifts (so rightly recognized by the King) than she; no one more deplored the unhappy international relations between England and Italy . . . Georgie briefly acknowledged Major Benjy's letter and said he had communicated its contents to his wife, who was greatly touched. Lucia thought that these letters had better not reach their recipients till after her party, and Mrs Simpson posted them later in the day.

Lucia was quite right about the husbands of expectant Mayoresses wanting a private word with Georgie that evening. Major Benjy and Elizabeth arrived first, a full ten minutes before dinner-time and explained to Foljambe that their clocks were fast, while Georgie in his new red velvet suit was putting the menu cards which Mrs Simpson had typed on the dinner-table. He incautiously put his head out of the dining-room door, while this explanation was going on, and Benjy spied him.

'Ha, a word with you, my dear old man,' he exclaimed, and joined Georgie, while Elizabeth was taken to the garden-room to wait for Lucia.

''Pon my soul, amazingly stupid of us to have come so early,' he said, closing the dining-room door behind him. 'I told Liz we should be too early – ah, our clocks were fast. Don't let me interrupt you; charming flowers, and, dear me, what a handsome suit. Just the colour of my wife's dress. However, that's neither here nor there. What I should like to urge on you is to persuade your wife to take advantage of Elizabeth's willingness to become Mayoress, for the good of the town. She's willing, I gather, to sacrifice her time and her leisure for that. Mrs Pillson and Mrs Mapp-Flint would be an alliance indeed. But Elizabeth feels that her offer can't remain open indefinitely, and she rather expected to have heard from your wife to-day.'

'But didn't you tell me, Major,' asked Georgie, 'that your wife knew nothing about your letter to me? I understood that it was only your opinion that if properly approached –'

There was a tap at the door, and Mr Wyse entered. He was dressed in a brand new suit, never before seen in Tilling, of sapphire blue velvet, with a soft pleated shirt, a sapphire solitaire and bright blue socks. The two looked like two middle-aged male mannequins.

Mr Wyse began bowing.

'Mr Georgie!' he said. 'Major Benjy! The noise of voices. It occurred to me that perhaps we men were assembling here according to that pretty Italian custom, for a glass of vermouth, so my wife went straight out to the garden-room. I am afraid we are some minutes early. The Royce makes nothing of the steep hill from Starling Cottage.'

Georgie was disappointed at the ruby velvet not being the only sartorial sensation of the evening, but he took it very well.

'Good evening,' he said. 'Well, I do call that a lovely suit. I was just finishing the flowers, when Major Benjy popped in. Let us go out to the garden-room, where we shall find some sherry.'

Once again the door opened.

'Eh, here be all the laddies,' said the Padre. 'Mr Wyse; a handsome costume, sir. Just the colour of the dress wee wifie's donned for this evening. She's ganged awa' to the garden-room. I wanted a bit word wi' ye, Mr Pillson, and your parlourmaid told me you were here.'

'I'm afraid we must go out now to the garden-room, Padre,' said Georgie, rather fussed. 'They'll all be waiting for us.'

It was difficult to get them to move, for each of the men stood aside to let the others pass, and thus secure a word with Georgie. Eventually the Church unwillingly headed the procession, followed by the Army, lured by the thought of sherry, and Mr Wyse deftly closed the dining-room door again and stood in front of it.

'A word, Mr Georgie,' he said. 'I had the honour yesterday to write a note to your wife about a private matter – not private from you, of course – and I wondered whether she had spoken to you about it. I have since ascertained from my dear Susan –'

The door opened again, and bumped against his heels and the back of his head with a dull thud. Foljambe's face looked in.

'Beg your pardon, sir,' she said. 'Thought I heard you go.'

'We must follow the others,' said Georgie. 'Lucia will wonder what's happened to us.'

The wives looked inquiringly into the faces of their husbands as they filed into the garden-room to see if there was any news. Georgie shook hands with the women and Lucia with the men. He saw how well his suit matched Elizabeth's gown, and Mr Wyse's might have been cut from the same piece as that of the Padre's wife. Another brilliant point of colour was furnished by Susan Wyse's budgerigar. The wing that had been flipped off yesterday had been re-stitched, and the head, as Diva had predicted, had been stuffed and completed the bird. She wore this notable decoration as a centrepiece on her ample bosom. Would it be tactful, wondered Georgie, to admire it, or would it be tearing open old wounds again? But surely when Susan displayed her wound so conspicuously, she would be disappointed if he appeared not to see it. He gave her a glass of sherry and moved aside with her.

'Perfectly charming, Mrs Wyse,' he said, looking pointedly at it. ' Lovely! Most successful!'

He had done right; Susan's great watery smile spread across her face.

'So glad you like it,' she said, 'and since I've worn it, Mr Georgie, I've felt comforted for Blue Birdie. He seems to be with me still. A very strong impression. Quite psychical.'

'Very interesting and touching,' said Georgie sympathetically.

'Is it not? I am hoping to get into rapport with him again. His pretty sweet ways! And may I congratulate you, too? Such a lovely suit!'

'Lucia's present to me,' said Georgie, 'though I chose it.'

'What a coincidence!' said Susan. 'Algernon's new suit is my present to him and he chose it. There are brain-waves everywhere, Mr Georgie, beyond the farthest stars.'

Foljambe announced dinner. Never before had conversation, even at Lucia's table, maintained so serious and solid a tone. The ladies in particular, though the word Mayoress was never mentioned, vied with each other in weighty observations bearing on municipal matters, in order to show the deep interest they took in them. It was as if they even engaged on a self-imposed viva voce examination to exhibit their qualifications for the unmentioned post. They addressed their answers to Lucia and of each other they were highly critical.

'No, dear Evie,' said Elizabeth, 'I cannot share your views about girl-guides. Boy-scouts I whole-heartedly support. All that drill teaches them discipline, but the best discipline for girls is to help mother at home. Cooking, housework, lighting the fire, father's slippers. Don't you agree, dear hostess?'

'Eh, Mistress Mapp-Flint,' said the Padre, strongly upholding his wife. 'Ye havena' the tithe of my Evie's experience among the bairns of the parish. Half the ailments o' the lassies come from being kept at home without enough exercise and air and chance to fend for themselves. Easy to have too much of mother's apron-strings, and as fur father's slippers I disapprove of corporal punishment for the young of whatever sex.'

'Oh, Padre, how could you think I meant that!' exclaimed Elizabeth.

'And as for letting a child light a fire,' put in Susan, 'that's most dangerous. No match-box should ever be allowed within a child's reach. I must say too, that I wish the fire-brigade in Tilling was better organized and more efficient. If once a fire broke out here the whole town would be burned to the ground.'

'Dear Susan, is it possible you haven't heard that there was a fire in Ford Place last week? Fancy! And you're strangely in error about the brigade's efficiency, for they were there in three minutes from the time the alarm was given, and the fire was extinguished in five minutes more.'

'Lucia, what is really wanted in Tilling,' said Susan, 'is better lighting of the streets. Coming home sometimes in the evening my Royce has to crawl down Porpoise Street.'

'More powerful lamps to your car would make that all right, dear,' said Elizabeth. 'Not a very great expense. The paving of the streets, to my mind, wants the most immediate attention. I nearly fell down the other day, stepping in a great hole. The roads, too: the road opposite my house is little better than a snipe-bog. Again and again I have written to the *Hampshire Argus* about it.'

Mr Wyse bowed across the table to her.

'I regret to say I have missed seeing your letters,' he said. 'Very careless of me. Was there one last week?'

Evie emitted the mouse-like squeak which denoted intense private amusement.

'I've missed them, too,' she said. 'I expect we all have. In any case, Elizabeth, Grebe is outside the parish boundaries. Nothing to do with Tilling. It's a County Council road you will find if you look at a map. Now the overcrowding in the town itself, Lucia, is another matter which does concern us. I have it very much at heart, as anybody must have who knows anything about it. And then there are the postal deliveries. Shocking. I wrote a letter the other day –'

This was one of the subjects which Susan Wyse had specially mugged up. By leaning forward and putting an enormous elbow on the table she interposed a mountain of healthy animal tissue between Evie and Lucia, and the mouse was obliterated behind the mountain.

'And only two posts a day, Lucia,' she said. 'You will find it terribly inconvenient to get only two and the second is never anything but circulars. There's not a borough in England so ill served. I'm told that if a petition is sent to the Postmaster-General signed by fifty per cent of the population he is bound by law to give us a third delivery. Algernon and I would be only too happy to get up this petition –'

Algernon from the other side of the table suddenly interrupted her.

'Susan, take care!' he cried. 'Your budgerigar: your raspberry soufflé!'

He was too late. The budgerigar dropped into the middle of Susan's bountifully supplied plate. She took it out, dripping with hot raspberry juice and wrapped it in her napkin, moaning softly to herself. The raspberry juice stained it red, as if Blue Birdie had been sat on again, and Foljambe very tactfully handed a plate to Susan on which she deposited it. After so sad and irrelevant an incident, it was hard to get back to high topics, and the Padre started on a lower level.

'A cosy little establishment will Mistress Diva Plaistow be running presently,' he said. 'She tells me that the opening of it will be the first function of our new Mayor. A fine send-off indeed.'

A simultaneous suspicion shot through the minds of the candidates present that Diva (incredible as it seemed) might be in the running. Like vultures they swooped on the absent prey.

'A little too cosy for my tastes,' said Elizabeth. 'If all the tables she means to put into her tea-room were full, sardines in a tin wouldn't be the word. Not to mention that the occupants of two of the tables would be being kippered up the chimney, and two others in a gale every time the door was opened. And are you going to open it officially, dear Lucia?'

'Certainly not,' said Lucia. 'I told her I would drink the first cup of tea with pleasure, but as Mrs Pillson, not as Mayor.'

'Poor Diva can't *make* tea,' squeaked Evie. 'She never could. It's either hot water or pure tannin.'

'And she intends to make all the fancy pastry herself,' said Susan sorrowfully. 'Much better to stick to bread and butter and a plain cake. Very ambitious, I call it, but nowadays Diva's like that. More plans for all we know.'

'And quite a reformer,' said Elizabeth. 'She talks about a quicker train service to London. She knows a brother-in-law of one of the directors. Of course the thing is as good as done with a word from Diva. It looks terribly like paranoia coming on.'

The ladies left. Major Benjy drunk off his port in a great hurry, so as to get a full glass when it came round again.

'A very good glass of port,' he said. 'Well, I don't mind if I fill up. The longer I live with my Liz, Pillson, the more I am astonished at her masculine grasp of new ideas.'

'My Susan's remarks about an additional postal delivery and lighting of the streets showed a very keen perception of the reforms of which our town most stands in need,' said Algernon. 'Her judgment is never at fault. I have often been struck –'

The Padre, speaking to Major Benjy, raised his voice for Georgie to hear and thumped the table.

'Wee wifie's energy is unbounded,' he said. 'Often I say to her: "Spare yourself a bitty" I've said, and always she's replied "Heaven fits the back to the burden" quo' she, and if there's more work and responsibility to be undertaken, Evie's ready for it.'

'You mustn't let her overtax herself, Padre,' said Benjy with great earnestness. 'She's got her hands over full already. Not so young as she was.'

'Eh, that's what ails all the ladies of Tilling,' retorted the Padre, 'an' she'll be younger than many I could mention. An abounding vitality. If they made me Lord Archbishop tomorrow, she'd be a mother in Israel to the province, and no mistake.'

This was too much for Benjy. It would have been a gross dereliction of duty not to let loose his withering powers of satire.

'No no, Padre,' he said. 'Tilling can't spare you. Canterbury must find someone else.'

'Eh, well, and if the War Office tries to entice you away, Major, you must say no. That'll be a bargain. But the point of my observation was that my Evie is aye ready and willing for any call that may come to her. That's what I'm getting at.'

'Ha, ha, Padre; let me know when you've got it, and then I'll talk to you. Well, if the port is standing idle in front of you –'

Georgie rose. He had had enough of these unsolicited testimonials, and when Benjy became satirical it was a symptom that he should have no more port.

'I think it's time we got to our bridge,' he said. 'Lucia will scold me if I keep you here too long.'

They marched in a compact body to the garden-room, where Lucia had been keeping hopeful Mayoresses at bay with music, and two tables were instantly formed. Georgie and Elizabeth, rubies, played against the sapphires, Mr Wyse and Evie, and the other table was drab in comparison. The evening ended unusually late, and it was on the stroke of midnight when the three pairs of guests, unable to get a private word with either of their hosts, moved sadly away like a vanquished army. The Royce conveyed the Wyses to Porpoise Street, just round the corner, with Susan, faintly suggesting Salome, holding the plate with the blood-stained handkerchief containing the budgerigar; a taxi that had long been ticking conveyed the Mapp-Flints to the snipe-bog, and two pairs of galoshes took the Padre and his wife to the Vicarage.

Lucia's tactful letters were received next morning. Mr Wyse thought that all was not yet lost, though it surprised him that Lucia had not taken Susan aside last night and implored her to be Mayoress. Diva, on the other hand, with a more correct estimate of the purport of Lucia's tact, was instantly sure that all was lost, and exclaiming, 'Drat it, so that's that,' gave Lucia's note to Paddy to worry, and started out for her morning's shopping. There were plenty of absorbing interests to distract her. Susan, with the budgerigar cockade in her hat, looked out of the window of the Royce, but to Diva's amazement the colour of the bird's plumage had changed; it was flushed with red like a stormy sunset with patches of blue sky behind. Could Susan, for some psychical reason, have dyed it? . . . Georgie and Lucia were approaching from Mallards, but Diva, after that tactful note, did not want to see her friend till she had thought of something pretty sharp to say. Turning towards the High Street she bumped baskets sharply with Elizabeth.

'Morning, dear!' said Elizabeth. 'Do you feel up to a chat?'

'Yes,' said Diva. 'Come in. I'll do my shopping afterwards. Any news?'

'Benjy and I dined with Worshipful last night. Wyses, Bartletts, bridge. We all missed you.'

'Wasn't asked,' said Diva. 'A good dinner? Did you win?'

'Partridges a little tough,' said Elizabeth musingly. 'Old birds are cheaper, of course. I won a trifle, but nothing like enough to pay for our taxi. An interesting, curious evening. Rather revolting at times, but one mustn't be captious. Evie and Susan – oh, a terrible thing happened. Susan wore the bird as a breastplate, and it fell into the raspberry soufflé. Plop!'

Diva gave a sigh of relief.

'*That* explains it,' she said. 'Saw it just now and it puzzled me. Go on, Elizabeth.'

'Revolting, I was saying. Those two women. One talked about boy-scouts, and the other about posts, and then one about overcrowding and the other about the fire-brigade. I just sat and listened and blushed for them both. So cheap and obvious.'

'But what's so cheap and obvious and blush-making?' asked Diva. 'It only sounds dull to me.'

'All that fictitious interest in municipal matters. What has Susan cared hitherto for postal deliveries, or Evie for over-crowding? In a nutshell, they were trying to impress Lucia, and get her to ask them, at least one of them, to be Mayoress. And from what Benjy told me, their husbands were just as barefaced when we went into the garden-room. An evening of intrigue and self-advertisement. Pah!'

'Pah indeed!' said Diva. 'How did Lucia take it?'

'I really hardly noticed. I was too disgusted at all these underground schemings. So transparent! Poor Lucia! I trust she will get someone who will be of use to her. She'll be sadly at sea without a woman of sense and experience to consult.'

'And was Mr Georgie's dinner-costume very lovely?' asked Diva.

Elizabeth half closed her eyes as if to visualize it.

'A very pretty colour,' she said. 'Just like the gown I had dyed red not long ago, if you happen to remember it. Of course he copied it.'

The front-door bell rang. It was quicker to answer it oneself, thought Diva, than to wait for Janet to come up from the kitchen, and she trundled off.

'Come in, Evie,' she said, 'Elizabeth's here.'

But Elizabeth would not wait, and Evie, in turn, gave her own impressions of the previous evening. They were on the same lines as Elizabeth's, only it had been Elizabeth and Susan who (instead of revolting her) had been so vastly comical with their sudden interest in municipal affairs:

'And, oh, dear me,' she said, 'Mr Wyse and Major Benjy were just as bad. It was like that musical thing where you have a tune in the treble, and the same tune next in the bass. Fugue; that's it. Those four were just like a Bach concert. Kenneth and I simply sat listening. And I'm much mistaken if Lucia and Mr Georgie didn't see through them all.'

Diva had now got a complete idea of what had taken place; clearly there had been a six-part fugue.

'But she's got to choose somebody,' she said. 'Wonder who it'll be.'

'Perhaps you, he, he!' squeaked Evie for a joke.

'That it won't,' cried Diva emphatically, looking at the fragments of Lucia's tactful note scattered about the room. 'Sooner sing songs in the gutter. Fancy being at Lucia's beck and call, whenever she wants something done which she doesn't want to do herself. Not worth living at that price. No, thank you!'

'Just my fun,' said Evie. 'I didn't mean it seriously. And then there were other surprises. Mr Georgie in a red –'

'I know; the colour of Elizabeth's dyed one,' put in Diva.

'– and Mr Wyse in sapphire velvet,' continued Evie. 'Just like my second-best, which I was wearing.'

'No! I hadn't heard that,' said Diva. 'Aren't the Tilling boys getting dressy?'

The tension increased during the next week to a point almost unbearable, for Lucia, like the Pythian Oracle in unfavourable circumstances, remained dumb, waiting for Elizabeth to implore her. The strain was telling and whenever the telephone-bell rang in the houses of any of the candidates she or her husband ran to it to see if it carried news of the nomination. But, as at an inconclusive sitting of the Conclave of Cardinals for the election of the Pontiff, no announcement came from the precinct; and every evening, since the weather was growing chilly, a column of smoke curled out of the chimney of the garden-room. Was it that Lucia, like the Cardinals, could not make up her mind, or had she possibly chosen her Mayoress and had enjoined silence till she gave the word? Neither supposition seemed likely, the first, because she was so very decisive a person; the second, because it was felt that the chosen candidate could not have kept it to herself.

Then a series of curious things happened, and to the over-wrought imagination of Tilling they appeared to be of the nature of omens. The church clock struck thirteen one noon, and then stopped with a jarring sound. That surely augured ill for the chances of the Padre's wife. A spring broke out in the cliff above the Mapp-Flint's house, and, flowing through the garden, washed the asparagus-bed away. That looked like Elizabeth's hopes being washed away too. Susan Wyse's Royce collided with a van in the High Street and sustained damage to a mud-guard; that looked bad for Susan. Then Elizabeth, distraught with anxiety, suddenly felt convinced that Diva had been chosen. What made this the more probable was that Diva had so emphatically denied to Evie that she would ever be induced to accept the post. It was like poor Diva to think that anybody would believe such a monstrous statement; it only convinced Elizabeth that she was telling a thumping lie, in order to conceal something. Probably she thought she was being Bismarckian, but that was an error. Bismarck had said that to tell the truth was a useful trick for a diplomatist, because others would conclude that he was not. But he had never said that telling lies would induce others to think that he was telling the truth.

The days went on, and Georgie began to have qualms as to whether Elizabeth would ever humble herself and implore the boon.

'Time's passing,' he said, as he and Lucia sat one morning in the garden-room. 'What on earth will you do, if she doesn't?'

'She will,' said Lucia, 'though I allow she has held out longer than I expected. I did not know how strong that false pride of hers was. But she's weakening. I've been sitting in the window most of the morning – such a multiplicity of problems to think over – and she has passed the house four times since breakfast. Once she began to cross the road to the front door, but then she saw me, and walked away again. The sight of me, poor thing, must have made more vivid to her what she had to do. But she'll come to it. Let us discuss something more important. That idea of mine about reviving the fishing in-dustry. The Royal Fish Express. I made a few notes –'

Lucia glanced once more out of the window.

'Georgie,' she cried. 'There's Elizabeth approaching again. That's the fifth time. Round and round like a squirrel in its cage.'

She glided to her ambush behind the curtain, and, peeping stealthily out, became like the reporter of the University boat-race on the wireless.

'She's just opposite, level with the front door,' she announced. 'She's crossing the road. She's quickening up. She's crossed the road. She's slowing down on the front-door steps. She's raised her hand to the bell. She's dropped it again. She turned half-round – no, I don't think she saw me. Poor woman, what a tussle! Just pride. Georgie, she's rung the bell. Foljambe's opened the door; she must have been dusting the hall. Foljambe's let her in, and has shut the door. She'll be out here in a minute.'

Foljambe entered.

'Mrs Mapp-Flint, ma'am,' she said. 'I told her you were probably engaged, but she much wants to see you for a few moments on a private matter of great importance.'

Lucia sat down in a great hurry, and spread some papers on the table in front of her.

'Go into the garden, will you, Georgie,' she said, 'for she'll never be able to get it out unless we're alone. Yes, Foljambe; tell her I can spare her five minutes.'

3

Five minutes later Elizabeth again stood on the doorstep of
Mallards, uncertain whether to go home to Grebe by the
Vicarage and tell inquisitive Evie the news, or *via* Irene and
Diva. She decided on the latter route, unconscious of the vast
issues that hung on this apparently trivial choice.

On this warm October morning, quaint Irene (having no
garden) was taking the air on a pile of cushions on her doorstep.
She had a camera beside her in case of interesting figures
passing by, and was making tentative jottings in her sketch-
book for her Victorian Venus in a tartan shawl. Irene noticed
something peculiarly buoyant about Elizabeth's gait, as she
approached, and with her Venus in mind she shouted to her:

'Stand still a moment, Mapp. Stand on one leg in a poised
attitude. I want that prancing action. One arm forward if you
can manage it without tipping up.'

Elizabeth would have posed for the devil in this triumphant
mood.

'Like that, you quaint darling?' she asked.

'Perfect. Hold it for a second while I snap you first.'

Irene focused and snapped.

'Now half a mo' more,' she said, seizing her sketch-book.
'Be on the point of stepping forward again.'

Irene dashed in important lines and curves.

'That'll do,' she said. 'I've got you. I never saw you so
lissom and elastic. What's up? Have you been successfully
seducing some young lad in the autumn of your life?'

'Oh, you shocking thing,' said Elizabeth. 'Naughty! But I've
just been having such a lovely talk with our sweet Lucia. Shall
I tell you about it, or shall I tease you?'

'Whichever you like,' said Irene, putting in a little shading.
'I don't care a blow.'

'Then I'll give you a hint. Make a pretty curtsey to the Mayoress.'

'Rubbish,' said Irene.

'No, dear. Not rubbish. Gospel.'

'My God, what an imagination you have,' said Irene. 'How do you *do* it? Does it just come to you like a dream?'

'Gospel, I repeat,' said Elizabeth. 'And such joy, dear, that you should be the first to hear about it, except Mr Georgie.'

Irene looked at her and was forced to believe. Unaffected bliss beamed in Mapp's face; she wasn't pretending to be pleased, she wallowed in a bath of exuberant happiness.

'Good Lord, tell me about it,' she said. 'Bring another cushion, Lucy,' she shouted to her six-foot maid, who was leaning out of the dining-room window, greedily listening.

'Well, dear, it was an utter surprise to me,' said Elizabeth. 'Such a notion had never entered my head. I was just walking up by Mallards: I often stroll by to look at the sweet old home that used to be mine –'

'You can cut all that,' said Irene.

'– and I saw Lucia at the window of the garden-room, looking, oh, so anxious and worn. She slipped behind a curtain and suddenly I felt that she needed me. A sort of presentiment. So I rang the bell – oh, and that was odd, too, for I'd hardly put my finger on it when the door was opened, as if kind Foljambe had been waiting for me – and I asked her if Lucia would like to see me.'

Elizabeth paused for a moment in her embroidery.

'So Foljambe went to ask her,' she continued, 'and came almost running back, and took me out to the garden-room. Lucia was sitting at her table apparently absorbed in some papers. Wasn't that queer, for the moment before she had been peeping out from behind the curtain? I could see she was thoroughly overwrought and she gave me such an imploring look that I was quite touched.'

A wistful smile spread over Elizabeth's face.

'And then it came,' she said. 'I don't blame her for holding back: a sort of pride, I expect, which she couldn't swallow. She begged me to fill the post, and I felt it was my duty to do so. A

dreadful tax, I am afraid, on my time and energies, and there
will be difficult passages ahead, for she is not always very easy
to lead. What Benjy will say to me I don't know, but I must do
what I feel to be right. What a blessed thing to be able to help
others!'

Irene was holding herself in, trembling slightly with the
effort.

Elizabeth continued, still wistfully.

'A lovely little talk,' she said, 'and then there was Mr
Georgie in the garden, and he came across the lawn to me with
such questioning eyes, for I think he guessed what we had
been talking about –'

Irene could contain herself no longer. She gave one maniac
scream.

'Mapp, you make me sick,' she cried. 'I believe Lucia has
asked you to be Mayoress, poor misguided darling, but it
didn't happen like that. It isn't true, Mapp. You've been
longing to be Mayoress: you've been losing weight, not a bad
thing either, with anxiety. You asked her: you implored her. I
am not arguing with you, I am telling you . . . Hullo, here they
both come. It will be pretty to see their gratitude to you. Don't
go, Mapp.'

Elizabeth rose. Dignity prevented her from making any
reply to these gutter-snipe observations. She did it very well.
She paused to kiss her hand to the approaching Lucia, and
walked away without hurrying. But once round the corner into
the High Street, she, like Foljambe, 'almost ran'.

Irene hailed Lucia.

'Come and talk for a minute, darling,' she said. 'First, is it
all too true, Mayoress Mapp, I mean? I see it is. You had far
better have chosen me or Lucy. And what a liar she is! Thank
God I told her so. She told me that you had at last swallowed
your pride, and asked her –'

'What?' cried Lucia.

'Just that; and that she felt it was her duty to help you.'

Lucia, though trembling with indignation, was magnificent.

'Poor thing!' she said. 'Like all habitual liars, she deceives
herself far more often than she deceives others.'

'But aren't you going to *do* anything?' asked Irene, dancing wild fandangoes on the doorstep. 'Not tell her she's a liar? Or, even better, tell her you never asked her to be Mayoress at all! Why not? There was no one there but you and she.'

'Dear Irene, you wouldn't want me to lower myself to her level?'

'Well, for once it wouldn't be a bad thing. You can become lofty again immediately afterwards. But I'll develop the snap-shot I made of her, and send it to the press as a photograph of our new Mayoress.'

Within an hour the news was stale. But the question of how the offer was made and accepted was still interesting, and fresh coins appeared from Elizabeth's mint: Lucia, it appeared had said 'Beloved friend, I could never have undertaken my duties without your support' or words to that effect, and Georgie had kissed the hand of the Mayoress-Elect. No repudiation of such sensational pieces came from head-quarters and they passed into a sort of doubtful currency. Lucia merely shrugged her shoulders, and said that her position forbade her directly to defend herself. This was thought a little excessive; she was not actually of Royal blood. A brief tranquillity followed, as when a kettle, tumultuously boiling, is put on the hob to cool off, and the *Hampshire Argus* merely stated that Mrs Elizabeth Mapp-Flint (née Mapp) would be Mayoress of Tilling for the ensuing year.

Next week the kettle began to lift its lid again, for in the same paper there appeared a remarkable photograph of the Mayoress. She was standing on one foot, as if skating, with the other poised in the air behind her. Her face wore a beckoning smile, and one arm was stretched out in front of her in eager solicitation. Something seemed bound to happen. It did.

Diva by this time had furnished her tea-room, and was giving dress-rehearsals, serving tea herself to a few friends and then sitting down with them, very hot and thirsty. To-day Georgie and Evie were being entertained, and the Padre was expected. Evie did not know why he was late: he had been out in the parish all day, and she had not seen him since after breakfast.

'Nothing like rehearsals to get things working smoothly,' said Diva, pouring her tea into her saucer and blowing on it. 'There are two jams, Mr Georgie, thick and clear, or is that soup?'

'They're both beautifully clear,' said Georgie politely, 'and such hot, crisp toast.'

'There should have been pastry-fingers as well,' said Diva, 'but they wouldn't rise.'

'Tarsome things,' said Georgie with his mouth full.

'Stuck to the tin and burned,' replied Diva. 'You must imagine them here even for a shilling tea. And cream for eighteen-penny teas with potted meat sandwiches. Choice of China or Indian. Tables for four can be reserved, but not for less . . . Ah, here's the Padre. Have a nice cup of tea, Padre, after all those funerals and baptisms.'

'Sorry I'm late, Mistress Plaistow,' said he, 'and I've a bit o' news, and what d'ye think that'll be about? Shall I tease you, as Mistress Mapp-Flint says?'

'You won't tease me,' said Georgie, 'because I know it's about that picture of Elizabeth in the *Hampshire Argus*. And I can tell you at once that Lucia knew nothing about it, whatever Elizabeth may say, till she saw it in the paper. Nothing whatever, except that Irene had taken a snap-shot of her.'

'Well, then, you know nowt o' my news. I was sitting in the Club for a bitty, towards noon, when in came Major Benjy, and picked up the copy of the *Hampshire Argus* where was the portrait of his guid wife. I heard a sort o' gobbling turkey-cock noise and there he was, purple in the face, wi' heathen expressions streaming from him like torrents o' spring. Out he rushed with the paper in his hand – Club-property, mind you, and not his at all – and I saw him pelting down the road to Grebe.'

'No!' cried Diva.

'Yes, Mistress Plaistow. A bit later as I was doing my parish visiting, I saw the Major again with the famous cane riding-whip in his hand, with which, we've all heard often enough, he hit the Indian tiger in the face while he snatched his gun to shoot him. "No one's going to insult my wife, while I'm above ground," he roared out, and popped into the office o' the *Hampshire Argus*.'

'Gracious! What a crisis!' squeaked Evie.

'And that's but the commencement, mem! The rest I've heard from the new Editor, Mr McConnell, who took over not a week ago. Up came a message to him that Major Mapp-Flint would like to see him at once. He was engaged, but said he'd see the Major in a quarter of an hour, and to pass the time wouldn't the Major have a drink. Sure he would, and sure he'd have another when he'd made short work of the first, and, to judge by the bottle, McConnell guessed he'd had a third, but he couldn't say for certain. Be that as it may, when he was ready to see the Major, either the Major had forgotten what he'd come about, or thought he'd be more prudent not to be so savage, for a big man is McConnell, a very big man indeed, and the Major was most affable, and said he'd just looked in to pay a call on the newcomer.'

'Well, that was a come-down,' ejaculated Georgie.

'And further to come down yet,' said the Padre, 'for they had another drink together, and the poor Major's mind must have got in a fair jumble. He'd come out, ye see, to give the man a thrashing, and instead they'd got very pleasant together, and now he began talking about bygones being bygones. That as yet was Hebrew-Greek to McConnell, for it was the Art Editor who'd been responsible for the picture of the Mayoress and McConnell had only just glanced at it, thinking there were some queer Mayoresses in Hampshire, and then, oh, dear me, if the Major didn't ask him to step round and have a bit of luncheon with him, and as for the riding-whip it went clean out of his head and he left it in the waiting-room at the office. There was Mistress Elizabeth when they got to Grebe, looking out o' the parlour window and waiting to see her brave Benjy come marching back with the riding-whip showing a bit of wear and tear, and instead there was the Major with no riding-whip at all, arm in arm with a total stranger saying as how this was his good friend Mr McConnell, whom he'd brought to take pot-luck with them. Dear, oh dear, what wunnerful things happen in Tilling, and I'll have a look at that red conserve.'

'Take it all,' cried Diva. 'And did they have lunch?'

'They did that,' said the Padre, 'though a sorry one it was. It soon came out that Mr McConnell was the Editor of the *Argus*, and then indeed there was a terrifying glint in the lady's eye. He made a hop and a skip of it when the collation was done, leaving the twa together, and he told me about it a' when I met him half an hour ago and 'twas that made me a bit late, for that's the kind of tale ye can't leave in the middle. God knows what'll happen now, and the famous riding-whip somewhere in the newspaper-office.'

The door-bell had rung while this epic was being related, but nobody noticed it. Now it was ringing again, a long, uninterrupted tinkle, and Diva rose.

'Shan't be a second,' she said. 'Don't discuss it too much till I get back.'

She hurried out.

'It must be Elizabeth herself,' she thought excitedly. 'Nobody else rings like that. Using up such a lot of current, instead of just dabbing now and then.'

She opened the door. Elizabeth was on the threshold smiling brilliantly. She carried in her hand the historic riding-whip. Quite unmistakable.

'Dear one!' she said. 'May I pop in for a minute. Not seen you for so long.'

Diva overlooked the fact that they had had a nice chat this morning in the High Street, for there was a good chance of hearing more. She abounded in cordiality.

'Do come in,' she said. 'Lovely to see you after all this long time. Tea going on. A few friends.'

Elizabeth sidled into the tea-room: the door was narrow for a big woman.

'Evie dearest! Mr Georgie! Padre!' she saluted. 'How de do everybody. How cosy! Yes, Indian, please, Diva.'

She laid the whip down by the corner of the fireplace. She beamed with geniality. What turn could this humiliating incident have taken, everybody wondered, to make her so jocund and gay? In sheer absorption of constructive thought the Padre helped himself to another dollop of red jam and ate it with his teaspoon. Clearly she had reclaimed the riding-whip from the *Argus* office but what next? Had she administered to Benjy the chastisement he had feared to inflict on another? Meantime, as puzzled eyes sought each other in perplexity, she poured forth compliments.

'What a banquet, Diva!' she exclaimed. 'What a pretty tablecloth! If this is the sort of tea you will offer us when you open, I shan't be found at home often. I suppose you'll charge two shillings at least, and even then you'll be turning people away.'

Diva recalled herself from her speculations.

'No: this will be only a shilling tea,' she said, 'and usually there'll be pastry as well.'

'Fancy! And so beautifully served. So dainty. Lovely flowers on the table. Quite like having tea in the garden with no earwigs . . . I had an unexpected guest to lunch to-day.'

Cataleptic rigidity seized the entire company.

'Such a pleasant fellow,' continued Elizabeth. 'Mr McConnell, the new Editor of the *Argus*. Benjy paid a morning call on him at the office and brought him home. He left his tiger riding-whip there, the forgetful boy, so I went and reclaimed it. Such a big man: Benjy looked like a child beside him.'

Elizabeth sipped her tea. The rigidity persisted.

'I never by any chance see the *Hampshire Argus*,' she said. 'Not set eyes on it for years, for it used to be very dull. All advertisements. But with Mr McConnell at the helm, I must take it in. He seemed so intelligent.'

Imperceptibly the rigidity relaxed, as keen brains dissected the situation . . . Elizabeth had sent her husband out to chastise McConnell for publishing this insulting caricature of herself. He had returned, rather tipsy, bringing the victim to lunch. Should the true version of what had happened become current, she would find herself in a very humiliating position with a craven husband and a monstrous travesty unavenged. But her version was brilliant. She was unaware that the *Argus* had contained any caricature of her, and Benjy had brought his friend to lunch. A perfect story, to the truth of which, no doubt, Benjy would perjure himself. Very clever! Bravo Elizabeth!

Of course there was a slight feeling of disappointment, for only a few minutes ago some catastrophic development seemed likely, and Tilling's appetite for social catastrophe was keen. The Padre sighed and began in a resigned voice 'A'weel, all's well that ends well', and Georgie hurried home to tell Lucia what had really happened and how clever Elizabeth had been. She sent fondest love to Worshipful, and as there were now four of them left, they adjourned to Diva's card-room for a rubber of bridge.

Diva's Janet came up to clear tea away, and with her the bouncing Irish terrier, Paddy, who had only got a little eczema. He scouted about the room, licking up crumbs from the floor and found the riding-whip. It was of agreeable texture for the teeth, just about sufficiently tough to make gnawing a pleasure as well as a duty. He picked it up, and, the back door being open, took it into the wood-shed and dealt with it. He went over it twice, reducing it to a wet and roughly minced sawdust. There was a silver cap on it, which he spurned and when he had triturated or swallowed most of the rest, he rolled in the debris and shook himself. Except for the silver cap, no murderer could have disposed of a corpse with greater skill.

Upstairs the geniality of the tea-table had crumbled over cards. Elizabeth had been losing and she was feeling hot. She said to Diva 'This little room – so cosy – is quite stifling, dear. May we have the window open?' Diva opened it as a deal was in progress, and the cards blew about the table: Elizabeth's remnant consisted of kings and aces, but a fresh deal was necessary. Diva dropped a card on the floor, face upwards, and put her foot on it so nimbly that nobody could see what it was. She got up to fetch the book of rules to see what ought to happen next, and, moving her foot disclosed an ace. Elizabeth demanded another fresh deal. That was conceded, but it left a friction. Then towards the end of a hand, Elizabeth saw that she had revoked, long, long ago, and detection was awaiting her. 'I'll give you the last trick,' she said, and attempted to jumble up together all the cards. 'Na, na, not so fast, Mistress,' cried the Padre, and he pounced on the card of error. 'Rather like cheating: rather like Elizabeth' was the unspoken comment, and everyone remembered how she had tried the same device about eighteen months ago. The atmosphere grew acid. The Padre and Evie had to hurry off for a choir-practice, for which they were already late, and Elizabeth finding she had not lost as much as she feared lingered for a chat.

'Seen poor Susan Wyse lately?' she asked Diva.

Diva was feeling abrupt. It *was* cheating to try to mix up the cards like that.

'This morning,' she said. 'But why "poor"? You're always calling people "poor". She's all right.'

'Do you think she's got over the budgerigar?' asked Elizabeth.

'Quite. Wearing it to-day. Still raspberry-coloured.'

'I wonder if she has got over it,' mused Elizabeth. 'If you ask me, I think the budgerigar has got over her.'

'Not the foggiest notion what you mean,' said Diva.

'Just what I say. She believes she is getting in touch with the bird's spirit. She told me so herself. She thinks that she hears that tiresome little squeak it used to make, only she now calls it singing.'

'Singing in the ears, I expect,' interrupted Diva. 'Had it sometimes myself. Wax. Syringe.'

'– and the flutter of its wings,' continued Elizabeth. 'She's trying to get communications from it by automatic script. I hope our dear Susan won't go dotty.'

'Rubbish!' said Diva severely, her thoughts going back again to that revoke. She moved her chair up to the fire, and extinguished Elizabeth by opening the evening paper.

The Mayoress bristled and rose.

'Well, we shall see whether it's rubbish or not,' she said. 'Such a lovely game of bridge, but I must be off. Where's Benjy's riding-whip?'

'Wherever you happened to put it, I suppose,' said Diva.

Elizabeth looked in the corner by the fireplace.

'That's where I put it,' she said. 'Who can have moved it?'

'You, of course. Probably took it into the card-room.'

'I'm perfectly certain I didn't,' said Elizabeth, hurrying there. 'Where's the switch, Diva?'

'Behind the door.'

'What an inconvenient place to put it. It ought to have been the other side.'

Elizabeth cannoned into the card-table and a heavy fall of cards and markers followed.

'Afraid I've upset something,' she said. 'Ah, I've got it.'

'I said you'd taken it there yourself,' said Diva. 'Pick those things up.'

'No, not the riding-whip; the switch,' she said.

Elizabeth looked in this corner and that, and under tables and chairs, but there was no sign of what she sought. She came out, leaving the light on.

'Not here,' she said. 'Perhaps the Padre has taken it. Or Evie.'

'Better go round and ask them,' said Diva.

'Thank you, dear. Or might I use your telephone? It would save me a walk.'

The call was made, but they were both at choir-practice.

'Or Mr Georgie, do you think?' asked Elizabeth. 'I'll just inquire.'

Now one of Diva's most sacred economies was the telephone. She would always walk a reasonable distance herself to avoid these outlays which, though individually small, mounted up so ruinously.

'If you want to telephone to all Tilling, Elizabeth,' she said, 'you'd better go home and do it from there.'

'Don't worry about that,' said Elizabeth effusively; 'I'll pay you for the calls now, at once.'

She opened her bag, dropped it, and a shower of coins of low denomination scattered in all directions on the parquet floor.

'Clumsy of me,' she said, pouncing on the bullion. 'Nine-pence in coppers, two sixpences and a shilling, but I know there was a threepenny bit. It must have rolled under your pretty sideboard. Might I have a candle, dear?'

'No,' said Diva firmly. 'If there's a threepenny bit, Janet will find it when she sweeps in the morning. You must get along without it till then.'

'There's no "if" about it, dear. There *was* a threepenny bit. I specially noticed it because it was a new one. With your permission I'll ring up Mallards.'

Foljambe answered. No; Mr Georgie had taken his umbrella when he went out to tea, and he couldn't have brought back a riding-whip by mistake . . . Would Foljambe kindly make sure by asking him . . . He was in his bath . . . Then would she just call through the door. Mrs Mapp-Flint would hold the line.

As Elizabeth waited for the answer, humming a little tune, Janet came in with Diva's glass of sherry. She put up two fingers and her eyebrows to inquire whether she should bring two glasses, and Diva shook her head. Presently Georgie came to the telephone himself.

'Wouldn't have bothered you for words, Mr Georgie,' said Elizabeth. 'Foljambe said you were in your bath. She must have made a mistake.'

'I was just going,' said Georgie rather crossly, for the water must be getting cold. 'What is it?'

'Benjy's riding-whip has disappeared most mysteriously, and I can't rest till I trace it. I thought you might possibly have taken it away by mistake.'

'What, the tiger one?' said Georgie, much interested in spite of the draught round his ankles. 'What a disaster. But I haven't got it. What a series of adventures it's had! I saw you bring it into Diva's; I noticed it particularly.'

'Thank you,' said Elizabeth, and rang off.

'And now for the police-station,' said Diva, sipping her delicious sherry. 'That'll be your fourth call.'

'Third, dear,' said Elizabeth, uneasily wondering what Georgie meant by the series of adventures. 'But that would be premature for the present. I must search a little more here, for it must be somewhere. Oh, here's Paddy. Good dog! Come to help Auntie Mayoress to find pretty riding-whip? Seek it, Paddy.'

Paddy, intelligently following Elizabeth's pointing hand, thought it must be a leaf of Diva's evening paper, which she had dropped on the floor, that Auntie Mayoress wanted. He pounced on it, and worried it.

'Paddy, you fool,' cried Diva. 'Drop it at once. Torn to bits and all wet. Entirely your fault, Elizabeth.' She rose, intensely irritated.

'You must give it up for the present,' she said to Elizabeth who was poking about among the logs in the wood-basket. 'All most mysterious, I allow, but it's close on my supper-time, and that interests me more.'

Elizabeth was most reluctant to return to Benjy with the news that she had called for the riding-whip at the office of the *Argus* and had subsequently lost it.

'But it's Benjy's most cherished relic,' she said. 'It was the very riding-whip with which he smacked the tiger over the face, while he picked up his rifle and then shot him.'

'Such a lot of legends aren't there?' said Diva menacingly. 'And if other people get talking there may be one or two more, just as remarkable. And I want my supper.'

Elizabeth paused in her search. This dark saying produced an immediate effect.

'Too bad of me to stop so long,' she said. 'And thanks, dear, for my delicious tea. It would be kind of you if you had another look round.'

Diva saw her off. The disappearance of the riding-whip was really very strange: positively spooky. And though Elizabeth had been a great nuisance, she deserved credit and sympathy for her ingenious version of the awkward incident . . . She looked for the pennies which Elizabeth had promised to pay at once for those telephone-calls, but there was no trace of them, and all her exasperation returned.

'Just like her,' she muttered. 'That's the sort of thing that really annoys me. So mean!'

It was Janet's evening out, and after eating her supper, Diva returned to the tea-room for a few games of patience. It was growing cold; Janet had forgotten to replenish the wood-basket, and Diva went out to the wood-shed with an electric torch to fetch in a few more logs. Something gleamed in the light, and she picked up a silver cap, which seemed vaguely familiar. A fragment of chewed wood projected from it, and looking more closely she saw engraved on it the initials B. F.

'Golly! It's it,' whispered the awe-struck Diva. 'Benjamin Flint, before he Mapped himself. But why here? And how?'

An idea struck her, and she called Paddy, but Paddy had no doubt gone out with Janet. Forgetting about fresh logs but with this relic in her hand, Diva returned to her room, and warmed herself with intellectual speculation.

Somebody had disposed of all the riding-whip except this metallic fragment. By process of elimination (for she acquitted Janet of having eaten it), it must be Paddy. Should she ring up Elizabeth and say that the riding-whip had been found? That would not be true, for all that had been found was a piece of overwhelming evidence that it never would be found. Besides, who could tell what Elizabeth had said to Benjy by this time? Possibly (even probably, considering what Elizabeth was) she would not tell him that she had retrieved it from the office of the *Argus*, and thus escape his just censure for having lost it.

'I believe,' thought Diva, 'that it might save developments which nobody can foresee, if I said nothing about it to anybody. Nobody knows except Paddy and me. *Silentio*, as Lucia says, when she's gabbling fit to talk your head off. Let them settle it between themselves, but nobody shall suspect *me* of having had anything to do with it. I'll bury it in the garden before Janet comes back. Rather glad Paddy ate it. I was tired of Major Benjy showing me the whip, and telling me about it over and over again. Couldn't be true, either. I'm killing a lie.'

With the help of a torch and a trowel Diva put the relic beyond reasonable risk of discovery. This was only just done when Janet returned with Paddy.

'Been strolling in the garden,' said Diva with chattering teeth. 'Such a mild night. Dear Paddy! Such a clever dog.'

Elizabeth pondered over the mystery as she walked briskly home, and when she came to discuss it with Benjy after dinner they presently became very friendly. She reminded him that he had behaved like a poltroon this morning, and, like a loyal wife, she had shielded him from exposure by her ingenious explanations. She disclosed that she had retrieved the riding-whip from the *Argus* office, but had subsequently lost it at

Diva's tea-rooms. A great pity, but it still might turn up. What they must fix firmly in their minds was that Benjy had gone to the office of the *Argus* merely to pay a polite call on Mr McConnell, and that Elizabeth had never seen the monstrous caricature of herself in that paper.

'That's settled then,' she said, 'and it's far the most dignified course we can take. And I've been thinking about more important things than these paltry affairs. There's an election to the Town Council next month. One vacancy. I shall stand.'

'Not very wise, Liz,' he said. 'You tried that once, and came in at the bottom of the poll.'

'I know that. Lucia and I polled exactly the same number of votes. But times have changed now. She's Mayor and I'm Mayoress. It's of her I'm thinking. I shall be much more assistance to her as a Councillor. I shall be a support to her at the meetings.'

'Very thoughtful of you,' said Benjy. 'Does she see it like that?'

'I've not told her yet. I shall be firm in any case. Well, it's bedtime; such an exciting day! Dear me, if I didn't forget to pay Diva for a few telephone-calls I made from her house. Dear Diva, and her precious economies!'

And in Diva's back-garden, soon to tarnish by contact with the loamy soil, there lay buried, like an unspent shell with all its explosive potentialities intact, the silver cap of the vanished relic.

Mayoring day arrived and Lucia, formally elected by the Town Council, assumed her scarlet robes. She swept them a beautiful curtsey and said she was their servant. She made a touching allusion to her dear friend the Mayoress, whose loyal and loving support would alone render her own immense responsibilities a joy to shoulder, and Elizabeth, wreathed in smiles, dabbed her handkerchief on the exact piece of her face where tears, had there been any, would have bedewed it. The Mayor then entertained a large party to lunch at the King's Arms Hotel, preceding them in state while church bells rang, dogs barked, cameras clicked, and the sun gleamed on the

massive maces borne before her. There were cheers for Lucia
led by the late Mayor and cheers for the Mayoress led by her
present husband.

In the afternoon Lucia inaugurated Diva's tea-shop, incognita as Mrs Pillson. The populace of Tilling was not quite
so thrilled as she had expected at the prospect of taking its tea
in the same room as the Mayor, and no one saw her drink the
first cup of tea except Georgie and Diva, who kept running to
the window on the look-out for customers. Seeing Susan in her
Royce, she tapped on the pane, and got her to come in so that
they could inaugurate the card-room with a rubber of bridge.
Then suddenly a torrent of folk invaded the tea-room and
Diva had to leave an unfinished hand to help Janet to serve
them.

'Wish they'd come sooner,' she said, 'to see the ceremony.
Do wait a bit; if they ease off we can finish our game.'

She hurried away. A few minutes afterwards she opened the
door and said in a thrilling whisper, 'Fourteen shilling ones,
and two eighteen-penny's.'

'Splendid!' said everybody, and Susan began telling them
about her automatic script.

'I sit there with my eyes shut and my pencil in my hand,' she
said, 'and Blue Birdie on the table by me. I get a sort of lost feeling,
and then Blue Birdie seems to say "Tweet, tweet," and I say
"Good morning dear." Then my pencil begins to move. I never
know what it writes. A queer, scrawling hand, not a bit like mine.'

The door opened and Diva's face beamed redly.

'Still twelve shilling ones,' she said, 'though six of the first
lot have gone. Two more eighteen-penny, but the cream is
getting low, and Janet's had to add milk.'

'Where had I got to?' said Susan. 'Oh, yes. It goes on
writing till Blue Birdie seems to say "Tweet, tweet" again, and
that means it's fnished and I say "Goodbye, dear".'

'What sort of things does it write?' asked Lucia.

'All sorts. This morning it kept writing *mère* over and over
again.'

'That's very strange,' said Lucia eagerly. 'Very. I expect
Blue Birdie wants to say something to me.'

'No,' said Susan. 'Not your sort of Mayor. The French word *mère*, just as if Blue Birdie said "Mummie". Speaking to me evidently.'

This did not seem to interest Lucia.

'And anything of value?' she asked.

'It's all of value,' said Susan.

A slight crash sounded from the tea-room.

'Only a teacup,' said Diva, looking in again. 'Rather like breaking a bottle of wine when you launch a ship.'

'Would you like me to show myself for a minute?' asked Lucia. 'I will gladly walk through the room if it would help.'

'So good of you, but I don't want any help except in handling things. Besides, I told the reporter of the *Argus* that you had had your tea, and were playing cards in here.'

'Oh, not quite wise, Diva,' said Lucia. 'Tell him I wasn't playing for money. Think of the example.'

'Afraid he's gone,' said Diva. 'Besides, it wouldn't be true. Two of your Councillors here just now. Shillings. Didn't charge them. Advertisement.'

The press of customers eased off, and, leaving Janet to deal with the remainder, Diva joined them, clinking a bag of bullion.

'Lots of tips,' she said. 'I never reckoned on that. Mostly twopences, but they'll add up. I must just count the takings, and then let's finish the rubber.'

The takings exceeded all expectation; quite a pile of silver; a pyramid of copper.

'What will you do with all that money now the banks are closed?' asked Georgie lightly. 'Such a sum to have in the house. I should bury it in the garden.'

Diva's hand gave an involuntary twitch as she swept the coppers into a bag. Odd that he should say that!

'Safe enough,' she replied. 'Paddy sleeps in my room, now that I know he hasn't got mange.'

The Mayoral banquet followed in the evening. Unfortunately, neither the Lord Lieutenant nor the Bishop nor the Member of Parliament were able to attend, but they sent charming letters of regret, which Lucia read before her Chaplain, the Padre, said Grace. She wore her Mayoral chain of office round her neck, and her chain of inherited seed-pearls in her hair, and Georgie, as arranged, sat alone on the other side of the table directly opposite her. He was disadvantageously placed with regard to supplies of food and drink, for the waiter had to go round the far end of the side-tables to get at him, but he took extra large helpings when he got the chance, and had all his wine-glasses filled. He wore on the lapel of his coat a fine green and white enamel star, which had long lain among his bibelots, and which looked like a foreign order. At the far end of the room was a gallery, from which ladies, as if in purdah, were allowed to look on. Elizabeth sat in the front row, and waggled her hand at the Mayor, whenever Lucia looked in her direction, in order to encourage her. Once, when a waiter was standing just behind Lucia, Elizabeth felt sure that she had caught her eye, and kissed her hand to her. The waiter promptly responded, and the Mayoress, blushing prettily, ceased to signal ... There were flowery speeches made and healths drunk, and afterwards a musical entertainment. The Mayor created a precedent by contributing to this herself and giving (as the *Hampshire Argus* recorded in its next issue) an exquisite rendering on the piano of the slow movement of Beethoven's 'Moonlight' Sonata. It produced a somewhat pensive effect, and she went back to her presiding place again amid respectful applause and a shrill, solitary cry of 'Encore!' from Elizabeth. The spirits of her guests revived under the spell of lighter melodies, and at the end 'Auld Lang Syne' was sung with crossed hands by all the company, with the exception of Georgie, who had no neighbours. Lucia swept regal curtsies to right and left, and a loop of the seed-pearls in her hair got loose and oscillated in front of her face.

The Mayor and her Prince Consort drove back to Mallards, Lucia strung up to the highest pitch of triumph, Georgie intensely fatigued. She put him through a catechism of self-glorification in the garden-room.

'I think I gave them a good dinner,' she said. 'And the wine was excellent, wasn't it?'

'Admirable,' said Georgie.

'And my speech. Not too long?'

'Not a bit. Exactly right.'

'I thought they drank my health very warmly. *Non e vero?*'

'Very. *Molto*,' said Georgie.

Lucia struck a chord on the piano before she closed it.

'Did I take the "Moonlight" a little too quick?' she asked.

'No. I never heard you play it better.'

'I felt the enthusiasm tingling round me,' she said. 'In the days of horse-drawn vehicles, I am sure they would have taken my horses out of the shafts and pulled us up home. But impossible with a motor.'

Georgie yawned.

'They might have taken out the carburetter,' he said wearily.

She glanced at some papers on her table.

'I must be up early to-morrow,' she said, 'to be ready for Mrs Simpson ... A new era, Georgie. I seem to see a new era for our dear Tilling.'

4

Lucia did not find her new duties quite as onerous as she expected, but she made them as onerous as she could. She pored over plans for new houses which the Corporation was building, and having once grasped the difference between section and elevation was full of ideas for tasteful weather-cocks, lightning conductors and balconies. With her previous experience in Stock Exchange transactions to help her, she went deeply into questions of finance and hit on a scheme of borrowing money at three and a half per cent for a heavy outlay for the renewal of drains, and investing it in some thoroughly sound concern that brought in four and a half per cent. She explained this masterpiece to Georgie.

'Say we borrow ten thousand pounds at three and a half,' she said, 'the interest on that will be three hundred and fifty pounds a year. We invest it, Georgie, – follow me closely here – at four and a half, and it brings us in four hundred and fifty pounds a year. A clear gain of one hundred pounds.'

'That does seem brilliant,' said Georgie. 'But wait a moment. If you re-invest what you borrow, how do you pay for the work on your drains?'

Lucia's face grew corrugated with thought.

'I see what you're driving at, Georgie,' she said slowly. 'Very acute of you. I must consider that further before I bring my scheme before the Finance Committee. But in my belief – of course this is strictly private – the work on the drains is not so very urgent. We might put it off for six months, and in the meantime reap our larger dividends. I'm sure there's something to be done on those lines.'

Then with a view to investigating the lighting of the streets, she took Georgie out for walks after dinner on dark and even rainy evenings.

'This corner now,' she said as the rain poured down on her umbrella. 'A most insufficient illumination. I should never forgive myself if some elderly person tripped up here in the dark and stunned himself. He might remain undiscovered for hours.'

'Quite,' said Georgie, 'but this is very cold-catching. Let's get home. No elderly person will come out on such a night. Madness.'

'It is a little wet,' said Lucia, who never caught cold. 'I'll go to look at that alley by Bumpus's buildings another night, for there's a memorandum on Town Development plans waiting for me, which I haven't mastered. Something about residential zones and industrial zones, Georgie. I mustn't permit a manufactory to be opened in a residential zone: for instance, I could never set up a brewery or a blacksmith's forge in the garden at Mallards –'

'Well, you don't want to, do you?' said Georgie.

'The principle, dear, is the interesting thing. At first sight it looks rather like a curtailment of the liberty of the individual, but if you look, as I am learning to do, below the surface, you will perceive that a blacksmith's forge in the middle of the lawn would detract from the tranquillity of adjoining residences. It would injure their amenities.'

Georgie plodded beside her, wishing Lucia was not so excruciatingly didactic, but trying between sneezes to be a good husband to the Mayor.

'And mayn't you reside in an industrial zone?' he asked.

'That I must look into. I should myself certainly permit a shoemaker to live above his shop. Then there's the general business zone. I trust that Diva's tea-rooms in the High Street are in order: it would be sad for her if I had to tell her to close them . . . Ah, our comfortable garden-room again! You were asking just now about residence in an industrial zone. I think I have some papers here which will tell you that. And there's a coloured map of zones somewhere, green for industrial, blue for residential and yellow for general business, which would fascinate you. Where is it now?'

'Don't bother about it to-night,' said Georgie. 'I can easily wait till to-morrow. What about some music? There's that Scarlatti duet.'

'*Ah, divino Scarlattino!*' said Lucia absently, as she turned over her papers. 'Eureka! Here it is! No, that's about slums, but also very interesting . . . What's a "messuage"?'

'Probably a misprint for message,' said he. 'Or massage.'

'No, neither makes sense: I must put a query to that.'

Georgie sat down at the piano, and played a few fragments of remembered tunes. Lucia continued reading: it was rather difficult to understand, and the noise distracted her.

'Delicious tunes,' she said, 'but would it be very selfish of me, dear, to ask you to stop while I'm tackling this? So important that I should have it at my fingers' ends before the next meeting, and be able to explain it. Ah, I see . . . no, that's green. Industrial. But in half an hour or so –'

Georgie closed the piano.

'I think I shall go to bed,' he said. 'I may have caught cold.'

'Ah, now I see,' cried Lucia triumphantly. 'You can reside in any zone. That is only fair: why should a chemist in the High Street be forced to live half a mile away? And very clearly put. I could not have expressed it better myself. Good night, dear. A few drops of camphor on a lump of sugar. Sleep well.'

The Mayoress was as zealous as the Mayor. She rang Lucia up at breakfast-time every morning, and wished to speak to her personally.

'Anything I can do for you, dear Worship?' she asked. 'Always at your service, as I needn't remind you.'

'Nothing whatever, thanks,' answered Lucia. 'I've a Council meeting this afternoon –'

'No points you'd like to talk over with me? Sure?'

'Quite,' said Lucia firmly.

'There are one or two bits of things I should like to bring to your notice,' said the baffled Elizabeth, 'for of course you can't keep in touch with everything. I'll pop in at one for a few minutes and chance finding you disengaged. And a bit of news.'

Lucia went back to her congealed bacon.

'She's got quite a wrong notion of the duties of a Mayoress, Georgie,' she said. 'I wish she would understand that if I want her help I shall ask for it. She has nothing to do with my official duties, and as she's not on the Town Council, she can't dip her oar very deep.'

'She's hoping to run you,' said Georgie. 'She hopes to have her finger in every pie. She will if she can.'

'I have got to be very tactful,' said Lucia thoughtfully. 'You see the only object of my making her Mayoress was to dope her malignant propensities, and if I deal with her too rigorously I should merely stimulate them . . . Ah, we must begin our regime of plain living. Let us go and do our marketing at once, and then I can study the agenda for this afternoon before Elizabeth arrives.'

Elizabeth had some assorted jobs for Worship to attend to. Worship ought to know that a car had come roaring down the hill into Tilling yesterday at so terrific a pace that she hadn't time to see the number. A van and Susan's Royce had caused a complete stoppage of traffic in the High Street; anyone with only a few minutes to spare to catch a train must have missed it. 'And far worse was a dog that howled all last night outside the house next Grebe,' said Elizabeth. 'Couldn't sleep a wink.'

'But I can't stop it,' said Lucia.

'No? I should have thought some threatening notice might be served on the owner. Or shall I write a letter to the *Argus*, which we both might sign. More weight. Or I would write a personal note to you which you might read to the Council. Whichever you like, Worship. You to choose.'

Lucia did not find any of these alternatives attractive, but made a business-like note of them all.

'Most valuable suggestions,' she said. 'But I don't feel that I could move officially about the dog. It might be a cat next, or a canary.'

Elizabeth was gazing out of the window with that kind, meditative smile which so often betokened some atrocious train of thought.

'Just little efforts of mine, dear Worship, to enlarge your

sphere of influence,' she said. 'Soon, perhaps, I may be able to support you more directly.'

Lucia felt a qualm of sickening apprehension.

'That would be lovely,' she said. 'But how, dear Elizabeth, could you do more than you are doing?'

Elizabeth focused her kind smile on dear Worship's face. A close up.

'Guess, dear!' she said.

'Couldn't,' said Lucia.

'Well, then, there's a vacancy in the Borough Council, and I'm standing for it. Oh, if I got in! At hand to support you in all your Council meetings. You and me! Just think!'

Lucia made one desperate attempt to avert this appalling prospect, and began to gabble.

'That would be wonderful,' she said, 'and how well I know that it's your devotion to me that prompts you. How I value that! But somehow it seems to me that your influence, your tremendous influence, would be lessened rather than the reverse, if you became just one out of my twelve Councillors. Your unique position as Mayoress would suffer. Tilling would think of you as one of a body. You, my right hand, would lose your independence. And then, unlikely, even impossible as it sounds, supposing you were not elected? A ruinous loss of prestige –'

Foljambe entered.

'Lunch,' she said, and left the door of the garden-room wide open.

Elizabeth sprang up with a shrill cry of astonishment.

'No idea it was lunch-time,' she cried. 'How naughty of me not to have kept my eye on the clock, but time passed so quickly, as it always does, dear, when I'm talking to you. But you haven't convinced me; far from it. I must fly; Benjy will call me a naughty girl for being so late.'

Lucia remembered that the era of plain living had begun. Hashed mutton and treacle pudding. Perhaps Elizabeth might go away if she knew that. On the other hand, Elizabeth had certainly come here at one o'clock in order to be asked to lunch, and it would be wiser to ask her.

'Ring him up and say you're lunching here,' she decided. 'Do.'

Elizabeth recollected that she had ordered hashed beef and marmalade pudding at home.

'I consider that a command, dear Worship,' she said. 'May I use your telephone?'

All these afflictions strongly reacted on Georgie. Mutton and Mapp and incessant conversation about municipal affairs were making home far less comfortable than he had a right to expect. Then Lucia sprang another conscientious surprise on him, when she returned that afternoon positively invigorated by a long Council meeting.

'I want to consult you, Georgie,' she said. 'Ever since the *Hampshire Argus* reported that I played bridge in Diva's card-room, the whole question has been on my mind. I don't think I ought to play for money.'

'You can't call threepence a hundred money,' said Georgie.

'It is not a large sum, but emphatically it *is* money. It's the principle of the thing. A very sad case – all this is very private – has just come to my notice. Young Twistevant, the grocer's son, has been backing horses, and is in debt with his last quarter's rent unpaid. Lately married and a baby coming. All the result of gambling.'

'I don't see how the baby is the result of gambling,' said Georgie. 'Unless he bet he wouldn't have one.'

Lucia gave the wintry smile that was reserved for jokes she didn't care about.

'I expressed myself badly,' she said. 'I only meant that his want of money, when he will need it more than ever, is the result of gambling. The principle is the same whether it's threepence or a starving baby. And bridge surely, with its call both on prudence and enterprise, is a sufficiently good game to play for love: for love of bridge. Let us set an example. When we have our next bridge-party, let it be understood that there are no stakes.'

'I don't think you'll get many bridge-parties if that's under-stood,' said Georgie. 'Everyone will go seven no-trumps at once.'

'Then they'll be doubled,' cried Lucia triumphantly.

'And redoubled. It wouldn't be any fun. Most monotonous. The dealer might as well pick up his hand and say seven no-trumps, doubled and redoubled, before he looked at it.'

'I hope we take a more intelligent interest in the game than *that*,' said Lucia. 'The judgment in declaring, the skill in the play of the cards, the various systems so carefully thought out – surely we shan't cease to practise them just because a few pence are no longer at stake? Indeed, I think we shall have far pleasanter games. They will be more tranquil, and on a loftier level. The question of even a few pence sometimes produces acrimony.'

'I can't agree,' said Georgie. 'Those acrimonies are the result of pleasant excitement. And what's the use of keeping the score, and wondering if you dare finesse, if it leads to nothing? You might try playing for twopence a hundred instead of threepence –'

'I must repeat that it's the principle,' interrupted Lucia. 'I feel that in my position it ought to be known that though I play cards, which I regard as quite a reasonable relaxation, I no longer play for money. I feel sure we should find it just as exciting. Let us put it to the test. I will ask the Padre and Evie to dine and play to-morrow, and we'll see how it goes.'

It didn't go. Lucia made the depressing announcement during dinner, and a gloom fell on the party as they cut for partners. For brief bright moments one or other of them forgot that there was nothing to be gained by astuteness except the consciousness of having been clever, but then he (or she) remembered, and the gleam faded. Only Lucia remained keen and critical. She tried with agonized anxiety to recollect if there was another trump in and decided wrong.

'Too stupid of me, Padre,' she said. 'I ought to have known. I should have drawn it, and then we made our contract. Quite inexcusable. Many apologies.'

'Eh, it's no matter; it's no matter whatever,' he said. 'Just nothing at all.'

Then came the adding-up. Georgie had not kept the score and everyone accepted Lucia's addition without a murmur. At half-past ten instead of eleven, it was agreed that it was wiser not to begin another rubber, and Georgie saw the languid guests to the door. He came back to find Lucia replaying the last hand.

'You could have got another trick, dear,' she said. 'Look; you should have discarded instead of trumping. A most interesting manoeuvre. As to our test, I think they were both quite as keen as ever, and for myself I never had a more enjoyable game.'

The news of this depressing evening spread apace through Tilling, and a small party assembled next day at Diva's for shilling teas and discussions.

'I winna play for nowt,' said the Padre. 'Such a mirthless evening I never spent. And by no means a well-furnished table at dinner. An unusual parsimony.'

Elizabeth chimed in.

'I got hashed mutton and treacle pudding for lunch a few days ago,' she said. 'Just what I should have had at home except that it was beef and marmalade.'

'Perhaps you happened to look in a few minutes before unexpectedly,' suggested Diva who was handing crumpets.

There was a nasty sort of innuendo about this.

'I haven't got any cream, dear,' retorted Elizabeth. 'Would you kindly –'

'It'll be an eighteen-penny tea then,' Diva warned her, 'though you'll get potted meat sandwiches as well. Shall it be eighteen-pence?'

Elizabeth ignored the suggestion.

'As for playing bridge for nothing,' she resumed, 'I won't. I've never played it before, and I'm too old to learn now. Dear Worship, of course, may do as she likes, so long as she doesn't do it with me.'

Diva finished her serving and sat down with her customers. Janet brought her cream and potted-meat sandwiches, for of course she could eat what she liked, without choosing between a shilling and an eighteen-penny tea.

'Makes it all so awkward,' she said. 'If one of us gives a

bridge-party, must the table at which Lucia plays do it for nothing?'

'The other table, too, I expect,' said Elizabeth bitterly, watching Diva pouring quantities of cream into her tea. 'Worship mightn't like to know that gambling was going on in her presence.'

'That I won't submit to,' cried Evie. 'I won't, I won't. She may be Mayor but she isn't Mussolini.'

'I see naught for it,' said the Padre, 'but not to ask her. I play my bridge for diversion and it doesna' divert me to exert my mind over the cards and not a bawbee or the loss of it to show for all my trouble.'

Other customers came in; the room filled up and Diva had to get busy again. The office-boy from the *Hampshire Argus* and a friend had a good blow-out, and ate an entire pot of jam, which left little profit on their teas. On the other hand, Evie and the Padre and Elizabeth were so concerned about the bridge crisis that they hardly ate anything. Diva presented them with their bills, and they each gave her a tip of twopence, which was quite decent for a shilling tea, but the office-boy and his friend, in the bliss of repletion, gave her threepence. Diva thanked them warmly.

Evie and the Padre continued the subject on the way home.

'Such hard luck on Mr Georgie,' she said. 'He's as bored as anybody with playing for love. I saw him yawn six times the other night and he never added up. I think I'll ask him to a bridge-tea at Diva's, just to see if he'll come without Lucia. Diva would be glad to play with us afterwards, but it would never do to ask her to tea first.'

'How's that?' asked the Padre.

'Why she would be making a profit by being our guest. And how could we tip her for four teas, when she had had one of them herself? Very awkward for her.'

'A'weel, then let her get her own tea,' said the Padre, 'though I don't think she's as delicate of feeling as all that. But ask the puir laddie by all means.'

Georgie was duly rung up and a slightly embarrassing moment followed. Evie thought she had said with sufficient emphasis 'So pleased if *you* will come to Diva's to-morrow for tea and bridge,' but he asked her to hold on while he saw if Lucia was free. Then Evie had to explain it didn't matter whether Lucia was free or not, and Georgie accepted.

'I felt sure it would happen,' he said to himself, 'but I think I shan't tell Lucia. Very likely she'll be busy.'

Vain was the hope of man. As they were moderately enjoying their frugal lunch next day, Lucia congratulated herself on having a free afternoon.

'Positively nothing to do,' she said. 'Not a committee to attend, nothing. Let us have one of our good walks, and pop in to have tea with Diva afterwards. I want to encourage her enterprise.'

'A walk would be lovely,' said Georgie, 'but Evie asked me to have tea at Diva's and play a rubber afterwards.'

'I don't remember her asking me,' said Lucia. 'Does she expect me?'

'I rather think Diva's making our fourth,' faltered Georgie.

Lucia expressed strong approval.

'A very sensible innovation,' she said. 'I remember telling you that it struck me as rather *bourgeois*, rather Victorian, always to have husbands and wives together. No doubt also, dear Evie felt sure I should be busy up till dinner-time. Really very considerate of her, not to give me the pain of refusing. How I shall enjoy a quiet hour with a book.'

'She doesn't like it all the same,' thought Georgie, as, rather fatigued with a six-mile tramp in a thick sea-mist, he tripped down the hill to Diva's, 'and I shouldn't wonder if she guessed the reason . . .' The tea-room was crowded, so that Diva could not have had tea with them even if she had been asked. She presented the bill to Evie herself (three eighteen-penny teas) and received the generous tip of fourpence a head.

'Thank you, dear Evie,' she said pocketing the extra shilling. 'I do call that handsome. I'll join you in the card-room as soon as ever I can.'

They had most exciting games at the usual stakes. It was impossible to leave the last rubber unfinished, and Georgie had to hurry over his dressing not to keep Lucia waiting. Her eye had that gimlet-like aspect, which betokened a thirst for knowledge.

'A good tea and a pleasant rubber?' she asked.

'Both,' said Georgie. 'I enjoyed myself.'

'So glad. And many people having tea?'

'Crammed. Diva couldn't join us till close on six.'

'How pleasant for Diva. And did you play for stakes, dear, or for nothing?'

'Stakes,' said Georgie. 'The usual threepence.'

'Georgie, I'm going to ask a favour of you,' she said. 'I want you to set an example – poor young Twistevant, you know – I want it to be widely known that I do not play cards for money. You diminish the force of my example, dear, if you continue to do so. The limelight is partially, at any rate, on you as well as me. I ask you not to.'

'I'm afraid I can't consent,' said Georgie. 'I don't see any harm in it – Naturally you will do as you like –'

'Thank you, dear,' said Lucia.

'No need to thank me. And I shall do as I like.'

Grosvenor entered.

'*Silentio!*' whispered Lucia. 'Yes, Grosvenor?'

'Mrs Mapp-Flint has rung up' – began Grosvenor.

'Tell her I can't attend to any business this evening,' said Lucia.

'She doesn't want you to, ma'am. She only wants to know if Mr Pillson will dine with her the day after to-morrow and play bridge.'

'Thank her,' said Georgie firmly. 'Delighted.'

Card-playing circles in Tilling remained firm: there was no slump. If, in view of her exemplary position, Worship declined to play bridge for money, far be it from us, said Tilling, to seek to persuade her against the light of conscience. But if Worship imagined that Tilling intended to follow her example, the sooner she got rid of that fond illusion the better. Lucia sent out invitations for another bridge-party at Mallards but everybody was engaged. She could not miss the significance of that, but she put up a proud front and sent for the latest book on bridge and studied it incessantly, almost to the neglect of her Mayoral duties, in order to prove that what she cared for was the game in itself. Her grasp of it, she declared, improved out of all knowledge, but she got no opportunities of demonstrating that agreeable fact. Invitations rained on Georgie, for it was clearly unfair that he should get no bridge because nobody would play with the Mayor, and he returned these hospitalities by asking his friends to have tea with him at Diva's rooms, with a rubber afterwards, for he could not ask three gamblers to dinner and leave Lucia to study bridge-problems by herself, while the rest of the party played. Other entertainers followed his example, for it was far less trouble to order tea at Diva's and find the card-room ready, and as Algernon Wyse expressed it, 'ye olde tea-house' became quite like Almack's. This was good business for the establishment, and Diva bitterly regretted that it had not occurred to her from the first to charge card-money. She put the question one day to Elizabeth.

'All those markers being used up so fast,' she said, 'and I shall have to get new cards so much oftener than I expected. Twopence, say, for card-money, don't you think?'

'I shouldn't dream of it, dear,' said Elizabeth very decidedly. 'You must be doing very well as it is. But I should recommend some fresh packs of cards. A little greasy, when last I played. More daintiness, clean cards, sharp pencils and so on are well worth while. But card-money, no!'

The approach of the election to the vacancy on the Town Council diverted the Mayor's mind from her abstract study of bridge. Up to within a few days of the date on which candidates' names must be sent in, Elizabeth was still the only aspirant. Lucia found herself faced by the prospect of her Mayoress being inevitably elected, and the thought of that filled her with the gloomiest apprehensions. She wondered if Georgie could be induced to stand. It was his morning for cleaning his bibelots, and she went up to his room with offers of help.

'I so often wish, dear,' she said pensively, attacking a

snuff-box, 'that you were more closely connected with me in my municipal work. And such an opportunity offers itself just now.'

'Do be careful with that snuff-box,' said he. 'Don't rub it hard. What's this opportunity?'

'The Town Council. There's a vacancy very soon. I'm convinced, dear, that with a little training, such as I could give you, you would make a marvellous Councillor, and you would find the work most absorbing.'

'I think it would bore me stiff,' he said. 'I'm no good at slums and drains.'

Lucia decided to disclose herself.

'Georgie, it's to help me,' she said. 'Elizabeth at present is the only candidate, and the idea of having her on the Council is intolerable. And with the prestige of your being my husband I don't doubt the result. Just a few days of canvassing; you with your keen interest in human nature will revel in it. It is a duty, it seems to me, that you owe to yourself. You would have an official position in the town. I have long felt it an anomaly that the Mayor's husband had none.'

Georgie considered. He had before now thought it would be pleasant to walk in Mayoral processions in a purple gown. And bored though he was with Lucia's municipal gabble, it would be different when, with the weight of his position to back him, he could say that he totally disagreed with her on some matter of policy, and perhaps defeat some project of hers at a Council meeting. Also, it would be a pleasure to defeat Elizabeth at the poll . . .

'Well, if you'll help me with the canvassing –' he began.

'Ah, if I only could!' she said. 'But, dear, my position precludes me from taking any active part. It is analogous to that of the King, who, officially, is outside politics. The fact that you are my husband – what a blessed day was that when our lives were joined – will carry immense weight. Everyone will know that your candidature has my full approval. I shouldn't wonder if Elizabeth withdrew when she learns you are standing against her.'

'Oh, very well,' said he. 'But you must coach me on what my programme is to be.'

'Thank you, dear, a thousand times! You must send in your name at once. Mrs Simpson will get you a form to fill up.'

Several horrid days ensued and Georgie wended his dripping way from house to house in the most atrocious weather. His ticket was better housing for the poorer classes, and he called at rows of depressing dwellings, promising to devote his best energies to procuring the tenants bathrooms, plumbing, bicycle-sheds and open spaces for their children to play in. A disagreeable sense oppressed him that the mothers, whose household jobs he was interrupting, were much bored with his visits, and took very little interest in his protestations. In reward for these distasteful exertions Lucia relaxed the Spartan commissariat – indeed, she disliked it very much herself and occasionally wondered if her example was being either followed or respected – and she gave him Lucullan lunches and dinners. Elizabeth, of course, at once got wind of his candidature and canvassing, but instead of withdrawing, she started a hurricane campaign of her own. Her ticket was the reduction of rates, instead of this rise in them which these idiotic schemes for useless luxuries would inevitably produce.

The result of the election was to be announced by the Mayor from the steps of the Town Hall. Owing to the howling gale, and the torrents of rain the street outside was absolutely empty save for the figure of Major Benjy clad in a sou'wester hat, a mackintosh and waders, crouching in the most sheltered corner he could find beneath a dripping umbrella. Elizabeth had had hard work to induce him to come at all: he professed himself perfectly content to curb his suspense in comfort at home by the fire till she returned with the news, and all the other inhabitants of Tilling felt they could wait till next morning ... Then Lucia emerged from the Town Hall with a candidate on each side of her, and in a piercing scream, to make her voice heard in this din of the elements, she announced the appalling figures. Mrs Elizabeth Mapp-Flint, she yelled, had polled eight hundred and five votes, and was therefore elected.

Major Benjy uttered a hoarse 'Hurrah!' and trying to clap his hands let go of his umbrella which soared into the gale and was seen no more . . . Mr George Pillson, screamed Lucia, had polled four hundred and twenty-one votes. Elizabeth, at the top of her voice, then warmly thanked the burgesses of Tilling for the confidence which they had placed in her, and which she would do her best to deserve. She shook hands with the Mayor and the defeated candidate, and instantly drove away with her husband. As there were no other burgesses to address, Georgie did not deliver the speech which he had prepared: indeed it would have been quite unsuitable, since he had intended to thank the burgesses of Tilling in similar terms. He and Lucia scurried to their car, and Georgie put up the window.

'Most mortifying,' he said.

'My dear, you did your best,' said Lucia, pressing his arm with a wet but sympathetic hand. 'In public life, one has to take these little reverses –'

'Most humiliating,' interrupted Georgie. 'All that trouble thrown away. Being triumphed over by Elizabeth when you led me to expect quite the opposite. She'll be far more swanky now than if I hadn't put up.'

'No, Georgie, there I can't agree,' said Lucia. 'If there had been no other candidate, she would have said that nobody felt he had the slightest chance against her. That would have been much worse. Anyhow she knows now that four hundred and – what was the figure?'

'Four hundred and twenty-one,' said Georgie.

'Yes, four hundred and twenty-one thoughtful voters in Tilling –'

'– against eight hundred and five thoughtless ones,' said Georgie. 'Don't let's talk any more about it. It's a loss of prestige for both of us. No getting out of it.'

Lucia hurried indoors to tell Grosvenor to bring up a bottle of champagne for dinner, and to put on to the fire the pretty wreath of laurel leaves which she had privily stitched together for the coronation of her new Town Councillor.

'What's that nasty smell of burning evergreen?' asked Georgie morosely, as they went into the dining-room.

In the opinion of friends the loss of prestige had been entirely

Lucia's. Georgie would never have stood for the Council unless she had urged him, and it was a nasty defeat which, it was hoped, might do the Mayor good. But the Mayoress's victory, it was feared, would have the worst effect on her character. She and Diva met next morning in the pouring rain to do their shopping.

'Very disagreeable for poor Worship,' said Elizabeth 'and not very friendly to me to put up another candidate –'

'Rubbish,' said Diva. 'She's made you Mayoress. Quite enough friendliness for one year, I should have thought.'

'And it was out of friendliness that I accepted. I wanted to be of use to her, and stood for the Council for the same reason –'

'Only she thought Mr Georgie would be of more use than you,' interrupted Diva.

'Somebody in her pocket – Take care, Diva. Susan's van.'

The Royce drew up close to them, and Susan's face loomed in the window.

'Good morning, Elizabeth,' she said. 'I've just heard –'

'Thanks, dear, for your congratulations,' said Elizabeth. 'But quite a walk-over.'

Susan's face showed no sign of comprehension.

'What did you walk over?' she asked. 'In this rain, too? – Oh, the election to the Town Council. How nice for you! When are you going to reduce the rates?'

A shrill whistle, and Irene's huge red umbrella joined the group.

'Hullo, Mapp!' she said. 'So you've got on the map again. Ha, ha! How dare you stand against Georgie when my Angel wanted him to get in?'

Irene's awful tongue always deflated Elizabeth.

'Dear quaint one!' she said. 'What a lovely umbrella.'

'I know that. But how dare you?'

Elizabeth was stung into sarcasm.

'Well, we don't all of us think that your Angel must always have her way, dear,' she replied, 'and that we must lie down flat for her to trample us into the mire.'

'But she raised you out of the mire, woman,' cried Irene,

'when she made you Mayoress. She took pity on your fruitless efforts to become somebody. Wait till you see my fresco.'

Elizabeth was sorry she had been so courageous!

'Painting a pretty fresco, dear?' she asked. 'How I shall look forward to seeing it!'

'It may be a disappointment to you,' said Irene. 'Do you remember posing for me on the day Lucia made you Mayoress? It came out in the *Hampshire Argus*. Well, it's going to come out again in my fresco. Standing on an oyster-shell with Benjy blowing you along. Wait and see.'

This was no brawl for an MBE to be mixed up in, and Susan called 'Home!' to her chauffeur, and shut the window. Even Diva thought she had better move on.

'Bye-bye,' she said. 'Must get back to my baking.'

Elizabeth turned on her with a frightful grin.

'Very wise,' she said. 'If you had got back earlier to your baking yesterday, we should have enjoyed your jam-puffs more.'

'That's too much!' cried Diva. 'You ate three.'

'And bitterly repented it,' said Elizabeth.

Irene hooted with laughter and went on down the street. Diva crossed it, and Elizabeth stayed where she was for a moment to recover her poise. Why did Irene always cause her to feel like a rabbit with a stoat in pursuit? She bewildered and disintegrated her; she drained her of all power of invective and retort. She could face Diva, and had just done so with signal success, but she was no good against Irene. She plodded home through the driving rain, menaced by the thought of that snap-shot being revived again in fresco.

5

Nobody was more conscious of this loss of prestige than Lucia herself, and there were losses in other directions as well. She had hoped that her renunciation of gambling would have induced card-playing circles to follow her example. That hope was frustrated; bridge-parties with the usual stakes were as numerous as ever, but she was not asked to them. Another worry was that the humiliating election rankled in Georgie's mind and her seeking his advice on municipal questions, which was intended to show him how much she relied on his judgment, left him unflattered. When they sat after dinner in the garden-room (where, alas, no eager gamblers now found the hours pass only too quickly) her lucid exposition of some administrative point failed to rouse any real enthusiasm in him.

'And if everything isn't quite clear,' she said, 'mind you interrupt me, and I'll go over it again.'

But no interruption ever came; occasionally she thought she observed that slight elongation of the face that betokens a suppressed yawn, and at the end, as likely as not, he made some comment which showed he had not listened to a word she was saying. To-night, she was not sorry he asked no questions about the contentious conduct of the catchment board, as she was not very clear about it herself. She became less municipal.

'How these subjects get between one and the lighter side of life!' she said. 'Any news to-day?'

'Only that turn-up between Diva and Elizabeth,' he said.

'Georgie, you never told me! What about?'

'I began to tell you at dinner,' said Georgie, 'only you changed the subject to the water-rate. It started with jam-puffs. Elizabeth ate three one afternoon at Diva's, and said

595

next morning that she bitterly repented it. Diva says she'll never serve her a tea again, until she apologizes, but I don't suppose she means it.'

'Tell me more!' said Lucia, feeling the old familiar glamour stealing over her. 'And how is her tea-shop getting on?'

'Flourishing. The most popular house in Tilling. All so pleasant and chatty, and a rubber after tea on most days. Quite a centre.'

Lucia wrestled with herself for an intense moment.

'There's a point on which I much want your advice,' she began.

'Do you know, I don't think I can hope to understand any more municipal affairs to-night,' said Georgie firmly.

'It's not that sort, dear,' she said, wondering how to express herself in a lofty manner. 'It is this: You know how I refused to play bridge any more for money. I've been thinking deeply over that decision. Deeply. It was meant to set an example, but if nobody follows an example, Georgie, one has to consider the wisdom of continuing to set it.'

'I always thought you'd soon find it very tarsome not to get your bridge,' said Georgie. 'You used to enjoy it so.'

'Ah, it's not *that*,' said Lucia, speaking in her best Oxford voice. 'I would willingly never see a card again if that was all, and indeed the abstract study of the game interests me far more. But I did find a certain value in our little bridge-parties quite apart from cards. Very suggestive discussions, sometimes, about local affairs, and now more than ever it is so important for me to be in touch with the social as well as the municipal atmosphere of the place. I regret that others have not followed my example, for I am sure our games would have been as thrilling as ever, but if others won't come into line with me, I will gladly step back into the ranks again. Nobody shall be able to say of me that I caused splits and dissensions. "One and all", as you know, is my favourite motto.'

Georgie didn't know anything of the sort, but he let it pass.

'Capital!' he said. 'Everybody will be very glad.'

'And it would give me great pleasure to reconcile that child-ish quarrel between Diva and Elizabeth,' continued Lucia. 'I'll ask Elizabeth and Benjy to have tea with us there to-morrow; dear Diva will not refuse to serve a guest of *mine*, and their little disagreement will be smoothed over. A rubber afterwards.'

Georgie looked doubtful.

'Perhaps you had better tell them that you will play for the usual stakes,' he said. 'Else they might say they were engaged again.'

Lucia, with her vivid imagination, visualized the horrid superior grin which, at the other end of the telephone, would spread over Elizabeth's face, when she heard that, and felt that she would scarcely be able to get the words out. But she steeled herself and went to the telephone.

Elizabeth and Benjy accepted, and, after a reconciliatory eighteen-penny tea, at which Elizabeth ate jam-puffs with gusto ('Dear Diva, what delicious, light pastry,' she said. ' I wonder it doesn't fly away.') the four retired into the card-room. As if to welcome Lucia back into gambling circles, the God of Chance provided most exciting games. There were slams declared and won, there was doubling and redoubling and rewards and vengeances. Suddenly Diva looked in with a teapot in her hand and a most anxious expression on her face. She closed the door.

'The Inspector of Police wants to see you, Lucia,' she whispered.

Lucia rose, white to the lips. In a flash there came back to her all her misgivings about the legality of Diva's permitting gambling in a public room, and now the police were raiding it. She pictured headlines in the *Hampshire Argus* and lurid paragraphs . . . Raid on Mrs Godiva Plaistow's gaming-rooms . . . The list of the gamblers caught there. The Mayor and Mayoress of Tilling . . . A retired Major. The Mayor's husband. The case brought before the Tilling magistrates with the Mayor in the dock instead of on the Bench. Exemplary fines. Her own resignation. Eternal infamy . . .

'Did he ask for me personally?' said Lucia.

'Yes. Knew that you were here,' wailed Diva. 'And my

tea-shop will be closed. Oh, dear me, if I'd only heeded your warning about raids! Or if we'd only joined you in playing bridge for nothing!'

Lucia rose to the topmost peak of magnanimity, and refrained from rubbing that in.

'Is there a back way out, Diva?' she asked. 'Then they could all go. I shall remain and receive my Inspector here. Just sitting here. Quietly.'

'But there's no back way out,' said Diva. 'And you can't get out of the window. Too small.'

'Hide the cards!' commanded Lucia, and they all snatched up their hands. Georgie put his in his breast-pocket. Benjy put his on the top of the large cupboard. Elizabeth sat on hers. Lucia thrust hers up the sleeve of her jacket.

'Ask him to come in,' she said. 'Now all talk!'

The door opened, and the Inspector stood majestically there with a blue paper in his hand.

'Indeed, as you say, Major Mapp-Flint,' said Lucia in an unwavering Oxford voice, 'the League of Nations has collapsed like a card-house – I should say a ruin – Yes, Inspector, did you want me?'

'Yes, Your Worship. I called at Mallards, and was told I should catch you here. There's a summons that needs your signature. I hope Your Worship will excuse my coming, but it's urgent.'

'Quite right, Inspector,' said Lucia. 'I am always ready to be interrupted on magisterial business. I see. On the dotted line. Lend me your fountain-pen, Georgie.'

As she held out her hand for it, all her cards tumbled out of her sleeve. A draught eddied through the open door and Benjy's *cache* on the cupboard fluttered into the air. Elizabeth jumped up to gather them, and the cards on which she was sitting fell on to the floor.

Lucia signed with a slightly unsteady hand, and gave the summons back to the Inspector.

'Thank you, Your Worship,' he said. 'Very sorry to interrupt your game, ma'am.'

'Not at all,' said Lucia. 'You were only doing your duty.'

He bowed and left the room.

'I must apologize to you all,' said Lucia without a moment's pause, 'but my good Inspector has orders to ask for me whenever he wants to see me on any urgent matter. Dear me! All my cards exposed on the table and Elizabeth's and Major Benjy's on the floor. I am afraid we must have a fresh deal.'

Nobody made any allusion to the late panic, and Lucia dealt again.

Diva looked in again soon, carrying a box of chocolates.

'Any more Inspectors, dear?' asked Elizabeth acidly. 'Any more raids? Your nerves seem rather jumpy.'

Diva was sorely tempted to retort that their nerves seemed pretty jumpy too, but it was bad for business to be sharp with patrons.

'No, and I'm giving him such a nice tea,' she said meekly. 'But it was a relief, wasn't it? A box of chocolates for you. Very good ones.'

The rubber came to an end, with everybody eating chocolates, and a surcharged chat on local topics succeeded. It almost intoxicated Lucia, who, now for weeks, had not partaken of that heady beverage, and she felt more than ever like Catherine the Great.

'A very recreative two hours,' she said to Georgie as they went up the hill homewards, 'though I still maintain that our game would have been just as exciting without playing for money. And that farcical interlude of my Inspector! Georgie, I don't mind confessing that just for one brief moment it *did* occur to me that he was raiding the premises –'

'Oh, I know that,' said Georgie. 'Why, you asked Diva if there wasn't a back way out, and told us to hide our cards and talk. I was the only one of us who knew how absurd it all was.'

'But how you bundled your cards into your pocket! We were all a little alarmed. All. I put it down to Diva's terror-stricken entrance with her teapot dribbling at the spout –'

'No! I didn't see that,' said Georgie.

'Quite a pool on the ground. And her lamentable outcry about her tea-rooms being closed. It was suggestion, dear. Very sensitive people like myself respond automatically to suggestion ... And most interesting about Susan and her automatic script. She thinks, Elizabeth tells me, that Blue Birdie controls her when she's in trance, and is entirely wrapped up in it.'

'She's hardly ever seen now,' said Georgie. 'She never plays bridge, nor comes to Diva's for tea, and Algernon usually does her marketing.'

'I must really go to one of her *séances*, if I can find a free hour sometime,' said Lucia. 'But my visit must be quite private. It would never do if it was known that the Mayor attended *séances* which do seem akin to necromancy. Necromancy, as you may know, is divining through the medium of a corpse.'

'But that's a human corpse, isn't it?' asked he.

'I don't think you can make a distinction – Oh! Take care!'

She pulled Georgie back, just as he was stepping on to the road from the pavement. A boy on a bicycle, riding without lights, flew down the hill, narrowly missing him.

'Most dangerous!' said Lucia. 'No lights and excessive speed. I must ring up my Inspector and report that boy – I wonder who he was.'

'I don't see how you can report him unless you know,' suggested Georgie.

Lucia disregarded such irrelevancy. Her eyes followed the boy as he curved recklessly round the sharp corner into the High Street.

'Really I feel more envious than indignant,' she said. 'It must be so exhilarating. Such speed! What Lawrence of Arabia always loved. I feel very much inclined to learn bicycling. Those smart ladies of the nineties used to find it very amusing. Bicycling-breakfasts in Battersea Park and all that. Our brisk walks, whenever I have time to take them, are so limited: in these short afternoons we can hardly get out into the country before it is time to turn again.'

The idea appealed to Georgie, especially when Lucia embellished it with mysterious and conspiratorial additions. No one must know that they were learning until they were accomplished enough to appear in the High Street in complete control of their machines. What a sensation that would cause! What envious admiration! So next day they motored out to a lonely stretch of road a few miles away, where a man from the bicycle-shop, riding a man's bicycle and guiding a woman's, had a clandestine assignation with them. He held Georgie on, while Cadman, Lucia's chauffeur, clung to her, and for the next few afternoons they wobbled about the road with incalculable swoopings. Lucia was far the quicker of the two in acquiring the precarious balance, and she talked all the time to Cadman.

'I'm beginning to feel quite secure,' she said. 'You might let go for one second. No: there's a cart coming. Better wait till it has passed. Where's Mr Georgie? Far behind, I suppose.'

'Yes, ma'am. Ever so far.'

'Oh, what a jolt!' she cried, as her front wheel went over a loose stone. 'Enough to unseat anybody. I put on the brake, don't I?'

After ringing the bell once or twice, Lucia found the brake. The bicycle stopped dead, and she stepped lightly off.

'So powerful,' she said remounting. 'Now both hands off for a moment, Cadman.'

The day came when Georgie's attendant still hovered close to him, but when Lucia outpaced Cadman altogether. A little way in front of her a man near the edge of the road, with a saucepan of tar bubbling over a pot of red-hot coals, was doctoring a telegraph-post. Then something curious happened to the co-ordination between Lucia's brain and muscles. The imperative need of avoiding the fire-pot seemed to impel her to make a bee-line for it. With her eyes firmly fixed on it, she felt in vain for that powerful brake, and rode straight into the fire-pot, upsetting the tar and scattering the coals.

'Oh, I'm so sorry,' she said to the operator. 'I'm rather new at it. Would half a crown? And then would you kindly hold my bicycle while I mount again?'

The road was quite empty after that, and Lucia sped prosperously along, wobbling occasionally for no reason, but rejoicing in the comparative swiftness. Then it was time to turn. This was impossible without dismounting, but she mounted again without much difficulty, and there was a lovely view of Tilling rising red-roofed above the level land. Telegraph-post after telegraph-post flitted past her, and then she caught sight of the man with the fire-pot again. Lucia felt that he was observing her, and once more something curious occurred to her co-ordinations, and with it the familiar sense of exactly the same situation having happened before. Her machine began to swoop about the road; she steadied it, and with the utmost precision went straight into the fire-pot again.

'You seem to make a practice of it,' remarked the operator severely.

'Too awkward of me,' said Lucia. 'It was the very last thing I wanted to do. Quite the last.'

'That'll be another half-crown,' said the victim, 'and now I come to look at you, it was you and your pals cocked up on the Bench, who fined me five bob last month, for not being half as unsteady as you.'

'Indeed! How small the world is,' said Lucia with great dignity and aloofness, taking out her purse. Indeed it was a strange coincidence that she should have disbursed to the culprit of last month exactly the sum that she had fined him for drunkenness. She thought there was something rather psychic about it, but she could not tell Georgie, for that would have disclosed to him that in the course of her daring, unac-companied ride she had twice upset a fire-pot and scattered tar and red-hot coals on the highway. Soon she met him still outward bound and he, too, was riding unsupported.

'I've made such strides to-day,' he called out. 'How have you got on?'

'Beautifully! Miles!' said Lucia, as they passed each other. But we must be getting back. Let me see you turn, dear, without dismounting. Not so difficult.'

The very notion of attempting that made Georgie unsteady, and he got off.

'I don't believe she can do it herself,' he muttered, as he turned his machine and followed her. The motor was waiting for them, and just as she was getting in, he observed a blob of tar on one of her shoes. She wiped it off on the grass by the side of the road.

Susan had invited them both to a necromantic *séance* after tea that evening. She exclaimed that she would not ask them to tea, because before these sittings she fasted and meditated in the dark for an hour. When they got home from their ride, Georgie went to his sitting-room to rest, but Lucia, fresh as a daisy, filled up time by studying a sort of catechism from the Board of the Southern Railway in answer to her suggestion of starting a Royal Fish Express with a refrigerating van to supply the Court. They did not seem very enthusiastic; they put a quantity of queries. Had Her Worship received a Royal command on the subject? Did she propose to run the RFE to Balmoral when the Court was in Scotland, because there were Scotch fishing-ports a little closer? Had she worked out the cost of a refrigerating van? Was the supply of fish at Tilling sufficient to furnish the Royal table as well as the normal requirements of the district? Did Her Worship –'

Grosvenor entered. Mr Wyse had called, and would much like, if quite convenient, to have a few words with Lucia before the *séance*. That seemed a more urgent call, for all these fish questions required a great deal of thought, and must be gone into with Mrs Simpson next morning, and she told Grosvenor that she could give him ten minutes. He entered, carrying a small parcel wrapped up in brown paper.

'So good of you to receive me,' he said. 'I am aware of the value of your time. A matter of considerable delicacy. My dear Susan tells me that you and your husband have graciously promised to attend her *séance* to-day.'

Lucia referred to her engagement-book.

'Quite correct,' she said. 'I found I could just fit it in. 5.30 p.m. is my entry.'

'I will speak but briefly of the ritual of these *séances*,' said Mr Wyse. 'My Susan sits at the table in our little dining-room, which you have, alas too rarely, honoured by your presence on what I may call less moribund occasions. It is furnished with a copious supply of scribbling-paper and of sharpened pencils,

for her automatic script. In front of her is a small shrine, I
may term it, of ebony – possibly ebonite – with white satin
curtains concealing what is within. At the commencement of
the *séance*, the lights are put out, and my Susan draws the
curtains aside. Within are the mortal remains – or such as
could be hygienically preserved – of her budgerigar. She used
to wear them in her hat or as a decoration for the bosom. They
once fell into a dish, a red dish, at your hospitable table.'

'I remember. Raspberry something,' said Lucia.

'I bow to your superior knowledge,' said Mr Wyse. 'Then
Susan goes into a species of trance, and these communications
through automatic script begin. Very voluminous sometimes,
and difficult to decipher. She spends the greater part of the
day in puzzling them out, not always successfully. Now, *ador-
abile Signora –*'

'Oh, Mr Wyse,' cried Lucia, slightly startled.

'Dear lady, I only meant Your Worship,' he explained.

'I see. Stupid of me,' she said. 'Yes?'

'I appeal to you,' continued he. 'To put the matter in a
nutshell, I fear my dear Susan will get unhinged, if this goes on.
Already she is sadly changed. Her strong common sense, her
keen appreciation of the comforts and interests of life, her fur
coat, her Royce, her shopping, her bridge; all these are tasteless
to her. Nothing exists for her except these communings.'

'But how can I help you?' asked Lucia . . .

Mr Wyse tapped the brown-paper parcel.

'I have brought here,' he said, 'the source of all our trouble:
Blue Birdie. I abstracted it from the shrine while my dear
Susan was meditating in the drawing-room. I want it to disappear in the hope that when she discovers it has gone, she will
have to give up the *séances*, and recover her balance. I would
not destroy it: that would be going too far. Would you therefore, dear lady, harbour the Object in some place unknown to
me, so that when Susan asks me, as she undoubtedly will, if I
know where it is, I may be able to tell her that I do not? A
shade jesuitical perhaps, but such jesuitry, I feel, is justifiable.'

Lucia considered this. 'I think it is, too,' she said. 'I will put
it somewhere safe. Anything to prevent our Susan becoming

unhinged. That must never happen. By the way, is there a slight odour?'

'A reliable and harmless disinfectant,' said Mr Wyse. 'There was a faint smell in the neighbourhood of the shrine which I put down to imperfect taxidermy. A thousand thanks, Worshipful Lady. One cannot tell what my Susan's reactions may be, but I trust that the disappearance of the Object may lead to a discontinuance of the *séances*. In fact, I do not see how they could be held without it.'

Lucia had ordered a stack of black japanned boxes to hold documents connected with municipal departments. The arms of the Borough and her name were painted on them, with the subject with which they were concerned. There were several empty ones, and when Mr Wyse had bowed himself out, she put Blue Birdie into the one labelled 'Museum', which seemed appropriate. 'Burial Board' would have been appropriate, too, but there was already an agenda-paper in that.

Presently she and Georgie set forth for Starling Cottage.

Susan and Algernon were ready for them in the dining-room. The shrine with drawn curtains was on the table. Susan had heated a shovel and was burning incense on it.

'Blue Birdie came from the Spice Islands,' she explained, waving the shovel in front of the shrine. 'Yesterday my hand wrote "sweet gums" as far as I could read it, over and over again, and I think that's what he meant. And I've put up a picture of St Francis preaching to the birds.'

Certainly Susan, as her husband had said, was much changed. She looked dotty. There was an ecstatic light in her eye, and a demented psychical smile on her mouth. She wore a wreath in her hair, a loose white gown, and reminded Lucia of an immense operatic Ophelia. But critical circumstances always developed Lucia's efficiency, and she nodded encouragingly to Algernon as Susan swept fragrantly about the room.

'So good of you to let us come, dear Susan,' she said. 'I have very great experience in psychical phenomena: adepts – do you remember the Guru at Riseholme, Georgie? – adepts always tell me that I should be a marvellous medium if I had time to devote myself to the occult.'

Susan held up her hand.

'Hush,' she whispered. 'Surely I heard "Tweet, tweet", which means Blue Birdie is here. Good afternoon, darling.'

She put the fire-shovel into the fender.

'Very promising,' she said. 'Blue Birdie doesn't usually make himself heard so soon, and it always means I'm going into trance. It must be you, Lucia, who have contributed to the psychic force.'

'Very likely,' said Lucia, 'the Guru always said I had immense power.'

'Turn out the lights then, Algernon, all but the little ruby lamp by my paper, and I will undraw the curtains of the shrine. Tweet, tweet! There it is again, and that lost feeling is coming over me.'

Lucia had been thinking desperately, while Ophelia got ready, with that intense concentration which, so often before, had smoothed out the most crumpled situations. She gave a silvery laugh.

'I heard it, I heard it,' she exclaimed to Algernon's great surprise. '*Buona sera*, Blue Birdie. Have you come to see Mummie and Auntie Lucia from Spicy Islands? . . . Oh, I'm sure I felt a little brush of soft feathers on my cheek.'

'No! did you really?' asked Susan with the slightest touch of jealousy in her voice. 'My pencil, Algernon.'

Lucia gave a swift glance at the shrine, as Susan drew the curtains, and was satisfied that the most spiritually enlightened eye could not see that it was empty. But dark though the room was, it was as if fresh candles were being profusely lit in her brain, as on some High Altar dedicated to Ingenuity. She kept her eyes fixed on Susan's hand poised over her paper. It was recording very little: an occasional dot or dash was all the inspiration Blue Birdie could give. For herself, she exclaimed now and then that she felt in the dark the brush of the bird's wing, or heard that pretty note. Each time she saw that the pencil paused. Then the last and the greatest candle was lit in her imagination, and she waited calm and composed for the conclusion of the *séance*, when Susan would see that the shrine was empty.

They sat in the dim ruby light for half an hour, and Susan, as if not quite lost, gave an annoyed exclamation.

'Very disappointing,' she said. 'Turn on the light, Algernon. Blue Birdie began so well and now nothing is coming through.'

Before he could get to the switch, Lucia, with a great gasp of excitement, fell back in her chair, and covered her eyes with her hands.

'Something wonderful has happened,' she chanted. 'Blue Birdie has left us altogether. What a manifestation!'

Still not even peeping, she heard Susan's voice rise to a scream.

'But the shrine's empty!' she cried. 'Where is Blue Birdie, Algernon?'

'I have no idea,' said the Jesuit. 'What has happened?'

Lucia still sat with covered eyes.

'Did I not tell you before the light was turned on that there had been a great manifestation?' she asked. 'I *knew* the shrine would be empty! Let me look for myself.'

'Not a feather!' she said. 'The dematerialization is complete. Oh, what would not the President of the Psychical Research have given to be present! Only a few minutes ago, Susan and I – did we not, Susan? – heard his little salutation, and I, at any rate, felt his feathers brush my cheek. Now no trace! Never, in all my experience, have I seen anything so perfect.'

'But what does it mean?' asked the distraught Susan, pulling the wreath from her dishevelled hair. Lucia waved her hands in a mystical movement.

'Dear Susan,' she said, beginning to gabble, 'Listen! All these weeks your darling's spirit has been manifesting itself to you and to me also to-night, with its pretty chirps and strokes of the wing, in order to convince you of its presence, earthbound and attached to its mortal remains. Now on the astral plane Blue Birdie has been able so to flood them with spiritual reality that they have been dissolved, translated – ah, how badly I put it – into spirit. Blue Birdie has been helping you all these weeks to realize that all is spirit. Now you have this final, supreme demonstration. Rapt with all of him that was mortal into a higher sphere!'

'But won't he ever come back?' asked Susan.

'Ah, you would not be so selfish as to wish that!' said Lucia. 'He is free; he is earth-bound no longer, and, by this miracle of dematerialization, has given you proof of that. Let me see what his last earthly communication with you was.'

Lucia picked up the sheet on which Susan had automatically recorded a few undecipherable scribbles.

'I knew it!' she cried. 'See, there is nothing but those few scrawled lines. Your sweet bird's spirit was losing connection with the material sphere; he was rising above it. How it all hangs together!'

'I shall miss him dreadfully,' said Susan in a faltering voice.

'But you mustn't, you mustn't. You cannot grudge him his freedom. And, oh, what a privilege to have assisted at such a demonstration! Ennobling! And if my small powers added to yours, dear, helped toward such a beautiful result, why that is *more* than a privilege.'

Georgie felt sure that there was hocus-pocus somewhere, and that Lucia had had a hand in it, but his probings, as they walked away, only elicited from her idiotic replies such as 'Too marvellous! What a privilege!'

It soon became known in marketing circles next morning that very remarkable necromancy had occurred at Starling Cottage, that Blue Birdie had fluttered about the darkened room, uttering his sharp cries, and had several times brushed against the cheek of the Mayor. Then, wonder of wonders, his mortal remains had vanished. Mr Wyse walked up and down the High Street, never varying his account of the phenomena, but unable to explain them, and for the first time for some days Susan appeared in her Royce, but without any cockade in her hat.

There was something mysterious and incredible about it all, but it did not usurp the entire attention of Tilling, for why did Elizabeth, from whom violent sarcasm might have been expected, seem to shun conversation? She stole rapidly from shop to shop, and, when cornered by Diva, coming out of the butcher's, she explained, scarcely opening her lips at all, that she had a relaxed throat, and must only breathe through her nose.

'I should open my mouth wide,' said Diva severely, 'and have a good gargle,' but Elizabeth only shook her head with an odd smile, and passed on. 'Looks a bit hollow-cheeked, too,' thought Diva. By contrast, Lucia was far from hollow-cheeked; she had a swollen face, and made no secret of her appointment with the dentist to have 'it' out. From there she went home, with the expectation of receiving, later in the day, a denture comprising a few molars with a fresh attachment added.

She ate her lunch, in the fashion of a rabbit, with her front teeth.

'Such a skilful extraction, Georgie,' she said, 'but a little sore.'

As she had a Council meeting that afternoon, Georgie went off alone in the motor for his assignation with the boy from the bicycle-shop. The *séance* last evening still puzzled him, but he felt more certain than ever that her exclamations that she heard chirpings and felt the brush of Birdie's wing were absolute rubbish; so, too, was her gabble that her psychic powers added to Susan's, had brought about the dematerialization. 'All bosh,' he said aloud in an annoyed voice, 'and it only confirms her complicity. It's very unkind of her not to tell me how she faked it, when she knows how I would enjoy it.'

His bicycle was ready for him; he mounted without the slightest difficulty, and the boy was soon left far behind. Then with secret trepidation he observed not far ahead a man with a saucepan of tar simmering over a fire-pot. As he got close, he was aware of a silly feeling in his head that it was exercising a sort of fascination over his machine, but by keeping his eye on the road he got safely by it, though with frightful wobbles, and dismounted for a short rest.

'Well, that's a disappointment,' observed the operator. 'You ain't a patch on the lady who knocked down my fire-pot twice yesterday.'

Suddenly Georgie remembered the dab of tar on Lucia's shoe, and illumination flooded his brain.

'No! Did she indeed?' he said with great interest. 'The same lady twice? That was bad riding!'

'Oh, something shocking. Not that I'd ever seek to hinder

her, for she gave me half a crown per upset. Ain't she coming to-day?'

As he rode home Georgie again meditated on Lucia's secretiveness. Why could she not tell him about her jugglings at the *séance* yesterday and about her antics with the fire-pot? Even to him she had to keep up this incessant flow of triumphant achievement both in occult matters and in riding a bicycle. Now that they were man and wife she ought to be more open with him. 'But I'll tickle her up about the fire-pot,' he thought vindictively.

When he got home he found Lucia just returned from a most satisfactory Council meeting.

'We got through our business most expeditiously,' she said, 'for Elizabeth was absent, and so there were fewer irrelevant interruptions. I wonder what ailed her: nothing serious I hope. She was rather odd in the High Street this morning. No smiles: she scarcely opened her mouth when I spoke to her. And did you make good progress on your bicycle this afternoon?'

'Admirable,' said he. 'Perfect steering. There was a man with a fire-pot tarring a telegraph-post –'

'Ah, yes,' interrupted Lucia. 'Tar keeps off insects that burrow into the wood. Let us go and have tea.'

'– and an odd feeling came over me,' he continued firmly, 'that just because I must avoid it, I should very likely run into it. Have you ever felt that? I suppose not.'

'Yes, indeed I have in my earlier stages,' said Lucia cordially. 'But I can give you an absolute cure for it. Fix your eyes straight ahead, and you'll have no bother at all.'

'So I found. The man was a chatty sort of fellow. He told me that some learner on a bicycle had knocked over the pot twice yesterday. Can you imagine such awkwardness? I am pleased to have got past that stage.'

Lucia did not show by the wink of an eyelid that this arrow had pierced her, and Georgie, in spite of his exasperation, could not help admiring such nerve.

'Capital!' she said. 'I expect you've quite caught me up by your practice to-day. Now after my Council meeting I think I must relax. A little music, dear?'

A melodious half-hour followed. They were both familiar with Beethoven's famous Fifth Symphony, as arranged for four hands on the piano, and played it with ravishing sensibility.

'*Caro*, how it takes one out of all petty carpings and schemings!' said Lucia at the end. 'How all our smallnesses are swallowed up in that broad cosmic splendour! And how beautifully you played, dear. Inspired! I almost stopped in order to listen to you.'

Georgie writhed under these compliments: he could hardly switch back to dark hints about *séances* and fire-pots after them. In strong rebellion against his kindlier feelings towards her, he made himself comfortable by the fire, while Lucia again tackled the catechism imposed on her by the Directors of the Southern Railway. Fatigued by his bicycle-ride, Georgie fell into a pleasant slumber.

Presently Grosvenor entered, carrying a small packet, neatly wrapped up and sealed. Lucia put her finger to her lip with a glance at her sleeping husband, and Grosvenor withdrew in tiptoe silence. Lucia knew what this packet must contain; she could slip the reconstituted denture into her mouth in a moment, and there would be no more rabbit-nibbling at dinner. She opened the packet and took out of the cotton-wool wrapping what it contained.

It was impossible to suppress a shrill exclamation, and Georgie awoke with a start. Beneath the light of Lucia's reading-lamp there gleamed in her hand something dazzling, something familiar.

'My dear, what *have* you got?' he cried. 'Why, it's Elizabeth's front teeth! It's Elizabeth's widest smile without any of her face! But how? Why? Blue Birdie's nothing to this.'

Lucia made haste to wrap up the smile again.

'Of course it is,' she said. 'I knew it was familiar, and the moment you said "smile" I recognized it. That explains Elizabeth's shut mouth this morning. An accident to her smile, and now by some extraordinary mistake the dentist has sent it back to me. Me of all people! What are we to do?'

'Send it back to Elizabeth,' suggested Georgie, 'with a polite note saying it was addressed to you, and that you opened it. Serve her right, the deceitful woman! How often has she said that she never had any bother with her teeth, and hadn't been to a dentist since she was a child, and didn't know what toothache meant. No wonder; that kind doesn't ache.'

'Yes, that would serve her right –' began Lucia.

She paused. She began to think intensely. If Elizabeth's entire smile had been sent to her, where, except to Elizabeth, had her own more withdrawn aids to mastication been sent? Elizabeth could not possibly identify those four hinterland molars, unless she had been preternaturally observant, but the inference would be obvious if Lucia personally sent her back her smile.

'No, Georgie; that wouldn't be kind,' she said. 'Poor Elizabeth would never dare to smile at me again, if she knew I knew. I don't deny she richly deserves it for telling all those lies, but it would be an unworthy action. It is by a pure accident that we know, and we must not use it against her. I shall instantly send this box back to the dentist's.'

'But how do you know who her dentist is?' asked Georgie.

'Mr Fergus,' said Lucia, 'who took my tooth so beautifully this morning; there was his card with the packet. I shall merely say that I am utterly at a loss to understand why this has been sent me, and not knowing what the intended destination was, I return it.'

Grosvenor entered again. She bore a sealed packet precisely similar to that which now again contained Elizabeth's smile.

'With a note, ma'am,' she said. 'And the boy is waiting for a packet left here by mistake.'

'Oh, do open it,' said Georgie gaily. 'Somebody else's teeth, I expect. I wonder if we shall recognize them. Quite a new game, and most exciting.'

Hardly were the words out of his mouth when he perceived what must have happened. How on earth could Lucia get out of such an awkward situation? But it took far more than that to disconcert the Mayor of Tilling. She gave Grosvenor the other packet.

'A sample or two of tea that I was expecting,' she said in her most casual voice. 'Yes, from Twistevant's.' And she put the sample into a drawer of her table.

Who could fail to admire, thought Georgie, this brazen composure?

6

Elizabeth's relaxed throat had completely braced itself by next morning, and at shopping-time she was profuse in her thanks to Diva.

'I followed your advice, dear, and gargled well when I got home,' she said, 'and not a trace of it this morning . . . Ah, here's Worship and Mr Georgie. I was just telling Diva how quickly her prescription cured my poor throat; I simply couldn't speak yesterday. And I hope you're better, Worship. It must be a horrid thing to have a tooth out.'

Lucia and Georgie scrutinized her smile . . . There was no doubt about it.

'Ah, you're one of the lucky ones,' said Lucia in tones of fervent congratulation. 'How I envied you your beautiful teeth when Mr Fergus said he must take one of mine out.'

'I envy you too,' said Georgie. 'We all do.'

These felicitations seemed to speed Elizabeth's departure. She shut off her smile, and tripped across the street to tell the Padre that her throat was well again, and that she would be able to sing alto as usual in the choir on Sunday. With a slightly puzzled face he joined the group she had just left.

'Queer doings indeed!' he said in a sarcastic voice. 'Everything in Tilling seems to be vanishing. There's Mistress Mapp-Flint's relaxed throat, her as couldn't open her mouth yesterday. And there's Mistress Wyse's little bird. Dematerialized, they say. Havers! And there's Major Benjy's riding-whip. Very strange indeed. I canna' make nothing of it a'.'

The subject did not lead to much. Lucia had nothing to say about Blue Birdie, nor Diva about the riding-whip. She turned to Georgie.

'My tulip-bulbs have just come for my garden,' she said.

'Do spare a minute and tell me where and how to plant them. Doing it all myself. No gardener. Going to have an open-air tea-place in the spring. Want it to be a bower.'

The group dispersed. Lucia went to the bicycle-shop to order machines for the afternoon. She thought it would be better to change the *venue* and appointed the broad, firm stretch of sands beyond the golf-links, where she and Georgie could practise turning without dismounting, and where there would be no risk of encountering fire-pots. Georgie went with Diva into her back-garden.

'Things,' explained Diva, 'can be handed out of the kitchen window. So convenient. And where shall I have the tulips?'

'All along that bed,' said Georgie. 'Give me a trowel and the bulbs. I'll show you.'

Diva stood admiringly by.

'What a neat hole!' she said.

'Press the bulb firmly down, but without force,' said Georgie.

'I see. And then you cover it up, and put the earth back again –'

'And the next about three inches away –'

'Oh dear, oh dear. What a quantity it will take!' said Diva. 'And *do* you believe in Elizabeth's relaxed throat. I don't. I've been wondering –'

Through the open window of the kitchen came the unmistakable sound of a kettle boiling over.

'Shan't be a minute,' she said. 'Stupid Janet. Must have gone to do the rooms and left it on the fire.'

She trundled indoors. Georgie dug another hole for a bulb, and the trowel brought up a small cylindrical object, blackish of hue, but of smooth, polished surface, and evidently no normal product of a loamy soil. It was metal, and a short stub of wood projected from it. He rubbed the soil off it, and engraved on it were two initials, B.F. Memory poised like a hawk and swooped.

'It's it!' he said to himself. 'Not a doubt about it. Benjamin Flint.'

He slipped it into his pocket while he considered what to do with it. No; it would never do to tell Diva what he had found. Relics did not bury themselves, and who but Diva could have buried this one? Evidently she wanted to get rid of it, and it would be heartless as well as unnecessary to let her know that she had not succeeded. Bury it again then? There are feats of which human nature is incapable, and Georgie dug a hole for the next tulip.

Diva whizzed out again, and went on talking exactly where she had left off before the kettle boiled over, but repeating the last word to give him the context.

'– wondering if it was not teeth in some way. She often says they're so marvellous, but people who have really got marvellous teeth *don't* speak about them. They let them talk for themselves. Or bite. Tilling's full of conundrums as the Padre said. Especially since Lucia's become Mayor. She's more dynamic than ever and makes things happen all round her. What a gift! Oh, dear me, I'm talking to her husband. You don't mind, Mr Georgie? She's so central.'

Georgie longed to tell her how central Lucia had been about Elizabeth's relaxed throat, but that wouldn't be wise.

'Mind? Not a bit,' he said. 'And she would love to know that you feel that about her. Well, good luck to the tulips, and don't dig them up to see how they're getting on. It doesn't help them.'

'Of course not. Won't it be a bower in the spring? And Irene is going to paint a sign-board for me. Sure to be startling. But nothing nude, I said, except hands and faces.'

Irene was doing physical jerks on her doorstep as Georgie passed her house on his way home.

'Come in, King of my heart,' she called. 'Oh, Georgie, you're a public temptation, you are, when you've got on your mustard-coloured cape and your blue tam-o'-shanter. Come in, and let me adore you for five minutes – only five – or shall I show you the new design for my fresco?'

'I should like that best,' said Georgie severely.

Irene had painted a large sketch in oils to take the place of that which the Town Surveying Department had prohibited.

Tilling, huddling up the hill and crowned by the church formed the background, and in front, skimming up the river was a huge oyster-shell, on which was poised a substantial Victorian figure in shawl and bonnet and striped skirt, instead of the nude, putty-coloured female. It reproduced on a large scale the snap-shot of Elizabeth which had appeared in the *Hampshire Argus*, and the face, unmistakably Elizabeth's, wore a rapturous smile. One arm was advanced, and one leg hung out behind, as if she was skating. An equally solid gentleman, symbolizing wind, sprawled, in a frock-coat and top-hat, on a cloud behind her and with puffed cheeks propelled her up-stream.

'Dear me, most striking!' said Georgie. 'But isn't it very like that photograph of Elizabeth in the *Argus*? And won't people say that it's Major Benjy in the clouds?'

'Why, of course they will, stupid, unless they're blind,' cried Irene. 'I've never forgiven Mapp for being Mayoress and standing against you for the Town Council. This will take her down a peg, and all for the sake of Lucia.'

'It's most devoted of you, Irene,' he said, 'and such fun, too, but do you think –'

'I never think,' cried Irene. 'I *feel*, and that's how I feel. I'm the only person in this petty, scheming world of Tilling who acts on impulse. Even Lucia schemes sometimes. And as you've introduced the subject –'

'I haven't introduced any subject yet,' said Georgie.

'Just like you. You wouldn't. But Georgie, what a glorious picture, isn't it? I almost think it has gained by being Victor-ianized; there's a devilish reserved force about the Victorians which mere nudity lacks. A nude has all its cards on the table. I've a good mind to send it to the Royal Academy instead of making a fresco of it. Just to punish the lousy Grundys of Tilling.'

'That would serve them right,' agreed Georgie.

The afternoon bicycling along the shore was a great success. The tide was low, exposing a broad strip of firm, smooth sand. Chapman and the bicycle-boy no longer ran behind, and, now that there was so much room for turning, neither of the athletes found the least difficulty in doing so, and their turns soon grew, as Lucia said, as sharp as a needle. The rocks and groins provided objects to be avoided, and they skimmed close by them without collision. They mounted and dismounted, masters of the arts of balance and direction; all those secret practisings suddenly flowered.

'It's time to get bicycles of our own,' said Lucia as they turned homewards. 'We'll order them to-day, and as soon as they come we'll do our morning shopping on them.'

'I shall be very nervous,' said Georgie.

'No need, dear. I pass you as being able to ride through any traffic, and to dismount quickly and safely. Just remember not to look at anything you want to avoid. The head turned well away.'

'I am aware of that,' said Georgie, much nettled by this patronage. 'And about you. Remember about your brake and your bell. You confuse them sometimes. Ring your bell, dear! Now put on your brake. That's better.'

They joined the car and drove back along Fire-Pot Road. Work was still going on there, and Lucia, in a curious fit of absence of mind, pointed to the bubbling saucepan of tar.

'And to think that only a few days ago,' she said, 'I actually – My dear, I'll confess, especially as I feel sure you've guessed. I upset that tar-pot. Twice.'

'Oh, yes, I knew that,' said Georgie. 'But I'm glad you've told me at last. I'll tell you something, too. Look at this. Tell me what it is.'

He took out of his pocket the silver top of Benjy's riding-whip, which he had excavated this morning. Foljambe had polished it up. Lucia's fine eyebrows knit themselves in re-collective agony.

'Familiar, somehow,' she mused. 'Ah! Initials. B.F. Why, it's Benjy's! Newspaper-office! Riding-whip! Disappearance! Georgie, how did you come by it?'

Georgie's account was punctuated by comments from Lucia.

'Only the depth of a tulip-bulb . . . Not nearly deep enough, such want of thoroughness . . . Diva must have buried it herself, I think . . . So you were quite right not to have told her; very humiliating. But how did the top come to be snapped off? Do you suppose she broke it off, and buried the rest somewhere else, like murderers cutting up their victims? And look at the projecting end! It looks as if it had been bitten off, and why should Diva do that? If it had been Elizabeth with her beautiful teeth, it would have been easier to understand.'

'All very baffling,' said Georgie, 'but anyhow I've traced the disappearances a step further. I shall turn my attention to Blue Birdie next.'

Lucia thought she had done enough confession for one day.

'Yes, do look into it, Georgie,' she said. 'Very baffling, too. But Mr Wyse is most happy about the effect of my explanation upon Susan. She has accepted my theory that Blue Birdie has gone to a higher sphere.'

'That seems to me a very bad sign,' said Georgie. 'It looks as if she was seriously deranged. And, candidly, do you believe it yourself?'

'So difficult, isn't it,' said Lucia in a philosophical voice, 'to draw hard and fast lines between what one rationally believes, and what one trusts is true, and what seems to admit of more than one explanation. We must have a talk about that some day. A wonderful sunset!'

The bicycles arrived a week later, nickel-plated and belled and braked; Lucia's had the Borough arms of Tilling brilliantly painted on the tool-bag behind her saddle. They were brought up to Mallards after dark; and next morning, before breakfast, the two rode about the garden paths, easily passing up the narrow path into the kitchen-garden, and making circles round the mulberry-tree on the lawn ('Here we go round the mulberry-tree' light-heartedly warbled Lucia) and proving themselves adepts. Lucia could not eat much breakfast with the first public appearance so close, and Georgie vainly hoped that tropical rain would begin. But the sun continued to shine, and at the shopping-hour they mounted and bumped slowly down the cobbles of the steep street into the High Street, ready to ring their bells. Irene was the first to see them, and she ran by Lucia's side.

'Marvellous, perfect person,' she cried, putting out her hand as if to lay it on Lucia's. 'What is there you can't do?'

'Yes, dear, but don't touch me,' screamed Lucia in panic. 'So rough just here.' Then they turned on to the smooth tarmac of the High Street.

Evie saw them next.

'Dear, oh, dear, you'll both be killed!' she squealed. 'There's a motor coming at such a pace. Kenneth, they're riding bicycles!'

They passed superbly on. Lucia dismounted at the post-office; Georgie, applying his brake with exquisite delicacy, halted at the poulterer's with one foot on the pavement. Elizabeth was in the shop and Diva came out of the post-office.

'Good gracious me,' she cried. 'Never knew you could. And all this traffic!'

'Quite easy, dear,' said Lucia. 'Order a chicken, Georgie, while I get some stamps.'

She propped her bicycle against the kerb; Georgie remained sitting till Mr Rice came out of the poulterer's with Elizabeth.

'What a pretty bicycle!' she said, green with jealousy. 'Oh, there's Worship, too. Well, this is a surprise! So accomplished!'

They sailed on again. Georgie went to the lending-library, and found that the book Lucia wanted had come, but he preferred to have it sent to Mallards: hands, after all, were meant to take hold of handles. Lucia went on to the grocer's, and by the time he joined her there, the world of Tilling had collected: the Padre and Evie, Elizabeth and Benjy and Mr Wyse, while Susan looked on from the Royce.

'Such a saving of time,' said Lucia casually to the admiring assembly. 'A little spin in the country, Georgie, for half an hour?'

They went unerringly down the High Street, leaving an amazed group behind.

'Well, there's a leddy of pluck,' said the Padre. 'See, how she glides along. A mistress of a' she touches.'

Elizabeth was unable to bear it, and gave an acid laugh.

'Dear Padre!' she said. 'What a fuss about nothing! When I

was a girl I learned to ride a bicycle in ten minutes. The easiest thing in the world.'

'Did ye, indeed, me'm,' said the Padre, 'and that was very remarkable, for in those days, sure, there was only those great high machines, which you rode straddle.'

'Years and years after that,' said Elizabeth, moving away.

He turned to Evie.

'A bicycle would be a grand thing for me in getting about the parish,' he said. 'I'll step into the bicycle-shop, and see if they've got one on hire for to learn on.'

'Oh, Kenneth, I should like to learn, too,' said Evie. 'Such fun!'

Meantime the pioneers, rosy with success, had come to the end of the High Street. From there the road sloped rapidly downhill. 'Now we can put on the pace a little, Georgie,' said Lucia, and she shot ahead. All her practisings had been on the level roads of the marsh or on the sea-shore, and at once she was travelling much faster than she had intended, and with eyes glued on the curving road, she fumbled for her brake. She completely lost her head. All she could find in her agitation was her bell, and, incessantly ringing it, she sped with ever increasing velocity down the short steep road towards the bridge over the railway. A policeman on point duty stepped forward, with the arresting arm of the law held out to stop her, but as she took no notice he stepped very hastily back again, for to commit suicide and possibly manslaughter, was a more serious crime than dangerous riding. Lucia's face was contorted with agonized apprehension, her eyes stared, her mouth was wide open, and all the young constable could do by way of identification was to notice, when the unknown female had whisked by him, that the bicycle was new and that there was the Borough coat of arms on the tool-bag. Lucia passed between a pedestrian and a van, just avoiding both: she switch-backed up and down the railway-bridge, still ringing her bell ... Then in front of her lay the long climb of the Tilling hill, and as the pace diminished she found her brake. She dismounted, and waited for Georgie. He had lost sight of her in the traffic, and followed her cautiously in icy expectation of finding her and that beautiful new bicycle flung shattered on the road. Then he had one glimpse of her swift swallow-flight up the steep incline of the railway-bridge. Thank God she was safe so far! He traversed it himself and then saw her a hundred yards ahead up the hill. Long before he reached her his impetus was exhausted, and he got off.

'Don't hurry, dear,' she called to him in a trembling voice. 'You were right, quite right to ride cautiously. Safety first *always*.'

'I felt very anxious about you,' said Georgie, panting as he joined her. 'You oughtn't to have gone so fast. You deserve to be summoned for dangerous riding.'

A vision, vague and bright, shot through Lucia's brain. She could not conceive a more enviable piece of publicity than, at her age, to be summoned for so athletic a feat. It was punishable, no doubt, by law, but like a *crime passionel*, what universal admiration it would excite! What a dashing Mayor!

'I confess I was going very fast,' she said, 'but I felt I had such complete control of my machine. And so exhilarating. I don't suppose anybody has ever ridden so fast down Landgate Street. Now, if you're rested, shall we go on?'

They had a long but eminently prudent ride, and after lunch a well-earned siesta. Lucia, reposing on the sofa in the garden-room, was awakened by Grosvenor's entry from a frightful nightmare that she was pedalling for all she was worth down Beachy Head into the arms of a policeman on the shore.

'Inspector Morrison, ma'am,' said Grosvenor. 'He'll call again if not convenient.'

Nightmare vanished: the vague vision grew brighter. Was it possible? . . .

'Certainly, at once,' she said springing up and Inspector Morrison entered.

'Sorry to disturb Your Worship,' he said, 'but one of my men has reported that about 11 a.m. to-day a new bicycle with the arms of Tilling on the tool-bag was ridden at a dangerous speed by a female down Landgate Street. He made inquiries at the bicycle-shop and found that a similar machine was sent to your house yesterday. I therefore ask your permission to question your domestics –'

'Quite right to apply to me, Inspector,' said Lucia. 'You did your duty. Certainly I will sign the summons.'

'But we don't know who it was yet, ma'am. I should like to ask your servants to account for their whereabouts at 11 a.m.'

'No need to ask them, Inspector,' said Lucia. 'I was the culprit. Please send the summons round here and I will sign it.'

'But, Your Worship –'

Lucia was desperately afraid that the Inspector might wriggle out of summoning the Mayor and that the case would never come into Court. She turned a magisterial eye on him.

'I will not have one law for the rich and another for the poor in Tilling,' she said. 'I was riding at a dangerous speed. It was very thoughtless of me, and I must suffer for it. I ask you to proceed with the case in the ordinary course.'

This one appearance of Lucia and Georgie doing their shopping on bicycles had been enough to kindle the spark of emulation in the breasts of the more mature ladies of Tilling. It looked so lissom, so gaily adolescent to weave your way in and out of traffic and go for a spin in the country, and surely if Lucia could, they could also. Her very casualness made it essential to show her that there was nothing remarkable about her unexpected feat. The bicycle-shop was besieged with inquiries for machines on hire and instructors. The Padre and Evie were the first in the field, and he put off his weekly visit to the workhouse that afternoon from half-past two till half-past three, and they hired the two bicycles which Lucia and Georgie no longer needed. Diva popped in next, and was chagrined to find that the only lady's bicycle was already bespoke, so she engaged it for an hour on the following morning. Georgie that day did quite complicated shopping alone, for Lucia was at a committee meeting at the Town Hall. She rode there – a distance of a hundred and fifty yards to save time, but the gain was not very great, for she had to dismount twice owing to the narrow passage between posts for the prevention of vehicular traffic. Georgie, having returned from his shopping, joined her at the Town Hall when her meeting was over, and, with brakes fully applied, they rode down into the High Street, *en route* for another dash into the country. Susan's Royce was drawn up at the bicycle-shop.

'Georgie, I shan't have a moment's peace,' said Lucia, 'until I know whether Susan has ambitions too. I must just pop in.'

Both the Wyses were there. Algernon was leaning over Susan's shoulder as she studied a catalogue of the newest types of tricycle . . .

The Mayoress alone remained scornful and aloof. Looking out from her window one morning, she observed Diva approaching very slowly up the trafficless road that ran past Grebe buttressed up by Georgie's late instructor, who seemed to have some difficulty in keeping her perpendicular. She hurried to the garden-gate, reaching it just as Diva came opposite.

'Good morning, dear,' she said. 'Sorry to see that you're down with it, too.'

'Good morning, dear,' echoed Diva, with her eyes glued to the road in front of her. 'I haven't the slightest idea what you mean.'

'But is it wise to take such strenuous exercise?' asked Elizabeth. 'A great strain surely on both of you.'

'Not a bit of a strain,' called Diva over her shoulder. 'And my instructor says I shall soon get on ever so quick.'

The bicycle gave a violent swerve.

'Oh, take care,' cried Elizabeth in an anxious voice, 'or you'll get off ever so quick.'

'We'll rest a bit,' said Diva to her instructor, and she stepped from her machine and went back to the gate to have it out with her friend. 'What's the matter with you,' she said to Elizabeth, 'is that you can't bear us following Lucia's lead. Don't deny it. Look in your own heart, and you'll find it's true, Elizabeth. Get over it, dear. Make an effort. Far more Christian!'

'Thank you for your kind interest in my character, Diva,' retorted Elizabeth. 'I shall know now where to come when in spiritual perplexity.'

'Always pleased to advise you,' said Diva. 'And now give me

a treat. You told us all you learned to ride in ten minutes when you were a girl. I'll give you my machine for ten minutes. See if you can ride at the end of it! A bit coy, dear? Not surprised. And rapid motion might be risky for your relaxed throat.'

There was a moment's pause. Then both ladies were so pleased at their own brilliant dialectic that Elizabeth said she would pop in to Diva's establishment for tea, and Diva said that would be charming.

In spite of Elizabeth (or perhaps even because of her) this revival of the bicycling nineties grew most fashionable. Major Benjy turned traitor and was detected by his wife surreptitiously practising with the gardener's bicycle on the cinder path in the kitchen-garden. Mr Wyse suddenly appeared on the wheel riding in the most elegant manner. Figgis, his butler, he said, happened to remember that he had a bicycle put away in the garage and had furbished it up. Mr Wyse introduced a new style: he was already an adept and instead of wearing a preoccupied expression, made no more of it than if he was strolling about on foot. He could take a hand off his handle-bar, to raise his hat to the Mayor, as if one hand was all he needed. When questioned about this feat, he said that it was not really difficult to take both hands off without instantly crashing, but Lucia, after several experiments in the garden, concluded that Mr Wyse, though certainly a very skilful performer, was wrong about that. To crown all, Susan, after a long wait at the corner of Porpoise Street, where a standing motor left only eight or nine feet of the roadway clear, emerged majestically into the High Street on a brand new tricycle. 'Those large motors,' she complained to the Mayor, 'ought not to be allowed in our narrow streets.'

The Town Hall was crowded to its utmost capacity on the morning that Lucia was summoned to appear before her own Court for dangerous riding. She had bicycled there, now negotiating the anti-vehicular posts with the utmost precision, and, wearing her semi-official hat, presided on the Borough Bench. She and her brother magistrates had two cases to try before hers came on, of which one was that of a motor-cyclist whose brakes were out of order. The Bench, consulting together, took a grave view of the offence, and imposed a penalty of twenty shillings. Lucia in pronouncing sentence, addressed some severe remarks to him: he would have been unable to pull up, she told him, in case of an emergency, and was endangering the safety of his fellow citizens. The magistrates gave him seven days in which to pay. Then came the great moment. The Mayor rose, and in a clear unfaltering voice, said:

'Your Worships, I am personally concerned in the next case, and will therefore quit my seat on the Bench. Would the senior of Your Worships kindly preside in my temporary absence?'

She descended into the body of the Town Hall.

'The next case before Your Worships,' said the Town Clerk, 'is one of dangerous riding of a push-bicycle on the part of Mrs Lucia Pillson. Mrs Lucia Pillson.'

She pleaded guilty in a voice of calm triumph, and the Bench heard the evidence. The first witness was a constable, who swore that he would speak the truth, the whole truth and nothing but the truth. He was on point duty by the railway-bridge at 11 a.m. on Tuesday the twelfth instant. He observed a female bicyclist approaching at a dangerous speed down Landgate Street, when there was a lot of traffic about. He put out his arm to stop her, but she dashed by him. He estimated her speed at twenty miles an hour, and she seemed to have no control over her machine. After she had passed, he observed a tool-bag on the back of the saddle emblazoned with the Borough coat of arms. He made inquiries at the bicycle-shop and ascertained that a machine of this description had been supplied the day before to Mrs Pillson of Mallards House. He reported to his superior.

'Have you any questions, Your Worsh – to ask the witness?' asked the Town Clerk.

'None,' said Lucia eagerly. 'Not one.'

The next witness was the pedestrian she had so nearly annihilated. Lucia was dismayed to see that he was the operator with the fire-pot. He began to talk about his experiences when tarring telegraph-posts some while ago, but, to her intense relief, was promptly checked and told he must confine himself to what occurred at 11 a.m. on Tuesday. He deposed that at that precise hour, as he was crossing the road by the railway-bridge, a female bicyclist dashed by him at a speed which he estimated at over twenty miles an hour. A gratified smile illuminated the Mayor's face, and she had no questions to ask him.

That concluded the evidence, and the Inspector of Police said there were no previous convictions against the accused.

The Bench consulted together: there seemed to be some difference of opinion as to the amount of the fine. After a little discussion the temporary Chairman told Lucia that she also would be fined twenty shillings. She borrowed it from Georgie, who was sitting near, and so did not ask for time in which to pay. With a superb air she took her place again on the Bench.

Georgie waited for her till the end of the sitting, and stood a little in the background, but well in focus, while Lucia posed on the steps of the Town Hall, in the act of mounting her bicycle, for the photographer of the *Hampshire Argus*. His colleague on the reporting staff had taken down every word uttered in this *cause célèbre* and Lucia asked him to send proofs to her, before it went to press. It was a slight disappointment that no reporters or photographers had come down from London, for Mrs Simpson had been instructed to inform the Central News Agency of the day and hour of the trial . . . But the Mayor was well satisfied with the local prestige which her reckless athleticism had earned for her. Elizabeth, indeed, had attempted to make her friends view the incident in a different light, and she had a rather painful scene on the subject with the Padre and Evie.

'All too terrible,' she said. 'I feel that poor Worship has utterly disgraced herself, and brought contempt on the dignified office she holds. Those centuries of honourable men who have been Mayors here must turn in their graves. I've been wondering whether I ought not, in mere self-respect, to resign from being Mayoress. It associates me with her.'

'That's not such a bad notion,' said the Padre, and Evie gave several shrill squeaks.

'On the other hand, I should hate to desert her in her trouble,' continued the Mayoress. 'So true what you said in your sermon last Sunday, Padre, that it's our duty as Christians always to stand by our friends, whenever they are in trouble and need us.'

'So because she needs you, which she doesn't an atom,' burst out Evie, 'you come and tell us that she's disgraced herself, and made everybody turn in their graves. Most friendly, Elizabeth.'

'And I'm of wee wifie's opinion, mem,' said the Padre, with the brilliant thought of Evie becoming Mayoress in his mind, 'and if you feel you canna' preserve your self-respect unless you resign, why, it's your Christian duty to do so, and I warrant that won't incommode her, so don't let the standing by your friends deter you. And if you ask me what I think of Mistress Lucia's adventure, 'twas a fine spunky thing to have gone flying down the Landgate Street at thirty miles an hour. You and I daurna do it, and peradventure we'd be finer folk if we daur. And she stood and said she was guilty like a God-fearing upstanding body and she deserves a medal, she does. Come awa', wifie: we'll get to our bicycle-lesson.'

The Padre's view was reflected in the town generally, and his new figure of thirty miles an hour accepted. Though it was a very lawless and dangerous feat, Tilling felt proud of having so spirited a Mayor. Diva indulged in secret visions of record-breaking when she had learned to balance herself, and Susan developed such a turn of speed on her tricycle that Algernon called anxiously after her 'Not so fast, Susan, I beg you. Supposing you met something.' The Padre scudded about his parish on the wheel, and, as the movement grew, Lucia offered to coach anybody in her garden. It became fashionable to career up and down the High Street after dark, when traffic was diminished, and the whole length of it resounded with tinkling bells and twinkled with bicycle-lamps. There were no collisions, for everyone was properly cautious, but on one chilly evening the flapping skirt of Susan's fur coat got so inextricably entangled in the chain of her tricycle that she had to shed it, and Figgis trundled coat and tricycle back to Porpoise Street in the manner of a wheelbarrow.

As the days grew longer and the weather warmer, picnic-parties were arranged to points of interest within easy distance, a castle, a church or a Martello tower, and they ate sandwiches and drank from their thermos-flasks in ruined dungeons or on tombstones or by the edge of a moat. The party, by reason of the various rates of progress which each found comfortable, could not start together, if they were to arrive fairly simultaneously, and Susan on her tricycle was always the first to leave Tilling, and Diva followed. There was some competition for the honour of being the last to leave: Lucia, with the *cachet* of furious riding to her credit, waited till she thought the Padre must have started, while he was sure that his normal pace was faster than hers. In consequence, they usually both arrived very late and very hot. They all wondered how they could ever have confined physical exercise within the radius of pedestrianism, and pitied Elizabeth for the pride that debarred her from joining in these pleasant excursions.

7

Lucia had failed to convince the Directors of the Southern Railway that the Royal Fish Train was a practicable scheme. 'Should Their Majesties' so ran the final communication 'express their Royal wish to be supplied with fish from Tilling, the Directors would see that the delivery was made with all expedition, but in their opinion the ordinary resources of the line will suffice to meet their requirements, of which at present no intimation has been received.'

'A sad want of enterprise, Georgie,' said the Mayor as she read this discouraging reply. 'A failure to think municipally and to see the distinction of bringing an Elizabethan custom up to date. I shall not put the scheme before my Council at all.' Lucia dropped this unenterprising ultimatum into the waste-paper basket. The afternoon post had just arrived and the two letters which it brought for her followed the ultimatum.

'My syllabus for a series of lectures at the Literary Institute is not making a good start,' she said. 'I asked Mr Desmond McCarthy to talk to us about the less known novelists of the time of William IV, but he has declined. Nor can Mr Noel Coward speak on the technique of the modern stage on any of the five nights I offered him. I am surprised that they should not have welcomed the opportunity to get more widely known.'

'Tarsome of them,' said Georgie sympathetically, 'such a chance for them.'

Lucia gave him a sharp glance, then mused for a while in silence over her scheme. Fresh ideas began to flood her mind so copiously that she could scarcely scribble them down fast enough to keep up with them.

'I think I will lecture on the Shakespearian drama myself,' she said. 'That should be the inaugural lecture, say April the

fifteenth. I don't seem to have any engagement that night, and
you will take the chair for me ... Georgie, we might act a
short scene together, without dresses or scenery to illustrate
the simplicity of the Elizabethan stage. Really, on reflection I
think my first series of lectures had much better be given by
local speakers. The Padre would address us one night on free
will or the origin of evil. Irene on the technique of fresco-
painting. Diva on catering for the masses. Then I ought to ask
Elizabeth to lecture on something, though I'm sure I don't
know on what subject she has any ideas of the slightest value.
Ah! Instead, Major Benjy on tiger-shooting. Then a musical
evening: the art of Beethoven, with examples. That would
make six lectures; six would be enough. I think it would be
expected of me to give the last as well as the first. Admission, a
shilling, or five shillings for the series. Official, I think, under
the patronage of the Mayor.'

'No,' said Georgie, going back to one of the earlier topics. 'I
won't act any Shakespearian scene with you to illustrate Elizabethan simplicity. And if you ask me I don't believe people
will pay a shilling to hear the Padre lecture on free will. They
can hear that sort of thing every Sunday morning for nothing
but the offertory.'

'I will consider that,' said Lucia, not listening and beginning
to draw up a schedule of the discourses. 'And if you won't do a
scene with me, I might do the sleep-walking from Macbeth by
myself. But you must help me with the Beethoven evening.
Extracts from the Fifth Symphony for four hands on the
piano. That glorious work contains, as I have always maintained, the key to the Master's soul. We must practise hard,
and get our extracts by heart.'

Georgie felt the sensation, that was now becoming odiously
familiar, of being hunted and harried. Life for him was losing
that quality of leisure, which gave one time to feel busy and
ready to take so thrilled an interest in the minute happenings
of the day. Lucia was poisoning that eager fount by this
infusion of Mayoral duties and responsibilities, and tedious
schemes for educational lectures and lighting of the streets.
True, the old pellucid spring gushed out sometimes: who, for

instance, but she could have made Tilling bicycle-crazy, or have convinced Susan that Blue Birdie had gone to a higher sphere? That was her real *métier*, to render the trivialities of life intense for others. But how her schemes for the good of Tilling bored him!

Lucia finished sketching out her schedule, and began gabbling again.

'Yes, Georgie, the dates seem to work out all right,' she said, 'though Mrs Simpson must check them for me. April the fifteenth: my inaugural lecture on Shakespeare. April the twenty-second: the Padre on free will which I am convinced will attract all serious people, for it is a most interesting subject, and I don't think any final explanation of it has yet been given. April the twenty-ninth: Irene on the technique of fresco-painting. May the sixth: Diva on tea-shops. I expect I shall have to write it for her. May the thirteenth: Major Benjy on tigers. May the twentieth: Beethoven, me again . . . I should like to see these little centres of enlightenment established everywhere in England, and I count it a privilege to be able, in my position, to set an example. The BBC, I don't deny, is doing good work, but lectures delivered viva voce are so much more vivid. Personal magnetism. I shall always entertain the lecturer and a few friends to a plain supper-party here after-wards, and we can continue the discussion in the garden-room. I shall ask some distinguished expert on the subject to come down and stay the night after each lecture: the Bishop when the Padre lectures on free will; Mr Gielgud when I speak about Shakespearian technique; Sir Henry Wood when we have our Beethoven night; and perhaps the Manager of Messrs Lyons after Diva's discourse. I shall send my Town Council complimentary seats in the first row for the inaugural lecture. How does that strike you for a rough sketch? You know how I value your judgment, and it is most important to get the initial steps right.'

Georgie was standing by her table, suppressing a yawn as he glanced at the schedule, and feeling in his waistcoat pocket for his gun-metal match-box with the turquoise latch. As he scooped for it, there dropped out the silver top of Major

Benjy's riding-whip, which he always kept on his person. It fell noiselessly on the piece of damp sponge which Mrs Simpson always preferred to use for moistening postage-stamps, rather than the less genteel human tongue. Simultaneously the telephone-bell rang, and Lucia jumped up.

'That incessant summons!' she said. 'A perfect slavery. I think I must take my name off the exchange, and give my number to just a few friends . . . Yes, yes, I am the Mayor of Tilling. Irene, is it? . . . My dear how colossal! I don't suppose anybody in Tilling has ever had a picture in the Royal Academy before. Is that the amended version of your fresco, Venus with no clothes on coming to Tilling? I'm sure this one is far nicer. How I wish I had seen it before you sent it in, but when the Academy closes you must show it at our picture-exhibition here. Oh, I've put you down to give a lecture in my Mayoral course of Culture on the technique of painting in fresco. And you're going up to London for varnishing day? Do take care. So many pictures have been ruined by being varnished too much.'

She rang off.

'Accepted, is it?' said Georgie in great excitement. 'There'll be wigs on the green if it's exhibited here. I believe I told you about it, but you were wrestling with the Royal Fish Express. Elizabeth, unmistakable, in a shawl and bonnet and striped skirt and button-boots, standing on an oyster-shell, and being blown into Tilling by Benjy in a top-hat among the clouds.'

'Dear me, that sounds rather dangerously topical,' said Lucia. 'But it's time to dress. The Mapp-Flints are dining, aren't they? What a coincidence!'

They had a most harmonious dinner, with never a mention of bicycles. Benjy readily consented to read a paper on tiger-shooting on May 13.

'Ah, what a joy,' said Lucia. 'I will book it. And some properties perhaps, to give vividness. The riding-whip with which you hit the tiger in the face. Oh, how stupid of me. I had forgotten about its mysterious disappearance which was never cleared up. Pass me the sugar, Georgie.'

There was a momentary pause, and Lucia grew very red in the face as she buried her orange in sugar. But that was soon over, and presently the Mayor and Mayoress went out to the garden-room with interlaced waists and arms. Lucia had told Georgie not to stop too long in the dining-room and Benjy made the most of his time and drank a prodigious quantity of a sound but inexpensive port. Elizabeth had eaten a dried fig for dessert, and a minute but adamantine fig-seed had lodged itself at the base of one of her beautiful teeth. She knew she would not have a tranquil moment till she had evicted it, and she needed only a few seconds unobserved.

'Dear Worship,' she said. 'Give me a treat, and let your hands just stray over the piano. Haven't heard you play for ever so long.'

Lucia never needed pressing and opened the lid of the instrument.

'I'm terribly rusty, I'm afraid,' she said, 'for I get no time for practising nowadays. Beethoven, dear, or a morsel of precious Mozart; whichever you like.'

'Oh, prettioth Mothart, pleath,' mumbled Elizabeth, who had effaced herself behind Lucia's business-table. A moment sufficed, and her eye, as she turned round towards the piano again and drank in precious Mozart, fell on Mrs Simpson's piece of damp sponge. Something small and bright, long-lost and familiar, gleamed there. Hesitation would have been mere weakness (besides, it belonged to her husband). She reached out a stealthy hand, and put it inside her bead-bag.

It was barely eleven when the party broke up, for Elizabeth was totally unable to concentrate on cards when her bag contained the lock, if not the key to the unsolved mystery, and she insisted that dear Worship looked very tired. But both she and Benjy were very tired before they had framed and been forced to reject all the hypotheses which could account for the reappearance in so fantastic a place of this fragment of the riding-whip. If the relic had come to light in one of Diva's jam-puffs, the quality of the mystery would have been less baffling, for at least it would have been found on the premises where it was lost, but how it had got to Lucia's table was as inexplicable as the doctrine of free will. They went over the ground five or six times.

'Lucia wasn't even present when it vanished,' said Elizabeth as the clock struck midnight. 'Often, as you know, I think Worship is not quite as above-board as I should wish a colleague to be, but here I do not suspect her.'

Benjy poured himself out some whisky. Finding that Elizabeth was far too absorbed in speculation to notice anything that was going on round her, he hastily drank it, and poured out some more.

'Pillson then,' he suggested.

'No; I rang him up that night from Diva's, as he was going to his bath,' said she, 'and he denied knowing anything about it. He's fairly truthful – far more truthful than Worship anyhow – as far as I've observed.'

'Diva then,' said Benjy, quietly strengthening his drink.

'But I searched and I searched, and she had not been out of my sight for five minutes. And where's the rest of it? One could understand the valuable silver cap disappearing – though I don't say for a moment that Diva would have stolen it – but it's just that part that has reappeared.'

'All mos' mysterious,' said Benjy. 'But wo'll you do next, Liz? There's the cruksh. Wo'll you do next?'

Benjy had not observed that the Mayoress was trembling slightly, like a motor-bicycle before it starts. Otherwise he would not have been so surprised when she sprang up with a loud crow of triumph.

'I have it,' she cried. 'Eureka! as Worship so often says when she's thought of nothing at all. Don't say a word to anybody, Benjy, about the silver cap, but have a fresh cane put into it, and use it as a property (isn't that the word?) at your tiger-talk, just as if it had never been lost. That'll be a bit of puzzle-work for guilty persons, whoever they may be. And it may lead to something in the way of discovery. The thief may turn pale or red or betray himself in some way . . . What a time of night!'

Puzzle-work began next morning.

'I can't make out what's happened to it,' said Georgie, in a state of fuss, as he came down very late to breakfast, 'and Foljambe can't either.'

Lucia gave an annoyed glance at the clock. It was five minutes to ten; Georgie was getting lazier and lazier in the morning. She gave the special peal of silvery laughter in which mirth played a minor part.

'Good afternoon, *caro*,' she said sarcastically. 'Quite rested? Capital!'

Georgie did not like her tone.

'No, I'm rather tired still,' he said. 'I shall have a nap after breakfast.'

Lucia abandoned her banter, as he did not seem to appreciate it.

'Well, I've finished,' she said. 'Poor Worship has got to go and dictate to Mrs Simpson. And what was it you and Foljambe couldn't find?'

'The silver top to Benjy's riding-whip. I was sure it was in my yesterday's waistcoat pocket, but it isn't, and Foljambe and I have been through all my suits. Nowhere.'

'Georgie, how very queer,' she said. 'When did you see it last?'

'Sometime yesterday,' he said, opening a letter. A bill.

'It'll turn up. Things do,' said Lucia.

He was still rather vexed with her.

'They seem to be better at vanishing,' he said. 'There was Blue Birdie –'

He opened the second of his letters, and the thought of riding-whip and Blue Birdie alike were totally expunged from his brain.

'My dear,' he cried. 'You'd never guess. Olga Bracely. She's back from her world-tour.'

Lucia pretended to recall distant memories. She actually had the most vivid recollection of Olga Bracely, and, not less, of Georgie's unbounded admiration of her in his bachelor days. She wished the world-tour had been longer.

'Olga Bracely?' she said vaguely. 'Ah, yes. Prima donna. Charming voice; some notes lovely. So she's got back. How nice!'

'– and she's going to sing at Covent Garden next month,' continued Georgie, deep in her letter. 'They're producing Cortese's opera, *Lucrezia*, on May the twentieth. Oh, she'll give us seats in her box. It's a gala performance. Isn't that too lovely? And she wants us to come and stay with her at Rise-holme.'

'Indeed, most kind of her,' said Lucia. 'The dear thing! But she doesn't realize how difficult it is for me to get away from Tilling while I am Mayor.'

'I don't suppose she has the slightest idea that you are Mayor,' said Georgie, beginning to read the letter over again.

'Ah, I forgot,' said Lucia. 'She has been on a world-tour, you told me. And as for going up to hear *Lucrezia* though it's very kind of her – I think we must get out of it. Cortese brought it down to Riseholme, I remember, as soon as he had finished it, and dear Olga begged me to come and hear her sing the great scene – I think she called it – and, oh, that cacophonous evening! Ah! Eureka! Did you not say the date was May the twentieth? – How providential! That's the very evening we have fixed for my lecture on Beethoven. Olga will understand how impossible it is to cancel that.'

'But that's quite easily altered,' said Georgie. 'You made out just the roughest schedule, and Benjy's tiger-slaying is the only date fixed. And think of hearing the gala performance in London! *Lucrezia*'s had the hugest success in America and Australia. And in Berlin and Paris.'

Lucia's decisive mind wavered. She saw herself sitting in a prominent box at Covent Garden, with all her seed-pearls and her Mayoral badge. Reporters would be eager to know who she was, and she would be careful to tell the box-attendant, so that they could find out without difficulty. And at Tilling, what *réclame* to have gone up to London on the prima donna's invitation to hear this performance of the world-famous *Lucrezia*. She might give an interview to the *Hampshire Argus* about it when she got back.

'Of course we must go,' continued Georgie. 'But she wants to know at once.'

Still Lucia hesitated. It would be almost as magnificent to

tell Tilling that she had refused Olga's invitation, except for the mortifying fact that Tilling would probably not believe her. And if she refused, what would Georgie do? Would he leave her to lecture on Beethoven all by herself, or would he loyally stand by her, and do his part in the four-handed pianoforte arrangement of the Fifth Symphony? He furnished the answer to that unspoken question.

'I'm sorry if you find it impossible to go,' he said quite firmly, 'but I shall go anyhow. You can play bits of the "Moonlight" by yourself. You've often said it was another key to Beethoven's soul.'

It suddenly struck Lucia that Georgie seemed not to care two hoots whether she went or not. Her sensitive ear could not detect the smallest regret in his voice, and the prospect of his going alone was strangely distasteful. She did not fear any temperamental disturbance; Georgie's passions were not volcanic, but there was glitter and glamour in opera houses and prima donnas which might upset him if he was unchaperoned.

'I'll try to manage it somehow, dear, for your sake,' she said, 'for I know how disappointed you would be if I didn't join you in Olga's welcome to London. Dear me; I've been keeping Mrs Simpson waiting a terrible time. Shall I take Olga's letter and dictate a grateful acceptance from both of us?'

'Don't bother,' said Georgie. 'I'll do it. You're much too busy. And as for that bit of Benjy's riding-whip, I dare say it will turn up.'

The prospectus of the Mayoral series of cultural lectures at the Literary Institute was re-cast, for the other lecturers, wildly excited at the prospect, found every night equally convenient. Mrs Simpson was supplied with packets of tickets, and books of receipts and counterfoils for those who sent a shilling for a single lecture or five shillings for the whole course. She arrived now at half-past nine o'clock so as to be ready for the Mayor's dictation of official correspondence at ten, and had always got through this additional work by that time. Complimentary tickets in the front row were sent to Town Councillors for Lucia's inaugural lecture, with the request that they should be returned if the recipient found himself unable to attend. Apart from these, the sale was very sluggish. Mr John Gielgud could not attend the lecture on Shakespearian technique, and previous engagements prevented the Bishop and Sir Henry Wood from listening to the Padre on free will and Lucia on Beethoven. But luckily the *Hampshire Argus* had already announced that they had received invitations.

'Charming letters from them all, Georgie,' said Lucia, tearing them up, 'and their evident disappointment at not being able to come really touches me. And I don't regret, far from it, that apparently we shall not have very large audiences. A small audience is more *intime*; the personal touch is more quickly established. And now for my sleep-walking scene in the first lecture. I should like to discuss that with you. I shall give that with Elizabethan realism.'

'Not pyjamas?' asked Georgie, in an awe-struck voice.

'Certainly not: it would be a gross anachronism. But I shall have all the lights in the room extinguished. Night.'

'Then they won't see you,' said Georgie. 'You would lose the personal touch.'

Lucia puzzled over this problem.

'Ah! I have it!' she said. 'An electric torch.'

'Wouldn't that be an anachronism, too?' interrupted Georgie.

'Rather a pedantic criticism, Georgie,' said Lucia.

'An electric torch: and as soon as the room is plunged in darkness, I shall turn it on to my face. I shall advance slowly, only my face visible suspended in the air, to the edge of the platform. Eyes open I think: I believe sleep-walkers often have their eyes open. Very wide, something like this, and unseeing. Filled with an expression of internal soul-horror. Have you half an hour to spare? Put the lights out, dear: I have my electric torch. Now.'

As the day for the inaugural lecture drew near and the bookings continued unsatisfactory except from the *intime* point of view, Lucia showered complimentary tickets right and left. Grosvenor and Foljambe received them and Diva's Janet. In fact, those who had purchased tickets felt defrauded, since so many were to be had without even asking for them. This discontent reached Lucia's ears, and in an ecstasy of fair-mindedness she paid Mrs Simpson the sum of one shilling for each complimentary ticket she had sent out. But even that did not silence the carpings of Elizabeth.

'What it really comes to, Diva,' she said, 'is that Worship is paying everybody to attend her lecture.'

'Nothing of the kind,' said Diva. 'She is taking seats for her lecture, and giving them to her friends.'

'Much the same thing,' said Elizabeth, 'but we won't argue. Of course she'll take the same number for Benjy's lecture and yours and all the others.'

'Don't see why, if, as you say, she's only paying people to go to hers. Major Benjy can pay people to go to his.'

Elizabeth softened at the thought of the puzzle that would rack the brains of Tilling when Benjy lectured.

'The dear boy is quite excited about it,' she said. 'He's going to have his tiger-skins hung up behind the platform to give local jungle-colour. He's copied out his lecture twice already and is thinking of having it typed. I dare say Worship would allow Mrs Simpson to do it for nothing to fill up her time a little. He read it to me: most dramatic. How I shuddered when he told how he had hit the man-slayer across the nose while he seized his rifle. Such a pity he can't whack that very tiger-skin with the riding-whip he used then. He's never quite got over its loss.'

Elizabeth eyed Diva narrowly and thought she looked very uncomfortable, as if she knew something about that loss. But she replied in the most spirited manner.

'Wouldn't be very wise of him,' she said. 'Might take a lot more of the fur off. Might hurt the dead tiger more than he hurt the live one.'

'Very droll,' said Elizabeth. 'But as the riding-whip vanished so mysteriously in your house, there's the end of it.'

Thanks to Lucia's prudent distribution of complimentary tickets, the room was very well filled at the inaugural lecture.

Georgie for a week past had been threatened with a nervous collapse at the thought of taking the chair, but he had staved this off by patent medicines, physical exercises and breakfast in bed. Wearing his ruby-coloured dinner-suit, he told the audience in a firm and audible voice that any introductory words from him were quite unnecessary, as they all knew the lecturer so well. He then revealed the astonishing fact that she was their beloved Mayor of Tilling, the woman whom he had the honour to call wife. She would now address them on the Technique of the Shakespearian Stage.

Lucia first gave them a brief and lucid definition of Drama as the audible and visible presentation of situations of human woe or weal, based on and developing from those dynamic individual forces which evoke the psychological clashes of temperament that give rise to action. This action (drama) being strictly dependent on the underlying motives which prompt it and on emotional stresses might be roughly summed up as Plot. It was important that her audience should grasp that quite clearly. She went on to say that anything that distracts attention from Plot or from the psychology of which it is the logical outcome, hinders rather than helps Drama, and therefore the modern craze for elaborate decorations and embellishments must be ruthlessly condemned. It was otherwise in Shakespeare's day. There was hardly any scenery for the setting of his masterpieces, and she ventured to put forward a theory which had hitherto escaped the acumen of more erudite Shakespearian scholars than she. Shakespeare was a staunch upholder of this simplicity and had unmistakably shown that in *Midsummer Night's Dream*. In that glorious masterpiece a play was chosen for the marriage festival at Athens, and the setting of it clearly proves Shakespeare's conviction that the less distraction of scenery there was on the stage, the better for Drama. The moon appeared in this play within a play. Modern *décor* would have provided a luminous disk moving slowly across the sky by some mechanical device. Not so Shakespeare. A man came on with a lantern, and told them that his lantern was the moon and he the man in the moon. There he was static and undistracting. Again the lovers Pyramus and Thisbe were separated by a wall. Modern *décor* would have furnished a convincing edifice covered with climbing roses. Not so Shakespeare. A man came out of the wings and said, 'I am the wall.' The lovers required a chink to talk through. The wall held up his hand and parted his fingers. Thus, in the guise of a jest the Master poured scorn on elaborate scenery.

'I will now,' said Lucia, 'without dress or scenery of any sort, give you an illustration of the technique of the Shakespearian Stage. Lady Macbeth in the sleep-walking scene.'

Foljambe, previously instructed, was sitting by the switch-board, and on a sign from Georgie, plunged the hall in darkness. Everybody thought that a fuse had gone. That fear was dispelled because Lucia, fumbling in the dark, could not find her electric torch, and Georgie called out 'Turn them on again, Foljambe.' Lucia found her torch and once more the lights went out. Then the face of the Mayor sprang into vivid illumination, suspended against the blackness, and her open, sleep-walking eyes gleamed with soul-horror in the focused light. A difficult moment came when she made the pantomimic washing of her hands for the beam went wobbling about all over the place and once fell full on Georgie's face, which much embarrassed him. He deftly took the torch from her and duly controlled its direction. At the end of the speech Foljambe restored the lights, and Lucia went on with her lecture.

Owing to the absence of distinguished strangers she did not give a supper-party afterwards, at which her subject could be further discussed and illuminated, but she was in a state of high elation herself as she and Georgie partook of a plain supper alone.

'From the first moment,' she said, waving a sandwich, 'I knew that I was in touch with my audience and held them in my hand. A delicious sensation of power and expansion, Georgie; it is no use my trying to describe it to you, for you have to experience it to understand it. I regret that the *Hampshire Argus* cannot have a verbatim report in its issue this week. Mr McConnell – how he enjoyed it – told me that it went to press to-night. I said I quite understood, and should not think of asking him to hold it up. I gave him the full typescript for next week, and promised to let him have a close-up photograph of Lady Macbeth; just my face with the background blacked out. He thanked me most warmly. And I thought, didn't you, that I did the sleep-walking scene at the right moment, just after I had been speaking of Shakespearian simplicity. A little earlier than I had meant, but I suddenly felt that it came there. I *knew* it came there.'

'The very place for it,' said Georgie, vividly recalling her catechism after the Mayoral banquet.

'And that little *contretemps* about the light going out before I had found my torch –'

'That wasn't my fault,' said he. 'You told me to signal to Foljambe, when you said "sleep-walking scene". That was my cue.'

'My dear, of course it wasn't your fault,' said Lucia warmly. 'You were punctuality itself. I was only thinking how fortunate that was. The audience knew what was coming, and that made the suspense greater. The rows of upturned faces, Georgie; the suspense; I could see the strain in their eyes. And in the speech, I think I got, didn't I, that veiled timbre in my voice suggestive of the unconscious physical mechanism, sinking to a strangled whisper at "Out, damned spot!" That, I expect, was not quite original, for I now remember when I was quite a child being taken to see Ellen Terry in the part and she veiled her voice like that. A subconscious impression coming to the surface.'

She rose.

'You must tell me more of what you thought to-morrow, dear,' she said, 'for I must go to bed. The emotional strain has quite worn me out, though it was well worth while. Mere mental or physical exertion –'

'I feel very tired too,' said Georgie.

He followed Lucia upstairs, waiting while she practised the Lady Macbeth face in front of the mirror on the landing.

Benjy's lecture took place a week later. There was a palm-tree beside his reading-desk and his three tiger-skins hung on the wall behind. 'Very effective, Georgie,' said Lucia, as they took their seats in the middle of the front row. 'Quite the Shakespearian tradition. It brings the jungle to us, the heat of the Indian noon-day, the buzz of insects. I feel quite stifled' . . . He marched on to the platform, carrying a rifle, and wearing a pith helmet and saluted the audience. He described himself as a plain old campaigner, who had seen a good deal of *shikarri* in his time, and read them a series of exciting adventures. Then (what a climax!) he took up from his desk a cane riding-whip with a silver top and pointed to the third of the skins.

'And that old villain,' he said, 'nearly prevented my having the honour to speak to you to-night. I had just sat down to a bite of tiffin, putting my rifle aside, when he was on me.'

He whisked round and gave the head of the tiger-skin a terrific whack. 'I slashed at him, just like that, with my riding-whip which I had in my hand, and that gave me the half-second I needed to snatch up my rifle. I fired point-blank at his heart, and he rolled over dead. And this, ladies and gentlemen, is what saved my life. It may interest you to see it, though it is familiar to some of you. I will pass it round.'

He bowed to the applause and drank some whisky and a little soda. Lucia took the riding-whip from him, and passed it to Georgie, Georgie passed it to Diva. They all carefully examined the silver top, and the initials B.F. that were engraved on it. There could be no doubt of its genuineness and they all became very still and thoughtful, forbearing to look at each other.

There was loud applause at the end of the lecture, and after making rather a long speech, thanking the lecturer, Lucia turned to Diva.

'Come to lunch to-morrow,' she whispered. 'Just us three. I am utterly puzzled . . . Ah, Major Benjy, marvellous! What a treat! I have never been so thrilled. Dear Elizabeth, how proud you must be of him. He ought to have that lecture printed, not a word, not a syllable altered, and read it to the Royal Zoological Society. They would make him an honorary member at once.'

*

Next day at a secret session in the garden-room Georgie and Diva contributed their personal share in the strange history of the relic (Paddy's being taken for granted, as no other supposition would fit the facts of the case) and thus the movements of the silver cap were accounted for up to the moment of its disappearance from Georgie's possession.

'I always kept it in my waistcoat pocket,' he concluded, 'and one morning it couldn't be found anywhere. You remember that, don't you, Lucia?'

A look of intense concentration dwelt in Lucia's eyes: Georgie did not expect much from that, because it so often led to nothing at all. Then she spoke in that veiled voice which had become rather common with her since the sleep-walking scene.

'Yes, yes,' she murmured. 'It comes back to me. And the evening before Elizabeth and Benjy had dined with us. Did it drop out of your pocket, do you think, Georgie? . . . She and I came into the garden-room after dinner, and . . . and she asked me to play to her, which is unusual. I am always unconscious of all else when I am playing . . .'

Lucia dropped the veiled voice which was hard to keep up and became very distinct.

'She sat all by herself at my table here,' she continued. 'What if she found it on the floor or somewhere? I seem to sense her doing that. And she had something on her mind when we played bridge. She couldn't attend at all, and she suggested stopping before eleven, because she said I looked so tired, though I was never fresher. Certainly we never saw the silver cap again till last night.'

'Well that is ingenious,' said Diva, 'and then I suppose they had another cane fitted to it, and Benjy said it was the real one. I do call that deceitful. How can we serve them out? Let's all think.'

They all thought. Lucia sat with her head on one side contemplating the ceiling, as was her wont when listening to music. Then she supplied the music, too, and laughed in the silvery ascending scale of an octave and a half.

'*Amichi,*' she said. 'If you will leave it to me, I think I can arrange something that will puzzle Elizabeth. She and her accomplice have thought fit to try to puzzle us. I will contrive to puzzle them.'

Diva glanced at the clock.

'How scrumptious!' she said. 'Do be quick and tell us, because I must get back to help Janet.'

'Not quite complete yet,' answered Lucia. 'A few finishing touches. But trust me.'

Diva trundled away down the hill at top-speed. A party of clerical tourists were spending a day of pilgrimage in Tilling, and after being shown round the church by the Padre were to refresh themselves at ye olde tea-house. The Padre would have his tea provided gratis as was customary with Couriers. She paused for a moment outside her house to admire the sign which quaint Irene had painted for her. There was nothing nude about it. Queen Anne in full regalia was having tea with the Archbishop of Canterbury, and decorum reigned. Diva plunged down the kitchen-stairs, and peeped into the garden where the tulips were now in flower. She wondered which tulip it was.

As often happened in Tilling, affairs of sensational interest overlapped. Georgie woke next morning to find Foljambe bringing in his early morning tea with the *Daily Mirror*.

'A picture this morning, sir, that'll make you jump,' she said. 'Lor', what'll happen?'

Off she went to fill his bath, and Georgie, still rather sleepy, began to look through the paper. On the third page was an article on the Royal Academy Exhibition, of which the Private View was to be held to-day.

'The Picture of the Year,' said our Art Editor, 'is already determined. For daring realism, for withering satire of the so-called Victorian age, for savage caricature of the simpering, guileless prettiness of such early Italian artists as Botticelli, Miss Irene Coles's –' Georgie read no more but turned to the centre-page of pictures. There it was. Simultaneously there came a rap on his door, and Grosvenor's hand, delicately inserted, in case he had got up, held a copy of *The Times*.

'Her Worship thought you might like to see the picture-page

of *The Times*,' she said. 'And could you spare her the *Daily Mirror*, if it's got it in.'

The transfer was effected. There again was Elizabeth on her oyster-shell being wafted by Benjy up the river to the quay at Tilling, and our Art Editor gave his most serious attention to this arresting piece. He was not sure whether it was justifiable to parody a noble work of art in order to ridicule an age, which, in spite of its fantastic prudery, was distinguished for achievement and progress. But no one could question the vigour, the daring, the exuberant vitality of this amazing canvas. Technically –

Georgie bounded out of bed. Thoughtful and suggestive though this criticism was, it was also lengthy, and the need for discussion with Lucia as to the reactions of Tilling was more immediate, especially since she had a committee meeting at ten. He omitted to have his bath at all, and nearly forgot about his *toupet*. She was already at breakfast when he got down, with the *Daily Mirror* propped up against the tea-pot in front of her, and seemed to continue aloud what she must have been saying to herself.

'– and in my position, I must – good morning, Georgie – be extremely careful. She *is* my Mayoress, and therefore, through me, has an official position, which I am bound to uphold if it is brought into ridicule. I should equally resent any ruthless caricature of the Padre, as he is my Chaplain. Of course you've seen the picture itself, Georgie, which, alas, I never did, and it's hard to form a reasoned judgment from a reduced reproduction. Is it really like poor Elizabeth?'

'The image,' said Georgie. 'You could tell it a hundred miles off. It's the image of Benjy, too, But that thing in his hand, which looks so like the neck of a bottle is really the top of his umbrella.'

'No! I thought it was a bottle,' said Lucia. 'I'm glad of that. The other would have been a sad lack of taste.'

'Oh, it's all a lack of taste,' said Georgie, 'though I don't quite feel the sadness. On the other hand it's being hailed as a masterpiece. That'll sweeten it for them a bit.'

Lucia held the paper up to get a longer focus, and Georgie got his tea.

'A wonderful pose,' she said. 'Really, there's something majestic and dominant about Elizabeth, which distinctly flatters her. And look at Benjy with his cheeks puffed out, as when he's declared three no-trumps, and knows he can't get them. A boisterous wind evidently, such as often comes roaring up the river. Waves tipped with foam. A slight want of perspective, I should have said, about the houses of Tilling . . . One can't tell how Elizabeth will take it –'

'I should have thought one could make a good guess,' said Georgie.

'But it's something, as you say, to have inspired a masterpiece.'

'Yes, but Irene's real object was to be thoroughly nasty. The critics seem to have found in the picture a lot she didn't intend to put there.'

'Ah, but who can tell about the artist's mind?' asked Lucia, with a sudden attack of high-brow. 'Did Messer Leonardo really see in the face of La Gioconda all that our wonderful Walter Pater found there? Does not the artist work in a sort of trance?'

'No; Irene wasn't in a trance at all,' insisted Georgie. 'Anything but. And as for your feeling that because Elizabeth is Mayoress you ought to resent it, that's thoroughly inconsistent with your theory that Art's got nothing to do with Life. But I'll go down to the High Street soon, and see what the general feeling is. You'll be late, dear, if you don't go off to your meeting at once. In fact, you're late already.'

Lucia mounted her bicycle in a great hurry and set off for the Town Hall. With every stroke of her pedals she felt growing pangs of jealousy of Elizabeth. Why, oh why, had not Irene painted her, the Mayor, the first woman who had ever been Mayor of Tilling, being wafted up the river, with Georgie blowing on her from the clouds?

Such a picture would have had a far greater historical interest, and she would not have resented the grossest caricature of herself if only she could have been the paramount figure in the

Picture of the Year. The town in the background would be widely recognized as Tilling, and Lucia imagined the eager comments of the crowd swarming round the masterpiece ... 'Why that's Tilling! We spent a week there this summer. Just like!' ... 'And who can that woman be? Clearly a portrait' ... 'Oh, that's the Mayor, Lucia Pillson: she was pointed out to me. Lives in a lovely family house called Mallards' ... 'And the man in the clouds with the Vandyck beard and the red dinner-suit (what a colour!) must be her husband' ...

'What fame!' thought Lucia with aching regret. 'What illimitable, immortal *réclame*. What publicity to be stared at all day by excited crowds!' At this moment the Private View would be going on, and Duchesses and Archbishops and Cabinet Ministers would soon be jostling to get a view of her, instead of Elizabeth and Benjy! 'I must instantly commission Irene to paint my portrait,' she said to herself as she dismounted at the steps of the Town Hall. 'A picture that tells a story I think. A sort of biography. In my robes by the front door at Mallards with my hand on my bicycle' ...

She gave but scant attention to the proceedings at her Committee, and mounting again rang the bell all the way down the hill into the High Street on a secret errand to the haberdashery-shop. By a curious coincidence she met Major Benjy on the threshold. He was carrying the reconstructed riding-whip and was in high elation.

'Good morning, your Worship,' he said. 'Just come to have my riding-whip repaired. I gave my old man-eater such a swipe at my lecture two nights ago, that I cracked it, by Jove.'

'Oh Major, what a pity!' said Lucia. 'But it was almost worth breaking it, wasn't it? You produced such a dramatic sensation.'

'And there's another sensation this morning,' chuckled Benjy. 'Have you seen the notice of the Royal Academy in *The Times*?'

Lucia still considered that the proper public line to take was her sense of the insult to her Mayoress, though certainly Benjy seemed very cheerful.

'I have,' she said indignantly. 'Oh, Major Benjy, it is monstrous! I was horrified: I should not have thought it of Irene. And the *Daily Mirror*, too –'

'No, really?' interrupted Benjy. 'I must get it.'

'Such a wanton insult to dear Elizabeth,' continued Lucia, 'and, of course, to you up in the clouds. Horrified! I shall write to Elizabeth as soon as I get home to convey my sympathy and indignation.'

'Don't you bother!' cried Benjy. 'Liz hasn't been so bucked up with anything for years. After all, to be the principal feature in the Picture of the Year is a privilege that doesn't fall to everybody. Such a leg up for our obscure little Tilling, too. We're going up to town next week to see it. Why, here's Liz herself.'

Elizabeth kissed her hand to Lucia from the other side of the street, and, waiting till Susan went ponderously by, tripped across, and kissed her (Lucia's) face.

'What a red-letter day, dear!' she cried. 'Quaint Irene suddenly becoming so world-wide, and your humble little Mayoress almost equally so. Benjy, it's in the *Daily Telegraph*, too. You'd better get a copy of every morning paper. Pop in, and tell them to mend your riding-whip, while I send a telegram of congratulation to Irene – I should think Burlington House, London, would find her now – and meet me at the paper-shop. And do persuade Irene, Worship, to let us have the picture for our exhibition here, when the Academy's over, unless the Chantrey Bequest buys it straight away.'

Benjy went into the haberdasher's to get the riding-whip repaired. This meeting with him just here made Lucia's errand much simpler. She followed him into the shop and became completely absorbed in umbrellas till he went out again. Then, with an eye on the door, she spoke to the shopman in a confidential tone.

'I want you,' she said, 'to make me an exact copy of Major Mapp-Flint's pretty riding-whip. Silver top with the same initials on it. Quite private, you understand: it's a little surprise for a friend. And send it, please, to me at Mallards House, as soon as it's ready.'

Lucia mounted her bicycle and rode thoughtfully homewards. Since Elizabeth and Benjy both took this gross insult to her Mayoress as the highest possible compliment, and longed to have quaint Irene's libel on them exhibited here, there was no need that she should make herself indignant or unhappy for their sakes. Indeed, she understood their elation, and her regret that Irene had not caricatured her instead of Elizabeth grew very bitter: she would have borne it with a magnanimity fully equal to theirs. It was a slight consolation to know that the replica of the riding-whip was in hand.

She went out into the garden-room where patient Mrs Simpson was waiting for her. There were invitations to be sent out for an afternoon-party next week to view the beauties of Lucia's spring-garden, for which she wanted to rouse the envious admiration of her friends, and the list must be written out. Then there was a letter to Irene of warm congratulation to be typed. Then the Committee of the Museum, of which the Mayor was Chairman was to meet on Friday, and she gave Mrs Simpson the key of the tin box labelled 'Museum'.

'Just look in it, Mrs Simpson,' she said, 'and see if there are any papers I ought to glance through. A mountain of work, I fear, to-day.'

Grosvenor appeared.

'Could you see Mrs Wyse for a moment?' she asked.

Lucia knitted her brows, and consulted her engagement-book.

'Yes, just for ten minutes,' she said. 'Ask her to come out here.'

Grosvenor went back into the house to fetch Susan, and simultaneously Mrs Simpson gave a shriek of horror.

'The corpse of a blue parrakeet,' she cried, 'and an awful smell.'

Lucia sprang from her seat. She plucked Blue Birdie, exhaling disinfectant and decay, from the Museum box, and scudding across the room thrust it into the fire. She poked and battered it down among the glowing embers, and even as she wrought she cursed herself for not having told Mrs Simpson to leave it where it was and lock the Museum box again, but it was too late for that. In that swift journey to cremation Blue Birdie had dropped a plume or two, and from the fire came a vivid smell of burned feathers. But she was just in time and had resumed her seat and taken up her pen as Susan came ponderously up the steps into the garden-room.

'Good morning, dear,' said Lucia. 'At my eternal tasks as usual, but charmed to see you.'

She rose in welcome, and to her horror saw a long blue tail-feather (slightly tinged with red) on the carpet. She planted her foot upon it.

'Good morning,' said Susan. 'What a horrid smell of burned feathers.'

Lucia sniffed, still standing firm.

'I do smell something,' she said. 'Gas, surely. I thought I smelt it the other day. I must send for my town surveyor. Do you not smell gas, Mrs Simpson?'

Lucia focused on her secretary the full power of her gimlet eye.

'Certainly, gas,' said that loyal woman, locking the Museum box.

'Most disagreeable,' said Lucia, advancing on Susan. 'Let us go into the garden and have our little talk there. I know what you've come about: Irene's picture. The Picture of the Year, they say. Elizabeth is famous at last, and is skipping for joy. I am so pleased for her sake.'

'I should certainly have said burned feathers,' repeated Susan.

Dire speculations flitted through Lucia's mind: would Susan's vague but retentive brain begin to grope after a connection between burned feathers and her vanished bird? A concentration of force and volubility was required, and taking another step forward on to another blue feather, she broke into a gabble of topics as she launched Susan, like a huge liner, down the slip of the garden-room stairs.

'No, Susan, gas,' she said. 'And have you seen the reproduction of Irene's picture in *The Times*? Mrs Simpson, would you kindly bring *The Times* into the garden. You must stroll across the lawn and have a peep at my daffodils in my *giardino segreto*. Never have I had such a show. Those lovely lines "dancing with the daffodils". How true! I saw you in the High Street this morning, dear, on your tricycle. And such wall-flowers; they will be in fullest bloom for my party next week, to which you and Mr Wyse must come. And Benjy in the clouds; so like, but Georgie says it isn't a bottle, but his umbrella. Tell me *exactly* what you think of it all. So important that I should know what Tilling feels.'

Unable to withstand such a cataract of subjects, Susan could hardly say 'burned feathers' again. She showed a tendency to drift towards the garden-room on their return, but Lucia, like a powerful tug, edged her away from that dangerous shoal and towed her out to the front door of Mallards, where she cast her adrift to propel her tricycle under her own steam. Then return-ing to the garden-room, she found that the admirable Mrs Simpson had picked up a few more feathers, which she had laid on Lucia's blotting-pad.

Lucia threw them into the fire and swept up some half-burned fragments from the hearth.

'The smell of gas seems quite gone, Mrs Simpson,' she said. 'No need, I think, to send for my town surveyor. It is such a pleasure to work with anyone who understands me as well as you . . . Yes, the list for my garden-party.'

The replica of the riding-whip was delivered, and looked identical. Lucia's disposition of it was singular. After she had retired for the night, she tied it safely up among the foliage of the *Clematis montana* which grew thickly up to the sill of her bedroom window. The silver top soon grew tarnished in this exposure, spiders spun threads about it, moisture dulled its varnished shaft, and it became a weathered object. 'About ripe,' said Lucia to herself one morning, and rang up Elizabeth and Benjy, inviting them to tea at ye olde tea-house next day, with bridge to follow. They had just returned from their visit to London to see the Picture of the Year, and accepted with pleasure.

Before starting for Diva's, Lucia took her umbrella up to her bedroom, and subsequently carried it to the tea-room, arriving there ten minutes before the others. Diva was busy in the kitchen, and she looked into the card-room. Yes: there was the heavy cupboard with claw feet standing in the corner; perfect. Her manoeuvres then comprised opening her umbrella and furling it again; and hearing Diva's firm foot on the kitchen-stairs she came softly back into the tea-room.

'Diva, *what* a delicious smell!' she said. 'Oh I want eighteen-penny teas. I came a few minutes early to tell you.'

'Reckoned on that,' said Diva. 'The smell is waffles. I've been practising. Going to make waffles at my lecture, as an illustration, if I can do them over a spirit-lamp. Hand them round to the front row. Good advertisement. Here are the others.'

The waffles were a greater success than Diva had anticipated, and the compliments hardly made up for the consumption. Then they adjourned to the card-room, and Lucia, leaning her umbrella against the wall let it slip behind the big cupboard.

'So clumsy!' she said, 'but never mind it now. We shall have to move the cupboard afterwards. Cut? You and I, Georgie. Families. Happy families.'

It was chatty bridge at first, rich in agreeable conversation.

'We only got back from London yesterday,' said Elizabeth, dealing. 'Such a rush, but we went to the Academy three times; one no-trump.'

'Two spades,' said Georgie. 'What did you think of the Picture?'

'Such a crowd round it! We had to scriggle in.'

'And I'm blest if I don't believe that they recognized Liz,' put in Major Benjy. 'A couple of women looked at her and then at the picture and back again, and whispered together, by Jove.'

'I'm sure they recognized me at our second visit,' said Elizabeth. 'The crowd was thicker than ever, and we got quite wedged in. Such glances and whisperings all round. Most entertaining, wasn't it, Benjy?'

Lucia tried to cork up her bitterness, but failed.

'I *am* glad you enjoyed it so much, dear,' she said. 'How I envy you your superb self-confidence. I should find such publicity quite insupportable. I should have scriggled out again at whatever cost.'

'Dear Worship, I don't think you would if you ever found yourself in such a position,' said Elizabeth. 'You would face it. So brave!'

'If we're playing bridge, two spades was what I said. Ever so long ago,' announced Georgie.

'Oh, Mr Georgie; apologies,' said Elizabeth. 'I'm such a chatterbox. What do you bid, Benjy? Don't be so slow.'

'Two no-trumps,' said Benjy. 'We made our third visit during lunch-time, when there were fewer people –'

'Three spades,' said Lucia. 'All I meant, dear Elizabeth, was that it is sufficient for me to tackle my little bit of public service, quietly and humbly and obscurely –'

'So like you, dear,' retorted Elizabeth, 'and I double three spades. That'll be a nice little bit for you to tackle quietly.'

Lucia made no reply, but the pleasant atmosphere was now charged with perilous stuff, for on the one side the Mayor was writhing with envy at the recognition of Elizabeth from the crowds round the Picture of the Year, while the Mayoress was writhing with exasperation at Lucia's pitiful assertion that she shunned publicity.

Lucia won the doubled contract and the game.

'So there's my little bit, Georgie,' she said, 'and you played it very carefully, though of course it was a sitter. I ought to have redoubled: forgive me.'

'Benjy, your finesse was idiotic,' said Elizabeth, palpably wincing. 'If you had played your ace, they'd have been two down. Probably more.'

'And what about your doubling?' asked Benjy. 'And what about your original no-trump?'

'Thoroughly justified, both of them,' said Elizabeth, 'if you hadn't finessed. Cut to me, please, Worship.'

'But you've just dealt, dear,' cooed Lucia.

'Haw, Haw. Well tried, Liz,' said Benjy.

Elizabeth looked so deadly at Benjy's gentle fun that at the end of the hand Lucia loaded her with compliments.

'Beautifully played, dear!' she said. 'Did you notice,

Georgie, how Elizabeth kept putting the lead with you? Masterly!'

Elizabeth was not to be appeased with that sort of blarney.

'Thank you, dear,' she said. 'I'm sorry, Benjy: I ought to have put the lead with Worship, and taken another trick.'

Diva came in as they were finishing the last rubber.

'Quite a lot of teas,' she said. 'But they all come in so late now. Hungrier, I suppose. Saves them supper. No more waffles for shilling teas. Not if I know it. Too popular.'

Lucia had won from the whole table, and with an indifferent air she swept silver and copper into her bag without troubling to count it.

'I must be off,' she said. 'I have pages of Borough expenditure to look through. Oh, my umbrella! I nearly forgot it.'

'Dear Worship,' asked Elizabeth. 'Do tell me what that means! Either you forget a thing, or you don't.'

'I let it slip behind your big cupboard, Diva,' said Lucia, not taking the slightest notice of her Mayoress.

'Catch hold of that end, Georgie, and we'll run it out from the wall.'

'Permit me,' said Benjy, taking Lucia's end. 'Now then, with a heave-ho, as they say in the sister service. One, two, three.'

He gave a tremendous tug. The cupboard, not so heavy as it looked, glided away from the wall with an interior rattle of crockery.

'Oh, my things!' cried Diva. 'Do be careful.'

'Here's your umbrella,' said Georgie. 'Covered with dust ... Why, what's this? Major Benjy's riding-whip, isn't it? Lost here ages ago. Well, that is queer!'

Diva simply snatched it from Georgie.

'But it is!' she cried. 'Initials, everything. Must have lain here all this time. But at your lecture the other day Major –'

Lucia instantly interrupted her.

'What a fortunate discovery!' she said. 'How glad you will be, Major, to get your precious relic back. Why it's half-past seven! Good night everybody.'

She and Georgie let themselves out into the street.

'But you *must* tell me,' said he, as they walked briskly up the hill. 'I shall die if you don't tell me. How did you do it?'

'I? What do you mean?' asked the aggravating woman.

'You're too tarsome,' said Georgie crossly. 'And it isn't fair. Diva told you how she buried the silver cap, and I told you how I dug it up, and you tell us nothing. Very miserly!'

Lucia was startled at the ill-humour in his voice.

'My dear, I was only teasing you –' she began.

'Well it doesn't amuse me to be teased,' he snapped at her. 'You're like Elizabeth sometimes.'

'Georgie, what a monstrous thing to say to me! Of course, I'll tell you, and Diva, too. Ring her up and ask her to pop in after dinner.'

She paused with her hand on the door of Mallards. 'But never hint to the poor Mapp-Flints,' she said, 'as Diva did just now, that the riding-whip Benjy used at his lecture couldn't have been the real one. They knew that quite well, and they knew we know it. Much more excruciating for them *not* to rub it in.'

8

Lucia, followed by Georgie, and preceded by an attendant, swept along the corridor behind the boxes on the grand tier at Covent Garden Opera House. They had dined early at their hotel and were in good time. She wore her seed-pearls in her hair, her gold Mayoral badge, like an Order, on her breast, and her gown was of a rich, glittering russet hue like cloth of copper. A competent-looking lady, hovering about with a small note-book and a pencil, hurried up to her as the attendant opened the door of the box.

'Name, please,' he said to Lucia.

'The Mayor of Tilling,' said Lucia, raising her voice for the benefit of the lady with the note-book.

He consulted his list.

'No such name, ma'am,' he said. 'Madam has given strict orders.'

'Mr and Mrs Pillson,' suggested Georgie.

'That's all right, sir'; and in they went.

The house was gleaming with tiaras and white shoulders, and loud with conversation. Lucia stood for a minute at the front of the box which was close to the stage, and nodded and smiled as she looked this way and that, as if recognizing friends . . . But, oh, to think that she might have been recognized, too, if only Irene had portrayed her in the Picture of the Year! They had been to see it this afternoon, and Georgie, also, had felt pangs of regret that it was not he with his Vandyck beard who sprawled windily among the clouds. But in spite of that he was very happy for in a few minutes now he would hear and see his adorable Olga again, and they were to lunch with her to-morrow at her hotel.

A burst of applause hailed the appearance of Cortese, composer, librettist and, to-night, conductor of *Lucrezia*. Lucia waggled her hand at him. He certainly bowed in her direction (for he was bowing in all directions), and she made up her mind to scrap her previous verdict on the opera and be enchanted with it.

The Royal party unfortunately invisible from Lucia's box arrived, and after the National Anthem the first slow notes of the overture wailed on the air.

'Divine!' she whispered to Georgie. 'How well I remember dear Signor Cortese playing it to me at Riseholme. I think he took it a shade faster . . . There! Lucrezia's motif, or is it the Pope's? Tragic splendour. The first composer in Europe.'

If Georgie had not known Lucia so well, he would scarcely have believed his ears. On that frightful evening, three years ago, when Olga had asked her to come and hear 'bits' of it, she had professed herself outraged at the hideous, modern stuff, but there were special circumstances on that occasion which conduced to pessimism. Lucia had let it be widely supposed that she talked Italian with ease and fluency, but when confronted with Cortese, it was painfully clear that she could not understand a word he said. An awful exposure . . . Now she was in a prominent box, guest of the prima donna, at this gala performance, she could not be called upon to talk to Cortese without annoying the audience very much, and she was fanatic in admiration. She pressed Georgie's hand, emotion drowning utterance; she rose in her place at the end of Olga's great song in the first act, crying 'Brava! Brava!' in the most correct Italian, and was convinced that she led the applause that followed.

During the course of the second act, the box was invaded by a large lady, clad in a magnificent tiara, but not much else, and a small man, who hid himself at the back. Lucia felt justly indignant at this interruption, but softened when the box-attendant appeared with another programme, and distinctly said 'Your Grace' to the large lady. That made a difference, and during the interval Lucia talked very pleasantly to her (for when strangers were thrown together stiffness was ridiculous) and told her how she had heard her beloved Olga run through some of her part before the opera was produced, and that she had prophesied a huge success for it. She was agonizing to know what the large lady was the Grace of, but could scarcely put so personal a question on such short acquaintance. She did not seem a brilliant conversationalist, but stared rather fixedly at Georgie ... At the end of the opera there was immense enthusiasm: Olga and Cortese were recalled again and again, and during these effusions, Her unidentified Grace and her companion left: Lucia presumed that they were husband and wife as they took no notice of each other. She regretted their disappearance, but consoled herself with the reflection that their names would appear in the dazzling list of those who would be recorded in the press to-morrow as having attended the first performance of *Lucrezia*. The competent female in the corridor would surely see to that.

Georgie lay long awake that night. The music had excited him, and, more than the music, Olga herself. What a voice, what an exquisite face and presence, what an infinite charm! He recalled his bachelor days at Riseholme, when Lucia had been undisputed Queen of that highly cultured village and he her *cavaliere servente*, whose allegiance had been seriously shaken by Olga's advent. He really had been in love with her, he thought, and the fact that she had a husband alive then, to whom she was devoted, allowed a moral man like him to indulge his emotions in complete security. It had thrilled him with daring joy to imagine that, had Olga been free, he would have asked her to marry him, but even in those flights of fancy he knew that her acceptance of him would have put him in a panic. Since then, of course, he had been married himself, but his union with Lucia had not been formidable, as they had agreed that no ardent tokens of affection were to mar their union. Marriage, in fact, with Lucia might be regarded as a vow of celibacy. Now, after three years, the situation was reversing itself in the oddest manner. Olga's husband had died and she was free, while his own marriage with Lucia protected him. His high moral principles would never suffer him to be unfaithful to his wife. 'I am not that sort of man,' he said to himself. 'I must go to sleep.'

He tossed and turned on his bed. Visions of Olga as he had

seen her to-night floated behind his closed eyelids. Olga as a mere girl at the fête of her infamous father Pope Alexander VI: Olga at her marriage in the Sistine Chapel to the Duke of Biseglia: his murder in her presence by the hired bravos of His Holiness and her brother. The scenery was fantastically gorgeous ('not Shakespearian at all, Georgie,' Lucia had whispered to him), but when Olga was on the stage, he was conscious of nothing but her. She outshone all the splendour, and never more so than when, swathed in black, she followed her husband's bier, and sang that lament – or was it a song of triumph? – 'Amore misterioso, celeste, profondo' . . . 'I believe I've got a very passionate nature,' thought Georgie, 'but I've always crushed it.'

It was impossible to get to sleep, and wheeling out of bed, he lit a cigarette and paced up and down his room. But it was chilly, and putting on a smart blue knitted pullover he got back into bed again. Once more he jumped up; he had no ashtray, but the lid of his soap-dish would do, and he reviewed Life.

'I know Tilling is very exciting,' he said to himself, 'for extraordinary things are always happening, and I'm very comfortable there. But I've no independence. I'm devoted to Lucia, but what with breakfast, lunch, tea and dinner, as well as a great deal in between . . . And then how exasperating she is as Mayor! What with her ceaseless jaw about her duties and position I get fed up. Those tin boxes with nothing in them! Mrs Simpson every morning with nothing to do! I want a change. Sometimes I almost sympathize with Elizabeth, when Lucia goes rolling along like the car of Juggernaut, squish-squash, whoever comes in her way. And yet it's she, I really believe, who makes things happen, just because she is Lucia, and I don't know where we should be without her. Good gracious, that's the second cigarette I've smoked in bed, and I had my full allowance before. Why didn't I bring up my embroidery? That often makes me sleepy. I shall be fit for nothing to-morrow, lying awake like this, and I must go shopping in the morning, and then we lunch with Olga, and catch the afternoon train back to That Hole. Damn everything!'

Georgie felt better in the morning after two cups of very hot tea brought him by Foljambe who had come up as their joint maid. He read his paper, breakfasting in his room, as in his comfortable bachelor days. There was a fervent notice of *Lucrezia*, but no indication, since there had been five Duchesses present, as to which their particular Grace was, who had rather embarrassed him by her fixed eye. But then Foljambe brought him another paper which Lucia wanted back. She had marked it with a blue pencil, and there he read that the Duke and Duchess of Sheffield and the Mayor of Tilling had attended the opera in Miss Bracely's box. That gave him great satisfaction, for all those folk who had looked at their box so much would now feel sure that he was the Mayor of Tilling . . . Then he went out alone for his shopping, as Lucia sent word that she had received some agenda for the next Council meeting, which she must study, and thoroughly enjoyed it. He found some very pretty new ties and some nice underwear, and he could linger by attractive windows, instead of going to some improving exhibition which Lucia would certainly have wished to do. Then in eager trepidation he went to the Ritz for lunch, and found that Lucia had not yet arrived. But there was Olga in the lounge, who hailed him on a high soprano note, so that everybody knew that he was Georgie, and might have guessed, from the *timbre*, that she was Olga.

'My dear, how nice to see you,' she cried. 'But a beard, Georgie! What does it mean? Tell me all about it. Where's your Lucia? She hasn't divorced you already, I hope? And have a cocktail? I insist, because it looks so bad for an elderly female to be drinking alone, and I am dying for one. And did you like the opera last night? I thought I sang superbly; even Cortese didn't scold me. How I love being in stuffy old London again; I'm off to Riseholme to-night for a week, and you must – Ah, here's Lucia! We'll go into lunch at once. I asked Cortese, but he can't come in till afterwards. Only Poppy Sheffield is coming, and she will probably arrive about tea-time. She'll be terribly taken up with Georgie, because she adores beards, and says they are getting so rare nowadays. Don't be alarmed, my lamb: she doesn't want to touch them, but the sight of them refreshes her in some psychic manner. Oh, of course, she was in your box last night. She hates music, and hears it only as a mortification of the flesh, of which she has plenty. Quite gaga, but so harmless.'

Olga was a long time getting to her table, because she made many greetings on the way, and Lucia began to hate her again. She was too casual, keeping the Mayor of Tilling standing about like this, and Lucia, who had strong views about *maquillage*, was distressed to see how many women, Olga included, were sadly made-up. And yet how marvellous to thread her way through the crowded restaurant with the prima donna, not waiting for a Duchess: if only some Tillingites had been there to see! *Per contra*, it was rather familiar of Olga to put her hand on Georgie's shoulder and shove him into his place. Lucia stored up in separate packets resentment and the deepest gratification.

Asparagus. Cold and very buttery. Olga picked up the sticks with her fingers and then openly sucked them. Lucia used a neat little holder which was beside her plate. Perhaps Olga did not know what it was for.

'And you and Georgie must come to Riseholme for the week-end,' she said. 'I get down to-night, so join me to-morrow.'

Lucia shook her head.

'Too sweet of you,' she said, 'but impossible, I'm afraid. So many duties. To-morrow is Friday, isn't it? Yes: a prize-giving to-morrow afternoon, and something in the evening, I fancy. Borough Bench on Monday at ten. One thing after another; no end to them, day after day. It was only by the rarest chance I was able to come up yesterday.'

Georgie knew that this was utter rubbish. Lucia had not had a single municipal engagement for four days, and had spent her time in bicycling and sketching and playing bridge. She just wanted to impress Olga with the innumerable duties of her position.

'Too bad!' said Olga. 'Georgie, you mustn't let her work herself to death like this. But you'll come, won't you, if we can't persuade her.'

Here was an opportunity for independent action. He strung himself up to take it.

'Certainly. Delighted. I should adore to,' he said with emphasis.

'Capital. That's settled then. But you must come, too, Lucia. How they would all love to see you again at Riseholme.'

Lucia wanted to go, especially since Georgie would otherwise go without her, and she would have been much disconcerted if her refusal had been taken as final. She pressed two fingers to her forehead.

'Let me think!' she said. 'I've nothing after Friday evening, have I, Georgie, till Monday's Council? I always try to keep Saturdays free. No: I don't think I have. I could come down with Georgie, on Saturday morning, but we shall have to leave again very early on Monday. Too tempting to refuse, dear Olga. The sweet place, and those busy days, or so they seemed then, but now, by comparison, what a holiday!'

Poppy appeared just as they had finished lunch, and Lucia was astonished to find that she had not the smallest idea that they had ever met before. When reminded, Poppy explained that when she went to hear music a total oblivion of all else seized her.

'Carried away,' she said. 'I don't know if I'm on my head or my heels.'

'If you were carried away you'd be on your back,' said Olga. 'What do you want to eat?'

'Dressed crab and plenty of black coffee,' said Poppy decidedly. 'That's what keeps me in perfect health.' She had just become conscious of Georgie, and had fixed her eye on his beard, when Cortese plunged into the restaurant and came, like a bore up the River Severn, to Olga's table, loudly lamenting in Italian that he had not been able to come to lunch. He kissed her hand, he kissed Poppy's hand, and after a short pause for recollection, he kissed Lucia's hand.

'*Si, si,*' he cried, 'it is the lady who came to hear the first trial of *Lucrezia* at your Riseholme, and spoke Italian with so pure an accent. *Come sta, signora?*' And he continued to prattle in Italian.

Lucia had a horrid feeling that all this had happened before, and that in a moment it would be rediscovered that she could not speak Italian. Lunch, anyhow, was over, and she could say a reluctant farewell. She summoned up a few words in that abhorred tongue.

'*Cara*,' she said to Olga, 'we must tear ourselves away. *A rivederci, non e vero, dopo domani*. But we must go to catch our train. A poor hard-worked Mayor must get back to the call of duty.'

'Oh, is he a Mayor?' asked Poppy with interest. 'How very distinguished.'

There was no time to explain; it was better that Georgie should be temporarily enthroned in Poppy's mind as Mayor, rather than run any further risks, and Lucia threaded her way through the narrow passage between the tables. After all she had got plenty of material to work up into noble narrative at Tilling. Georgie followed and slammed the door of the taxi quite crossly.

'I can't think why you were in such a hurry,' he said. 'I was enjoying myself, and we shall only be kicking our heels at the station.'

'Better to run no risk of missing our train,' she said. 'And we have to pick up Foljambe and our luggage.'

'Not at all,' said Georgie. 'We particularly arranged that she should meet us with it at Victoria.'

'Georgie, how stupid of me!' said the shameless Lucia. 'Forgive me.'

Lucia found that she had no engagement for the next evening, and got up a party for dinner and bridge in order casually to disseminate these magnificent experiences. Mr Wyse and Diva (Susan being indisposed), the Mapp-Flints and the Padre and Evie were her guests. It rather surprised her that nobody asked any questions at dinner, about her visit to London, but, had she only known it, Tilling had seen in the paper that she and a Duke and Duchess had been in Olga's box, and had entered into a fell conspiracy, for Lucia's good, not to show the slightest curiosity about it. Thus, though her guests were starving for information, conversation at dinner had been entirely confined to other topics, and whenever Lucia made a casual allusion to the opera, somebody spoke loudly about something else. But when the ladies retired into the garden-room the strain on their curiosity began to tell, and Lucia tried again.

'So delightful to get back to peaceful Tilling,' she said, as if she had been away for thirty-six weeks instead of thirty-six hours, 'though I fear it is not for long. London was such a terrible rush. Of course the first thing we did was to go to the Academy to see the Picture of the Year, dear Elizabeth.'

That was crafty: Elizabeth could not help being interested in that.

'And could you get near it, dear?' she asked.

'Easily. Not such a great crowd. Technically I was a wee bit disappointed. Very vigorous, of course, and great *bravura* –'

'What does that mean?' asked Diva.

'How shall I say it? Dash, sensational effect, a too obvious dexterity,' said Lucia, gesticulating like a painter doing bold brush-work. 'I should have liked more time to look at it, for Irene will long to know what I think about it, but we had to dress and dine before the opera. Dear Olga had given us an excellent box, a little too near the stage perhaps.'

It was more than flesh and blood could stand: the conspiracy of silence broke down.

'I saw in the paper that the Duke and Duchess of Sheffield were there, too,' said Evie.

'In the paper was it?' asked Lucia with an air of great surprise. 'How the press ferrets things out! He and Poppy Sheffield came in in the middle of the second act. I was rather cross, I'm afraid, for I hate such interruptions.'

Elizabeth was goaded into speech.

'Most inconsiderate,' she said. 'I hope you told her so, Worship.'

Lucia smiled indulgently.

'Ah, people who aren't *really* musical – poor Poppy Sheffield is not – have no idea of the pain they give. And what has happened here since Georgie and I left?'

'Seventeen to tea yesterday,' said Diva. 'What was the opera like?'

'Superb. Olga sang the great scene to me years ago and I confess I did not do it justice. A little modern for my classical taste, but a very great work. Very. And her voice is still magnificent; perhaps a little sign of forcing in the top register, but then I am terribly critical.'

The conspiracy of silence had become a cross-examination of questions. These admissions were being forced from her.

'And then did you go out to supper?' asked Evie.

'Ah no! Music takes too much out of me. Back to the hotel and so to bed, as Pepys says.'

'And next morning, Worship, after such an exciting evening?' asked Elizabeth.

'Poor me! A bundle of agenda for the Council meeting on Monday. I had to slave at them until nearly lunch-time.'

'You and Mr Georgie in your hotel?' asked Diva.

'No: dear Olga insisted that we should lunch with her at the Ritz,' said Lucia in the slow drawling voice which she adopted when her audience were on tenterhooks. 'No party, just the four of us.'

'Who was the fourth?'

'The Duchess. She was very late, just as she had been at the opera. A positive obsession with her. So we didn't wait.'

Not waiting for a Duchess produced a stunning effect.

Diva recovered first.

'Good food?' she asked.

'Fair, I should have called it. Or do you mean Poppy's food? How you will laugh! A dressed crab and oceans of black coffee. The only diet on which she feels really well.'

'Sounds most indigestible,' said Diva. 'What an odd sort of stomach. And then?'

'How you all catechize me! Then Cortese came in. He is the composer, I must explain, of *Lucrezia*, and conducted it. Italian, with all the vivaciousness of the South –'

'So you had a good talk in Italian to him, dear,' said Elizabeth viciously.

'Alas, no. We had to rush off almost immediately to catch
our train. Hardly a word with him.'

'What a pity!' said Elizabeth. 'And just now you told us you
were not going to be here long. Gadding off again?'

'Alas, yes; though how ungrateful of me to say "alas",' said
Lucia still drawling. 'Dear Olga implored Georgie and me to
spend the week-end with her at Riseholme. She would not take
a refusal. It will be delicious to see the dear old place again. I
shall make her sing to us. These great singers are always at
their best with a small *intime* sympathetic audience.'

'And will there be some Duchesses there?' asked Elizabeth,
unable to suppress her bitterness.

'*Chi lo sa?*' said Lucia with superb indifference. 'Ah, here
come the men. Let us get to our bridge.'

The men, who were members of this conspiracy, had shown
a stronger self-control than the women, and had not asked
Georgie a single question about high-life, but they knew now
about his new ties. Evie could not resist saying in an aside to
her husband:

'Fancy, Kenneth, the Duchess of Sheffield lives on dressed
crab and black coffee.'

Who could resist such an alluring fragment? Certainly not
the Padre.

'Eh, that's a singular diet,' he said, 'and has Mistress Mayor
been telling you a' about it? An' what does she do when there's
no crab to be had?'

From the eagerness in his voice, Lucia instantly guessed that
the men had heard nothing, and were consumed with curiosity.

'Enough of my silly tittle-tattle,' she said. 'More important
matters lie before us. Elizabeth, will you and the Padre and Mr
Wyse play at my table?'

For a while cards overrode all other interest, but it was
evident that the men were longing to know all that their vow of
self-control had hidden from them: first one and then another,
during the deals, alluded to shellfish and Borgias. But Lucia
was adamant: they had certainly conspired to show no interest
in the great events of the London visit, and they must be

punished. But when the party broke up, Mr Wyse insisted on driving Diva back in the Royce, and plied her with questions, and Major Benjy and the Padre, by the time they got home, knew as much as their wives.

Lucia and Georgie, with Grosvenor as maid (for it was only fair that she should have her share in these magnificent excursions) motored to Riseholme next morning. Lucia took among her luggage the tin box labelled 'Housing', in order to keep abreast of municipal work, but in the hurry of departure forgot to put any municipal papers inside it. She would have liked to take Mrs Simpson as well, but Grosvenor occupied the seat next her chauffeur, and three inside would have been uncomfortable. Olga gave a garden-party in her honour in the afternoon, and Lucia was most gracious to all her old friends, in the manner of a Dowager Queen who has somehow come into a far vaster kingdom, but who has a tender remembrance of her former subjects, however humble, and she had a kind word for them all. After the party had dispersed, she and Georgie and Olga sat on in the garden, and her smiles were touched with sadness.

'Such a joy to see all the dear, quaint folk again,' she said, 'but what a sad change has come over the place! Riseholme, which in old days used to be seething with every sort of interest, has become just like any other vegetating little village –'

'I don't agree at all,' said Georgie loudly. 'It's seething still. Daisy Quantock's got a French parlourmaid who's an atheist, and Mrs Antrobus has learned the deaf and dumb alphabet, as she's got so deaf that the most expensive ear-trumpet isn't any use to her. Everybody has been learning it, too, and when Mrs Boucher gave a birthday-party for her only last week, they all talked deaf and dumb to each other, so that Mrs Antrobus could understand what was being said. I call that marvellous manners.'

The old flame flickered for a moment in Lucia's breast.

'No!' she cried. 'What else?'

'I haven't finished this yet,' said Georgie. 'And they were all using their hands so much to talk, that they couldn't get on with their dinner, and it took an hour and a half, though it was only four courses.'

'Georgie, how thrilling!' said Olga. 'Go on.'

Georgie turned to the more sympathetic listener.

'You see, they couldn't talk fast, because they were only learning, but when Mrs Antrobus replied, she was so quick, being an expert, that nobody except Piggie and Goosie –'

Lucia tilted her head sideways, with a sidelong glance at Olga, busy with a looking-glass and lipstick.

'Ah; I recollect. Her daughters,' she said.

'Yes, of course. They could tell you what she said if they were looking, but if they weren't looking you had to guess, like when somebody talks fast in a foreign language which you don't know much of, and you make a shot at what he's saying.'

Lucia gave him a gimlet glance. But of course, Georgie couldn't have been thinking of her and the Italian crisis.

'Their dear, funny little ways!' she said. 'But everyone I talked to was so eager to hear about Tilling and my Mayoral work, that I learned nothing about what was going on here. How they besieged me with questions! What else, Georgie?'

'Well, the people who have got your house now have made a swimming-bath in the garden and have lovely mixed bathing-parties.'

Lucia repressed a pang of regret that she had never thought of doing that, and uttered a shocked sort of noise.

'Oh, what a sad desecration!' she said. 'Where is it? In my pleached alley, or in Perdita's garden?'

'In the pleached alley, and it's a great success. I wish I'd brought my bathing-suit.'

'And do they keep up my tableaux and Elizabethan fêtes and literary circles?' she asked.

'I didn't hear anything about them, but there's a great deal going on. Very gay, and lots of people come down for week-ends from town.'

Lucia rose.

'And cocktail-parties, I suppose,' she said. 'Well, well, one must expect one's traces to be removed by the hand of time.

That wonderful sonnet of Shakespeare's about it. *Olga mia*, will you excuse me till dinner-time? Some housing plans I have got to study, or I shall never be able to face my Council on Monday.'

Lucia came down to dinner steeped in the supposed contents of her tin box and with a troubled face.

'Those riband-developments!' she said. 'They form one of the greatest problems I have to tackle.'

Olga looked utterly bewildered.

'Ribands?' she asked. 'Things in hats.'

Lucia gave a bright laugh.

'Stupid of me not to explain, dear,' she said. 'How could you know? Building developments: dreadful hideous dwellings along the sweet country roads leading into Tilling. Red-brick villas instead of hedges of hawthorn and eglantine. It seems such desecration.'

Georgie sighed. Lucia had already told him what she meant to say to her Council on Monday afternoon, and would assuredly tell him what she had said on Monday evening.

'Caterpillars!' she cried with a sudden inspiration. 'I shall compare those lines of houses to caterpillars, hungry red caterpillars wriggling out across the marsh and devouring its verdant loveliness. A vivid metaphor like that is needed. But I know, dear Olga, that nothing I say to you will go any further. My Councillors have a right to know my views before anybody else.'

'My lips are sealed,' said Olga.

'And yet we must build these new houses,' said the Mayor, putting both her elbows on the table and disregarding her plate of chicken. 'We must abolish the slums in Tilling, and that means building on the roads outside. Such a multiplicity of conflicting interests.'

'I suppose the work is tremendous,' said Olga.

'Yes, I think we might call it tremendous, mightn't we, Georgie?' asked Lucia.

Georgie was feeling fearfully annoyed with her. She was only putting it on in order to impress Olga, but the more fervently he agreed, the sooner, it might be hoped, she would stop.

'Overwhelming. Incessant,' he asserted.

The hope was vain.

'No, dear, not overwhelming,' she said, eating her chicken in a great hurry. 'I am not overwhelmed by it. Working for others enlarges one's capacity for work. For the sake of my dear Tilling I can undertake without undue fatigue, what would otherwise render me a perfect wreck. *Ich Dien*. Of course I have to sacrifice other interests. My reading? I scarcely open a book. My painting? I have done nothing since I made a sketch of some gorgeous dahlias in the autumn which Georgie didn't think too bad.'

'Lovely,' said Georgie in a voice of wood.

'Thank you, dear. My music? I have hardly played a note. But as you must know so well, dear Olga, music makes an imperishable store of memories within one: morsels of Mozart: bits of Beethoven all audible to the inward ear.'

'How well I remember you playing the slow movement of the "Moonlight Sonata,"' said Olga, seeking, like Georgie to entice her away from Mayoral topics. But the effect of this was appalling. Lucia assumed her rapt music-face, and with eyes fixed on the ceiling, indicated slow triplets on the tablecloth. Her fingers faltered, they recovered, and nobody could guess how long she would continue: probably to the end of the movement, and yet it seemed rude to interrupt this symbolic recital. But presently she sighed.

'Naughty fingers,' she said, as if shaking the triplets off. 'So forgetful of them!'

Somehow she had drained the life out of the others, but dinner was over, and they moved into Olga's music-room. The piano stood open, and Lucia, as if walking in sleep, like Lady Macbeth, glided on to the music-stool. The naughty fingers became much better, indeed they became as good as they had ever been. She dwelt long on the last note of the famous slow movement, gazing wistfully up, and they all sighed, according to the traditional usage when Lucia played the 'Moonlight'.

'Thank you, dear,' said Olga. 'Perfect.'

Lucia suddenly sprang off the music-stool with a light laugh.

'Better than I had feared,' she said, 'but far from perfect. And now, dear Olga, dare I? Might we? One little song. Shall I try to accompany you?'

Olga thought she could accompany herself and Lucia seated herself on a sort of throne close beside her and resumed her rapt expression, as Olga sang the 'Ave' out of *Lucrezia*. That solemn strain seemed vaguely familiar to Lucia, but she could not place it. Was it Beethoven? Was it from *Fidelio* or from *Creation Hymn*? Perhaps it was wiser only to admire with emotion without committing herself to the composer.

'That wonderful old tune!' she said. 'What a treat to hear it again. Those great melodies are the very foundation-stone of music.'

'But isn't it the prayer in *Lucrezia*?' asked Georgie. Lucia instantly remembered that it was.

'Yes, of course it is, Georgie,' she said. 'But in the plain-song mode. I expressed myself badly.'

'She hadn't the smallest idea what it was,' thought Olga, 'but she could wriggle out of a thumb-screw.' Then aloud:

'Yes, that was Cortese's intention,' she said. 'He will be pleased to know you think he has caught it. By the way, he rang up just before dinner to ask if he and his wife might come down to-morrow afternoon for the night. I sent a fervent "yes".'

'My dear, you spoil us!' said Lucia ecstatically. 'That will be too delightful.'

In spite of her ecstasy, this was grave news, and as she went to bed she pondered it. There would be Cortese, whose English was very limited (though less circumscribed than her own Italian), there would be Olga, who, though she said she spoke Italian atrociously, was fluent and understood it perfectly, and possibly Cortese's wife knew no English at all. If she did not, conversation must be chiefly conducted in Italian, and Lucia's vivid imagination pictured Olga translating to her what they were all saying, and re-translating her replies to them. Then no doubt he would play to them, and she would have to guess whether he was playing Beethoven or Mozart or plainsong or Cortese. It would be an evening full of hazards and humiliations. Better perhaps, in view of a pretended engagement on Monday morning, to leave on Sunday afternoon, before these dangerous foreigners arrived. 'If only I could bring myself to say that I can neither speak nor understand Italian, and know nothing about music!' thought Lucia. 'But I can't after all these years. It's wretched to run away like this, but I couldn't bear it.'

Georgie came down very late to breakfast. He had had dreams of Olga trying through a song to his accompaniment. She stood behind him with her hands on his shoulders, and her face close to his. Then he began singing, too, and their voices blended exquisitely . . . Dressing was a festival with his tiled bathroom next door, and he debated as to which of his new ties Olga would like best. Breakfast, Grosvenor had told him, would be on the verandah, but it was such a warm morning there was no need for his cape.

The others were already down.

'Georgie, this will never do,' said Olga, as he came out. 'Lucia says she must go back to Tilling this afternoon. Keep her in order. Tell her she shan't.'

'But what's happened, Lucia?' he asked. 'If we start early to-morrow we shall be in heaps of time for your Council meeting.'

Lucia began to gabble.

'I'm too wretched about it,' she said, 'But when I went upstairs last night, I looked into those papers again which I brought down with me, and I find there is so much I must talk over with my Town Clerk if I am to be equipped for my Council in the afternoon. You know what Monday morning is, Georgie. I must not neglect my duties though I have to sacrifice my delicious evening here. I must be adamant.'

'Too sad,' said Olga. 'But there's no reason why you should go, Georgie. I'll drive you back to-morrow. My dear, what a pretty tie!'

'I shall stop then,' said he. 'I've nothing to do at Tilling. I thought you'd like my tie.'

Lucia had never contemplated this, and she did not like it. But having announced herself as adamant, she could not instantly turn to putty. Just one chance of getting him to come with her remained.

'I shall have to take Grosvenor with me,' she said.

Georgie pictured a strange maid bringing in his tea, and getting his bath ready, with the risk of her finding his *toupet*, and other aids to juvenility. He faced it: it was worth it.

'That doesn't matter,' he replied. 'I shall be able to manage perfectly.'

9

Lucia was in for a run of bad luck, and it began that very afternoon. Ten minutes before she started with Grosvenor for Tilling, Cortese and his wife arrived. The latter was English and knew even less Italian than she did. And Cortese brought with him the first act of his new opera. It was too late to change her plans and she drove off after a most affectionate parting from Olga, whom she charged to come and stay at Tilling any time at a moment's notice. Just a telephone-message to say she was coming, and she could start at once sure of the fondest welcome ... But it was all most tiresome, for no doubt Cortese would run through the first act of his opera to-night, and the linguistic panic which had caused her to flee from Riseholme as from a plague-stricken village, leaving her nearest and dearest there, had proved to be utterly foundationless.

For the present that was all she knew: had she known what was to occur half an hour after she had left, she would certainly have turned and gone back to the plague-stricken village again, trusting to her unbounded ingenuity to devise some reason for her reappearance. A phone-call from the Duchess of Sheffield came for Madame Cortese.

'Poor mad Cousin Poppy,' she said. 'What on earth can she want?'

'Dressed crab,' screamed Olga after her as she went to the telephone, 'Cortese, you darling, let's have a go at your *Diane de Poictiers* after dinner. I had no idea you were near the end of the first act.'

'Nor I also. It has come as smooth as margarine,' said Cortese, who had been enjoined by Madame to learn English with all speed, and never to dare to speak Italian in her presence. 'And such an aria for you. When you hear it, you will jump for joy. I jump, you jumps, they jumpino. Dam' good.'

Madame returned from the telephone.

'Poppy asked more questions in half a minute than were ever asked before in that time,' she said. 'I took the first two or three and told her to wait. First, will we go to her awful old Castle to-morrow, to dine and stay the night. Second: who is here. Olga, I told her, and Cortese, and Mr Pillson of Tilling. "Why, of course I know him," said Poppy. "He's the Mayor of Tilling, and I met him at *Lucrezia*, and at lunch at the Ritz. Such a lovely beard." Thirdly –'

'But I'm not the Mayor of Tilling,' cried Georgie. 'Lucia's the Mayor of Tilling, and she hasn't got a beard –'

'Georgie, don't be pedantic,' said Olga. 'Evidently she means you –'

'*La barba e mobile*,' chanted Cortese. '*Una barba per due. Scusi.* Should say "A beard for two," my Dorothea.'

'It isn't *mobile*,' said Georgie, thinking about his *toupet*.

'Of course it isn't,' said Olga. 'It's a fine, natural beard. Well, what about Poppy? Let's all go to-morrow afternoon.'

'No: I must get back to Tilling,' said Georgie. 'Lucia expects me –'

'Aha, you are a hen-peck,' cried Cortese. 'And I am also a hen-peck. Is it not so, my Dorothea?'

'You're coming with us, Georgie,' said Olga. 'Ring up Lucia in the morning and tell her so. Just like that. And tell Poppy that we'll all four come, Dorothy. So that's settled.'

Lucia, for all her chagrin, was thrilled at the news, when Georgie rang her up next morning. He laid special stress on the Mayor of Tilling having been asked, for he felt sure she would enjoy that. Though it was agonizing to think what she had missed by her precipitate departure yesterday, Lucia cordially gave him leave to go to Sheffield Castle, for it was something that Georgie should stay there, though not she, and she sent her love and regrets to Poppy. Then after presiding at the Borough Bench (which lasted exactly twenty seconds, as there were no cases) instead of conferring with her Town

Clerk, she hurried down to the High Street to release the news like a new film.

'Back again, dear Worship,' cried Elizabeth, darting across the street. 'Pleasant visit?'

'Delicious,' said Lucia in the drawling voice. 'Dear Riseholme! How pleased they all were to see me. No party at Olga's; just Cortese and his wife, *très intime*, but such music. I got back last night to be ready for my duties to-day.'

'And not Mr Georgie?' asked Elizabeth.

'No. I insisted that he should stop. Indeed, I don't expect him till to-morrow, for he has just telephoned that Duchess Poppy — a cousin of Madame Cortese — asked the whole lot of us to go over to Sheffield to-day to dine and sleep. Such short notice, and impossible for me, of course, with my Council meeting this afternoon. The dear thing cannot realize that one has duties which must not be thrown over.'

'What a pity. So disappointing for you, dear,' said Elizabeth, writhing under a sudden spasm of colic of the mind. 'But Sheffield's a long way to go for one night. Does she live in the town?'

Lucia emitted the musical trill of merriment.

'No, it's Sheffield Castle,' she said. 'Not a long drive from Riseholme, in one of Olga's Daimlers. A Norman tower. A moat. It was in *Country Life* not long ago ... Good morning Padre.'

'An' where's your guid man?' asked the Padre.

Lucia considered whether she should repeat the great news. But it was more exalted not to, especially since the dissemination of it, now that Elizabeth knew, was as certain as if she had it proclaimed by the town crier.

'He joins me to-morrow,' she said. 'Any news here?'

'Such a lovely sermon from Reverence yesterday,' said Elizabeth, for the relief of her colic. 'All about riches and position in the world being only dross. I wish you could have heard it, Worship.'

Lucia could afford to smile at this pitiable thrust, and proceeded with her shopping, not ordering any special delicacies for herself because Georgie would be dining with a

Duchess. She felt that fate had not been very kind to her personally, though most thoughtful for Georgie. It was cruel that she had not known the nationality of Cortese's wife, and her rooted objection to his talking Italian, before she had become adamant about returning to Tilling, and this was doubly bitter, because in that case she would have still been on the spot when Poppy's invitation arrived, and it might have been possible (indeed, she would have made it possible) for the deputy Mayor to take her place at the Council meeting to-day, at which her presence had been so imperative when she was retreating before the Italians.

She began to wonder whether she could not manage to join the ducal party after all. There was actually very little business at the Council meeting; it would be over by half-past four, and if she started then she would be in time for dinner at Sheffield Castle. Or perhaps it would be safer to telephone to the deputy Mayor, asking him to take her place, as she had been called away unexpectedly. The deputy Mayor very willingly consented. He hoped it was not bad news and was reassured. All that there remained was to ring up Sheffield Castle, and say that the Mayor of Tilling was delighted to accept Her Grace's invitation to dine and sleep, conveyed to Her Worship by Mr Pillson. The answer was returned that the Mayor of Tilling was expected. 'And just for a joke,' thought Lucia, 'I won't tell them at Riseholme that I'm coming. Such a lovely surprise for them, if I get there first. I can start soon after lunch, and take it quietly.'

She recollected, with a trivial pang of uneasiness, that she had told Elizabeth that her duties at Tilling would have prevented her in any case from going to Sheffield Castle, but that did not last long. She would live it down or deny having said it, and she went into the garden-room to release Mrs Simpson, and, at the same time, to provide for the propagation of the tidings that she was going to her Duchess.

'I shall not attend the Council meeting this afternoon, Mrs Simpson,' she said, 'as there's nothing of the slightest importance. It will be a mere formality, so I am playing truant. I shall be leaving Tilling after lunch, to dine and sleep at the Duchess of Sheffield's, at Sheffield Castle. A moat and I think a drawbridge. Ring me up there if anything occurs that I must deal with personally, and I will give it my attention. There seems nothing that need detain you any more to-day. One of our rare holidays.'

On her way home Mrs Simpson met Diva's Janet, and told her the sumptuous news. Janet scuttled home and plunged down into the kitchen to tell her mistress who was making buns. She had already heard about Georgie from Elizabeth.

'Don't believe a word of it,' said Diva. 'You've mixed it up, Janet. It's Mr Georgie, if anybody, who's going to Sheffield Castle.'

'Beg your pardon, ma'am,' said Janet hotly, 'but I've mixed nothing up. Mrs Simpson told me direct that the Mayor was going, and talking of mixing you'd better mix twice that lot of currants, if it's going to be buns.'

The telephone-bell rang in the tea-room above, and Diva flew up the kitchen-stairs, scattering flour.

'Diva, is that Diva?' said Lucia's voice. 'My memory is shocking; did I say I would pop in for tea to-day?'

'No. Why?' said Diva.

'That is all right then,' said Lucia. 'I feared that I might have to put it off. I'm joining Georgie on a one-night's visit to a friend. I couldn't get out of it. Back to-morrow.'

Diva replaced the receiver.

'Janet, you're quite right,' she called down the kitchen-stairs. 'Just finish the buns. Must go out and tell people.'

Lucia's motor came round after lunch. Foljambe (it was Foljambe's turn, and Georgie felt more comfortable with her) was waiting in the hall with the jewel-case and a camera, and Lucia was getting the 'Slum Clearance' tin box from the garden-room to take with her, when the telephone-bell rang. She had a faint presage of coming disaster as she said, 'Who is it?' in as steady a voice as she could command.

'Sheffield Castle speaking. Is that the Mayor of Tilling.'

'Yes,'

'Her Grace's maid speaking, Your Worship. Her Grace partook of her usual luncheon to-day –'

'Dressed crab?' asked Lucia in parenthesis.

'Yes, Your Worship, and was taken with internal pains.'

'I am terribly sorry,' said Lucia. 'Was it tinned?'

'Fresh, I understand, and the party is put off.'

Lucia gave a hollow moan into the receiver, and Her Grace's maid offered consolation.

'No anxiety at all, Your Worship,' she said, 'but she thought she wouldn't feel up to a party.'

The disaster evoked in Lucia the exercise of her utmost brilliance. There was such a fearful lot at stake over this petty indigestion.

'I don't mind an atom about the dislocation of my plans,' she said, 'but I am a little anxious about Her dear Grace. I quite understand about the party being put off; so wise to spare her fatigue. It would be such a relief if I might come just to reassure myself. I was on the point of starting, my maid, my luggage all ready. I would not be any trouble. My maid would bring me a tray instead of dinner. Is it possible?'

'I'll see,' said her Grace's maid, touched by this devotion. 'Hold on.'

She held on; she held on, it seemed, as for life itself, till, after an interminable interval the reply came.

'Her Grace would be very happy to see the Mayor of Tilling, but she's putting off the rest of the party,' said the angelic voice.

'Thank you, thank you,' called Lucia. 'So good of her. I will start at once.'

She picked up 'Slum Clearance' and went into the house only to be met by a fresh ringing of the telephone in the hall. A panic seized her lest Poppy should have changed her mind.

'Let it ring, Grosvenor,' she said. 'Don't answer it at all. Get in, Foljambe. Be quick.'

She leaped into the car.

'Drive on, Cadman,' she called.

The car rocked its way down to the High Street, and Lucia let down the window and looked out, in case there were any friends about. There was Diva at the corner, and she stopped the car.

'Just off, Diva,' she said. 'Duchess Poppy not very well, so I've just heard.'

'No! Crab?' asked Diva.

'Apparently, but not tinned, and there is no need for me to feel anxious. She insisted on my coming just the same. Such a lovely drive in front of me. Taking some work with me.'

Lucia pulled up the window again and pinched her finger but she hardly regarded that for there was so much to think about. Olga at Riseholme, for instance, must have been informed by now that the party was off, and yet Georgie had not rung up to say that he would be returning to Tilling to-day. A disagreeable notion flitted through her mind that, having got leave to go to Sheffield Castle, he now meant to stay another night with Olga, without telling her, and it was with a certain relief that she remembered the disregarded telephone-call which had hurried her departure. Very likely that was Georgie ringing up to tell her that he was coming back to Tilling to-day. It would be a sad surprise for him not to find her there.

Her route lay through Riseholme, and passing along the edge of the village green, she kept a sharp look-out for familar figures. She saw Piggie and Goosie with Mrs Antrobus: they were all three gesticulating with their hands in a manner that seemed very odd until she remembered that they must be speaking in deaf and dumb alphabet: she saw a very slim elegant young woman whom she conjectured to be Daisy Quantock's atheistic French maid, but there was no sign of Georgie or Olga. She debated a moment as to whether she should call at Olga's to find out for certain that he had gone, but dismissed the idea as implying a groundless suspicion. Beyond doubt the telephone-call which she had so narrowly evaded was to say that he had done so, and she steadily backed away from the familiar scene in order to avoid seeing him if he was still here ... Then came less familiar country, a belt of woods, a stretch of heathery upland glowing in the afternoon sun, positively demanding to be sketched in water-colours, and presently a turning with a sign-post 'To Sheffield Bottom'. Trees again, a small village of grey stone houses, and facing her a great castellated wall with a tower above a gateway and a bridge over a moat leading to it. Lucia stopped the car and got out, camera in hand.

'What a noble façade,' she said to herself. 'I wonder if my room will be in that tower.'

She took a couple of photographs, and getting back into the car, she passed over the bridge and through the gateway.

Inside lay a paved courtyard in a state of indescribable neglect. Weeds sprouted between the stones, a jungle of neglected flower-beds lay below the windows, here and there were moss-covered stone seats. On one of these close beside the huge discoloured door of blistered paint sat Poppy with her mouth open, fast asleep. As Lucia stepped out, she awoke, and looked at her with a dazed expression of strong disfavour.

'Who are you?' asked Poppy.

'Dear Duchess, so good of you to let me come,' said Lucia, thinking that she was only half-awake. 'Lucia Pillson, the Mayor of Tilling.'

'That you aren't,' said Poppy. 'It's a man, and he's got a beard.'

Lucia laughed brightly.

'Ah, you're thinking of my husband,' she said. 'Such a vivid description of him. It fits him exactly. But I'm the Mayor. We met at dear Olga's opera-box, and at the Ritz next day.'

Poppy gave a great yawn, and sat silent, assimilating this information.

'I'm afraid there's been a complete muddle,' she said. 'I thought it was he who was coming. You see I was much flattered at his eagerness to spend a quiet evening with me and my stomach-ache, and so I said yes. No designs on him of any kind I assure you. All clean as a whistle: he'd have been as safe with me as with his grandmother, if she's still alive. My husband's away, and I just wanted a pleasant companion. And to think that it was you all the while. That never entered my head. Fancy!'

It did not require a mind of Lucia's penetrative power to perceive that Poppy did not want her, and did not intend that she should stop. Her next remarks removed any possibility of doubt.

'But you'll have some tea first, *won't* you?' she asked. 'Indeed I insist on your having some tea unless you prefer coffee. If you ring the door-bell, somebody will probably come. Oh, I see you've got a camera. Do take some photographs. Would you like to begin with me, though I'm not looking my best.'

In spite of the nightmarish quality of the situation, Lucia kept her head, and it was something to be given tea and to take photographs. Perhaps there was a scoop here, if she handled it properly, and first she photographed Poppy and the dismal courtyard, and then went to Poppy's bedroom to tidy herself for tea and snapped her washing-stand and the corner of her Elizabethan bed. After tea Poppy took her to the dining-room and the gaunt picture-gallery and through a series of decayed drawing-rooms, and all the time Lucia babbled rapturous comments.

'Magnificent tapestry,' she said, 'ah, and a glimpse of the Park from the window. Would you stand there, Duchess, looking out with your dog on the window-seat? What a little love! Perfect. And this noble hall: the panelling by that lovely oriel window would make a lovely picture. And that refectory-table.'

But now Poppy had had enough, and she walked firmly to the front door and shook hands.

'Charmed to have seen you,' she said, 'though I've no head for names. You will have a pleasant drive home on this lovely evening. Good-bye, or perhaps *au revoir*.'

'That would be much nicer,' said Lucia, cordial to the last.

She drove out of the gateway she had entered three-quarters of an hour before, and stopped the car to think out her plans. Her first idea was to spend the night at the Ambermere Arms at Riseholme, and return to Tilling next morning laden with undeveloped photographs of Sheffield Castle and Poppy, having presumably spent the night there. But that was risky: it could hardly help leaking out through Foljambe that she had done nothing of the sort, and the exposure, coupled with the loss of prestige, would be infinitely painful. 'I must think of something better that that,' she said to herself, and suddenly a great illumination shone on her. 'I shall tell the truth,' she heroically determined, 'in all essentials. I shall say that Poppy's maid told me that I, the Mayor of Tilling was expected. That, though the party was abandoned, she still wanted me to come. That I found her asleep in a weedy courtyard, looking ghastly. That she evidently didn't feel up to entertaining me, but insisted that I should have tea. That I took photographs all over the place. All gospel truth, and no necessity for saying anything about that incredible mistake of hers in thinking that Georgie was the Mayor of Tilling.'

She tapped on the window.

'We'll just have dinner at the Ambermere Arms, at Riseholme, Cadman,' she called, 'and then go back to Tilling.'

It was about half-past ten when Lucia's car drew up at the door of Mallards. She could scarcely believe that it was still the same day as that on which she had awoken here, regretful that she had fled from Riseholme on a false alarm, had swanked about Georgie staying at Sheffield Castle, had shirked the Council meeting to which duty had called her, had wangled an invitation to the Castle herself, had stayed there for quite three-quarters of an hour, and had dined at Riseholme. 'Quite like that huge horrid book by Mr James Joyce, which all happens in one day,' she reflected, as she stepped out of the car.

Looking up, she saw that the garden-room was lit, and simultaneously she heard the piano: Georgie therefore must have come home. Surely (this time) she recognized the tune: it was the prayer in *Lucrezia*. He was playing that stormy introduction with absolute mastery, and he must be playing it by heart, for he could not have the score, nor, if he had, could he have read it. And then that unmistakable soprano voice (though a little forced in the top register) began to sing. The wireless? Was Olga singing *Lucrezia* in London to-night? Impossible; for only a few hours ago during this interminable day, she was engaged to dine and sleep at Poppy's Castle. Besides, if this was relayed from Covent Garden, the orchestra, not the piano, would be accompanying her. Olga must be singing in the garden-room, and Georgie must be here, and nobody else could be here ... There seemed to be material for another huge horrid book by Mr James Joyce before the day was done.

'I shall be perfectly calm and lady-like whatever happens,' thought Lucia, and concentrating all her power on this genteel feat she passed through the hall and went out to the garden-room. But before entering, she paused, for in her reverence for Art, she felt she could not interrupt so superb a performance: Olga had never sung so gloriously as now when she was singing to Georgie all alone ... She perched on the final note pianissimo. She held it with gradual crescendo till she was singing fortissimo. She ceased, and it was as if a great white flame had been blown out.

Lucia opened the door. Georgie was sitting in the window: his piece of needlework had dropped from his hand, and he was gazing at the singer. 'Too marvellous,' he began, thinking that Grosvenor was coming in with drinks. Then, by some sixth sense, he knew it wasn't Grosvenor, and turning, he saw his wife.

In that moment he went through a selection of emotions that fully equalled hers. The first was blank consternation. A sense of baffled gallantry succeeded, and was followed by an over-whelming thankfulness that it was baffled. All evening he had been imagining himself delightfully in love with Olga, but had been tormented by the uneasy thought that any man of spirit would make some slight allusion to her magnetic charm. That would be a most perilous proceeding. He revelled in the feeling that he was in love with her, but to inform her of that might be supposed to lead to some small practical demonstration of his passion, and the thought made him feel cold with apprehension. She might respond (it was not likely but it was possible, for he had lately been reading a book by a very clever writer, which showed how lightly ladies in artistic professions take an adorer's caresses), and he was quite convinced that he was no good at that sort of thing. On the other hand she might snub him, and that would wound his tenderest sensibilities. Whatever happened, in fact, it would entirely mar their lovely evening. Taking it all in all, he had never been so glad to see Lucia.

Having pierced him with her eye, she turned her head calmly and gracefully towards Olga.

'Such a surprise!' she said. 'A delightful one, of course. And you, no doubt, are equally surprised to see me.'

Lucia was being such a perfect lady that Olga quaked and quivered with suppressed laughter.

'Georgie, explain at once,' she said. 'It's the most wonderful muddle that ever happened.'

'Well, it's like this,' said Georgie carefully. 'As I telephoned you this morning, we were all invited to go to Poppy's for the night. Then she was taken ill after lunch and put us off. So I rang up in order to tell you that I was coming back here and bringing Olga. You told her to propose herself whenever she felt inclined, and just start –'

Lucia bestowed a polite bow on Olga.

'Quite true,' she said. 'But I never received that message. Oh –'

'I know you didn't,' said Georgie. 'I couldn't get any answer. But I knew you would be delighted to see her, and when we got here not long before dinner, Grosvenor said you'd gone to dine and sleep at Poppy's. Why didn't you answer my telephone? And why didn't you tell us you were going away? In fact, what about you?'

During this brief but convincing narrative, the thwarted Muse of Tragedy picked up her skirts and fled. Lucia gave a little trill of happy laughter.

'Too extraordinary,' she said. 'A comedy of errors. Georgie, you told me this morning, very distinctly, that Poppy had invited the Mayor of Tilling. Very well. I found that there was nothing that required my presence at the Council meeting, and I rang up Sheffield Castle to say I could manage to get away. I was told that I was expected. Then just as I was starting there came a message that poor Poppy was ill and the party was off.'

Lucia paused a moment to review her facts as already rehearsed, and resumed in her superior, drawling voice.

'I felt a little uneasy about her,' she said, 'and as I had no further engagement this afternoon, I suggested that though the party was off, I would run over – the motor was actually at the door – and stay the night. She said she would be so happy to see me. She gave me such a pleasant welcome, but evidently she was far from well, and I saw she was not up to entertaining me. So I just had tea; she insisted on that, and she took me round the Castle and made me snap a quantity of photographs. Herself, her bedroom, the gallery, that noble oriel window in the hall. I must remember to send her prints. A delicious hour or two, and then I left her. I think my visit had done her good. She seemed brighter. Then a snack at the Ambermere Arms; I saw your house was dark, dear Olga, or I should have popped in. And here we are. That lovely prayer from *Lucrezia* to welcome me. I waited entranced on the doorstep till it was over.'

It was only by strong and sustained effort that Olga restrained herself from howling with laughter. She hadn't been singing the prayer from *Lucrezia* this time, but 'Les feux magiques', by Berlioz; Lucia seemed quite unable – though of course she had been an agitated listener – to recognize the prayer when she heard it. But she was really a wonderful woman. Who but she would have had the genius to take advantage of Poppy's delusion that Georgie was the Mayor of Tilling? Then what about Lucia's swift return from the Castle? Without doubt Poppy had sent her away when she saw her female, beardless guest, and the clever creature had made out that it was she who had withdrawn as Poppy was so unwell, with a gallery of photographs to prove she had been there. Then she recalled Lucia's face when she entered the garden-room a few minutes ago, the face of a perfect lady who, unexpectedly returns home to find a wanton woman, bent on seduction, alone with her husband. Or was Georgie's evident relief at her advent funnier still? Impossible to decide, but she must not laugh till she could bury her face in her pillow. Lucia had a few sandwiches to refresh her after her drive, and they went up to bed. The two women kissed each other affectionately. Nobody kissed Georgie.

Tilling next morning, unaware of Lucia's return, soon began to sprout with a crop of conjectures which, like mushrooms, sprang up all over the High Street. Before doing any shopping at all, Elizabeth rushed into Diva's tea-shop to obtain confirmation that Diva had actually seen Lucia driving away with Foljambe and luggage on the previous afternoon *en route* for Sheffield Castle.

'Certainly I did,' said Diva. 'Why?'

Elizabeth contracted her brows in a spasm of moral anguish.

'I wish I could believe,' she said, 'that it was all a blind, and that Worship didn't go to Sheffield Castle at all, but only wanted to make us think so, and returned home after a short drive by another route. Deceitful though that would be, it would be far, far better than what I fear may have happened.'

'I suppose you're nosing out some false scent as usual,' said Diva. 'Get on.'

Elizabeth made a feint of walking towards the door at this rude speech, but gave it up.

'It's too terrible, Diva,' she said. 'Yesterday evening, it might have been about half-past six, I was walking up the street towards Mallards. A motor passed me, laden with luggage, and it stopped there.'

'So I suppose you stopped, too,' said Diva.

'– and out of it got Mr Georgie and a big, handsome – yes, she was very handsome – woman, though, oh, so common. She stood on the doorstep a minute looking round, and sang out, "Georgino! How *divino*!" Such a screech! I judge so much by voice. In they went, and the luggage was taken in after them, and the door shut. Bang. And Worship, you tell me, had gone away.'

'Gracious me!' said Diva.

'You may well say that. And you may well say that I stopped. I did, for I was rooted to the spot. It was enough to root anybody. At that moment the Padre had come round the corner, and he was rooted too. As I didn't know then for certain whether Worship had actually gone – it might only have been one of her grand plans of which one hears no more – I said nothing to him, because it is so wicked to start any breath of scandal, until one has one's facts. It looks to me very black, and I shouldn't have thought it of Mr Georgie. Whatever his faults – we all have faults – I did think he was a man of clean life. I still hope it may be so, for he has always conducted himself with propriety, as far as I know, to the ladies of Tilling, but I don't see how it possibly can.'

Diva gave a hoarse laugh.

'Not much temptation,' she said, 'from us old hags. But it is queer that he brought a woman of that sort to stay at Mallards on the very night Lucia was away. And then there's another thing. She told us all that *he* was going to stay at Poppy's last night –'

'I can't undertake to explain all that Worship tells us,' said Elizabeth. 'That is asking too much of me.'

'– but he was here,' said Diva. 'Yet I shouldn't wonder if you'd got hold of the wrong end of the stick somehow. Habit of yours, Elizabeth. After all, the woman may have been a friend of Lucia's –'

'– and so Mr Georgie brought her when Lucia was away. I see,' said Elizabeth.

Her pensive gaze wandered to the window, and she stiffened like a pointing setter, for down the street from Mallards was coming Georgie with the common, handsome, screeching woman. Elizabeth said nothing to Diva, for something might be done in the way of original research, and she rose.

'Very dark clouds,' she said, 'but we must pray that they will break. I've done no shopping yet. I suppose Worship will be back sometime to-day with a basket of strawberry leaves, if Poppy can spare her. Otherwise, the municipal life of Tilling will be suspended. Not that it matters two straws whether she's here or not. Quite a cypher in the Council.'

'Now that's not fair,' shouted Diva angrily after her. 'You can't have it both ways. Why she ever made you Mayoress –' but Elizabeth had shut the door.

Diva went down to her kitchen with an involuntary glow of admiration for Georgie, which was a positive shock to her moral principles. He and his *petit point*, and his little cape, and his old-maidish ways – was it possible that these cloaked a passionate temperament? Who could this handsome, common female be? Where had he picked her up? Perhaps in the hotel when he and Lucia had stayed in London, for Diva seemed to have heard that voluptuous assignations were sometimes made in the most respectable places. What a rogue! And how frightful for Lucia, if she got to know about it. 'I'm sure I hope she won't,' thought Diva, 'but it wouldn't be bad for her to be taken down a peg or two, though I should pity her at the same time. However, one mustn't rush to conclusions. But it's shocking that I've got a greater respect for Mr Georgie than I ever had before. Can't make it out.'

Diva got to work with her pastry-making, but some odd undercurrent of thought went trickling on. What a starvation diet for a man of ardent temperament, as Georgie now appeared, must his life in Tilling have been, where all the women were so very undecorative. If there had only been a woman with a bit of brilliance about her, whom he could admire and flirt with just a little, all this might have been averted. She left Janet to finish the shortbread, and went out to cull developments.

Elizabeth meantime had sighted her prey immediately, and from close at hand observed the guilty pair entering the photographer's. Were the shameless creatures, she wondered, going to be photographed together? That was the sort of bemused folly that sinning couples often committed, and bitterly rued it afterwards. She glided in after them, but Georgie was only giving the shopman a roll of negatives to be developed and printed and sent up to Mallards as soon as possible. He took off his hat to her very politely, but left the shop without introducing her to his companion which was only natural and showed good feeling. Certainly she was remarkably handsome. Beautifully dressed. A row of pearls so large that they could not be real. Hatless with waved hair. Rouge. Lipstick . . . She went in pursuit again. They passed the Padre and his wife, who turned completely round to look at them; they passed Susan in her Royce (she had given up tricycling in this hot weather) who held her head out of the window till foot-passengers blocked her view of them, and Diva, standing on her doorstep with her market-basket, was rooted to the spot as firmly as Elizabeth had been the night before. The woman was a dream of beauty with her brilliant colouring and her high, arched eyebrows. Recovering her powers of locomotion, Diva went into the hairdressing and toilet saloon.

Elizabeth bought some parsnips at Twistevant's, deep in thought. Bitter moralist though she was, she could not withhold her admiration for the anonymous female. Diva had rudely alluded to the ladies of Tilling as old hags, and was there not a grain of truth in it? They did not make the best of themselves. What brilliance that skilfully applied rouge and lipstick gave a face! Without it the anonymous might have looked ten years older and far less attractive. 'Hair, too,' thought Elizabeth, 'that soft brown, so like a natural tint. But finger-nails, dripping with bright arterial blood: never!'

She went straight to the hairdressing and toilet establishment. Diva was just coming out of the shop carrying a small packet.

'Little titivations, dear?' asked Elizabeth, reading her own thoughts unerringly.

'Tooth-powder,' said Diva without hesitation, and scooted across the road to where Susan was still leaning out of the window of her Royce and beckoning to her.

'I've seen her,' she said (there was no need to ask who 'she' was). 'And I recognized her at once from her picture in the *Tatler*. You'd never guess.'

'No, I know I shouldn't,' said Diva impatiently. 'Who?'

'The great prima donna. Dear me, I've forgotten her name. But the one Lucia went to hear sing in London,' said Susan. 'Bracelet, wasn't it?'

'Bracely? Olga Bracely?' cried Diva. 'Are you *quite* sure?'

'Positive. Quite lovely, and such hair.'

That was enough, and Diva twinkled back across the road to intercept Elizabeth who was just coming out of the hairdressing and toilet shop with a pink packet in her hand, which she instantly concealed below the parsnips.

'Such a screechy voice, didn't you say, Elizabeth?' she asked.

'Yes, frightful. It went right through me like a railway whistle. Why?'

'It's the prima donna, Olga Bracely. That's all,' said Diva. 'Voice must have gone. Sad for her. Glad to have told you who she is.'

Very soon all Tilling knew who was the lovely *maquillée* woman with the pearls, who had stayed the night alone with Georgie at Mallards. Lucia had not been seen at all this morning, and it was taken for granted that she was still away on that snobbish expedition for which she had thrown over her Council meeting. Though Olga (so she said) was a dear friend, it would certainly be a surprise to her, when she returned to find her dear friend staying with her husband at her own house, when she had told Tilling that both Georgie and Olga were staying that night at Poppy's Castle. Or would Olga leave Tilling again before Lucia returned? Endless interpretations could be put on this absorbing incident, but Tilling was too dazzled with the prima donna herself, her pearls, her beauty, her reputation as the Queen of Song to sit in judgment on her.

What a dream of charm and loveliness she was with her delicately rouged cheeks and vermilion mouth, and that air of joyous and unrepentant paganism! For Evie her blood-red nails had a peculiar attraction, and she too went to the hairdressing and toilet establishment, and met Susan just coming out.

Lucia meantime had spent a municipal morning in the garden-room without showing herself even for a moment at the window. Her departmental boxes were grouped round her, but she gave them very little attention. She was completely satisfied with the explanation of the strange adventures which had led to the staggering discovery of Olga and Georgie alone in her house the night before, and was wondering whether Tilling need ever know how very brief her visit to Poppy had been. It certainly was not her business to tell her friends that a cup of tea had been the only hospitality she had received. Then her photographs (if they came out) would be ready by to-morrow, and if she gave a party in the evening she would leave her scrap-book open on the piano. She would not call attention to it, but there it would be, furnishing unshakable ocular evidence of her visit . . .

After lunch, accordingly, she rang up all her more intimate circle, and, without definitely stating that she had this moment returned to Tilling from Sheffield Castle, let it be understood that such was the case. It had been such a lovely morning: she had enjoyed her drive so much: she had found a mass of arrears waiting for her, and she asked them all to dine next night at eight. She apologized for such short notice, but her dear friend Olga Bracely, who was here on a short visit, would be leaving the day after – a gala night at the opera – and it would give her such pleasure to meet them all. But, as she and Olga went up to dress next evening, she told Olga that dinner would be at eightish: say ten minutes past eight. There was a subtle reason for this, for the photographs of Sheffield Castle had arrived and she had pasted them into her scrap-book. Tilling would thus have time to admire and envy before Olga appeared: Lucia felt that her friends would not take much interest in them if she was there.

Never had any party in Tilling worn so brilliant and un-expected an appearance as that which assembled in the garden-room the following night. Evie and the Padre arrived first: Evie's finger-nails looked as if she had pinched them all, except one, in the door, causing the blood to flow freely underneath each. She had forgotten about that one, and it looked frost-bitten. Elizabeth and Benjy came next: Elizabeth's cheeks were like the petals of wild roses, but she had not the nerve to incarnadine her mouth, which, by contrast, appeared to be afflicted with the cyanosis which precedes death. Diva, on the other hand, had been terrified at the aspect of blooming youth which rouge gave her, and she had wiped it off at the last moment, retaining the Cupid's bow of a vermilion mouth, and two thin arched eyebrows in charcoal. Susan, wearing the Order of the British Empire, had had her grey hair waved, and it resembled corrugated tin roofing: Mr Wyse and Georgie wore their velvet suits. It took them all a few minutes to get used to each other, for they were like butterflies which had previously only known each other in the caterpillar or chrysalis stage, and they smiled and simpered like new acquaintances in the most polite circles, instead of old and censorious friends.

Olga had not yet appeared, and so they had time to study Lucia's album of snap-shots which lay open on the piano, and she explained in a casual manner what the latest additions were.

'A corner of the courtyard of Sheffield Castle,' she said. 'Not come out very well. The Norman tower. The dining-hall. The Duchess's bedroom; wonderful Elizabethan bed. The picture-gallery. She is standing looking out of the window with her Pekingese. Such a sweet. It jumped up on the window-seat just before I snapped. The Duchess at the tea-table –'

'What a big cake!' interrupted Diva professionally. 'Sugared, too. So she does eat something besides dressed crab. Hope she didn't have much cake after her indigestion.'

'But what a shabby court-yard,' said Evie. 'I should have thought a Duke would have liked his Castle to look tidier. Why doesn't he tell his gardener to weed it?'

Elizabeth felt she would burst unless she put in a venomous word.

'Dear Worship, when you write to thank Her Grace for your pleasant visit, you must say, just in fun, of course, that you expect the courtyard to be tidied up before you come next.'

Lucia was perfectly capable of dealing with such clumsy sarcasm.

'What a good idea!' she said. 'You always think of the right thing, Elizabeth. Certainly I will. Remind me, Georgie.'

So the photographs did their work. Tilling could not doubt that Lucia had been wrapped in the Norman embrace of Sheffield Castle, and determined silently and sternly never again to allude to the painful subject. That suited Lucia admirably, for there were questions that might be asked about her visit which would involve regrettable admissions if she was to reply quite truthfully. Just as her friends were turning surfeited and sad from the album a step was heard outside and Olga appeared in the doorway. A white gown, high at the neck, reeking of Molyneux and simplicity. A scarlet girdle, and pearls as before.

'Dear Lucia,' she cried, 'I see I'm late. Forgive me.'

'My own! I always forgive you as soon as I see you, only

there is never anything to forgive,' said Lucia effusively. 'Now I needn't say who you are, but this is Mrs Bartlett and our Padre, and here are Mr and Mrs Wyse, and this is Diva Plaistow, and here's my beloved Mayoress, Elizabeth Mapp-Flint and Major Mapp-Flint –'

Olga looked from Benjy to Elizabeth and back again.

'But surely I recognize them,' she said. 'That marvellous picture, which everybody raves about –'

'Yes, little me,' said the beaming Elizabeth, 'and my Benjy in the clouds. What an eye you've got, Miss Bracely!'

'And this is my husband,' went on Lucia with airy humour, 'who says he thinks he has met you before –'

'I believe we did meet somewhere, but ages ago, and he won't remember me,' said Olga. 'Oh, Georgie, I mustn't drink sherry, but as you've poured it out for me –'

'Dinner,' said Grosvenor rather sternly.

In the hard overhead light of the dining-room, the ladies of Tilling, novices in *maquillage*, looked strangely spurious, but the consciousness in each of her rejuvenated appearance, combined with Olga's gay presence, made them feel exceptionally brilliant. All round the table conversation was bright and eager, and they all talked at her, striving to catch her attention. Benjy, sitting next her, began telling her one of his adventures with a tiger, but instantly Susan raised her voice and spoke of her tricycle. Her husband chipped in, and with an eye on Olga told Lucia that his sister the Contessa di Faraglione was a passionate student of the age of Lucrezia Borgia. Diva, longing to get Olga to come to ye old tea-house, spoke loudly about her new recipe for sardine tartlets, but Lucia overrode so commercial a subject by the introduction of the Mayoral Motif coupled with slums. Olga herself chattered and laughed, the only person present who was not anxious to make a favourable impression. She lit a cigarette long before dinner was over, and though Elizabeth had once called that 'a disgusting foreign habit' she lit one, too. Olga ate a cherry beginning with the end of the stalk and at once Benjy was trying to do the same, ejaculating, as it dropped into his finger-bowl, 'Not so easy, by Jove.' There was no bridge to-night, but by incessant harping on antique dances, Lucia managed to get herself asked to tread a minuet with Georgie. Olga accompanied them, and as she rose from the piano, she became aware that they were all looking at her with the expectant air of dogs that hope to be taken out for a walk.

'Yes, certainly if you want me to,' she said.

She sat down at the piano again. And she sang.

10

Though Tilling remained the same at heart, Olga's brief visit had considerably changed the decorative aspect of its leading citizenesses. The use of powder on the face on very hot days when prominent features were apt to turn crimson, or on very cold ones, when prominent features were apt to turn mauve, had always been accepted, but that they should embellish themselves with rouge and lipstick and arched eyebrows was a revolution indeed. They had always considered such aids to loveliness as typical of women who shamelessly advertised their desire to capture the admiration of males, and that was still far from their intentions. But Diva found that arched eyebrows carefully drawn where there were none before gave her a look of high-bred surprise: Elizabeth that the rose-mantled cheeks she now saw in her looking-glass made her feel (not only appear) ten years younger: Susan that her corrugated hair made her look like a French *marquise*. Irene, who had been spending a fortnight of lionization in London, was amazed at the change when she returned, and expressed her opinion of it, by appearing in the High Street with the tip of her nose covered with green billiard-chalk.

She at once got to work on the portrait which Lucia had commissioned. She had amplified Lucia's biographical suggestion, and it represented her in full Mayoral robes and chain and a three-cornered hat playing the piano in the garden-room. Departmental boxes were piled in the background, a pack of cards and a paint-box lay on the lid of the piano, and her bicycle leaned against it.

'Symbols, beloved,' said the artist, 'indicating your marvellous many-sidedness. I know you don't ride your bicycle in the garden-room, nor play cards on your piano, nor wear your robes when you're at your music, but I group your completeness round you. Ah! Hold that expression of indulgent disdain for the follies of the world for a moment. Think of the Tilling hags and their rouge.'

'Like that?' asked Lucia, curling her upper lip.

'No, not at all like that. Try another. Be proud and calm. Think of spending an evening with your Duchess – darling, why are you such a snob? – or just think of yourself with all your faults and splendours. Perfect!'

Irene stepped back from her easel.

'And I've got it!' she cried. 'There's not a living artist and very few dead ones who could have seized that so unerringly. How monstrous that my work should be hated just because I am a woman!'

'But your picture was the picture of the year,' said Lucia, 'and all the critics cracked it up.'

'Yes, but I felt the undercurrent of hostility. Men are such self-centred brutes. Wait till I publish my memoirs.'

'But aren't you rather young for that?'

'No, I'm twenty-five, and by that age everyone has experienced all that matters, or anyhow has imagined it. Oh, tell me the truth about what all the painted hags are whispering. Georgie and Olga Bracely being alone here. What happened really? Did you arrange it all for them? How perfect of you! Nobody but you would be so modern and open-minded. And Tilling's respect for Georgie has gone up enormously.'

Lucia stared at her a moment, assimilating this monstrous suggestion, then sprang to her feet with a gasp of horror.

'Oh, the poisonous tongues!' she cried 'Oh, the asps. And besides –'

She stopped. She found herself entangled in the web she herself had woven, and never had any spider known to natural history so completely encircled itself. She had told Tilling that she was going to dine and sleep at Poppy's Castle, and had shown everybody those elegant photographs as tacit evidence that she had done so. Tilling therefore, had concluded that Olga and Georgie had spent the night alone at Mallards, and here was Irene intolerably commending her for her open-mindedness not only in condoning but in promoting this assignation. The fair fame, the unsullied morality of herself and Georgie, not to mention Olga, was at stake, and (oh, how it hurt!) she would be forced to give the utmost publicity to the fact that she had come back to Tilling the same evening. That would be a frightful loss of prestige, but there was no choice. She laughed scornfully.

'Foolish of me to have been indignant for a single moment at such an idea!' she said. 'I never heard such rubbish. I found poor Poppy very unwell, so I just had tea with her, cheered her up and took some photographs and came home at once. Tilling is really beyond words!'

'Darling, what a disappointment!' said Irene. 'It would have been so colossal of you. And what a come-down for poor Georgie. Just an old maid again.'

The news was very soon known, and Tilling felt that Lucia and Georgie had let them down. Everything had been so exciting and ducal and compromising, and there was really nothing left of it. Elizabeth and Diva lost no time in discussing it in Diva's tea-room next morning when marketing was done, and were severe.

'The deceitfulness of it is what disgusts me most,' said the Mayoress. 'Far worse than the snobbishness. Worship let it be widely known that she was staying the night with Poppy, and then she skulks back, doesn't appear at all next morning to make us think that she was still away –'

'And shows us all those photographs,' chimed in Diva, 'as a sort of . . . what's the word?'

'Can't say, dear,' said Elizabeth, regarding her rose-leaf cheeks with high approval in the looking-glass over the mantelpiece.

'Affidavit, that's it, as testifying that she had stayed with Poppy. Never told us she hadn't.'

'My simple brain can't follow her conjuring tricks,' said Elizabeth, ' and I should be sorry if it could. But I'm only too thankful she did come back. It will be a great relief to the Padre, I expect, to be told that. I wonder, if you insist on knowing what I think, whether Mr Georgie somehow decoyed that lovely creature to Tilling, telling her that Lucia was here. That's only my guess, and if so we must try to forgive him, for if anything is certain in this bad business, it is that he's madly in love with her. I know myself how a man looks –'

Diva gave a great gasp, but her eyebrows could not express any higher degree of astonishment.

'Oh! Elizabeth!' she cried. 'Was a man ever madly in love with you? Who was it? Do tell me!'

'There are things one can't speak of even to an old friend like you,' said Elizabeth. 'Yes, he's madly in love with her, and I think Worship knows it. Did you notice her demonstrations of affection to sweet Olga? She was making the best of it, I believe; putting on a brazen – no, let us say a brave face. How worn and anxious she looked the other night when we were all so gay. That pitiful little minuet! I'm sorry for her. When she married Mr Georgie, she thought life would be so safe and comfortable. A sad awakening, poor thing . . . Oh, another bit of news. Quaint Irene tells me she is doing a portrait of Worship. Quite marvellous, she says, and it will be ready for our summer exhibition. After that Lucia means to present it to the Borough, and have it hung in the Town Hall. And Irene's Academy picture of Benjy and me will be back in time for our exhibition, too. Interesting to compare them.'

Lucia bore her loss of prestige with characteristic gallantry. Indeed, she seemed to be quite unconscious that she had lost any, and continued to let her album of snap-shots remain open on the piano at the Sheffield Castle page, and airily talked about the Florentine mirror which just did not come into the photograph of Poppy's bedroom. Occasionally a tiresome moment occurred, as when Elizabeth, being dummy at a bridge-party in the garden-room, pored over the Castle page, and came back to her place, saying,

'So clever of you, Worship, to take so many pretty photographs in so short a time.'

Lucia was not the least disconcerted.

'They were all very short exposures, dear,' she said. 'I will explain that to you sometime.'

Everybody thought that a very fit retort, for now the Poppy-crisis was no longer recent, and it was not the custom of

Tilling to keep such incidents alive too long: it was not generous or kind, and besides, they grew stale. But Lucia paid her back in her own coin, for next day, when playing bridge at the Mapp-Flints, she looked long and earnestly at Benjy's tiger-whip, which now hung in its old place among bead-aprons and Malayan creases.

'Is that the one he broke at his interesting lecture, dear Elizabeth,' she asked, 'or the one he lost at Diva's tea-rooms?'

Evie continued to squeak in a disconcerting manner during the whole of the next hand, and the Poppy-crisis (for the present) was suffered to lapse.

The annual Art Exhibition moved into the foreground of current excitements, and the Tilling artists sent in their contributions: Lucia her study of dahlias, entitled *'Belli fiori'*, and a sketch of the courtyard of Sheffield Castle, which she had weeded for purposes of Art. She called it 'From Memory', though it was really from her photograph, and, without specifying the Castle, she added the motto

'The splendour falls on Castle walls'.

Elizabeth sent in 'A misty morning on the Marsh'. She was fond of misty mornings, because the climatic conditions absolutely prohibited defined draughtsmanship. Georgie (without any notion of challenging her) contributed 'A sunny morning on the Marsh', with sheep and dykes and clumps of ragwort very clearly delineated: Mr Wyse, one of his usual still-life studies of a silver tankard, a glass half-full of (probably) Capri wine, and a spray of nasturtiums: Diva another piece of still-life, in pastel, of two buns and a tartlet (probably sardine) on a plate. This was perhaps an invasion of Mr Wyse's right to reproduce still-life, but Diva had to be in the kitchen so much, waiting for kettles to boil and buns to rise, that she had very little leisure for landscape. Susan Wyse sent a mystical picture of a budgerigar with a halo above its head, and rays of orange light emanating from the primary feathers of its spread wings: 'Lost Awhile' was the touching title. But in spite of these gems, the exhibition was really Irene's show. She had been elected an honorary member of the hanging committee, and at their meetings she showed that she fully appreciated this fact.

'My birth of Venus,' she stated, 'must be hung quite by itself at one end of the room, with all the studies I made for it below. They are of vast interest. Opposite it, also by itself, must be my picture of Lucia. There were no studies for that; it was an inspiration, but none of your potty little pictures must be near it. Hang them where you like – oh, darling Lucia, you don't mind your dahlias and your Castle walls being quite out of range, do you? But those are my terms, and if you don't like them, I shall withdraw my pictures. And the walls behind them must be painted duck's-egg green. Take it or leave it. Now I can't bother about settling about the rest, so I shall go away. Let me know what you decide.'

There was no choice. To reject the Picture of the Year and that which Irene promised them should be the picture of next year was inconceivable. The end-walls of the studio where the exhibition was held were painted duck's-egg green, a hydrangea and some ferns were placed beneath each, and in front of them a row of chairs. Lucia, as Mayor, opened the show and made an inaugural speech, tracing the history of pictorial Art from earliest times, and, coming down to the present, alluded to the pictures of all her friends, the poetical studies of the marsh, the loving fidelity of the still-life exhibits, the spiritual uplift of the budgerigar. 'Of the two great works of Miss Coles,' she concluded, 'which will make our exhibition so ever-memorable, I need not speak. One has already acquired world-wide fame, and I hope it will not be thought egotistic of me if I confidently prophesy that the other will also. I am violating no secrets if I say that it will remain in Tilling in some conspicuous and public place, the cherished possession for ever of our historic town.'

She bowed, she smiled, she accepted a special copy of the catalogue, which Georgie had decorated with a blue riband, and, very tactfully, instead of looking at the picture of herself, sat down with him in front of that of Elizabeth and Benjy, audibly pointing out its beauties to him.

'Wonderful brush-work,' she said, waving her catalogue as if it was a paint-brush. 'Such life and movement! The waves. Venus's button-boots. Quite Dutch. But how Irene has developed since then! Presently we will look at the picture of me with this fresh in our minds.'

Elizabeth and Benjy were compelled, by the force of Lucia's polite example, to sit in front of her picture, and they talked quietly behind their catalogues.

'Can't make head or tail of it,' murmured Benjy. 'I never saw such a jumble.'

'A little puzzling at first,' said Elizabeth, 'but I'm beginning to grasp it. Seated at her piano you see, to show how divinely she plays. Scarlet robe and chain, to show she's Mayor. Cards littered about for her bridge. Rather unkind. Bicycle leaning against the piano. Her paint-box because she's such a great artist. A pity the whole thing looks like a jumble-sale, with Worship as auctioneer. And such a sad falling off as a work of Art. I'm afraid success has gone to Irene's head.'

'Time we looked at our own picture,' said Benjy. 'Fancy this daub in the Town Hall, if that's what she meant by some conspicuous and public place.'

'It hasn't got there yet,' whispered Elizabeth. 'As a Councillor, I shall have something to say to that.'

They crossed over to the other side of the room, passing Lucia and Georgie on the way, as if in some figure of the Lancers. Evie and the Padre were standing close in front of the Venus and Evie burst into a series of shrill squeaks.

'Oh, dear me! Did you ever, Kenneth!' she said. 'Poor Elizabeth. What a face and so like!'

'Well indeed!' said Kenneth. 'Surely the puir oyster-shell canna' bear that weight, and down she'll go and get a ducking. An' the Major up in the clouds wi' his wee bottle . . . Eh, and here's Mistress Mapp-Flint herself and her guid man. A proud day for ye. Come along wifie.'

Irene had not been at the opening, but now she entered in her shorts and scarlet jersey. Her eye fell on the hydrangea below the Venus.

'Take that foul thing away,' she screamed. 'It kills my picture. What, another of them under my Lucia! Throw them into the street, somebody. By whose orders were they put there? Where's the hanging committee? I summon the hanging committee.'

The offending vegetables were borne away by Georgie and the Padre, and Irene, having cooled down, joined Benjy and Elizabeth by the Venus. She looked from it to them and from them to it.

'My God, how I've improved since I did that!' she said. 'I think I must repaint some of it, and put more character into your faces.'

'Don't touch it, dear,' said Elizabeth nervously. 'It's perfect as it is. Genius.'

'I know that,' said Irene, 'but a few touches would make it more scathing. There's rouge on your cheeks now, Mapp, and that would give your face a hungry impropriety. I'll see to that this afternoon when the exhibition closes for the day.'

'But not while it's on view, quaint one,' argued Elizabeth. 'The committee accepted it as it was. Most irregular.'

'They'll like it far better when I've touched it up,' said Irene. 'You'll see.' And she joined Lucia and Georgie.

'Darling, it's not unworthy of you, is it?' she asked. 'And how noble you are to give it to the Borough for the Town Hall. It must hang just above the Mayor's chair. That's the only place for it.'

'There'll be no difficulty about that,' said Lucia.

She announced her gift to the Town Council at their next meeting, coupled with the artist's desire that it should be hung on the wall behind the Mayor's chair. Subdued respectful applause followed her gracious speech and an uncomfortable silence, for most of her Councillors had already viewed the work of Art with feelings of bewildered stupefaction. Then she was formally thanked for her generous intention and the Town Clerk intimated that before the Borough accepted any gift, a small committee was always appointed to inspect it. Apart from Elizabeth, who said she would be honoured to serve on it, some diffidence was shown; several Councillors explained that they had no knowledge of the pictorial art, but eventually two of them said they would do their best.

This committee met next morning at the exhibition, and sat in depressed silence in front of the picture. Then Elizabeth sighed wistfully and said 'Tut, tut' and the two others looked to her for a lead. She continued to gaze at the picture.

'Me to say something, gentlemen?' she asked, suddenly conscious of their scrutiny, 'Well, if you insist. I trust you will disagree with what I feel I'm bound to say, for otherwise I fear a very painful duty lies in front of us. So generous of our beloved Mayor, and so like her, isn't it? But I don't see how it is possible for us to recommend the Council to accept her gift. I wouldn't for the world set up my opinion against yours, but that's what I feel. Most distressing for me, you will well understand, being so intimate a friend of hers, but private affection cannot rank against public responsibility.' A slight murmur of sympathy followed this speech, and the committee found that they were of one mind in being conscientiously unable to recommend the Council to accept the Mayor's gift.

'Very sad,' said Elizabeth, shaking her head. 'Our proceedings, I take it, are confidential until we communicate them officially to the Council.'

When her colleagues had gone, the Mayoress strolled round the gallery. A misty morning on the marsh really looked very well: its vague pearly opalescence seemed to emphasize the faulty drawing in Georgie's sunny morning on the marsh and Diva's tartlets. Detaching herself from it, she went to the Venus, and a horrified exclamation burst from her. Quaint Irene had carried out her awful threat, had tinged her cheeks with unnatural colour, and had outlined her mouth with a thin line of vermilion, giving it a coyly beckoning expression. So gross a parody of her face and indeed of her character could not be permitted to remain there: something must be done, and, leaving the gallery in great agitation, she went straight to Mallards, for no one but Lucia had the smallest influence with that quaint and venomous young person.

The Mayor had snatched a short respite from her incessant work, and was engaged on a picture of some fine hollyhocks in her garden. She was feeling very buoyant, for the Poppy-crisis seemed to be quite over, and she knew that she had guessed correctly the purport of her Mayoress's desire to see her on urgent business. Invisible to mortal eye, there was a brazier of coals of fire on the lawn beside her, which she would presently pour on to the Mayoress's head.

'Good morning, dear Elizabeth,' she said. 'I've just snatched half an hour while good Mrs Simpson is typing some letters for me. Susan and Mr Wyse have implored me to do another little flower-study for our *esposizione*, to fill up the vacant place by my dahlias. I shall call it "Jubilant July". As you know, I am always at your disposal. What good wind blows you here?'

'Lovely of you to spare the time,' said Elizabeth. 'I've just been to the *esposizione*, and I felt it was my duty to see you at once. Quaint Irene has done something too monstrous. She's altered my face; she's given it a most disgusting expression. The picture can't be allowed to remain there in its present condition. I wondered if you with your great influence –'

Lucia half-closed her eyes, and regarded her sketch with intolerable complacency.

'Yes: that curious picture of Irene's,' she said at length. 'What a Puck-like genius! I went with her to our gallery a couple of hours ago, to see what she had done to the Venus: she was so eager to know what I thought about her little altera-tions.'

'An outrage, an abomination!' cried Elizabeth.

'I should not put it quite as strongly as that,' said Lucia, returning to her hollyhocks and putting in a vein on one of the leaves with exquisite delicacy. 'But I told her that I could not approve of those new touches. They introduced, to my mind, a note of farce into her satire, which was out of place, though amusing in itself. She agreed with me after a little argument into which I need not go. She will remove them again during the lunch-hour.'

'Oh thank you, dear,' said Elizabeth effusively. 'I always say what a true friend you are. I was terribly upset.'

'Nothing at all,' said Lucia sucking her paint-brush. 'Quite easy.'

Elizabeth turned her undivided attention to the hollyhocks.

'What a lovely sketch!' she said. 'How it will enrich our exhibition. Thank you, dear, again. I won't keep you from your work any longer. How you find time for all you do is a constant amazement to me.'

She ambled swiftly away. It would have been awkward if, at such a genial moment, Lucia had asked whether the artistic committee appointed by the Council had inspected Irene's other masterpiece yet.

The holiday months of August and September were at hand, when the ladies of Tilling were accustomed to let their houses and move into smaller houses themselves at a cheaper rent than what they received. Diva, for instance, having let her own house, was accustomed to move into Irene's who took a remote cottage on the marsh, where she could pursue her art and paint nude studies of herself in a looking-glass. But this year Diva refused to quit ye olde tea-house, when, with the town full of visitors, she would be doing so roaring a business; the Wyses decided not to go to Italy to stay with the Contessa, since international relations were so strained, and Lucia felt it her duty as Mayor, to remain in Tilling. The only letting done, in fact, was by the Padre, who left his curate in charge, while he and Evie took a prolonged holiday in bonnie Scotland, and let the Vicarage to the Mapp-Flints who had a most exciting tenant. This was a Miss Susan Leg, who, so Tilling was thrilled to learn from an interview she gave to a London paper, was none other than the world-wide novelist, Rudolph da Vinci. Miss Leg (so she stated in this piece of self-revelation) never took a holiday. 'I shall not rest,' she finely observed, 'till the shadows of life's eventide close round me,' and she went on to explain that she would be studying, in view of a future book, this little centre of provincial English life. 'I am well aware,' said Miss Leg, 'that my readers expect of me an aristocratic setting for my romances, but I intend to prove to them that life is as full of human interest in any simple, humble country village as in Belgravia and the country houses of the nobility.'

Lucia read this interview aloud to Georgie. It seemed to suggest possibilities. She veiled these in her usual manner.

'Rudolph da Vinci,' she said musingly. 'I have heard her name now I come to think of it. She seems to expect us all to be yokels and bumpkins. I fancy she will have to change her views a little. No doubt she will get some introduction to me, and I shall certainly ask her to tea. If she is as uppish and superior as she appears to be, that would be enough. We don't want best-sellers to write up our cultured vivid life here. So cheap and vulgarizing; not in accordance with our traditions.'

There was nothing, Georgie knew, that would fill Lucia with deeper pride than that traditions should be violated and life vulgarized, and even while she uttered these high sentiments a vision rose in her mind of Rudolph da Vinci writing a best-seller, with the scene laid in Tilling, and with herself, quite undisguised, as head of its social and municipal activities.

'Yet one must not prejudge her,' she went on, as this vision grew brighter. 'I must order a book of hers and read it, before I pass judgment on her work. And we may find her a very pleasant sort of woman. Perhaps I had better call on her, Georgie, for I should not like her to think that I slighted her, and then I will ask her to dine with us, *très intime*, just you and she and I. I should be sorry if her first impressions of Tilling were not worthy of us. Diva, for instance; it would be misleading if she saw Diva with those extraordinary eyebrows, bringing up teas from the kitchen, purple in the face, and thought her representative of our social life. Or if Elizabeth with her rouged cheeks asked her to dine at the Vicarage, and Benjy told his tiger-stories. Yes, I will call on her as soon as she arrives, and get hold of her. I will take her to our Art Exhibition, allow her to sign the Mayor's book as a distinguished visitor, and make her free of my house without ceremony. We will show her our real, inner life. Perhaps she plays bridge: I will ascertain that when I call. I might almost meet her at the station, if I can find out when she arrives. Or it might be better if you met her at the station as representing me, and I would call on her at Grebe half an hour afterwards. That would be more regular.'

'Elizabeth told me that she arrives by the three twenty-five to-day,' said Georgie. 'And she has hired a motor and is meeting her.'

It did not require so keen a nose as Lucia's to scent rivalry, but she gave no hint of that.

'Very proper,' she said. 'Elizabeth no doubt will drive her to Grebe, and show her tenant the house.'

Lucia bicycled to Grebe about tea-time, but found that Miss Leg had driven into the town, accompanied by the Mayoress, to have tea. She left her official card, as Mayor of Tilling, and went straight to the Vicarage. But Elizabeth was also out, and Lucia at once divined that she had taken Miss Leg to have tea at Diva's. She longed to follow and open operations at once, but decided to let the Mayoral card do its work. On her way home she bought a copy of the 25th edition of the novelist's *Kind Hearts and Coronets*, and dipped into it. It was very sumptuous. On the first page there was a Marchioness who had promised to open a village bazaar and was just setting off to do so, when a telephone-message arrived that a Royal Princess would like to visit her that afternoon. 'Tell her Royal Highness,' said that kind-hearted woman, 'that I have a long-standing engagement, and cannot disappoint my people. I will hurry back as soon as the function is over . . .' Lucia pictured herself coming back rather late to entertain Miss Leg at lunch – Georgie would be there to receive her – because it was her day for reading to the inmates of the workhouse. She would return with a copy of *Kind Hearts and Coronets* in her hand, explaining that the dear old bodies implored her to finish the chapter. The idea of Miss Leg writing a best-seller about Tilling became stupefyingly sweet.

Georgie came in, bringing the evening post.

'A letter from Olga,' he said, 'and she's written to me too, so it's sure to be the same. She wants us to go to Riseholme to-morrow for two days, as she's got music. A string quartette coming down.'

Lucia read her letter.

'Yes, most kind of her,' she said. 'But how can I get away? Ah, she anticipates that, and says that if I'm too busy she will understand. And it would look so marked if I went away directly after Miss Leg had arrived.'

'That's for you to judge,' he said. 'If you think she matters, I expect you're right, because Elizabeth's getting a pretty firm hold. I've been introduced to her: Elizabeth brought her in to tea at Diva's.'

'I imagined that had happened,' said Lucia. 'What about her?'

'A funny little round red thing, rather like Diva. Swanky. She's brought a butler and a footman, she told us, and her new Daimler will get down late to-night. And she asked if any of the nobility had got country seats near Tilling –'

'Did you tell her that I dined and slept – that Duchess Poppy asked me to dine and sleep at the Castle?' interrupted Lucia.

'No,' said Georgie. 'I thought of it, but then I judged it was wiser not to bring it up again. She ate a whole lot of buns, and she was very gracious to Diva (which Diva didn't like much), and told her she would order her *chef* – her very words – to send her a recipe for cream-wafers. Elizabeth's toadying her like anything. She said "Oh, how kind, Miss Leg. You are lucky, dear Diva." And they were going on to see the church afterwards, and Leg's dining with the Mapp-Flints to-morrow.'

Lucia reviewed this rather sinister intelligence.

'I hate to disappoint dear Olga,' she said, 'but I think I had better stop here. What about you?'

'Of course I shall go,' said Georgie.

Georgie had to leave for Riseholme next morning without a maid, for in view of the entertainment that might be going on at Mallards, Lucia could not spare either Foljambe or Grosvenor. She spent a long time at the garden-room window that afternoon, and told her cook to have a good tea ready to be served at a moment's notice, for Miss Leg would surely return her call to-day. Presently a large car came bouncing up the street: from its size Lucia thought at first that it was Susan's, but there was a man in livery sitting next the chauffeur, and at once she guessed. The car stopped at Mallards, and from behind her curtain Lucia could see that Elizabeth and another woman were inside. A podgy little hand was thrust out of the window, holding a card, which the man-servant thrust into the letter-box. He rang the bell, but before it was answered he mounted again, and the car drove on. A hundred pages of stream-of-consciousness fiction could not have explained the situation more exhaustively to Lucia than her own flash of insight. Elizabeth had evidently told the novelist that it would be quite sufficient to leave a card on the Mayor and have done with her. What followed at the Vicarage that evening when Miss Leg dined with the Mapp-Flints bore out the accuracy of Lucia's intuition.

'A very plain simple dinner, dear Miss Leg,' said Elizabeth as they sat down. 'Just pot-luck, as I warned you, so I hope you've got a country appetite.'

'I know I have, Liz,' said Benjy heartily. 'A round of golf makes me as hungry as I used to be after a day's tiger-shooting in the jungle.'

'Those are trophies of yours at Grebe, then,' said Miss Leg. 'I consider tiger-shooting a manly pursuit. That's what I mean by sport, taking your life in your hand instead of sitting in an armchair and firing into flocks of hand-reared pheasants. That kind of "sportsman" doesn't even load his own gun, I believe. Butchers and poulterers; that's what I called them in one of my books.'

'Withering! scathing!' cried Elizabeth. 'And how well deserved! Benjy gave such a wonderful lecture here the other day about his hair-breadth escapes. You could have heard a pin drop.'

'Ah, that's an old story now,' said Benjy. 'My *shikarri* days are over. And there's not a man in Tilling who's even seen a tiger except through the bars at the Zoo. Georgie Pillson, for instance –'

'Whom I presented to you at tea yesterday, Miss Leg,' put in Elizabeth. 'Husband of our dear Mayor. Pointed beard. Sketches quite prettily, and does exquisite needlework. My wicked Benjy once dubbed him Miss Milliner Michael-Angelo.'

'And that was very withering too,' said Miss Leg, eating lumps of expensive middle-cut salmon with a country appetite.

'Well, well, not very kind, I'm afraid, but I like a man to be a man,' said Benjy. 'I'll take a bit more fish, Liz. A nice fresh-run fish. And what are you going to give us next?'

'Just a brace of grouse,' said Elizabeth.

'Ah, yes. A few old friends with Scotch moors haven't quite forgotten me yet, Miss Leg. Dear old General!'

'Your Miss Milliner has gone away, Benjy,' said Elizabeth. 'Staying with Miss Olga Bracely. Probably you know her, Miss Leg. The prima donna. Such a fascinating woman.'

'Alone? Without his wife?' asked Miss Leg. 'I do not approve of that. A wife's duty, Mayor or not, is to be always with her husband and vice versa. If she can't leave her home, she ought to insist on his stopping with her.'

'Dear Lucia is a little slack in these ways,' said Elizabeth regretfully. 'But she gives us to understand that they're all old friends.'

'The older the better,' said Miss Leg epigrammatically, and they all laughed very much.

'Tell me more about your Lucia,' she ordered, when their mirth subsided.

'I don't fancy you would find very much in common with her,' said Elizabeth thoughtfully. 'Rather prone we think, to plot and intrigue in a way we regret. And a little superior at times.'

'It seems to have gone to her head to be Mayor,' put in Benjy. 'She'd have made a sad mess of things without you to steady her, Liz.'

'I do my best,' sighed Elizabeth, 'though it's uphill work sometimes. I am her Mayoress and a Councillor, Miss Leg, and she does need assistance and support. Oh, her dear, funny little ways! She's got a curious delusion that she can play the piano, and she gives us a treat sometimes, and one doesn't know which way to look. And not long ago – how you'll scream, Miss Leg, she told us all, several times over, that she was going to stay with the Duchess of Sheffield, and when she came back she showed us quantities of photographs of the Castle to prove she had been there –'

'I went to a Charity Concert of the Duchess's in her mansion

in Grosvenor Square not long ago,' said Miss Leg. 'Five-
guinea seats. Does she live near here?'

'No, many miles away. There's the cream of it. It turned out
that Worship only went to tea. A three-hours' drive each way
to get a cup of tea! So odd. I almost suspect that she was never
asked at all really; some mistake. And she always alludes to her
as Poppy; whether she calls her that to her face is another question.'

'Evidently a snob,' said Miss Leg. 'If there's one thing I
hate it's snobbishness.'

'Oh, you mustn't call her a snob,' cried Elizabeth. 'I should
be so vexed with myself if I had conveyed that impression.'

'And is that a family house of her husband's where I left my
card to-day?' asked Miss Leg.

Elizabeth sighed.

'Oh, what a tragic question!' she said. 'No, they're quite
parvenus in Tilling; that beautiful house – such a garden –
belonged to my family. I couldn't afford to live there, and I
had to sell it. Lucia gave me a pitiful price for it, but beggars
can't be choosers. A cruel moment!'

'What a shame,' said Miss Leg. 'All the old homes of
England are going to upstarts and interlopers. I hope you
never set foot in it.'

'It's a struggle to do so,' said Elizabeth, 'but I feel that both
as Mayoress and as a friend of Lucia, I must be neighbourly.
Neither officially nor socially must I fail to stand by her.'

They made plans for next day. Elizabeth was very sarcastic
and amusing about the morning shopping of her friends.

'Such fun!' she said. 'Quite a feature of life here, you must
not miss it. You'll see Diva bolting in and out of shops like a
rabbit, Benjy says, when a ferret's after it, and Susan Wyse
perhaps on a tricycle, and Lucia and quaint Irene Coles who
painted the Picture of the Year, which is in our exhibition
here; you must see that. Then we could pop in at the Town
Hall, and I would show you our ancient charters and our
wonderful Elizabethan plate. And would you honour us by
signing your name in the Mayor's book for distinguished visitors?'

'Certainly, very glad,' said Miss Leg, 'though I don't often give my autograph.'

'Oh, that is kind. I would be ready for you at ten – not too early? and take you round. Must you really be going? Benjy, see if Miss Leg's beautiful Daimler is here. Au reservoir!'

'O what?' asked Miss Leg.

'Some of the dear folk here say "au reservoir" instead of "*au revoir*",' explained Elizabeth.

'Why do they do that?' asked Miss Leg.

Lucia, as she dined alone, had been thinking over the hostilities which she felt were imminent. She was quite determined to annex Miss Leg with a view to being the central figure in her next best-seller, but Elizabeth was determined to annex her too, and Lucia was aware that she and her Mayoress could not run in harness over this job; the feat was impossible. Her pride forbade her to get hold of Miss Leg through Elizabeth, and Elizabeth, somehow or other, must be detached. She sat long that night meditating in the garden-room, and when next morning the Mayoress rang her up as usual at breakfast-time, she went to the telephone ready for anything.

'Good morning, dear Worship,' said that cooing voice. 'What a beautiful day.'

'Lovely!' said Lucia.

'Nothing I can do for you, dear?'

'Nothing, thanks,' said Lucia, and waited.

'I'm taking Miss Leg –'

'Who?' asked Lucia.

'Susan Leg: Rudolph da Vinci: my tenant,' explained Elizabeth.

'Oh, yes. She left a card on me yesterday, Foljambe told me. So kind. I hope she will enjoy her visit.'

'I'm taking her to the Town Hall this morning. So would you be a very sweet Worship and tell the Serjeant to get out the Corporation plate, which she would like to see. We shall be there by half-past ten, so if it is ready by a quarter past there'll be no delay. And though she seldom gives her autograph, she's promised to sign her name in Worship's book.'

Lucia gave a happy sigh. She had not dared to hope for such a rash move.

'My dear, how very awkward,' she said. 'You see, the Corporation plate is always on view to the public on Tuesdays at 3 p.m. – or it may be 2 p.m.; you had better make certain – and it is such a business to get it out. One cannot do that for any casual visitor. And the privilege of signing the Mayor's book is reserved for really distinguished strangers, whose visit it is an honour to record. Olga, for instance.'

'But, dear Worship,' said Elizabeth. 'I've already promised to show her the plate.'

'Nothing simpler. At 2 p.m. or 3 p.m., whichever it is, on Tuesday afternoon.'

'And the Mayor's book: I've asked her to sign it.'

Lucia laughed gaily.

'Start a Mayoress's book, dear,' she said. 'You can get anybody you like to sign that.'

Lucia remained a moment in thought after ringing off. Then she rang up the Town Hall.

'Is that the Serjeant?' she said. 'The Mayor speaking. Serjeant, do not get out the Corporation plate or produce my visitors' book without direct orders from me. At present I have given none. What a lovely morning.'

Lucia gave Mrs Simpson a holiday, as there was nothing for her to do, and went down to the High Street for her marketing. Her mind resembled a modern army attended by an air force and all appliances. It was ready to scout and skirmish, to lay an ambush, to defend or to attack an enemy with explosive from its aircraft or poison gas (which would be only a reprisal, for she was certain it had been used against her). Diva was watching at her window, evidently waiting for her, and threw it open.

'Have you seen her?' she asked.

There was only one 'her' just now.

'Only her hand,' said Lucia. 'She put it out of her motor – a podgy sort of hand – yesterday afternoon. She left a card on me, or rather her footman popped it into my letter-box, without asking if I was in. Elizabeth was with her. They drove on.'

'Well, I do call that rude,' said Diva, warmly. 'High and lofty, that's what she is. She told me her *chef* would send me a recipe for cream-wafers. I tried it. Muck. I gave one to Paddy, and he was sick. And she rang me up just now to go to tea with her this afternoon. Did she think I was going out to Grebe, just when I was busiest, to eat more muck? Not I. She dined at Elizabeth's last night, and Janet heard from Elizabeth's parlour-maid what they had. Tomato soup, middle-cut of salmon sent over from Hornbridge, a brace of grouse from Rice's, Melba peaches, but only bottled with custard instead of cream, and tinned caviare. And Elizabeth called it pot-luck! I never had such luck there, pot or unpot. Elizabeth's meaning to run her, that's what it is. Let 'em run! I'll come out with you and do my shopping. Just see how Paddy is, but I think he's got rid of it. Cream-wafers, indeed! Wait a sec.'

While Lucia waited a sec., Susan Wyse's Royce, with her husband and herself inside, hooted its ponderous way into the High Street. As it drew up at the fishmonger's, Lucia's eagle eye spied Elizabeth and a round, fat little woman, of whose identity there could be no doubt, walking towards it. Mr Wyse had got out and Elizabeth clearly introduced him to her companion. He stood hatless, as was his polite habit when he talked to ladies under God's blue sky, or even in the rain, and then led her towards the open door of the Royce, where Elizabeth was chatting to Susan.

Lucia strolled towards them, but the moment Elizabeth saw her, she wheeled round without smile or greeting, and, detaching Miss Leg, moved away up the street to where Irene in her usual shorts and scarlet pullover, had just set up her easel at the edge of the pavement.

'Good morning, dear Susan,' called Lucia. 'Oh, Mr Wyse, pray put your hat on; such a hot sun. Who was that odd little woman with my Mayoress, who spoke to you just now?'

'I think your Mayoress said Miss Leg,' observed Mr Wyse. 'And she told my Susan that if she asked Miss Leg to dine to-night she would probably accept. Did you ask her, dear? If so, we must order more fish.'

'Certainly I didn't,' said Susan. 'Who is this Leg? Why should Elizabeth foist her friends on me? Most unheard of.'

'Leg? Leg?' said Lucia vaguely. 'Ah, of course. Elizabeth's tenant. The novelist. Does she not call herself Rudolph da Vinci?'

'A very self-satisfied little woman, whatever she calls herself,' said Susan with unusual severity, 'and she's not going to dine with me. She can dine with Elizabeth.'

Diva had trundled up and overheard this.

'She did. Last night,' she said. 'All most sumptuous and grand. But fancy her leaving a card on Lucia without even asking whether she was at home! So rude.'

'Did she indeed?' asked Mr Wyse in a shocked voice. 'We are not accustomed to such want of manners in Tilling. You were very right, Susan, not to ask her to dine. Your intuition served you well.'

'I thought it strange,' said Lucia, 'but I dare say she's a very decent, homely little woman, when left to herself. Elizabeth was with her, when she honoured me with her card.'

'That accounts for it,' interrupted Diva and Susan simultaneously.

'– and Elizabeth rang me up at breakfast and asked to give orders that the Corporation plate should be ready for her little friend's inspection this morning at 10.30. And the Mayor's book for her to sign.'

'Well, I never!' said Diva. 'And the church bells ringing, I suppose. And the Town Band playing the Italian National Anthem for Rudolph da Vinci. What did you say?'

'Very polite regrets.'

Irene's voice from a few yards away, loud and emphatic, broke in on their conversation.

'No, Mapp!' she cried. 'I will not come to the exhibition to show you and your friend – I didn't catch her name – my pictures. And I can't bear being looked over when I'm sketching. Trot along.'

There seemed nothing else for them to do, and Lucia walked on to Irene.

'Did you hear?' asked Irene. 'I sent Mapp and her friend about their business. Who is the little guy?'

'A Miss Leg, I am told,' said Lucia. 'She writes novels

under some foreign name. Elizabeth's tenant: she seems to have taken her up with great warmth.'

'Poor wretch. Mapp-kissed, like raisins. But the most exciting news, beloved. The Directors of the Carlton Gallery in Bond Street have asked me if I will let them have my Venus for their autumn exhibition. Also an inquiry from an American collector, if it's for sale. I'm asking a thumping price for it. But I shall show it at the Carlton first, and I shall certainly put back Mapp's rouge and her cocotte smile. May I come up presently to Mallards?'

'Do dear. I have a little leisure this morning.'

Lucia passed on with that ever-recurring sense of regret that Irene had not painted her on the oyster-shell and Georgie in the clouds, and, having finished her shopping, strolled home by the Town Hall. The Serjeant was standing on the steps, looking a little flushed.

'The Mayoress and a friend have just been here, Your Worship,' he said. 'She told me to get out the Corporation plate and Your Worship's book. I said I couldn't without direct orders from you. She was a bit threatening.'

'You did quite right, Serjeant,' said Lucia very graciously. 'The same reply always, please.'

Meantime Elizabeth and Miss Leg, having been thwarted at the Town Hall, passed on to the exhibition where Elizabeth demanded free admittance for her as a distinguished visitor. But the door-keeper was as firm as the Serjeant had been, and Elizabeth produced a sixpence and six coppers. They went first to look at the Venus, and Elizabeth had a most disagreeable surprise, for the eminent novelist highly disapproved of it.

'An irreverent parody of that great Italian picture by Botticello,' she said. 'And look at that old hag on the oyster-shell and that boozy navvy in a top-hat. Most shocking! I am astonished that you allowed it to be exhibited. And by that rude unsexed girl in shorts? Her manners and her painting are on a par.'

After this pronouncement Elizabeth did not feel equal to disclosing that she was the hag and Benjy the navvy, but she

was pleased that Miss Leg was so severe on the art of the rude
girl in shorts, and took her to the portrait of Lucia.

'There's another picture of Miss Coles's,' she said, 'which is
much worse than the other. Look: it reminds me of an auctioneer
at a jumble-sale. Bicycle, piano, old packs of cards, paint-box –'

Miss Leg burst into loud cries of pleasure and admiration.

'A magnificent work!' she said. 'That's something to look at.
Glorious colour, wonderful composition. And what an interesting face. Who is it?'

'Our Mayor: our dear Lucia whom we chatted about last
night,' said Elizabeth.

'Your chat misled me. That woman has great character.
Please ask her to meet me, and the artist too. She has real
talent in spite of her other picture. I could dine with you this
evening: just a plain little meal as we had last night. I never
mind what I eat. Or tea. Tea would suit me as well.'

Agitated thoughts darted through the Mayoress's mind. She
was still desperately anxious to retain her proprietary rights
over Miss Leg, but another plain little meal could not be
managed. Moreover it could not be expected that even the
most exalted Christian should forgive, to the extent of asking
Lucia to dinner, her monstrous rudeness about the Corporation
plate and the Mayor's book, and it would take a very good
Christian to forgive Irene. Tea was as far as she could go, and
there was always the hope that they would refuse.

'Alas, Benjy and I are both engaged to-night,' she said. 'But
I'll ask them to tea as soon as I get home.'

They strayed round the rest of the gallery: the misty morning
on the marsh, Elizabeth thought, looked very full of poetry.

'The usual little local daubs,' observed Miss Leg, walking
by it without a glance. But the hollyhocks are charming, and so
are the dahlias. By Miss Coles, too, I suppose.'

Elizabeth simply could not bear that she should know who
the artist was.

'She does exquisite flower-studies,' she said.

Irene was in the garden-room with Lucia when Elizabeth's call
came through.

'Just been to the exhibition, dear Worship, with Miss Leg. She's so anxious to know you and quaint Irene. Would you pop in for a cup of tea this afternoon? She will be there.'

'So kind!' said Lucia. 'I must consult my engagement-book.'

She covered the receiver with her hand, and thought intensely for a moment.

'Irene,' she whispered. 'Elizabeth asks us both to go to tea with her and meet Miss Leg. I think I won't. I don't want to get at her *via* Elizabeth. What about you?'

'I don't want to get at Leg *via* anybody,' said Irene.

Lucia uncovered the receiver.

'Alas!' she said. 'As I feared I am engaged. And Irene is with me and regrets she can't come either. Such a pity. Good-bye.'

'Why my regrets?' asked Irene. 'And what's it all about?'

Lucia sighed. 'All very tiresome,' she said, 'but Elizabeth forces me, in mere self-defence, to descend to little schemings and intrigues. How it bores me!'

'Darling, it's the breath of your life!' said Irene, 'and you do it so beautifully!'

In the course of that day and the next Miss Leg found that she was not penetrating far into the life of Tilling. She attended shopping-parade next morning by herself. Diva and the Wyses were talking together, but gave her no more than cold polite smiles, and when she had passed, Irene joined them and there was laughter. Further on Lucia, whom she recognized from Irene's portrait was walking with a tall man with a Vandyck beard, whom she guessed to be the truant husband returned. Elizabeth was approaching, all smiles; surely they would have a few words together, and she would introduce them, but Lucia and the tall man instantly crossed the road. It was all very odd: Lucia and Irene would not come to tea at the Mapp-Flints, and the Wyses had not asked her to dinner, and Diva had refused to go to tea at Grebe, and Elizabeth had not produced the Corporation plate and the Mayor's book. She began to wonder whether the Mapp-Flints were not some species of pariah whom nobody would know. This was a dreadful thought; perhaps she had got into wrong hands, and, while they clutched her, Tilling held aloof. She remembered quite a large percentage of Elizabeth's disparaging remarks about Lucia at the plain little meal, and of Benjy's comments on Georgie, and now they assumed a different aspect. Were they prompted by malice and jealousy, and impotence to climb into Tilling society? 'I've not got any copy at present,' thought Miss Leg. 'I must do something. Perhaps Mrs Mapp-Flint has had a past, though it doesn't look likely.'

It was a very hot day, and Georgie and Lucia settled to go bicycling after tea. The garden-room, till then, was the coolest place and after lunch they played the piano and sat in the window overlooking the street. He had had two lovely days at Riseholme, and enlarged on them with more enthusiasm than tact.

'Olga was too wonderful,' he said. 'Singing divinely and inspiring everybody. She enjoys herself simply by giving enjoyment to other people. A concert both evenings at seven, with the Spanish quartette and a few songs by Olga. Just an hour and a half and then a delicious supper in the garden, with everybody in Riseholme asked, and no Duchesses and things at all. Just for Riseholme: that's so like her: she doesn't know what the word 'snob' means. And I had the room I had before, with a bathroom next door, and my breakfast on the balcony. And none of those plots and intrigues we used to be always embroiled in. It *was* a change.'

A certain stoniness had come into Lucia's face, which Georgie, fired with his subject, did not perceive.

'And she asked down a lot of the supers from Covent Garden,' he went on, 'and put them up at the Ambermere Arms. And her kindness to all her old friends: dull old me, for instance. She's taken a villa at Le Touquet now, and she's asked me there for a week. I shall cross from Seaport, and there are some wonderful anti-sick tablets –'

'Did dearest Olga happen to mention if she was expecting me as well?' asked Lucia in a perfectly calm voice.

Georgie descended, like an aeroplane with engine-trouble, from these sunlit spaces. He made a bumpy landing.

'I can't remember her doing so,' he said.

'Not a thing you would be likely to forget,' said Lucia. 'Your wonderful memory.'

'I dare say she doesn't want to bother you with invitations,' said Georgie artfully. 'You see, you did rub it in a good deal how difficult it was for you to get away, and how you had to bring tin boxes full of municipal papers with you.'

Lucia's face brightened.

'Very likely that is it,' she said.

'And you promised to spend Saturday till Monday with her a few weeks ago,' continued Georgie, 'and then left on Sunday because of your Council meeting, and then you couldn't leave Tilling the other day because of Miss Leg. Olga's beginning to realize, don't you think, how busy you are – What's the matter?'

Lucia had sprung to her feet.

'Leg's motor coming up the street,' she said. 'Georgie, stand at the door, and, if I waggle my thumb at you, fly into the house and tell Grosvenor I'm at home. If I turn it down – those Roman gladiators – still fly, but tell her I'm out. It all depends on whether Elizabeth is with her. I'll explain afterwards.'

Lucia slid behind the window-curtain, and Georgie stood at the door, to fly. There came a violent waggling of his wife's thumb, and he sped into the house. He came flying back again, and Lucia motioned him to the piano, on the music-stand of which she had already placed a familiar Mozart duet. 'Quick! Top of the page,' she said. '*Uno, due, tre.* Pom. Perfect!'

They played half a dozen brilliant bars, and Grosvenor opened the door and said, 'Miss Leg.' Lucia took no notice but continued playing, till Grosvenor said 'Miss Leg!' much louder, and then, with a musical exclamation of surprise, she turned and rose from her seat.

'Ah, Miss Leg, so pleased!' she said, drawling frightfully. 'How-de-do? Have you met Miss Leg, Georgie? Ah, yes, I think you saw her at Diva's one afternoon. Georgie, tell somebody that Miss Leg – you will, won't you – will stop to tea . . . My little garden-room, which you may have noticed from outside. I'm told that they call it the Star Chamber –'.

Miss Leg looked up at the ceiling, as if expecting to see the hosts of heaven depicted there.

'Indeed. Why do they call it that?' she asked.

Lucia had, of course, just invented that name for the garden-room herself. She waved her hand at the pile of Departmental tin boxes.

'Secrets of municipal business,' she said lightly. 'The Cabal, you know: Arlington, Bolingbroke . . . Shall we go out into the garden, until tea is ready? A tiny little plot, but so dear to me, the red-brick walls, the modest little house.'

'You bought it quite lately from Mrs Mapp-Flint, I understand,' said Miss Leg.

Clever Lucia at once guessed that Elizabeth had given her version of that.

'Yes, poor thing,' she said. 'I was so glad to be able to get her out of her difficulties. It used to belong to an aunt of hers by marriage. What a state it was in! The garden a jungle of weeds, but I am reclaiming it. And here's my little secret garden: when I am here and the door is shut, I am not to be disturbed by anybody. Busy folk, like you and me, you with your marvellous creative work, and me with my life so full of interruptions, must have some inviolable sanctuary, must we not? . . . Some rather fine hollyhocks.'

'Charming!' said Miss Leg, who was disposed to hate Lucia with her loftiness and her Star Chamber, but still thought she might be the Key to Tilling. 'I have a veritable grove of them at my little cottage in the country. There was a beautiful study of hollyhocks at your little exhibition. By Miss Coles, I think Mrs Mapp-Flint said.'

Lucia laughed gaily.

'Oh, my sweet, muddle-headed Mayoress!' she cried. 'Georgie, did you hear? Elizabeth told Miss Leg that my picture of hollyhocks was by Irene. So like her. Tea ready?'

Harmony ripened. Miss Leg expressed her great admiration for Irene's portrait of Lucia, and her withering scorn for the Venus, and promised to pay another visit to study the features of the two principal figures: she had been so disgusted with the picture that one glance was enough. Before she had eaten her second bun, Lucia had rung up the Serjeant at the Town Hall, and asked him to get out the Corporation plate and the Mayor's book, for she would be bringing round a distinguished visitor very shortly: and before Miss Leg had admired the plate and signed the book ('Susan Leg' and below, 'Rudolph da Vinci'), she had engaged herself to dine at Mallards next day. 'Just a few friends,' said Lucia, 'who would be so much honoured to meet you.' She did not ask Elizabeth and Benjy, for Miss Leg had seen so much of them lately, but, for fear they should feel neglected, she begged them to come in afterwards for a cup of coffee and a chat. Elizabeth interpreted this as an insult rather than an invitation, and she and Benjy had coffee and a vivacious chat by themselves.

The party was very gay, and a quantity of little anecdotes were told about the absentees. At the end of most of them Lucia cried out:

'Ah, you mustn't be so ill-natured about them,' and sometimes she told another. It was close on midnight when the gathering broke up, and they were all bidden to dine with Miss Leg the next night.

'Such a pleasant evening, may I say "Lucia"?' said she on the doorstep, as she put up her round red face for the Mayor to deal with as she liked.

'Indeed do, dear Susan,' she said. 'But I think you must be Susanna. Will you? We have one dear Susan already.'

They kissed.

Georgie continued to be tactless about Olga's manifold perfections, and though his chaste passion for her did not cause Lucia the smallest anxiety (she knew Georgie too well for that) she wondered what Tilling would make of his coming visit to Le Touquet without her. Her native effrontery had lived the Poppy-crisis down, but her rescue of Susan Leg, like some mature Andromeda, from the clutches of her Mayoress, had raised the deepest animosity of the Mapp-Flints, and she was well aware that Elizabeth would embrace every opportunity to be nasty. She was therefore prepared for trouble, but, luckily for her peace of mind, she had no notion what a tempest of tribulation was gathering . . . Georgie and Foljambe left by a very early train for Seaport so that he might secure a good position amidships on the boat, for the motion was felt less there, before the continental express from London arrived, and each of them had a tube of *cachets* preventive of sea-sickness.

Elizabeth popped into Diva's for a chat that morning.

'They've gone,' she said. 'I've just met Worship. She was looking very much worried, poor thing, and I'm sure I don't wonder.'

Diva had left off her eyebrows. They took too long, and she was tired of always looking surprised when, as on this occasion, she was not surprised.

'I suppose you mean about Mr Georgie going off alone,' she said.

'Among other worries. Benjy and I both grieve for her. Mr Georgie's infatuation is evidently increasing. First of all there was that night here – '

'No: Lucia came back,' said Diva.

'Never quite cleared up, I think. And then he's been staying

at Riseholme without her, unless you're going to tell me that
Worship went over every evening and returned at cock-crow
for her duties here.'

'Olga asked them both, anyhow,' said Diva.

'So we've been told, but did she? And this time Lucia's
certainly not been asked. It's mounting up, and it must be
terrible for her. All that we feared at first is coming true, as I
knew it would. And I don't believe for a moment that he'll
come back at the end of a week.'

'That would be humiliating,' said Diva.

'Far be it from me to insinuate that there's anything wrong,'
continued Elizabeth emphatically, 'but if I was Lucia I
shouldn't like it, any more than I should like it if you and
Benjy went for a week and perhaps more to Le Touquet.'

'And I shouldn't like it either,' said Diva. 'But I'm sorry for
Lucia, too.'

'I dare say she'll need our sympathy before long,' said Elizabeth darkly. 'And how truly grateful I am to her for taking
that Leg woman off my hands. Such an incubus. How she
managed it I don't inquire. She may have poisoned Leg's
mind about me, but I should prefer to be poisoned than see
much more of her.'

'Now you're getting mixed, Elizabeth,' protested Diva. 'It
was Leg's mind you suggested was poisoned, not you.'

'That's a quibble, dear,' said Elizabeth decidedly. 'You'll
hardly deny that Benjy and I were most civil to the woman. I
even asked Lucia and Irene to meet her, which was going a
long way considering Lucia's conduct about the Corporation
plate and the Mayor's book. But I couldn't have stood Leg
much longer, and I should have had to drop her . . . I must be
off; so busy to-day, like Worship. A Council meeting this
afternoon.'

Lucia always enjoyed her Council meetings. She liked presiding, she liked being suave and gracious and deeply conscious of
her own directing will. As she took her seat to-day, she glanced
at the wall behind her, where before long Irene's portrait of
her would be hanging. Minutes of the previous meeting were

read, reports from various committees were received, discussed and adopted. The last of these was that of the committee which had been appointed to make its recommendation to the Council about her portrait. She had thought over a well-turned sentence or two: she would say what a privilege it was to make this work of genius the permanent possession of the Borough. Miss Coles, she need hardly remind the Council was a Tillingite of whom they were all proud, and the painter also of the Picture of the Year, in which there figured two of Tilling's most prominent citizens, one being a highly honoured member of the Council. ('And then I shall bow to Elizabeth,' thought Lucia, 'she will appreciate that.')

She looked at the agenda.

'And now we come to our last business, ladies and gentlemen,' she said. 'To receive the report of the Committee on the Mayor's offer of a portrait of herself to the Council, to be hung in the Town Hall.'

Elizabeth rose.

'As Chairman of this Committee,' she said, 'it is my duty to say that we came to the unanimous conclusion that we cannot recommend the Council to accept the Mayor's most generous gift.'

The gracious sovereignty of Lucia's demeanour did not suffer the smallest diminution.

'Those in favour of accepting the findings of the Committee?' she asked. 'Unanimous, I think.'

Never, in all Lucia's triumphant career, had she suffered so serious a reverse, nor one out of which it seemed more impossible to reap some incidental advantage. She had been dismissed from Sheffield Castle at the shortest notice, but she had got a harvest of photographs. Out of her inability to find the brake on her bicycle, thus madly scorching through a crowded street, she had built herself a monument for dash and high athletic prowess. She always discovered silver linings to the blackest of clouds, but now, scrutinize them as she might, she could detect in them none but the most sombre hues. Her imagination had worked out a dazzling future for this portrait.

It would hang on the wall behind her; the Corporation, at her request, would lend it (heavily insured) to the Royal Academy exhibition next May, where it would be universally acclaimed as a masterpiece far outshining the Venus of the year before. It would be lithographed or mezzo-tinted, and she would sign the first fifty pulls. Visitors would flock to the Town Hall to see it; they would recognize her as she flashed by them on her bicycle or sat sketching at some picturesque corner; admiring the mellow front of Mallards, the ancestral home of the Mayor, they would be thrilled to know that the pianist, whose exquisite strains floated out of the open window of the garden-room, was the woman whose portrait they had just seen above her official chair. Such thoughts as these were not rigidly defined but floated like cloud-castles in the sky, forming and shifting and always elegant.

Now of those fairy edifices there was nothing left. The Venus was to be exhibited at the Carlton Gallery and then perhaps to form a gem in the collection of some American millionaire, and Elizabeth would go out into all lands and Benjy to the ends of the earth, while her own rejected portrait would be returned to Mallards, with the best thanks of the committee, like Georgie's sunny morning on the marsh, and Susan's budgerigar, and Diva's sardine tartlet. (And where on earth should she hang this perpetual reminder of defeated dreams?) . . . Another aspect of this collapse struck her. She had always thought of herself as the beneficent director of municipal action, but now the rest of her Council had expressed unanimous agreement with the report of a small malignant committee, instead of indignantly rallying round her and expressing their contempt of such base ingratitude. This was a snub to which she saw no possible rejoinder except immediate resignation of her office, but that would imply that she felt the snub, which was not to be thought of. Besides, if her resignation was accepted, there would be nothing left at all.

Her pensive steps, after the Council meeting was over, had brought her to the garden-room, and the bright japanned faces of tin boxes labelled 'Museum', 'Fire Brigade' or 'Burial Board' gave her no comfort: their empty expressions seemed to mock her. Had Georgie been here, she could have confided the tragedy to him without loss of dignity. He would have been sympathetic in the right sort of way: he would have said 'My dear, how tarsome! That foul Elizabeth: of course she was at the bottom of it. Let's think of some plan to serve her out.' But without that encouragement she was too flattened out to think of Elizabeth at all. The only thing she could do was to maintain, once more, her habitual air of prosperous self-sufficiency. She shuddered at the thought of Tilling being sorry for her, because, communing with herself, she seemed to sense below this superficial pity, some secret satisfaction that she had had a knock. Irene, no doubt, would be wholly sincere, but though her prestige as an artist had suffered indignity, what difference would it make to her that the Town Council of Tilling had rejected her picture, when the Carlton Gallery in London had craved the loan of her Venus, and an American millionaire was nibbling for its purchase? Irene would treat it as a huge joke; perhaps she would design a Christmas card showing Mapp, as a nude, mature, female Cupid, transfixing Benjy's heart with a riding-whip. For a moment, as this pleasing fantasy tickled Lucia's brain, she smiled wanly. But the smile faded again: not the grossest insult to Elizabeth would mend matters. A head held high and a total unconsciousness that anything disagreeable had happened was the only course worthy of the Mayor.

The council meeting had been short, for no reports from committees (especially the last) had raised controversy, and Lucia stepped briskly down the hill to have tea in public at Diva's, and exhibit herself as being in cheerful or even exuberant spirits. Just opposite the door was drawn up a monstrous motor, behind which was strapped a dress-basket and other substantial luggage with the initials P.S. on them. 'A big postscript,' thought Lucia, lightening her heavy heart with humorous fancies, and she skirted round behind this ponderous conveyance, and so on to the pavement. Two women were just stepping out of ye olde tea-house: one was Elizabeth dripping with unctuous smiles, and the other was Poppy Sheffield.

'And here's sweet Worship herself,' said Elizabeth. 'Just in time to see you. How fortunate!'

Some deadly misgiving stirred in Lucia's heart as Poppy turned on her a look of blank unrecognition. But she managed to emit a thin cry of welcome.

'Dear Duchess!' she said. 'How naughty of you to come to my little Tilling without letting me know. It was *au revoir* when we parted last.'

Poppy still seemed puzzled, and then (unfortunately, perhaps) she began to remember.

'Why, of course!' she said. 'You came to see me at the Castle, owing to some stupid misunderstanding. My abominable memory. Do tell me your name.'

'Lucia Pillson,' said the wretched woman. 'Mayor of Tilling.'

'Yes, how it all comes back,' said Poppy, warmly shaking hands. 'That was it. I thought your husband was the Mayor of Tilling, and I was expecting him. Quite. So stupid of me. And then tea and photographs, wasn't it? I trust they came out well.'

'Beautifully. Do come up to my house – only a step – and I'll show you them.'

'Alas! not a moment to spare. I've spent such a long time chatting to all your friends. Somebody – somebody called Leg, I think – introduced them to me. She said she had been to my house in London which I dare say was quite true. One never can tell. But I'm catching, at least I hope so, the evening boat at Seaport on my way to stay with Olga Bracely at Le Touquet. Such a pleasure to have met you again.'

Lucia presented a brave front.

'Then do come and dine and sleep here to break your journey on your return,' she said. 'I shall expect you to propose yourself at any time, like all my friends. Just a wire or a telephone-call. Georgie and I are sure to be here. Impossible for me to get away in these crowded months –'

'That *would* be nice,' said Poppy. 'Good-bye: Mrs Pillson, isn't it? Quite. Charmed, I'm sure: so pleasant. Drive straight on to the quay at Seaport,' she called to her chauffeur.

Lucia kissed her hand after the car.

'How lucky just to have caught her for a moment,' she drawled to Elizabeth, as they went back into ye olde tea-house.

'Naughty of her not to have let me know. How dreadfully bad her memory is becoming.'

'Shocking,' said Elizabeth. 'You should persuade her to see somebody about it.'

Lucia turned on the full horse-power of her courage for the coming encounter in ye olde tea-house. The moment she saw the faces of her friends assembled there, Evie and Leg and Diva, she knew she would need it all.

'You've just missed an old friend, Lucia,' said Susanna. (Was there in her words a touch of the irony for which Rudolph da Vinci was celebrated?)

'Too unfortunate, dear Susanna,' said Lucia. 'But I just got a word with her. Off to stay at Le Touquet, she said. Ah! I never told her she would find Georgie there. My memory is getting as bad as hers. Diva, may I have a one and sixpenny?'

Diva usually went down to the kitchen to see to the serving of a one and sixpenny, but she only called the order down the stairs to Janet. And her face lacked its usual cordiality.

'You've missed such a nice chat,' she said.

There was a silence pregnant with trouble. It was impossible, thought Lucia, that her name should not have figured in the nice chat, or that Poppy should not have exhibited that distressing ignorance about her which had been so evident outside. In any case Elizabeth would soon promulgate the news with the addition of that hideous detail, as yet undiscovered, that she had been asked to Sheffield Castle only because Poppy thought that Georgie was Mayor of Tilling. Brave cheerfulness was the only possible demeanour.

'Too unfortunate,' she repeated, 'and I could have been here half an hour ago, for we had quite a short Council meeting. Nothing controversial: all went so smoothly –'

The memory of that uncontroversial rejection of her portrait brought her up short. Then the sight of Elizabeth's wistful, softly smiling face lashed her forward again.

'How you will laugh, Susanna,' she said brightly, 'when I tell you that the Council unanimously refused to accept my gift of the portrait Irene painted of me which you admired so much. A small committee advised them against it. And *ecco*!'

Susanna's laugh lacked the quality of scorn and contempt for the Council, for which Lucia had hoped. It sounded amused.

'Well, that was a pity,' she said. 'They just didn't like it. But you can't get people to like what they don't like by telling them that they ought to.'

The base desertion was a shock. Lucia looked without favour at the sumptuous one and sixpenny Janet had brought her, but her voice remained calm.

'I think I was wrong to have offered it them at all,' she said. 'I ought to have known that they could not understand it. What fun Irene and I will have over it when I tell her. I can hear her scream "Philistines! Vandals!" and burst into shrieks of laughter. And what a joy to have it back at Mallards again!'

Elizabeth continued to smile.

'No place like home is there, dear?' she said. 'Where will you hang it?'

Lucia gave up the idea of eating her sardine tartlet. She had intended to stay on, until Susanna and Elizabeth left, and find out from Diva what had been said about her before she came in. She tried a few light topics of general interest, evoking only short replies of paralysing politeness. This atmosphere of veiled hostility was undermining her. She knew that if she went first, Elizabeth would pour out all that Poppy had let slip on the doorstep, but perhaps the sooner that was known the better. After drinking her tea and scalding her mouth she rose.

'I must be off,' she said. 'See you again very soon, Susanna. One and sixpence, Diva? Such a lovely tea.'

Elizabeth continued smiling till the door closed.

'Such odd things happened outside,' she said. 'Her Poppy didn't recognize her. She asked her who she was. And Worship wasn't invited to Sheffield Castle at all. Poppy thought that Mr Georgie was the Mayor, and the invitation was for him. That was why Worship came back so soon.'

'Gracious, what a crash!' said Diva.

'It always comes in time,' said Elizabeth thoughtfully. 'Poor thing, we must be very gentle with her, but what a lot of things we must avoid talking about!'

She enumerated them on her plump fingers.

'Duchesses, Castles, photographs – I wonder if they were picture-postcards – prima donnas, for I'm sure she'd have gone to Le Touquet, if she had been asked – portraits – it was my duty to recommend the Council not to accept that daub – gadabout husbands – I haven't got enough fingers. Such a lot of subjects that would tear old wounds open, and she's brought it all on herself, which makes it so much more bitter for her.'

Diva, who hated waste (and nothing would keep in this hot weather) ate Lucia's sardine tartlet.

'Don't gloat, Elizabeth!' she commanded. 'You may say sympathetic things, but there's a nasty tone in the way you say them. I'm really rather sorry for her.'

'Which is just what I have been trying to express,' retorted Elizabeth.

'Then you haven't expressed it well. Not that impression at all. Goodness, here's a fresh party coming in. Janet!'

Lucia passed by the fishmonger's, and some stir of subconscious cerebration prompted her to order a dressed crab that she saw in the window. Then she went home and out into the garden-room. This second blow falling so fast on the heels of the first, caused her to reel. To all the dismal reflections occasioned by the rejection of her portrait there were added those appropriate to the second, and the composite mental picture presented by the two was appalling. Surely some malignant Power, specially dedicated to the service of her discomfiture, must have ordained the mishaps (and their accurate timing) of this staggering afternoon: the malignant Power was a master of stage-craft. Who could stand up against a relentless tragedian? Lucia could not, and two tears of self-pity rolled down her cheeks. She was much surprised to feel their tickling progress, for she had always thought herself incapable of such weakness, but there they were. The larger one fell on to her blotting-pad, and she dashed the smaller aside.

She pulled herself together. Whatever humiliations were heaped on her, her resolve to continue sprightly and dominant and unsubdued was as firm as ever, and she must swallow pity or contempt without apparently tasting them. She went to her piano, and through a slightly blurred vision had a good practice at the difficult treble part of the duet Georgie and she had run through before his departure. She did a few bracing physical exercises, and a little deep-breathing. 'I have lost a great deal of prestige,' she said to herself as she held her breath and puffed it out again, 'but that shall not upset me. I shall recover it all. In a fortnight's time, if not less, I shall be unable to believe that I could ever have felt so abject and have behaved so weakly. *Sursum corda!* I shall –'

Her telephone-bell rang. It required a strong call on her courage to answer it, for who could tell what fresh calamity might not be sprung on her? When she heard the name of the speaker, she nearly rang off, for it seemed so impossible. Probably some infamous joke was being played on her. But she listened.

'I've just missed my boat,' said the voice, 'and sleeping in a hotel makes me ill for a week. Would you be wonderfully kind and let me dine and sleep? You were so good as to suggest that this afternoon. Then I can catch the early boat to-morrow.'

A sob of joy rose in Lucia's throat.

'Delighted, Duchess,' she answered. 'So glad you took me at my word and proposed yourself.'

'Many thanks. I shall be with you in an hour or so.'

Lucia skipped to the bell, and kept her finger on it till Grosvenor came running out.

'Grosvenor, the Duchess of Sheffield will be here in about an hour to dine and sleep,' cried Lucia, still ringing. 'What is there for dinner?'

'Couldn't say, except for a dressed crab that's just come in –' began Grosvenor.

'Yes, I ordered it,' cried Lucia excitedly, ceasing to ring. 'It was instinctive, Grosvenor, it was a leading. Things like that often happen to me. See what else, and plenty of strong coffee.'

Grosvenor went into the house, and the music of triumphant meditations poured through Lucia's brain.

'Shall I ask Benjy and Elizabeth?' she thought. 'That would crush Elizabeth for ever, but I don't really wish her such a

fate. Diva? No. A good little thing, but it might seem odd to
Poppy to meet at dinner a woman to whom she had paid a
shilling for her tea, or perhaps eighteen-pence. Susanna Leg?
No: she was not at all kind about the picture. Shall I send for
the Mayor's book and get Poppy to write in it? Again, no. It
would look as if I wanted to record her visit officially, whereas
she only just drops in. We will be alone, I think. Far more
chic.'

Grosvenor returned with the modest menu, and Lucia added
a savoury.

'And I shan't dress, Grosvenor,' she said. 'Her Grace (rich
words!) will be leaving very early, and she won't want to
unpack, I expect.'

Her Grace arrived. She seemed surprised not to find Georgie
there, but was pleased to know that he was staying with Olga
at Le Touquet. She went to bed very soon after dinner, and
left at eight next morning. Never had Lucia waited so impatiently for the shopping-hour, when casually, drawlingly,
she would diffuse the news.

The first person she met was Elizabeth herself, who hurried
across the street with an odious smile of kindly pity on her face.

'So lonely for you, Worship, all by yourself without Mr
Georgie,' she said. 'Pop in and dine with us tonight.'

Lucia could have sung aloud to think how soon that kindly
pity would be struck from the Mayoress's face. She pressed a
finger to her forehead.

'Let me think,' she said. 'I'm afraid . . . No, that's to-morrow
. . . Yes, I am free. Charmed.' She paused, prolonging the
anticipation of the wonderful disclosure.

'And I had such a queer little surprise last night,' she
drawled. 'I went home after tea at Diva's – of course you were
there – and played my piano a while. Then the eternal telephone rang. Who do you think it was who wanted to dine and
sleep at such short notice?'

Elizabeth curbed her longing to say 'Duchess Poppy,' but
that would have been too unkind and sarcastic.

'Tell me, dear,' she said.

'The Duchess,' said Lucia. 'I begged her, do you remember, when we three met for a minute yesterday, just to propose herself . . . And an hour afterwards, she did. Dear vague thing! She missed her boat and can't bear hotels and telephoned. A pleasant quiet evening. She went off again very early to-day, to catch the morning boat. I wonder if she'll succeed this time. Eight o'clock this evening then? I shall look forward to it.'

Lucia went into a shop, leaving Elizabeth speechless on the pavement, with her mouth wide open. Then she closed it, and it assumed its grimmest aspect. She began to cross the street, but leaped back to the pavement again on the violent hooting, almost in her ear, of Susan's Royce.

'So sorry if it made you jump,' said Susan, putting her face out of the window, 'but I hear that Lucia's Duchess was here yesterday and didn't know her from Adam. Or Eve. Either of them. Can it be true?'

'I was there,' said Elizabeth. 'She hadn't the slightest idea who Worship was.'

'That's odd, considering all those photographs.'

'There's something odder yet,' said Elizabeth. 'Worship has just told me she had a visitor to dine and sleep, who left very early this morning. Guess who that was!'

'I never can guess, as you know,' said Susan. 'Who?'

'She!' cried Elizabeth shrilly. 'And Lucia had the face to tell me so!'

Mr Wyse, concealed behind the immense bulk of his wife, popped his head round the corner of her shoulder. The Mayoress's savage countenance so terrified him that he popped it back again.

'How Worship's conscience will let her tell such whoppers, is her concern and not mine, thank God,' continued the Mayoress. 'What I deplore is that she should think me idiotic enough to believe them. Does one woman ask another woman, whom she doesn't know by sight, to let her dine and sleep? *Does* she?'

Mr Wyse always refused to be drawn into social crises. 'Drive on,' he said in a low voice down the speaking-tube, and the car hooted and moved away. Elizabeth screamed '*Does* she,' after it.

The news spread fast, and there was only one verdict on it. Obviously Lucia had invented the story to counter the mortification of being unrecognized by Poppy the day before. 'So silly,' said Diva, when Elizabeth plunged into the tea-house and told her. 'Much better to have lived it down. We've all got to live things down sometimes. She's only made it much harder for herself. What's the good of telling lies which nobody can believe? When you and I tell lies, Elizabeth, it's in the hope anyhow – What is it Janet?'

'Please ma'am, Grosvenor's just told me there was a visitor at Mallards last night, and who do you think –'

'Yes, I've heard,' said Diva. 'I'll be down in the kitchen in a minute.'

'And making poor Grosvenor her accomplice,' said Elizabeth. 'Come and dine to-night, Diva. I've asked Worship, and you must help Benjy and me to get through the evening. You must help us to keep her off the subject, or I shall lose my self-control and forget that I'm a lady and tell her she's a liar.'

Lucia spent a wonderfully happy day. She came straight home after telling Elizabeth her news, for it was far more lofty not to spread it herself and give the impression that she was gratified, and devoted herself to her music and her reading, as there was no municipal business to occupy her. Long before evening everyone would know, and she would merely make casual allusions at dinner to her visitor, and inflame their curiosity. She went out wearing her seed-pearls in the highest spirits.

'Dear host and hostess,' she said as she swept in. 'So sweet of you to take compassion on my loneliness. No, Major Benjy, no sherry thanks, though I really deserve some after my long day. Breakfast at half-past seven –'

'Fancy! That was early!' interrupted Elizabeth. Diva entered.

'So sorry,' she said. 'A bit late. Fearfully busy afternoon. Worn out. Yes, Major Benjy: just half a glass.'

'I was just saying that I had had a long day, too,' said Lucia. 'My guest was off at eight to catch the early boat at Seaport –'

'Such a good service,' put in Benjy. 'Liz and I went by that route on our honeymoon.'

'– and would get to Le Touquet in time for lunch.'

'Well, dinner, dinner,' said Benjy, and in they went.

'I've not seen Susan Leg to-day,' remarked Diva. 'She usually drops in to tea now.'

'She's been writing hard,' said Elizabeth. 'I popped in for a minute. She's got some material *now*, she told me.'

This dark saying had a bright lining for Lucia. Her optimistic mind concluded that Susanna knew about her visitor, and she laughed gaily as dressed crab was handed to her.

'Such a coincidence,' she said. 'Last night I had ordered dressed crab before – dear Elizabeth, I never get tired of it – before I was rung up from Seaport. Was not that lucky? Her favourite food.'

'And how many teas did you say you served to-day, Diva?' asked Elizabeth.

'Couldn't tell you yet. Janet hadn't finished counting up. People still in the garden when I left.'

'I heard from Georgie to-day,' said Lucia. 'He'll be back from Le Touquet on Saturday. The house was quite full already, he said, and he didn't know where Olga would put another guest.'

'Such lovely September weather,' said Elizabeth. 'So good for the crops.'

Lucia was faintly puzzled. They had all been so eager to hear about her visit to Sheffield Castle, and now whenever she brought up kindred topics, Elizabeth or Diva changed the subject with peculiar abruptness. Very likely Elizabeth was a little jealous, a little resentful that Lucia had not asked her to dine last night. But she could explain that.

'It was too late, alas,' she said, 'to get up a small party,' she said, 'as I should have so much liked to do. Simply no time. We didn't even dress.'

Elizabeth rose.

'Such a short visit,' she said, 'and breakfast at half-past seven. Fancy! Let us have a rubber, as we needn't get up so early to-morrow.'

*

Lucia walked home in the bright moonlight, making benevolent plans. If Poppy broke her return journey by staying a night here she must certainly have a party. She vaguely regretted not having done so last night: it would have given pleasure, and she ought to welcome all opportunities of making treats for her friends ... They were touchy folk; to-night they had been harsh with each other over bridge, but to her they had been scrupulously polite, receiving all her criticisms of their play in meek silence. Perhaps they were beginning to perceive at last that she was a different class of player from them. As she caressed this vainglorious thought, she stopped to admire the chaste whiteness of the moonlight on the church tower, which seemed to point skywards as if towards her own serene superiority among the stars. Then quite suddenly a violent earthquake happened in her mind, and it collapsed.

'They don't believe that Poppy ever stayed with me at all,' she moaned. 'They think I invented it. Infamous!'

12

For the whole of the next day no burgess of Tilling except Mrs Simpson and the domestic staff, set eyes on the Mayor. By a strong effort of will Lucia took up her market-basket after breakfast with the intention of shopping, but looking out from the window of her hall, she saw Elizabeth on the pavement opposite, sketching the front of the ancestral house of her aunt by marriage. She could not face Elizabeth yet, for that awful mental earthquake in the churchyard last night had shattered her nerve. The Mayor was a self-ordained prisoner in her own house, as Popes had been at the Vatican.

She put down her basket and went back into the garden-room. She must show Elizabeth though not by direct encounter, that she was happy and brilliant and busy. She went to her piano and began practising scales. Arpeggios and roulades of the most dazzling kind followed. Slightly exhausted by this fine display she crept behind the curtain and peered out. Elizabeth was still there, and, in order to continue the impression of strenuous artistic activity, Lucia put on a gramophone record of the 'Moonlight' Sonata. At the conclusion of that she looked out again; Elizabeth had gone. It was something to have driven that baleful presence away from the immediate neighbourhood, but it had only taken its balefulness elsewhere. She remembered how Susanna had said with regard to the rejected portrait (which no longer seemed to matter an atom) 'You can't get people to like what they don't like by telling them that they ought to;' and now a parallel aphorism suggested itself to Lucia's harassed brain.

'You can't get people to believe what they won't believe by telling them that it's true,' she whispered to herself. 'Yet Poppy did stay here: she did, she did! And it's too unfair that I should lose more prestige over that, when I ought to have recovered all that I had lost . . . What is it, Grosvenor?'

Grosvenor handed her a telegram.

'Mr Georgie won't be back till Monday instead of Saturday,' said Lucia in a toneless voice. 'Anything else?'

'Shall Cook do the shopping, ma'am, if you're not going out? It's early closing.'

'Yes. I shall be alone for lunch and dinner,' said Lucia, wishing that it were possible for all human affairs to shut down with the shops.

She glanced at Georgie's telegram again, amazed at its light-heartedness. 'Having such fun,' it ran. 'Olga insists I stop till Monday. Know you won't mind. Devoted Georgie.'

She longed for devoted Georgie, and fantastic ideas born of pure misery darted through her head. She thought of replying: 'Come back at once and stand by me. Nobody believes that Poppy slept here.' She thought of asking the BBC to broadcast an SOS: 'Will George Pillson last heard of to-day at Le Touquet, return at once to Tilling where his wife the Mayor –' No, she could not say she was dangerously ill. That would alarm him; besides he would find on arrival that she was perfectly well. He might even come by air, and then the plane might crash and he would be burned to death. She realized that such thoughts were of the most morbid nature, and wondered if a glass of sherry would disperse them. But she resisted. 'I won't risk becoming like Major Benjy,' she said to herself, 'and I've got to stick it alone till Monday.'

The hours crept dismally by: she had lunch, tea and dinner by herself. One fragment of news reached her through Grosvenor and that was not encouraging. Her cook had boasted to Elizabeth's parlourmaid that she had cooked dinner for a Duchess, and the parlourmaid with an odd laugh, had advised her not to be so sure about that. Cook had returned in a state of high indignation, which possibly she had expressed by saturating Lucia's soup with pepper, and putting so much mustard into her devilled chicken that it might have been used as a plaster for the parlourmaid. Perhaps these fiery substances helped to kindle Lucia again materially, and all day psychical stimulants were at work: pride which refused to surrender, the extreme boredom of being alone, and the consciousness of rectitude. So next morning, after making sure that Elizabeth was not lurking about, Lucia set forth with her market-basket. Irene was just coming out of her house, and met her with a grave and sympathetic face.

'Darling, I am so sorry about it,' she said.

Lucia naturally supposed that she was referring to the rejection of the portrait.

'Don't give it another thought,' she said. 'It will be such a joy to have it at Mallards. They're all Goths and Vandals and Elizabeths.'

'Oh that!' said Irene. 'Who cares? Just wait till I've touched up Elizabeth and Benjy for the Carlton Gallery. No, about this septic Duchess. Why did you do it? So unwise!'

Lucia wondered if some fresh horror had ripened, and her mouth went dry.

'Why did I do what?' she asked.

'Say that she'd been to stay with you, when she didn't even know you by sight. So futile!'

'But she did stay with me!' cried Lucia.

'No, no,' said Irene soothingly. 'Don't go on saying it. It wounds me. Naturally, you were vexed at her not recognizing you. You *had* seen her before somewhere, hadn't you!'

'But this is preposterous!' cried Lucia. 'You *must* believe me. We had dressed crab for dinner. She went to bed early. She slept in the spare room. She snored. We breakfasted at half-past seven –'

'Darling, we won't talk about it any more,' said Irene. 'Whenever you want me, I'll come to you. Just send for me.'

'I shall want you,' said Lucia with awful finality, 'when you beg my pardon for not believing me.'

Irene uttered a dismal cry, and went back into her house. Lucia with a face of stone went on to the High Street. As she was leaving the grocer's her basket bumped against Diva's, who was entering.

'Sorry,' said Diva. 'Rather in a hurry. My fault.'

It was as if an iceberg, straight from the North Pole, had apologized. Mr Wyse was just stepping on to the pavement, and he stood hatless as she hailed him.

'Lovely weather, isn't it?' she said. 'Georgie writes to me that they're having the same at Le Touquet. We must have some more bridge-parties when he gets back.'

'You enjoy your bridge so much, and play it so beautifully,' said Mr Wyse with a bow. 'And, believe me, I shall never forget your kindness over Susan's budgerigar.'

In Lucia's agitated state, this sounded dreadfully like an assurance that, in spite of all, she hadn't lost his friendship. Then with an accession of courage, she determined to stick to her guns.

'The Duchess's visit to me was at such short notice,' she said, 'that there was literally not time to get a few friends together. She would so much have liked to see you and Susan.'

'Very good of you to say so. I – I heard that she had spent the night under your hospitable roof. Ah! I see Susan beckoning to me.'

Lucia's shopping had not raised her spirits, and when she went up the street again towards Mallards, there was Elizabeth on the pavement opposite, at her easel. But now the sight of her braced Lucia. It flashed through her mind that her dear Mayoress had selected this subject for her sketch in order to keep an eye on her, to observe, as through a malicious microscope, her joyless exits and entrances and report to her friends how sad and wan she looked: otherwise Elizabeth would never have attempted anything which required the power to draw straight lines and some knowledge, however elementary, of perspective. All the more reason, then, that Lucia should be at her very best and brightest and politest and most withering.

Elizabeth out of the corner of her eye saw her approaching and kissed the top end of her paint-brush to her.

'Good morning, dear Worship,' she said. 'Been shopping and chatting with all your friends? Any news?'

'Good morning, *sindaca mia*,' she said. 'That means Mayoress, dear. Oh, what a promising sketch! But have you quite got the mellow tone of the bricks in my garden-room? I should suggest just a touch of brown-madder.'

Elizabeth's paint-brush began to tremble.

'Thank you, dear,' she said. 'Brown-madder. I must remember that.'

'Or a little rose-madder mixed with burnt sienna would do as well,' continued Lucia. 'Just stippled on. You will find that will give the glowing effect you want.'

Elizabeth wondered whether Lucia could have realized that nobody in Tilling believed that Poppy had ever stayed with her and yet remain so complacent and superior. She hoped to find an opportunity of introducing that topic. But she could find something to say on the subject of Art first.

'So lovely for quaint Irene to have had this great success with her picture of me,' she said. 'The Carlton Gallery, she tells me, and then perhaps an American purchaser. Such a pity that masterpieces have to leave the country. Luckily her picture of you is likely to remain here.'

'That was a terrible set-back for Irene,' said Lucia, as glibly as if she had learned this dialogue by heart, 'when your Committee induced the Council to reject it.'

'Impossible to take any other view,' said Elizabeth. 'A daub. We couldn't have it in our beautiful Town Hall. And it didn't do you justice, dear.'

'How interesting that you should say that!' said Lucia. 'Dear Irene felt just that about her picture of you. She felt she had not put enough character into your face. She means to make some little alterations in it before she sends it to the Carlton Galleries.'

That was alarming: Elizabeth remembered the 'little alterations' Irene had made before. But she did not allow that to unnerve her.

'Sometimes I am afraid she will never rise to the level of her Venus again,' she sighed. 'Her high-water mark. Her picture of you, for instance. It might have been out of Mr Wyse's pieces of still-life: bicycle, piano, packs of cards.'

'Some day when I can find time, I will explain to you the principles of symbolism,' Lucia promised.

Elizabeth saw her way to the desired topic.

'Thank you, dear,' she said fervently. 'That would be a treat. But I know how busy you are with all your duties and all your entertaining. Have you had any more visitors to dine and sleep and go away very early next morning before they had seen anything of our lovely Tilling?'

The blow was wholly unexpected and it shook Lucia. She pulled herself together.

'Let me think,' she said. 'Such a succession of people dropping in. No! I think the dear Duchess was my last guest.'

'What a lovely evening you must have had,' said Elizabeth. 'Two old friends together. How I love a *tête-à-tête*, just like what we're having now with nobody to interrupt. Roaming over all sorts of subjects, like bees sipping at flowers. How much you always teach me, Worship. Rose-madder and burnt sienna to give luminousness –'

Lucia clutched at the return of this topic, and surveyed Elizabeth's sketch.

'So glad to have given you that little tip,' she said. 'Immense improvement, isn't it? How the bricks glow now –'

'I haven't put any madder on yet, brown or rose,' cooed Elizabeth, 'but so glad to know about it. And is poor Duchess's memory really as bad as it seemed? How dreadful for you if she had forgotten her own name as well as yours.'

Quite suddenly Lucia knew that she had no more force left in her. She could only just manage a merry laugh.

'What a delicious social crisis that would be!' she said. 'You ought to send it to some comic paper. And what a pleasant talk we have had! I could stay here all morning chatting, but alas, I have a hundred arrears to get through. *Addio, cara sindaca.*'

She walked without hurrying up the steps to her door and tottered out into the garden-room. Presently she crept to the observation-post behind the curtain and looked out. Benjy had joined the Mayoress, and something she said caused him to laugh very heartily . . . And even devoted Irene did not believe that Poppy had ever stayed here.

Next day was Sunday. As Lucia listened to the joyful peal of the bells she wondered whether, without Georgie, she could meet the fresh ordeal that awaited her, when after the service Tilling society assembled outside the south porch of the church for the Sunday morning chat which took the place of the weekday shopping. To shirk that would be a tacit confession that she could not face her friends: she might just as well, from the social point of view, not go to church at all. But though the *débâcle* appeared so complete, she knew that her essential spirit was unbroken: it would be 'given her', she felt, to make that manifest in some convincing manner.

She sang very loud in the hymns and psalms, she winced when the organist had a slight misunderstanding with the choir, she let ecclesiastical smiles play over her face when she found herself in sympathy with the doctrine of the curate's sermon, she gave liberally to the offertory. When the service was over she waited outside the south porch. Elizabeth followed close behind, and behind Elizabeth were other familiar faces. Lucia felt irresistibly reminded of the hymn she had just been singing about the hosts of Midian who 'prowled and prowled around' . . . So much the worse for the hosts of Midian.

'Good morning, dear,' said Elizabeth. 'No Mr Georgie in church? Not ill I hope?'

'No, particularly well,' said Lucia, 'and enjoying himself so much at Le Touquet that he's staying till Monday.'

'Sweet of you to allow him,' responded Elizabeth, 'for you must be so lonely without him.'

At that precise moment there took possession of Lucia an emotion to which hitherto she had been a stranger, namely sheer red rage. In all the numerous crises of her career her brain had always been occupied with getting what she wanted and with calm triumph when she got it, or with devising plans to extricate herself from tight places and with scaring off those who had laid traps for her. Now all such insipidities were swept away; rage at the injustice done her thrilled every fibre of her being, and she found the sensation delicious. She began rather gently.

'Lonely?' she asked. 'I don't know the word. How could I be lonely with my books and my music and my work, above all with so many loving loyal friends like yourself, dear Elizabeth, so close about me?'

'That's the stuff to give her. That made her wince,' she thought, and opening the furnace doors she turned to the group of loving loyal friends, who had emerged from church, and were close about her.

'I'm still the deserted wife, you see,' she said gaily. 'My

Georgie can't tear himself away from the sirens at Le Touquet, Olga and Poppy and the rest. Oh, Mr Wyse, what a cold you've got! You must take care of yourself: your sister the Contessa Amelia di Faraglione would never have allowed you to come out! Dear Susan! No Royce? Have you actually walked all the way from Porpoise Street? You mustn't overdo it! Diva, how is Paddy? He's not been sick again, I hope, after eating one of your delicious sardine tartlets. Yes, Georgie's not back yet. I am thinking of going by aeroplane to Le Touquet this afternoon, just to dine and sleep – like Poppy – and return with him to-morrow. And Susanna! I hear you've been so busy with your new story about Tilling. I do hope you will get someone to publish it when it's finished. Dear Diva, what a silly mistake I've made: of course it was the recipe for cream-wafers which Susanna's *chef* gave you which made Paddy so unwell. Irene? You in church? Was it not a lovely sermon, all about thinking evil of your friends? Good morning, Major Benjy. You must get poor Mr Wyse to try your favourite cure for colds. A tumbler of whisky, isn't it, every two hours with a little boiling water according to taste. *Au revoir*, dear ones: See you all to-morrow I hope.'

She smiled and kissed her hand, and walked off without turning her head, a little out of breath with this shattering eloquence, but rejoicing and rejuvenated.

'That *was* a pleasure,' she said to herself, 'and to think that I was ever terrified of meeting them! What a coward! I don't think I left anybody out: I insulted each one in the presence of all the rest. That's what they get for not believing that Poppy stayed here, and for thinking that I was down and out. I've given them something else to think about. I've paid them back, thank God, and now we'll see what will happen next.'

Lucia, of course, had no intention of flying to Le Touquet, but she drove to Seaport next morning to meet Georgie. He was wearing a new French yachting costume with a double-breasted jacket and brass buttons.

'My dear, how delightful of you to come and meet me!' he said. 'Quite a smooth crossing. Do you like my clothes?'

'Too smart for anything, Georgie, and I am so glad to see you again. Such a lot to tell you which I couldn't write.'

'Elizabeth been behaving well?' he asked.

'Fiendishly. A real crisis, Georgie, and you've come into the middle of it. I'll tell you all about it as we go.'

Lucia gave an unbiased and lucid sketch of what had happened, peppered by indignant and excited comments from him:

'Poppy's imbecile – yes I call her Poppy to her face, she asked me to – Fancy her forgetting you: just the sort of thing for that foul Mapp to make capital of – And so like her to get the Council to reject the picture of you – My dear, you cried? What a shame, and how very unlike you – And they don't believe Poppy stayed with you? Why of course she did! She talked about it – Even Irene? – How utterly poisonous of them all! – Hurray, I'm glad you gave it them hot after church. Capital! We'll do something stunning, now that we can put our heads together about it. I must hear it all over again bit by bit. And here we are in the High Street. There's Mapp, grinning like a Cheshire cat. We'll cut her anyhow, just to make a beginning: we can't go wrong over that.'

Georgie paused a moment.

'And, do you know, I'm very glad to be back,' he said. 'Olga was perfectly sweet, as she always is, but there were other things. It would have been far better if I'd come home on Saturday.'

'Georgie, how thrilling!' cried Lucia, forgetting her own crisis for a brief second. 'What is it?'

'I'll tell you afterwards. Hullo, Grosvenor, how are you? Yes, I think I'll have a warm bath after my journey and then rest till tea-time.'

They had tea in his sitting-room after he had rested, where he was arranging his bibelots, for Grosvenor had not put them back, after dusting them, exactly as he wished. This done, he took up his needlework and his narration.

'It's been rather upsetting,' he said. 'Poppy was terribly ill on her crossing, and I didn't see her till next day, after I had settled to stop at Olga's over the Sunday, as I telegraphed.

And then she was very queer. She took hold of my hand under the table at dinner, and trod on my foot and smiled at me most oddly. She wouldn't play bridge, but came and sat close up against me. One thing after another –'

'Georgie, what a horrid woman,' said Lucia. 'How could she dare? Did she try –'

'No,' said Georgie hastily. 'Nothing important. Olga assured me she didn't mean anything of the sort, but that she always behaved like that to people with beards. Olga wasn't very sympathetic about it: in fact she came to my room one night, and simply went into fits of laughter.'

'Your bedroom, Georgie?' asked Lucia.

'Yes. She often did when we went upstairs and talked for a bit. But Poppy was very embarrassing. I'm not good at that sort of thing. And yesterday, she made me go for a walk with her along the beach, and wanted to paddle with me. But I was quite firm about that. I said I should go inland at once if she went on about it.'

'Quite right, dear. Just what I should have done myself,' said Lucia appreciatively.

'And so those last two days weren't so pleasant. I was uncomfortable. I wished I'd come back on Saturday.'

'Very tiresome for you, dear,' said Lucia. 'But it's all over now.'

'That's just what I'm not so sure about,' said he. 'She's leaving Olga's to-morrow, and she's going to telegraph to you, asking if you would let her stay here for a couple of nights. Apparently you begged her to propose herself. You must really say your house is full or that you're away. Though Olga says she means no harm, it's most disagreeable.'

Lucia sprang from her chair.

'Georgie, how absolutely providential!' she cried. 'If only she came, it would kill that despicable scandal that she hadn't stayed here before. They would be forced to believe that she had. Oh! What a score!'

'Well, I couldn't stop here if she came,' said Georgie firmly. 'It got on my nerves. It made me feel very jumpy.'

'But then she mightn't stop if she found you weren't here,'

pleaded Lucia. 'Besides, as Olga says, she doesn't mean anything, I shall be with you; surely that will be sufficient protection, and I won't leave you alone with her a minute all day.
And if you're nervous, you may sleep in my room. Just while
she's here, of course.'

'Oh, I don't think either of us would like that,' said Georgie,
'and Foljambe would think it so odd.'

'Well, you could lock your door. Oh, Georgie, it isn't really
much to ask, and it will put me on a higher pinnacle than ever,
far, far above their base insinuations. They will eat their hearts
out with shame.'

Grosvenor entered.

'A telegram for you, ma'am. Prepaid.'

With trembling hands Lucia tore it open, and, for Grosvenor's benefit, assumed her drawling voice.

'From the Duchess, dear,' she said. 'She wants to come here
to-morrow for two nights, on her way back from Le Touquet. I
suppose I had better say yes, as I did ask her to propose herself.'

'Oh, very well,' said Georgie.

Lucia scribbled a cordial reply, and Grosvenor took it away
with the tea-tray.

'Georgino, you're an angel,' said she. 'My dear, all the time
that I was so wretched here, I knew it would all come right as
soon as you got back, and see what has happened! Now let us
make our plans at once. I think we'll ask nobody the first night
she is here –'

'Nor the second either I should hope,' said Georgie. 'Give
them a good lesson. Besides, after the way you talked to them
yesterday after church, they probably wouldn't come. That
would be a knock.'

Lucia regarded an angle of the ceiling with that far-away
abstracted expression with which she listened to music.

'About their coming, dear,' she said, 'I will wager my knowledge of human nature that they will without exception. As to
my asking them, you know how I trust your judgment, but
here I'm not sure that I agree. Don't you think that to forgive
them all, and to behave as if nothing had happened, would be

the most devastating thing I could do? There's nothing that stings so much as contemptuous oblivion. I have often found that.'

'You don't mean to say that you'll ask Elizabeth Mapp-Flint to dine?' asked Georgie.

'I think so, Georgie, poor soul. If I don't she will feel that she has hurt me, that I want to pay her out. I shouldn't like her to feel that. I don't want to leave her a leg to stand on. Up till now I have never desired quite to crush her, but I feel I have been too lenient. If she is to become a better woman, I must give her a sharper lesson than merely ignoring her. I may remind her by some little impromptu touch of what she tried to do to me, but I shall trust to the inspiration of the moment about that.'

Georgie came round to Lucia's view of the value of vindictive forgiveness, while for himself he liked the idea of calling a Duchess by her Christian name before Mapp and Co. He would not even mind her holding his hand if there were plenty of people there.

'It ought to be a wonderful party,' he said. 'Even better than the party you gave for Olga. I'm beginning to look forward to it. Shall I help you with writing the invitations?'

'Not necessary, dear, thank you,' said Lucia. 'I shall ask them all quite casually by telephone on the afternoon of our dinner. Leave it to me.'

Poppy arrived next evening, again prostrated by sea-sickness and far from amorous. But a good night restored her, and the three took a morning stroll in the High Street, so that everybody saw them. Lucia, absolutely certain that there would be a large dinner-party at Mallards that night, ordered appropriate provisions. In the afternoon they went for a motor-drive: just before starting Lucia directed Foljambe to ring up the whole circle of friends, asking them to excuse such short notice and take pot-luck with her, and not a word was Foljambe to say about Duchesses. They knew.

While the ducal party traversed the country roads, the telephone-bells of Tilling were ringing merrily. For the Wyses were engaged to dine and play bridge with the Mapp-Flints, and Susan, feeling certain that she would not meet the Mapp-Flints anyhow at Mallards, rang up Elizabeth to say that she was not feeling at all well and regretted not being able to come. Algernon, she said, did not like to leave her. To her surprise Elizabeth was all cordiality: dear Susan must not think of going out, it was no inconvenience at all, and they would arrange another night. So, with sighs of relief, they both rang up Mallards, and found that the line was engaged, for Susan Leg, having explained to Diva that she had made a stupid mistake, and had meant to ask her for to-morrow not for to-night, was telling Foljambe that she would be charmed to come. Diva got the line next, and fussing with this delay, Elizabeth sent Benjy round to Mallards to say how pleased. Then to make certain, they all wrote formal notes of acceptance. As for Irene, she was so overcome with remorse at having ever doubted Lucia's word, and so overwhelmed by her nobility in forgiving her, that she burst into tears, and forgot to answer at all.

Poppy was very late for dinner, and all Lucia's guests had arrived before she appeared. They were full of a timid yet eager cordiality, as if scarcely believing that such magnanimity was possible, and their hostess was graciousness itself. She was particularly kind to Elizabeth and made inquiries about her sketch. Then as Poppy still lingered she said to Georgie: 'Run up to Poppy's room, dear, and tell her she must be quick.' She had hardly got that pleasant sentence out when Poppy entered.

'Naughty!' said Lucia, and took her arm to introduce the company. 'Mr and Mrs Wyse, Miss Leg (Rudolph da Vinci, you know, dear), Miss Irene Coles – the Picture of the Year – and Mrs Plaistow: didn't you have one of her delicious teas when you were here? And my Mayoress, Mrs Mapp-Flint, I don't think you met her when you stayed with me last week. And Major Mapp-Flint. Now everybody knows everybody. Sherry, dear Poppy?'

Georgie kept his hands on the table during dinner, and Poppy intermittently caressed the one nearest her in a casual manner; with so many witnesses and in so bright a light,

Georgie liked it rather than otherwise. Her attempt to stroll with him alone in the garden afterwards was frustrated, for Lucia, as bound by her promise, instantly joined them, and brought them back to the garden-room. She was induced to play to them, and Poppy, sitting close to Georgie on the sofa, fell into a refreshing slumber. At the cessation of the music, she woke with a start and asked what the time was. A most distinguished suavity prevailed, and though the party lacked the gaiety and lightness of the Olga-festival, its quality was far more monumental. Then the guests dispersed; Lucia had a kind word for each and she thanked them all for having excused her giving them such short notice.

Elizabeth walked home in silence with Benjy. Her exaltation evaporated in the night air like the fumes of wine, leaving behind an irritated depression.

'Well, there's no help for it,' she said bitterly, as he fumbled with the latch-key of the Vicarage. 'But I dare say before long – Do be quick.'

Half an hour later at Mallards, Lucia, having seen Poppy well on the way to bed, tapped discreetly at Georgie's door. That gave him a terrible fright, till he remembered he had locked it.

'No, you can't come in,' he said. 'Good night, Poppy. Sleep well.'

'It's me, Georgie,' said Lucia in a low voice. 'Open the door: only a chink. She isn't here.'

Georgie unlocked it.

'Perfect!' she whispered. 'Such a treat for them all! They will remember this evening. Perfect.'

refresh yourself at penguin.co.uk

Visit penguin.co.uk for exclusive information and interviews with
bestselling authors, fantastic give-aways and the
inside track on all our books, from the Penguin Classics
to the latest bestsellers.

BE FIRST ▼

first chapters, first editions, first novels

EXCLUSIVES ▼

author chats, video interviews, biographies, special
features

EVERYONE'S A WINNER ▼

give-aways, competitions, quizzes, ecards

READERS GROUPS ▼

exciting features to support existing groups and
create new ones

NEWS ▼

author events, bestsellers, awards, what's new

EBOOKS ▼

books that click – download an ePenguin today

BROWSE AND BUY ▼

thousands of books to investigate – search, try
and buy the perfect gift online – or treat yourself!

ABOUT US ▼

job vacancies, advice for writers and company
history

Get Closer To Penguin . . . www.penguin.co.uk